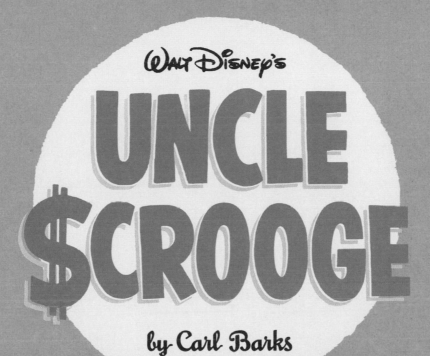

Walt Disney's

UNCLE $CROOGE

by Carl Barks

Publisher and Executive Editor: GARY GROTH
Senior Editor: J. MICHAEL CATRON
Color Editor: JUSTIN ALLAN-SPENCER
Colorists: RICH TOMMASO, GARY LEACH, SUSAN DAIGLE-LEACH, TOM ZIUKO
Series Design: JACOB COVEY
Cover Design: KEELI MCCARTHY
Volume Design: JUSTIN ALLAN-SPENCER
Production: PAUL BARESH
Associate Publisher: ERIC REYNOLDS

- -

Fantagraphics Books, Inc.
7563 Lake City Way NE
Seattle WA 98115
(800) 657-1100

Visit us at fantagraphics.com. Follow us on Twitter at @fantagraphics
and on Facebook at facebook.com/fantagraphics.

Special thanks to Joakim Gunnarsson, David Gerstein, Thomas Jensen, and Kim Weston.

First printing, June 2019
ISBN 978-1-68396-187-1

Printed in Malaysia
Library of Congress Control Number: 2018949829

Now available in this series:

Boxed sets of some titles are available at select locations.

- -

Now available in the *Disney Masters* series:

Also available:

Walt Disney's

UNCLE $CROOGE

"The Mines of King Solomon"

---

by Carl Barks

FANTAGRAPHICS BOOKS
SEATTLE

Contents

All comics stories written and drawn by Carl Barks.

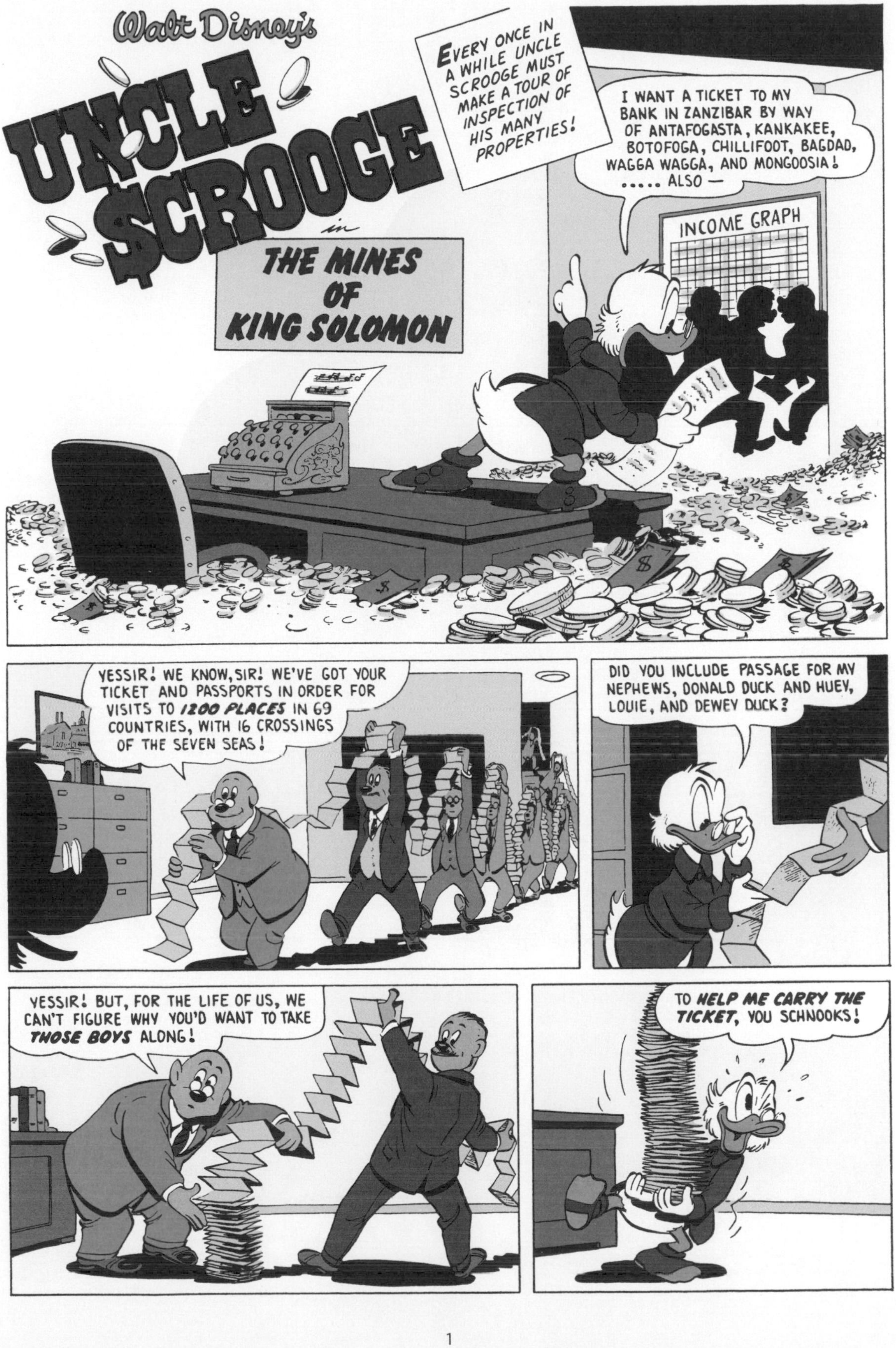
Walt Disney's
UNCLE $CROOGE
in
THE MINES OF KING SOLOMON
EVERY ONCE IN A WHILE UNCLE SCROOGE MUST MAKE A TOUR OF INSPECTION OF HIS MANY PROPERTIES!
I WANT A TICKET TO MY BANK IN ZANZIBAR BY WAY OF ANTAFOGASTA, KANKAKEE, BOTOFOGA, CHILLIFOOT, BAGDAD, WAGGA WAGGA, AND MONGOOSIA! ..... ALSO —
INCOME GRAPH
YESSIR! WE KNOW, SIR! WE'VE GOT YOUR TICKET AND PASSPORTS IN ORDER FOR VISITS TO 1200 PLACES IN 69 COUNTRIES, WITH 16 CROSSINGS OF THE SEVEN SEAS!
DID YOU INCLUDE PASSAGE FOR MY NEPHEWS, DONALD DUCK AND HUEY, LOUIE, AND DEWEY DUCK?
YESSIR! BUT, FOR THE LIFE OF US, WE CAN'T FIGURE WHY YOU'D WANT TO TAKE THOSE BOYS ALONG!
TO HELP ME CARRY THE TICKET, YOU SCHNOOKS!

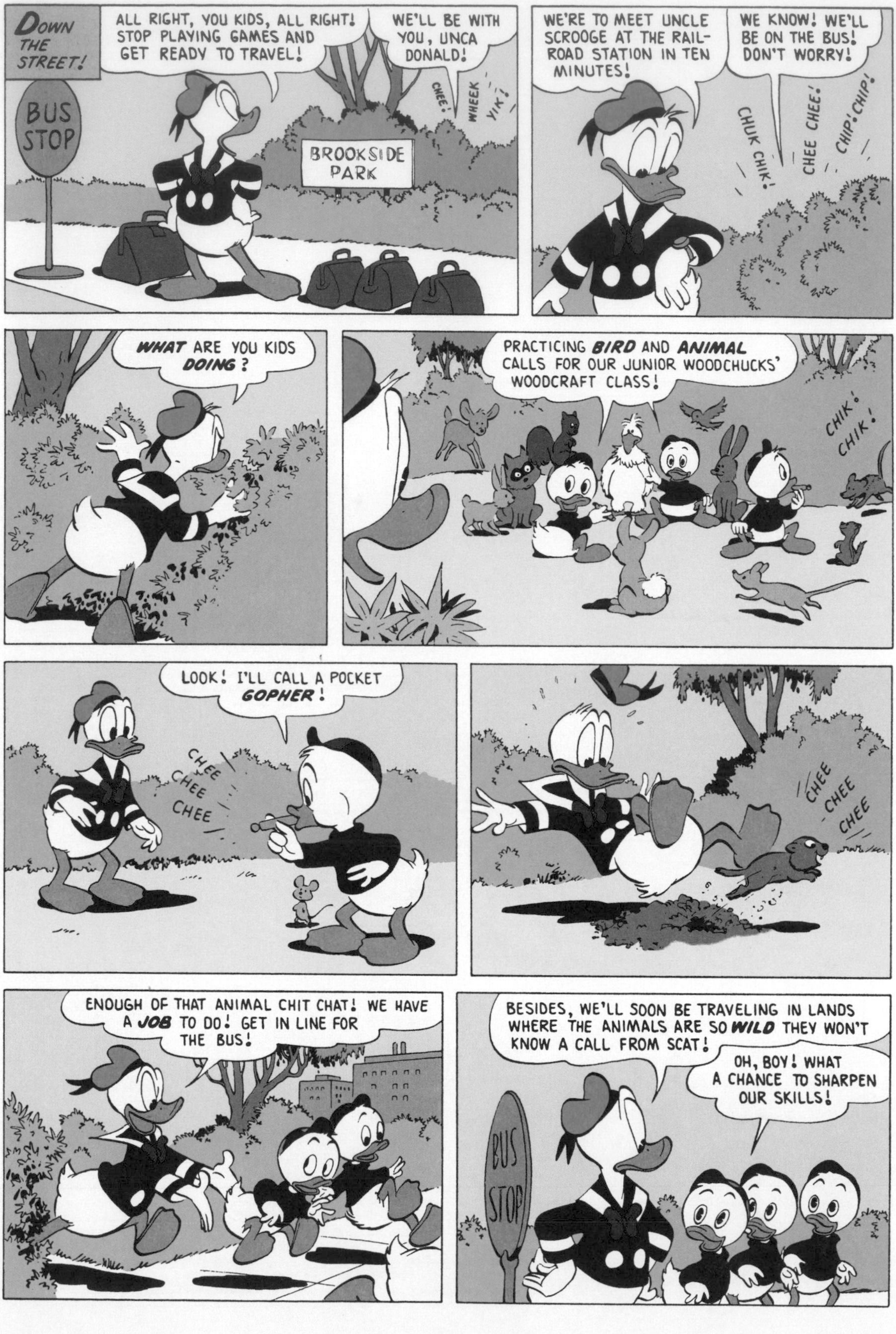
DOWN THE STREET!
ALL RIGHT, YOU KIDS, ALL RIGHT! STOP PLAYING GAMES AND GET READY TO TRAVEL!
WE'LL BE WITH YOU, UNCA DONALD!
CHEE!
WHEEK
YIK!
BUS STOP
BROOKSIDE PARK
WE'RE TO MEET UNCLE SCROOGE AT THE RAIL-ROAD STATION IN TEN MINUTES!
WE KNOW! WE'LL BE ON THE BUS! DON'T WORRY!
CHUK CHIK!
CHEE CHEE!
CHIP! CHIP!
WHAT ARE YOU KIDS DOING?
PRACTICING BIRD AND ANIMAL CALLS FOR OUR JUNIOR WOODCHUCKS' WOODCRAFT CLASS!
CHIK! CHIK!
LOOK! I'LL CALL A POCKET GOPHER!
CHEE CHEE CHEE
CHEE CHEE CHEE
ENOUGH OF THAT ANIMAL CHIT CHAT! WE HAVE A JOB TO DO! GET IN LINE FOR THE BUS!
BESIDES, WE'LL SOON BE TRAVELING IN LANDS WHERE THE ANIMALS ARE SO WILD THEY WON'T KNOW A CALL FROM SCAT!
OH, BOY! WHAT A CHANCE TO SHARPEN OUR SKILLS!
BUS STOP

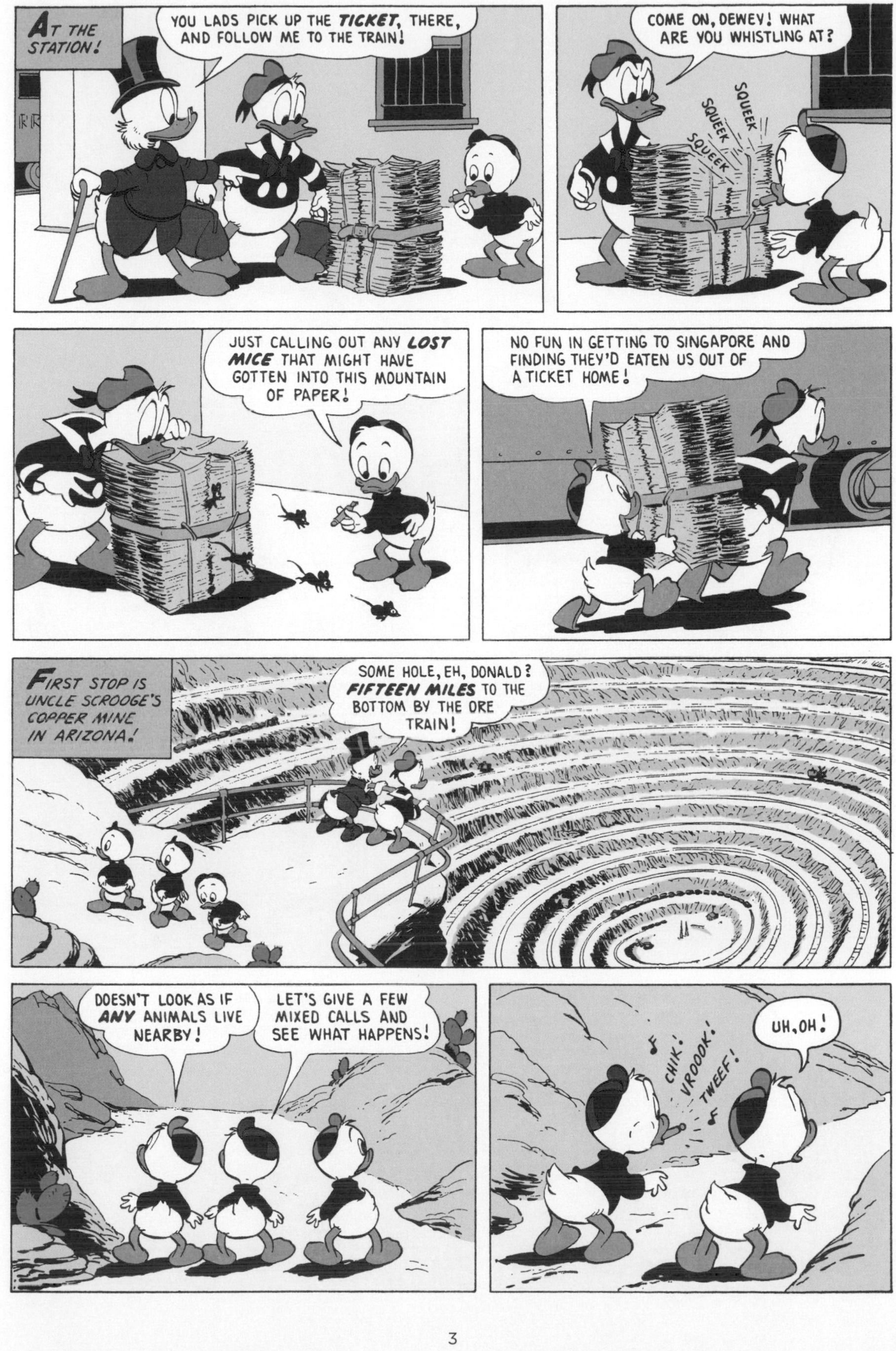
AT THE STATION!
YOU LADS PICK UP THE TICKET, THERE, AND FOLLOW ME TO THE TRAIN!
COME ON, DEWEY! WHAT ARE YOU WHISTLING AT?
SQUEEK
SQUEEK
SQUEEK
JUST CALLING OUT ANY LOST MICE THAT MIGHT HAVE GOTTEN INTO THIS MOUNTAIN OF PAPER!
NO FUN IN GETTING TO SINGAPORE AND FINDING THEY'D EATEN US OUT OF A TICKET HOME!
FIRST STOP IS UNCLE SCROOGE'S COPPER MINE IN ARIZONA!
SOME HOLE, EH, DONALD? FIFTEEN MILES TO THE BOTTOM BY THE ORE TRAIN!
DOESN'T LOOK AS IF ANY ANIMALS LIVE NEARBY!
LET'S GIVE A FEW MIXED CALLS AND SEE WHAT HAPPENS!
CHIK! VROOOK! TWEEF!
UH, OH!

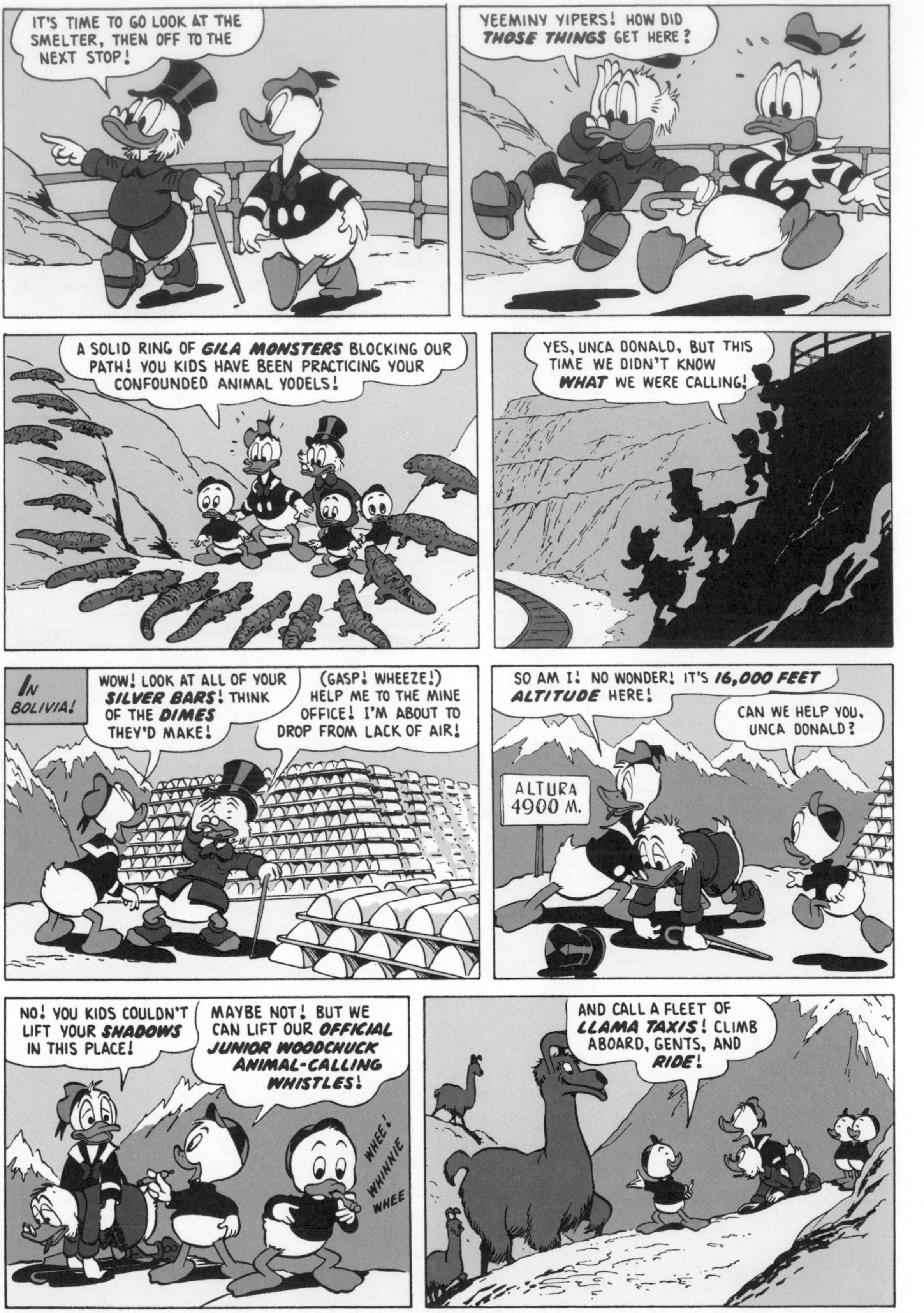
IT'S TIME TO GO LOOK AT THE SMELTER, THEN OFF TO THE NEXT STOP!
YEEMINY YIPERS! HOW DID THOSE THINGS GET HERE?
A SOLID RING OF GILA MONSTERS BLOCKING OUR PATH! YOU KIDS HAVE BEEN PRACTICING YOUR CONFOUNDED ANIMAL YODELS!
YES, UNCA DONALD, BUT THIS TIME WE DIDN'T KNOW WHAT WE WERE CALLING!
IN BOLIVIA!
WOW! LOOK AT ALL OF YOUR SILVER BARS! THINK OF THE DIMES THEY'D MAKE!
(GASP! WHEEZE!) HELP ME TO THE MINE OFFICE! I'M ABOUT TO DROP FROM LACK OF AIR!
SO AM I! NO WONDER! IT'S 16,000 FEET ALTITUDE HERE!
ALTURA 4900 M.
CAN WE HELP YOU, UNCA DONALD?
NO! YOU KIDS COULDN'T LIFT YOUR SHADOWS IN THIS PLACE!
MAYBE NOT! BUT WE CAN LIFT OUR OFFICIAL JUNIOR WOODCHUCK ANIMAL-CALLING WHISTLES!
WHEE! WHINNIE WHEE
AND CALL A FLEET OF LLAMA TAXIS! CLIMB ABOARD, GENTS, AND RIDE!

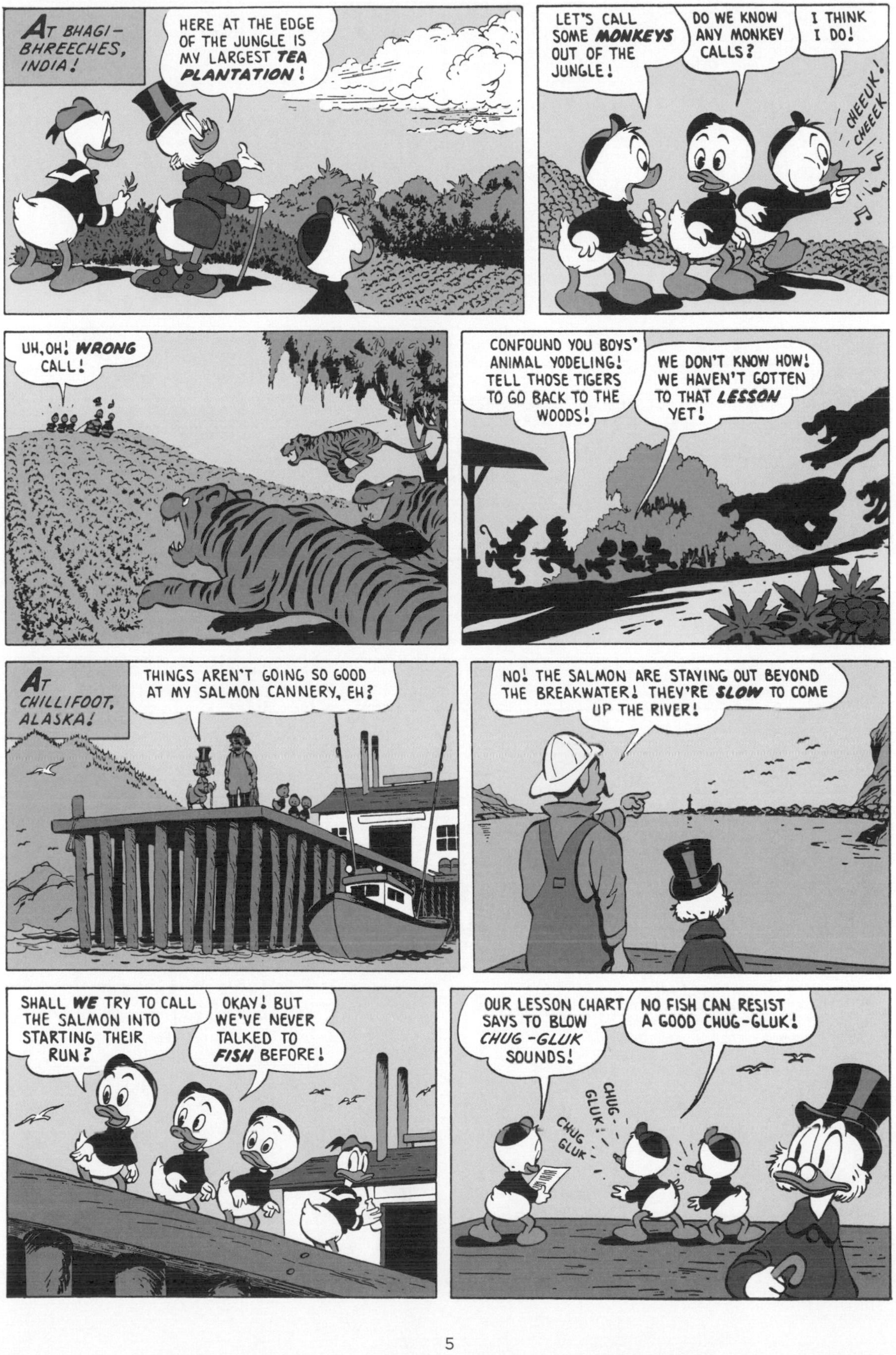

AT BHAGI-BHREECHES, INDIA!
HERE AT THE EDGE OF THE JUNGLE IS MY LARGEST TEA PLANTATION!
LET'S CALL SOME MONKEYS OUT OF THE JUNGLE!
DO WE KNOW ANY MONKEY CALLS?
I THINK I DO!
CHEEUK! CHEEEK
UH, OH! WRONG CALL!
CONFOUND YOU BOYS' ANIMAL YODELING! TELL THOSE TIGERS TO GO BACK TO THE WOODS!
WE DON'T KNOW HOW! WE HAVEN'T GOTTEN TO THAT LESSON YET!
AT CHILLIFOOT, ALASKA!
THINGS AREN'T GOING SO GOOD AT MY SALMON CANNERY, EH?
NO! THE SALMON ARE STAYING OUT BEYOND THE BREAKWATER! THEY'RE SLOW TO COME UP THE RIVER!
SHALL WE TRY TO CALL THE SALMON INTO STARTING THEIR RUN?
OKAY! BUT WE'VE NEVER TALKED TO FISH BEFORE!
OUR LESSON CHART SAYS TO BLOW CHUG-GLUK SOUNDS!
NO FISH CAN RESIST A GOOD CHUG-GLUK!
CHUG-GLUK!
CHUG GLUK

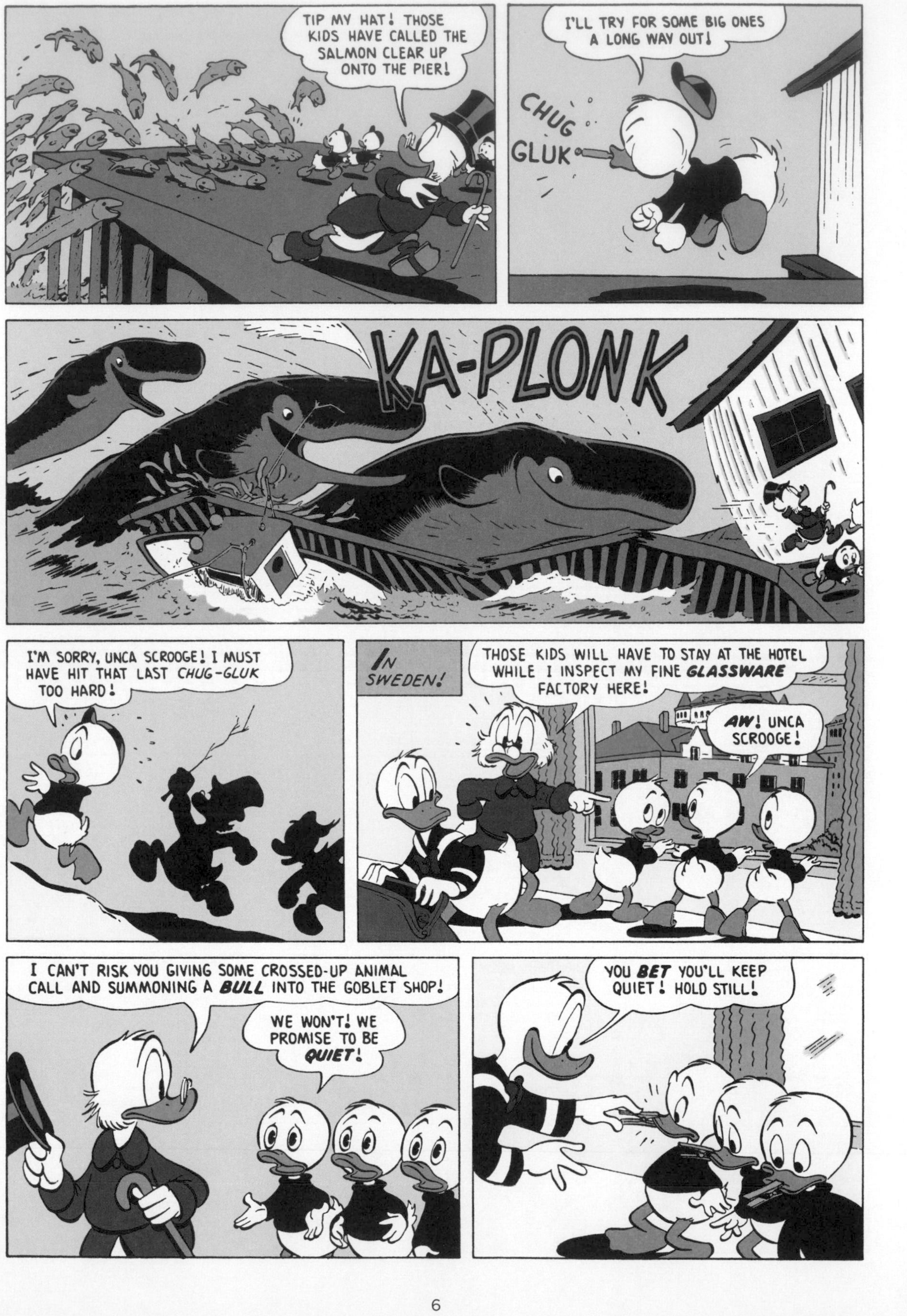
TIP MY HAT! THOSE KIDS HAVE CALLED THE SALMON CLEAR UP ONTO THE PIER!
I'LL TRY FOR SOME BIG ONES A LONG WAY OUT!
CHUG
GLUK
KA-PLONK
I'M SORRY, UNCA SCROOGE! I MUST HAVE HIT THAT LAST CHUG-GLUK TOO HARD!
IN SWEDEN!
THOSE KIDS WILL HAVE TO STAY AT THE HOTEL WHILE I INSPECT MY FINE GLASSWARE FACTORY HERE!
AW! UNCA SCROOGE!
I CAN'T RISK YOU GIVING SOME CROSSED-UP ANIMAL CALL AND SUMMONING A BULL INTO THE GOBLET SHOP!
WE WON'T! WE PROMISE TO BE QUIET!
YOU BET YOU'LL KEEP QUIET! HOLD STILL!

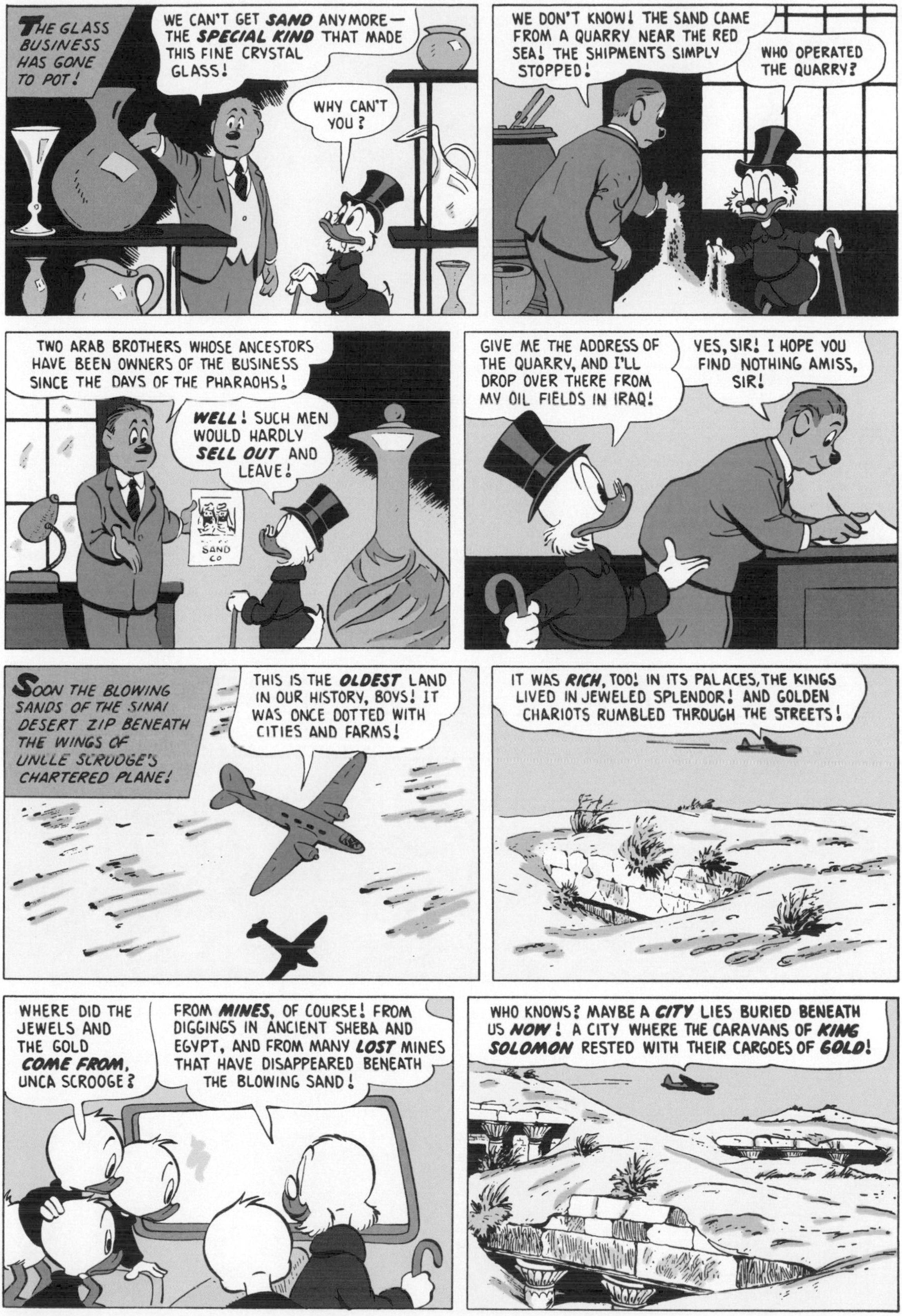
THE GLASS BUSINESS HAS GONE TO POT!
WE CAN'T GET SAND ANYMORE— THE SPECIAL KIND THAT MADE THIS FINE CRYSTAL GLASS!
WHY CAN'T YOU?
WE DON'T KNOW! THE SAND CAME FROM A QUARRY NEAR THE RED SEA! THE SHIPMENTS SIMPLY STOPPED!
WHO OPERATED THE QUARRY?
TWO ARAB BROTHERS WHOSE ANCESTORS HAVE BEEN OWNERS OF THE BUSINESS SINCE THE DAYS OF THE PHARAOHS!
WELL! SUCH MEN WOULD HARDLY SELL OUT AND LEAVE!
SAND CO
GIVE ME THE ADDRESS OF THE QUARRY, AND I'LL DROP OVER THERE FROM MY OIL FIELDS IN IRAQ!
YES, SIR! I HOPE YOU FIND NOTHING AMISS, SIR!
SOON THE BLOWING SANDS OF THE SINAI DESERT ZIP BENEATH THE WINGS OF UNCLE SCROOGE'S CHARTERED PLANE!
THIS IS THE OLDEST LAND IN OUR HISTORY, BOYS! IT WAS ONCE DOTTED WITH CITIES AND FARMS!
IT WAS RICH, TOO! IN ITS PALACES, THE KINGS LIVED IN JEWELED SPLENDOR! AND GOLDEN CHARIOTS RUMBLED THROUGH THE STREETS!
WHERE DID THE JEWELS AND THE GOLD COME FROM, UNCA SCROOGE?
FROM MINES, OF COURSE! FROM DIGGINGS IN ANCIENT SHEBA AND EGYPT, AND FROM MANY LOST MINES THAT HAVE DISAPPEARED BENEATH THE BLOWING SAND!
WHO KNOWS? MAYBE A CITY LIES BURIED BENEATH US NOW! A CITY WHERE THE CARAVANS OF KING SOLOMON RESTED WITH THEIR CARGOES OF GOLD!

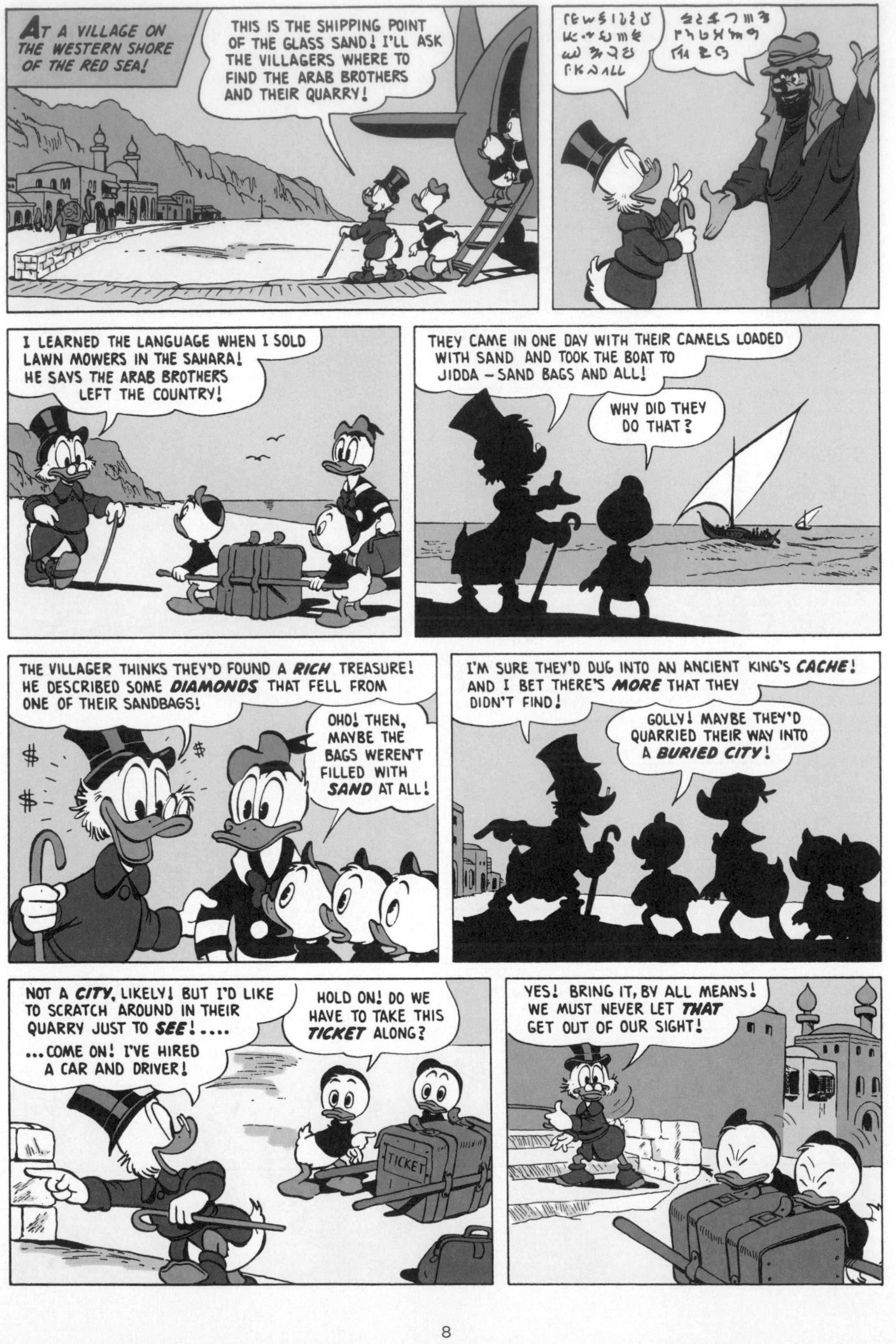
AT A VILLAGE ON THE WESTERN SHORE OF THE RED SEA!
THIS IS THE SHIPPING POINT OF THE GLASS SAND! I'LL ASK THE VILLAGERS WHERE TO FIND THE ARAB BROTHERS AND THEIR QUARRY!
I LEARNED THE LANGUAGE WHEN I SOLD LAWN MOWERS IN THE SAHARA! HE SAYS THE ARAB BROTHERS LEFT THE COUNTRY!
THEY CAME IN ONE DAY WITH THEIR CAMELS LOADED WITH SAND AND TOOK THE BOAT TO JIDDA — SAND BAGS AND ALL!
WHY DID THEY DO THAT?
THE VILLAGER THINKS THEY'D FOUND A RICH TREASURE! HE DESCRIBED SOME DIAMONDS THAT FELL FROM ONE OF THEIR SANDBAGS!
OHO! THEN, MAYBE THE BAGS WEREN'T FILLED WITH SAND AT ALL!
I'M SURE THEY'D DUG INTO AN ANCIENT KING'S CACHE! AND I BET THERE'S MORE THAT THEY DIDN'T FIND!
GOLLY! MAYBE THEY'D QUARRIED THEIR WAY INTO A BURIED CITY!
NOT A CITY, LIKELY! BUT I'D LIKE TO SCRATCH AROUND IN THEIR QUARRY JUST TO SEE!....
...COME ON! I'VE HIRED A CAR AND DRIVER!
HOLD ON! DO WE HAVE TO TAKE THIS TICKET ALONG?
TICKET
YES! BRING IT, BY ALL MEANS! WE MUST NEVER LET THAT GET OUT OF OUR SIGHT!

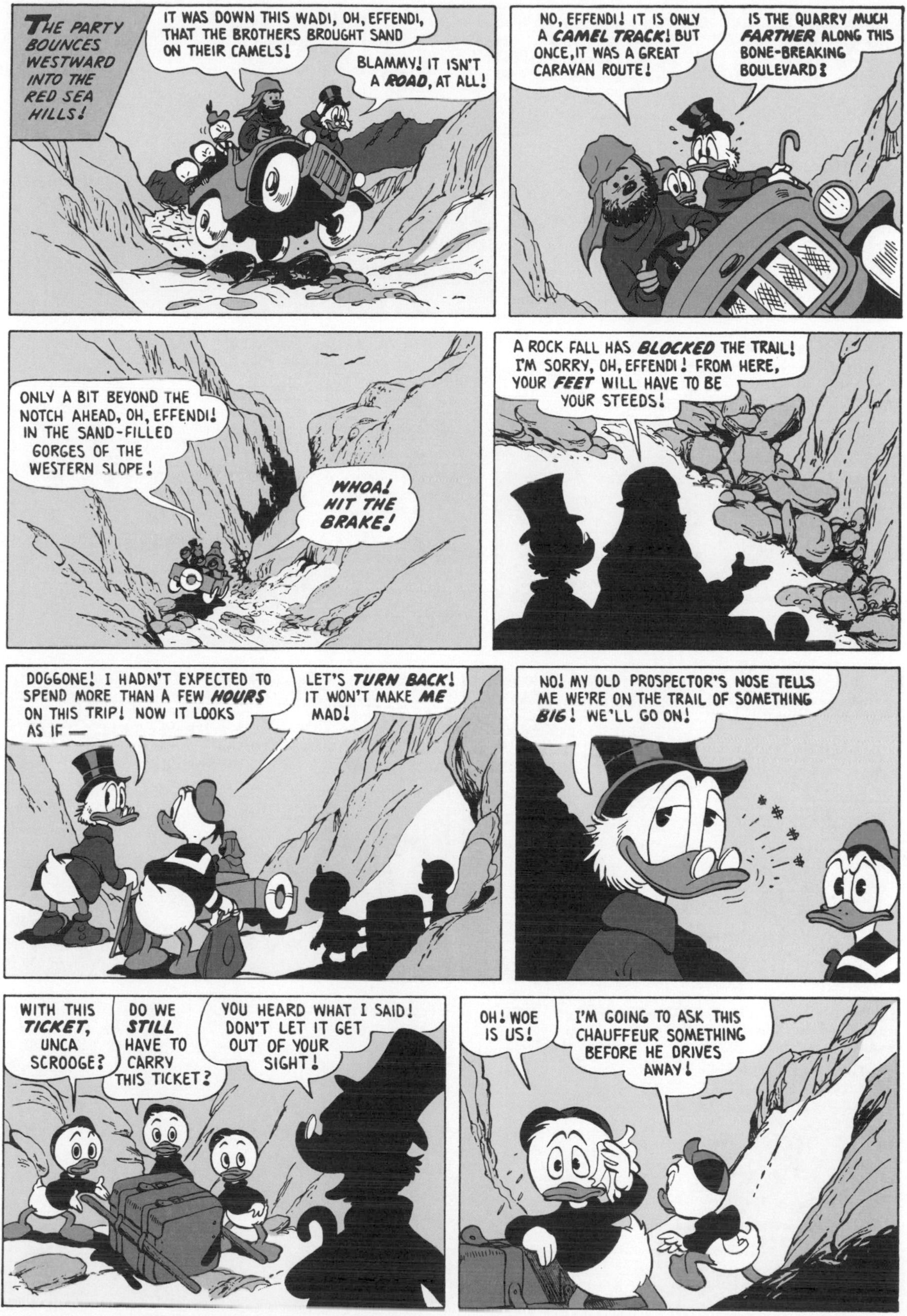
THE PARTY BOUNCES WESTWARD INTO THE RED SEA HILLS!
IT WAS DOWN THIS WADI, OH, EFFENDI, THAT THE BROTHERS BROUGHT SAND ON THEIR CAMELS!
BLAMMY! IT ISN'T A ROAD, AT ALL!
NO, EFFENDI! IT IS ONLY A CAMEL TRACK! BUT ONCE, IT WAS A GREAT CARAVAN ROUTE!
IS THE QUARRY MUCH FARTHER ALONG THIS BONE-BREAKING BOULEVARD?
ONLY A BIT BEYOND THE NOTCH AHEAD, OH, EFFENDI! IN THE SAND-FILLED GORGES OF THE WESTERN SLOPE!
WHOA! HIT THE BRAKE!
A ROCK FALL HAS BLOCKED THE TRAIL! I'M SORRY, OH, EFFENDI! FROM HERE, YOUR FEET WILL HAVE TO BE YOUR STEEDS!
DOGGONE! I HADN'T EXPECTED TO SPEND MORE THAN A FEW HOURS ON THIS TRIP! NOW IT LOOKS AS IF —
LET'S TURN BACK! IT WON'T MAKE ME MAD!
NO! MY OLD PROSPECTOR'S NOSE TELLS ME WE'RE ON THE TRAIL OF SOMETHING BIG! WE'LL GO ON!
WITH THIS TICKET, UNCA SCROOGE?
DO WE STILL HAVE TO CARRY THIS TICKET?
YOU HEARD WHAT I SAID! DON'T LET IT GET OUT OF YOUR SIGHT!
OH! WOE IS US!
I'M GOING TO ASK THIS CHAUFFEUR SOMETHING BEFORE HE DRIVES AWAY!

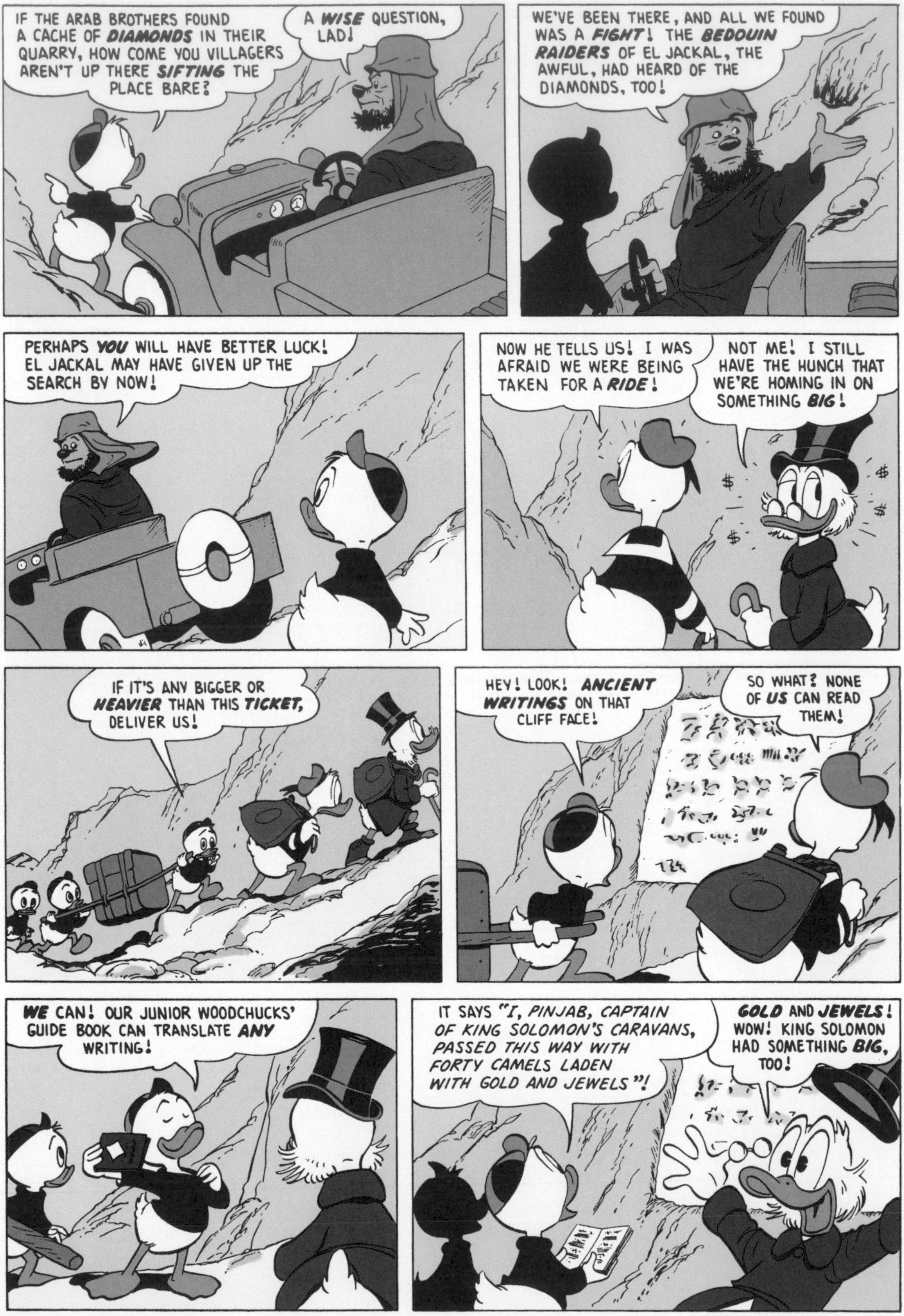
IF THE ARAB BROTHERS FOUND A CACHE OF DIAMONDS IN THEIR QUARRY, HOW COME YOU VILLAGERS AREN'T UP THERE SIFTING THE PLACE BARE?
A WISE QUESTION, LAD!
WE'VE BEEN THERE, AND ALL WE FOUND WAS A FIGHT! THE BEDOUIN RAIDERS OF EL JACKAL, THE AWFUL, HAD HEARD OF THE DIAMONDS, TOO!
PERHAPS YOU WILL HAVE BETTER LUCK! EL JACKAL MAY HAVE GIVEN UP THE SEARCH BY NOW!
NOW HE TELLS US! I WAS AFRAID WE WERE BEING TAKEN FOR A RIDE!
NOT ME! I STILL HAVE THE HUNCH THAT WE'RE HOMING IN ON SOMETHING BIG!
IF IT'S ANY BIGGER OR HEAVIER THAN THIS TICKET, DELIVER US!
HEY! LOOK! ANCIENT WRITINGS ON THAT CLIFF FACE!
SO WHAT? NONE OF US CAN READ THEM!
WE CAN! OUR JUNIOR WOODCHUCKS' GUIDE BOOK CAN TRANSLATE ANY WRITING!
IT SAYS "I, PINJAB, CAPTAIN OF KING SOLOMON'S CARAVANS, PASSED THIS WAY WITH FORTY CAMELS LADEN WITH GOLD AND JEWELS"!
GOLD AND JEWELS! WOW! KING SOLOMON HAD SOMETHING BIG, TOO!

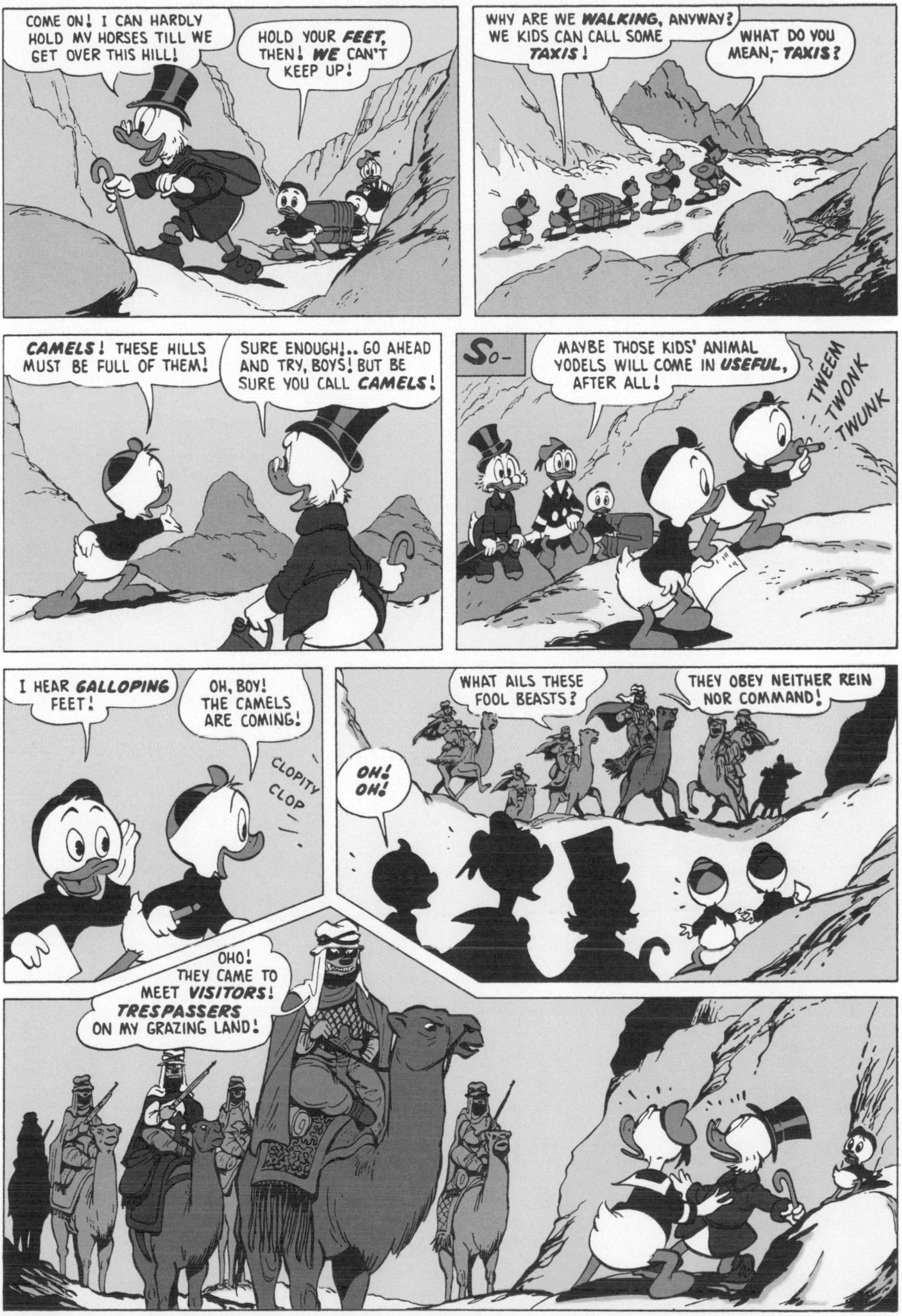
COME ON! I CAN HARDLY HOLD MY HORSES TILL WE GET OVER THIS HILL!
HOLD YOUR FEET, THEN! WE CAN'T KEEP UP!
WHY ARE WE WALKING, ANYWAY? WE KIDS CAN CALL SOME TAXIS!
WHAT DO YOU MEAN,- TAXIS?
CAMELS! THESE HILLS MUST BE FULL OF THEM!
SURE ENOUGH!.. GO AHEAD AND TRY, BOYS! BUT BE SURE YOU CALL CAMELS!
SO-
MAYBE THOSE KIDS' ANIMAL YODELS WILL COME IN USEFUL, AFTER ALL!
TWEEM
TWONK
TWUNK
I HEAR GALLOPING FEET!
OH, BOY! THE CAMELS ARE COMING!
CLOPITY
CLOP
WHAT AILS THESE FOOL BEASTS?
THEY OBEY NEITHER REIN NOR COMMAND!
OH! OH!
OHO! THEY CAME TO MEET VISITORS! TRESPASSERS ON MY GRAZING LAND!

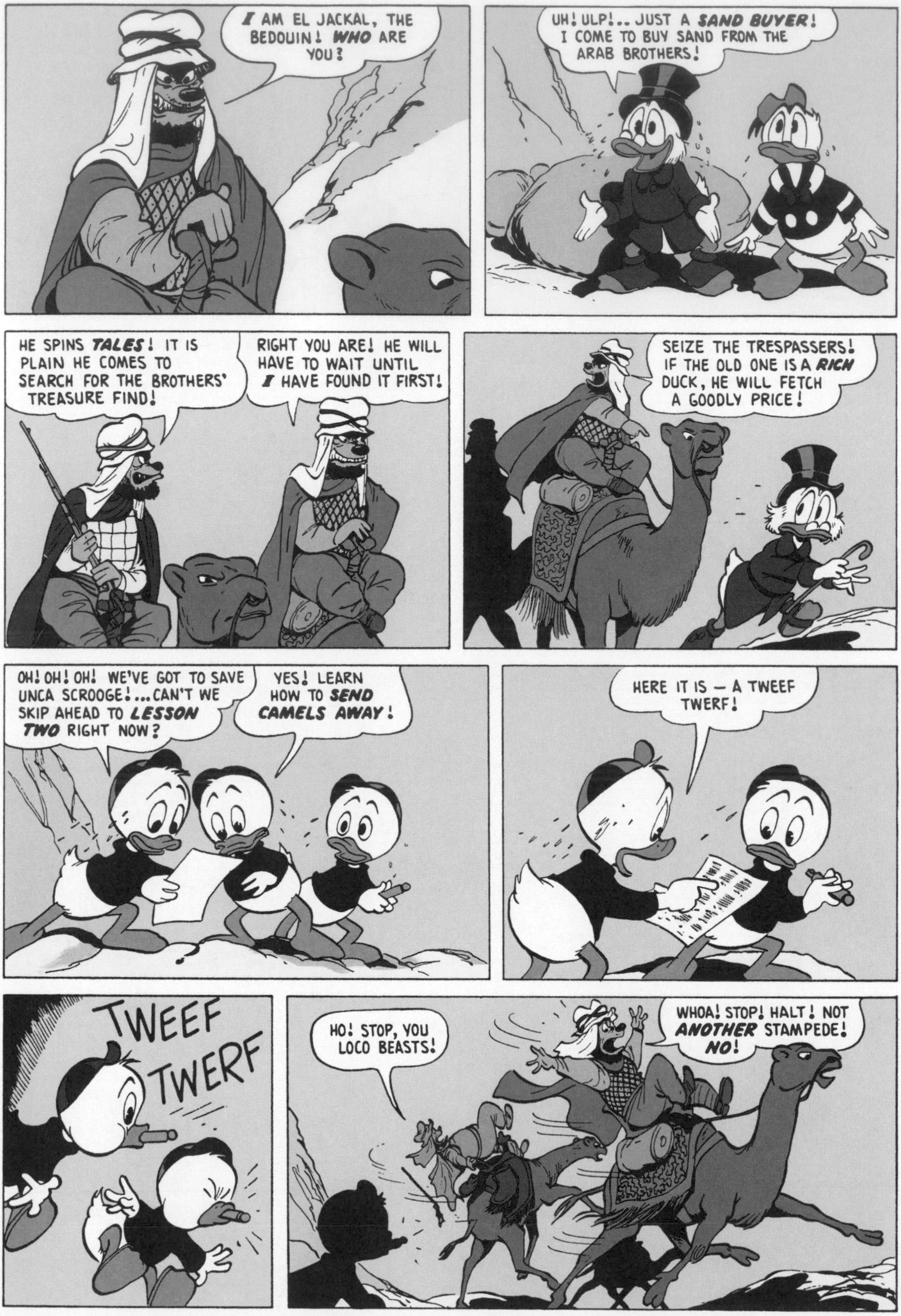
I AM EL JACKAL, THE BEDOUIN! WHO ARE YOU?
UH! ULP!.. JUST A SAND BUYER! I COME TO BUY SAND FROM THE ARAB BROTHERS!
HE SPINS TALES! IT IS PLAIN HE COMES TO SEARCH FOR THE BROTHERS' TREASURE FIND!
RIGHT YOU ARE! HE WILL HAVE TO WAIT UNTIL I HAVE FOUND IT FIRST!
SEIZE THE TRESPASSERS! IF THE OLD ONE IS A RICH DUCK, HE WILL FETCH A GOODLY PRICE!
OH! OH! OH! WE'VE GOT TO SAVE UNCA SCROOGE!...CAN'T WE SKIP AHEAD TO LESSON TWO RIGHT NOW?
YES! LEARN HOW TO SEND CAMELS AWAY!
HERE IT IS — A TWEEF TWERF!
TWEEF TWERF
HO! STOP, YOU LOCO BEASTS!
WHOA! STOP! HALT! NOT ANOTHER STAMPEDE! NO!

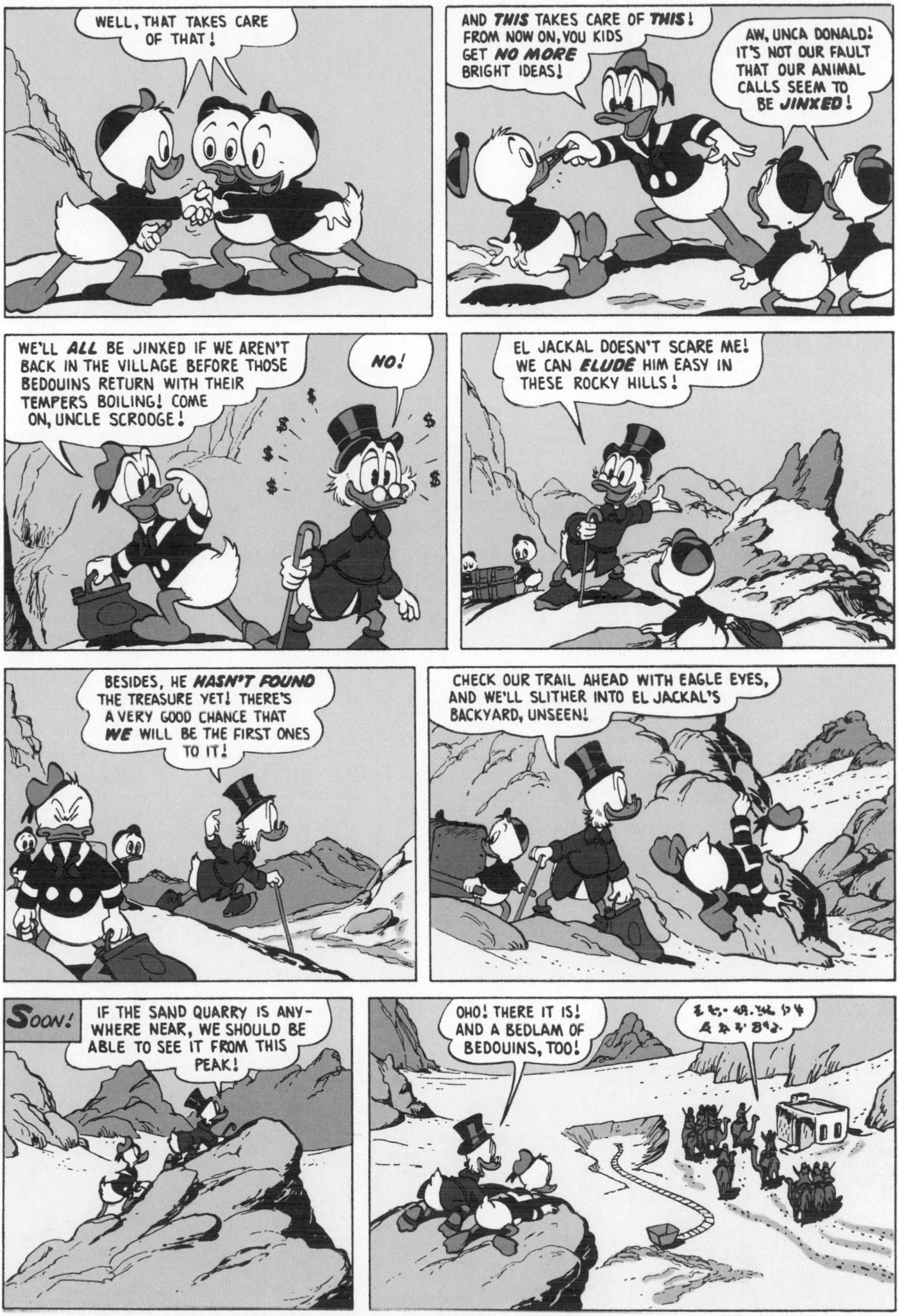
WELL, THAT TAKES CARE OF THAT!
AND THIS TAKES CARE OF THIS! FROM NOW ON, YOU KIDS GET NO MORE BRIGHT IDEAS!
AW, UNCA DONALD! IT'S NOT OUR FAULT THAT OUR ANIMAL CALLS SEEM TO BE JINXED!
WE'LL ALL BE JINXED IF WE AREN'T BACK IN THE VILLAGE BEFORE THOSE BEDOUINS RETURN WITH THEIR TEMPERS BOILING! COME ON, UNCLE SCROOGE!
NO!
EL JACKAL DOESN'T SCARE ME! WE CAN ELUDE HIM EASY IN THESE ROCKY HILLS!
BESIDES, HE HASN'T FOUND THE TREASURE YET! THERE'S A VERY GOOD CHANCE THAT WE WILL BE THE FIRST ONES TO IT!
CHECK OUR TRAIL AHEAD WITH EAGLE EYES, AND WE'LL SLITHER INTO EL JACKAL'S BACKYARD, UNSEEN!
SOON!
IF THE SAND QUARRY IS ANYWHERE NEAR, WE SHOULD BE ABLE TO SEE IT FROM THIS PEAK!
OHO! THERE IT IS! AND A BEDLAM OF BEDOUINS, TOO!

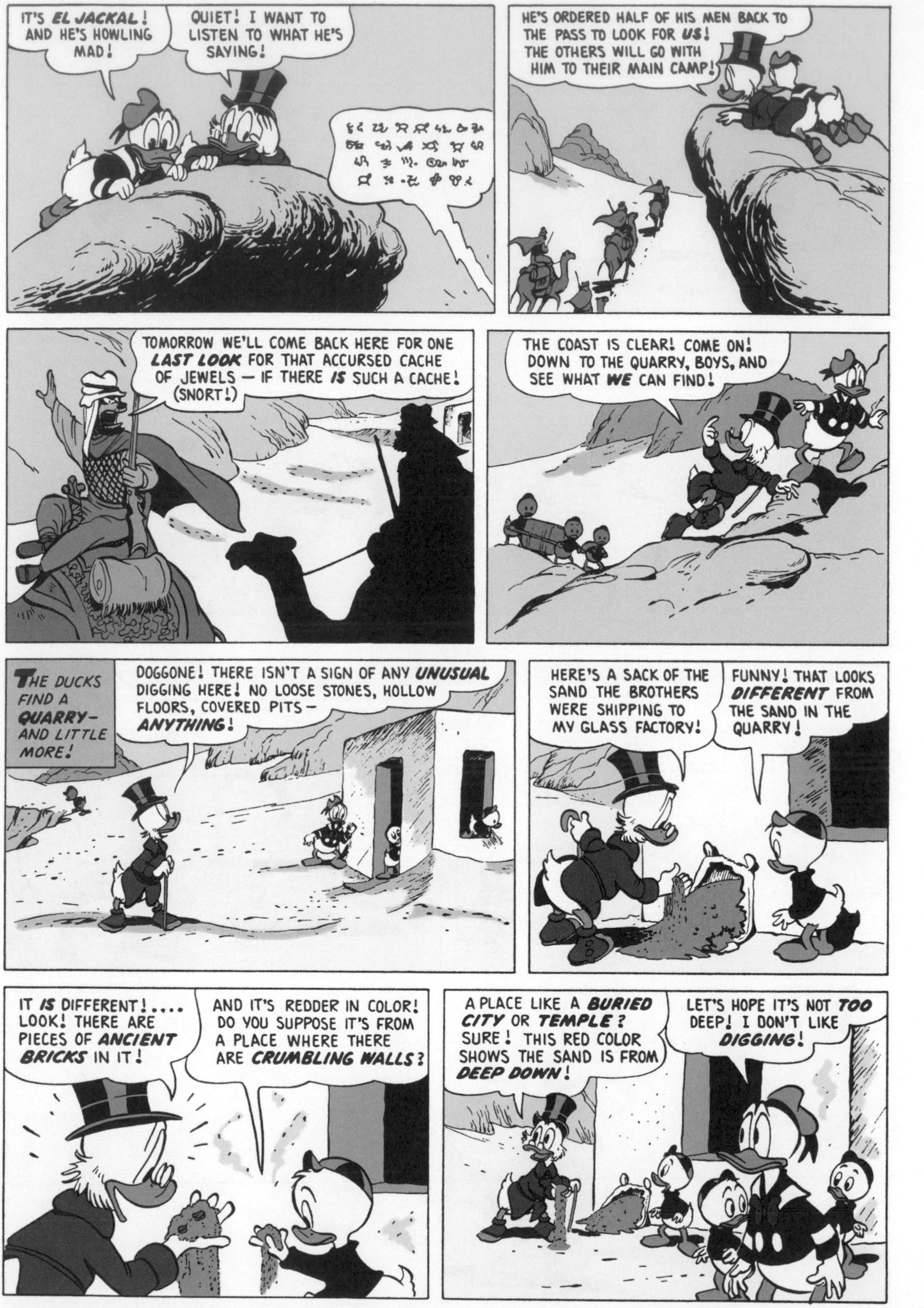
IT'S EL JACKAL! AND HE'S HOWLING MAD!
QUIET! I WANT TO LISTEN TO WHAT HE'S SAYING!
HE'S ORDERED HALF OF HIS MEN BACK TO THE PASS TO LOOK FOR US! THE OTHERS WILL GO WITH HIM TO THEIR MAIN CAMP!
TOMORROW WE'LL COME BACK HERE FOR ONE LAST LOOK FOR THAT ACCURSED CACHE OF JEWELS — IF THERE IS SUCH A CACHE! (SNORT!)
THE COAST IS CLEAR! COME ON! DOWN TO THE QUARRY, BOYS, AND SEE WHAT WE CAN FIND!
THE DUCKS FIND A QUARRY— AND LITTLE MORE!
DOGGONE! THERE ISN'T A SIGN OF ANY UNUSUAL DIGGING HERE! NO LOOSE STONES, HOLLOW FLOORS, COVERED PITS — ANYTHING!
HERE'S A SACK OF THE SAND THE BROTHERS WERE SHIPPING TO MY GLASS FACTORY!
FUNNY! THAT LOOKS DIFFERENT FROM THE SAND IN THE QUARRY!
IT IS DIFFERENT!.... LOOK! THERE ARE PIECES OF ANCIENT BRICKS IN IT!
AND IT'S REDDER IN COLOR! DO YOU SUPPOSE IT'S FROM A PLACE WHERE THERE ARE CRUMBLING WALLS?
A PLACE LIKE A BURIED CITY OR TEMPLE? SURE! THIS RED COLOR SHOWS THE SAND IS FROM DEEP DOWN!
LET'S HOPE IT'S NOT TOO DEEP! I DON'T LIKE DIGGING!

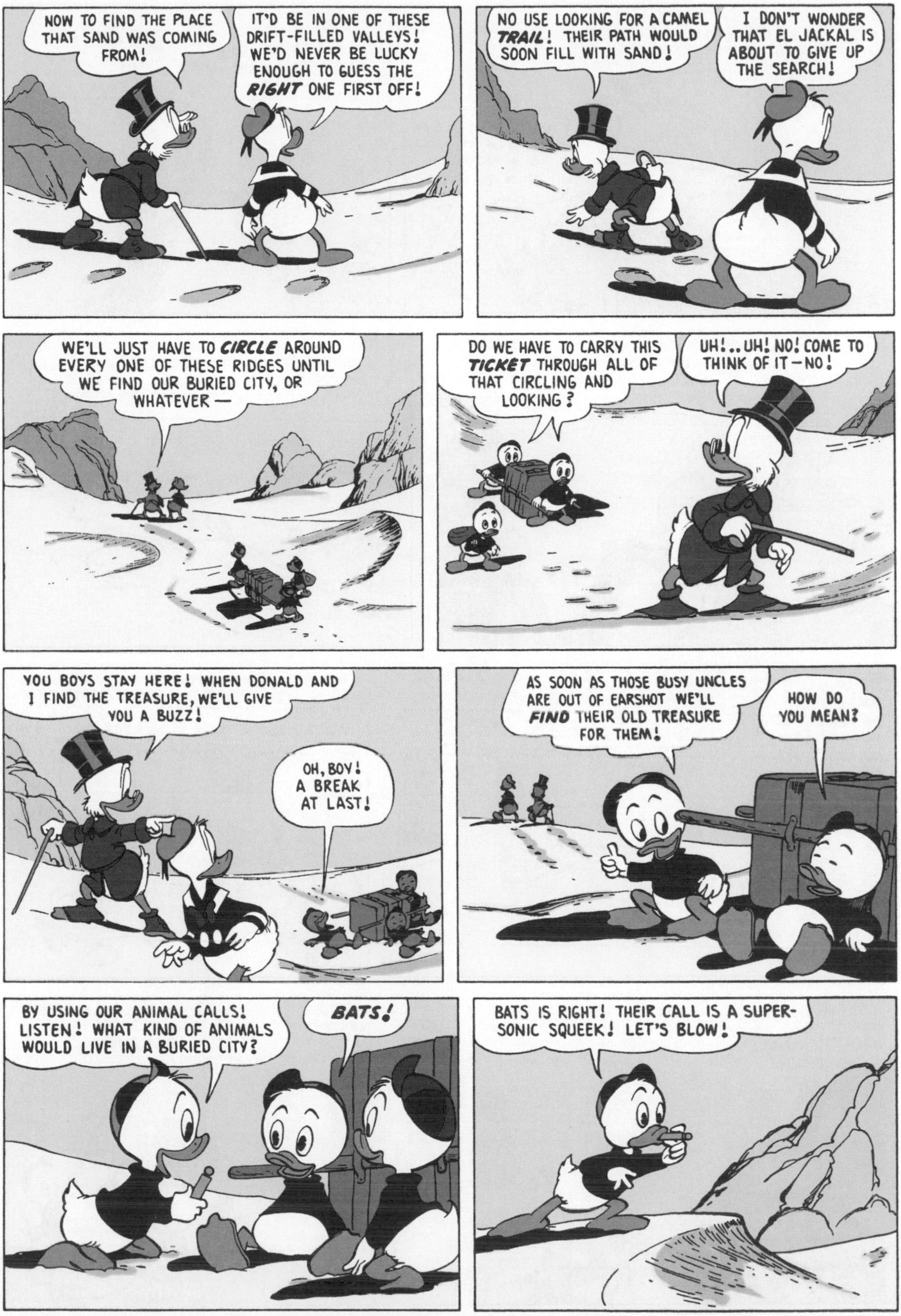
NOW TO FIND THE PLACE THAT SAND WAS COMING FROM!
IT'D BE IN ONE OF THESE DRIFT-FILLED VALLEYS! WE'D NEVER BE LUCKY ENOUGH TO GUESS THE RIGHT ONE FIRST OFF!
NO USE LOOKING FOR A CAMEL TRAIL! THEIR PATH WOULD SOON FILL WITH SAND!
I DON'T WONDER THAT EL JACKAL IS ABOUT TO GIVE UP THE SEARCH!
WE'LL JUST HAVE TO CIRCLE AROUND EVERY ONE OF THESE RIDGES UNTIL WE FIND OUR BURIED CITY, OR WHATEVER —
DO WE HAVE TO CARRY THIS TICKET THROUGH ALL OF THAT CIRCLING AND LOOKING?
UH!..UH! NO! COME TO THINK OF IT — NO!
YOU BOYS STAY HERE! WHEN DONALD AND I FIND THE TREASURE, WE'LL GIVE YOU A BUZZ!
OH, BOY! A BREAK AT LAST!
AS SOON AS THOSE BUSY UNCLES ARE OUT OF EARSHOT WE'LL FIND THEIR OLD TREASURE FOR THEM!
HOW DO YOU MEAN?
BY USING OUR ANIMAL CALLS! LISTEN! WHAT KIND OF ANIMALS WOULD LIVE IN A BURIED CITY?
BATS!
BATS IS RIGHT! THEIR CALL IS A SUPER-SONIC SQUEEK! LET'S BLOW!

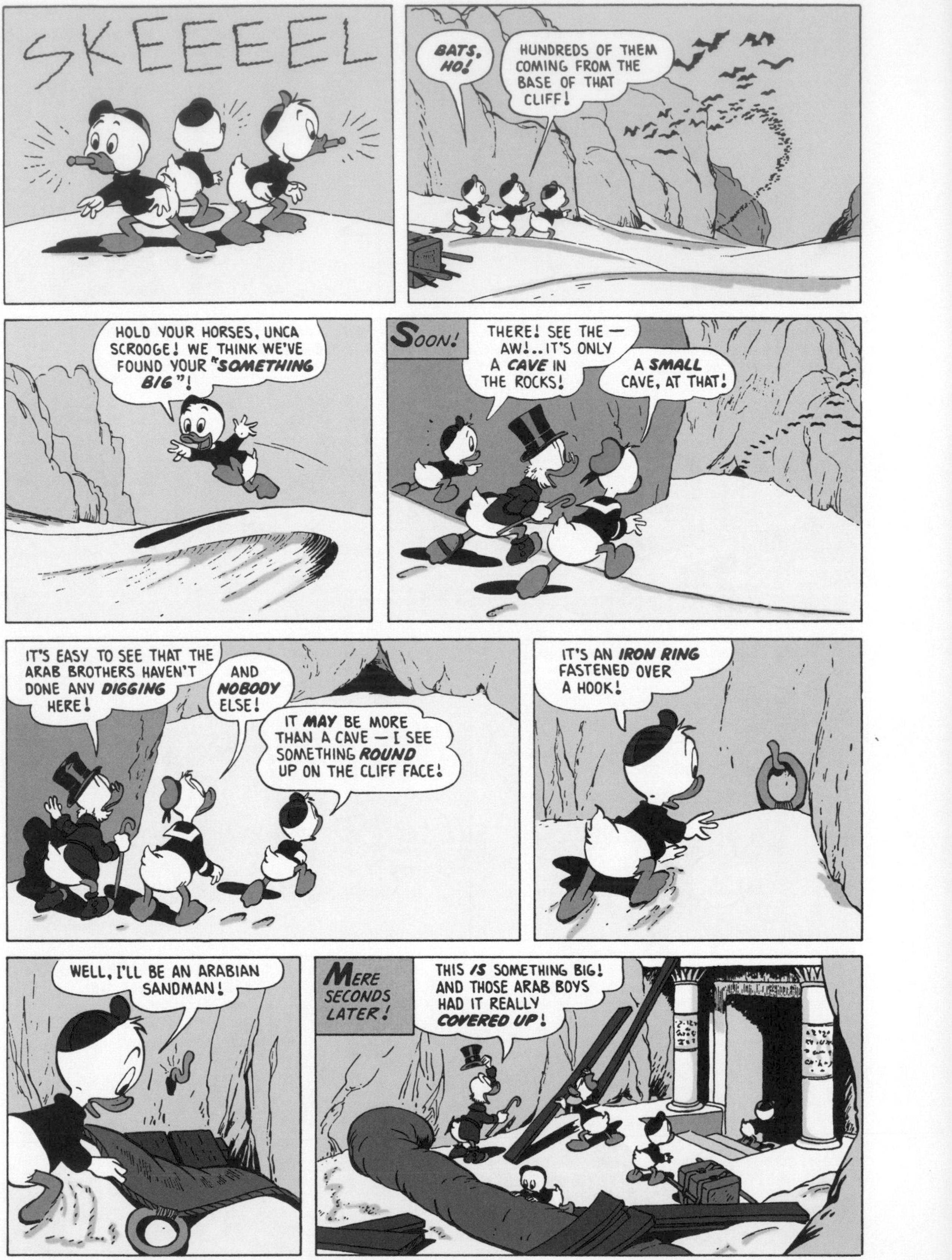
SKEEEEL
BATS, HO!
HUNDREDS OF THEM COMING FROM THE BASE OF THAT CLIFF!
HOLD YOUR HORSES, UNCA SCROOGE! WE THINK WE'VE FOUND YOUR "SOMETHING BIG"!
SOON!
THERE! SEE THE — AW!..IT'S ONLY A CAVE IN THE ROCKS!
A SMALL CAVE, AT THAT!
IT'S EASY TO SEE THAT THE ARAB BROTHERS HAVEN'T DONE ANY DIGGING HERE!
AND NOBODY ELSE!
IT MAY BE MORE THAN A CAVE — I SEE SOMETHING ROUND UP ON THE CLIFF FACE!
IT'S AN IRON RING FASTENED OVER A HOOK!
WELL, I'LL BE AN ARABIAN SANDMAN!
MERE SECONDS LATER!
THIS IS SOMETHING BIG! AND THOSE ARAB BOYS HAD IT REALLY COVERED UP!

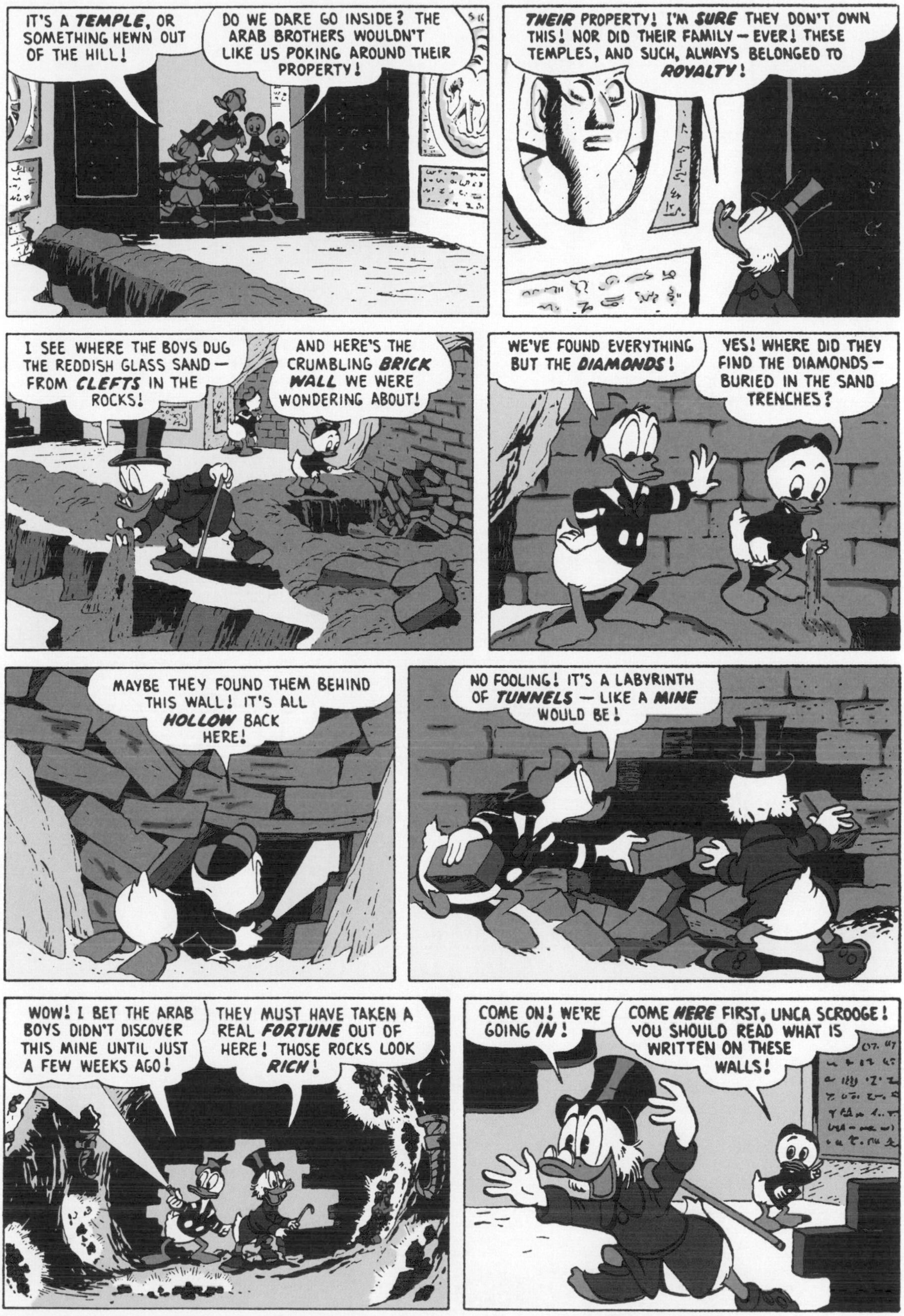
IT'S A TEMPLE, OR SOMETHING HEWN OUT OF THE HILL!
DO WE DARE GO INSIDE? THE ARAB BROTHERS WOULDN'T LIKE US POKING AROUND THEIR PROPERTY!
THEIR PROPERTY! I'M SURE THEY DON'T OWN THIS! NOR DID THEIR FAMILY — EVER! THESE TEMPLES, AND SUCH, ALWAYS BELONGED TO ROYALTY!
I SEE WHERE THE BOYS DUG THE REDDISH GLASS SAND — FROM CLEFTS IN THE ROCKS!
AND HERE'S THE CRUMBLING BRICK WALL WE WERE WONDERING ABOUT!
WE'VE FOUND EVERYTHING BUT THE DIAMONDS!
YES! WHERE DID THEY FIND THE DIAMONDS — BURIED IN THE SAND TRENCHES?
MAYBE THEY FOUND THEM BEHIND THIS WALL! IT'S ALL HOLLOW BACK HERE!
NO FOOLING! IT'S A LABYRINTH OF TUNNELS — LIKE A MINE WOULD BE!
WOW! I BET THE ARAB BOYS DIDN'T DISCOVER THIS MINE UNTIL JUST A FEW WEEKS AGO!
THEY MUST HAVE TAKEN A REAL FORTUNE OUT OF HERE! THOSE ROCKS LOOK RICH!
COME ON! WE'RE GOING IN!
COME HERE FIRST, UNCA SCROOGE! YOU SHOULD READ WHAT IS WRITTEN ON THESE WALLS!

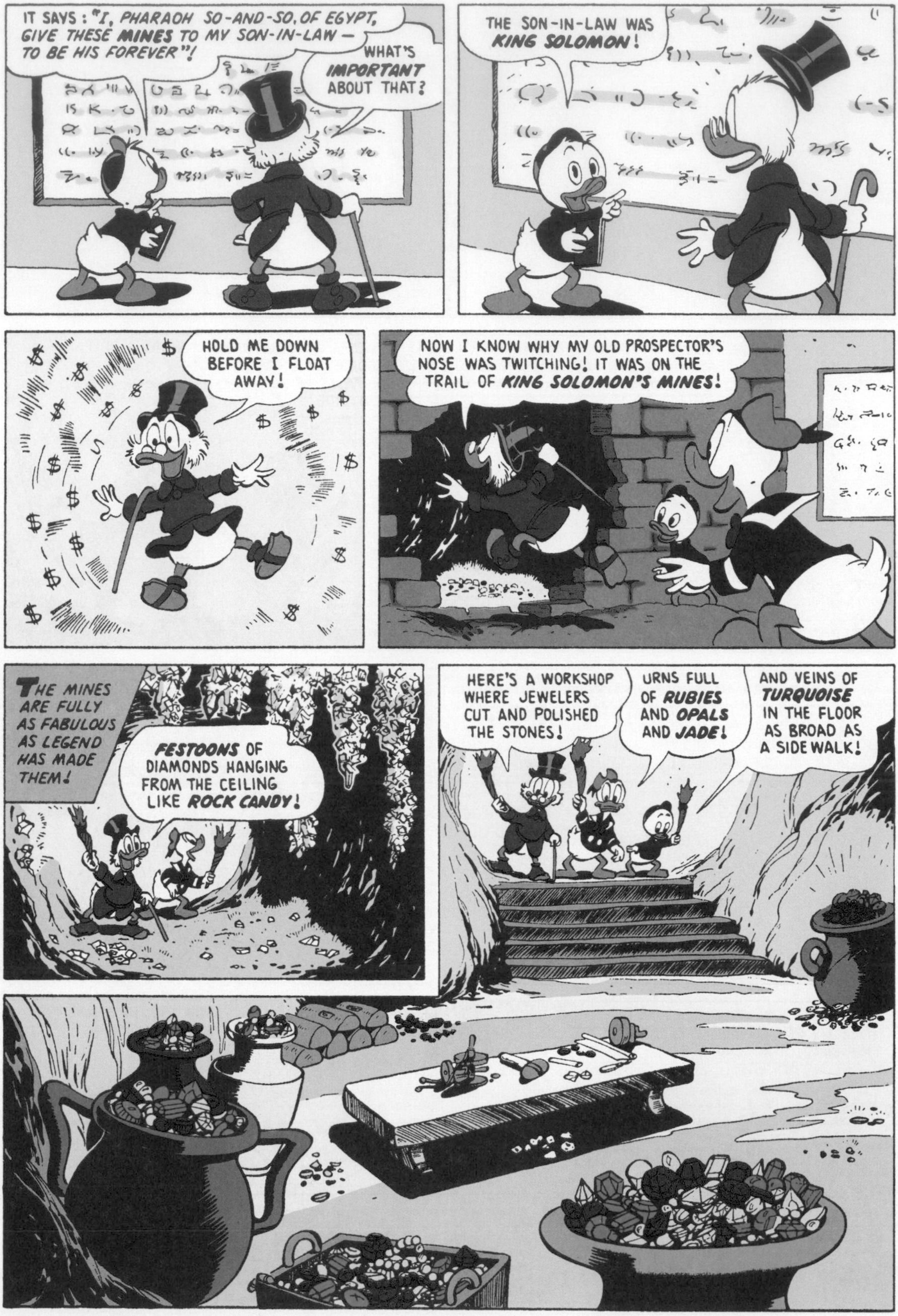
IT SAYS: "I, PHARAOH SO-AND-SO, OF EGYPT, GIVE THESE MINES TO MY SON-IN-LAW — TO BE HIS FOREVER"!
WHAT'S IMPORTANT ABOUT THAT?
THE SON-IN-LAW WAS KING SOLOMON!
HOLD ME DOWN BEFORE I FLOAT AWAY!
NOW I KNOW WHY MY OLD PROSPECTOR'S NOSE WAS TWITCHING! IT WAS ON THE TRAIL OF KING SOLOMON'S MINES!
THE MINES ARE FULLY AS FABULOUS AS LEGEND HAS MADE THEM!
FESTOONS OF DIAMONDS HANGING FROM THE CEILING LIKE ROCK CANDY!
HERE'S A WORKSHOP WHERE JEWELERS CUT AND POLISHED THE STONES!
URNS FULL OF RUBIES AND OPALS AND JADE!
AND VEINS OF TURQUOISE IN THE FLOOR AS BROAD AS A SIDEWALK!

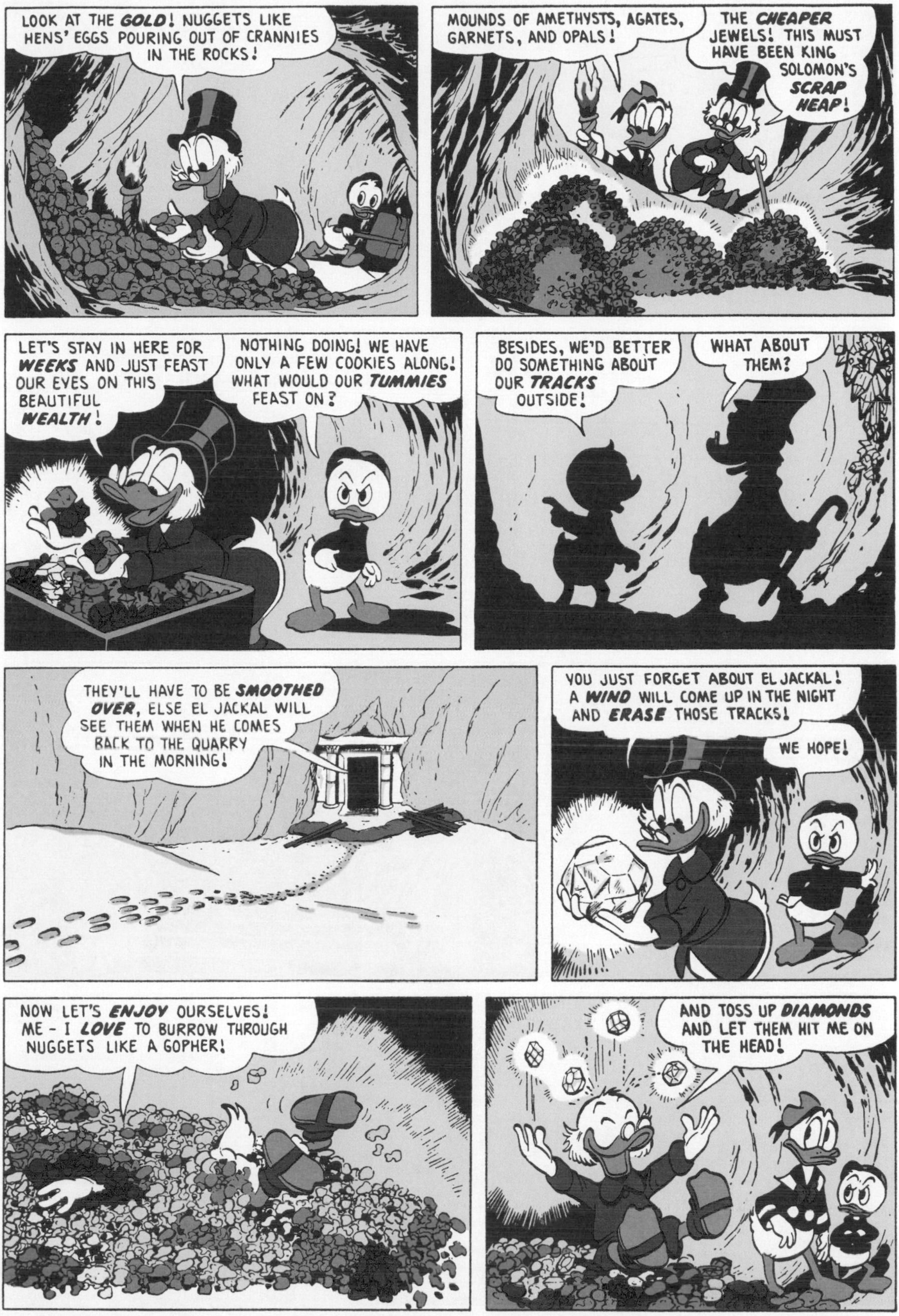

LOOK AT THE GOLD! NUGGETS LIKE HENS' EGGS POURING OUT OF CRANNIES IN THE ROCKS!
MOUNDS OF AMETHYSTS, AGATES, GARNETS, AND OPALS!
THE CHEAPER JEWELS! THIS MUST HAVE BEEN KING SOLOMON'S SCRAP HEAP!
LET'S STAY IN HERE FOR WEEKS AND JUST FEAST OUR EYES ON THIS BEAUTIFUL WEALTH!
NOTHING DOING! WE HAVE ONLY A FEW COOKIES ALONG! WHAT WOULD OUR TUMMIES FEAST ON?
BESIDES, WE'D BETTER DO SOMETHING ABOUT OUR TRACKS OUTSIDE!
WHAT ABOUT THEM?
THEY'LL HAVE TO BE SMOOTHED OVER, ELSE EL JACKAL WILL SEE THEM WHEN HE COMES BACK TO THE QUARRY IN THE MORNING!
YOU JUST FORGET ABOUT EL JACKAL! A WIND WILL COME UP IN THE NIGHT AND ERASE THOSE TRACKS!
WE HOPE!
NOW LET'S ENJOY OURSELVES! ME - I LOVE TO BURROW THROUGH NUGGETS LIKE A GOPHER!
AND TOSS UP DIAMONDS AND LET THEM HIT ME ON THE HEAD!

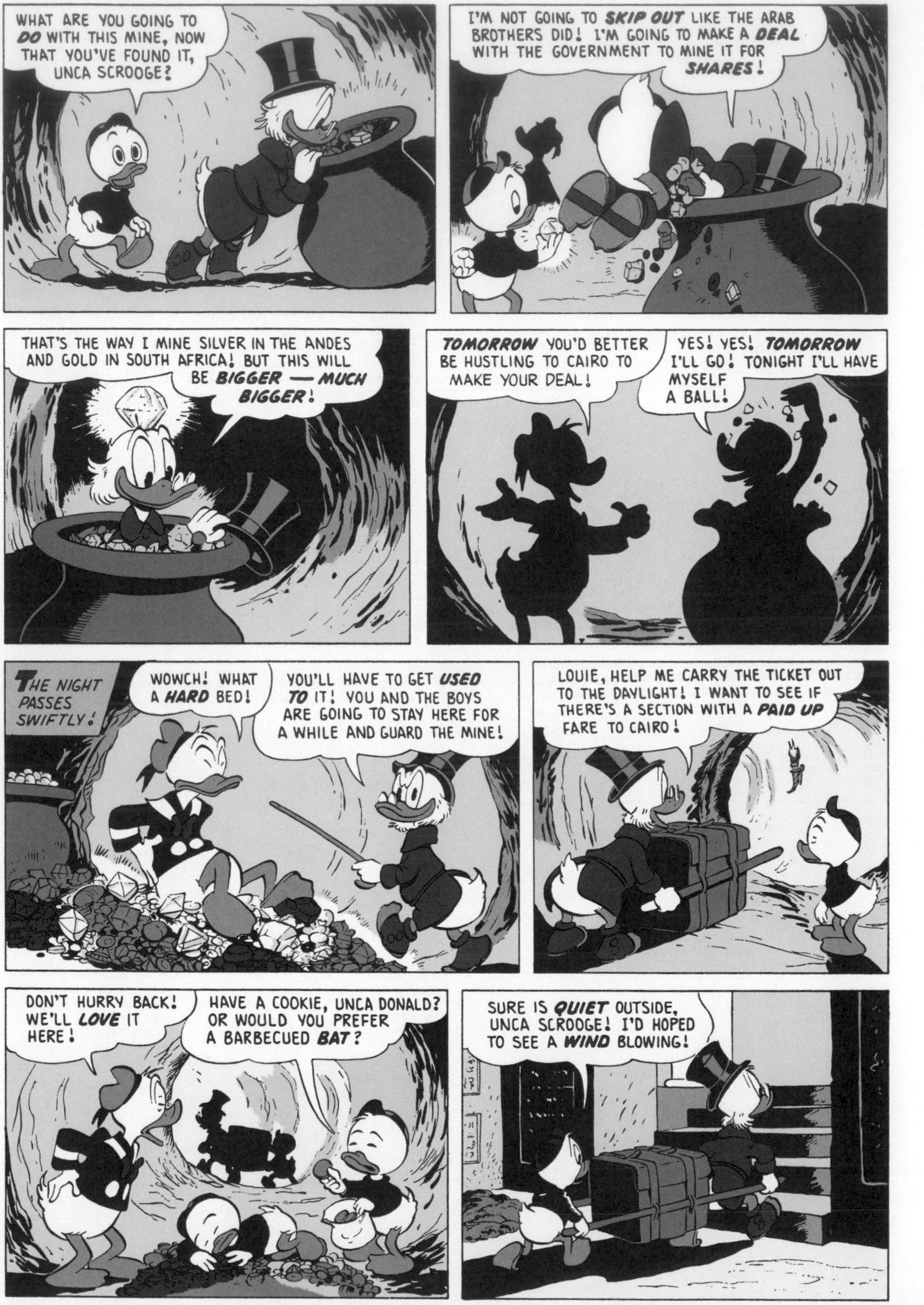
WHAT ARE YOU GOING TO DO WITH THIS MINE, NOW THAT YOU'VE FOUND IT, UNCA SCROOGE?
I'M NOT GOING TO SKIP OUT LIKE THE ARAB BROTHERS DID! I'M GOING TO MAKE A DEAL WITH THE GOVERNMENT TO MINE IT FOR SHARES!
THAT'S THE WAY I MINE SILVER IN THE ANDES AND GOLD IN SOUTH AFRICA! BUT THIS WILL BE BIGGER — MUCH BIGGER!
TOMORROW YOU'D BETTER BE HUSTLING TO CAIRO TO MAKE YOUR DEAL!
YES! YES! TOMORROW I'LL GO! TONIGHT I'LL HAVE MYSELF A BALL!
THE NIGHT PASSES SWIFTLY!
WOWCH! WHAT A HARD BED!
YOU'LL HAVE TO GET USED TO IT! YOU AND THE BOYS ARE GOING TO STAY HERE FOR A WHILE AND GUARD THE MINE!
LOUIE, HELP ME CARRY THE TICKET OUT TO THE DAYLIGHT! I WANT TO SEE IF THERE'S A SECTION WITH A PAID UP FARE TO CAIRO!
DON'T HURRY BACK! WE'LL LOVE IT HERE!
HAVE A COOKIE, UNCA DONALD? OR WOULD YOU PREFER A BARBECUED BAT?
SURE IS QUIET OUTSIDE, UNCA SCROOGE! I'D HOPED TO SEE A WIND BLOWING!

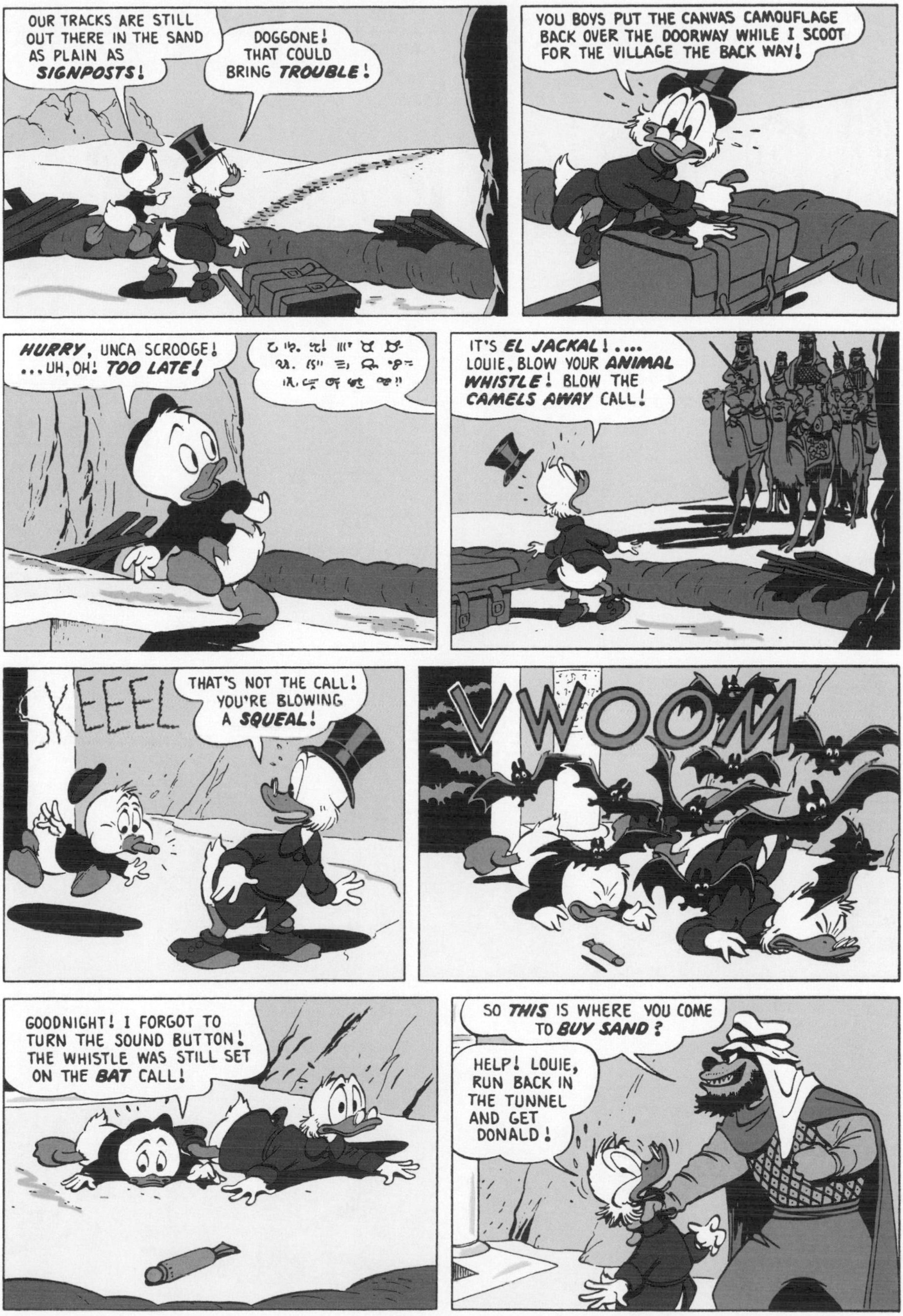

OUR TRACKS ARE STILL OUT THERE IN THE SAND AS PLAIN AS SIGNPOSTS!
DOGGONE! THAT COULD BRING TROUBLE!
YOU BOYS PUT THE CANVAS CAMOUFLAGE BACK OVER THE DOORWAY WHILE I SCOOT FOR THE VILLAGE THE BACK WAY!
HURRY, UNCA SCROOGE! ...UH, OH! TOO LATE!
IT'S EL JACKAL!.... LOUIE, BLOW YOUR ANIMAL WHISTLE! BLOW THE CAMELS AWAY CALL!
SKEEEL
THAT'S NOT THE CALL! YOU'RE BLOWING A SQUEAL!
VWOOM
GOODNIGHT! I FORGOT TO TURN THE SOUND BUTTON! THE WHISTLE WAS STILL SET ON THE BAT CALL!
SO THIS IS WHERE YOU COME TO BUY SAND?
HELP! LOUIE, RUN BACK IN THE TUNNEL AND GET DONALD!

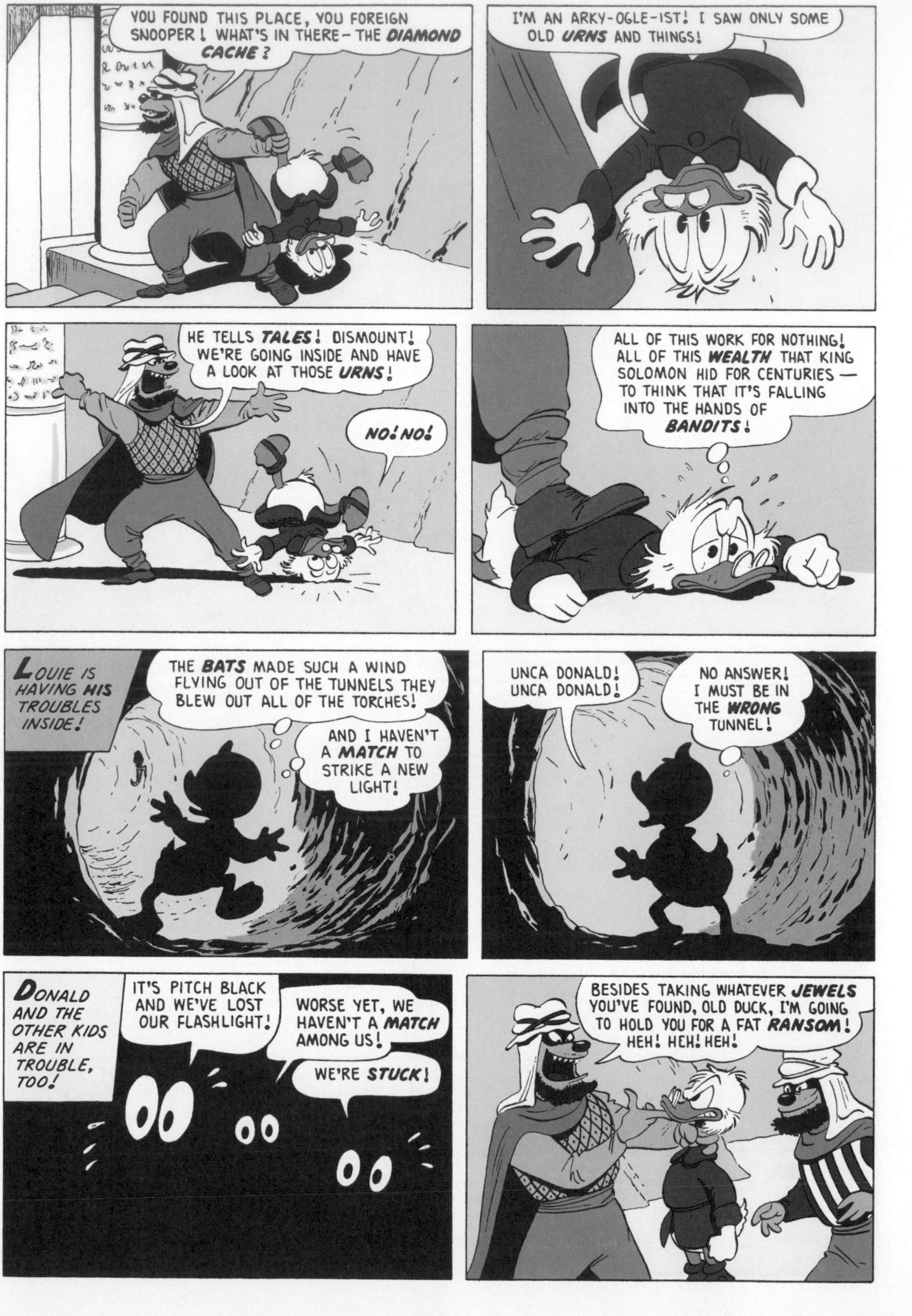
YOU FOUND THIS PLACE, YOU FOREIGN SNOOPER! WHAT'S IN THERE– THE DIAMOND CACHE?
I'M AN ARKY-OGLE-IST! I SAW ONLY SOME OLD URNS AND THINGS!
HE TELLS TALES! DISMOUNT! WE'RE GOING INSIDE AND HAVE A LOOK AT THOSE URNS!
NO! NO!
ALL OF THIS WORK FOR NOTHING! ALL OF THIS WEALTH THAT KING SOLOMON HID FOR CENTURIES — TO THINK THAT IT'S FALLING INTO THE HANDS OF BANDITS!
LOUIE IS HAVING HIS TROUBLES INSIDE!
THE BATS MADE SUCH A WIND FLYING OUT OF THE TUNNELS THEY BLEW OUT ALL OF THE TORCHES!
AND I HAVEN'T A MATCH TO STRIKE A NEW LIGHT!
UNCA DONALD! UNCA DONALD!
NO ANSWER! I MUST BE IN THE WRONG TUNNEL!
DONALD AND THE OTHER KIDS ARE IN TROUBLE, TOO!
IT'S PITCH BLACK AND WE'VE LOST OUR FLASHLIGHT!
WORSE YET, WE HAVEN'T A MATCH AMONG US!
WE'RE STUCK!
BESIDES TAKING WHATEVER JEWELS YOU'VE FOUND, OLD DUCK, I'M GOING TO HOLD YOU FOR A FAT RANSOM! HEH! HEH! HEH!

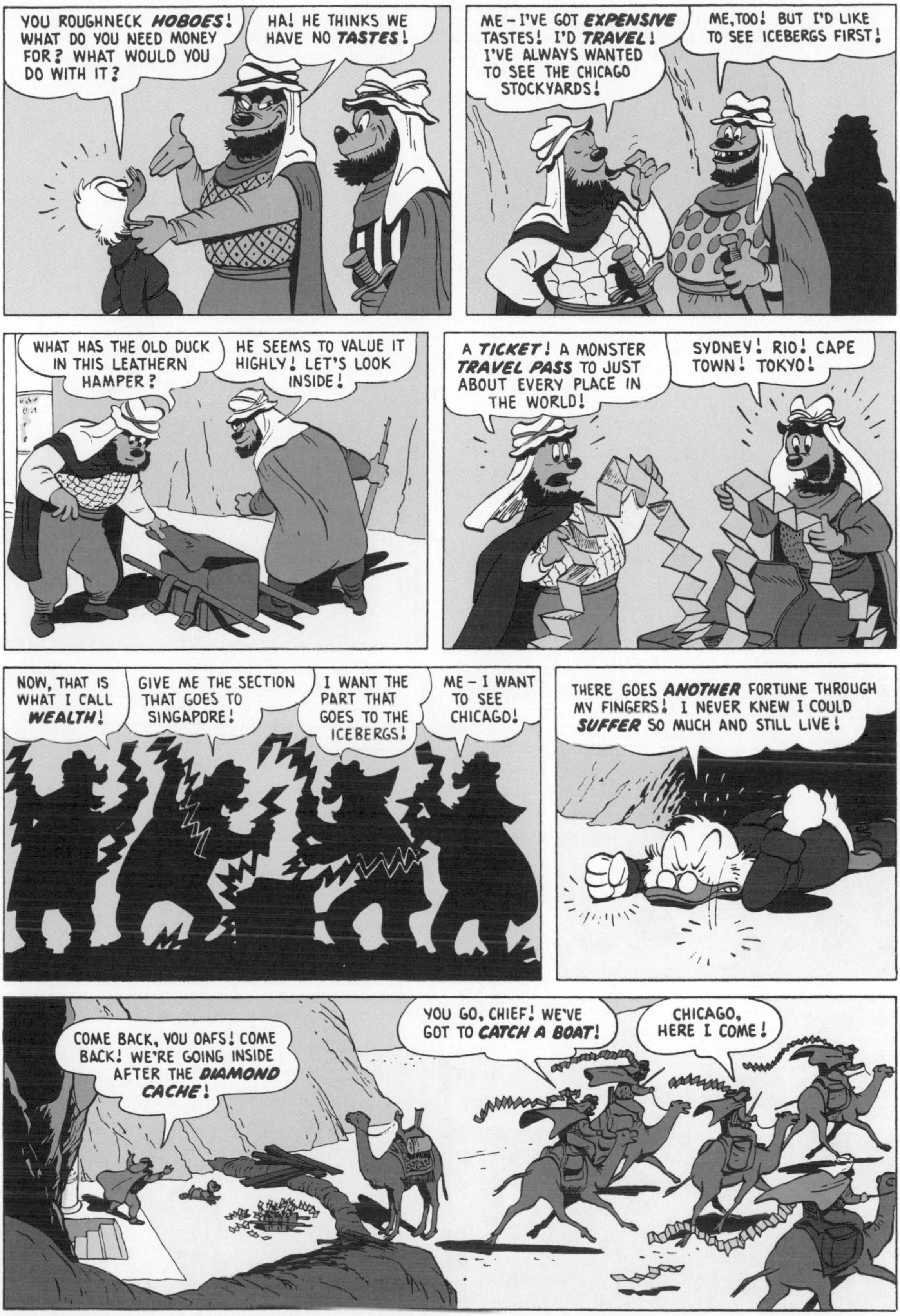
YOU ROUGHNECK HOBOES! WHAT DO YOU NEED MONEY FOR? WHAT WOULD YOU DO WITH IT?
HA! HE THINKS WE HAVE NO TASTES!
ME - I'VE GOT EXPENSIVE TASTES! I'D TRAVEL! I'VE ALWAYS WANTED TO SEE THE CHICAGO STOCKYARDS!
ME, TOO! BUT I'D LIKE TO SEE ICEBERGS FIRST!
WHAT HAS THE OLD DUCK IN THIS LEATHERN HAMPER?
HE SEEMS TO VALUE IT HIGHLY! LET'S LOOK INSIDE!
A TICKET! A MONSTER TRAVEL PASS TO JUST ABOUT EVERY PLACE IN THE WORLD!
SYDNEY! RIO! CAPE TOWN! TOKYO!
NOW, THAT IS WHAT I CALL WEALTH!
GIVE ME THE SECTION THAT GOES TO SINGAPORE!
I WANT THE PART THAT GOES TO THE ICEBERGS!
ME - I WANT TO SEE CHICAGO!
THERE GOES ANOTHER FORTUNE THROUGH MY FINGERS! I NEVER KNEW I COULD SUFFER SO MUCH AND STILL LIVE!
COME BACK, YOU OAFS! COME BACK! WE'RE GOING INSIDE AFTER THE DIAMOND CACHE!
YOU GO, CHIEF! WE'VE GOT TO CATCH A BOAT!
CHICAGO, HERE I COME!

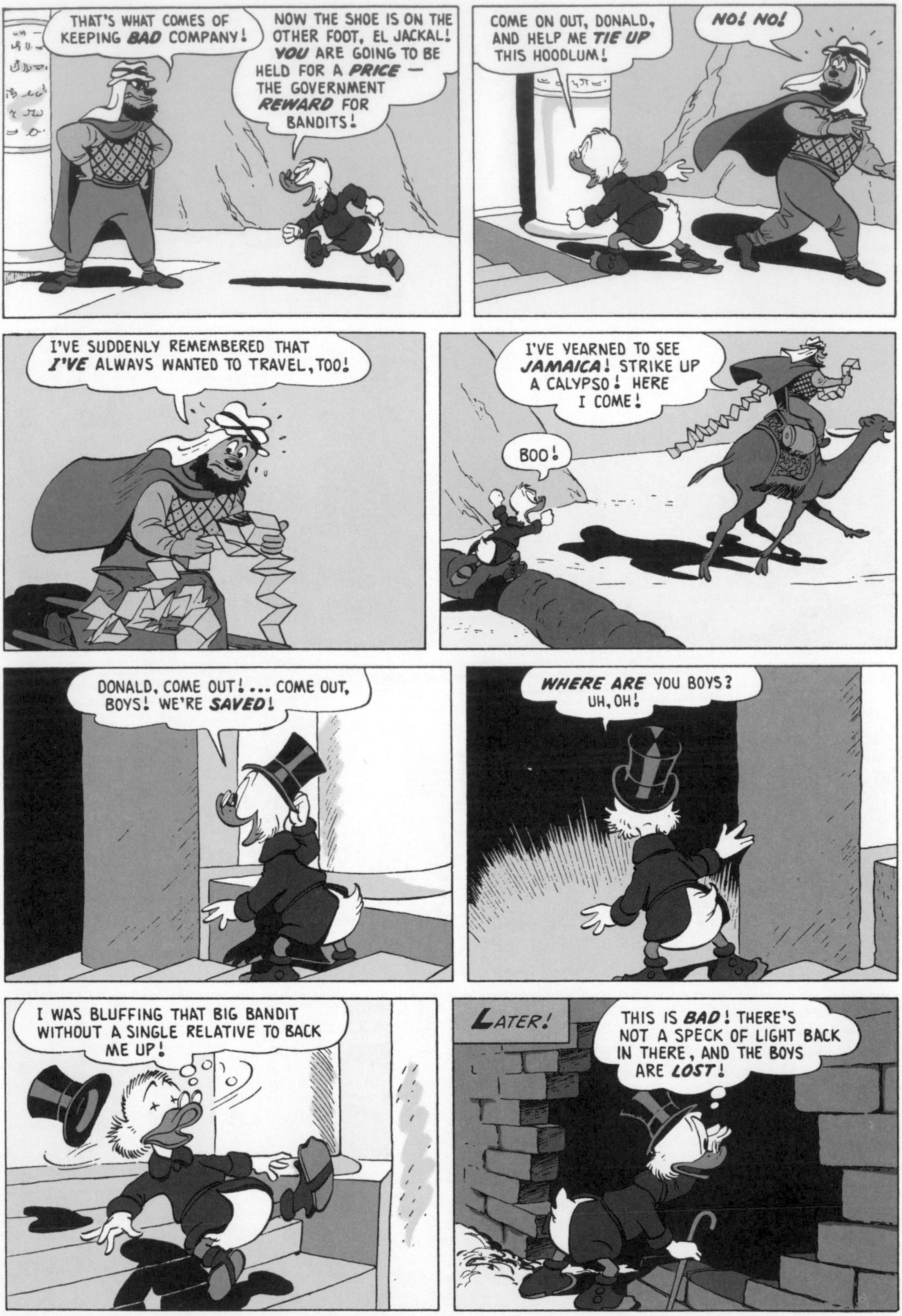
THAT'S WHAT COMES OF KEEPING BAD COMPANY!
NOW THE SHOE IS ON THE OTHER FOOT, EL JACKAL! YOU ARE GOING TO BE HELD FOR A PRICE — THE GOVERNMENT REWARD FOR BANDITS!
COME ON OUT, DONALD, AND HELP ME TIE UP THIS HOODLUM!
NO! NO!
I'VE SUDDENLY REMEMBERED THAT I'VE ALWAYS WANTED TO TRAVEL, TOO!
I'VE YEARNED TO SEE JAMAICA! STRIKE UP A CALYPSO! HERE I COME!
BOO!
DONALD, COME OUT! ... COME OUT, BOYS! WE'RE SAVED!
WHERE ARE YOU BOYS? UH, OH!
I WAS BLUFFING THAT BIG BANDIT WITHOUT A SINGLE RELATIVE TO BACK ME UP!
LATER!
THIS IS BAD! THERE'S NOT A SPECK OF LIGHT BACK IN THERE, AND THE BOYS ARE LOST!

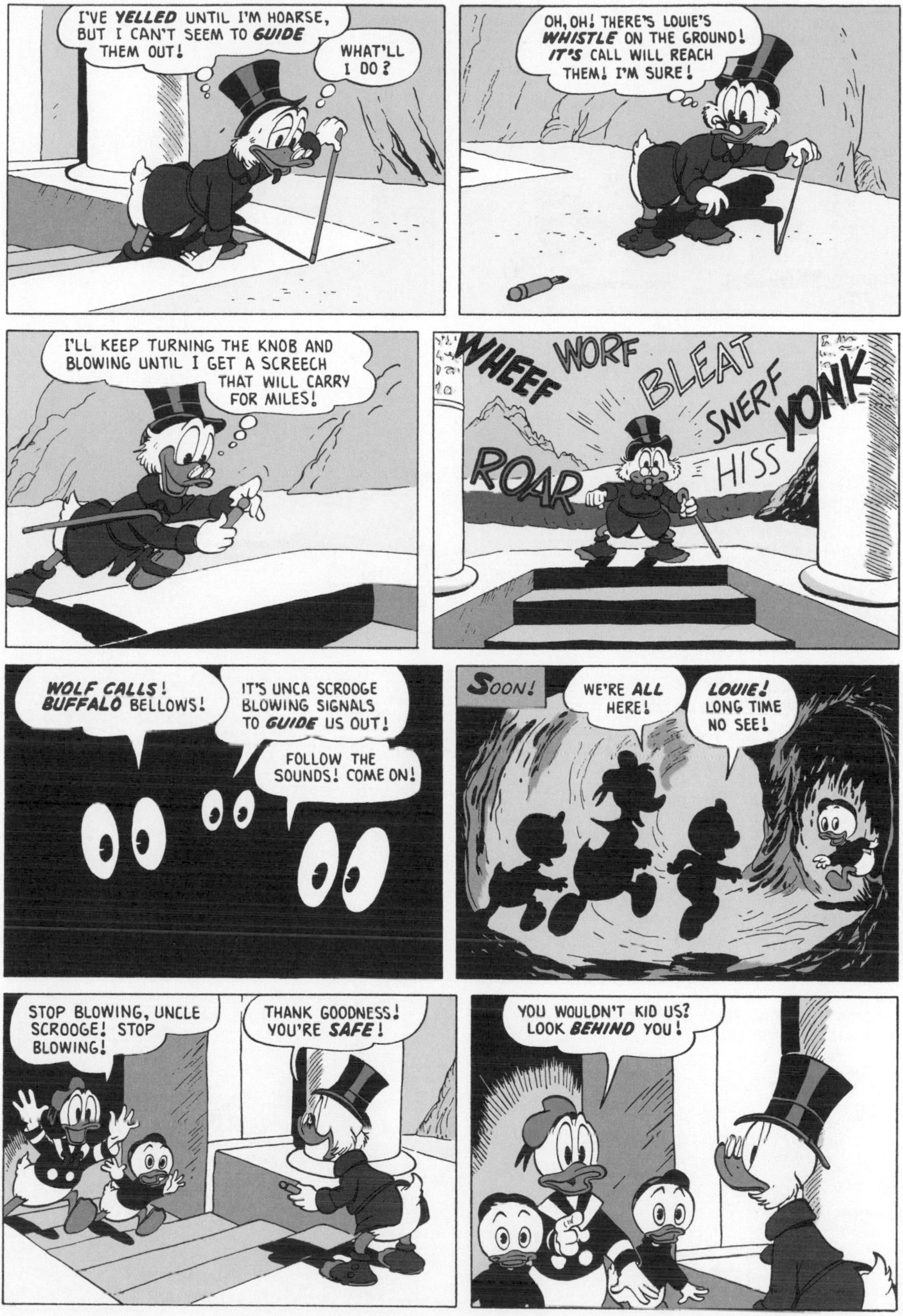
I'VE YELLED UNTIL I'M HOARSE, BUT I CAN'T SEEM TO GUIDE THEM OUT!
WHAT'LL I DO?
OH, OH! THERE'S LOUIE'S WHISTLE ON THE GROUND! IT'S CALL WILL REACH THEM! I'M SURE!
I'LL KEEP TURNING THE KNOB AND BLOWING UNTIL I GET A SCREECH THAT WILL CARRY FOR MILES!
WHEEF
WORF
BLEAT
SNERF
YONK
ROAR
HISS
WOLF CALLS! BUFFALO BELLOWS!
IT'S UNCA SCROOGE BLOWING SIGNALS TO GUIDE US OUT!
FOLLOW THE SOUNDS! COME ON!
SOON!
WE'RE ALL HERE!
LOUIE! LONG TIME NO SEE!
STOP BLOWING, UNCLE SCROOGE! STOP BLOWING!
THANK GOODNESS! YOU'RE SAFE!
YOU WOULDN'T KID US? LOOK BEHIND YOU!

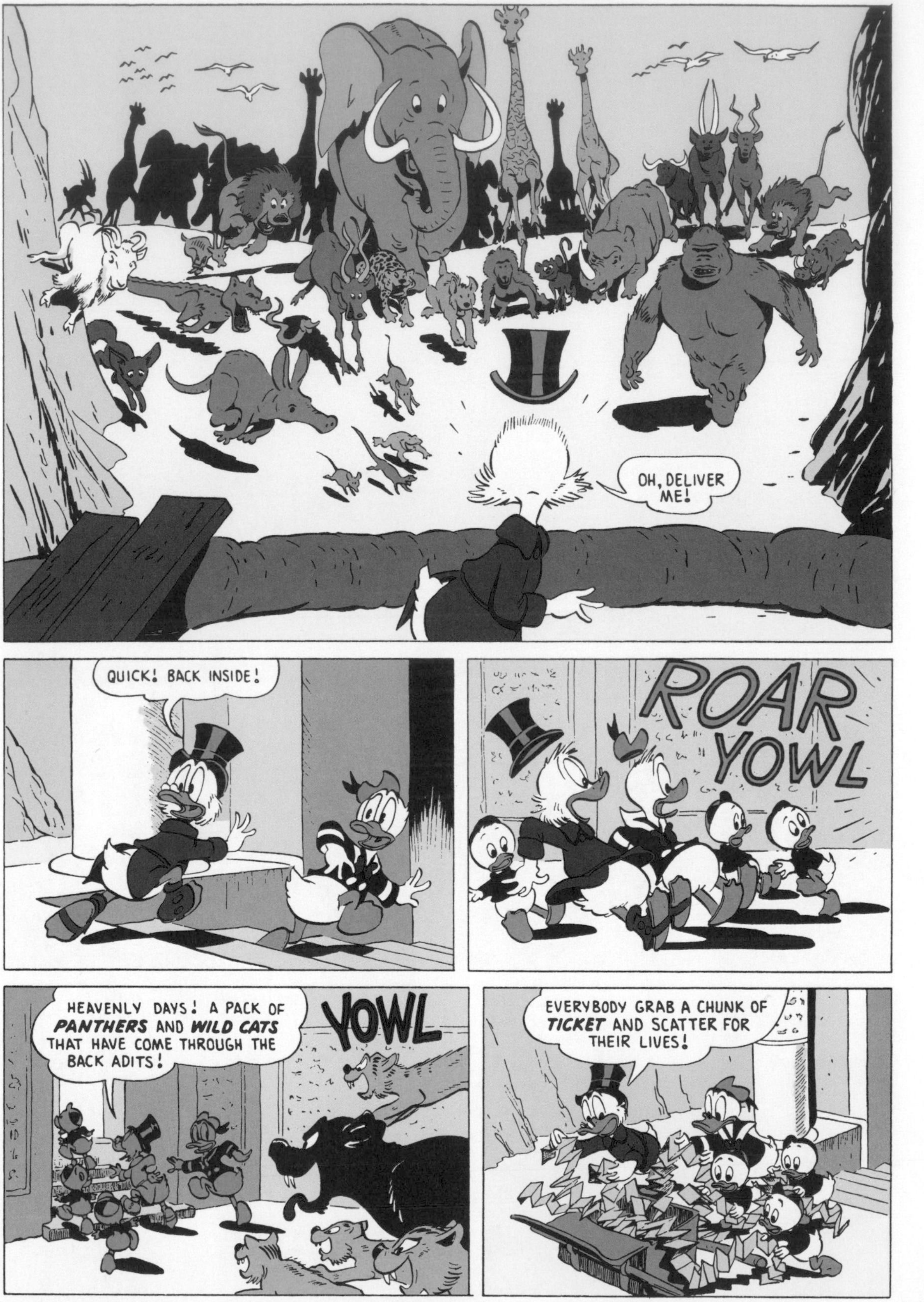
OH, DELIVER ME!
QUICK! BACK INSIDE!
ROAR
YOWL
HEAVENLY DAYS! A PACK OF PANTHERS AND WILD CATS THAT HAVE COME THROUGH THE BACK ADITS!
YOWL
EVERYBODY GRAB A CHUNK OF TICKET AND SCATTER FOR THEIR LIVES!

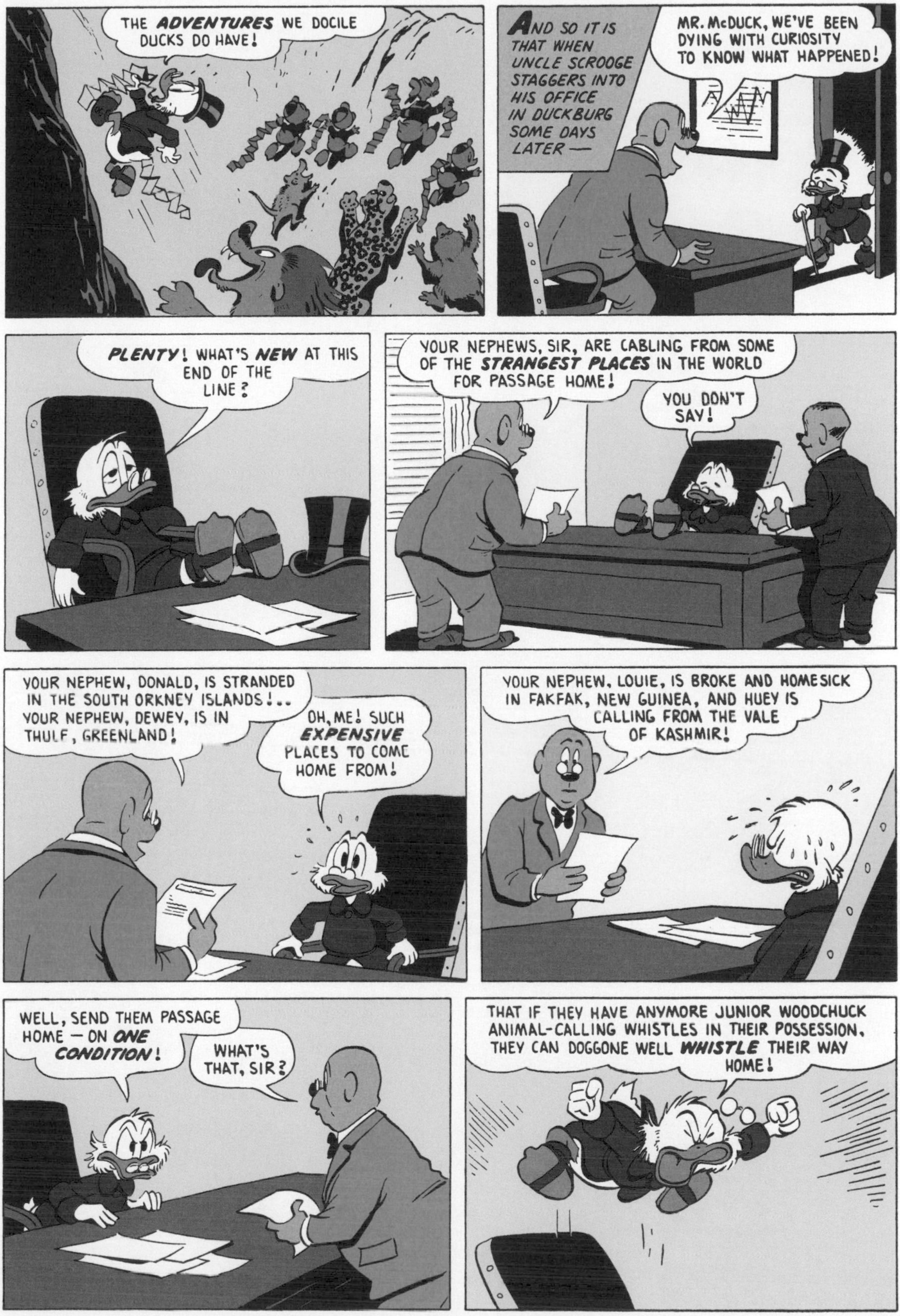
THE ADVENTURES WE DOCILE DUCKS DO HAVE!
AND SO IT IS THAT WHEN UNCLE SCROOGE STAGGERS INTO HIS OFFICE IN DUCKBURG SOME DAYS LATER —
MR. McDUCK, WE'VE BEEN DYING WITH CURIOSITY TO KNOW WHAT HAPPENED!
PLENTY! WHAT'S NEW AT THIS END OF THE LINE?
YOUR NEPHEWS, SIR, ARE CABLING FROM SOME OF THE STRANGEST PLACES IN THE WORLD FOR PASSAGE HOME!
YOU DON'T SAY!
YOUR NEPHEW, DONALD, IS STRANDED IN THE SOUTH ORKNEY ISLANDS!.. YOUR NEPHEW, DEWEY, IS IN THULE, GREENLAND!
OH, ME! SUCH EXPENSIVE PLACES TO COME HOME FROM!
YOUR NEPHEW, LOUIE, IS BROKE AND HOMESICK IN FAKFAK, NEW GUINEA, AND HUEY IS CALLING FROM THE VALE OF KASHMIR!
WELL, SEND THEM PASSAGE HOME — ON ONE CONDITION!
WHAT'S THAT, SIR?
THAT IF THEY HAVE ANYMORE JUNIOR WOODCHUCK ANIMAL-CALLING WHISTLES IN THEIR POSSESSION, THEY CAN DOGGONE WELL WHISTLE THEIR WAY HOME!

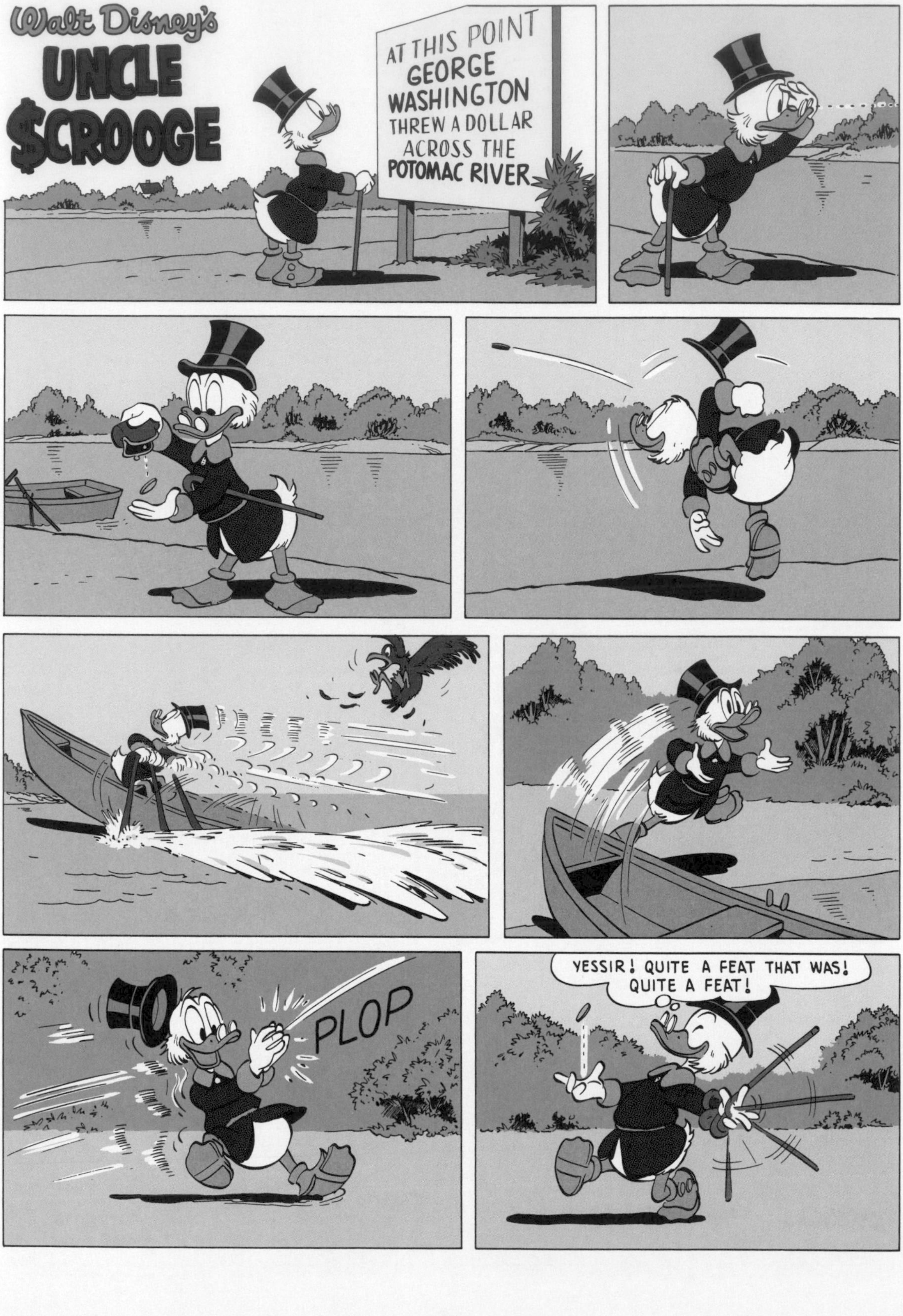
Walt Disney's
UNCLE $CROOGE
AT THIS POINT GEORGE WASHINGTON THREW A DOLLAR ACROSS THE POTOMAC RIVER
PLOP
YESSIR! QUITE A FEAT THAT WAS! QUITE A FEAT!

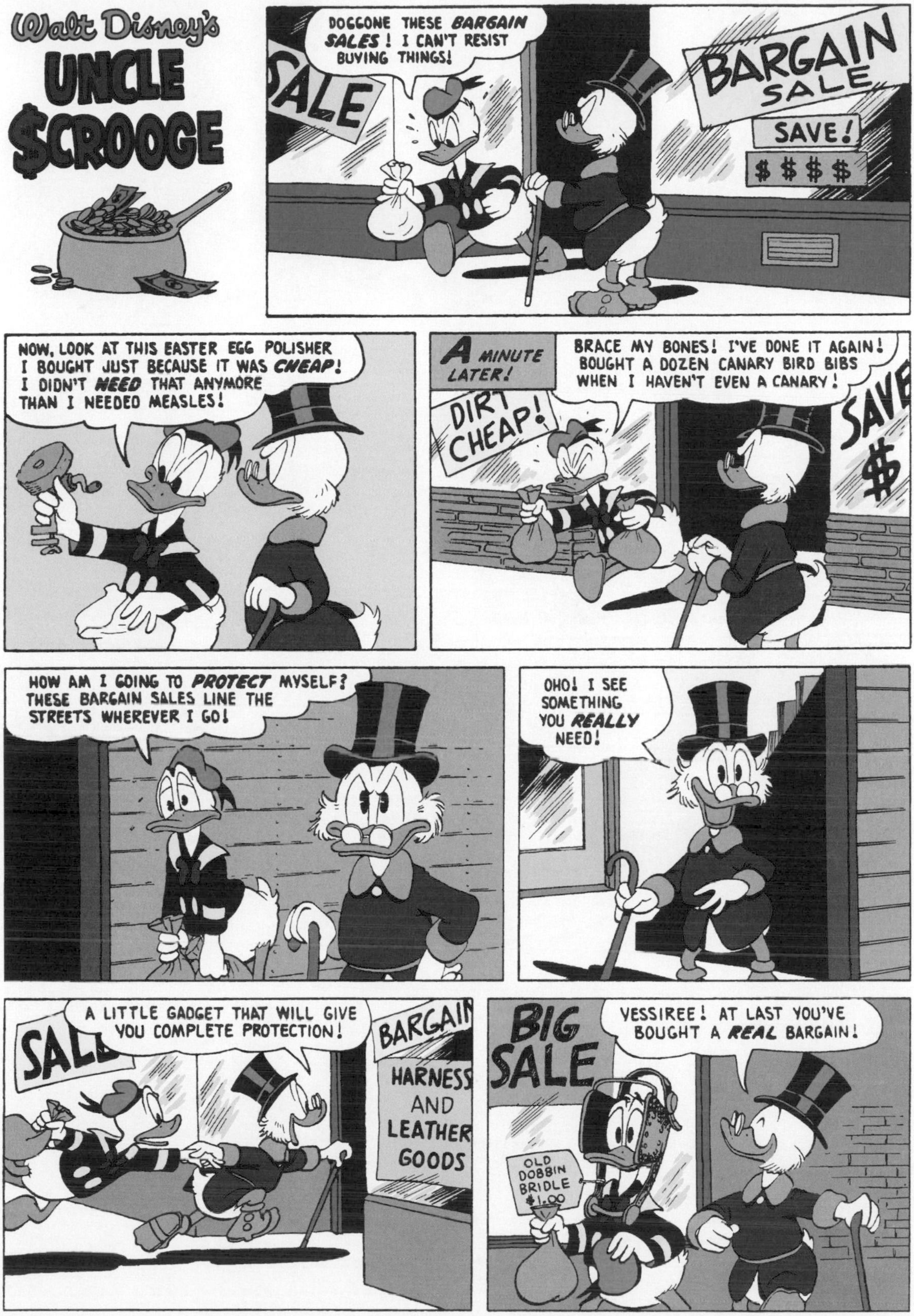
Walt Disney's
UNCLE $CROOGE
DOGGONE THESE BARGAIN SALES! I CAN'T RESIST BUYING THINGS!
SALE
BARGAIN SALE
SAVE!
$ $ $ $
NOW, LOOK AT THIS EASTER EGG POLISHER I BOUGHT JUST BECAUSE IT WAS CHEAP! I DIDN'T NEED THAT ANYMORE THAN I NEEDED MEASLES!
A MINUTE LATER!
BRACE MY BONES! I'VE DONE IT AGAIN! BOUGHT A DOZEN CANARY BIRD BIBS WHEN I HAVEN'T EVEN A CANARY!
DIRT CHEAP!
HOW AM I GOING TO PROTECT MYSELF? THESE BARGAIN SALES LINE THE STREETS WHEREVER I GO!
OHO! I SEE SOMETHING YOU REALLY NEED!
A LITTLE GADGET THAT WILL GIVE YOU COMPLETE PROTECTION!
HARNESS AND LEATHER GOODS
BIG SALE
YESSIREE! AT LAST YOU'VE BOUGHT A REAL BARGAIN!
OLD DOBBIN BRIDLE $1.00

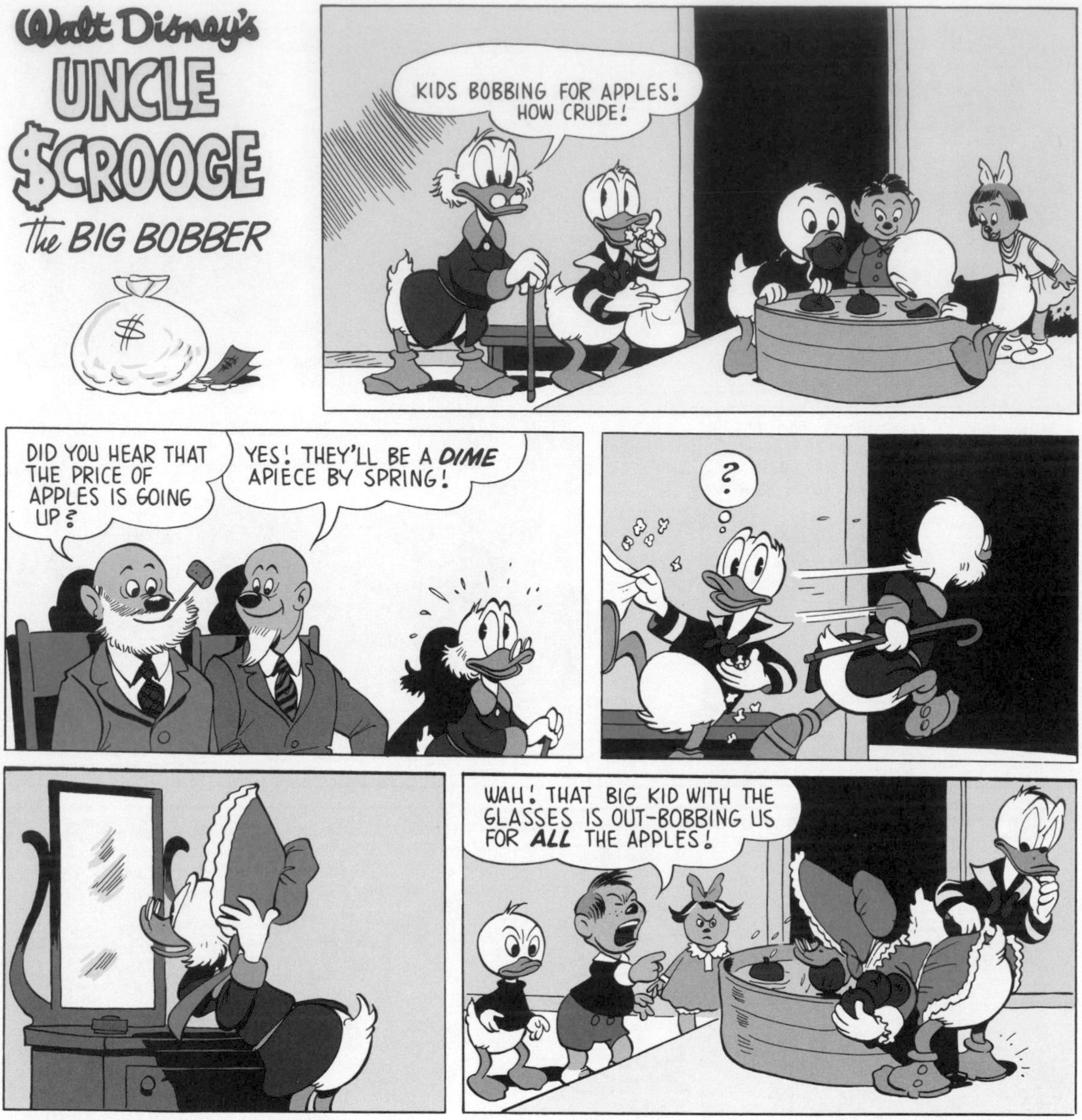
Walt Disney's
UNCLE $CROOGE
The BIG BOBBER
KIDS BOBBING FOR APPLES! HOW CRUDE!
DID YOU HEAR THAT THE PRICE OF APPLES IS GOING UP?
YES! THEY'LL BE A *DIME* APIECE BY SPRING!
?
WAH! THAT BIG KID WITH THE GLASSES IS OUT-BOBBING US FOR **ALL** THE APPLES!

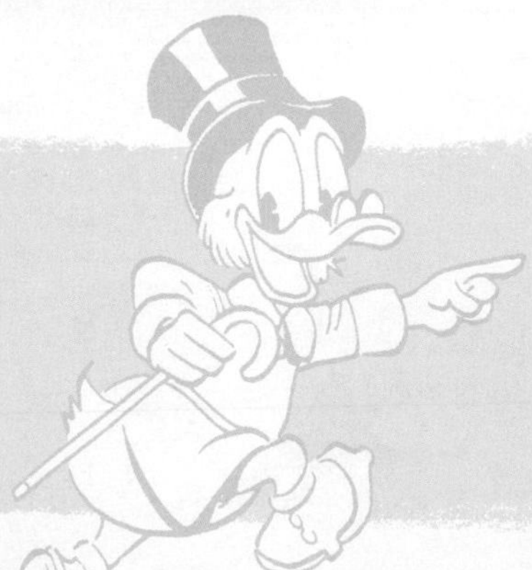

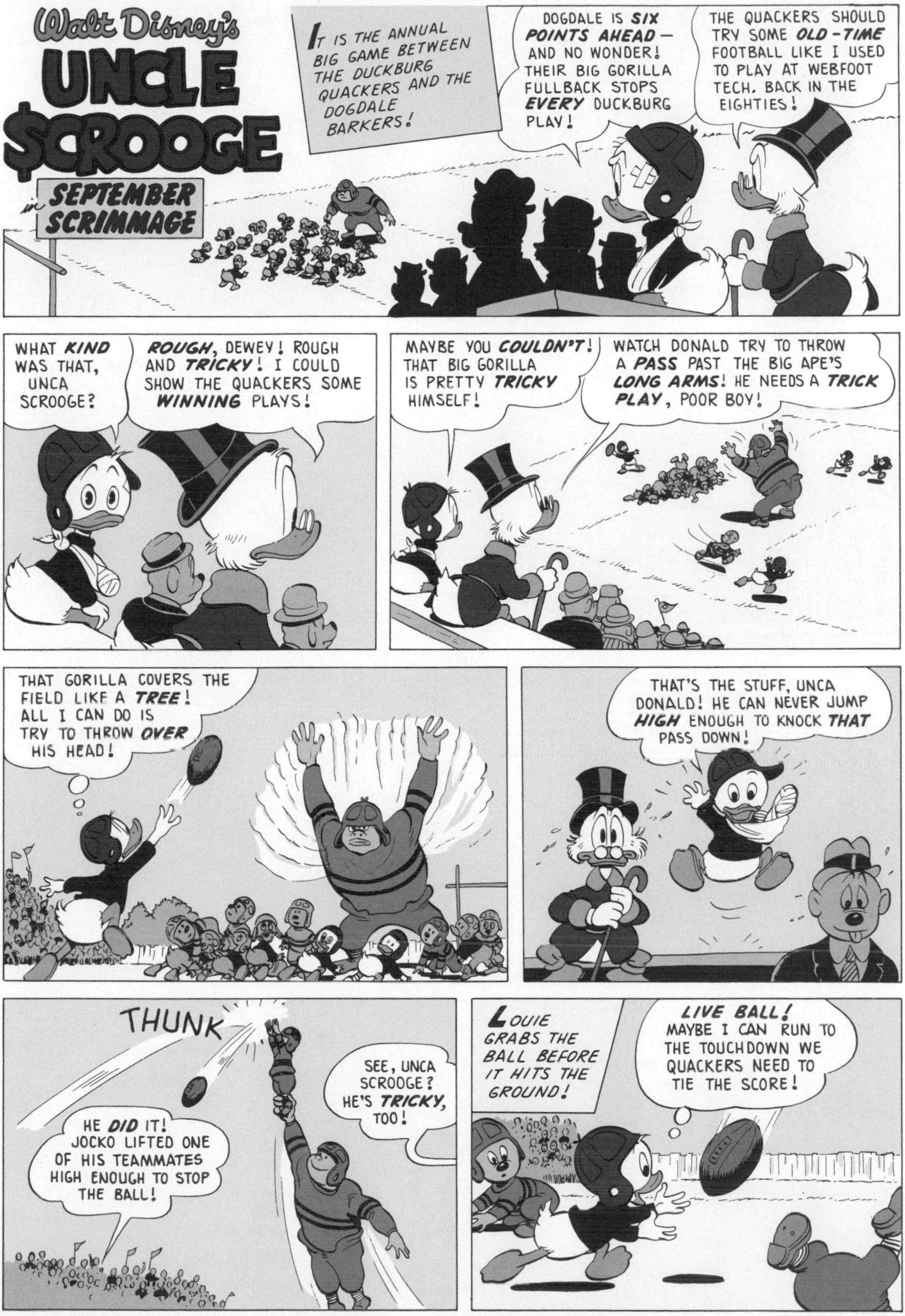
Walt Disney's
UNCLE $CROOGE
in SEPTEMBER SCRIMMAGE
IT IS THE ANNUAL BIG GAME BETWEEN THE DUCKBURG QUACKERS AND THE DOGDALE BARKERS!
DOGDALE IS SIX POINTS AHEAD — AND NO WONDER! THEIR BIG GORILLA FULLBACK STOPS EVERY DUCKBURG PLAY!
THE QUACKERS SHOULD TRY SOME OLD-TIME FOOTBALL LIKE I USED TO PLAY AT WEBFOOT TECH. BACK IN THE EIGHTIES!
WHAT KIND WAS THAT, UNCA SCROOGE?
ROUGH, DEWEY! ROUGH AND TRICKY! I COULD SHOW THE QUACKERS SOME WINNING PLAYS!
MAYBE YOU COULDN'T! THAT BIG GORILLA IS PRETTY TRICKY HIMSELF!
WATCH DONALD TRY TO THROW A PASS PAST THE BIG APE'S LONG ARMS! HE NEEDS A TRICK PLAY, POOR BOY!
THAT GORILLA COVERS THE FIELD LIKE A TREE! ALL I CAN DO IS TRY TO THROW OVER HIS HEAD!
THAT'S THE STUFF, UNCA DONALD! HE CAN NEVER JUMP HIGH ENOUGH TO KNOCK THAT PASS DOWN!
THUNK
SEE, UNCA SCROOGE? HE'S TRICKY, TOO!
HE DID IT! JOCKO LIFTED ONE OF HIS TEAMMATES HIGH ENOUGH TO STOP THE BALL!
LOUIE GRABS THE BALL BEFORE IT HITS THE GROUND!
LIVE BALL! MAYBE I CAN RUN TO THE TOUCHDOWN WE QUACKERS NEED TO TIE THE SCORE!

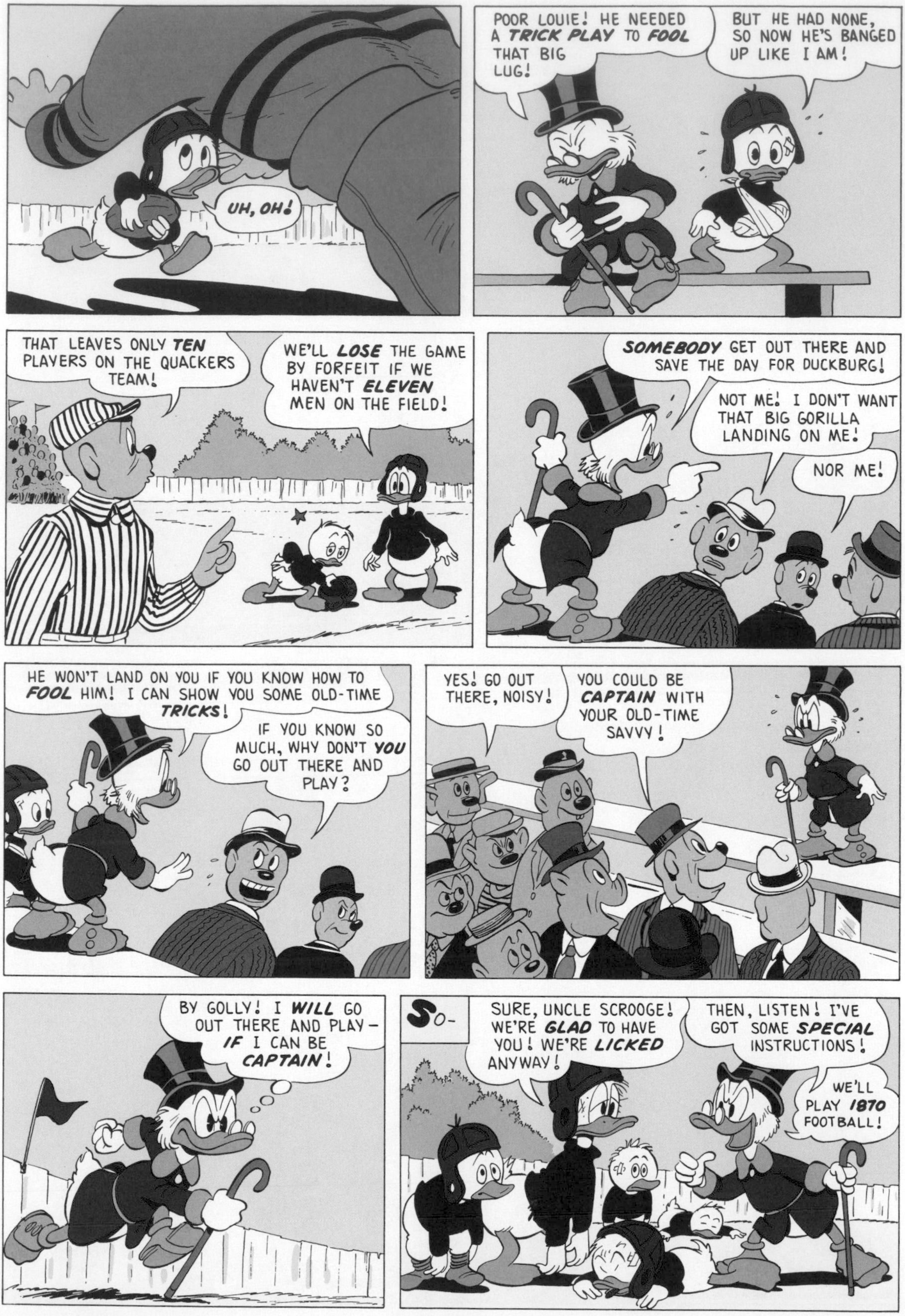
UH, OH!
POOR LOUIE! HE NEEDED A TRICK PLAY TO FOOL THAT BIG LUG!
BUT HE HAD NONE, SO NOW HE'S BANGED UP LIKE I AM!
THAT LEAVES ONLY TEN PLAYERS ON THE QUACKERS TEAM!
WE'LL LOSE THE GAME BY FORFEIT IF WE HAVEN'T ELEVEN MEN ON THE FIELD!
SOMEBODY GET OUT THERE AND SAVE THE DAY FOR DUCKBURG!
NOT ME! I DON'T WANT THAT BIG GORILLA LANDING ON ME!
NOR ME!
HE WON'T LAND ON YOU IF YOU KNOW HOW TO FOOL HIM! I CAN SHOW YOU SOME OLD-TIME TRICKS!
IF YOU KNOW SO MUCH, WHY DON'T YOU GO OUT THERE AND PLAY?
YES! GO OUT THERE, NOISY!
YOU COULD BE CAPTAIN WITH YOUR OLD-TIME SAVVY!
BY GOLLY! I WILL GO OUT THERE AND PLAY— IF I CAN BE CAPTAIN!
SO-
SURE, UNCLE SCROOGE! WE'RE GLAD TO HAVE YOU! WE'RE LICKED ANYWAY!
THEN, LISTEN! I'VE GOT SOME SPECIAL INSTRUCTIONS!
WE'LL PLAY 1870 FOOTBALL!

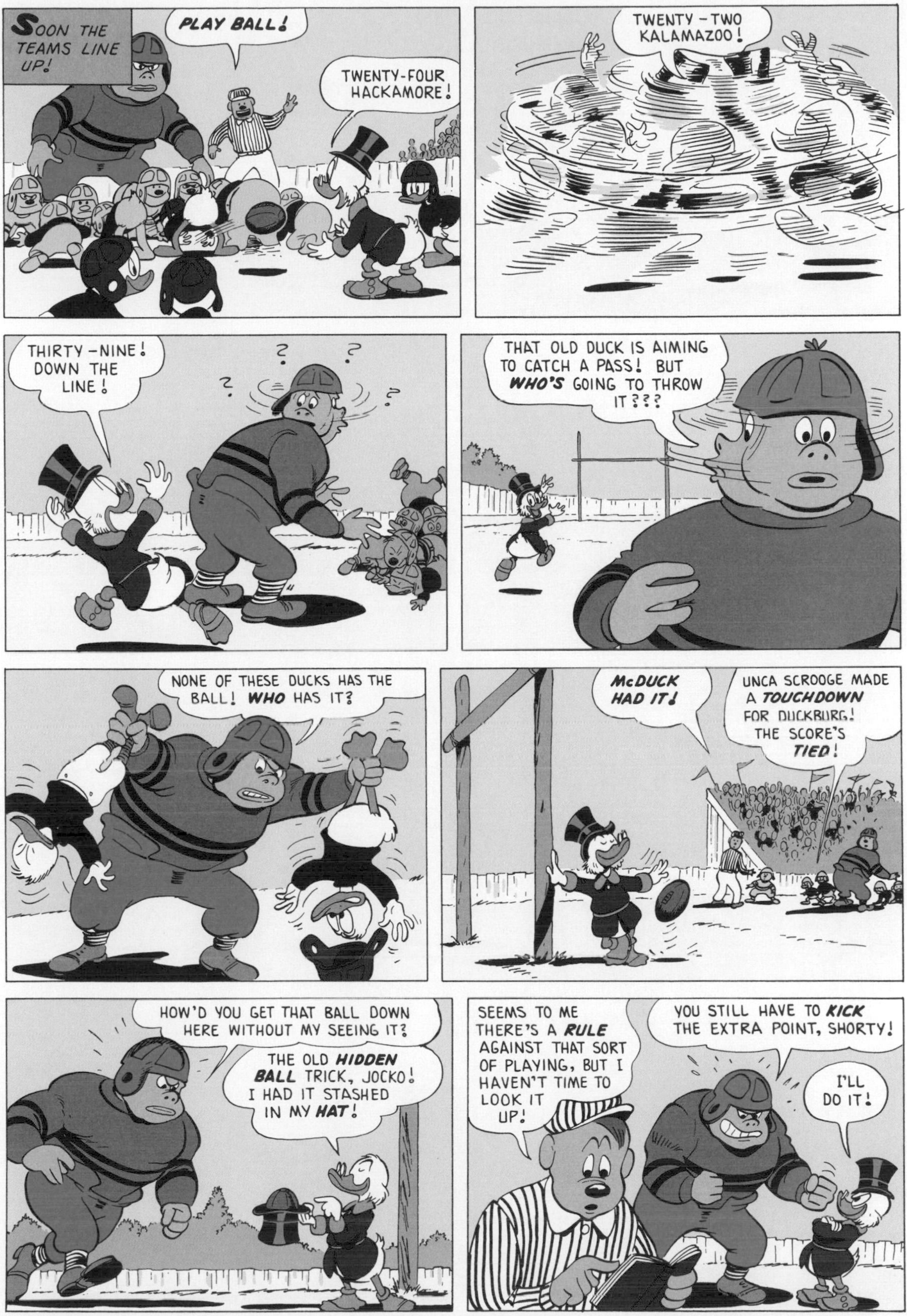
SOON THE TEAMS LINE UP!
PLAY BALL!
TWENTY-FOUR HACKAMORE!
TWENTY-TWO KALAMAZOO!
THIRTY-NINE! DOWN THE LINE!
? ? ? ?
THAT OLD DUCK IS AIMING TO CATCH A PASS! BUT WHO'S GOING TO THROW IT???
NONE OF THESE DUCKS HAS THE BALL! WHO HAS IT?
McDUCK HAD IT!
UNCA SCROOGE MADE A TOUCHDOWN FOR DUCKBURG! THE SCORE'S TIED!
HOW'D YOU GET THAT BALL DOWN HERE WITHOUT MY SEEING IT?
THE OLD HIDDEN BALL TRICK, JOCKO! I HAD IT STASHED IN MY HAT!
SEEMS TO ME THERE'S A RULE AGAINST THAT SORT OF PLAYING, BUT I HAVEN'T TIME TO LOOK IT UP!
YOU STILL HAVE TO KICK THE EXTRA POINT, SHORTY!
I'LL DO IT!

UNCA SCROOGE SENT ME FOR THESE *PIGEONS* AND SOME *CORN*! HE'S GOT ANOTHER *TRICK* UP HIS SLEEVE!

YES! HE TOLD ME WHAT WE'RE TO DO WITH THEM!

SOON!

BE SURE YOU SET THE BALL *JUST SO* FOR MY KICK!

YOU'VE GOT SOME *CORN* TIED TO THE BALL! WHAT'S THAT FOR?

YOU'LL SEE!

NOW WATCH THAT *PIGEON*!

GLOM

HEY! A PIGEON'S CARRYING THE BALL OVER THE GOAL! THAT ISN'T *FAIR*!

CRASH

HERE, PIDGY, PIDGY! *MORE* CORN!

THE EXTRA POINT PUTS DUCKBURG AHEAD *SEVEN* TO *SIX*!

BUT WAIT! THERE'S A *BEEF*! THE GAME'S *OVER*!

I'LL SAY IT IS! THE OFFICIALS ARE CHASING SCROOGE McDUCK AND THE GORILLA OFF THE FIELD!

AND THEY'RE *THROWING THE RULE BOOKS* AT BOTH OF THEM!

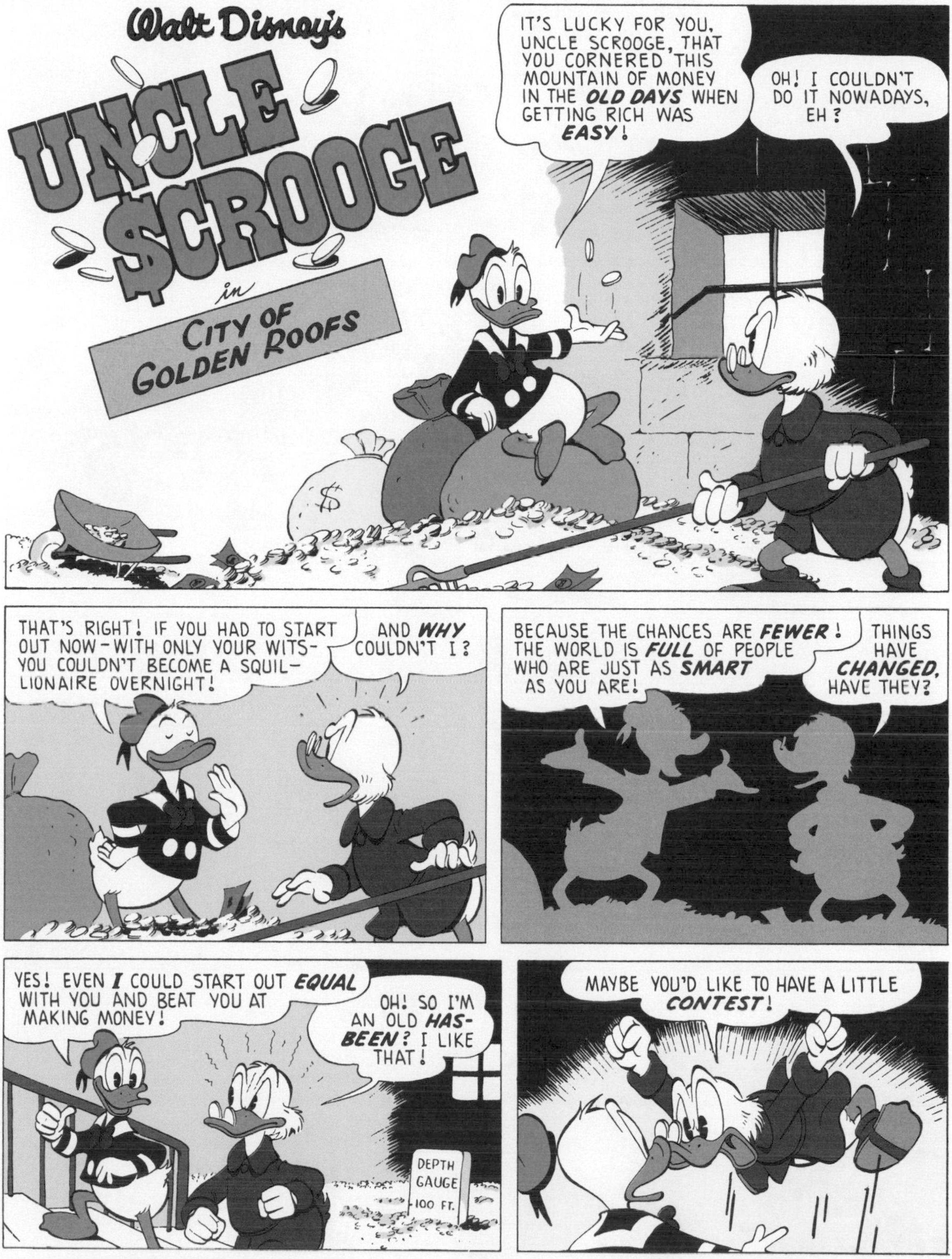
Walt Disney's
UNCLE $CROOGE
in
CITY OF GOLDEN ROOFS
IT'S LUCKY FOR YOU, UNCLE SCROOGE, THAT YOU CORNERED THIS MOUNTAIN OF MONEY IN THE OLD DAYS WHEN GETTING RICH WAS EASY!
OH! I COULDN'T DO IT NOWADAYS, EH?
$
THAT'S RIGHT! IF YOU HAD TO START OUT NOW—WITH ONLY YOUR WITS—YOU COULDN'T BECOME A SQUIL-LIONAIRE OVERNIGHT!
AND WHY COULDN'T I?
BECAUSE THE CHANCES ARE FEWER! THE WORLD IS FULL OF PEOPLE WHO ARE JUST AS SMART AS YOU ARE!
THINGS HAVE CHANGED, HAVE THEY?
YES! EVEN I COULD START OUT EQUAL WITH YOU AND BEAT YOU AT MAKING MONEY!
OH! SO I'M AN OLD HAS-BEEN? I LIKE THAT!
DEPTH GAUGE 100 FT.
MAYBE YOU'D LIKE TO HAVE A LITTLE CONTEST!

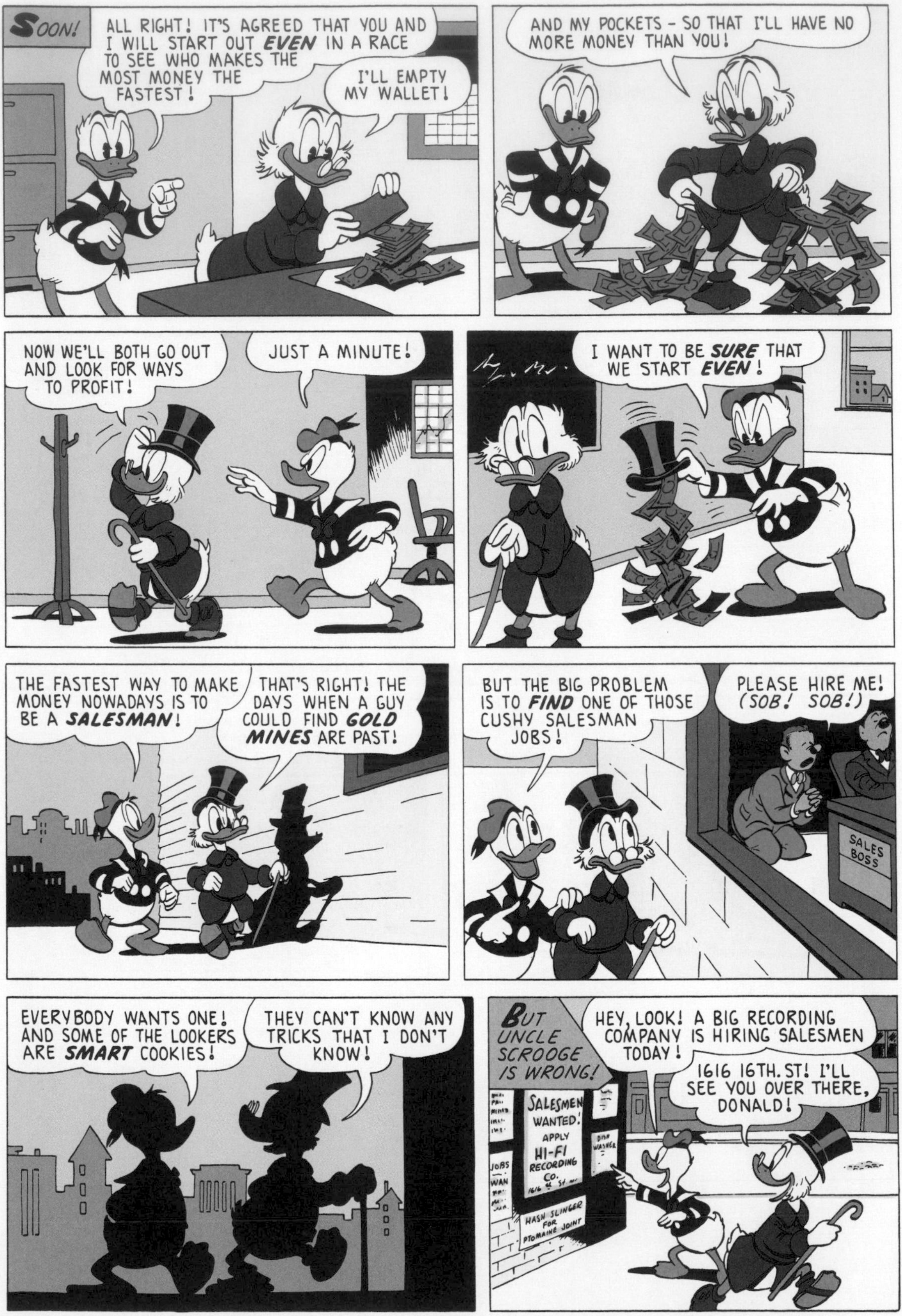
SOON!
ALL RIGHT! IT'S AGREED THAT YOU AND I WILL START OUT EVEN IN A RACE TO SEE WHO MAKES THE MOST MONEY THE FASTEST!
I'LL EMPTY MY WALLET!
AND MY POCKETS - SO THAT I'LL HAVE NO MORE MONEY THAN YOU!
NOW WE'LL BOTH GO OUT AND LOOK FOR WAYS TO PROFIT!
JUST A MINUTE!
I WANT TO BE SURE THAT WE START EVEN!
THE FASTEST WAY TO MAKE MONEY NOWADAYS IS TO BE A SALESMAN!
THAT'S RIGHT! THE DAYS WHEN A GUY COULD FIND GOLD MINES ARE PAST!
BUT THE BIG PROBLEM IS TO FIND ONE OF THOSE CUSHY SALESMAN JOBS!
PLEASE HIRE ME! (SOB! SOB!)
SALES BOSS
EVERYBODY WANTS ONE! AND SOME OF THE LOOKERS ARE SMART COOKIES!
THEY CAN'T KNOW ANY TRICKS THAT I DON'T KNOW!
BUT UNCLE SCROOGE IS WRONG!
HEY, LOOK! A BIG RECORDING COMPANY IS HIRING SALESMEN TODAY!
1616 16TH. ST! I'LL SEE YOU OVER THERE, DONALD!
SALESMEN WANTED! APPLY HI-FI RECORDING CO.
DISH WASHER
HASH SLINGER FOR PTOMAINE JOINT
JOBS WAN

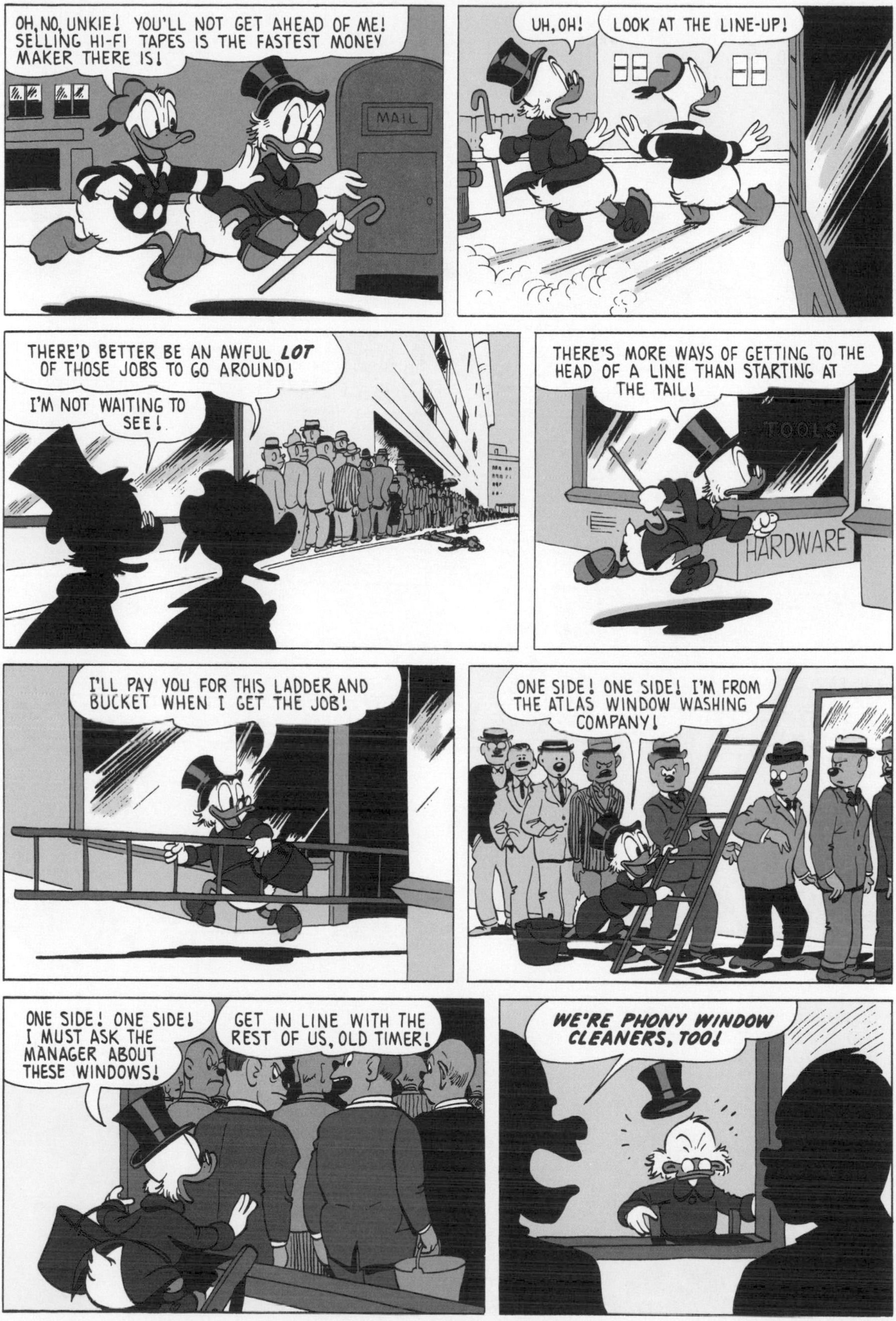
OH, NO, UNKIE! YOU'LL NOT GET AHEAD OF ME! SELLING HI-FI TAPES IS THE FASTEST MONEY MAKER THERE IS!
MAIL
UH, OH!
LOOK AT THE LINE-UP!
THERE'D BETTER BE AN AWFUL LOT OF THOSE JOBS TO GO AROUND!
I'M NOT WAITING TO SEE!
THERE'S MORE WAYS OF GETTING TO THE HEAD OF A LINE THAN STARTING AT THE TAIL!
TOOLS
HARDWARE
I'LL PAY YOU FOR THIS LADDER AND BUCKET WHEN I GET THE JOB!
ONE SIDE! ONE SIDE! I'M FROM THE ATLAS WINDOW WASHING COMPANY!
ONE SIDE! ONE SIDE! I MUST ASK THE MANAGER ABOUT THESE WINDOWS!
GET IN LINE WITH THE REST OF US, OLD TIMER!
WE'RE PHONY WINDOW CLEANERS, TOO!

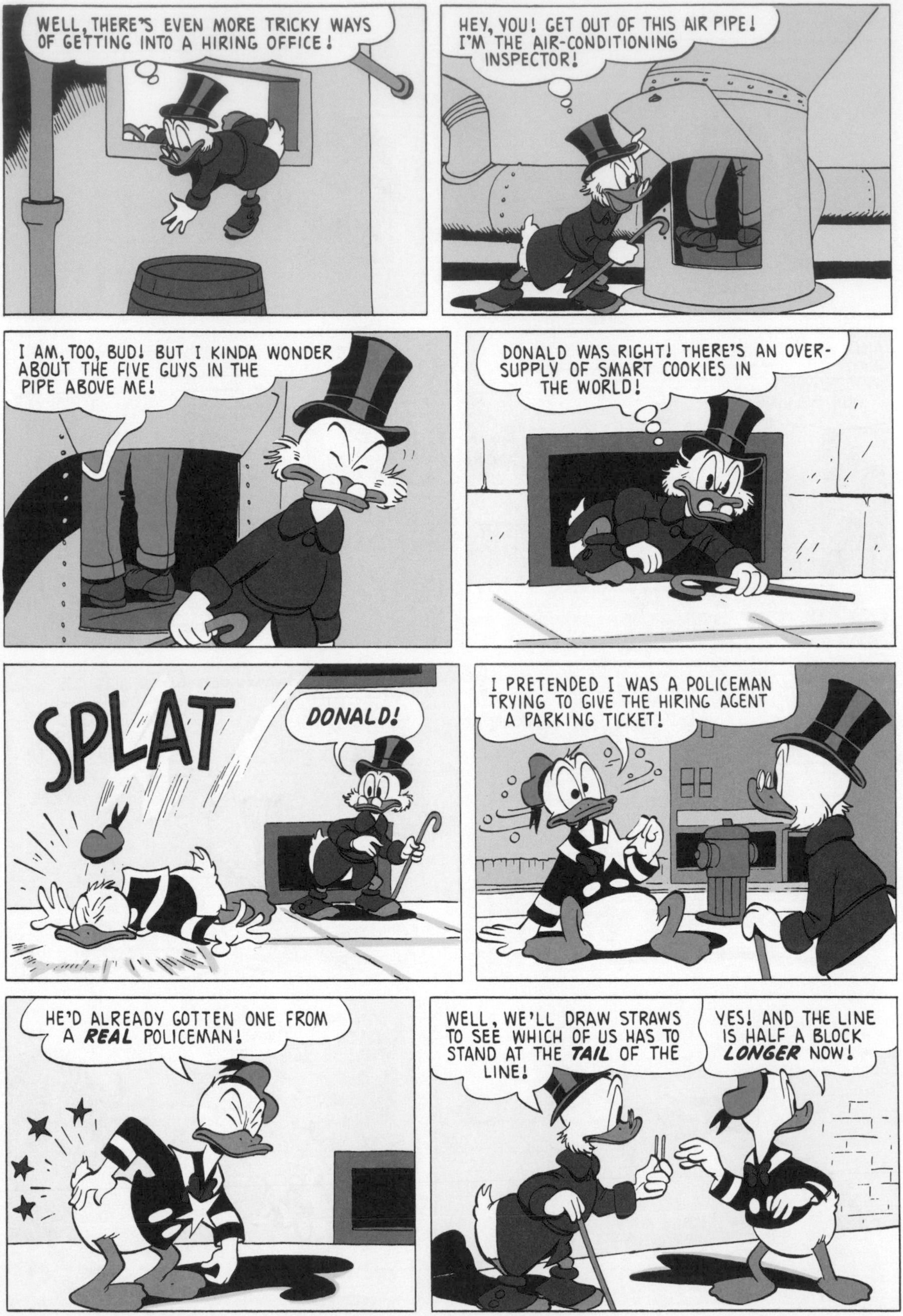
WELL, THERE'S EVEN MORE TRICKY WAYS OF GETTING INTO A HIRING OFFICE!
HEY, YOU! GET OUT OF THIS AIR PIPE! I'M THE AIR-CONDITIONING INSPECTOR!
I AM, TOO, BUD! BUT I KINDA WONDER ABOUT THE FIVE GUYS IN THE PIPE ABOVE ME!
DONALD WAS RIGHT! THERE'S AN OVER-SUPPLY OF SMART COOKIES IN THE WORLD!
SPLAT
DONALD!
I PRETENDED I WAS A POLICEMAN TRYING TO GIVE THE HIRING AGENT A PARKING TICKET!
HE'D ALREADY GOTTEN ONE FROM A **REAL** POLICEMAN!
WELL, WE'LL DRAW STRAWS TO SEE WHICH OF US HAS TO STAND AT THE **TAIL** OF THE LINE!
YES! AND THE LINE IS HALF A BLOCK **LONGER** NOW!

HOURS LATER UNCLE SCROOGE AND DONALD REACH THE CHARMED DOOR!

THERE IS ONLY **ONE** SELLING JOB LEFT

IT'LL DO! I'LL TAKE IT!

HIRING OFFICE

NOT SO FAST, OLD TIMER! YOU FIRST HAVE TO PASS A LITTLE TEST!

AND, BESIDES, YOU MIGHT NOT WANT THE JOB WHEN YOU SEE WHERE YOU'VE GOT TO DO YOUR SELLING!

AFTER ALL THIS TROUBLE, I'D SELL SALT IN A SALT MINE!

SAMPLE

DO YOU KNOW WHAT THAT IS, SIR?

NO!

YOU'VE **FLUNKED** THE TEST!

SEND THE NEXT GUY IN!

?

DO **YOU** KNOW WHAT THAT IS?

YES, SIR! IT'S A MIDGET HI-FI TAPE RECORDER! EVERYBODY AROUND IS DYING TO OWN ONE!

YOU'LL DO! -- NOW, THE ONLY SPOT IN THE WORLD WHERE WE HAVEN'T A SALESMAN IS IN —

I DON'T CARE WHERE IT IS! I'M HAVING A **RACE** WITH MY UNCLE, AND I HAVEN'T TIME TO BE CHOOSEY!

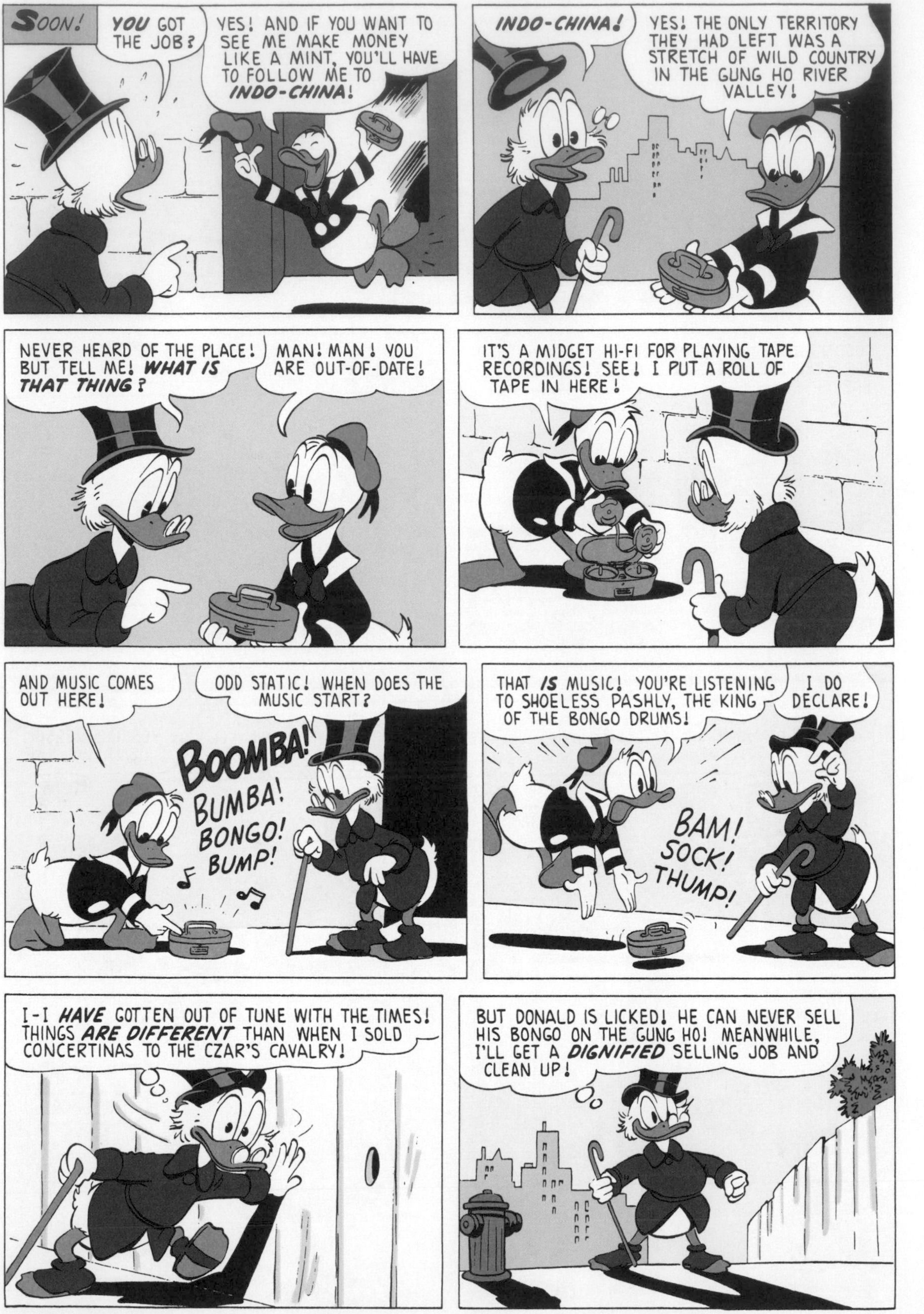
SOON!
YOU GOT THE JOB?
YES! AND IF YOU WANT TO SEE ME MAKE MONEY LIKE A MINT, YOU'LL HAVE TO FOLLOW ME TO INDO-CHINA!
INDO-CHINA!
YES! THE ONLY TERRITORY THEY HAD LEFT WAS A STRETCH OF WILD COUNTRY IN THE GUNG HO RIVER VALLEY!
NEVER HEARD OF THE PLACE! BUT TELL ME! WHAT IS THAT THING?
MAN! MAN! YOU ARE OUT-OF-DATE!
IT'S A MIDGET HI-FI FOR PLAYING TAPE RECORDINGS! SEE! I PUT A ROLL OF TAPE IN HERE!
AND MUSIC COMES OUT HERE!
ODD STATIC! WHEN DOES THE MUSIC START?
BOOMBA! BUMBA! BONGO! BUMP!
THAT IS MUSIC! YOU'RE LISTENING TO SHOELESS PASHLY, THE KING OF THE BONGO DRUMS!
I DO DECLARE!
BAM! SOCK! THUMP!
I-I HAVE GOTTEN OUT OF TUNE WITH THE TIMES! THINGS ARE DIFFERENT THAN WHEN I SOLD CONCERTINAS TO THE CZAR'S CAVALRY!
BUT DONALD IS LICKED! HE CAN NEVER SELL HIS BONGO ON THE GUNG HO! MEANWHILE, I'LL GET A DIGNIFIED SELLING JOB AND CLEAN UP!

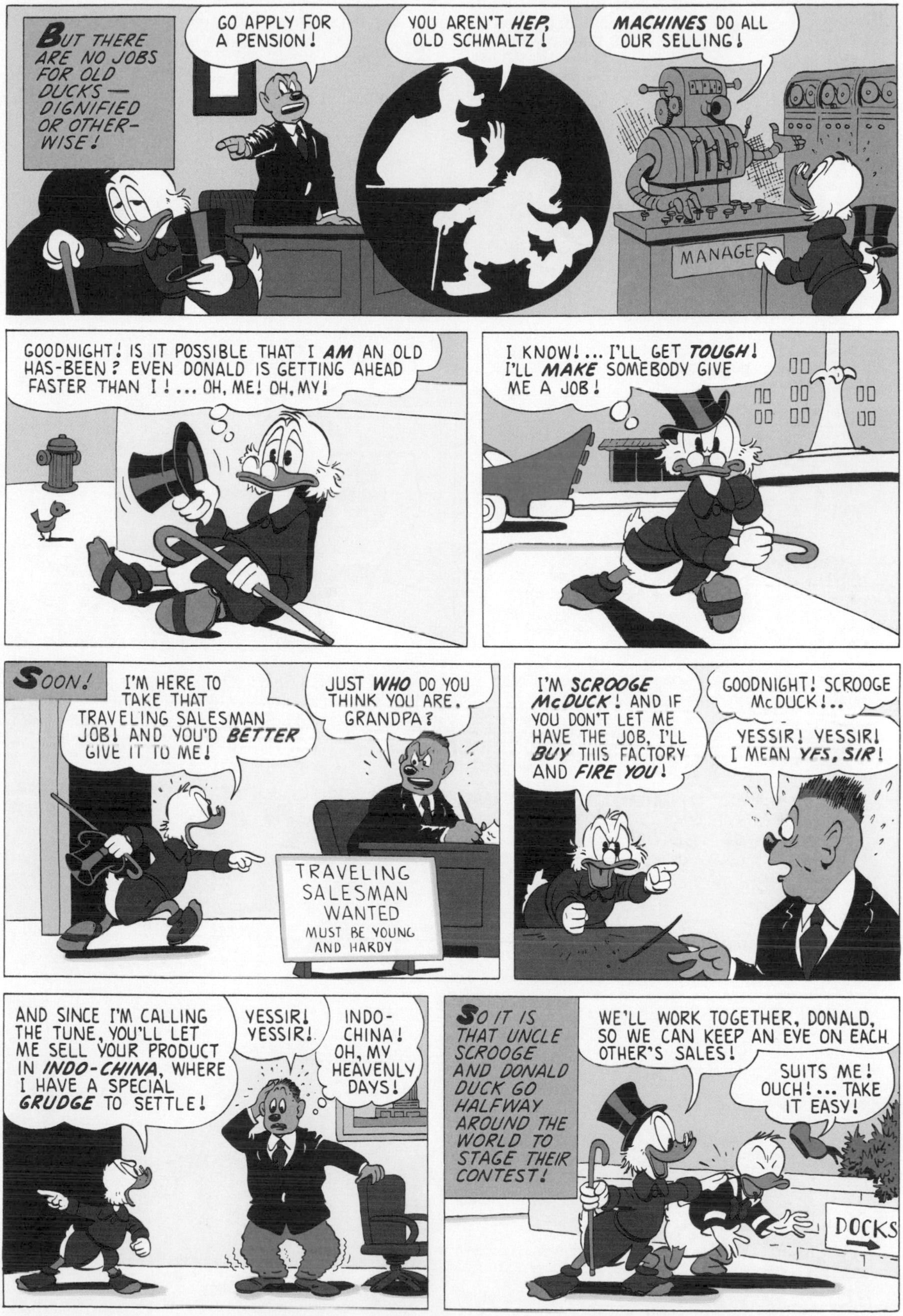
BUT THERE ARE NO JOBS FOR OLD DUCKS— DIGNIFIED OR OTHER-WISE!
GO APPLY FOR A PENSION!
YOU AREN'T HEP, OLD SCHMALTZ!
MACHINES DO ALL OUR SELLING!
MANAGER
GOODNIGHT! IS IT POSSIBLE THAT I AM AN OLD HAS-BEEN? EVEN DONALD IS GETTING AHEAD FASTER THAN I! ... OH, ME! OH, MY!
I KNOW! ... I'LL GET TOUGH! I'LL MAKE SOMEBODY GIVE ME A JOB!
SOON!
I'M HERE TO TAKE THAT TRAVELING SALESMAN JOB! AND YOU'D BETTER GIVE IT TO ME!
JUST WHO DO YOU THINK YOU ARE, GRANDPA?
TRAVELING SALESMAN WANTED MUST BE YOUNG AND HARDY
I'M SCROOGE McDUCK! AND IF YOU DON'T LET ME HAVE THE JOB, I'LL BUY THIS FACTORY AND FIRE YOU!
GOODNIGHT! SCROOGE McDUCK! ..
YESSIR! YESSIR! I MEAN YES, SIR!
AND SINCE I'M CALLING THE TUNE, YOU'LL LET ME SELL YOUR PRODUCT IN INDO-CHINA, WHERE I HAVE A SPECIAL GRUDGE TO SETTLE!
YESSIR! YESSIR!
INDO-CHINA! OH, MY HEAVENLY DAYS!
SO IT IS THAT UNCLE SCROOGE AND DONALD DUCK GO HALFWAY AROUND THE WORLD TO STAGE THEIR CONTEST!
WE'LL WORK TOGETHER, DONALD, SO WE CAN KEEP AN EYE ON EACH OTHER'S SALES!
SUITS ME! OUCH! ... TAKE IT EASY!
DOCKS

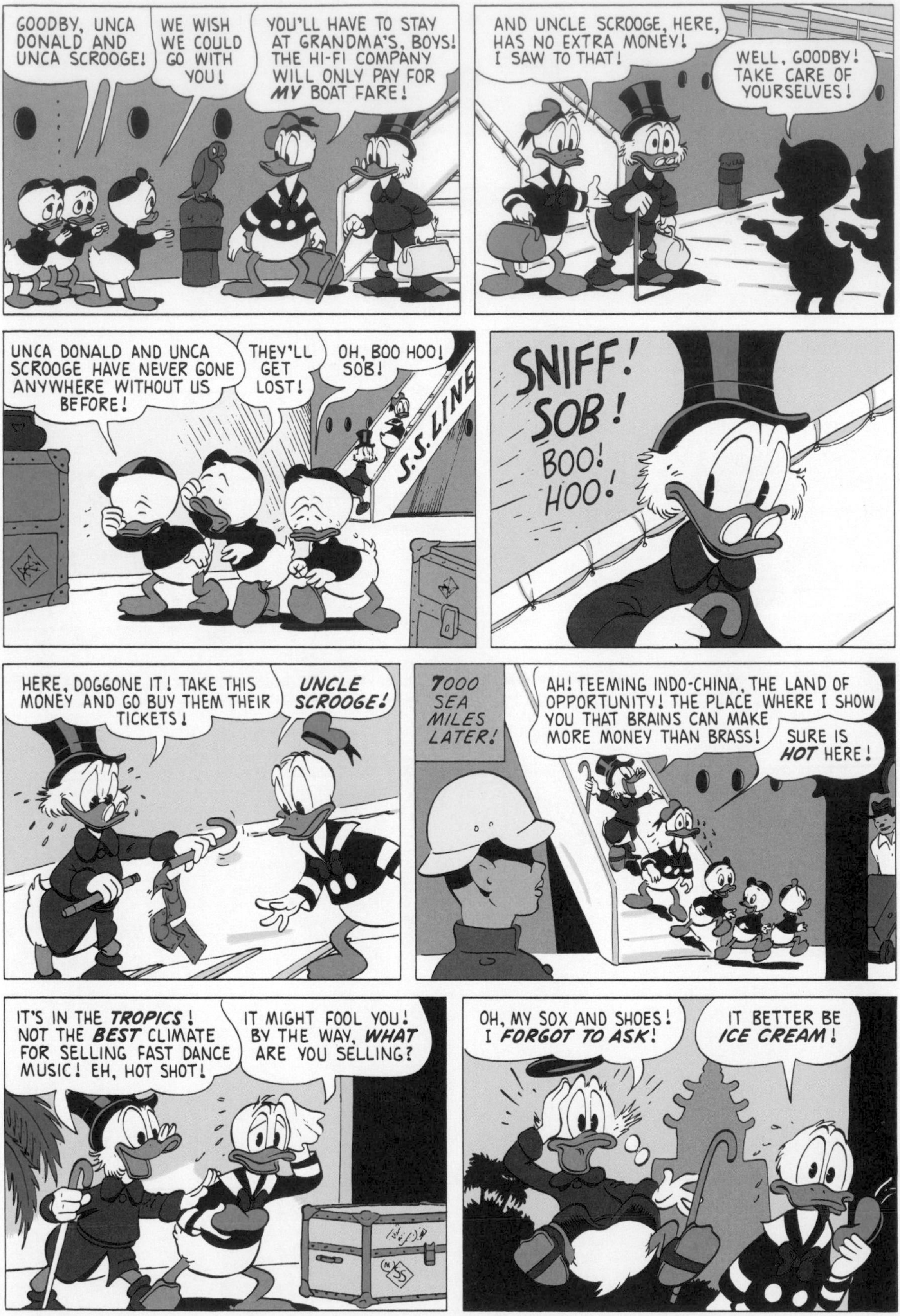
GOODBY, UNCA DONALD AND UNCA SCROOGE!
WE WISH WE COULD GO WITH YOU!
YOU'LL HAVE TO STAY AT GRANDMA'S, BOYS! THE HI-FI COMPANY WILL ONLY PAY FOR MY BOAT FARE!
AND UNCLE SCROOGE, HERE, HAS NO EXTRA MONEY! I SAW TO THAT!
WELL, GOODBY! TAKE CARE OF YOURSELVES!
UNCA DONALD AND UNCA SCROOGE HAVE NEVER GONE ANYWHERE WITHOUT US BEFORE!
THEY'LL GET LOST!
OH, BOO HOO! SOB!
S.S. LINE
SNIFF! SOB! BOO! HOO!
HERE, DOGGONE IT! TAKE THIS MONEY AND GO BUY THEM THEIR TICKETS!
UNCLE SCROOGE!
7000 SEA MILES LATER!
AH! TEEMING INDO-CHINA, THE LAND OF OPPORTUNITY! THE PLACE WHERE I SHOW YOU THAT BRAINS CAN MAKE MORE MONEY THAN BRASS!
SURE IS HOT HERE!
IT'S IN THE TROPICS! NOT THE BEST CLIMATE FOR SELLING FAST DANCE MUSIC! EH, HOT SHOT!
IT MIGHT FOOL YOU! BY THE WAY, WHAT ARE YOU SELLING?
OH, MY SOX AND SHOES! I FORGOT TO ASK!
IT BETTER BE ICE CREAM!

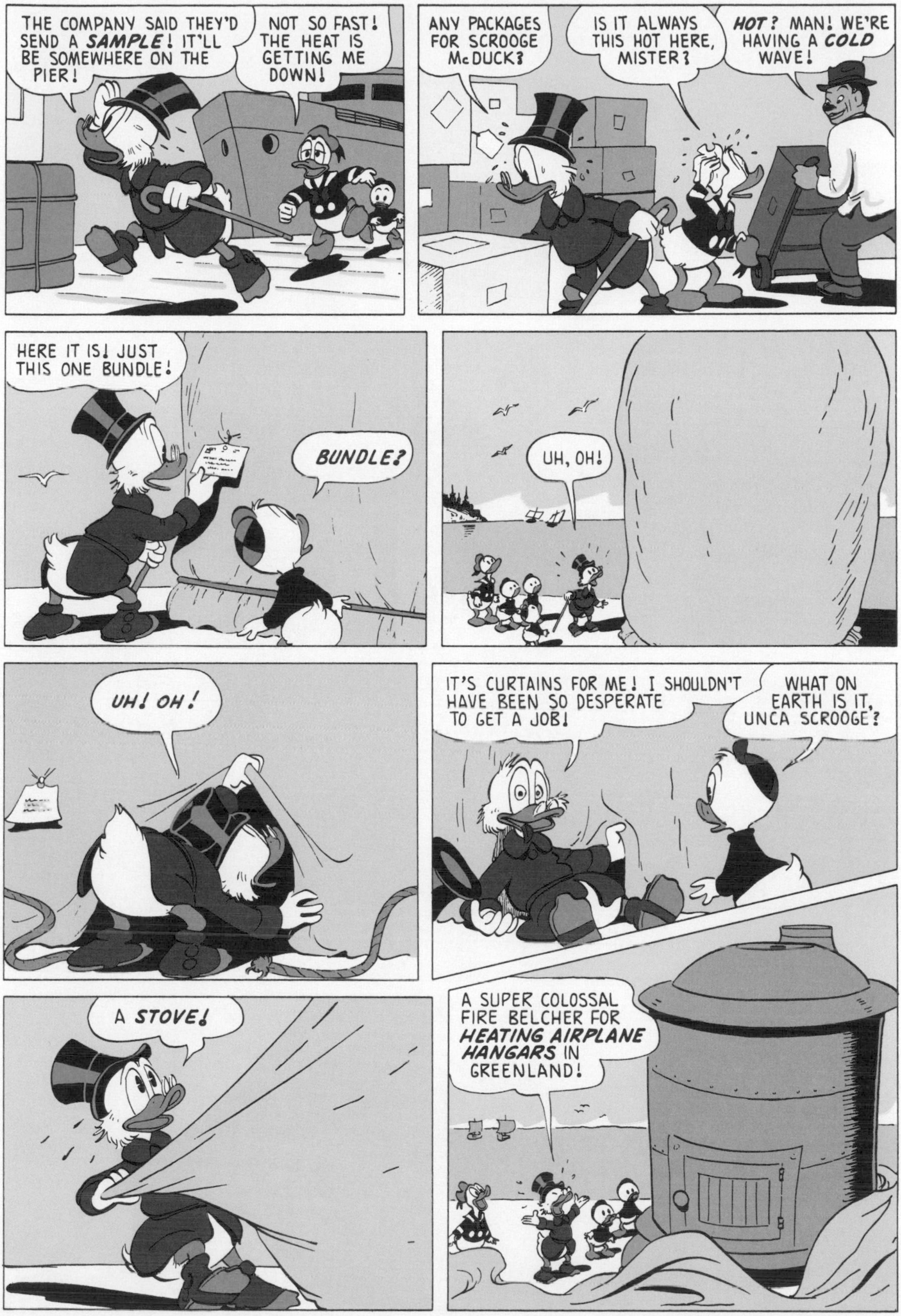
THE COMPANY SAID THEY'D SEND A SAMPLE! IT'LL BE SOMEWHERE ON THE PIER!
NOT SO FAST! THE HEAT IS GETTING ME DOWN!
ANY PACKAGES FOR SCROOGE McDUCK?
IS IT ALWAYS THIS HOT HERE, MISTER?
HOT? MAN! WE'RE HAVING A COLD WAVE!
HERE IT IS! JUST THIS ONE BUNDLE!
BUNDLE?
UH, OH!
UH! OH!
IT'S CURTAINS FOR ME! I SHOULDN'T HAVE BEEN SO DESPERATE TO GET A JOB!
WHAT ON EARTH IS IT, UNCA SCROOGE?
A STOVE!
A SUPER COLOSSAL FIRE BELCHER FOR HEATING AIRPLANE HANGARS IN GREENLAND!

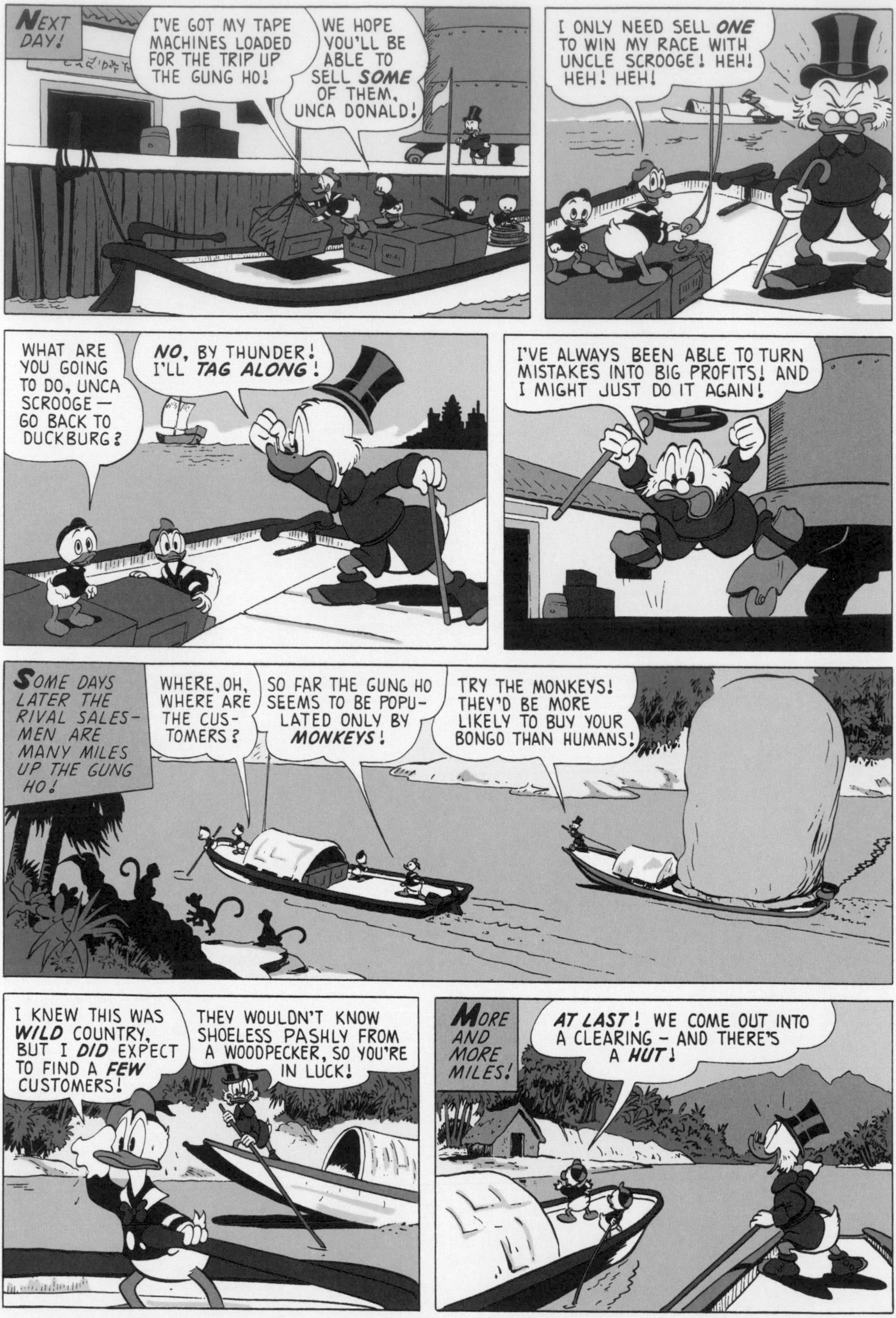
NEXT DAY!
I'VE GOT MY TAPE MACHINES LOADED FOR THE TRIP UP THE GUNG HO!
WE HOPE YOU'LL BE ABLE TO SELL SOME OF THEM, UNCA DONALD!
I ONLY NEED SELL ONE TO WIN MY RACE WITH UNCLE SCROOGE! HEH! HEH! HEH!
WHAT ARE YOU GOING TO DO, UNCA SCROOGE — GO BACK TO DUCKBURG?
NO, BY THUNDER! I'LL TAG ALONG!
I'VE ALWAYS BEEN ABLE TO TURN MISTAKES INTO BIG PROFITS! AND I MIGHT JUST DO IT AGAIN!
SOME DAYS LATER THE RIVAL SALES-MEN ARE MANY MILES UP THE GUNG HO!
WHERE, OH, WHERE ARE THE CUS-TOMERS?
SO FAR THE GUNG HO SEEMS TO BE POPU-LATED ONLY BY MONKEYS!
TRY THE MONKEYS! THEY'D BE MORE LIKELY TO BUY YOUR BONGO THAN HUMANS!
I KNEW THIS WAS WILD COUNTRY, BUT I DID EXPECT TO FIND A FEW CUSTOMERS!
THEY WOULDN'T KNOW SHOELESS PASHLY FROM A WOODPECKER, SO YOU'RE IN LUCK!
MORE AND MORE MILES!
AT LAST! WE COME OUT INTO A CLEARING - AND THERE'S A HUT!

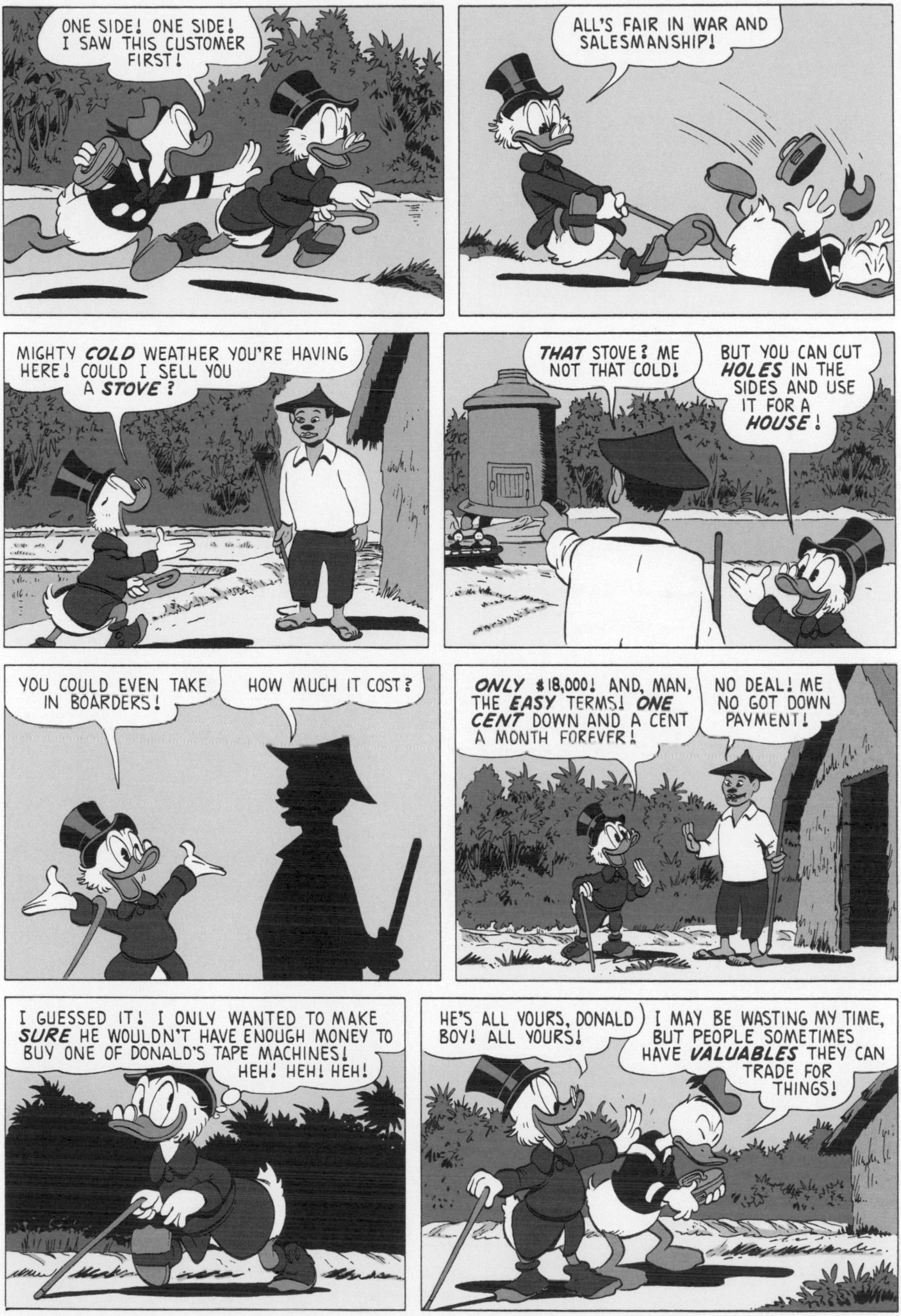
ONE SIDE! ONE SIDE! I SAW THIS CUSTOMER FIRST!
ALL'S FAIR IN WAR AND SALESMANSHIP!
MIGHTY COLD WEATHER YOU'RE HAVING HERE! COULD I SELL YOU A STOVE?
THAT STOVE? ME NOT THAT COLD!
BUT YOU CAN CUT HOLES IN THE SIDES AND USE IT FOR A HOUSE!
YOU COULD EVEN TAKE IN BOARDERS!
HOW MUCH IT COST?
ONLY $18,000! AND, MAN, THE EASY TERMS! ONE CENT DOWN AND A CENT A MONTH FOREVER!
NO DEAL! ME NO GOT DOWN PAYMENT!
I GUESSED IT! I ONLY WANTED TO MAKE SURE HE WOULDN'T HAVE ENOUGH MONEY TO BUY ONE OF DONALD'S TAPE MACHINES! HEH! HEH! HEH!
HE'S ALL YOURS, DONALD BOY! ALL YOURS!
I MAY BE WASTING MY TIME, BUT PEOPLE SOMETIMES HAVE VALUABLES THEY CAN TRADE FOR THINGS!

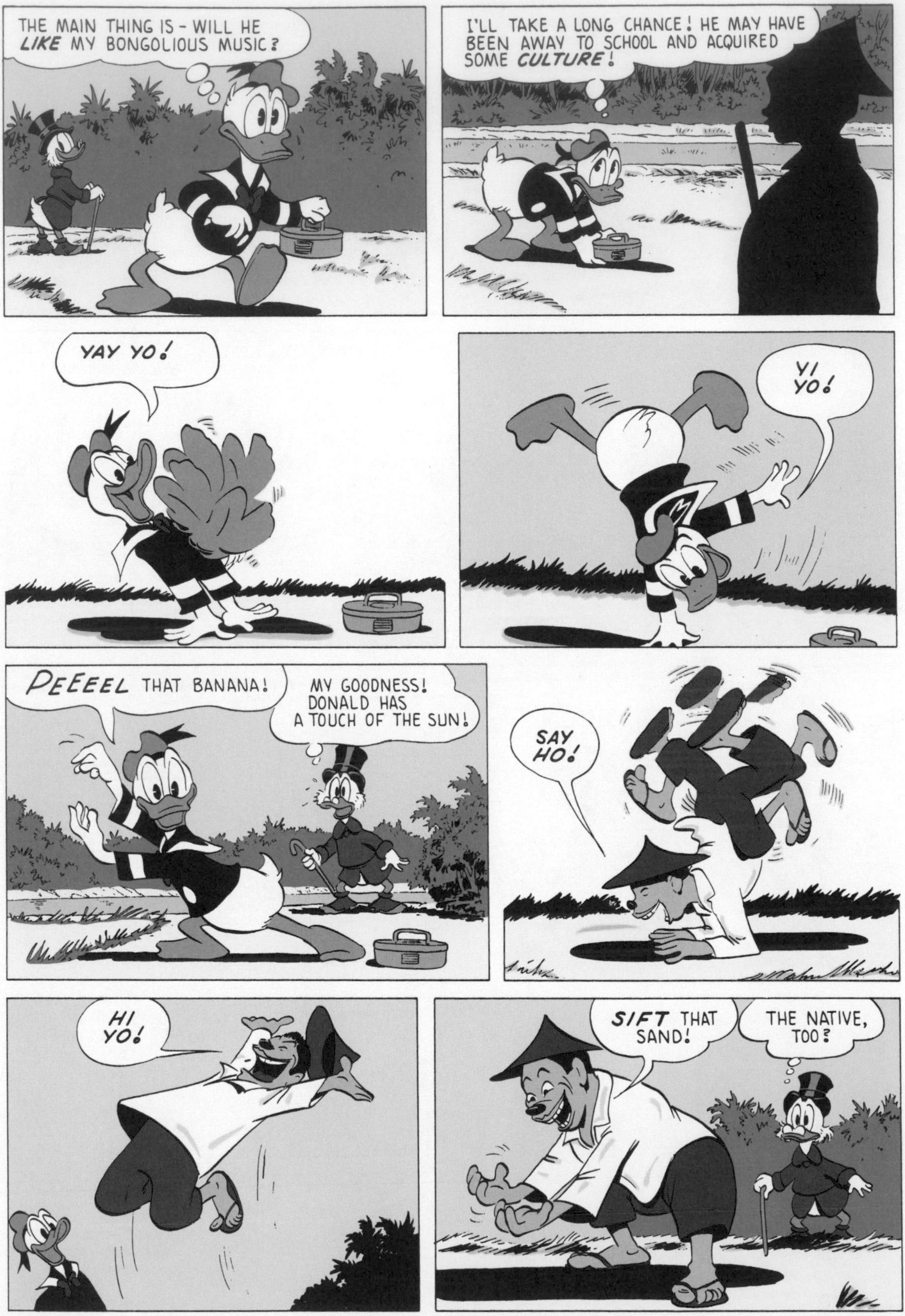
THE MAIN THING IS - WILL HE LIKE MY BONGOLIOUS MUSIC?
I'LL TAKE A LONG CHANCE! HE MAY HAVE BEEN AWAY TO SCHOOL AND ACQUIRED SOME CULTURE!
YAY YO!
YI YO!
PEEEEL THAT BANANA!
MY GOODNESS! DONALD HAS A TOUCH OF THE SUN!
SAY HO!
HI YO!
SIFT THAT SAND!
THE NATIVE, TOO?

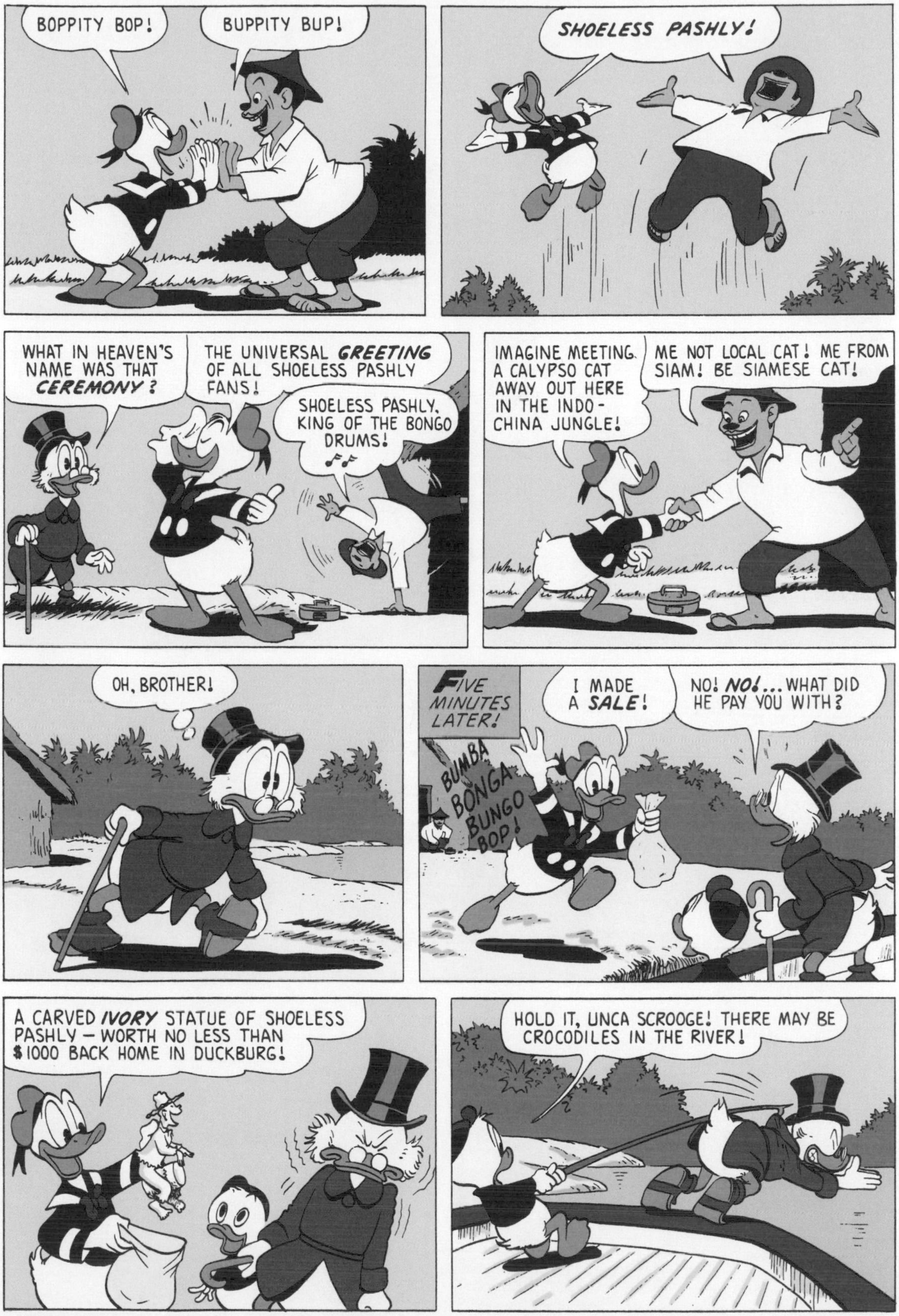
BOPPITY BOP!
BUPPITY BUP!
SHOELESS PASHLY!
WHAT IN HEAVEN'S NAME WAS THAT CEREMONY?
THE UNIVERSAL GREETING OF ALL SHOELESS PASHLY FANS!
SHOELESS PASHLY, KING OF THE BONGO DRUMS!
IMAGINE MEETING A CALYPSO CAT AWAY OUT HERE IN THE INDO-CHINA JUNGLE!
ME NOT LOCAL CAT! ME FROM SIAM! BE SIAMESE CAT!
OH, BROTHER!
FIVE MINUTES LATER!
I MADE A SALE!
NO! NO!... WHAT DID HE PAY YOU WITH?
BUMBA BONGA BUNGO BOP!
A CARVED IVORY STATUE OF SHOELESS PASHLY — WORTH NO LESS THAN $1000 BACK HOME IN DUCKBURG!
HOLD IT, UNCA SCROOGE! THERE MAY BE CROCODILES IN THE RIVER!

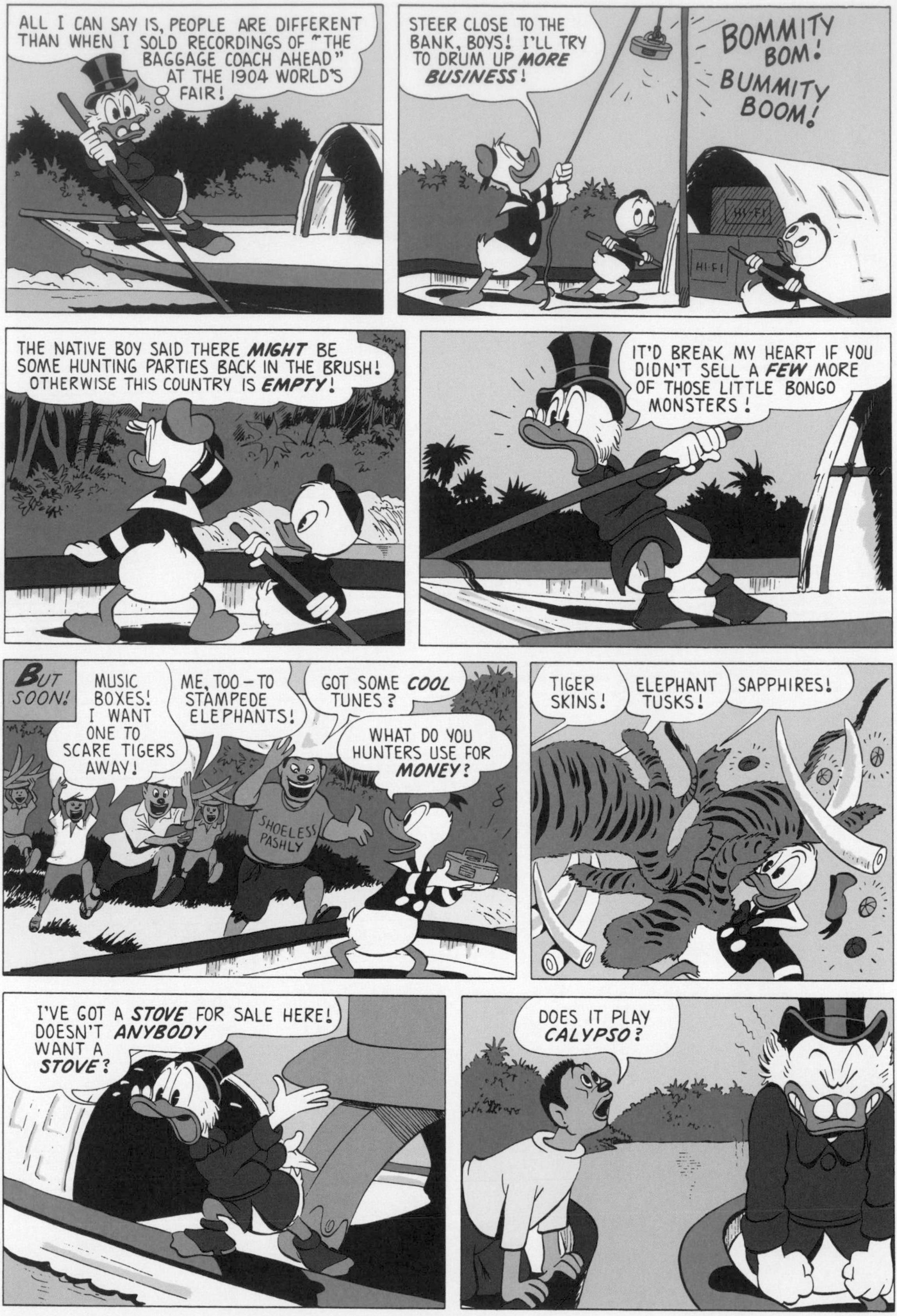
ALL I CAN SAY IS, PEOPLE ARE DIFFERENT THAN WHEN I SOLD RECORDINGS OF "THE BAGGAGE COACH AHEAD" AT THE 1904 WORLD'S FAIR!
STEER CLOSE TO THE BANK, BOYS! I'LL TRY TO DRUM UP MORE BUSINESS!
BOMMITY BOM! BUMMITY BOOM!
HI-FI
HI-FI
THE NATIVE BOY SAID THERE MIGHT BE SOME HUNTING PARTIES BACK IN THE BRUSH! OTHERWISE THIS COUNTRY IS EMPTY!
IT'D BREAK MY HEART IF YOU DIDN'T SELL A FEW MORE OF THOSE LITTLE BONGO MONSTERS!
BUT SOON!
MUSIC BOXES! I WANT ONE TO SCARE TIGERS AWAY!
ME, TOO—TO STAMPEDE ELEPHANTS!
GOT SOME COOL TUNES?
WHAT DO YOU HUNTERS USE FOR MONEY?
SHOELESS PASHLY
TIGER SKINS!
ELEPHANT TUSKS!
SAPPHIRES!
I'VE GOT A STOVE FOR SALE HERE! DOESN'T ANYBODY WANT A STOVE?
DOES IT PLAY CALYPSO?

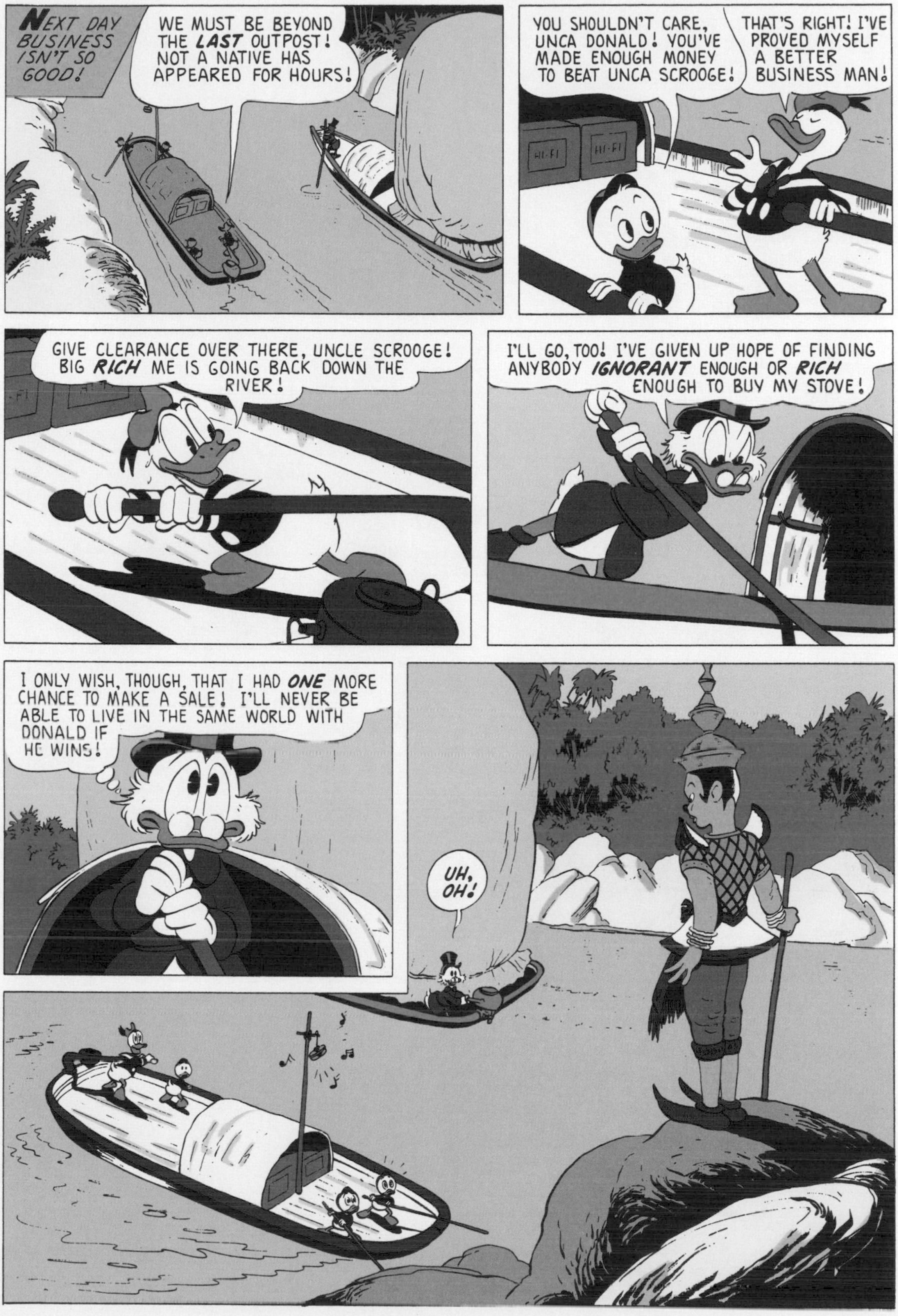
NEXT DAY BUSINESS ISN'T SO GOOD!
WE MUST BE BEYOND THE LAST OUTPOST! NOT A NATIVE HAS APPEARED FOR HOURS!
YOU SHOULDN'T CARE, UNCA DONALD! YOU'VE MADE ENOUGH MONEY TO BEAT UNCA SCROOGE!
THAT'S RIGHT! I'VE PROVED MYSELF A BETTER BUSINESS MAN!
HI-FI
HI-FI
GIVE CLEARANCE OVER THERE, UNCLE SCROOGE! BIG RICH ME IS GOING BACK DOWN THE RIVER!
I'LL GO, TOO! I'VE GIVEN UP HOPE OF FINDING ANYBODY IGNORANT ENOUGH OR RICH ENOUGH TO BUY MY STOVE!
I ONLY WISH, THOUGH, THAT I HAD ONE MORE CHANCE TO MAKE A SALE! I'LL NEVER BE ABLE TO LIVE IN THE SAME WORLD WITH DONALD IF HE WINS!
UH, OH!

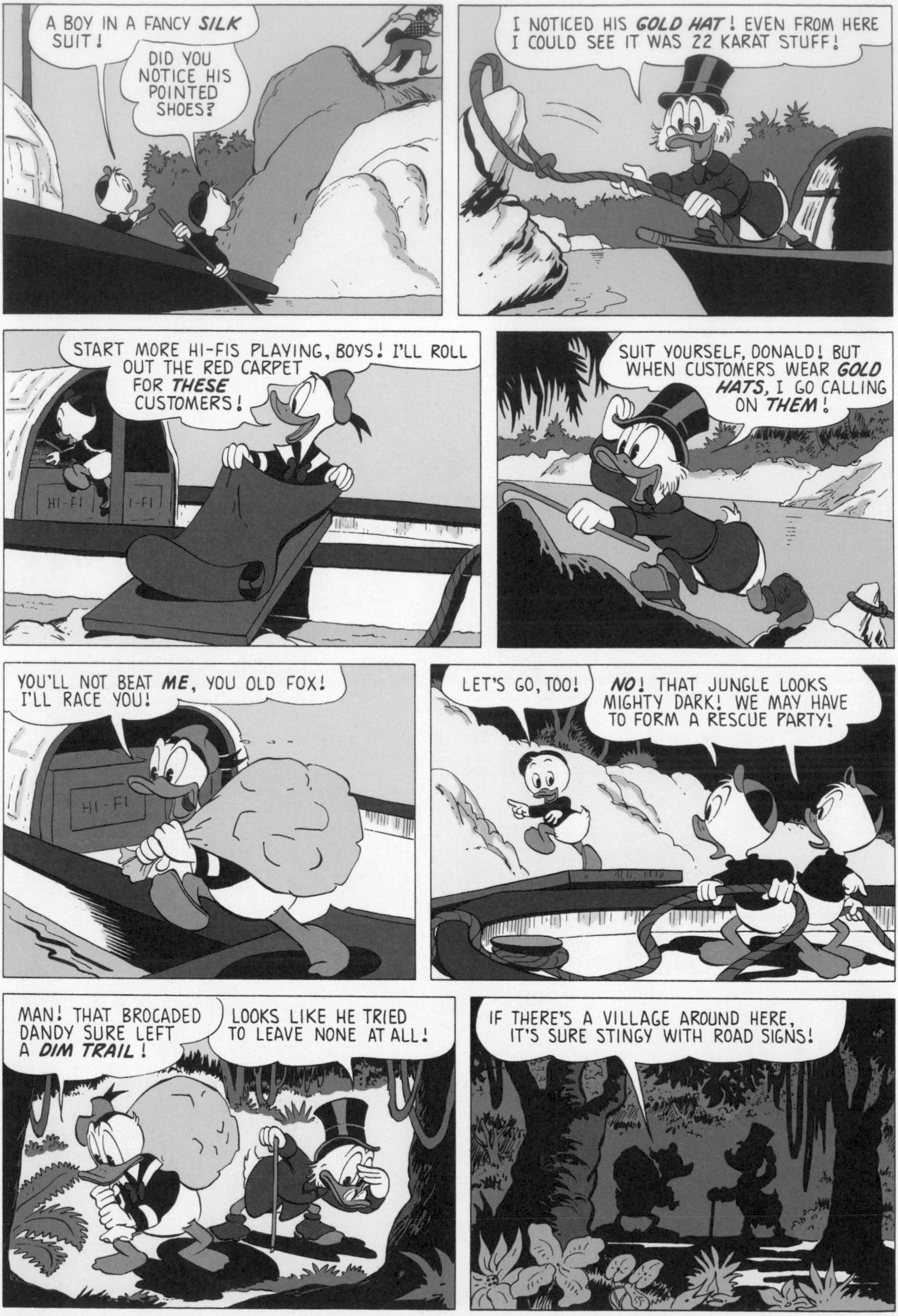
A BOY IN A FANCY SILK SUIT!
DID YOU NOTICE HIS POINTED SHOES?
I NOTICED HIS GOLD HAT! EVEN FROM HERE I COULD SEE IT WAS 22 KARAT STUFF!
START MORE HI-FIS PLAYING, BOYS! I'LL ROLL OUT THE RED CARPET FOR THESE CUSTOMERS!
HI-FI
I-FI
SUIT YOURSELF, DONALD! BUT WHEN CUSTOMERS WEAR GOLD HATS, I GO CALLING ON THEM!
YOU'LL NOT BEAT ME, YOU OLD FOX! I'LL RACE YOU!
HI-FI
LET'S GO, TOO!
NO! THAT JUNGLE LOOKS MIGHTY DARK! WE MAY HAVE TO FORM A RESCUE PARTY!
MAN! THAT BROCADED DANDY SURE LEFT A DIM TRAIL!
LOOKS LIKE HE TRIED TO LEAVE NONE AT ALL!
IF THERE'S A VILLAGE AROUND HERE, IT'S SURE STINGY WITH ROAD SIGNS!

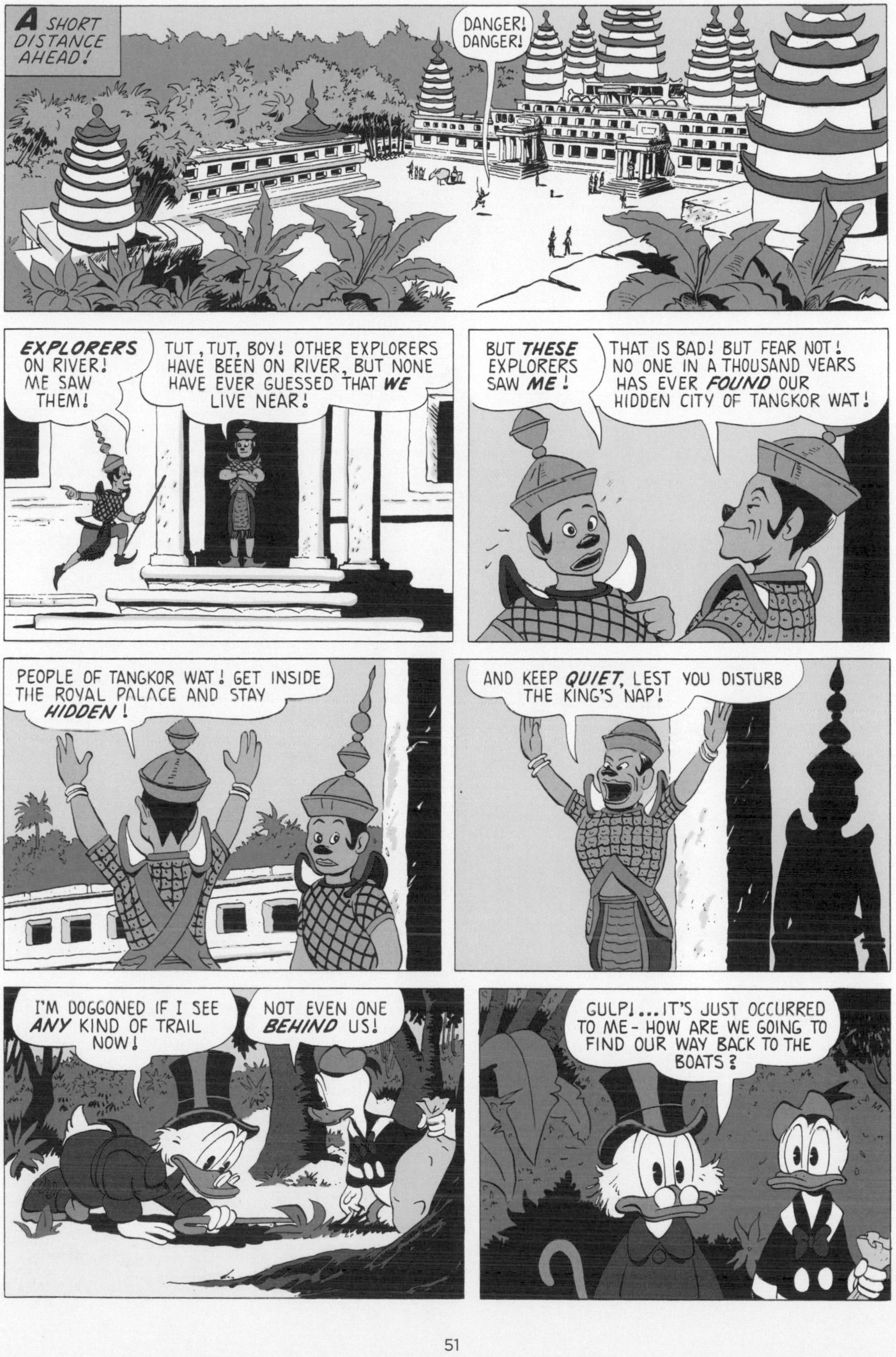

A SHORT DISTANCE AHEAD!
DANGER! DANGER!
EXPLORERS ON RIVER! ME SAW THEM!
TUT, TUT, BOY! OTHER EXPLORERS HAVE BEEN ON RIVER, BUT NONE HAVE EVER GUESSED THAT WE LIVE NEAR!
BUT THESE EXPLORERS SAW ME!
THAT IS BAD! BUT FEAR NOT! NO ONE IN A THOUSAND YEARS HAS EVER FOUND OUR HIDDEN CITY OF TANGKOR WAT!
PEOPLE OF TANGKOR WAT! GET INSIDE THE ROYAL PALACE AND STAY HIDDEN!
AND KEEP QUIET, LEST YOU DISTURB THE KING'S NAP!
I'M DOGGONED IF I SEE ANY KIND OF TRAIL NOW!
NOT EVEN ONE BEHIND US!
GULP! ...IT'S JUST OCCURRED TO ME– HOW ARE WE GOING TO FIND OUR WAY BACK TO THE BOATS?

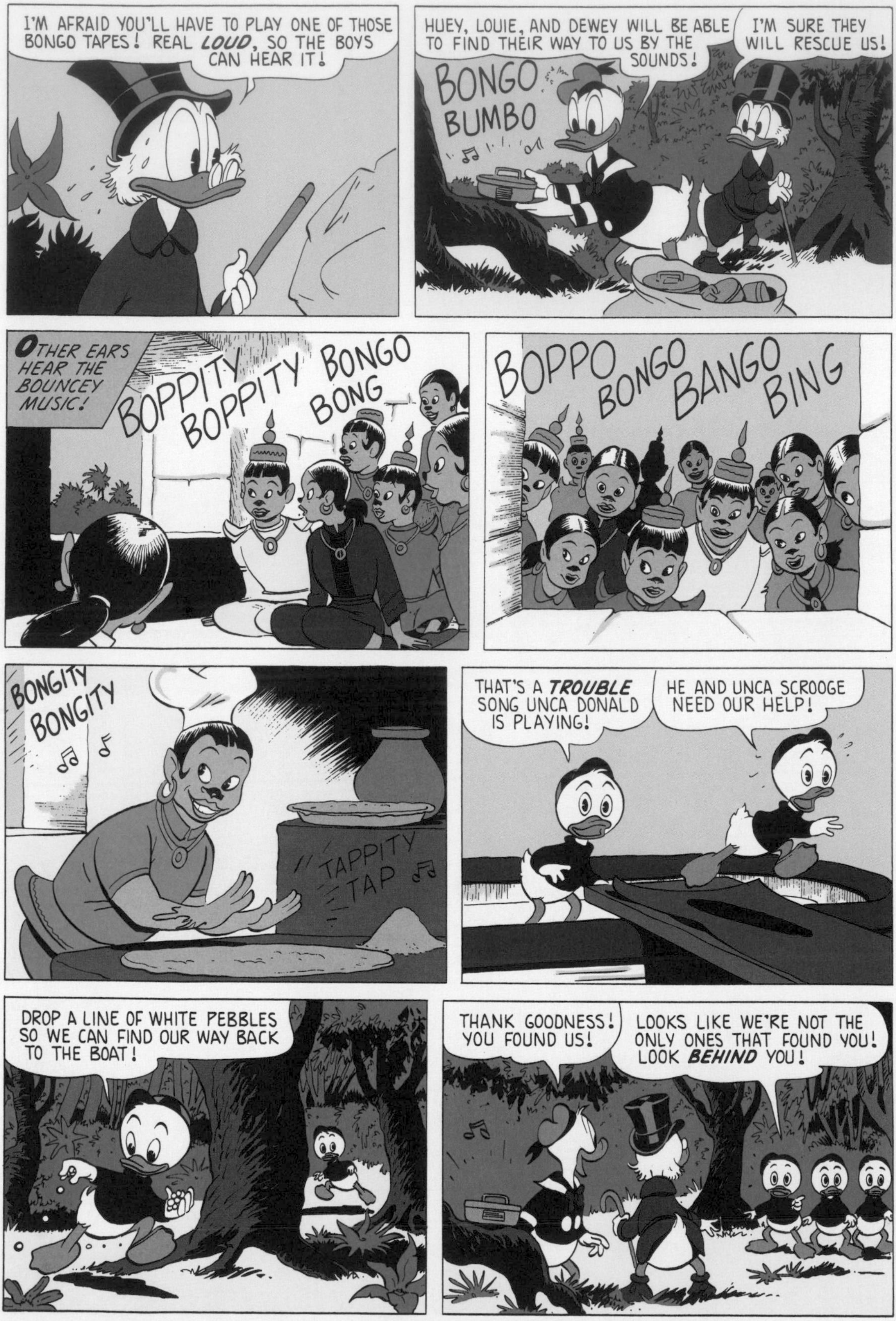
I'M AFRAID YOU'LL HAVE TO PLAY ONE OF THOSE BONGO TAPES! REAL LOUD, SO THE BOYS CAN HEAR IT!
HUEY, LOUIE, AND DEWEY WILL BE ABLE TO FIND THEIR WAY TO US BY THE SOUNDS!
I'M SURE THEY WILL RESCUE US!
BONGO BUMBO
OTHER EARS HEAR THE BOUNCEY MUSIC!
BOPPITY BOPPITY BONGO BONG
BOPPO BONGO BANGO BING
BONGITY BONGITY
TAPPITY TAP
THAT'S A TROUBLE SONG UNCA DONALD IS PLAYING!
HE AND UNCA SCROOGE NEED OUR HELP!
DROP A LINE OF WHITE PEBBLES SO WE CAN FIND OUR WAY BACK TO THE BOAT!
THANK GOODNESS! YOU FOUND US!
LOOKS LIKE WE'RE NOT THE ONLY ONES THAT FOUND YOU! LOOK BEHIND YOU!

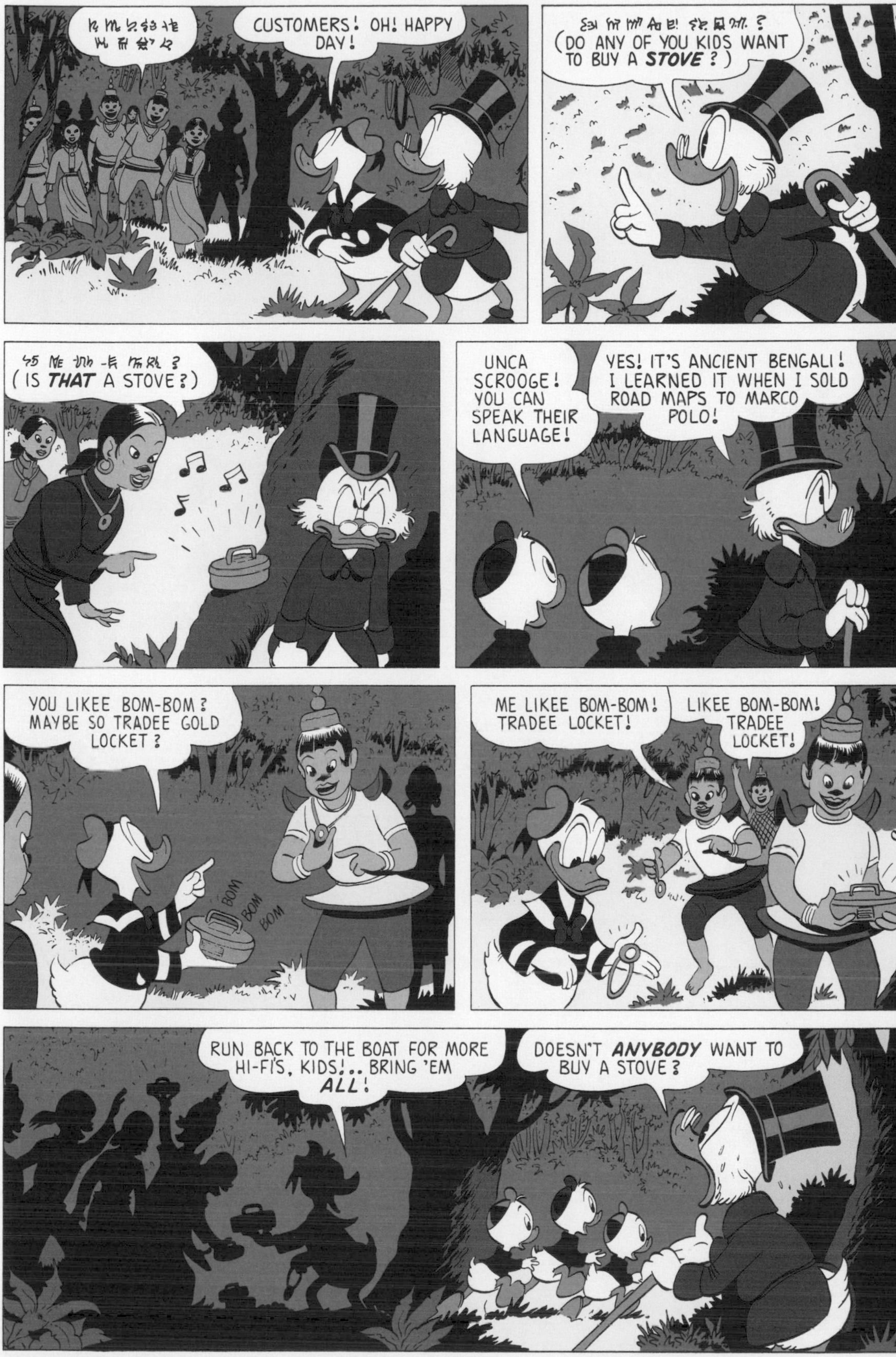
CUSTOMERS! OH! HAPPY DAY!
(DO ANY OF YOU KIDS WANT TO BUY A STOVE?)
(IS THAT A STOVE?)
UNCA SCROOGE! YOU CAN SPEAK THEIR LANGUAGE!
YES! IT'S ANCIENT BENGALI! I LEARNED IT WHEN I SOLD ROAD MAPS TO MARCO POLO!
YOU LIKEE BOM-BOM? MAYBE SO TRADEE GOLD LOCKET?
BOM
BOM
BOM
ME LIKEE BOM-BOM! TRADEE LOCKET!
LIKEE BOM-BOM! TRADEE LOCKET!
RUN BACK TO THE BOAT FOR MORE HI-FI'S, KIDS!.. BRING 'EM ALL!
DOESN'T ANYBODY WANT TO BUY A STOVE?

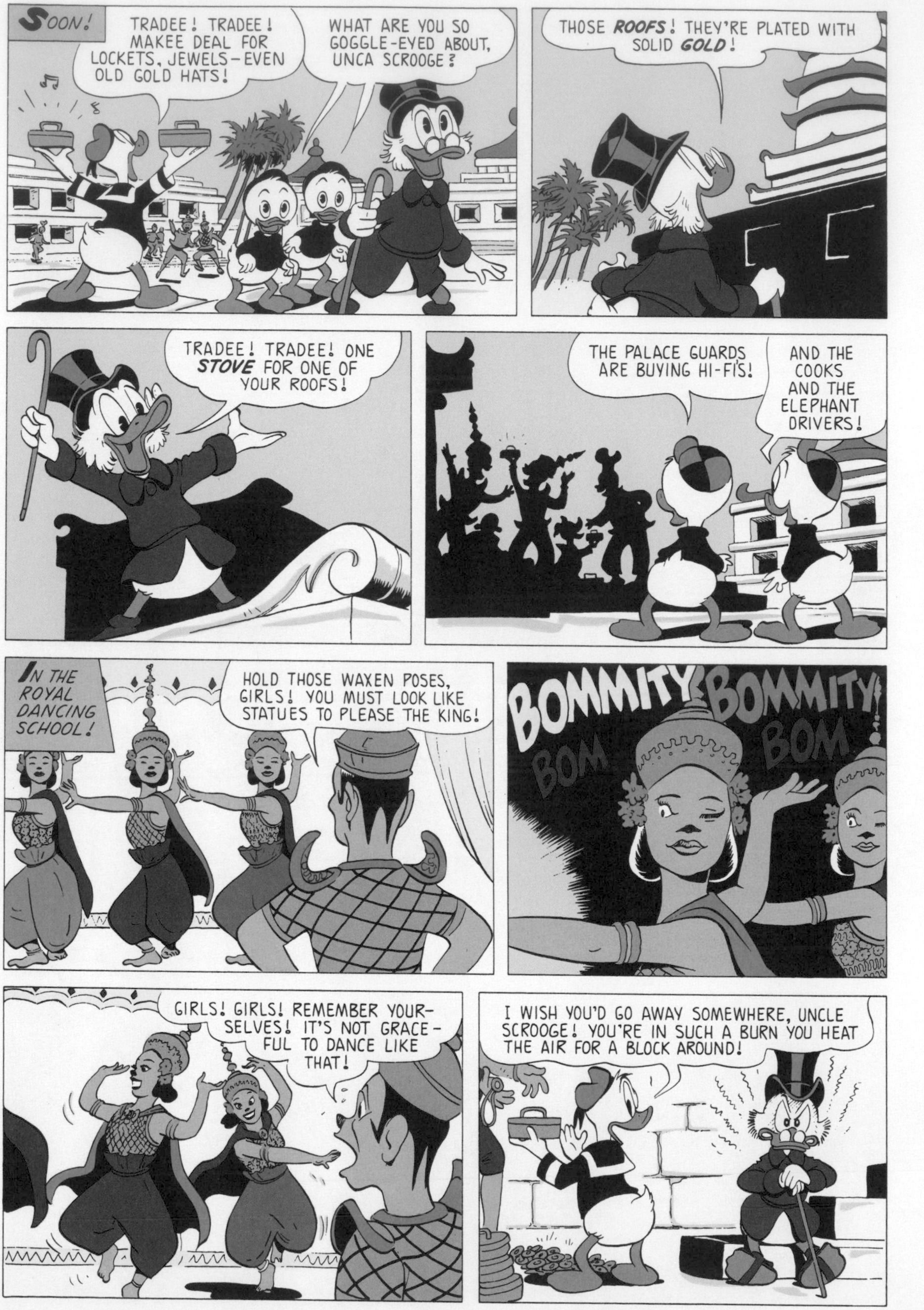
SOON!
TRADEE! TRADEE! MAKEE DEAL FOR LOCKETS, JEWELS—EVEN OLD GOLD HATS!
WHAT ARE YOU SO GOGGLE-EYED ABOUT, UNCA SCROOGE?
THOSE ROOFS! THEY'RE PLATED WITH SOLID GOLD!
TRADEE! TRADEE! ONE STOVE FOR ONE OF YOUR ROOFS!
THE PALACE GUARDS ARE BUYING HI-FI'S!
AND THE COOKS AND THE ELEPHANT DRIVERS!
IN THE ROYAL DANCING SCHOOL!
HOLD THOSE WAXEN POSES, GIRLS! YOU MUST LOOK LIKE STATUES TO PLEASE THE KING!
BOMMITY BOMMITY
BOM BOM
GIRLS! GIRLS! REMEMBER YOURSELVES! IT'S NOT GRACEFUL TO DANCE LIKE THAT!
I WISH YOU'D GO AWAY SOMEWHERE, UNCLE SCROOGE! YOU'RE IN SUCH A BURN YOU HEAT THE AIR FOR A BLOCK AROUND!

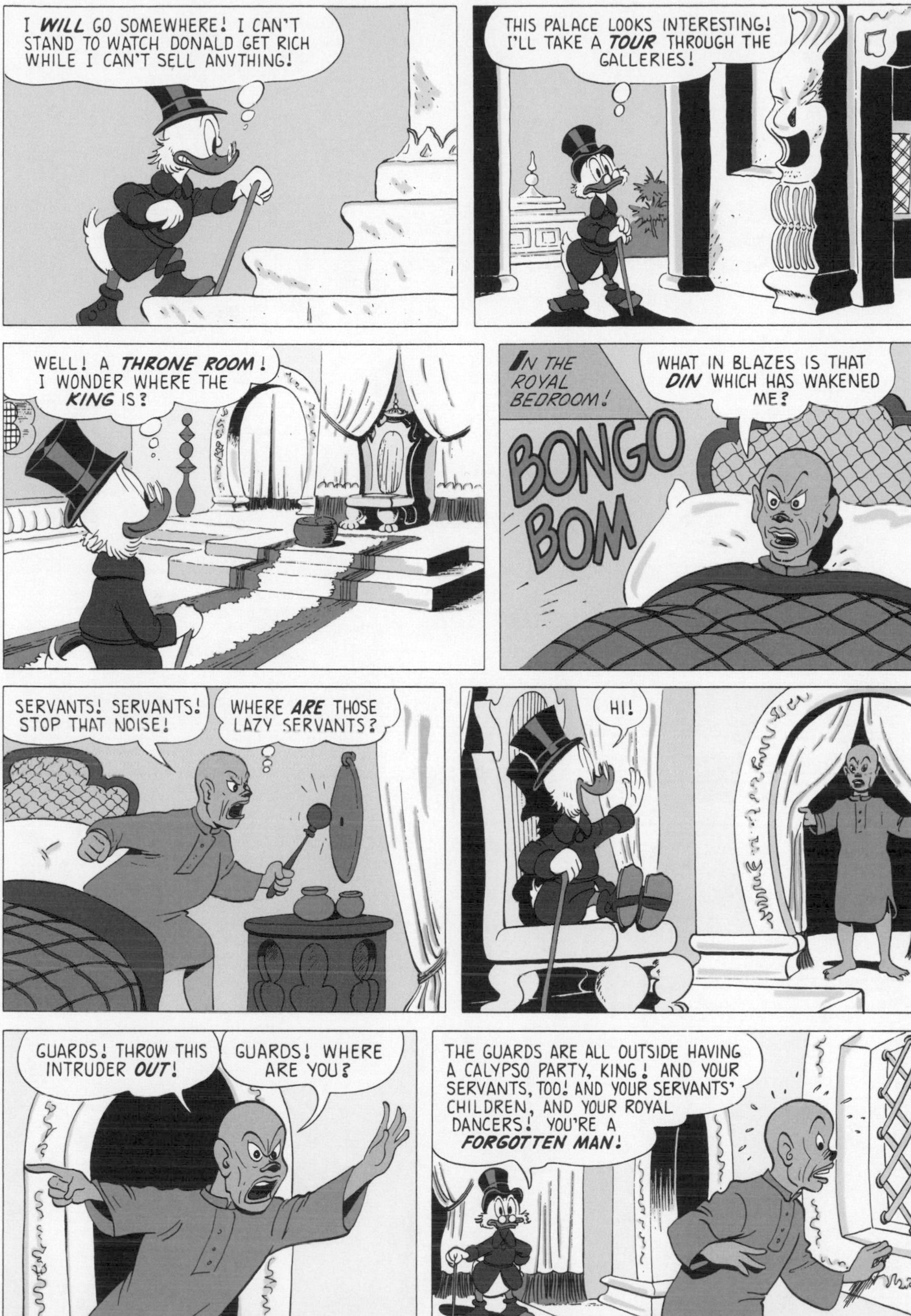
I WILL GO SOMEWHERE! I CAN'T STAND TO WATCH DONALD GET RICH WHILE I CAN'T SELL ANYTHING!
THIS PALACE LOOKS INTERESTING! I'LL TAKE A TOUR THROUGH THE GALLERIES!
WELL! A THRONE ROOM! I WONDER WHERE THE KING IS?
IN THE ROYAL BEDROOM!
WHAT IN BLAZES IS THAT DIN WHICH HAS WAKENED ME?
BONGO BOM
SERVANTS! SERVANTS! STOP THAT NOISE!
WHERE ARE THOSE LAZY SERVANTS?
HI!
GUARDS! THROW THIS INTRUDER OUT!
GUARDS! WHERE ARE YOU?
THE GUARDS ARE ALL OUTSIDE HAVING A CALYPSO PARTY, KING! AND YOUR SERVANTS, TOO! AND YOUR SERVANTS' CHILDREN, AND YOUR ROYAL DANCERS! YOU'RE A FORGOTTEN MAN!

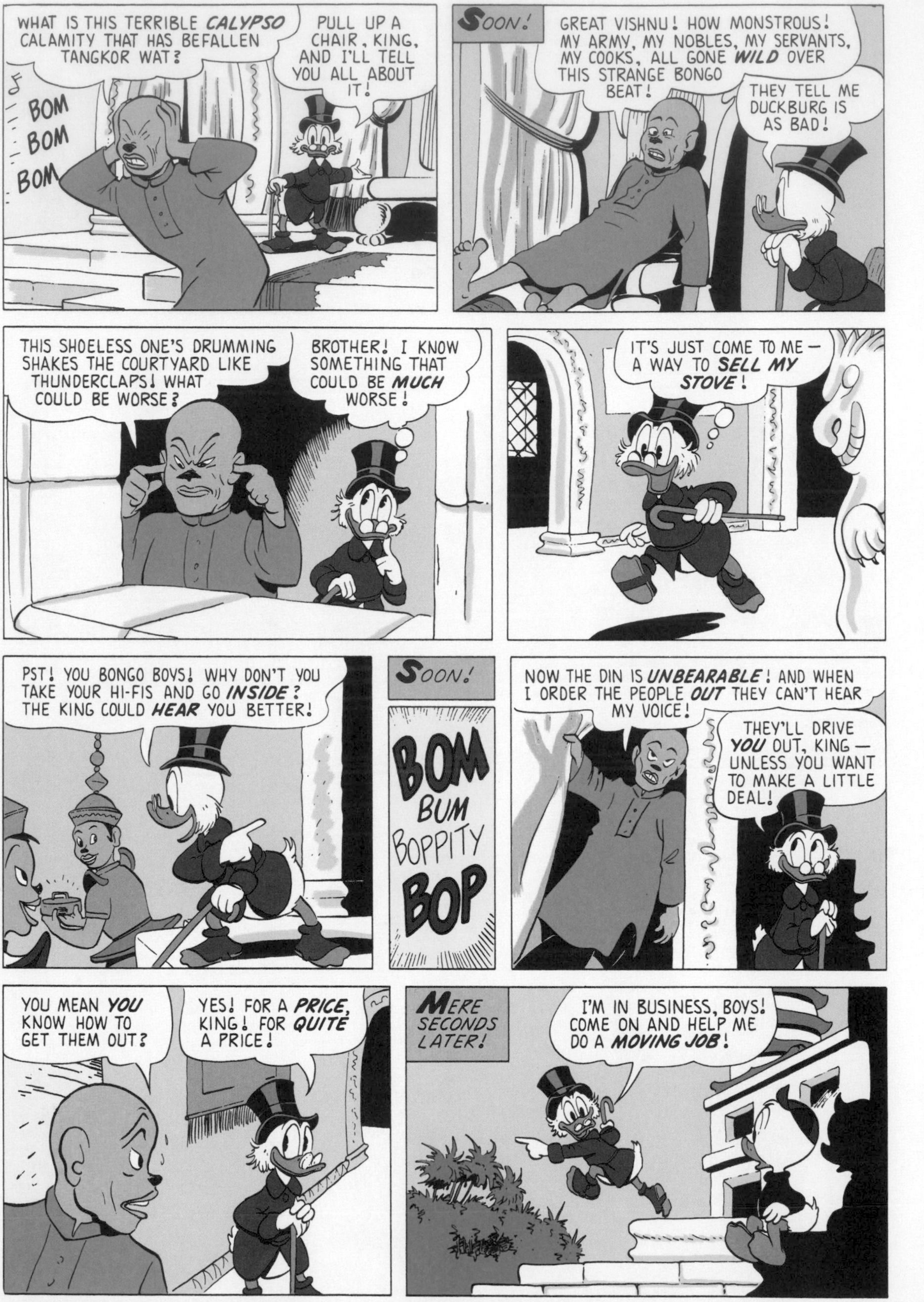
WHAT IS THIS TERRIBLE CALYPSO CALAMITY THAT HAS BEFALLEN TANGKOR WAT?
PULL UP A CHAIR, KING, AND I'LL TELL YOU ALL ABOUT IT!
BOM BOM BOM
SOON!
GREAT VISHNU! HOW MONSTROUS! MY ARMY, MY NOBLES, MY SERVANTS, MY COOKS, ALL GONE WILD OVER THIS STRANGE BONGO BEAT!
THEY TELL ME DUCKBURG IS AS BAD!
THIS SHOELESS ONE'S DRUMMING SHAKES THE COURTYARD LIKE THUNDERCLAPS! WHAT COULD BE WORSE?
BROTHER! I KNOW SOMETHING THAT COULD BE MUCH WORSE!
IT'S JUST COME TO ME — A WAY TO SELL MY STOVE!
PST! YOU BONGO BOYS! WHY DON'T YOU TAKE YOUR HI-FIS AND GO INSIDE? THE KING COULD HEAR YOU BETTER!
SOON!
BOM BUM BOPPITY BOP
NOW THE DIN IS UNBEARABLE! AND WHEN I ORDER THE PEOPLE OUT THEY CAN'T HEAR MY VOICE!
THEY'LL DRIVE YOU OUT, KING — UNLESS YOU WANT TO MAKE A LITTLE DEAL!
YOU MEAN YOU KNOW HOW TO GET THEM OUT?
YES! FOR A PRICE, KING! FOR QUITE A PRICE!
MERE SECONDS LATER!
I'M IN BUSINESS, BOYS! COME ON AND HELP ME DO A MOVING JOB!

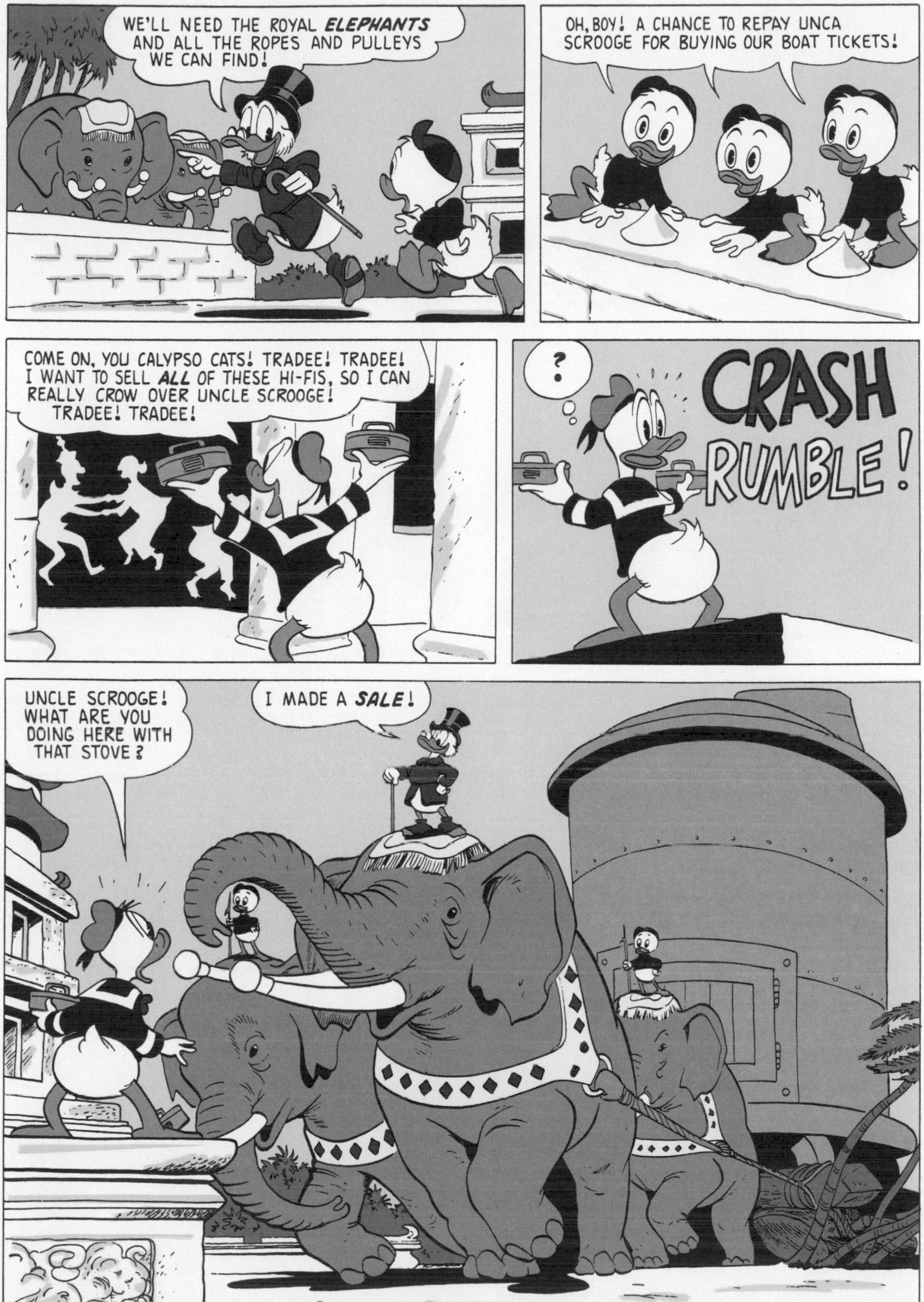

WE'LL NEED THE ROYAL ELEPHANTS AND ALL THE ROPES AND PULLEYS WE CAN FIND!
OH, BOY! A CHANCE TO REPAY UNCA SCROOGE FOR BUYING OUR BOAT TICKETS!
COME ON, YOU CALYPSO CATS! TRADEE! TRADEE! I WANT TO SELL ALL OF THESE HI-FIS, SO I CAN REALLY CROW OVER UNCLE SCROOGE! TRADEE! TRADEE!
?
CRASH
RUMBLE!
UNCLE SCROOGE! WHAT ARE YOU DOING HERE WITH THAT STOVE?
I MADE A SALE!

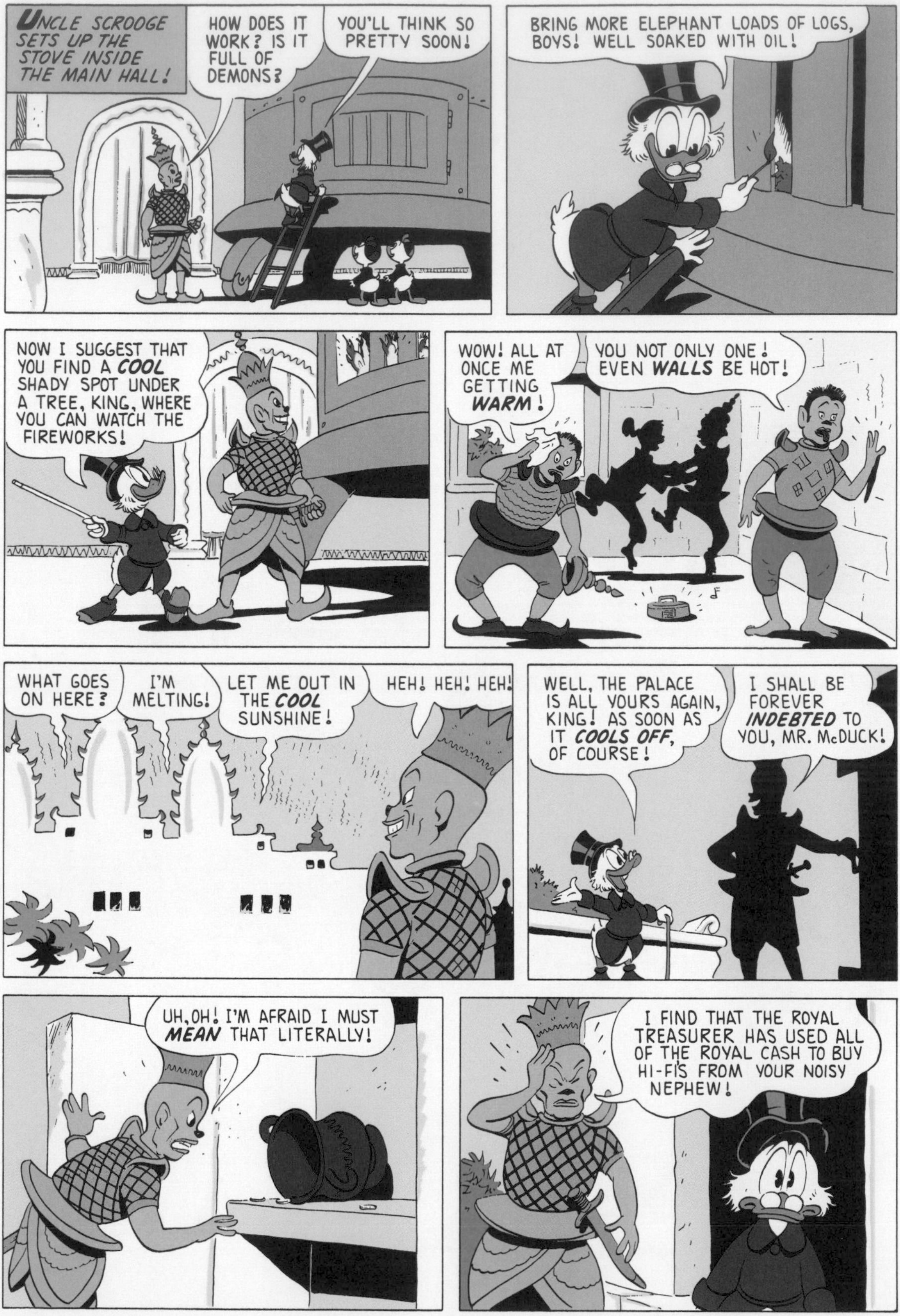
UNCLE SCROOGE SETS UP THE STOVE INSIDE THE MAIN HALL!
HOW DOES IT WORK? IS IT FULL OF DEMONS?
YOU'LL THINK SO PRETTY SOON!
BRING MORE ELEPHANT LOADS OF LOGS, BOYS! WELL SOAKED WITH OIL!
NOW I SUGGEST THAT YOU FIND A COOL SHADY SPOT UNDER A TREE, KING, WHERE YOU CAN WATCH THE FIREWORKS!
WOW! ALL AT ONCE ME GETTING WARM!
YOU NOT ONLY ONE! EVEN WALLS BE HOT!
WHAT GOES ON HERE?
I'M MELTING!
LET ME OUT IN THE COOL SUNSHINE!
HEH! HEH! HEH!
WELL, THE PALACE IS ALL YOURS AGAIN, KING! AS SOON AS IT COOLS OFF, OF COURSE!
I SHALL BE FOREVER INDEBTED TO YOU, MR. McDUCK!
UH, OH! I'M AFRAID I MUST MEAN THAT LITERALLY!
I FIND THAT THE ROYAL TREASURER HAS USED ALL OF THE ROYAL CASH TO BUY HI-FI'S FROM YOUR NOISY NEPHEW!

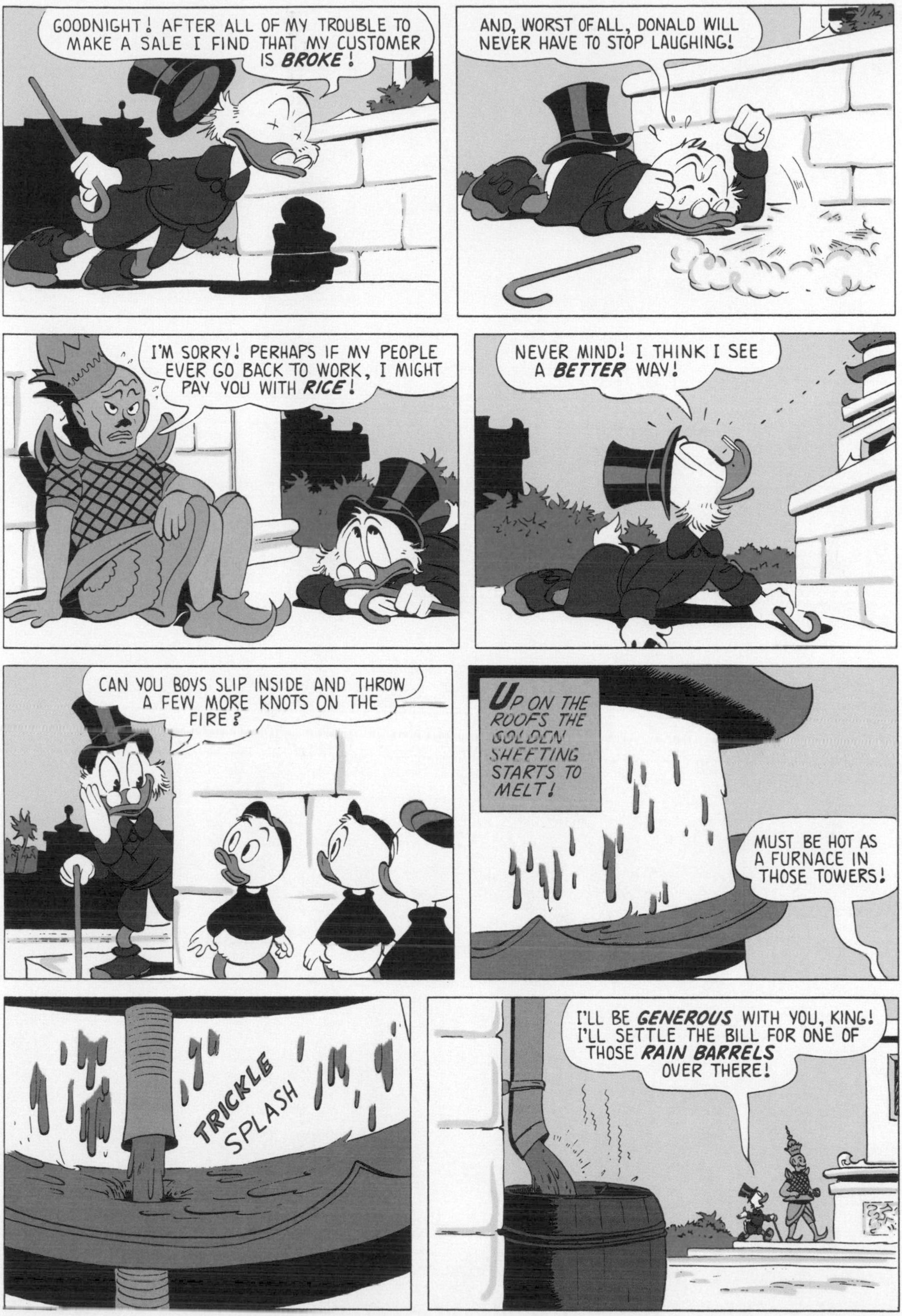
GOODNIGHT! AFTER ALL OF MY TROUBLE TO MAKE A SALE I FIND THAT MY CUSTOMER IS BROKE!
AND, WORST OF ALL, DONALD WILL NEVER HAVE TO STOP LAUGHING!
I'M SORRY! PERHAPS IF MY PEOPLE EVER GO BACK TO WORK, I MIGHT PAY YOU WITH RICE!
NEVER MIND! I THINK I SEE A BETTER WAY!
CAN YOU BOYS SLIP INSIDE AND THROW A FEW MORE KNOTS ON THE FIRE?
UP ON THE ROOFS THE GOLDEN SHEFTING STARTS TO MELT!
MUST BE HOT AS A FURNACE IN THOSE TOWERS!
TRICKLE
SPLASH
I'LL BE GENEROUS WITH YOU, KING! I'LL SETTLE THE BILL FOR ONE OF THOSE RAIN BARRELS OVER THERE!

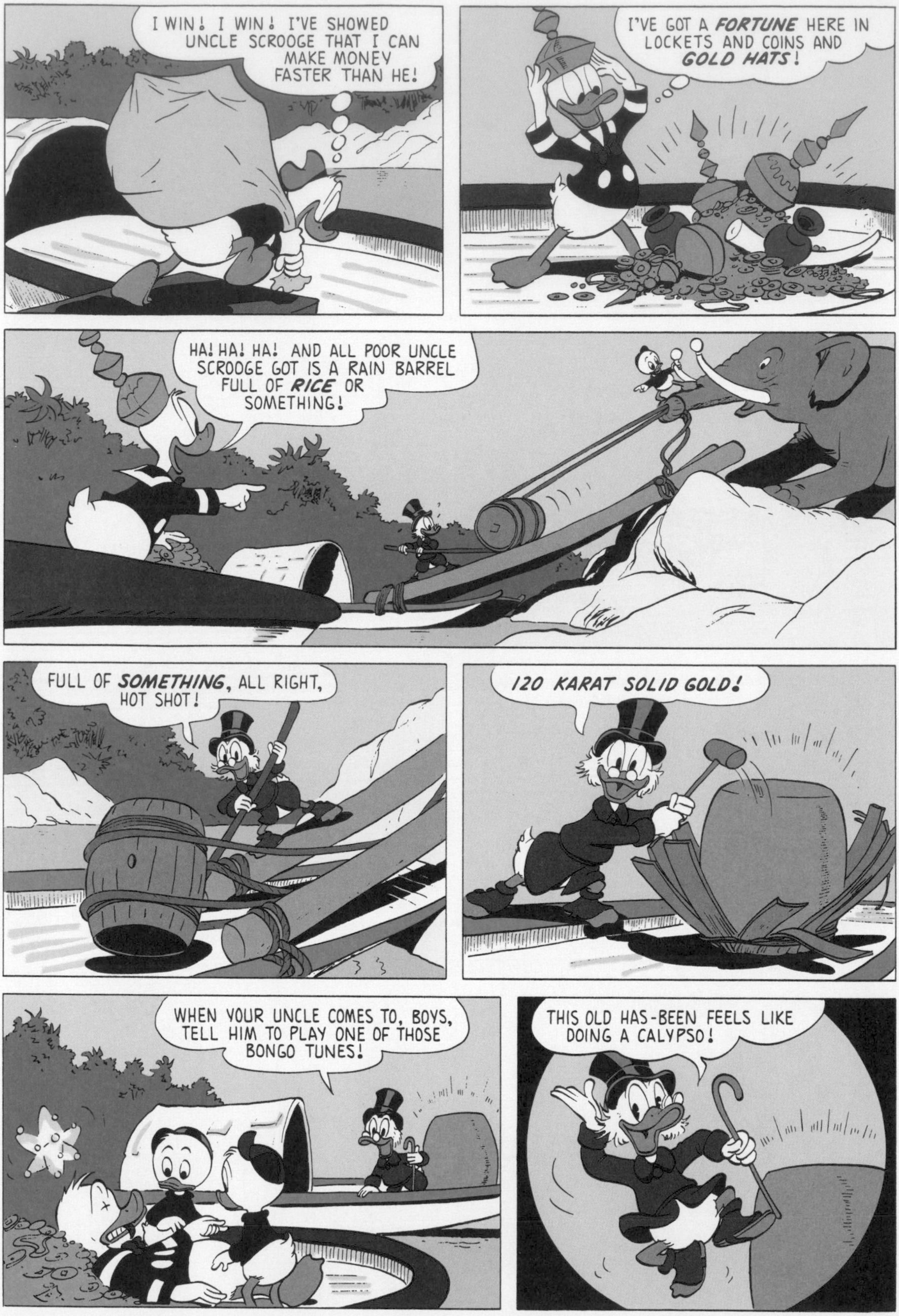
I WIN! I WIN! I'VE SHOWED UNCLE SCROOGE THAT I CAN MAKE MONEY FASTER THAN HE!
I'VE GOT A FORTUNE HERE IN LOCKETS AND COINS AND GOLD HATS!
HA! HA! HA! AND ALL POOR UNCLE SCROOGE GOT IS A RAIN BARREL FULL OF RICE OR SOMETHING!
FULL OF SOMETHING, ALL RIGHT, HOT SHOT!
120 KARAT SOLID GOLD!
WHEN YOUR UNCLE COMES TO, BOYS, TELL HIM TO PLAY ONE OF THOSE BONGO TUNES!
THIS OLD HAS-BEEN FEELS LIKE DOING A CALYPSO!

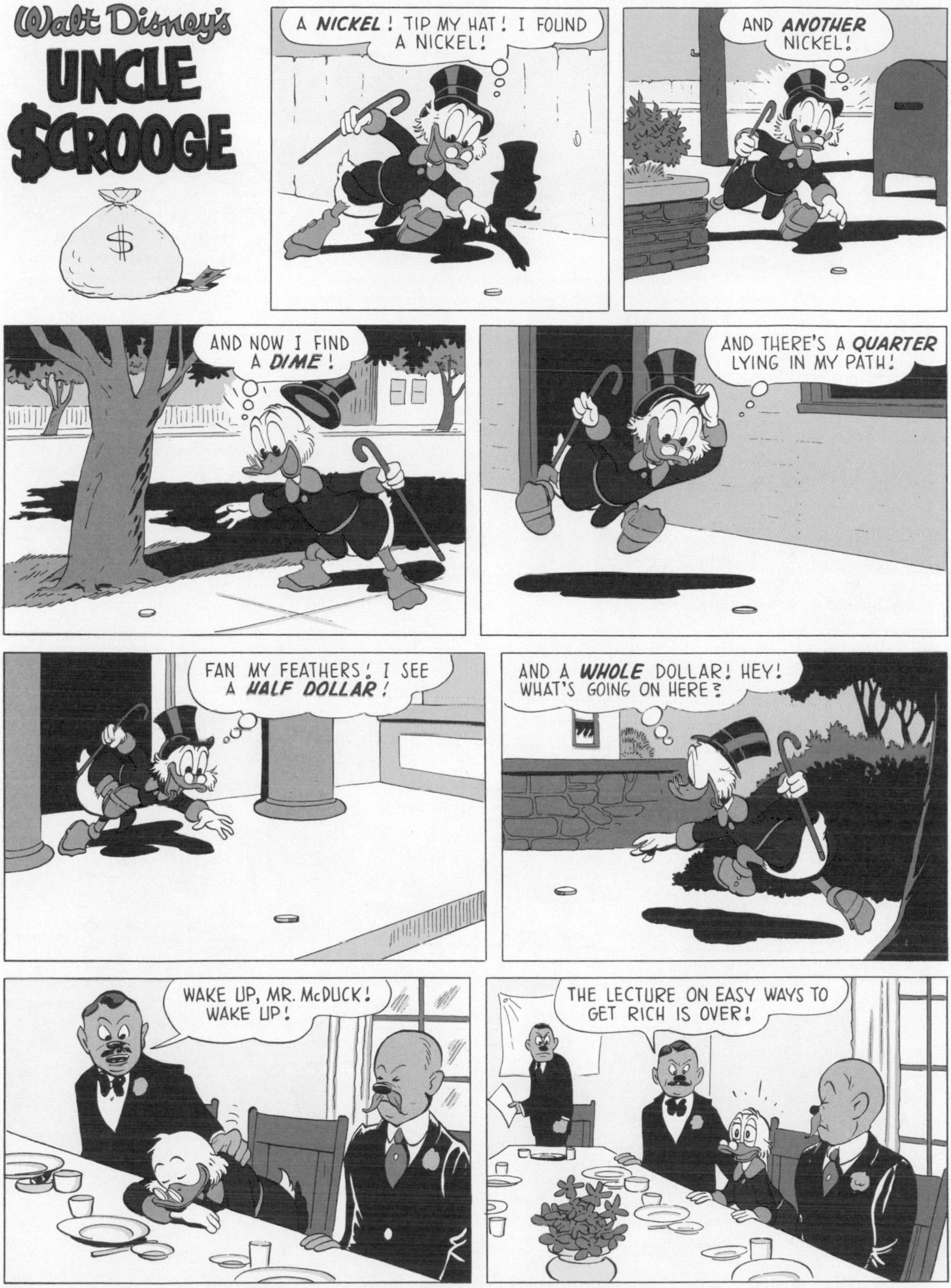
Walt Disney's
UNCLE $CROOGE
A NICKEL! TIP MY HAT! I FOUND A NICKEL!
AND ANOTHER NICKEL!
AND NOW I FIND A DIME!
AND THERE'S A QUARTER LYING IN MY PATH!
FAN MY FEATHERS! I SEE A HALF DOLLAR!
AND A WHOLE DOLLAR! HEY! WHAT'S GOING ON HERE?
WAKE UP, MR. McDUCK! WAKE UP!
THE LECTURE ON EASY WAYS TO GET RICH IS OVER!

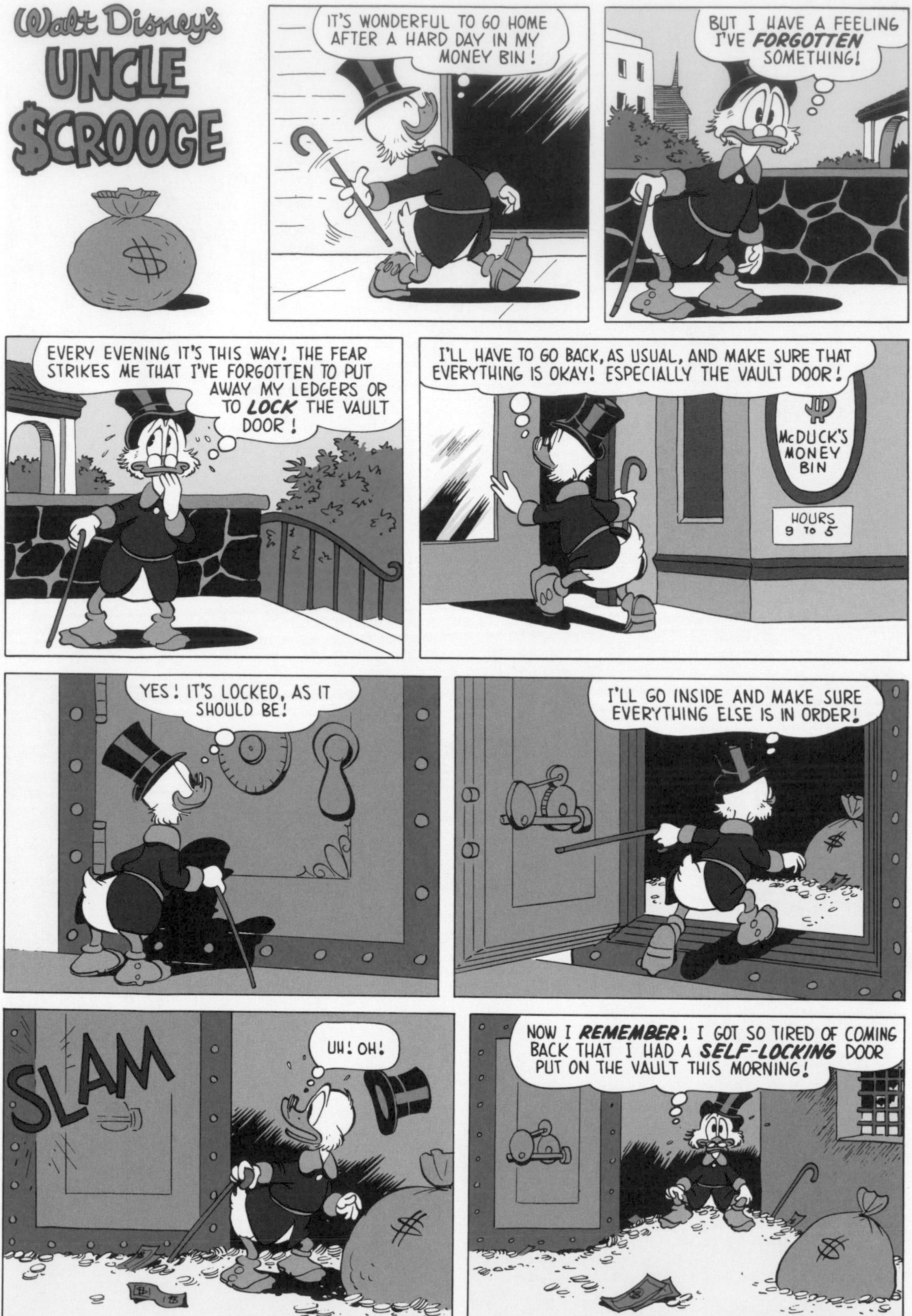
Walt Disney's
UNCLE $CROOGE
IT'S WONDERFUL TO GO HOME AFTER A HARD DAY IN MY MONEY BIN!
BUT I HAVE A FEELING I'VE FORGOTTEN SOMETHING!
EVERY EVENING IT'S THIS WAY! THE FEAR STRIKES ME THAT I'VE FORGOTTEN TO PUT AWAY MY LEDGERS OR TO LOCK THE VAULT DOOR!
I'LL HAVE TO GO BACK, AS USUAL, AND MAKE SURE THAT EVERYTHING IS OKAY! ESPECIALLY THE VAULT DOOR!
McDUCK'S MONEY BIN
HOURS 9 TO 5
YES! IT'S LOCKED, AS IT SHOULD BE!
I'LL GO INSIDE AND MAKE SURE EVERYTHING ELSE IS IN ORDER!
SLAM
UH! OH!
NOW I REMEMBER! I GOT SO TIRED OF COMING BACK THAT I HAD A SELF-LOCKING DOOR PUT ON THE VAULT THIS MORNING!

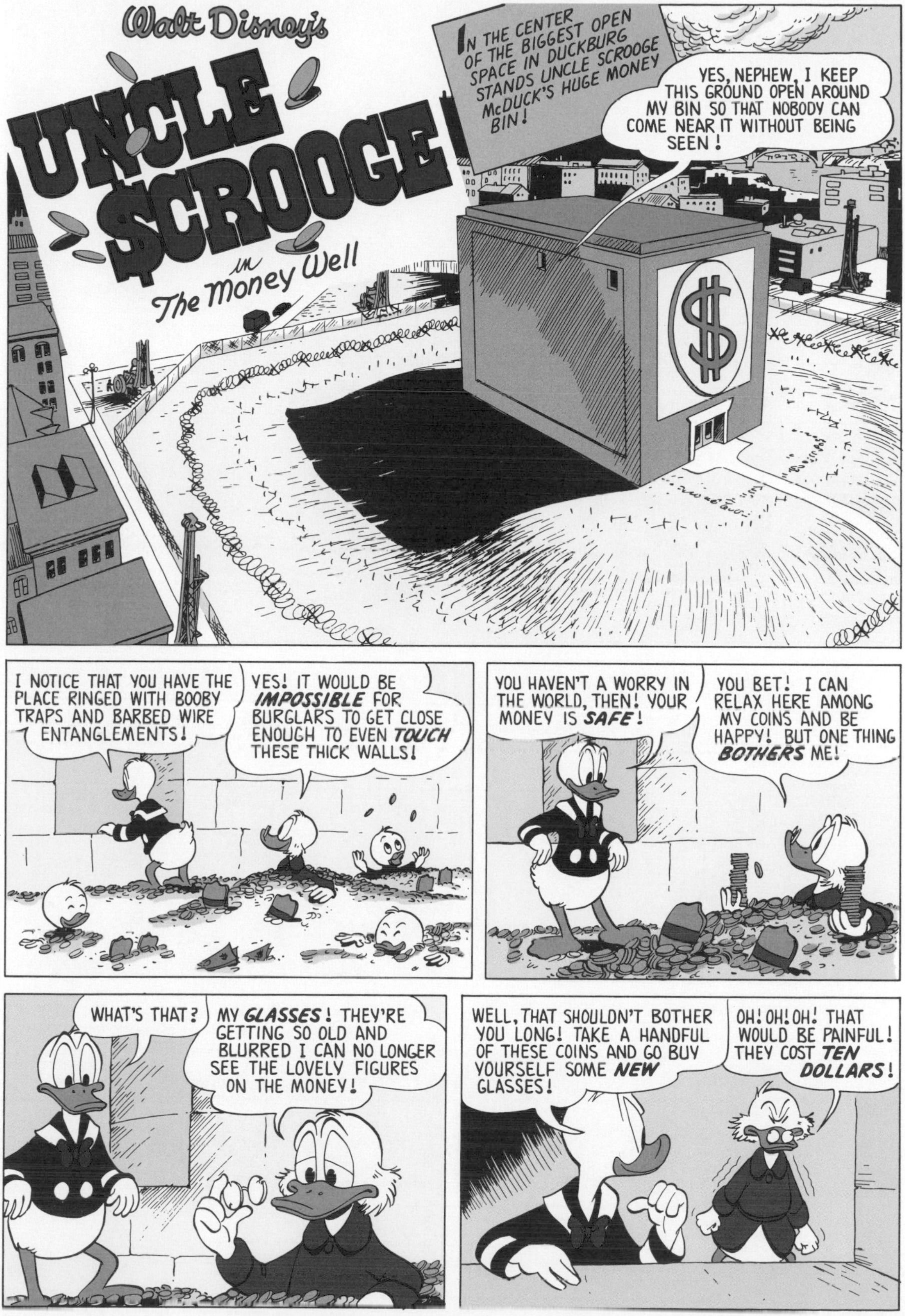
Walt Disney's
UNCLE $CROOGE
in
The Money Well
IN THE CENTER OF THE BIGGEST OPEN SPACE IN DUCKBURG STANDS UNCLE SCROOGE McDUCK'S HUGE MONEY BIN!
YES, NEPHEW, I KEEP THIS GROUND OPEN AROUND MY BIN SO THAT NOBODY CAN COME NEAR IT WITHOUT BEING SEEN!
I NOTICE THAT YOU HAVE THE PLACE RINGED WITH BOOBY TRAPS AND BARBED WIRE ENTANGLEMENTS!
YES! IT WOULD BE IMPOSSIBLE FOR BURGLARS TO GET CLOSE ENOUGH TO EVEN TOUCH THESE THICK WALLS!
YOU HAVEN'T A WORRY IN THE WORLD, THEN! YOUR MONEY IS SAFE!
YOU BET! I CAN RELAX HERE AMONG MY COINS AND BE HAPPY! BUT ONE THING BOTHERS ME!
WHAT'S THAT?
MY GLASSES! THEY'RE GETTING SO OLD AND BLURRED I CAN NO LONGER SEE THE LOVELY FIGURES ON THE MONEY!
WELL, THAT SHOULDN'T BOTHER YOU LONG! TAKE A HANDFUL OF THESE COINS AND GO BUY YOURSELF SOME NEW GLASSES!
OH! OH! OH! THAT WOULD BE PAINFUL! THEY COST TEN DOLLARS!

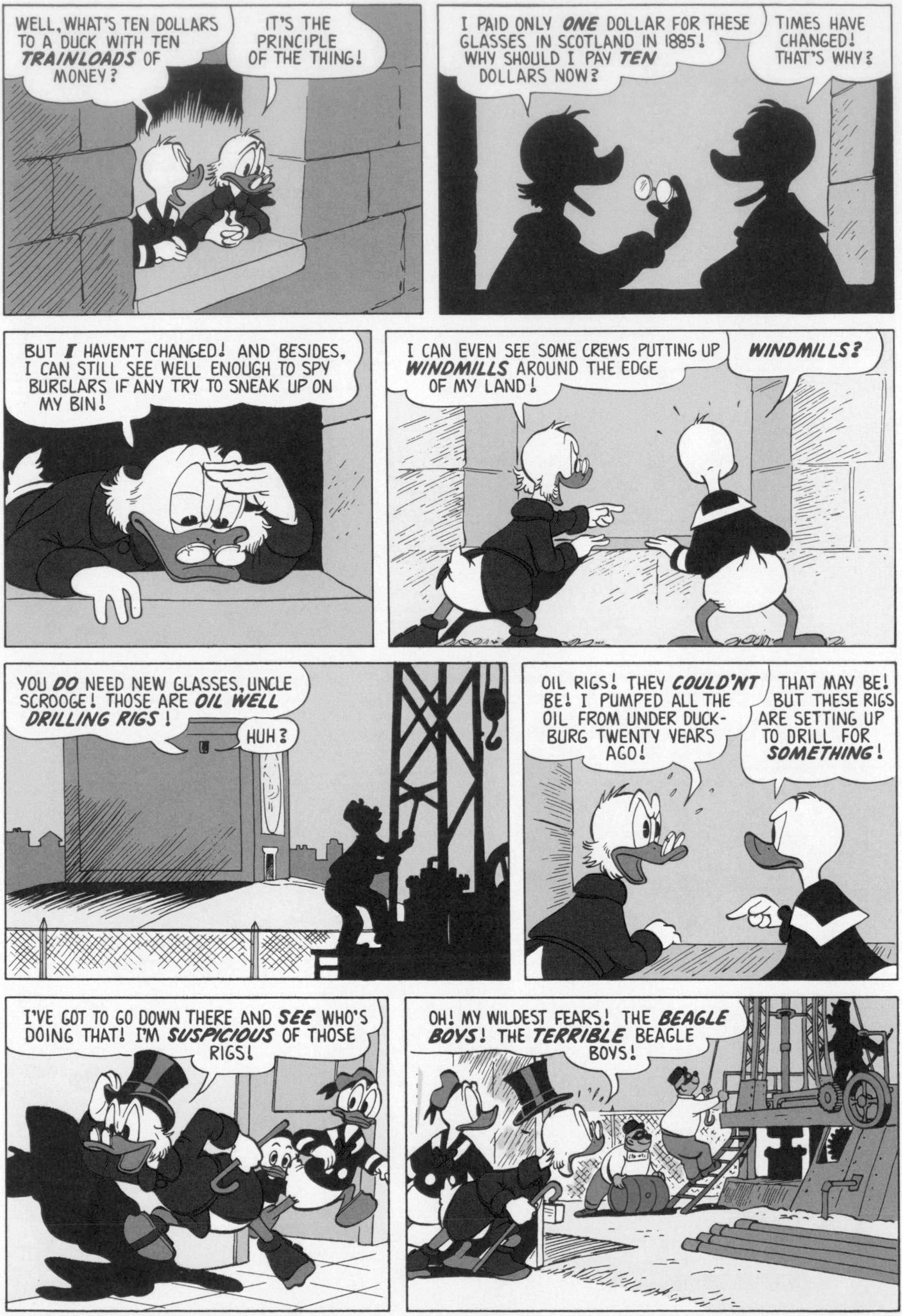
WELL, WHAT'S TEN DOLLARS TO A DUCK WITH TEN TRAINLOADS OF MONEY?
IT'S THE PRINCIPLE OF THE THING!
I PAID ONLY ONE DOLLAR FOR THESE GLASSES IN SCOTLAND IN 1885! WHY SHOULD I PAY TEN DOLLARS NOW?
TIMES HAVE CHANGED! THAT'S WHY?
BUT I HAVEN'T CHANGED! AND BESIDES, I CAN STILL SEE WELL ENOUGH TO SPY BURGLARS IF ANY TRY TO SNEAK UP ON MY BIN!
I CAN EVEN SEE SOME CREWS PUTTING UP WINDMILLS AROUND THE EDGE OF MY LAND!
WINDMILLS?
YOU DO NEED NEW GLASSES, UNCLE SCROOGE! THOSE ARE OIL WELL DRILLING RIGS!
HUH?
OIL RIGS! THEY COULD'NT BE! I PUMPED ALL THE OIL FROM UNDER DUCK-BURG TWENTY YEARS AGO!
THAT MAY BE! BUT THESE RIGS ARE SETTING UP TO DRILL FOR SOMETHING!
I'VE GOT TO GO DOWN THERE AND SEE WHO'S DOING THAT! I'M SUSPICIOUS OF THOSE RIGS!
OH! MY WILDEST FEARS! THE BEAGLE BOYS! THE TERRIBLE BEAGLE BOYS!

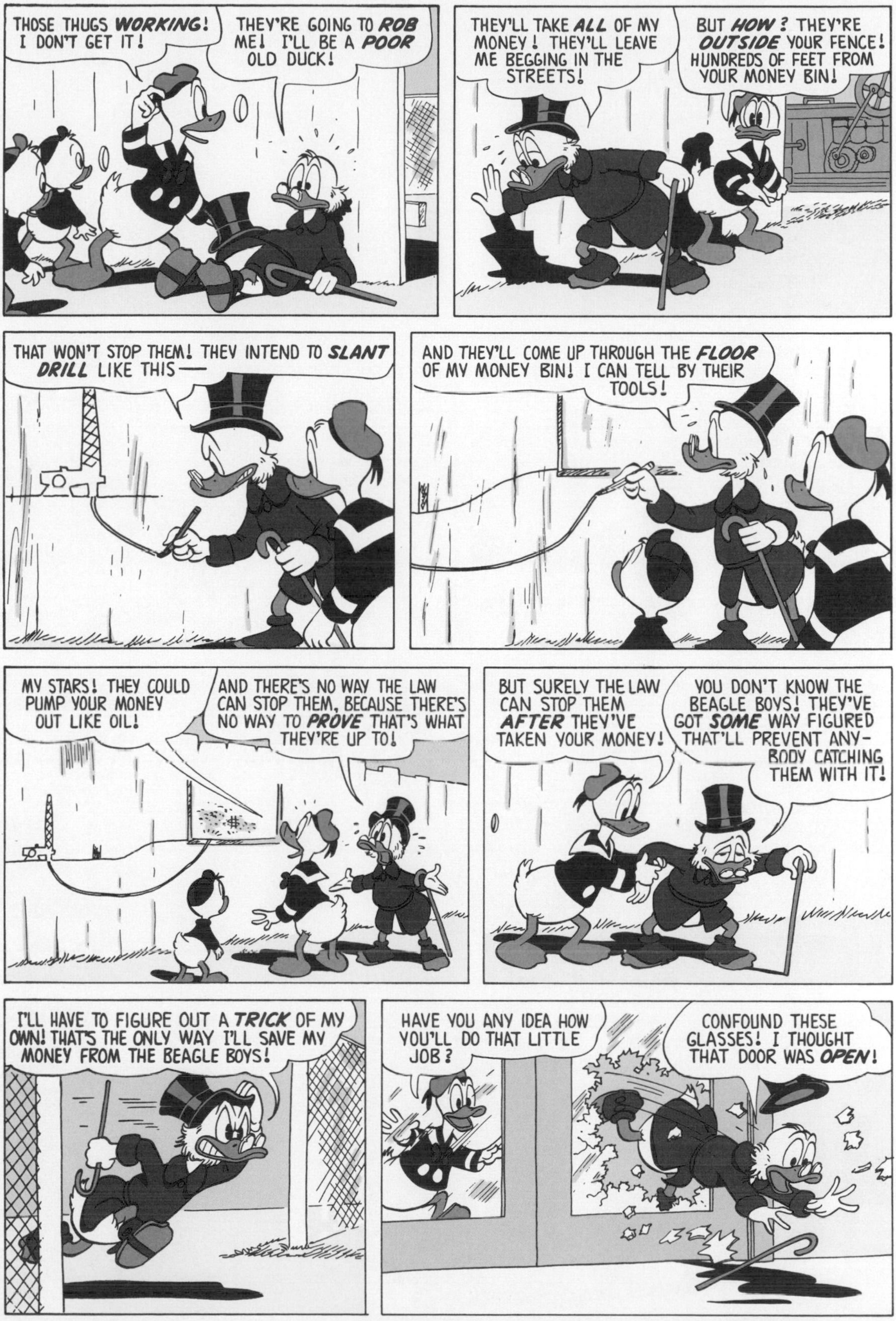
THOSE THUGS WORKING! I DON'T GET IT!
THEY'RE GOING TO ROB ME! I'LL BE A POOR OLD DUCK!
THEY'LL TAKE ALL OF MY MONEY! THEY'LL LEAVE ME BEGGING IN THE STREETS!
BUT HOW? THEY'RE OUTSIDE YOUR FENCE! HUNDREDS OF FEET FROM YOUR MONEY BIN!
THAT WON'T STOP THEM! THEY INTEND TO SLANT DRILL LIKE THIS—
AND THEY'LL COME UP THROUGH THE FLOOR OF MY MONEY BIN! I CAN TELL BY THEIR TOOLS!
MY STARS! THEY COULD PUMP YOUR MONEY OUT LIKE OIL!
AND THERE'S NO WAY THE LAW CAN STOP THEM, BECAUSE THERE'S NO WAY TO PROVE THAT'S WHAT THEY'RE UP TO!
BUT SURELY THE LAW CAN STOP THEM AFTER THEY'VE TAKEN YOUR MONEY!
YOU DON'T KNOW THE BEAGLE BOYS! THEY'VE GOT SOME WAY FIGURED THAT'LL PREVENT ANY-BODY CATCHING THEM WITH IT!
I'LL HAVE TO FIGURE OUT A TRICK OF MY OWN! THAT'S THE ONLY WAY I'LL SAVE MY MONEY FROM THE BEAGLE BOYS!
HAVE YOU ANY IDEA HOW YOU'LL DO THAT LITTLE JOB?
CONFOUND THESE GLASSES! I THOUGHT THAT DOOR WAS OPEN!

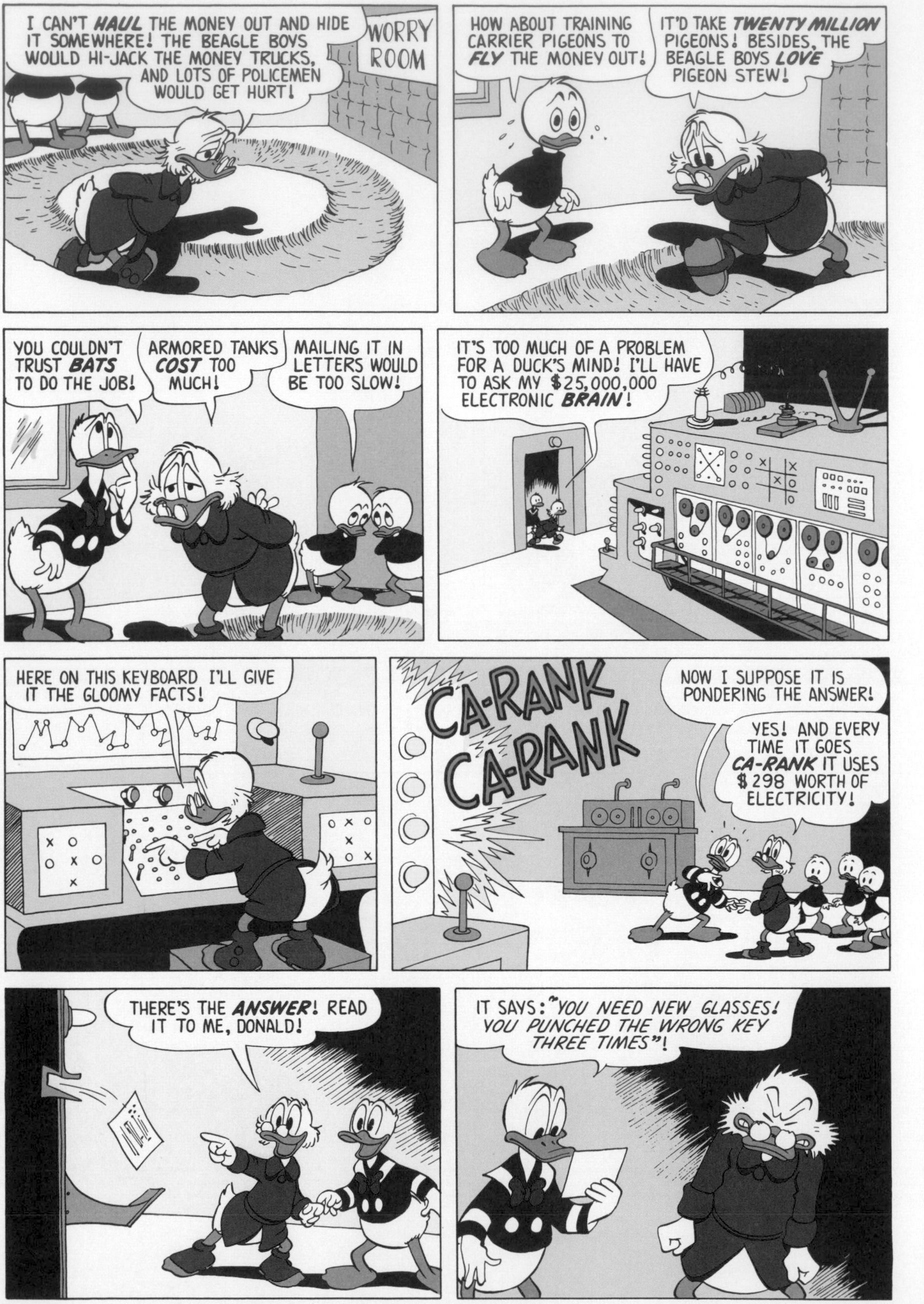
I CAN'T HAUL THE MONEY OUT AND HIDE IT SOMEWHERE! THE BEAGLE BOYS WOULD HI-JACK THE MONEY TRUCKS, AND LOTS OF POLICEMEN WOULD GET HURT!
WORRY ROOM
HOW ABOUT TRAINING CARRIER PIGEONS TO FLY THE MONEY OUT!
IT'D TAKE TWENTY MILLION PIGEONS! BESIDES, THE BEAGLE BOYS LOVE PIGEON STEW!
YOU COULDN'T TRUST BATS TO DO THE JOB!
ARMORED TANKS COST TOO MUCH!
MAILING IT IN LETTERS WOULD BE TOO SLOW!
IT'S TOO MUCH OF A PROBLEM FOR A DUCK'S MIND! I'LL HAVE TO ASK MY $25,000,000 ELECTRONIC BRAIN!
HERE ON THIS KEYBOARD I'LL GIVE IT THE GLOOMY FACTS!
CA-RANK
CA-RANK
NOW I SUPPOSE IT IS PONDERING THE ANSWER!
YES! AND EVERY TIME IT GOES CA-RANK IT USES $298 WORTH OF ELECTRICITY!
THERE'S THE ANSWER! READ IT TO ME, DONALD!
IT SAYS: "YOU NEED NEW GLASSES! YOU PUNCHED THE WRONG KEY THREE TIMES"!

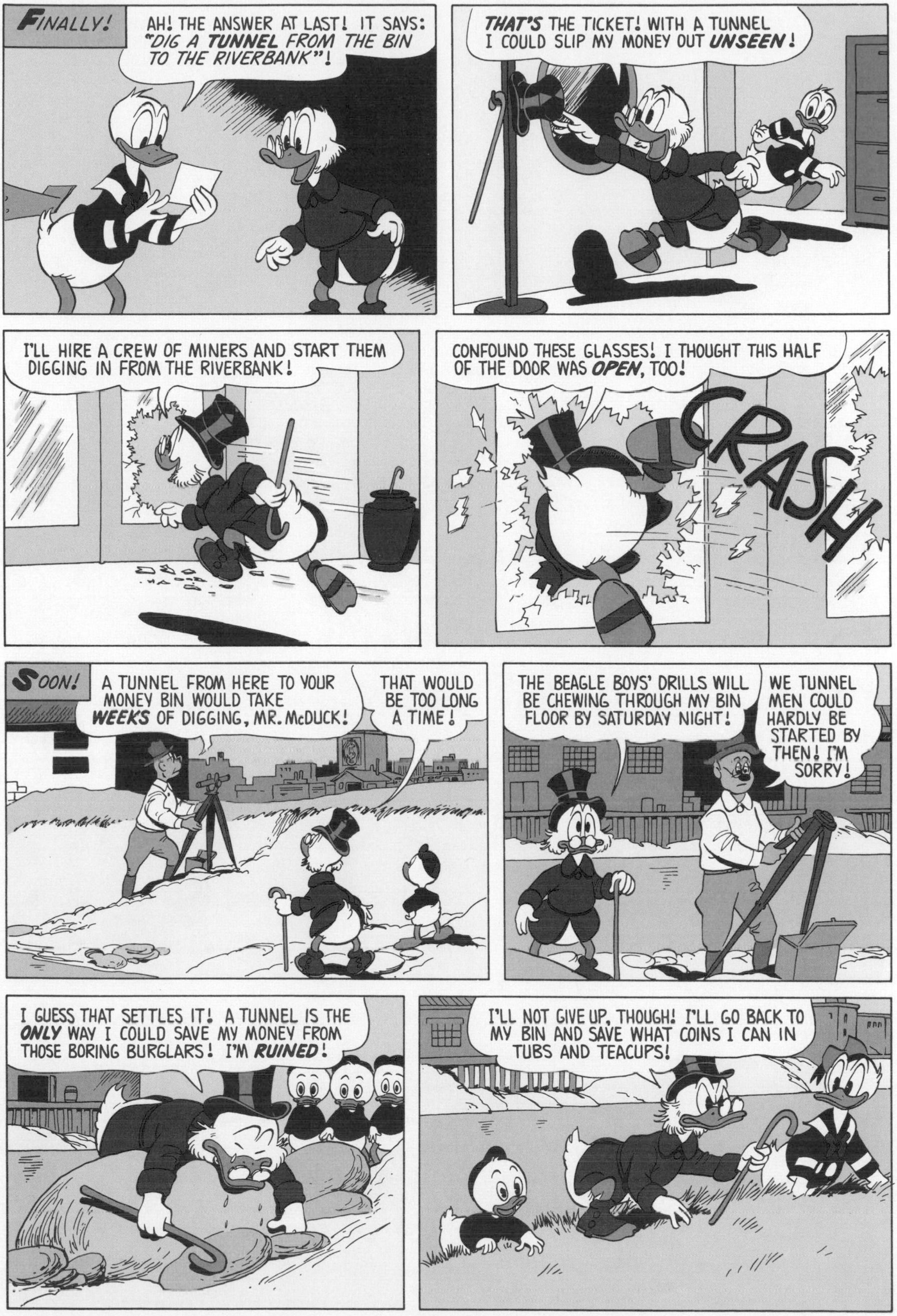
FINALLY!
AH! THE ANSWER AT LAST! IT SAYS: "DIG A TUNNEL FROM THE BIN TO THE RIVERBANK"!
THAT'S THE TICKET! WITH A TUNNEL I COULD SLIP MY MONEY OUT UNSEEN!
I'LL HIRE A CREW OF MINERS AND START THEM DIGGING IN FROM THE RIVERBANK!
CONFOUND THESE GLASSES! I THOUGHT THIS HALF OF THE DOOR WAS OPEN, TOO!
CRASH
SOON!
A TUNNEL FROM HERE TO YOUR MONEY BIN WOULD TAKE WEEKS OF DIGGING, MR. McDUCK!
THAT WOULD BE TOO LONG A TIME!
THE BEAGLE BOYS' DRILLS WILL BE CHEWING THROUGH MY BIN FLOOR BY SATURDAY NIGHT!
WE TUNNEL MEN COULD HARDLY BE STARTED BY THEN! I'M SORRY!
I GUESS THAT SETTLES IT! A TUNNEL IS THE ONLY WAY I COULD SAVE MY MONEY FROM THOSE BORING BURGLARS! I'M RUINED!
I'LL NOT GIVE UP, THOUGH! I'LL GO BACK TO MY BIN AND SAVE WHAT COINS I CAN IN TUBS AND TEACUPS!

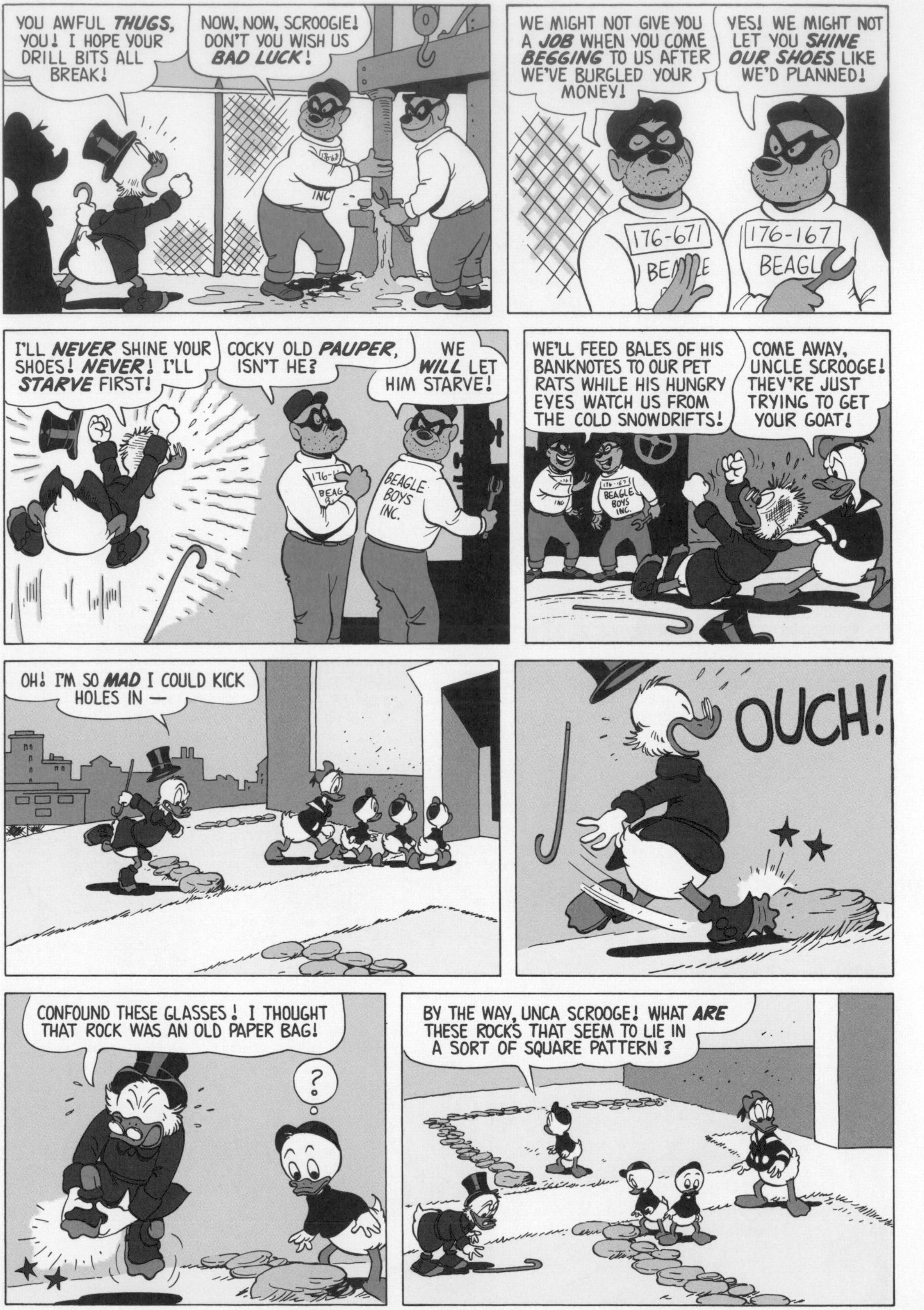

YOU AWFUL THUGS, YOU! I HOPE YOUR DRILL BITS ALL BREAK!
NOW, NOW, SCROOGIE! DON'T YOU WISH US BAD LUCK!
WE MIGHT NOT GIVE YOU A JOB WHEN YOU COME BEGGING TO US AFTER WE'VE BURGLED YOUR MONEY!
YES! WE MIGHT NOT LET YOU SHINE OUR SHOES LIKE WE'D PLANNED!
176-671
176-167
I'LL NEVER SHINE YOUR SHOES! NEVER! I'LL STARVE FIRST!
COCKY OLD PAUPER, ISN'T HE?
WE WILL LET HIM STARVE!
BEAGLE BOYS INC.
WE'LL FEED BALES OF HIS BANKNOTES TO OUR PET RATS WHILE HIS HUNGRY EYES WATCH US FROM THE COLD SNOWDRIFTS!
COME AWAY, UNCLE SCROOGE! THEY'RE JUST TRYING TO GET YOUR GOAT!
OH! I'M SO MAD I COULD KICK HOLES IN —
OUCH!
CONFOUND THESE GLASSES! I THOUGHT THAT ROCK WAS AN OLD PAPER BAG!
?
BY THE WAY, UNCA SCROOGE! WHAT ARE THESE ROCKS THAT SEEM TO LIE IN A SORT OF SQUARE PATTERN?

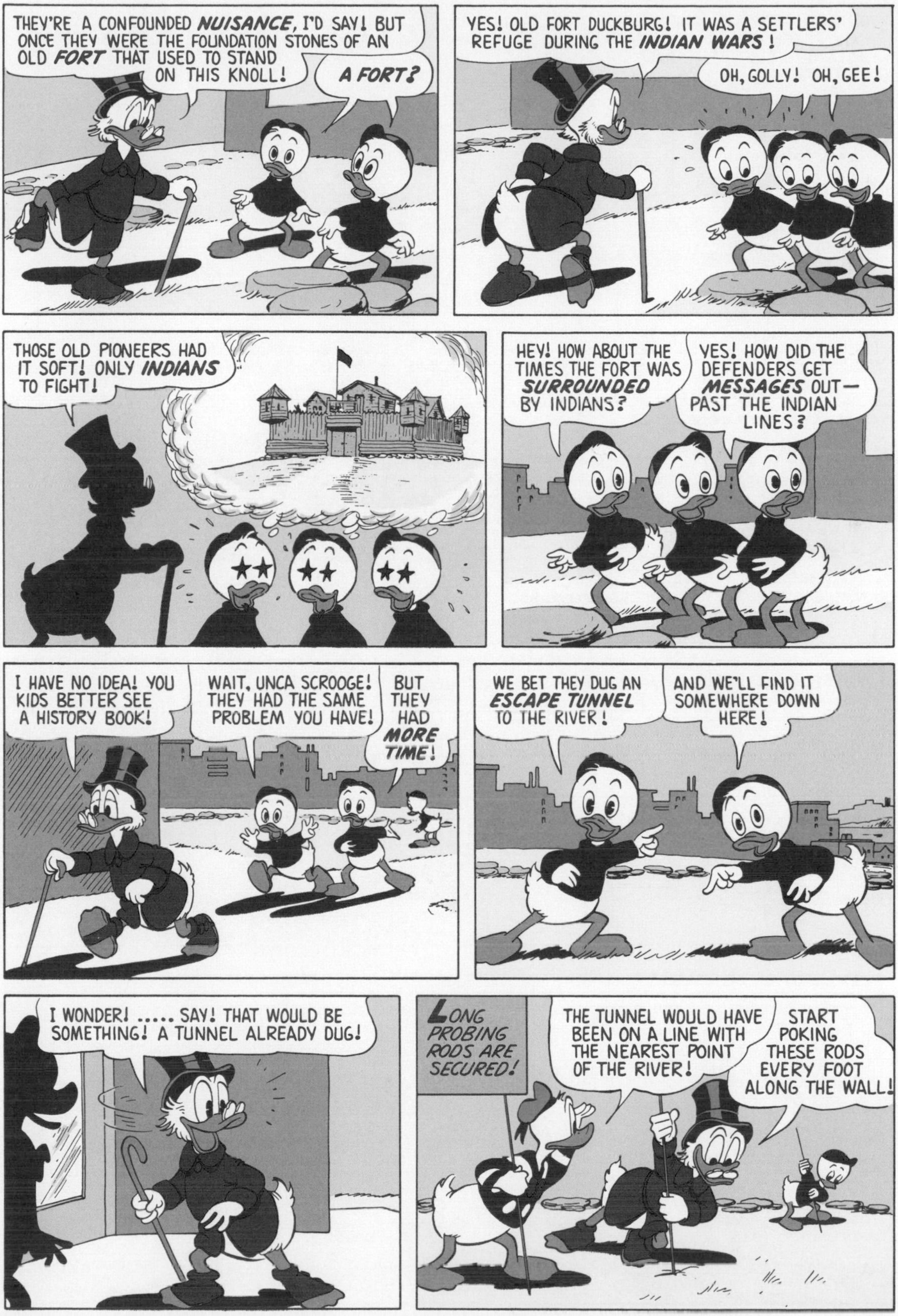

THEY'RE A CONFOUNDED NUISANCE, I'D SAY! BUT ONCE THEY WERE THE FOUNDATION STONES OF AN OLD FORT THAT USED TO STAND ON THIS KNOLL!
A FORT?
YES! OLD FORT DUCKBURG! IT WAS A SETTLERS' REFUGE DURING THE INDIAN WARS!
OH, GOLLY! OH, GEE!
THOSE OLD PIONEERS HAD IT SOFT! ONLY INDIANS TO FIGHT!
HEY! HOW ABOUT THE TIMES THE FORT WAS SURROUNDED BY INDIANS?
YES! HOW DID THE DEFENDERS GET MESSAGES OUT— PAST THE INDIAN LINES?
I HAVE NO IDEA! YOU KIDS BETTER SEE A HISTORY BOOK!
WAIT, UNCA SCROOGE! THEY HAD THE SAME PROBLEM YOU HAVE!
BUT THEY HAD MORE TIME!
WE BET THEY DUG AN ESCAPE TUNNEL TO THE RIVER!
AND WE'LL FIND IT SOMEWHERE DOWN HERE!
I WONDER! ..... SAY! THAT WOULD BE SOMETHING! A TUNNEL ALREADY DUG!
LONG PROBING RODS ARE SECURED!
THE TUNNEL WOULD HAVE BEEN ON A LINE WITH THE NEAREST POINT OF THE RIVER!
START POKING THESE RODS EVERY FOOT ALONG THE WALL!

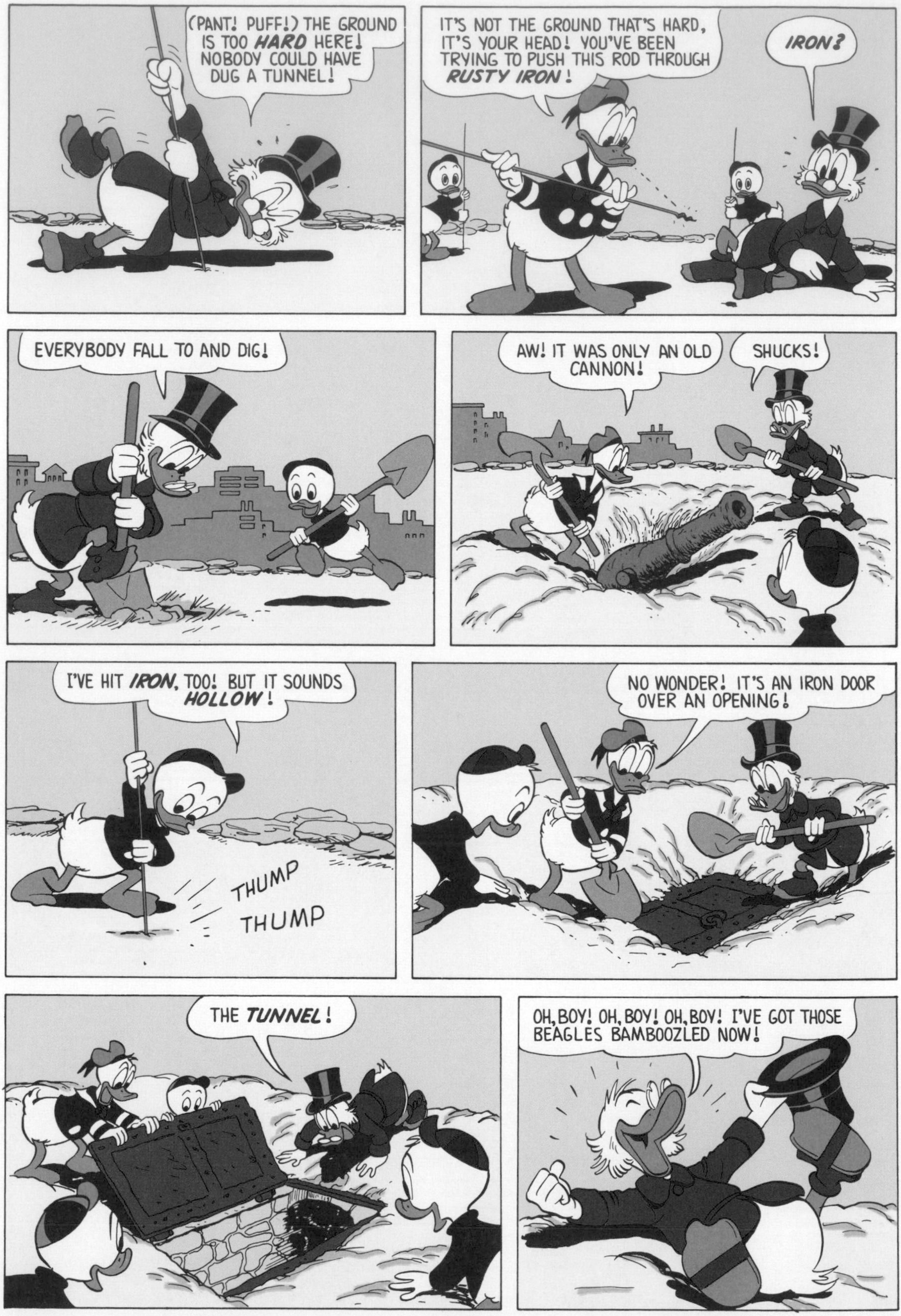
(PANT! PUFF!) THE GROUND IS TOO HARD HERE! NOBODY COULD HAVE DUG A TUNNEL!
IT'S NOT THE GROUND THAT'S HARD, IT'S YOUR HEAD! YOU'VE BEEN TRYING TO PUSH THIS ROD THROUGH RUSTY IRON!
IRON?
EVERYBODY FALL TO AND DIG!
AW! IT WAS ONLY AN OLD CANNON!
SHUCKS!
I'VE HIT IRON, TOO! BUT IT SOUNDS HOLLOW!
THUMP
THUMP
NO WONDER! IT'S AN IRON DOOR OVER AN OPENING!
THE TUNNEL!
OH, BOY! OH, BOY! OH, BOY! I'VE GOT THOSE BEAGLES BAMBOOZLED NOW!

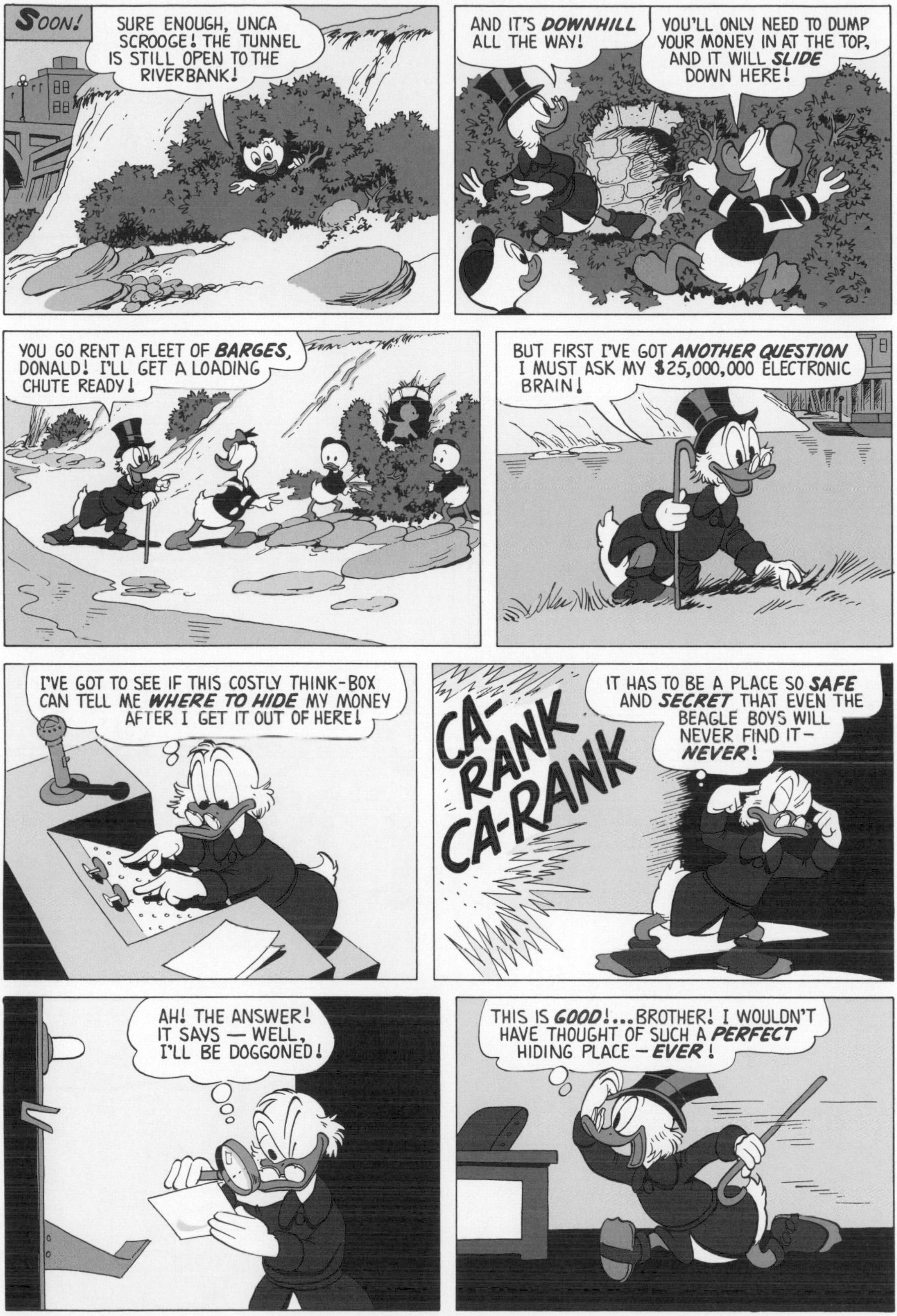
SOON!
SURE ENOUGH, UNCA SCROOGE! THE TUNNEL IS STILL OPEN TO THE RIVERBANK!
AND IT'S DOWNHILL ALL THE WAY!
YOU'LL ONLY NEED TO DUMP YOUR MONEY IN AT THE TOP, AND IT WILL SLIDE DOWN HERE!
YOU GO RENT A FLEET OF BARGES, DONALD! I'LL GET A LOADING CHUTE READY!
BUT FIRST I'VE GOT ANOTHER QUESTION I MUST ASK MY $25,000,000 ELECTRONIC BRAIN!
I'VE GOT TO SEE IF THIS COSTLY THINK-BOX CAN TELL ME WHERE TO HIDE MY MONEY AFTER I GET IT OUT OF HERE!
CA-RANK CA-RANK
IT HAS TO BE A PLACE SO SAFE AND SECRET THAT EVEN THE BEAGLE BOYS WILL NEVER FIND IT— NEVER!
AH! THE ANSWER! IT SAYS — WELL, I'LL BE DOGGONED!
THIS IS GOOD!...BROTHER! I WOULDN'T HAVE THOUGHT OF SUCH A PERFECT HIDING PLACE — EVER!

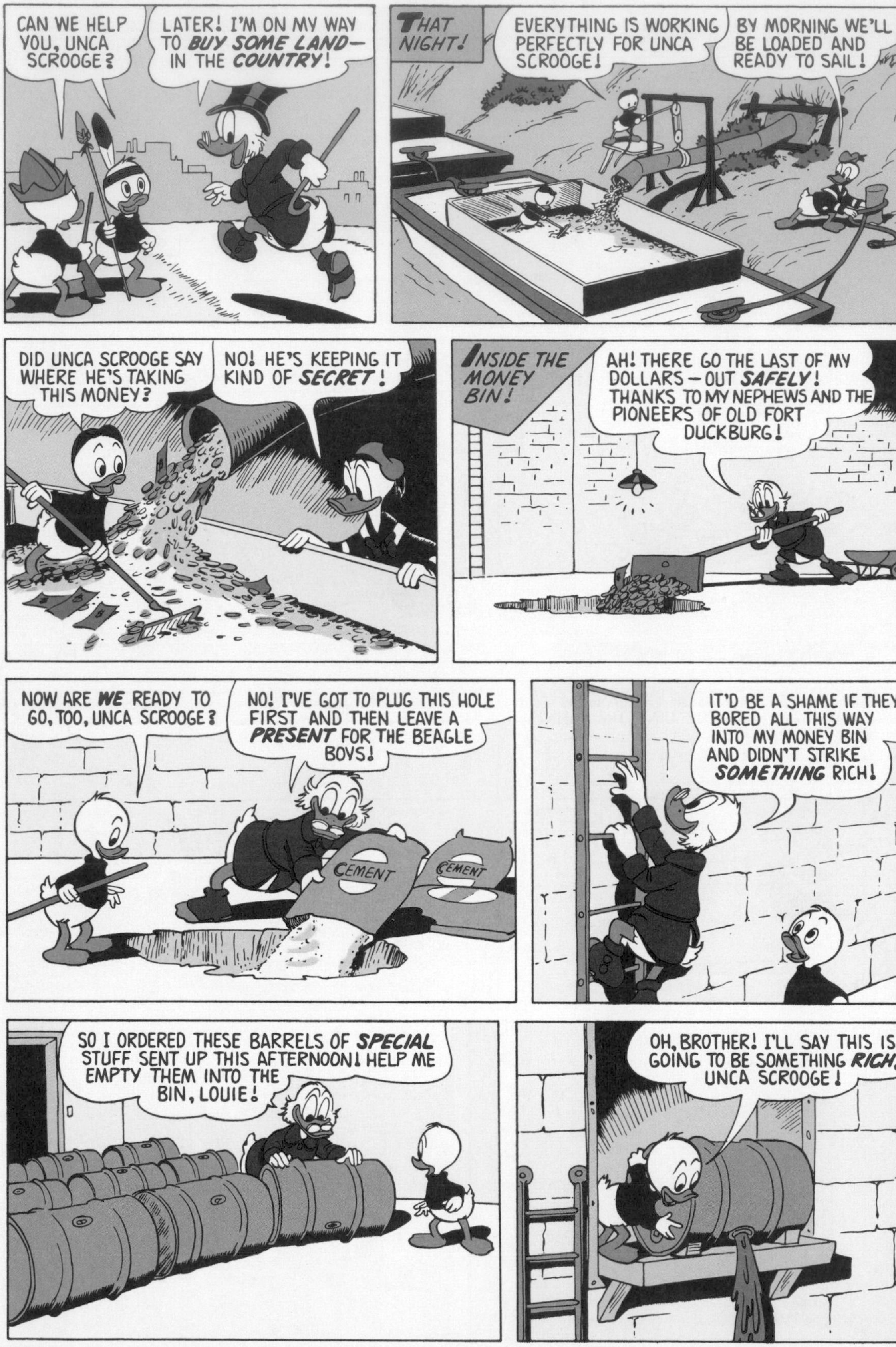
CAN WE HELP YOU, UNCA SCROOGE?
LATER! I'M ON MY WAY TO BUY SOME LAND— IN THE COUNTRY!
THAT NIGHT!
EVERYTHING IS WORKING PERFECTLY FOR UNCA SCROOGE!
BY MORNING WE'LL BE LOADED AND READY TO SAIL!
DID UNCA SCROOGE SAY WHERE HE'S TAKING THIS MONEY?
NO! HE'S KEEPING IT KIND OF SECRET!
INSIDE THE MONEY BIN!
AH! THERE GO THE LAST OF MY DOLLARS — OUT SAFELY! THANKS TO MY NEPHEWS AND THE PIONEERS OF OLD FORT DUCKBURG!
NOW ARE WE READY TO GO, TOO, UNCA SCROOGE?
NO! I'VE GOT TO PLUG THIS HOLE FIRST AND THEN LEAVE A PRESENT FOR THE BEAGLE BOYS!
CEMENT
CEMENT
IT'D BE A SHAME IF THEY BORED ALL THIS WAY INTO MY MONEY BIN AND DIDN'T STRIKE SOMETHING RICH!
SO I ORDERED THESE BARRELS OF SPECIAL STUFF SENT UP THIS AFTERNOON! HELP ME EMPTY THEM INTO THE BIN, LOUIE!
OH, BROTHER! I'LL SAY THIS IS GOING TO BE SOMETHING RICH, UNCA SCROOGE!

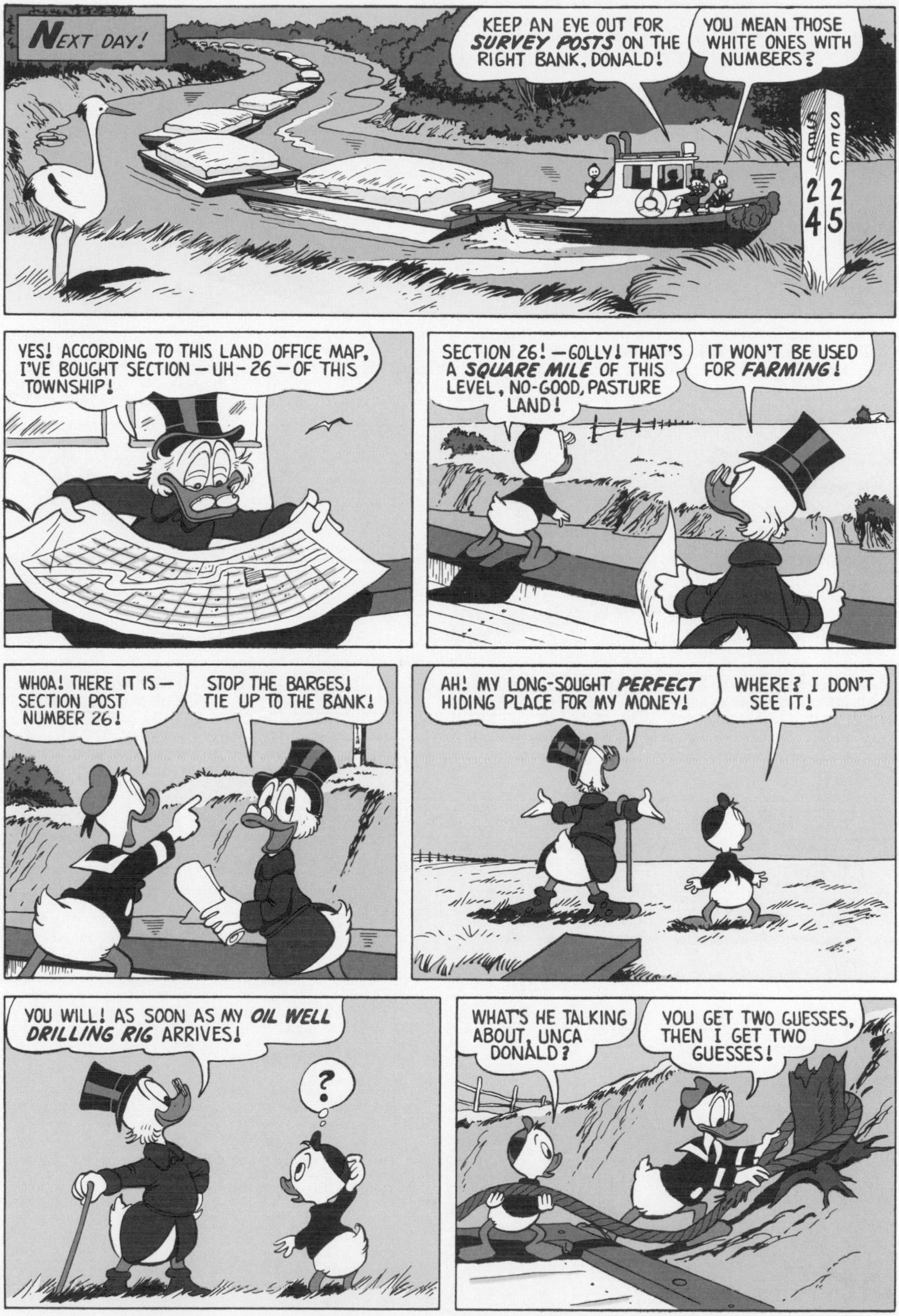
NEXT DAY!
KEEP AN EYE OUT FOR SURVEY POSTS ON THE RIGHT BANK, DONALD!
YOU MEAN THOSE WHITE ONES WITH NUMBERS?
SEC 24
SEC. 25
YES! ACCORDING TO THIS LAND OFFICE MAP, I'VE BOUGHT SECTION — UH — 26 — OF THIS TOWNSHIP!
SECTION 26! — GOLLY! THAT'S A SQUARE MILE OF THIS LEVEL, NO-GOOD, PASTURE LAND!
IT WON'T BE USED FOR FARMING!
WHOA! THERE IT IS — SECTION POST NUMBER 26!
STOP THE BARGES! TIE UP TO THE BANK!
AH! MY LONG-SOUGHT PERFECT HIDING PLACE FOR MY MONEY!
WHERE? I DON'T SEE IT!
YOU WILL! AS SOON AS MY OIL WELL DRILLING RIG ARRIVES!
?
WHAT'S HE TALKING ABOUT, UNCA DONALD?
YOU GET TWO GUESSES, THEN I GET TWO GUESSES!

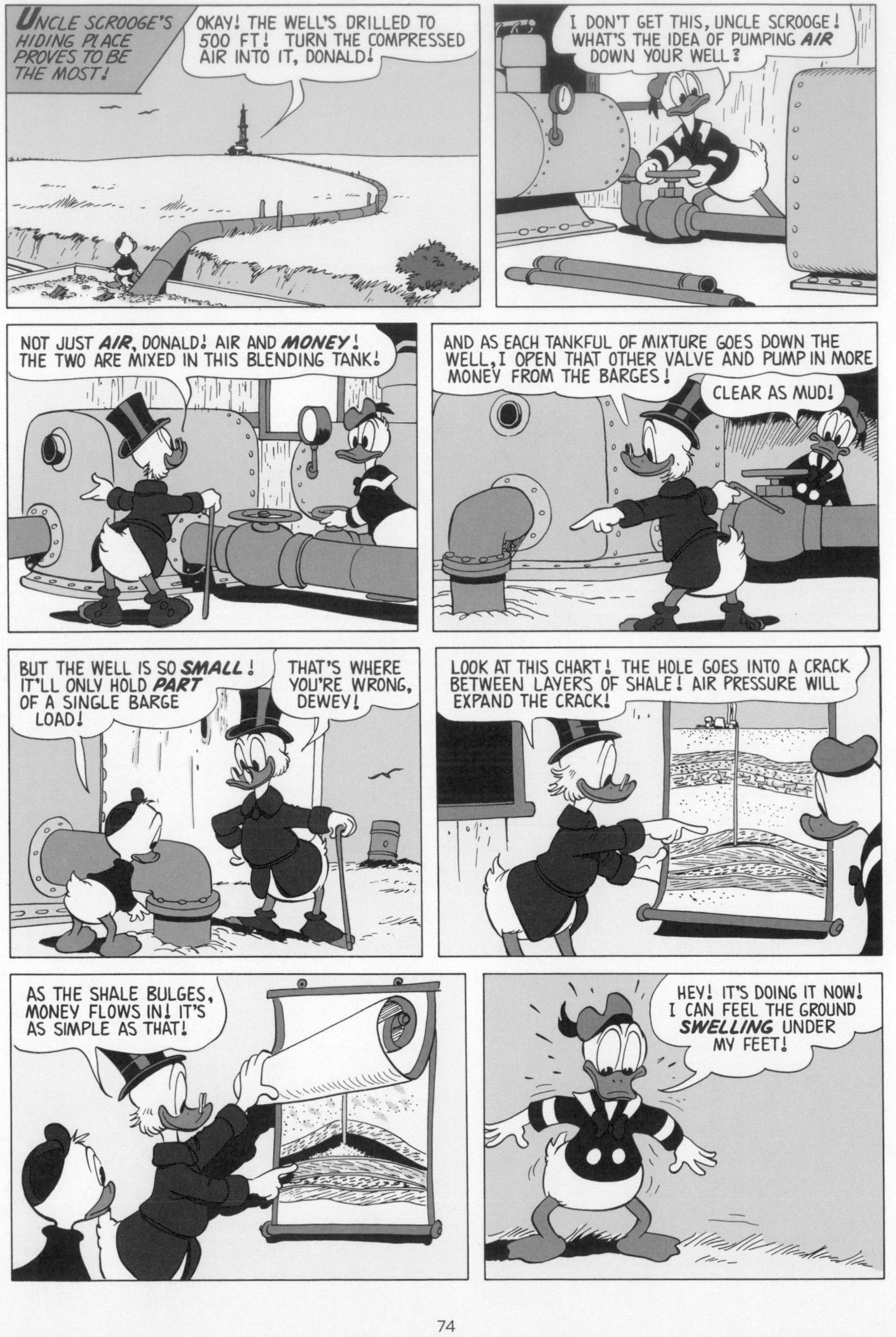
UNCLE SCROOGE'S HIDING PLACE PROVES TO BE THE MOST!
OKAY! THE WELL'S DRILLED TO 500 FT! TURN THE COMPRESSED AIR INTO IT, DONALD!
I DON'T GET THIS, UNCLE SCROOGE! WHAT'S THE IDEA OF PUMPING AIR DOWN YOUR WELL?
NOT JUST AIR, DONALD! AIR AND MONEY! THE TWO ARE MIXED IN THIS BLENDING TANK!
AND AS EACH TANKFUL OF MIXTURE GOES DOWN THE WELL, I OPEN THAT OTHER VALVE AND PUMP IN MORE MONEY FROM THE BARGES!
CLEAR AS MUD!
BUT THE WELL IS SO SMALL! IT'LL ONLY HOLD PART OF A SINGLE BARGE LOAD!
THAT'S WHERE YOU'RE WRONG, DEWEY!
LOOK AT THIS CHART! THE HOLE GOES INTO A CRACK BETWEEN LAYERS OF SHALE! AIR PRESSURE WILL EXPAND THE CRACK!
AS THE SHALE BULGES, MONEY FLOWS IN! IT'S AS SIMPLE AS THAT!
HEY! IT'S DOING IT NOW! I CAN FEEL THE GROUND SWELLING UNDER MY FEET!

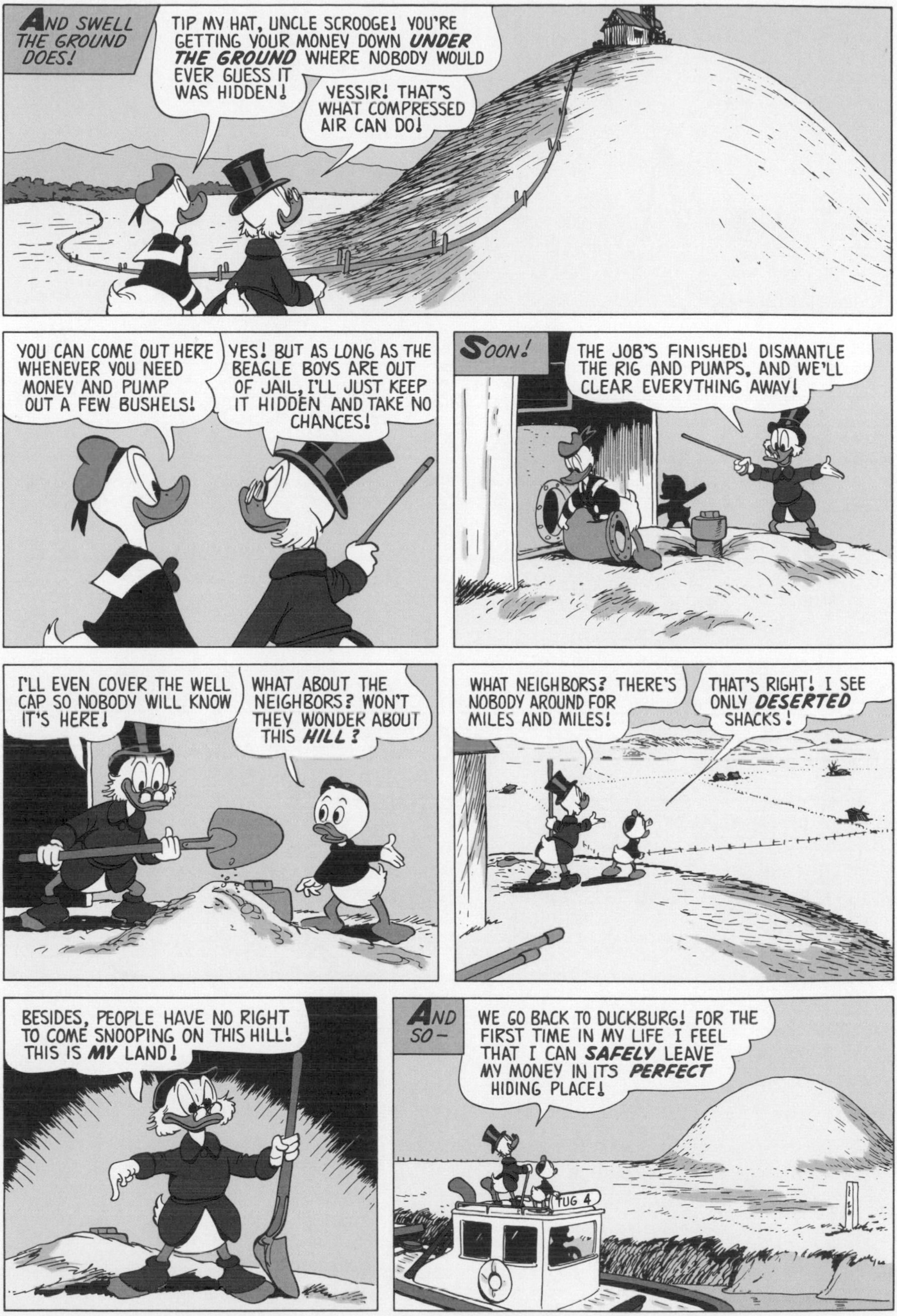
AND SWELL THE GROUND DOES!
TIP MY HAT, UNCLE SCROOGE! YOU'RE GETTING YOUR MONEY DOWN UNDER THE GROUND WHERE NOBODY WOULD EVER GUESS IT WAS HIDDEN!
YESSIR! THAT'S WHAT COMPRESSED AIR CAN DO!
YOU CAN COME OUT HERE WHENEVER YOU NEED MONEY AND PUMP OUT A FEW BUSHELS!
YES! BUT AS LONG AS THE BEAGLE BOYS ARE OUT OF JAIL, I'LL JUST KEEP IT HIDDEN AND TAKE NO CHANCES!
SOON!
THE JOB'S FINISHED! DISMANTLE THE RIG AND PUMPS, AND WE'LL CLEAR EVERYTHING AWAY!
I'LL EVEN COVER THE WELL CAP SO NOBODY WILL KNOW IT'S HERE!
WHAT ABOUT THE NEIGHBORS? WON'T THEY WONDER ABOUT THIS HILL?
WHAT NEIGHBORS? THERE'S NOBODY AROUND FOR MILES AND MILES!
THAT'S RIGHT! I SEE ONLY DESERTED SHACKS!
BESIDES, PEOPLE HAVE NO RIGHT TO COME SNOOPING ON THIS HILL! THIS IS MY LAND!
AND SO—
WE GO BACK TO DUCKBURG! FOR THE FIRST TIME IN MY LIFE I FEEL THAT I CAN SAFELY LEAVE MY MONEY IN ITS PERFECT HIDING PLACE!
TUG 4

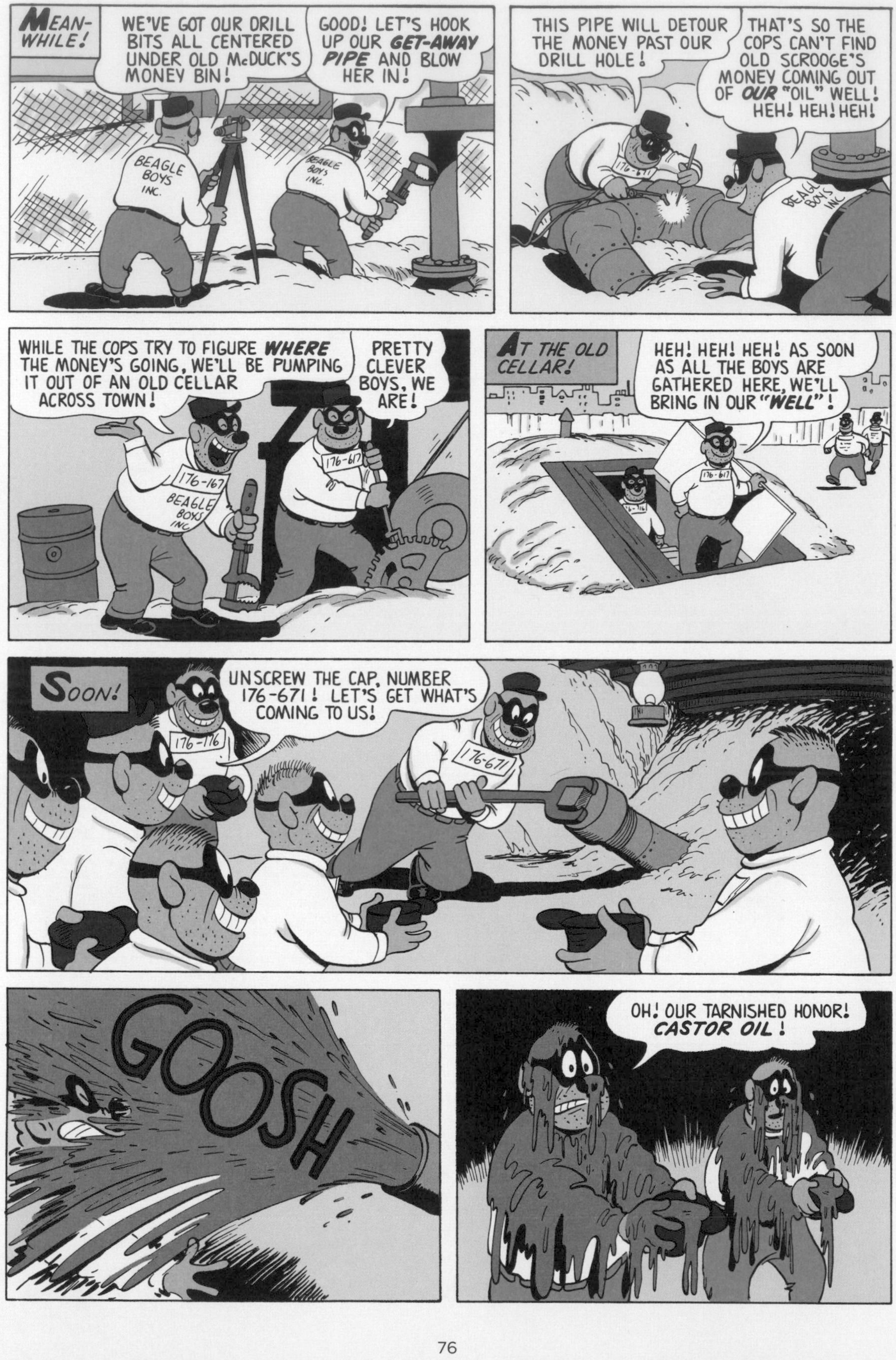
MEAN-WHILE!
WE'VE GOT OUR DRILL BITS ALL CENTERED UNDER OLD McDUCK'S MONEY BIN!
GOOD! LET'S HOOK UP OUR GET-AWAY PIPE AND BLOW HER IN!
BEAGLE BOYS INC.
THIS PIPE WILL DETOUR THE MONEY PAST OUR DRILL HOLE!
THAT'S SO THE COPS CAN'T FIND OLD SCROOGE'S MONEY COMING OUT OF OUR "OIL" WELL! HEH! HEH! HEH!
WHILE THE COPS TRY TO FIGURE WHERE THE MONEY'S GOING, WE'LL BE PUMPING IT OUT OF AN OLD CELLAR ACROSS TOWN!
PRETTY CLEVER BOYS, WE ARE!
176-167
176-617
AT THE OLD CELLAR!
HEH! HEH! HEH! AS SOON AS ALL THE BOYS ARE GATHERED HERE, WE'LL BRING IN OUR "WELL"!
SOON!
UNSCREW THE CAP, NUMBER 176-671! LET'S GET WHAT'S COMING TO US!
176-176
176-671
GOOSH
OH! OUR TARNISHED HONOR! CASTOR OIL!

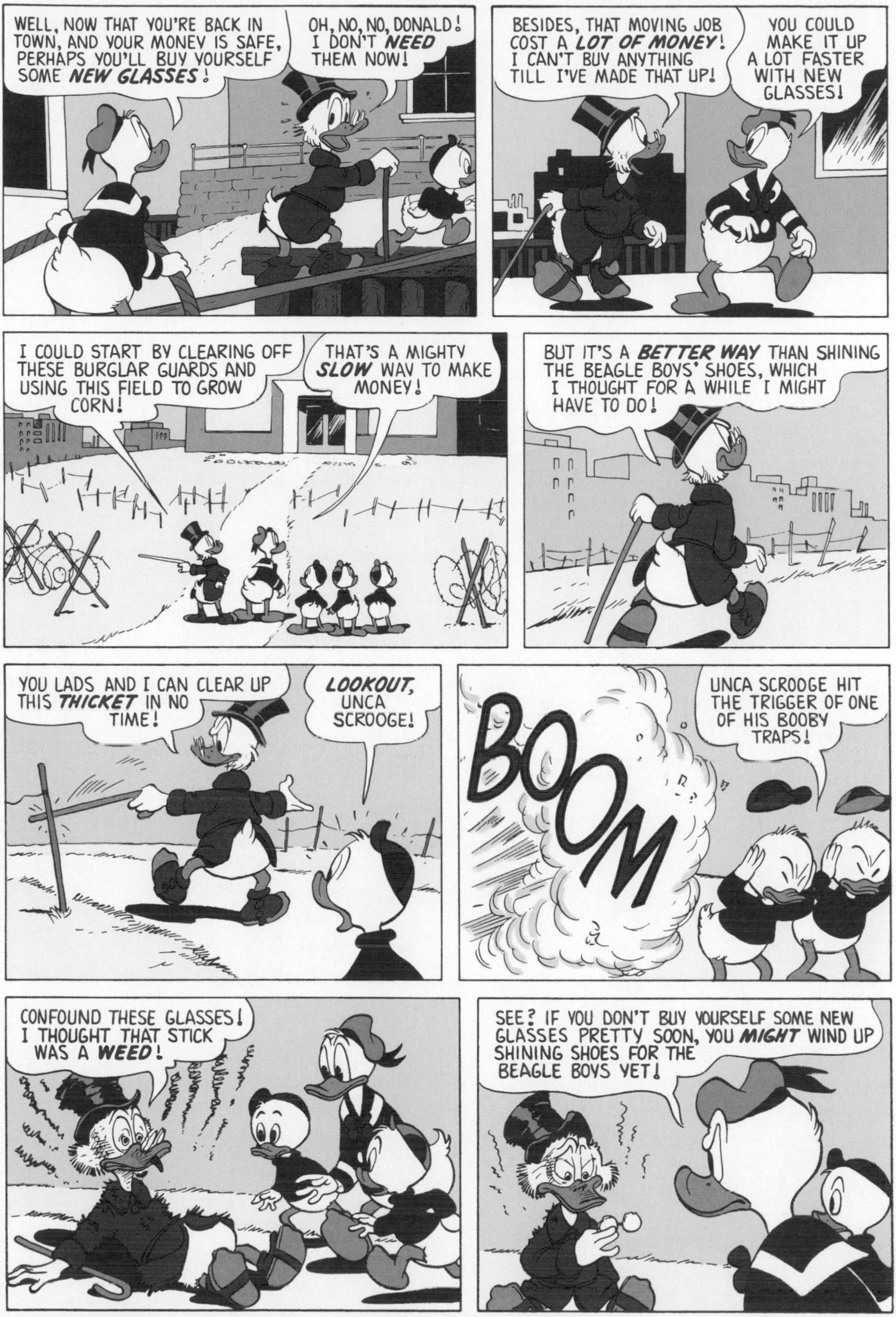

WELL, NOW THAT YOU'RE BACK IN TOWN, AND YOUR MONEY IS SAFE, PERHAPS YOU'LL BUY YOURSELF SOME **NEW GLASSES**!
OH, NO, NO, DONALD! I DON'T **NEED** THEM NOW!
BESIDES, THAT MOVING JOB COST A **LOT OF MONEY**! I CAN'T BUY ANYTHING TILL I'VE MADE THAT UP!
YOU COULD MAKE IT UP A LOT FASTER WITH NEW GLASSES!
I COULD START BY CLEARING OFF THESE BURGLAR GUARDS AND USING THIS FIELD TO GROW CORN!
THAT'S A MIGHTY **SLOW** WAY TO MAKE MONEY!
BUT IT'S A **BETTER WAY** THAN SHINING THE BEAGLE BOYS' SHOES, WHICH I THOUGHT FOR A WHILE I MIGHT HAVE TO DO!
YOU LADS AND I CAN CLEAR UP THIS **THICKET** IN NO TIME!
LOOKOUT, UNCA SCROOGE!
BOOM
UNCA SCROOGE HIT THE TRIGGER OF ONE OF HIS BOOBY TRAPS!
CONFOUND THESE GLASSES! I THOUGHT THAT STICK WAS A **WEED**!
SEE? IF YOU DON'T BUY YOURSELF SOME NEW GLASSES PRETTY SOON, YOU **MIGHT** WIND UP SHINING SHOES FOR THE BEAGLE BOYS YET!

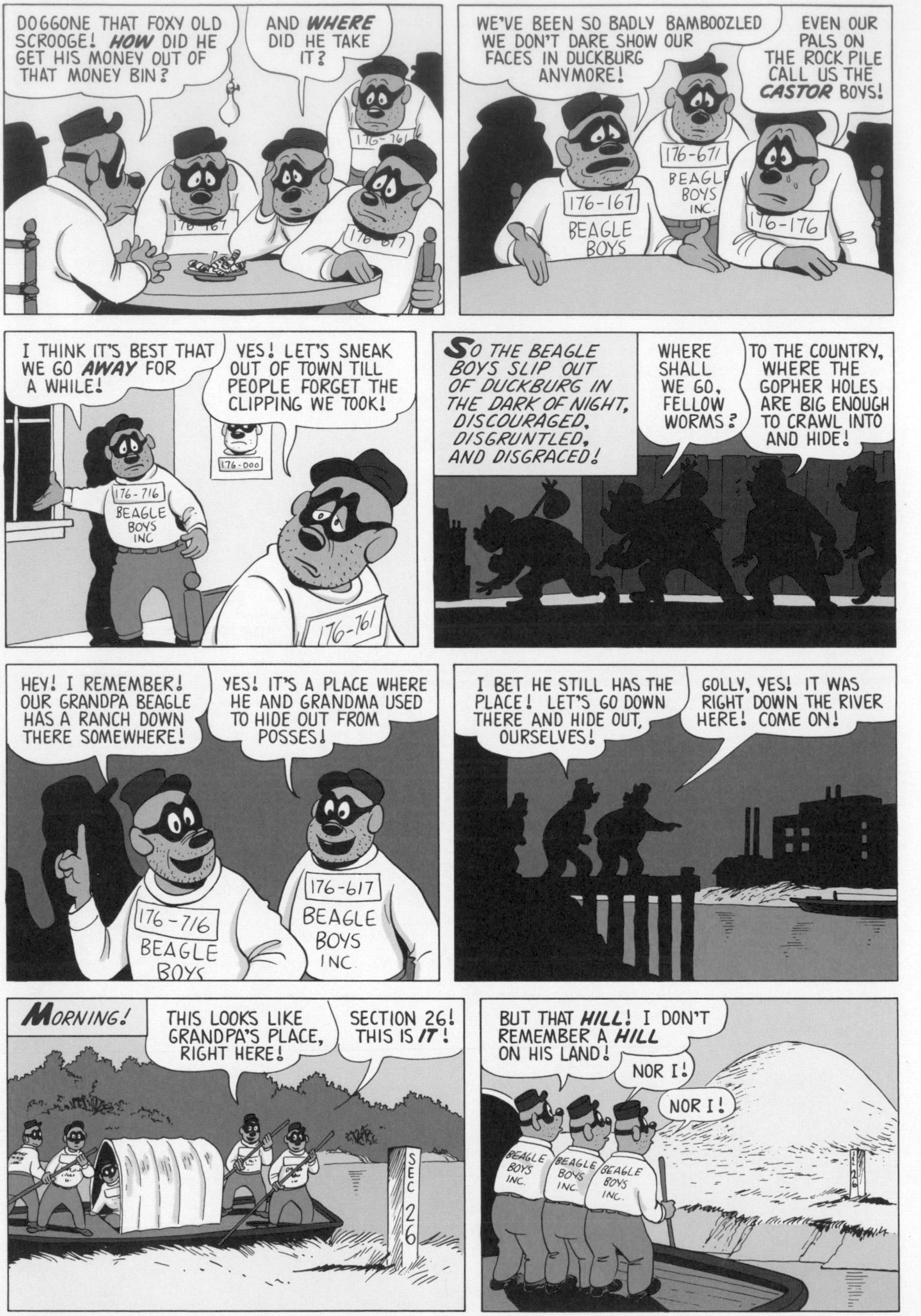
DOGGONE THAT FOXY OLD SCROOGE! HOW DID HE GET HIS MONEY OUT OF THAT MONEY BIN?
AND WHERE DID HE TAKE IT?
176-761
176-167
176-617
WE'VE BEEN SO BADLY BAMBOOZLED WE DON'T DARE SHOW OUR FACES IN DUCKBURG ANYMORE!
EVEN OUR PALS ON THE ROCK PILE CALL US THE CASTOR BOYS!
176-671 BEAGLE BOYS INC.
176-167 BEAGLE BOYS
176-176
I THINK IT'S BEST THAT WE GO AWAY FOR A WHILE!
YES! LET'S SNEAK OUT OF TOWN TILL PEOPLE FORGET THE CLIPPING WE TOOK!
176-000
176-716 BEAGLE BOYS INC
176-761
SO THE BEAGLE BOYS SLIP OUT OF DUCKBURG IN THE DARK OF NIGHT, DISCOURAGED, DISGRUNTLED, AND DISGRACED!
WHERE SHALL WE GO, FELLOW WORMS?
TO THE COUNTRY, WHERE THE GOPHER HOLES ARE BIG ENOUGH TO CRAWL INTO AND HIDE!
HEY! I REMEMBER! OUR GRANDPA BEAGLE HAS A RANCH DOWN THERE SOMEWHERE!
YES! IT'S A PLACE WHERE HE AND GRANDMA USED TO HIDE OUT FROM POSSES!
176-716 BEAGLE BOYS
176-617 BEAGLE BOYS INC.
I BET HE STILL HAS THE PLACE! LET'S GO DOWN THERE AND HIDE OUT, OURSELVES!
GOLLY, YES! IT WAS RIGHT DOWN THE RIVER HERE! COME ON!
MORNING!
THIS LOOKS LIKE GRANDPA'S PLACE, RIGHT HERE!
SECTION 26! THIS IS IT!
SEC 26
BUT THAT HILL! I DON'T REMEMBER A HILL ON HIS LAND!
NOR I!
NOR I!
BEAGLE BOYS INC.
BEAGLE BOYS INC.
BEAGLE BOYS INC.

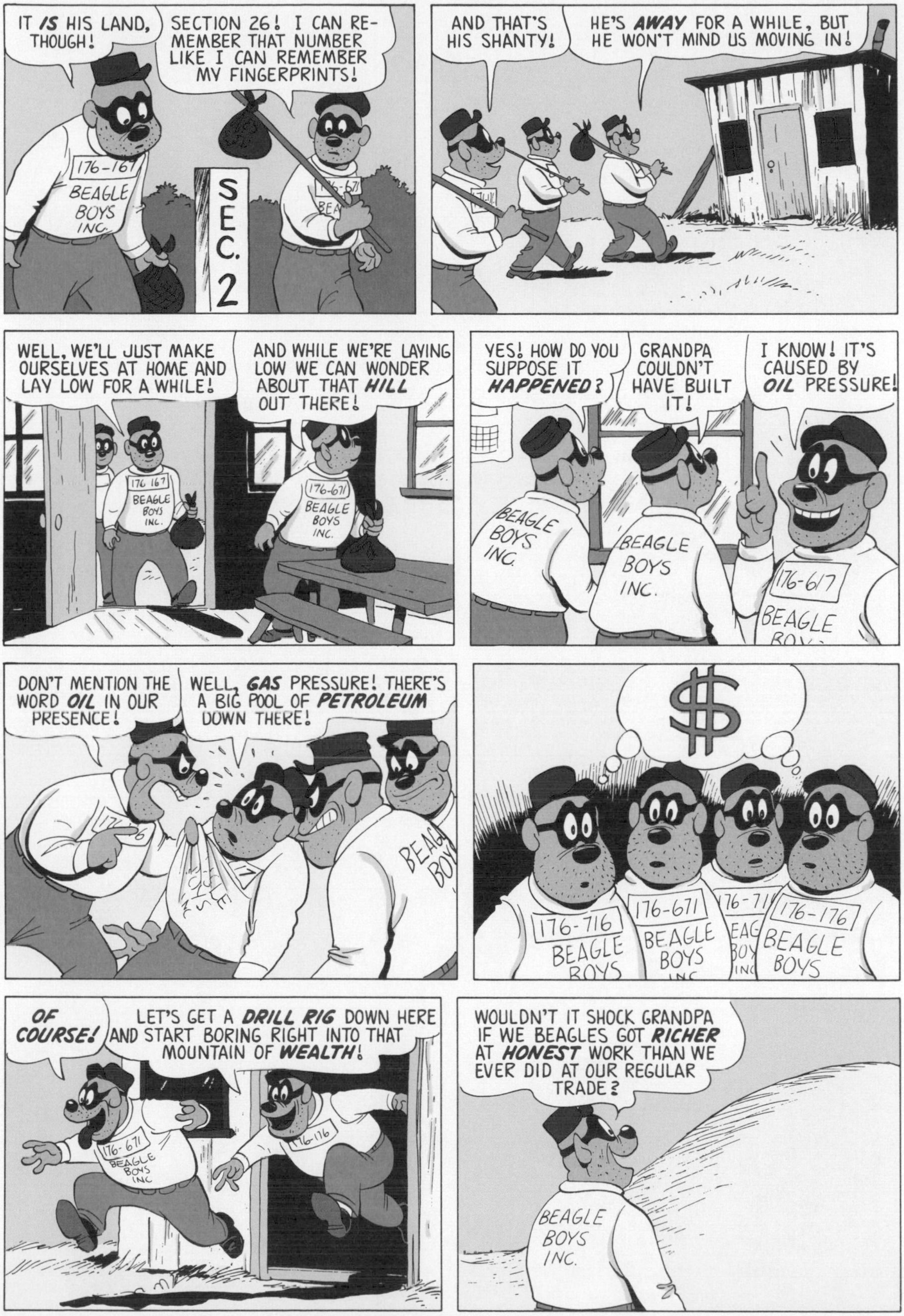
IT *IS* HIS LAND, THOUGH!
SECTION 26! I CAN REMEMBER THAT NUMBER LIKE I CAN REMEMBER MY FINGERPRINTS!
SEC. 2
176-167
BEAGLE BOYS INC.
AND THAT'S HIS SHANTY!
HE'S *AWAY* FOR A WHILE, BUT HE WON'T MIND US MOVING IN!
WELL, WE'LL JUST MAKE OURSELVES AT HOME AND LAY LOW FOR A WHILE!
AND WHILE WE'RE LAYING LOW WE CAN WONDER ABOUT THAT *HILL* OUT THERE!
176-167
BEAGLE BOYS INC.
176-671
BEAGLE BOYS INC.
YES! HOW DO YOU SUPPOSE IT *HAPPENED*?
GRANDPA COULDN'T HAVE BUILT IT!
I KNOW! IT'S CAUSED BY *OIL* PRESSURE!
BEAGLE BOYS INC.
BEAGLE BOYS INC.
176-617
DON'T MENTION THE WORD *OIL* IN OUR PRESENCE!
WELL, *GAS* PRESSURE! THERE'S A BIG POOL OF *PETROLEUM* DOWN THERE!
$
176-716
BEAGLE BOYS
176-671
BEAGLE BOYS
176-176
BEAGLE BOYS
OF COURSE!
LET'S GET A *DRILL RIG* DOWN HERE AND START BORING RIGHT INTO THAT MOUNTAIN OF *WEALTH*!
176-671
BEAGLE BOYS INC
176-116
WOULDN'T IT SHOCK GRANDPA IF WE BEAGLES GOT *RICHER* AT *HONEST* WORK THAN WE EVER DID AT OUR REGULAR TRADE?
BEAGLE BOYS INC.

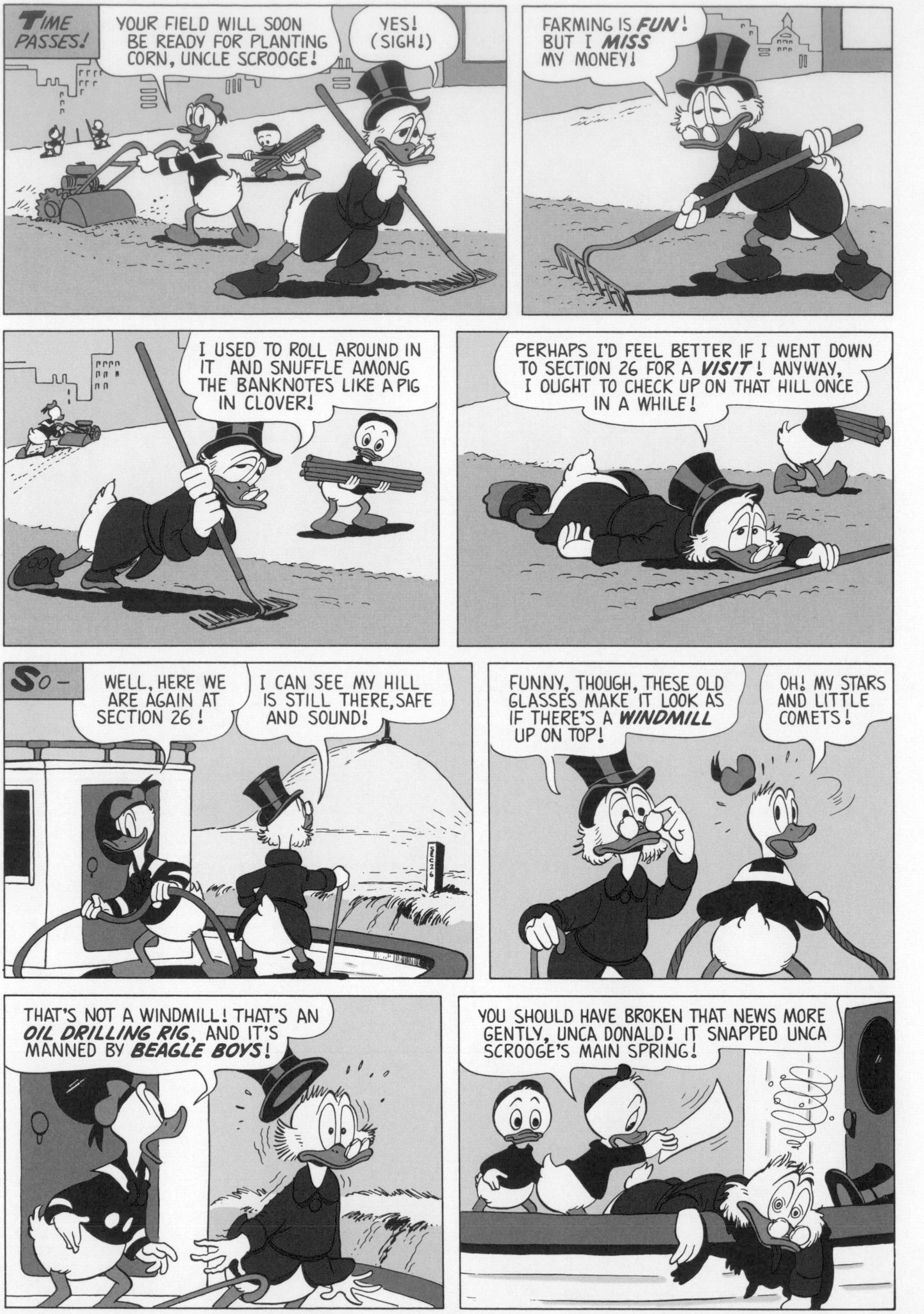
TIME PASSES!
YOUR FIELD WILL SOON BE READY FOR PLANTING CORN, UNCLE SCROOGE!
YES! (SIGH!)
FARMING IS FUN! BUT I MISS MY MONEY!
I USED TO ROLL AROUND IN IT AND SNUFFLE AMONG THE BANKNOTES LIKE A PIG IN CLOVER!
PERHAPS I'D FEEL BETTER IF I WENT DOWN TO SECTION 26 FOR A VISIT! ANYWAY, I OUGHT TO CHECK UP ON THAT HILL ONCE IN A WHILE!
SO-
WELL, HERE WE ARE AGAIN AT SECTION 26!
I CAN SEE MY HILL IS STILL THERE, SAFE AND SOUND!
FUNNY, THOUGH, THESE OLD GLASSES MAKE IT LOOK AS IF THERE'S A WINDMILL UP ON TOP!
OH! MY STARS AND LITTLE COMETS!
THAT'S NOT A WINDMILL! THAT'S AN OIL DRILLING RIG, AND IT'S MANNED BY BEAGLE BOYS!
YOU SHOULD HAVE BROKEN THAT NEWS MORE GENTLY, UNCA DONALD! IT SNAPPED UNCA SCROOGE'S MAIN SPRING!

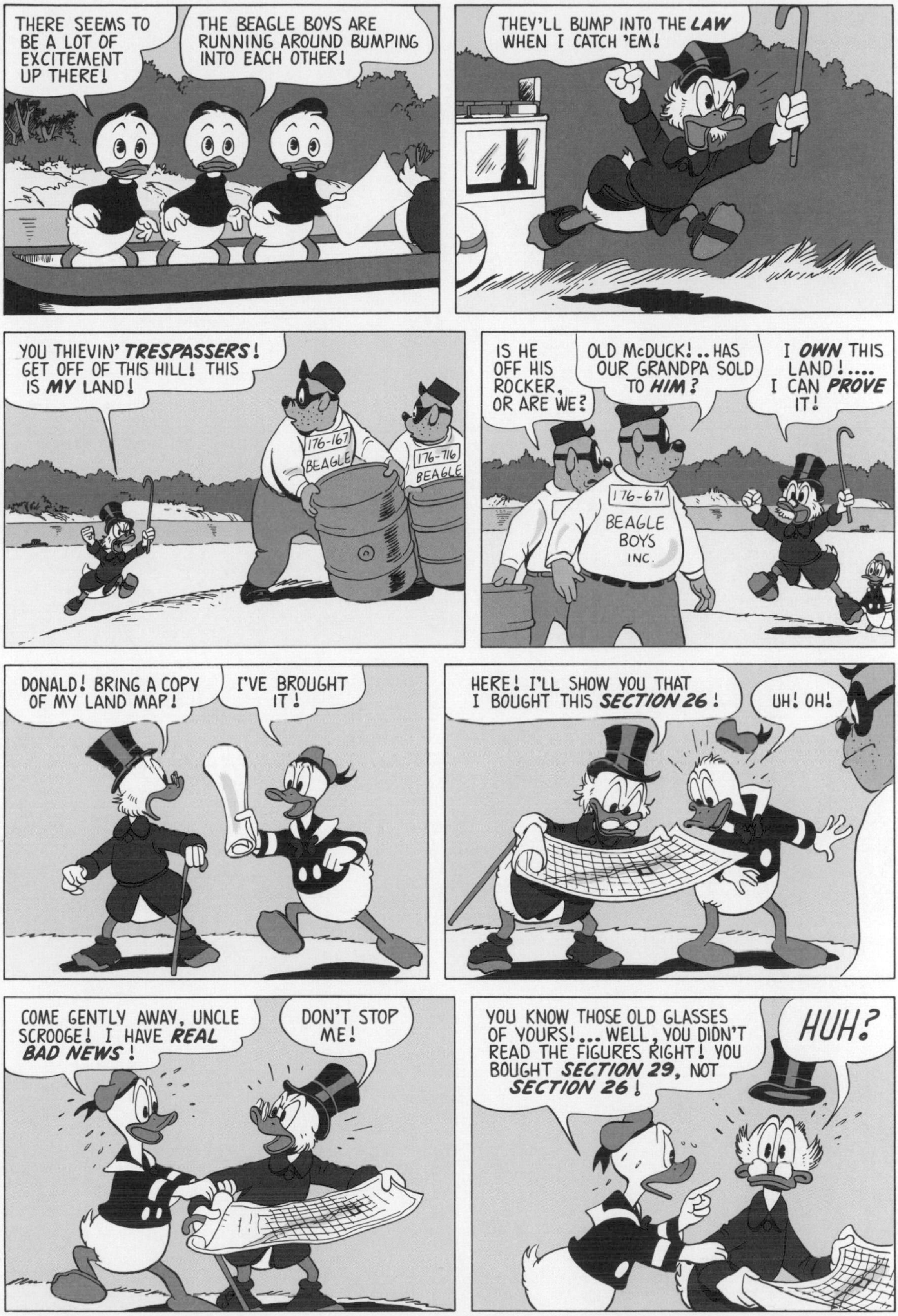
THERE SEEMS TO BE A LOT OF EXCITEMENT UP THERE!
THE BEAGLE BOYS ARE RUNNING AROUND BUMPING INTO EACH OTHER!
THEY'LL BUMP INTO THE **LAW** WHEN I CATCH 'EM!
YOU THIEVIN' **TRESPASSERS**! GET OFF OF THIS HILL! THIS IS **MY** LAND!
176-167 BEAGLE
176-716 BEAGLE
IS HE OFF HIS ROCKER, OR ARE WE?
OLD McDUCK!.. HAS OUR GRANDPA SOLD TO **HIM**?
I **OWN** THIS LAND!.... I CAN **PROVE** IT!
176-671 BEAGLE BOYS INC.
DONALD! BRING A COPY OF MY LAND MAP!
I'VE BROUGHT IT!
HERE! I'LL SHOW YOU THAT I BOUGHT THIS **SECTION 26**!
UH! OH!
COME GENTLY AWAY, UNCLE SCROOGE! I HAVE **REAL BAD NEWS**!
DON'T STOP ME!
YOU KNOW THOSE OLD GLASSES OF YOURS!... WELL, YOU DIDN'T READ THE FIGURES RIGHT! YOU BOUGHT **SECTION 29**, NOT **SECTION 26**!
HUH?

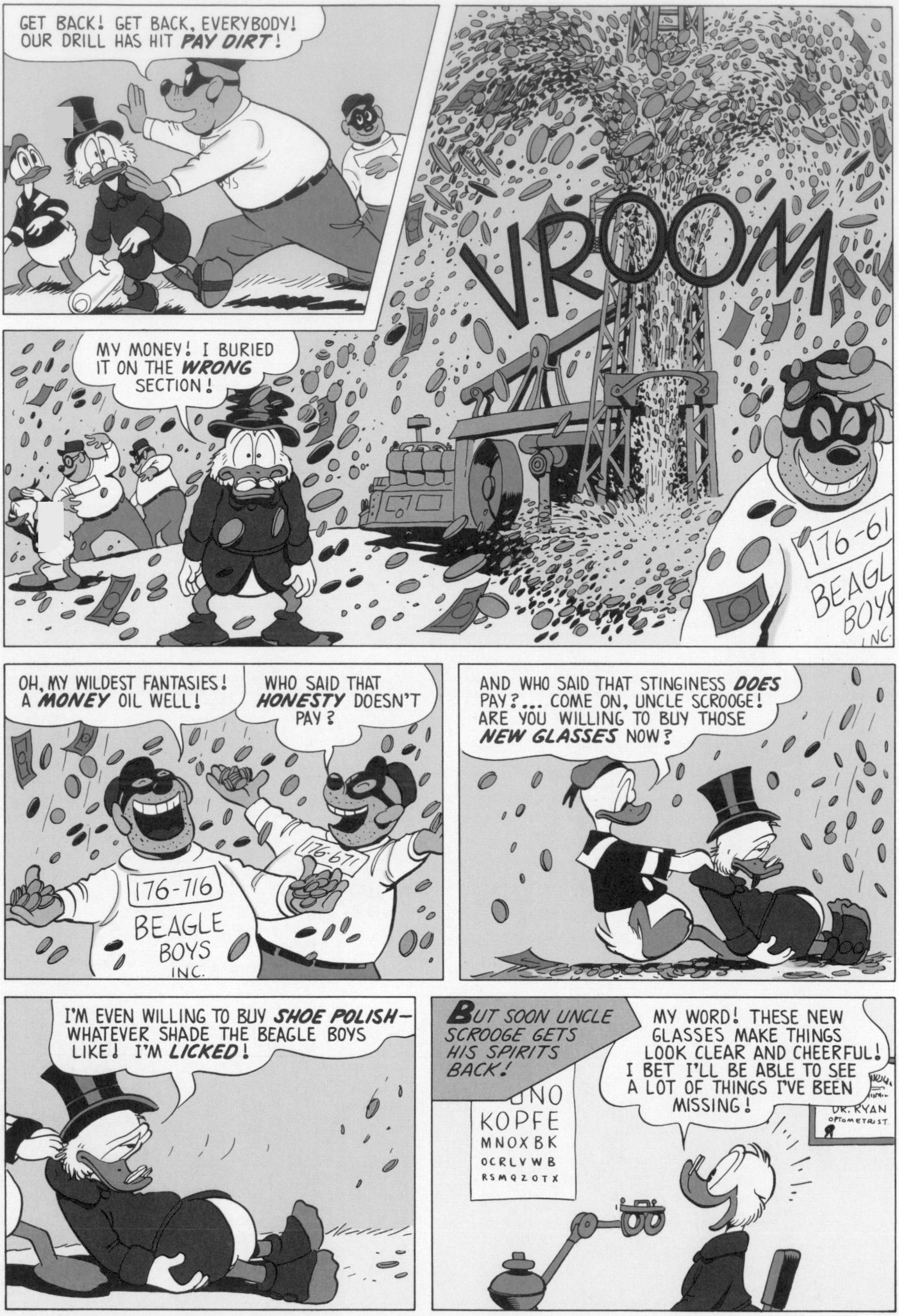
GET BACK! GET BACK, EVERYBODY! OUR DRILL HAS HIT *PAY DIRT*!
VROOM
MY MONEY! I BURIED IT ON THE *WRONG* SECTION!
176-61 BEAGL BOYS INC.
OH, MY WILDEST FANTASIES! A *MONEY* OIL WELL!
WHO SAID THAT *HONESTY* DOESN'T PAY?
176-716 BEAGLE BOYS INC.
176-671
AND WHO SAID THAT STINGINESS *DOES* PAY?... COME ON, UNCLE SCROOGE! ARE YOU WILLING TO BUY THOSE *NEW GLASSES* NOW?
I'M EVEN WILLING TO BUY *SHOE POLISH*— WHATEVER SHADE THE BEAGLE BOYS LIKE! I'M *LICKED*!
BUT SOON UNCLE SCROOGE GETS HIS SPIRITS BACK!
MY WORD! THESE NEW GLASSES MAKE THINGS LOOK CLEAR AND CHEERFUL! I BET I'LL BE ABLE TO SEE A LOT OF THINGS I'VE BEEN MISSING!
KOPFE
MNOXBK
OCRLVWB
RSMQZOTX
DR. RYAN OPTOMETRIST

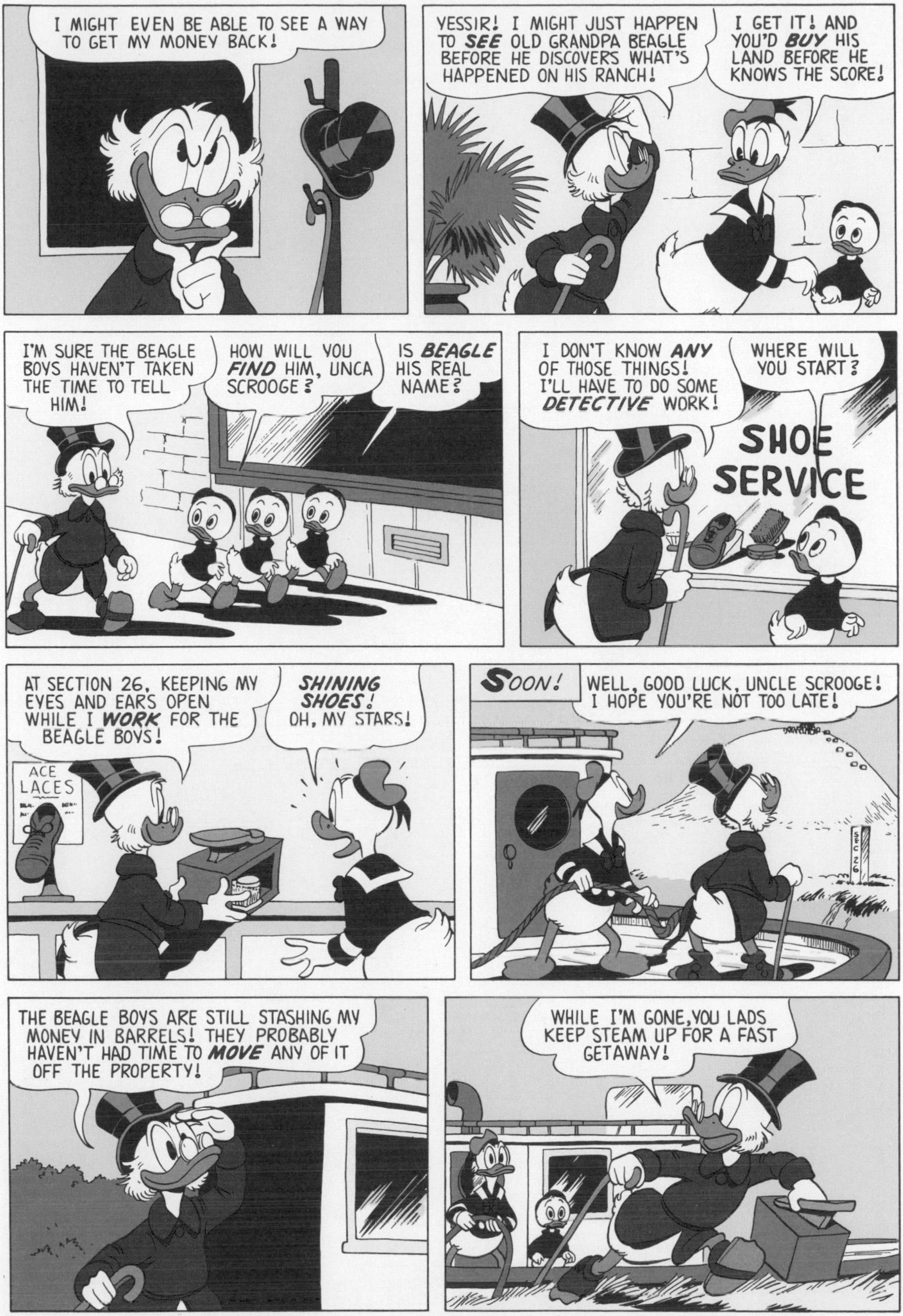
I MIGHT EVEN BE ABLE TO SEE A WAY TO GET MY MONEY BACK!
YESSIR! I MIGHT JUST HAPPEN TO **SEE** OLD GRANDPA BEAGLE BEFORE HE DISCOVERS WHAT'S HAPPENED ON HIS RANCH!
I GET IT! AND YOU'D **BUY** HIS LAND BEFORE HE KNOWS THE SCORE!
I'M SURE THE BEAGLE BOYS HAVEN'T TAKEN THE TIME TO TELL HIM!
HOW WILL YOU **FIND** HIM, UNCA SCROOGE?
IS **BEAGLE** HIS REAL NAME?
I DON'T KNOW **ANY** OF THOSE THINGS! I'LL HAVE TO DO SOME **DETECTIVE** WORK!
WHERE WILL YOU START?
SHOE SERVICE
AT SECTION 26, KEEPING MY EYES AND EARS OPEN WHILE I **WORK** FOR THE BEAGLE BOYS!
ACE LACES
SHINING SHOES! OH, MY STARS!
SOON!
WELL, GOOD LUCK, UNCLE SCROOGE! I HOPE YOU'RE NOT TOO LATE!
SEC 26
THE BEAGLE BOYS ARE STILL STASHING MY MONEY IN BARRELS! THEY PROBABLY HAVEN'T HAD TIME TO **MOVE** ANY OF IT OFF THE PROPERTY!
WHILE I'M GONE, YOU LADS KEEP STEAM UP FOR A FAST GETAWAY!

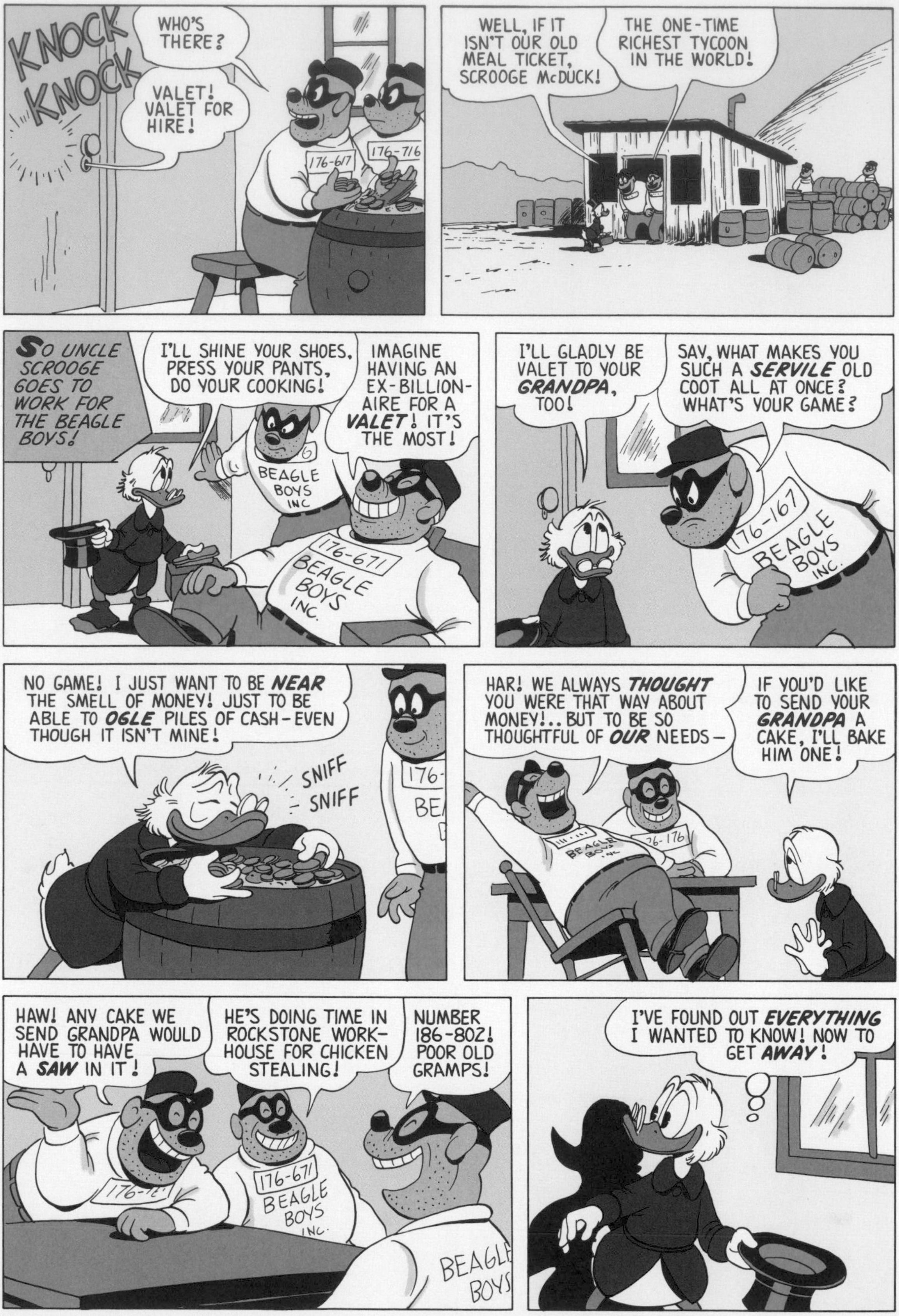
KNOCK KNOCK
WHO'S THERE?
VALET! VALET FOR HIRE!
WELL, IF IT ISN'T OUR OLD MEAL TICKET, SCROOGE McDUCK!
THE ONE-TIME RICHEST TYCOON IN THE WORLD!
SO UNCLE SCROOGE GOES TO WORK FOR THE BEAGLE BOYS!
I'LL SHINE YOUR SHOES, PRESS YOUR PANTS, DO YOUR COOKING!
IMAGINE HAVING AN EX-BILLIONAIRE FOR A VALET! IT'S THE MOST!
I'LL GLADLY BE VALET TO YOUR GRANDPA, TOO!
SAY, WHAT MAKES YOU SUCH A SERVILE OLD COOT ALL AT ONCE? WHAT'S YOUR GAME?
NO GAME! I JUST WANT TO BE NEAR THE SMELL OF MONEY! JUST TO BE ABLE TO OGLE PILES OF CASH—EVEN THOUGH IT ISN'T MINE!
SNIFF SNIFF
HAR! WE ALWAYS THOUGHT YOU WERE THAT WAY ABOUT MONEY!.. BUT TO BE SO THOUGHTFUL OF OUR NEEDS—
IF YOU'D LIKE TO SEND YOUR GRANDPA A CAKE, I'LL BAKE HIM ONE!
HAW! ANY CAKE WE SEND GRANDPA WOULD HAVE TO HAVE A SAW IN IT!
HE'S DOING TIME IN ROCKSTONE WORK-HOUSE FOR CHICKEN STEALING!
NUMBER 186-802! POOR OLD GRAMPS!
I'VE FOUND OUT EVERYTHING I WANTED TO KNOW! NOW TO GET AWAY!

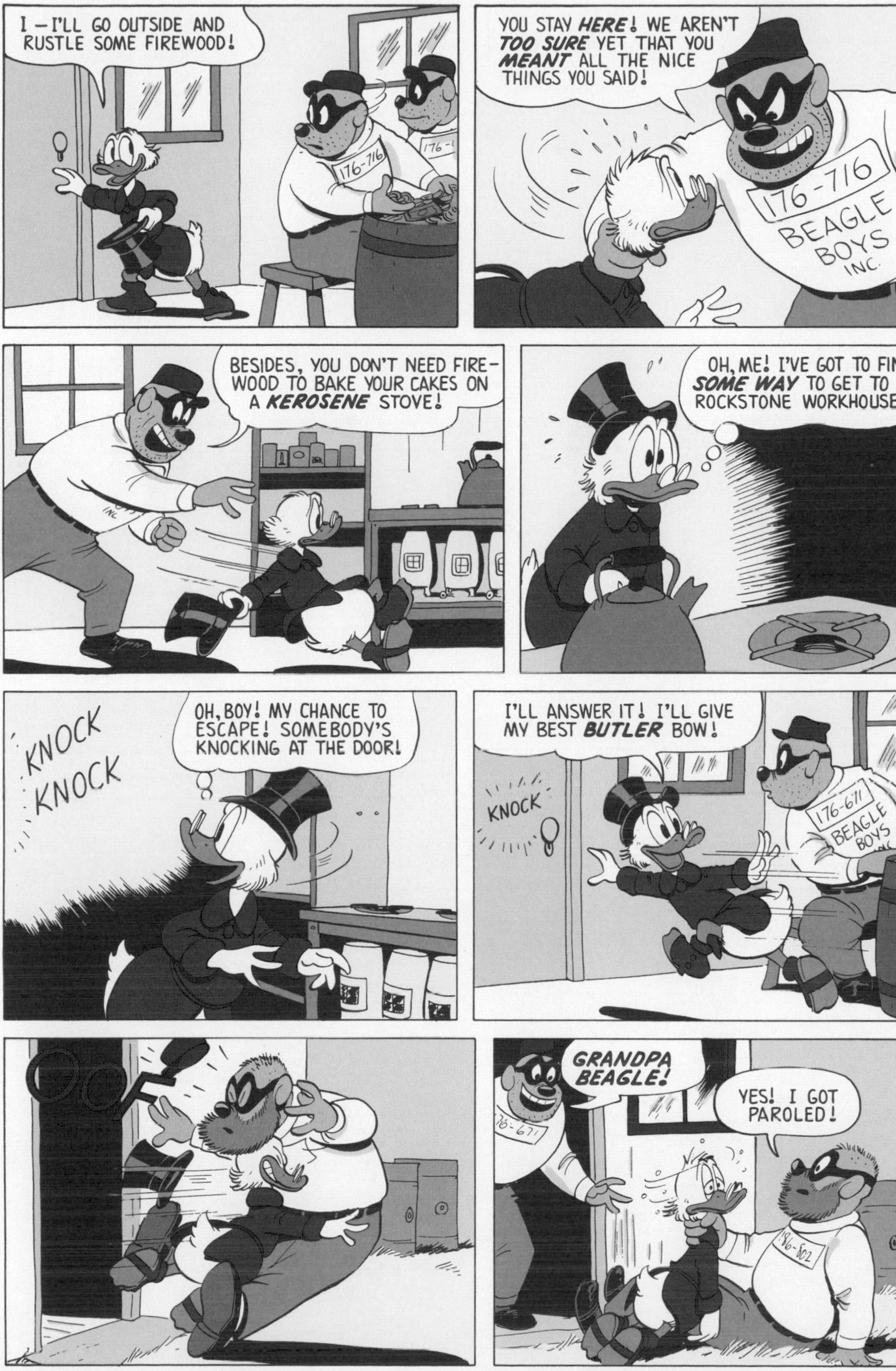

I—I'LL GO OUTSIDE AND RUSTLE SOME FIREWOOD!
176-716
YOU STAY HERE! WE AREN'T TOO SURE YET THAT YOU MEANT ALL THE NICE THINGS YOU SAID!
176-716 BEAGLE BOYS INC.
BESIDES, YOU DON'T NEED FIRE-WOOD TO BAKE YOUR CAKES ON A KEROSENE STOVE!
OH, ME! I'VE GOT TO FIND SOME WAY TO GET TO ROCKSTONE WORKHOUSE!
KNOCK KNOCK
OH, BOY! MY CHANCE TO ESCAPE! SOMEBODY'S KNOCKING AT THE DOOR!
I'LL ANSWER IT! I'LL GIVE MY BEST BUTLER BOW!
KNOCK
176-671 BEAGLE BOYS
GRANDPA BEAGLE!
YES! I GOT PAROLED!
176-671
186-802

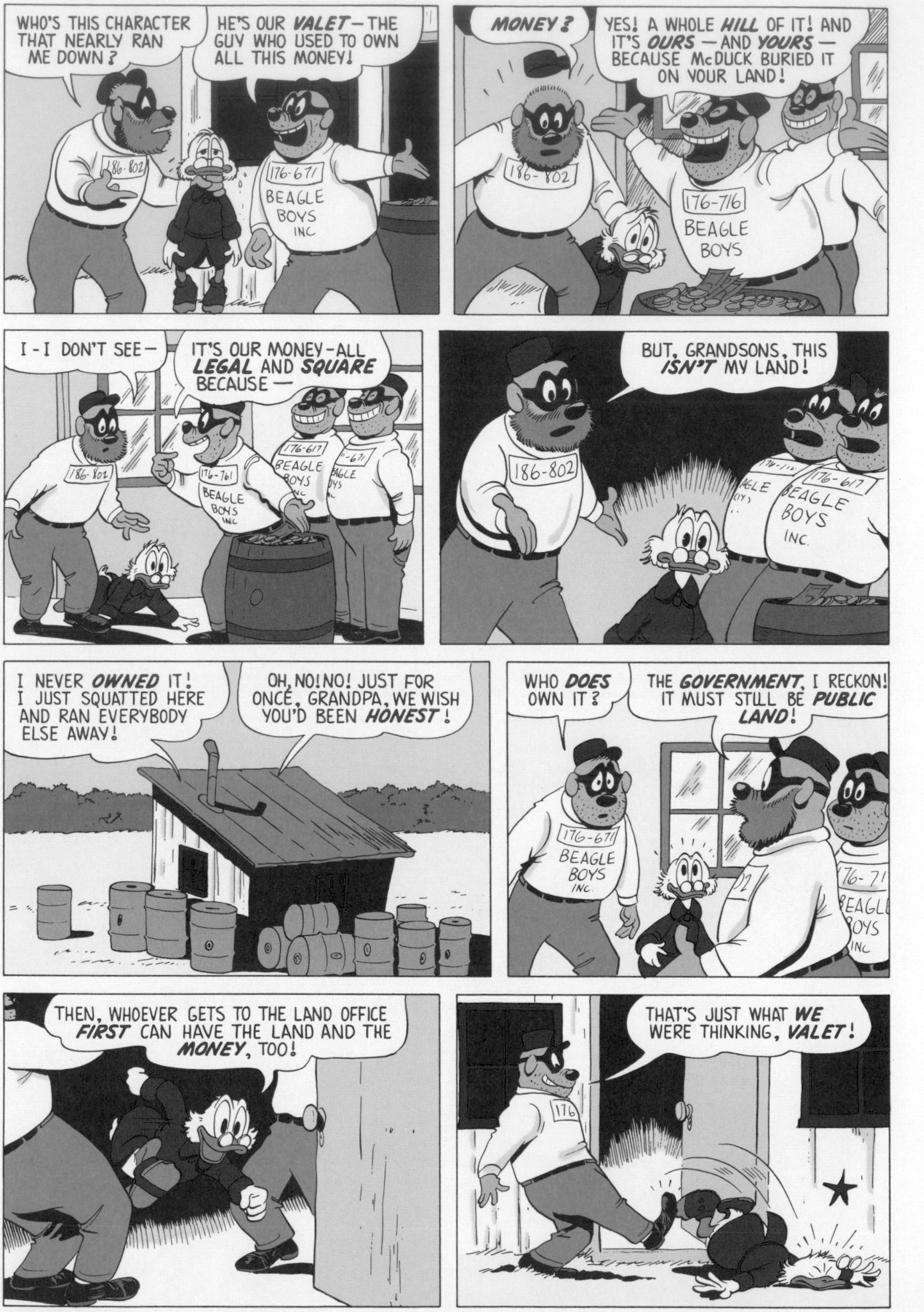
WHO'S THIS CHARACTER THAT NEARLY RAN ME DOWN?
HE'S OUR VALET — THE GUY WHO USED TO OWN ALL THIS MONEY!
186-802
176-671 BEAGLE BOYS INC
MONEY?
YES! A WHOLE HILL OF IT! AND IT'S OURS — AND YOURS — BECAUSE McDUCK BURIED IT ON YOUR LAND!
186-802
176-716 BEAGLE BOYS
I-I DON'T SEE—
IT'S OUR MONEY-ALL LEGAL AND SQUARE BECAUSE —
186-802
176-761 BEAGLE BOYS INC
176-617 BEAGLE BOYS
BUT, GRANDSONS, THIS ISN'T MY LAND!
186-802
176-617 BEAGLE BOYS INC.
I NEVER OWNED IT! I JUST SQUATTED HERE AND RAN EVERYBODY ELSE AWAY!
OH, NO! NO! JUST FOR ONCE, GRANDPA, WE WISH YOU'D BEEN HONEST!
WHO DOES OWN IT?
THE GOVERNMENT, I RECKON! IT MUST STILL BE PUBLIC LAND!
176-671 BEAGLE BOYS INC.
THEN, WHOEVER GETS TO THE LAND OFFICE FIRST CAN HAVE THE LAND AND THE MONEY, TOO!
THAT'S JUST WHAT WE WERE THINKING, VALET!

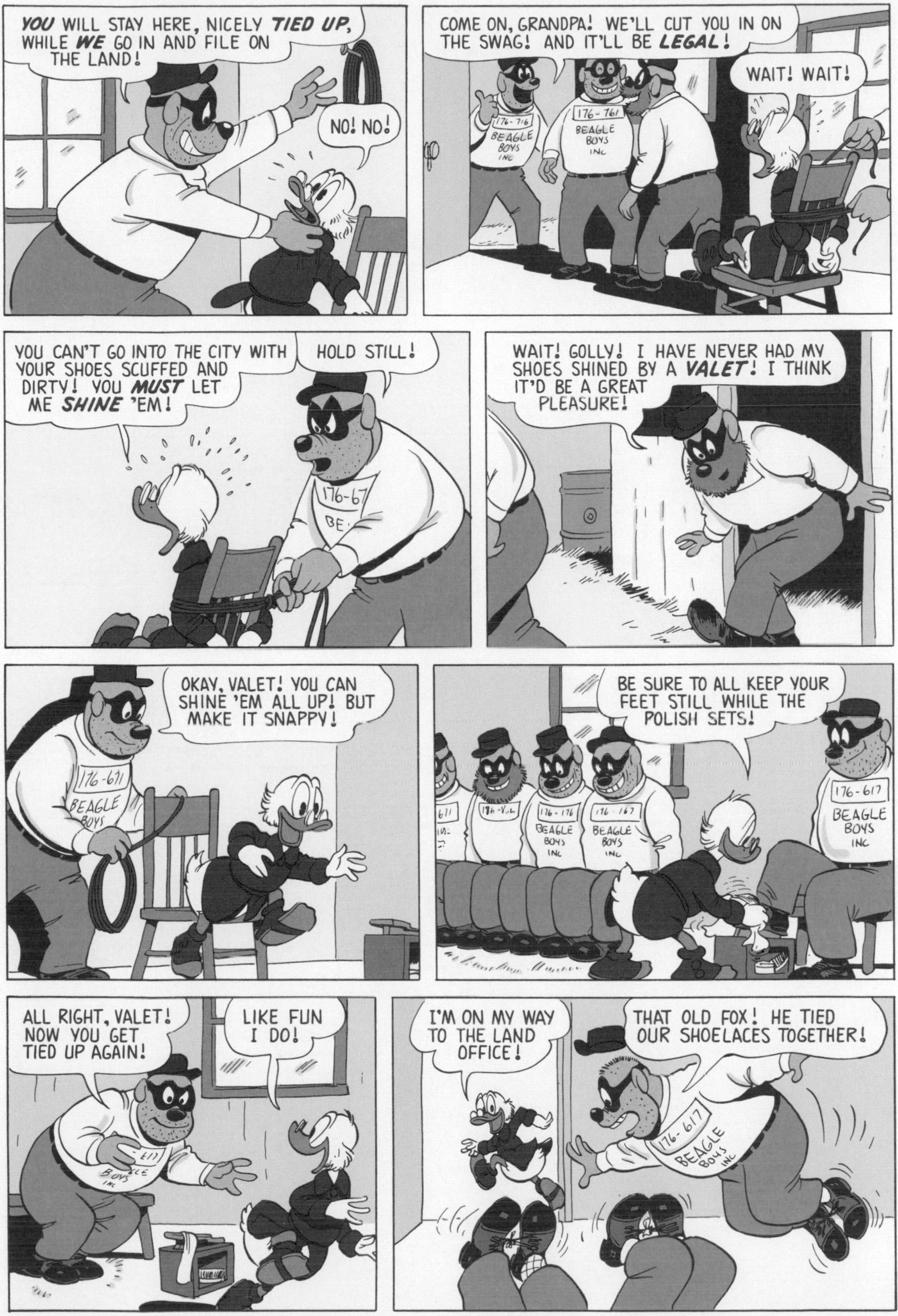
YOU WILL STAY HERE, NICELY TIED UP, WHILE WE GO IN AND FILE ON THE LAND!
NO! NO!
COME ON, GRANDPA! WE'LL CUT YOU IN ON THE SWAG! AND IT'LL BE LEGAL!
WAIT! WAIT!
YOU CAN'T GO INTO THE CITY WITH YOUR SHOES SCUFFED AND DIRTY! YOU MUST LET ME SHINE 'EM!
HOLD STILL!
WAIT! GOLLY! I HAVE NEVER HAD MY SHOES SHINED BY A VALET! I THINK IT'D BE A GREAT PLEASURE!
OKAY, VALET! YOU CAN SHINE 'EM ALL UP! BUT MAKE IT SNAPPY!
BE SURE TO ALL KEEP YOUR FEET STILL WHILE THE POLISH SETS!
ALL RIGHT, VALET! NOW YOU GET TIED UP AGAIN!
LIKE FUN I DO!
I'M ON MY WAY TO THE LAND OFFICE!
THAT OLD FOX! HE TIED OUR SHOELACES TOGETHER!

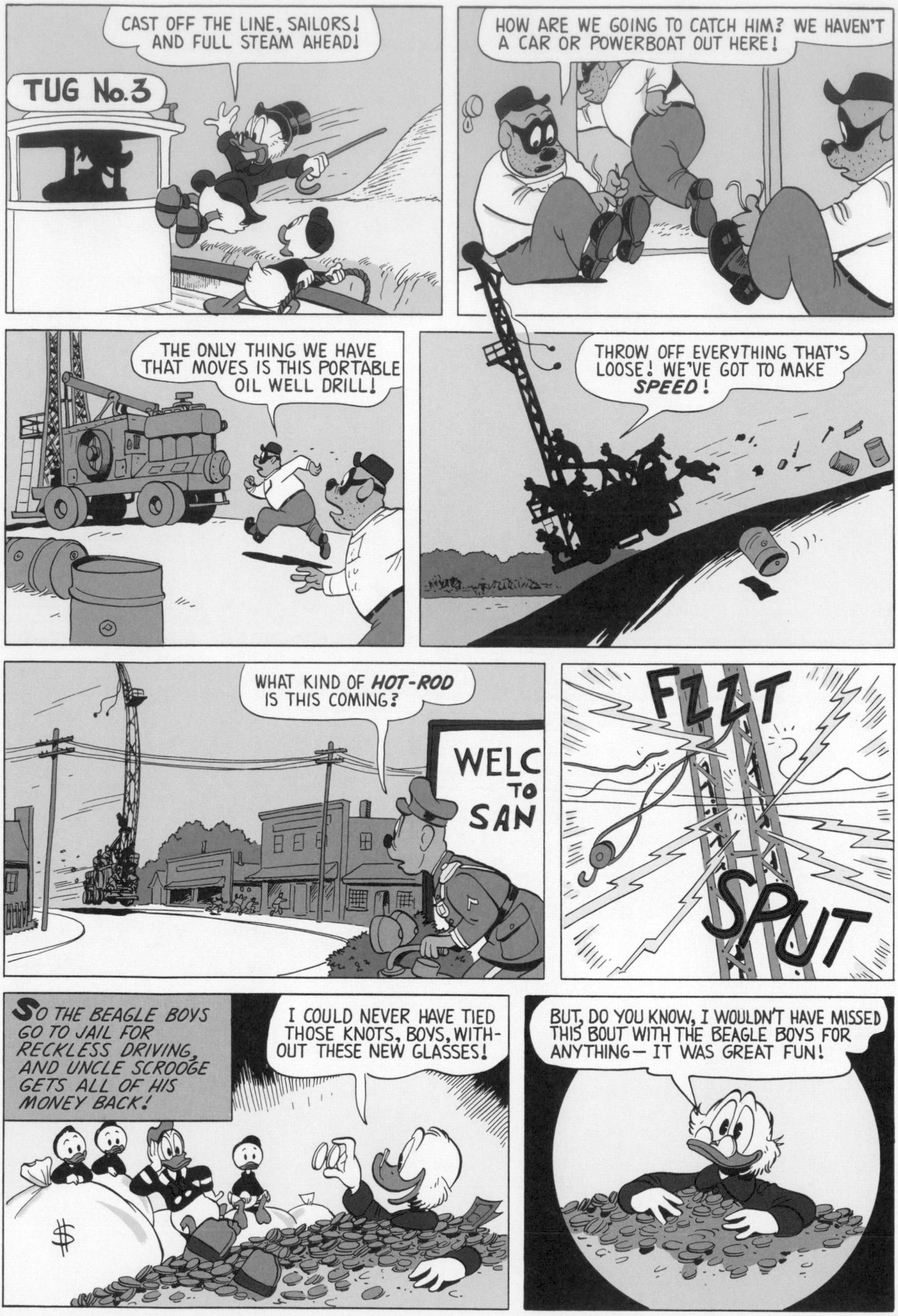
CAST OFF THE LINE, SAILORS! AND FULL STEAM AHEAD!
TUG No.3
HOW ARE WE GOING TO CATCH HIM? WE HAVEN'T A CAR OR POWERBOAT OUT HERE!
THE ONLY THING WE HAVE THAT MOVES IS THIS PORTABLE OIL WELL DRILL!
THROW OFF EVERYTHING THAT'S LOOSE! WE'VE GOT TO MAKE SPEED!
WHAT KIND OF HOT-ROD IS THIS COMING?
WELC TO SAN
FZZT
SPUT
SO THE BEAGLE BOYS GO TO JAIL FOR RECKLESS DRIVING, AND UNCLE SCROOGE GETS ALL OF HIS MONEY BACK!
I COULD NEVER HAVE TIED THOSE KNOTS, BOYS, WITHOUT THESE NEW GLASSES!
BUT, DO YOU KNOW, I WOULDN'T HAVE MISSED THIS BOUT WITH THE BEAGLE BOYS FOR ANYTHING— IT WAS GREAT FUN!

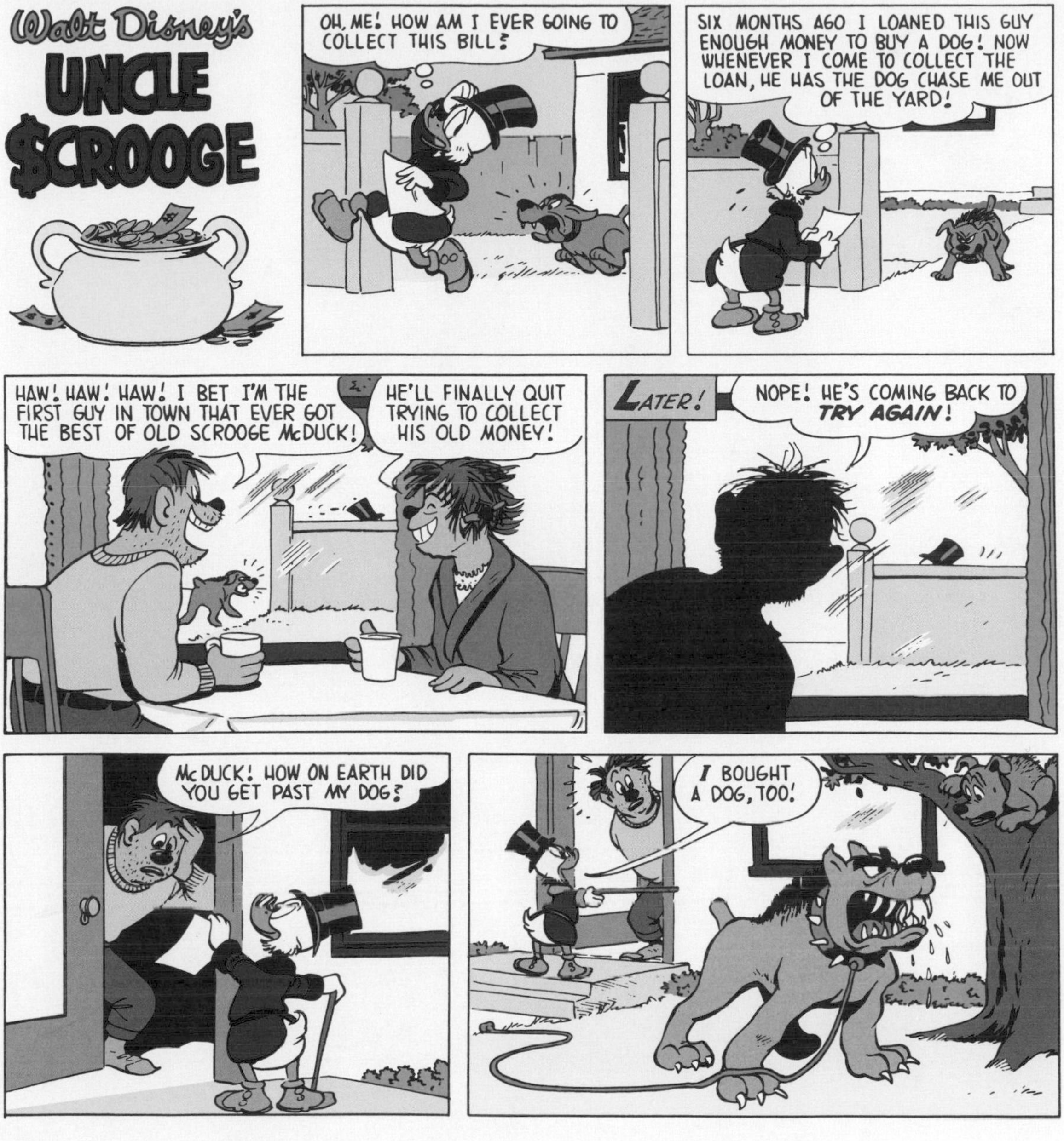
Walt Disney's
UNCLE $CROOGE
OH, ME! HOW AM I EVER GOING TO COLLECT THIS BILL?
SIX MONTHS AGO I LOANED THIS GUY ENOUGH MONEY TO BUY A DOG! NOW WHENEVER I COME TO COLLECT THE LOAN, HE HAS THE DOG CHASE ME OUT OF THE YARD!
HAW! HAW! HAW! I BET I'M THE FIRST GUY IN TOWN THAT EVER GOT THE BEST OF OLD SCROOGE McDUCK!
HE'LL FINALLY QUIT TRYING TO COLLECT HIS OLD MONEY!
LATER!
NOPE! HE'S COMING BACK TO TRY AGAIN!
McDUCK! HOW ON EARTH DID YOU GET PAST MY DOG?
I BOUGHT A DOG, TOO!

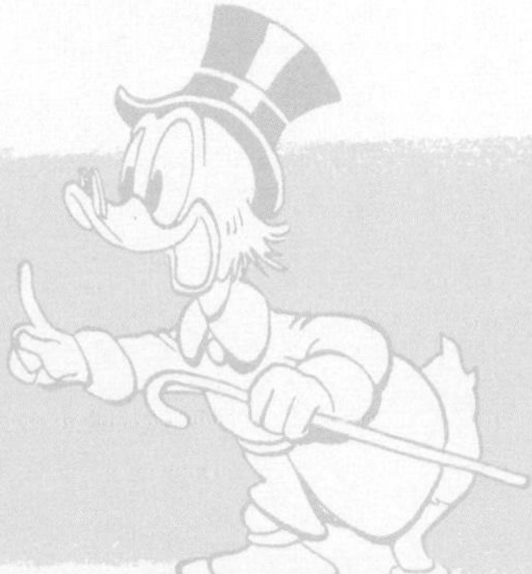

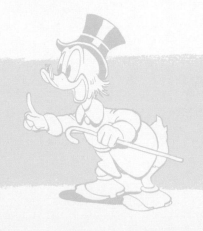

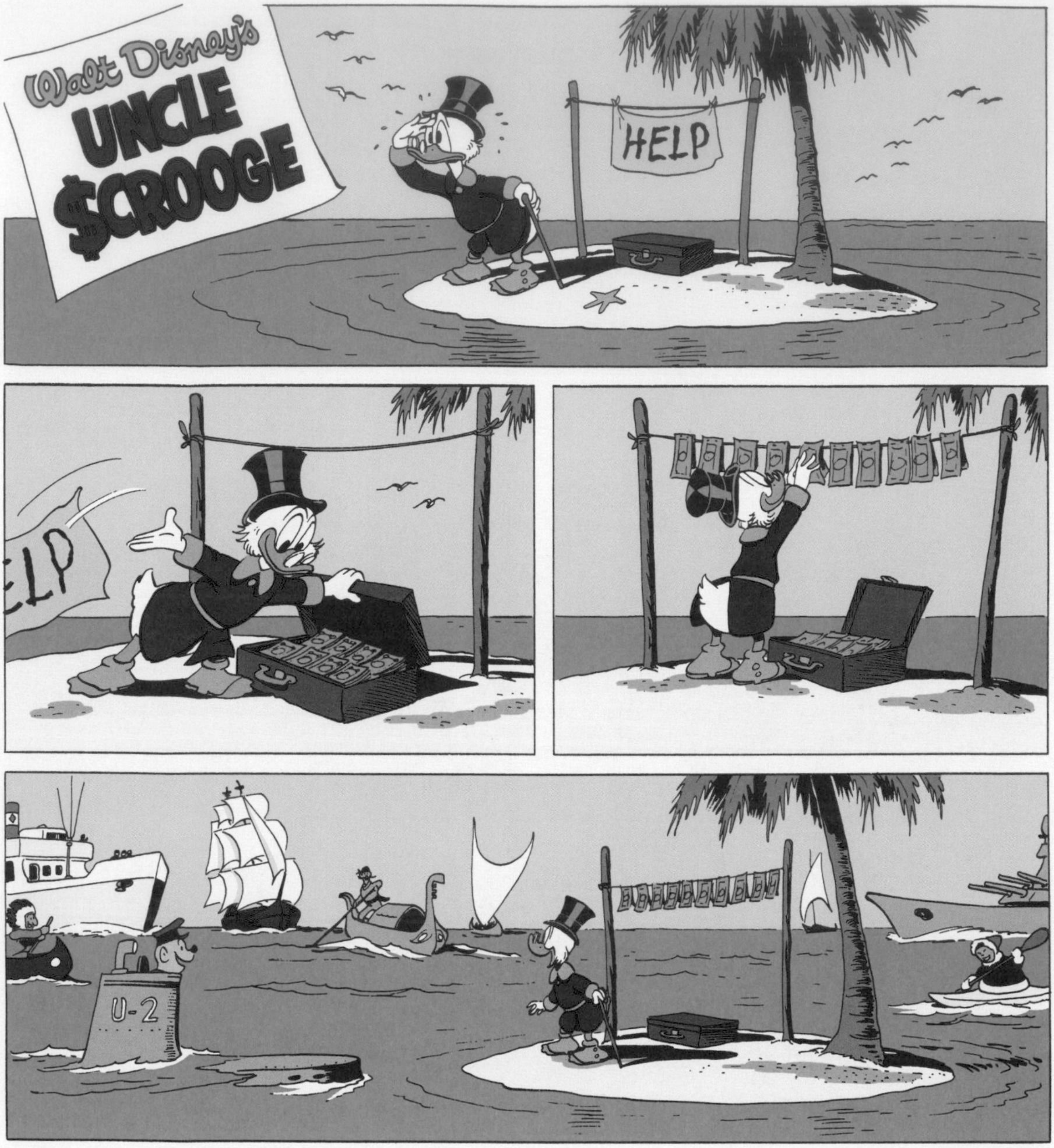
Walt Disney's
UNCLE
$CROOGE
HELP
ELP
U-2

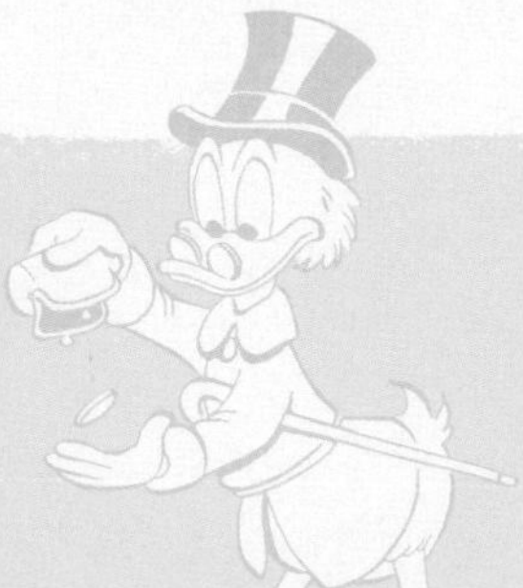

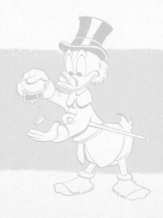

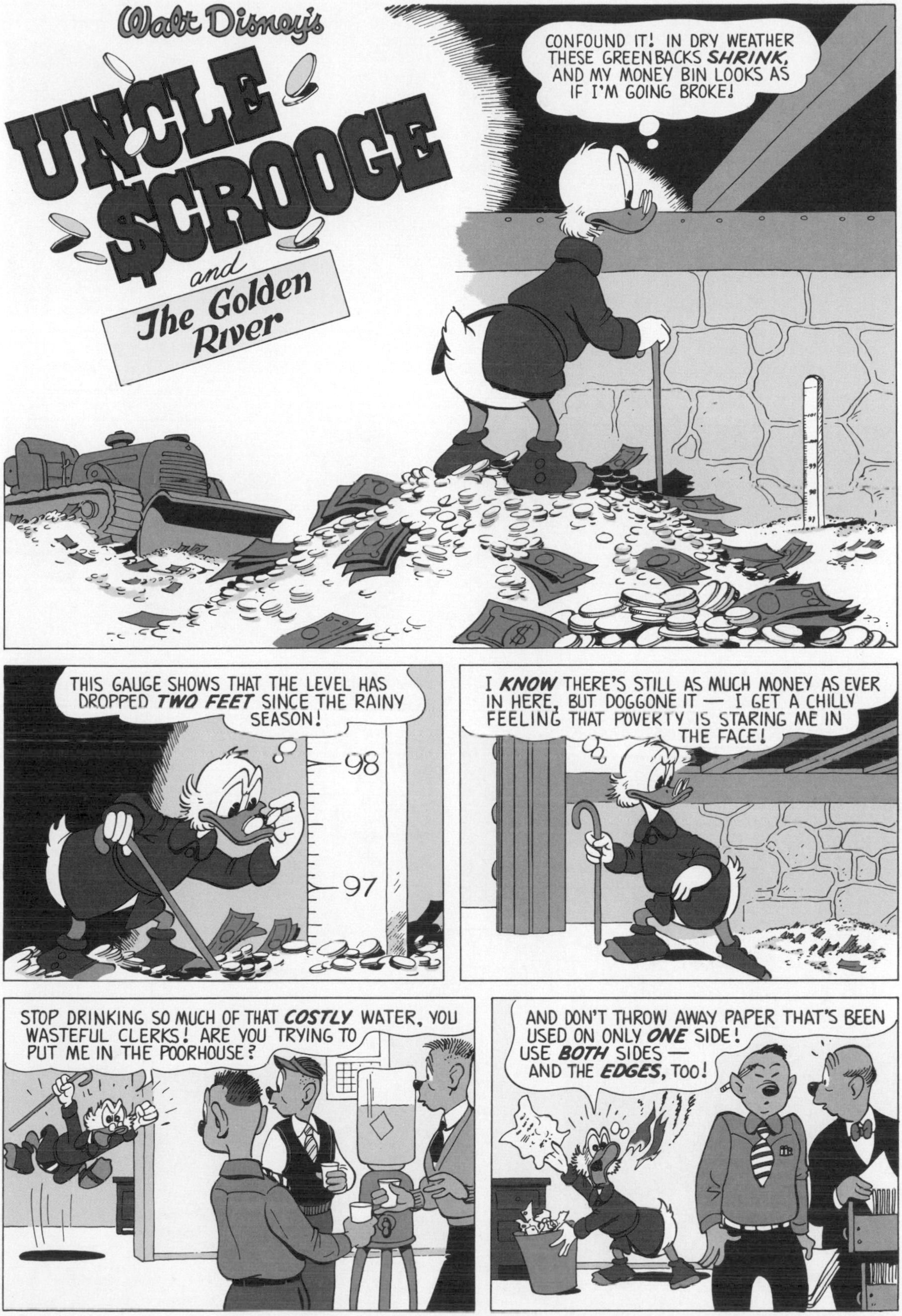
Walt Disney's
UNCLE $CROOGE
and
The Golden River
CONFOUND IT! IN DRY WEATHER THESE GREENBACKS SHRINK, AND MY MONEY BIN LOOKS AS IF I'M GOING BROKE!
THIS GAUGE SHOWS THAT THE LEVEL HAS DROPPED TWO FEET SINCE THE RAINY SEASON!
98
97
I KNOW THERE'S STILL AS MUCH MONEY AS EVER IN HERE, BUT DOGGONE IT — I GET A CHILLY FEELING THAT POVERTY IS STARING ME IN THE FACE!
STOP DRINKING SO MUCH OF THAT COSTLY WATER, YOU WASTEFUL CLERKS! ARE YOU TRYING TO PUT ME IN THE POORHOUSE?
AND DON'T THROW AWAY PAPER THAT'S BEEN USED ON ONLY ONE SIDE! USE BOTH SIDES — AND THE EDGES, TOO!

AND LOOK AT THE WORN-OUT *ERASERS*! IF YOU MADE FEWER *MISTAKES*, YOU'D ALSO USE *FEWER* PENCILS!

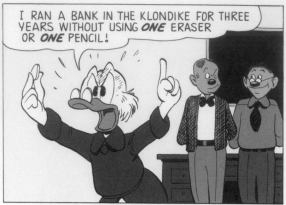

I RAN A BANK IN THE KLONDIKE FOR THREE YEARS WITHOUT USING *ONE* ERASER OR *ONE* PENCIL!

THAT WAS WHEN HE DID HIS FIGURING WITH A WALRUS TUSK ON A BLOCK OF ICE!

HE TELLS US ABOUT IT EVERY SPRING WHEN THE DRY WEATHER STARTS SHRINKING HIS MONEY!

I WANT SOME *ECONOMY* AROUND HERE! THERE'S GOING TO BE MONEY *SAVED* — EVEN IF I HAVE TO NAIL IT TO THE FLOOR!

MY *MONEY*! I WENT COLD AND HUNGRY AND SLEEPLESS TO SCRAPE IT TOGETHER! IT BREAKS MY HEART TO SEE IT SHRINKING CLEAR DOWN TO THE *NINETY FOOT* MARK ON THE DEPTH GAUGE!

OUTSIDE!

McDUCK BLDG

I HOPE UNCA SCROOGE IS IN A *GOOD* MOOD THIS MORNING!

WE'VE GOT TO ASK HIM FOR FIVE DOLLARS FOR OUR JUNIOR WOODCHUCKS' PLAYGROUND FUND!

HE IS THE ONLY PERSON IN DUCKBURG WHO HASN'T GIVEN TO HELP BUY A PLAYGROUND FOR THE WOODCHUCKS!

HI, UNCLE SCROOGE!

I CAN TELL BY YOUR TRILLY GREETING THAT YOU'RE HERE TO ASK FOR *MONEY*!

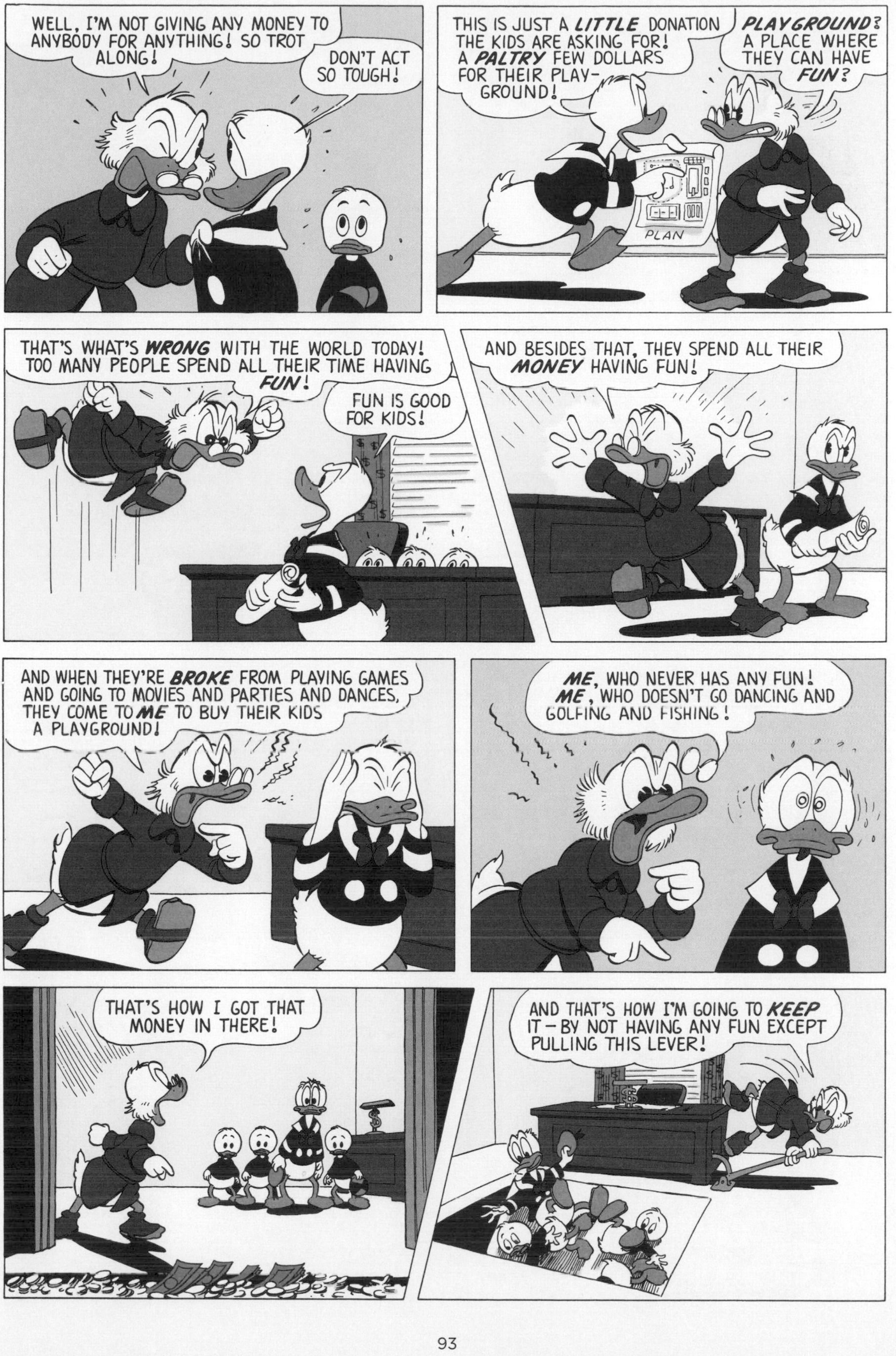
WELL, I'M NOT GIVING ANY MONEY TO ANYBODY FOR ANYTHING! SO TROT ALONG!
DON'T ACT SO TOUGH!
THIS IS JUST A LITTLE DONATION THE KIDS ARE ASKING FOR! A PALTRY FEW DOLLARS FOR THEIR PLAY-GROUND!
PLAN
PLAYGROUND? A PLACE WHERE THEY CAN HAVE FUN?
THAT'S WHAT'S WRONG WITH THE WORLD TODAY! TOO MANY PEOPLE SPEND ALL THEIR TIME HAVING FUN!
FUN IS GOOD FOR KIDS!
AND BESIDES THAT, THEY SPEND ALL THEIR MONEY HAVING FUN!
AND WHEN THEY'RE BROKE FROM PLAYING GAMES AND GOING TO MOVIES AND PARTIES AND DANCES, THEY COME TO ME TO BUY THEIR KIDS A PLAYGROUND!
ME, WHO NEVER HAS ANY FUN! ME, WHO DOESN'T GO DANCING AND GOLFING AND FISHING!
THAT'S HOW I GOT THAT MONEY IN THERE!
AND THAT'S HOW I'M GOING TO KEEP IT — BY NOT HAVING ANY FUN EXCEPT PULLING THIS LEVER!

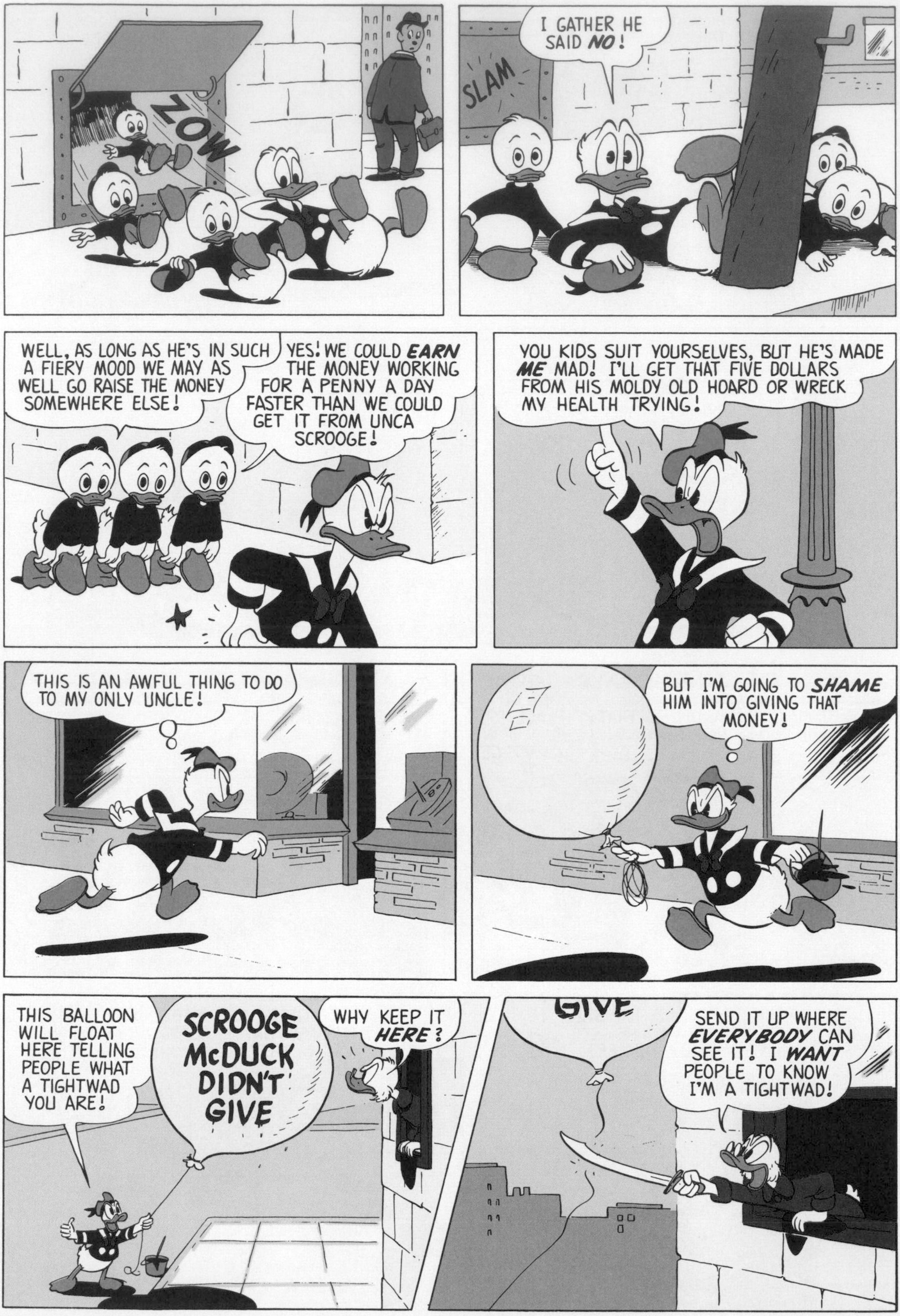

ZOW
I GATHER HE SAID NO!
SLAM
WELL, AS LONG AS HE'S IN SUCH A FIERY MOOD WE MAY AS WELL GO RAISE THE MONEY SOMEWHERE ELSE!
YES! WE COULD EARN THE MONEY WORKING FOR A PENNY A DAY FASTER THAN WE COULD GET IT FROM UNCA SCROOGE!
YOU KIDS SUIT YOURSELVES, BUT HE'S MADE ME MAD! I'LL GET THAT FIVE DOLLARS FROM HIS MOLDY OLD HOARD OR WRECK MY HEALTH TRYING!
THIS IS AN AWFUL THING TO DO TO MY ONLY UNCLE!
BUT I'M GOING TO SHAME HIM INTO GIVING THAT MONEY!
THIS BALLOON WILL FLOAT HERE TELLING PEOPLE WHAT A TIGHTWAD YOU ARE!
SCROOGE McDUCK DIDN'T GIVE
WHY KEEP IT HERE?
GIVE
SEND IT UP WHERE EVERYBODY CAN SEE IT! I WANT PEOPLE TO KNOW I'M A TIGHTWAD!

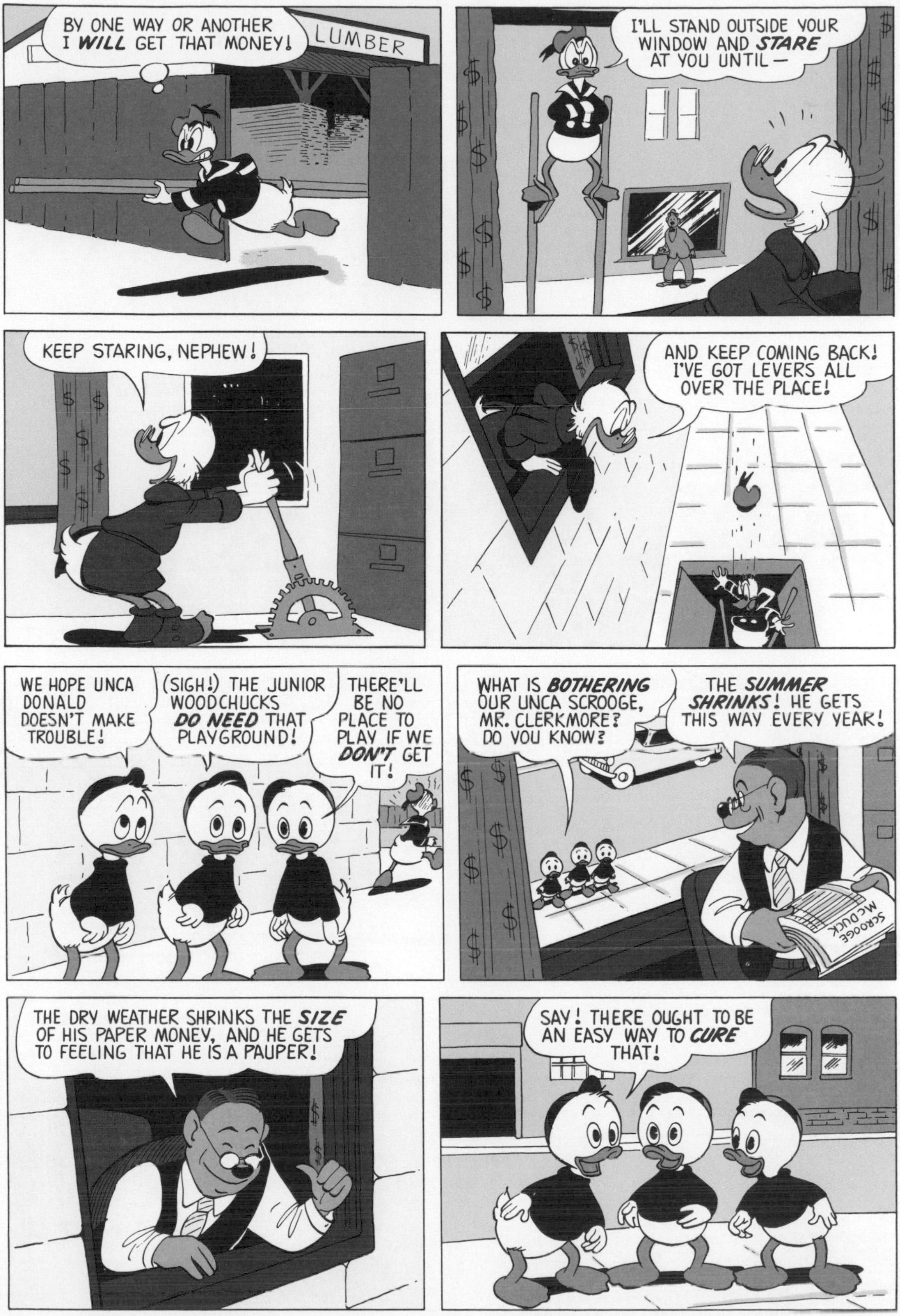
BY ONE WAY OR ANOTHER I WILL GET THAT MONEY!
LUMBER
I'LL STAND OUTSIDE YOUR WINDOW AND STARE AT YOU UNTIL—
KEEP STARING, NEPHEW!
AND KEEP COMING BACK! I'VE GOT LEVERS ALL OVER THE PLACE!
WE HOPE UNCA DONALD DOESN'T MAKE TROUBLE!
(SIGH!) THE JUNIOR WOODCHUCKS DO NEED THAT PLAYGROUND!
THERE'LL BE NO PLACE TO PLAY IF WE DON'T GET IT!
WHAT IS BOTHERING OUR UNCA SCROOGE, MR. CLERKMORE? DO YOU KNOW?
THE SUMMER SHRINKS! HE GETS THIS WAY EVERY YEAR!
SCROOGE MC DUCK
THE DRY WEATHER SHRINKS THE SIZE OF HIS PAPER MONEY, AND HE GETS TO FEELING THAT HE IS A PAUPER!
SAY! THERE OUGHT TO BE AN EASY WAY TO CURE THAT!

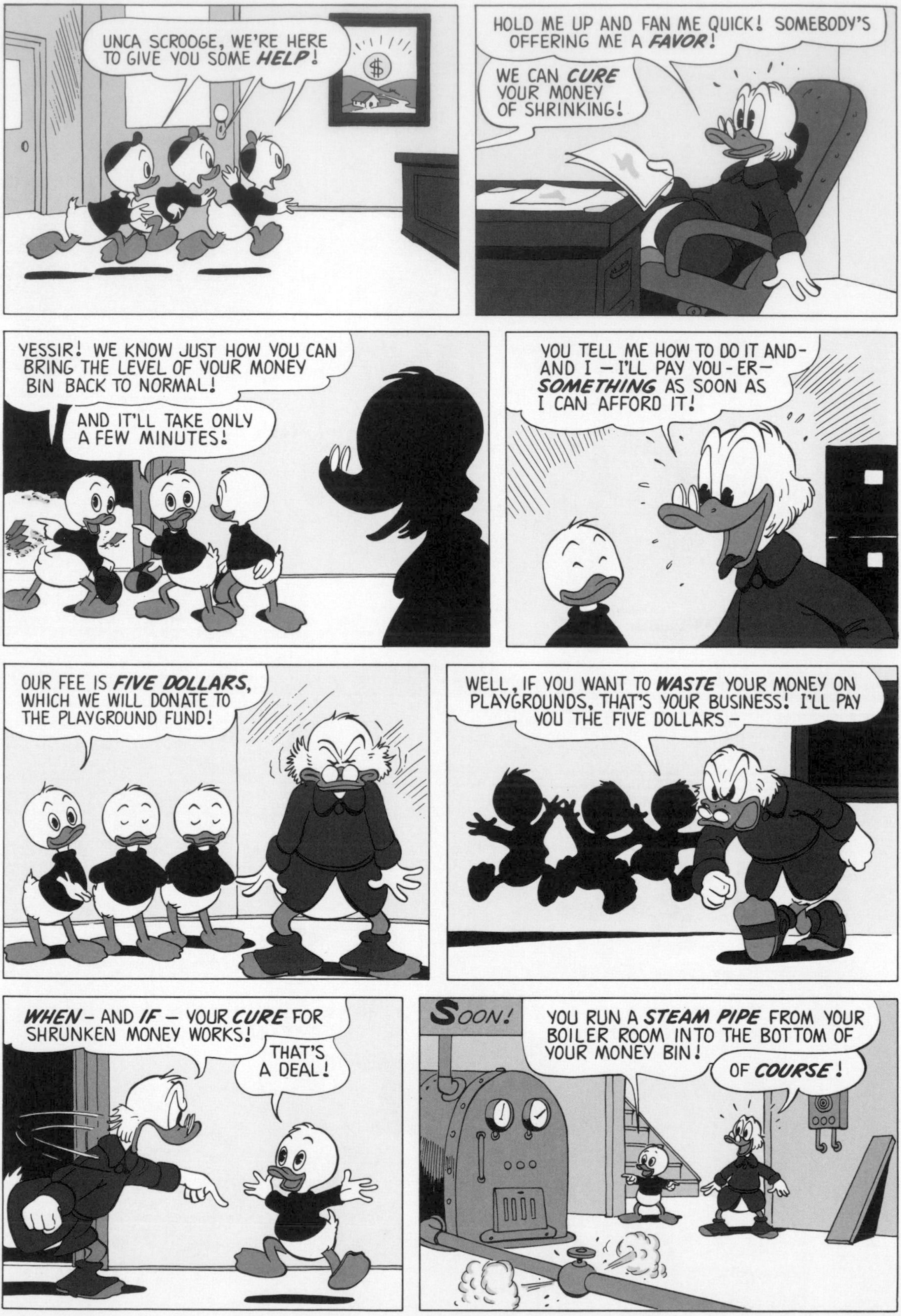
UNCA SCROOGE, WE'RE HERE TO GIVE YOU SOME HELP!
HOLD ME UP AND FAN ME QUICK! SOMEBODY'S OFFERING ME A FAVOR!
WE CAN CURE YOUR MONEY OF SHRINKING!
YESSIR! WE KNOW JUST HOW YOU CAN BRING THE LEVEL OF YOUR MONEY BIN BACK TO NORMAL!
AND IT'LL TAKE ONLY A FEW MINUTES!
YOU TELL ME HOW TO DO IT AND-AND I — I'LL PAY YOU - ER— SOMETHING AS SOON AS I CAN AFFORD IT!
OUR FEE IS FIVE DOLLARS, WHICH WE WILL DONATE TO THE PLAYGROUND FUND!
WELL, IF YOU WANT TO WASTE YOUR MONEY ON PLAYGROUNDS, THAT'S YOUR BUSINESS! I'LL PAY YOU THE FIVE DOLLARS -
WHEN - AND IF — YOUR CURE FOR SHRUNKEN MONEY WORKS!
THAT'S A DEAL!
SOON!
YOU RUN A STEAM PIPE FROM YOUR BOILER ROOM INTO THE BOTTOM OF YOUR MONEY BIN!
OF COURSE!

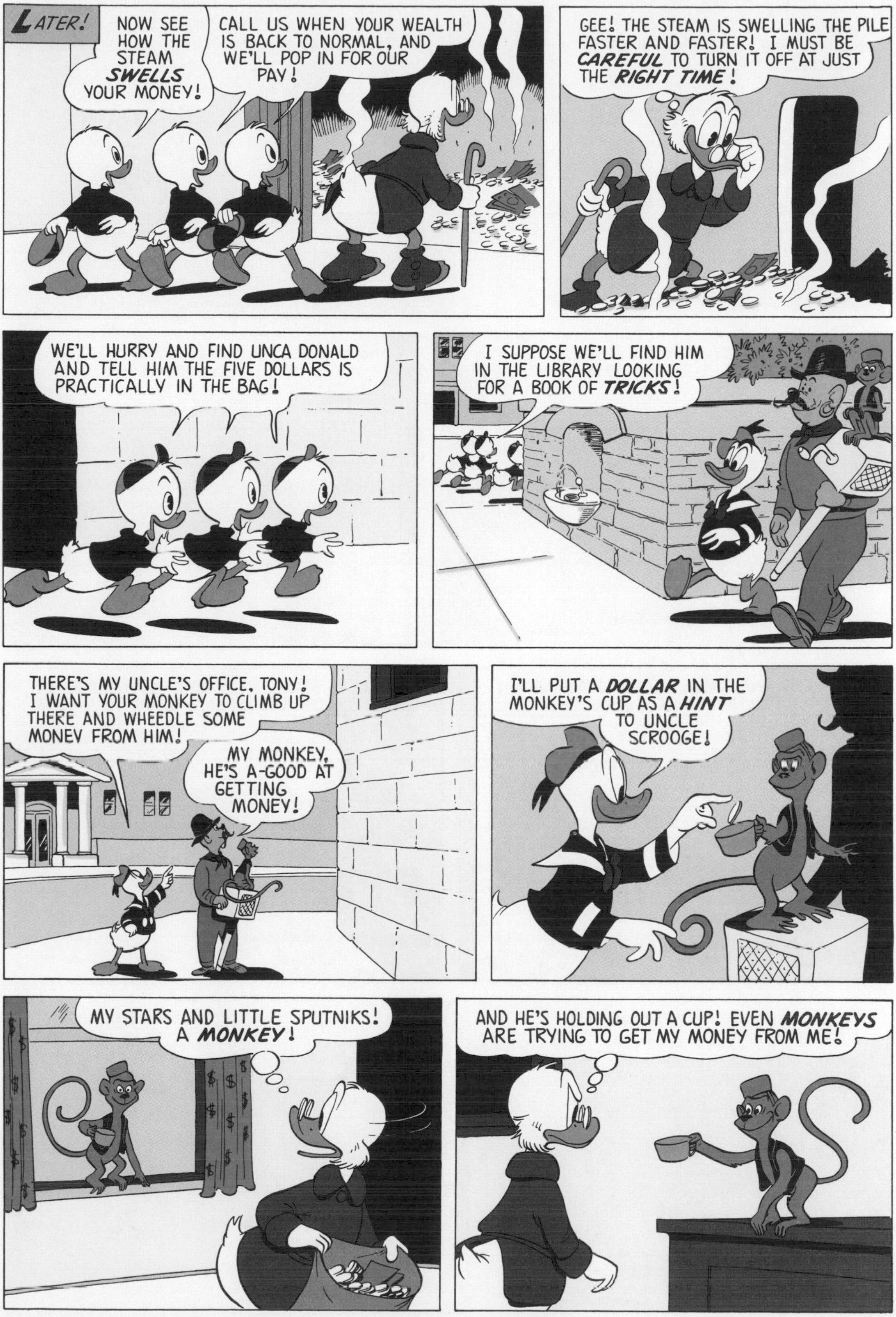
LATER!
NOW SEE HOW THE STEAM SWELLS YOUR MONEY!
CALL US WHEN YOUR WEALTH IS BACK TO NORMAL, AND WE'LL POP IN FOR OUR PAY!
GEE! THE STEAM IS SWELLING THE PILE FASTER AND FASTER! I MUST BE CAREFUL TO TURN IT OFF AT JUST THE RIGHT TIME!
WE'LL HURRY AND FIND UNCA DONALD AND TELL HIM THE FIVE DOLLARS IS PRACTICALLY IN THE BAG!
I SUPPOSE WE'LL FIND HIM IN THE LIBRARY LOOKING FOR A BOOK OF TRICKS!
THERE'S MY UNCLE'S OFFICE, TONY! I WANT YOUR MONKEY TO CLIMB UP THERE AND WHEEDLE SOME MONEV FROM HIM!
MY MONKEY, HE'S A-GOOD AT GETTING MONEY!
I'LL PUT A DOLLAR IN THE MONKEY'S CUP AS A HINT TO UNCLE SCROOGE!
MY STARS AND LITTLE SPUTNIKS! A MONKEY!
AND HE'S HOLDING OUT A CUP! EVEN MONKEYS ARE TRYING TO GET MY MONEY FROM ME!

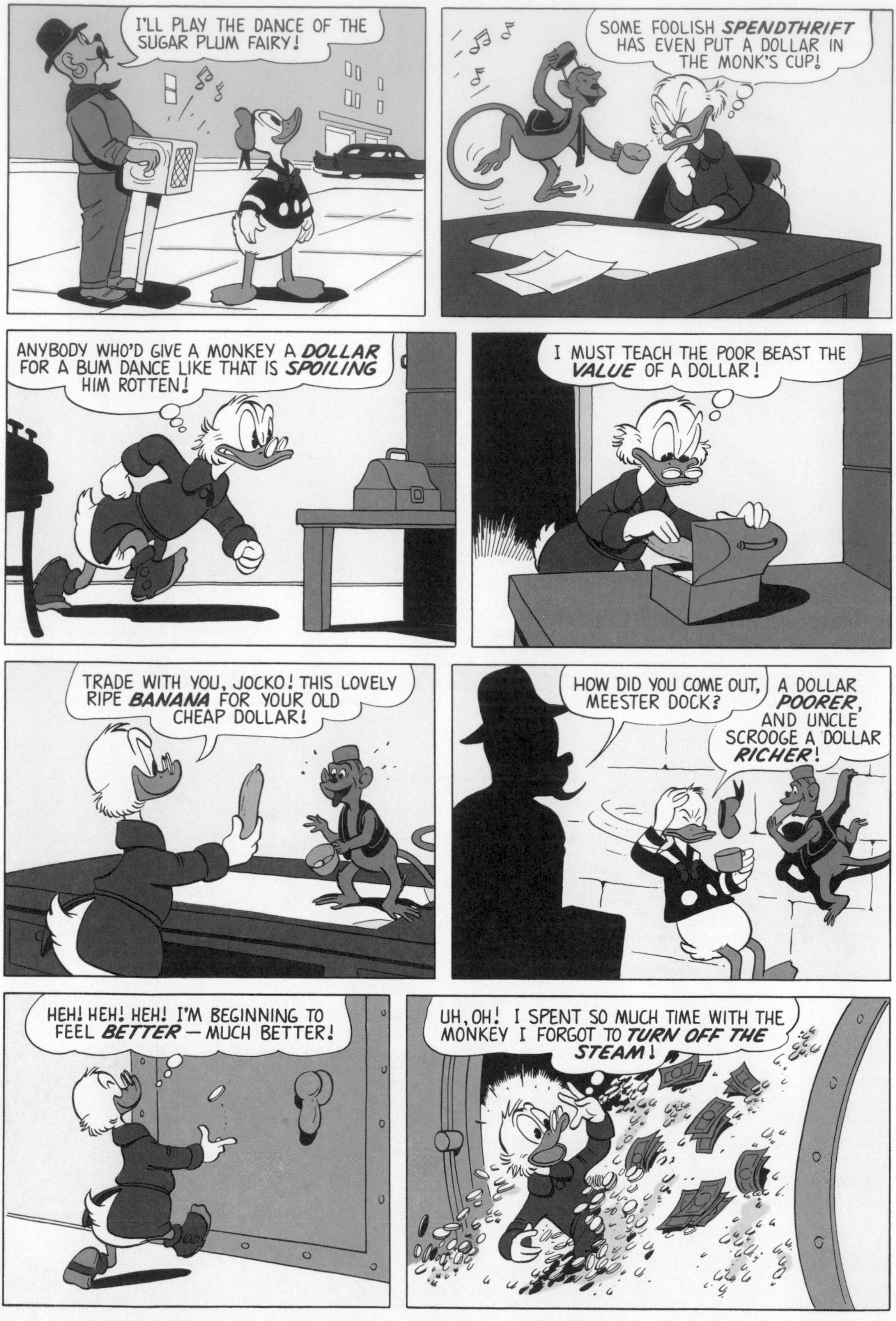
I'LL PLAY THE DANCE OF THE SUGAR PLUM FAIRY!
SOME FOOLISH SPENDTHRIFT HAS EVEN PUT A DOLLAR IN THE MONK'S CUP!
ANYBODY WHO'D GIVE A MONKEY A DOLLAR FOR A BUM DANCE LIKE THAT IS SPOILING HIM ROTTEN!
I MUST TEACH THE POOR BEAST THE VALUE OF A DOLLAR!
TRADE WITH YOU, JOCKO! THIS LOVELY RIPE BANANA FOR YOUR OLD CHEAP DOLLAR!
HOW DID YOU COME OUT, MEESTER DOCK?
A DOLLAR POORER, AND UNCLE SCROOGE A DOLLAR RICHER!
HEH! HEH! HEH! I'M BEGINNING TO FEEL BETTER — MUCH BETTER!
UH, OH! I SPENT SO MUCH TIME WITH THE MONKEY I FORGOT TO TURN OFF THE STEAM!

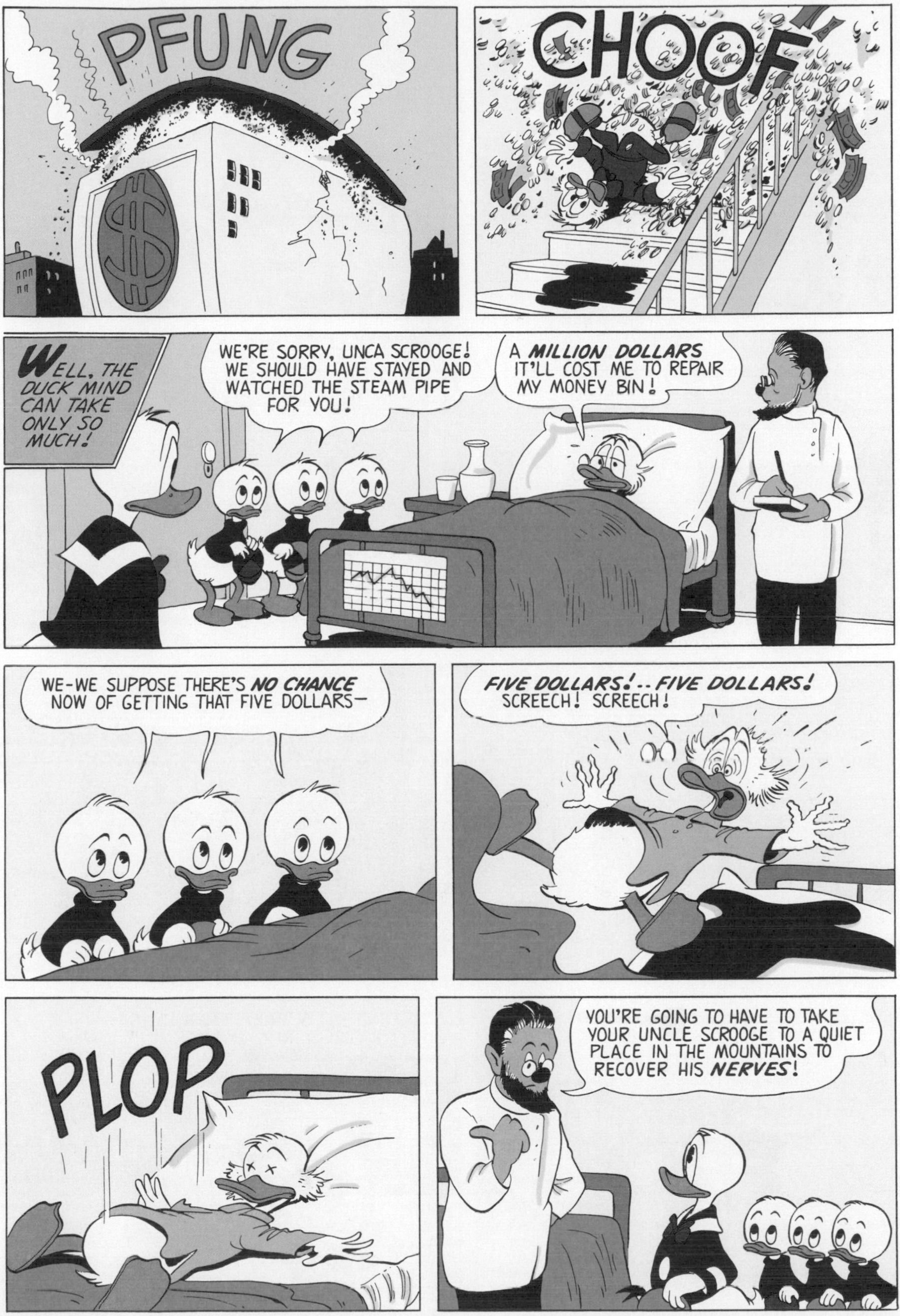
PFUNG
CHOOF
WELL, THE DUCK MIND CAN TAKE ONLY SO MUCH!
WE'RE SORRY, UNCA SCROOGE! WE SHOULD HAVE STAYED AND WATCHED THE STEAM PIPE FOR YOU!
A MILLION DOLLARS IT'LL COST ME TO REPAIR MY MONEY BIN!
WE-WE SUPPOSE THERE'S NO CHANCE NOW OF GETTING THAT FIVE DOLLARS—
FIVE DOLLARS!.. FIVE DOLLARS! SCREECH! SCREECH!
PLOP
YOU'RE GOING TO HAVE TO TAKE YOUR UNCLE SCROOGE TO A QUIET PLACE IN THE MOUNTAINS TO RECOVER HIS NERVES!

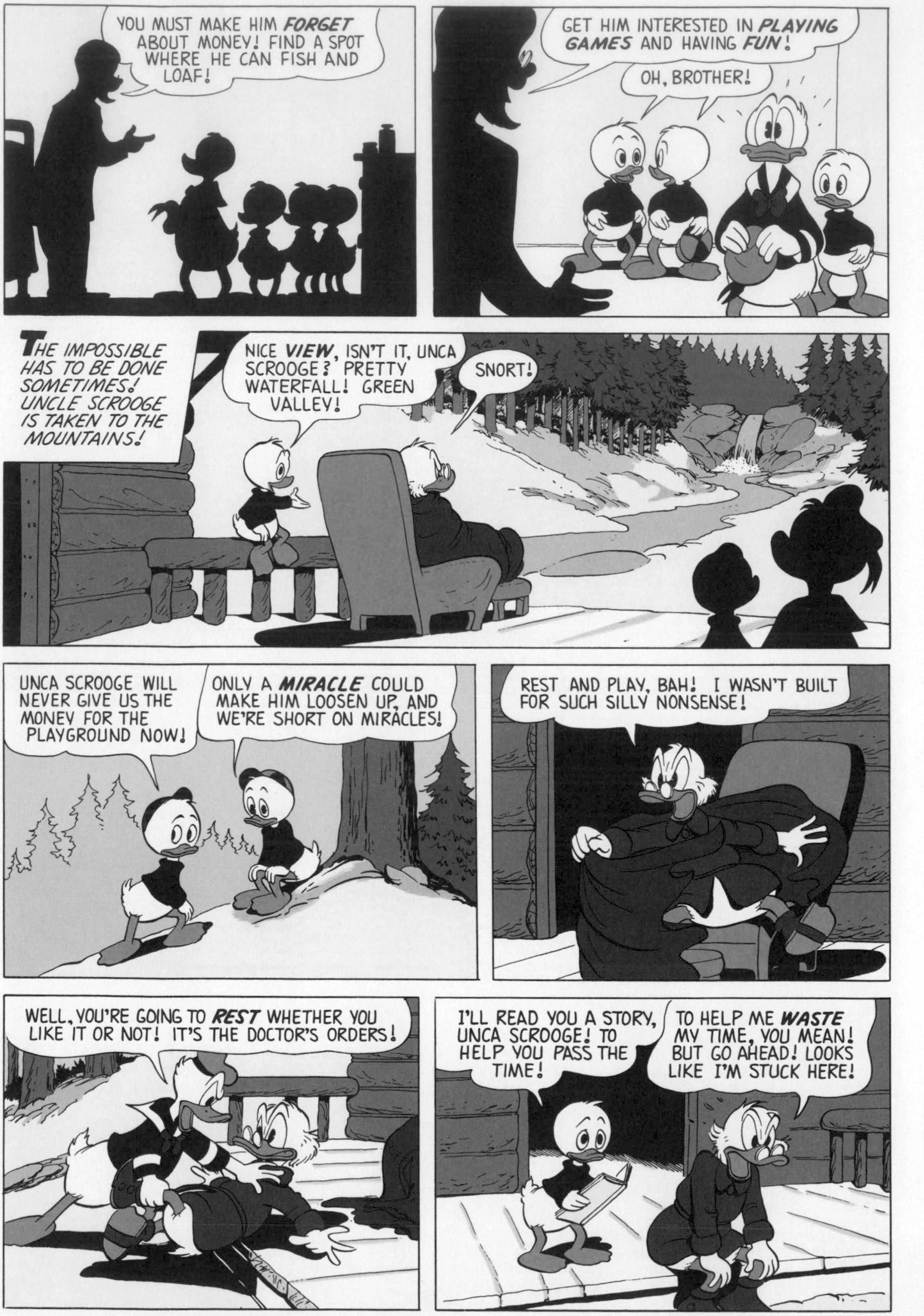
YOU MUST MAKE HIM FORGET ABOUT MONEY! FIND A SPOT WHERE HE CAN FISH AND LOAF!
GET HIM INTERESTED IN PLAYING GAMES AND HAVING FUN!
OH, BROTHER!
THE IMPOSSIBLE HAS TO BE DONE SOMETIMES! UNCLE SCROOGE IS TAKEN TO THE MOUNTAINS!
NICE VIEW, ISN'T IT, UNCA SCROOGE? PRETTY WATERFALL! GREEN VALLEY!
SNORT!
UNCA SCROOGE WILL NEVER GIVE US THE MONEY FOR THE PLAYGROUND NOW!
ONLY A MIRACLE COULD MAKE HIM LOOSEN UP, AND WE'RE SHORT ON MIRACLES!
REST AND PLAY, BAH! I WASN'T BUILT FOR SUCH SILLY NONSENSE!
WELL, YOU'RE GOING TO REST WHETHER YOU LIKE IT OR NOT! IT'S THE DOCTOR'S ORDERS!
I'LL READ YOU A STORY, UNCA SCROOGE! TO HELP YOU PASS THE TIME!
TO HELP ME WASTE MY TIME, YOU MEAN! BUT GO AHEAD! LOOKS LIKE I'M STUCK HERE!

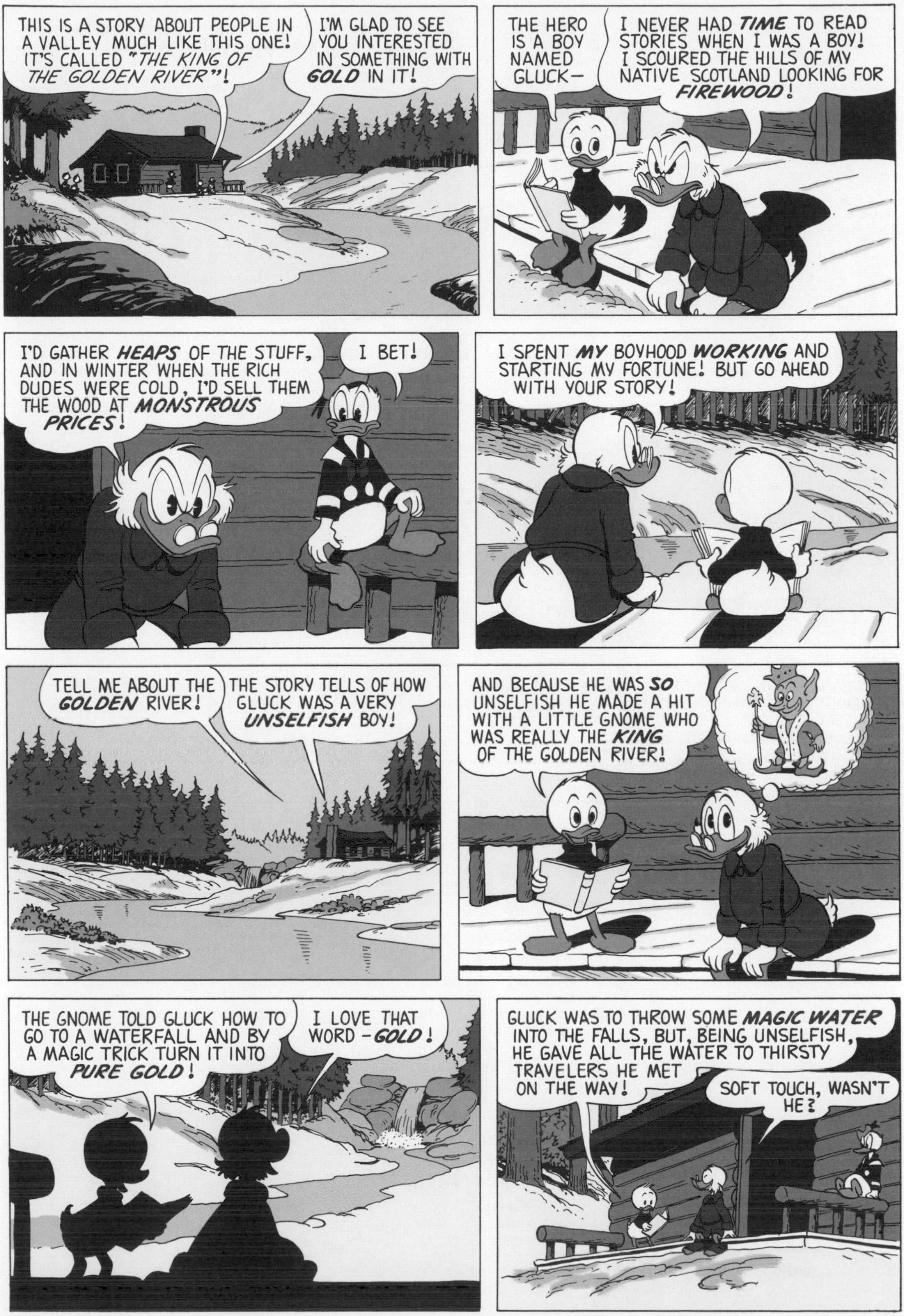

THIS IS A STORY ABOUT PEOPLE IN A VALLEY MUCH LIKE THIS ONE! IT'S CALLED "THE KING OF THE GOLDEN RIVER"!
I'M GLAD TO SEE YOU INTERESTED IN SOMETHING WITH GOLD IN IT!
THE HERO IS A BOY NAMED GLUCK—
I NEVER HAD TIME TO READ STORIES WHEN I WAS A BOY! I SCOURED THE HILLS OF MY NATIVE SCOTLAND LOOKING FOR FIREWOOD!
I'D GATHER HEAPS OF THE STUFF, AND IN WINTER WHEN THE RICH DUDES WERE COLD, I'D SELL THEM THE WOOD AT MONSTROUS PRICES!
I BET!
I SPENT MY BOYHOOD WORKING AND STARTING MY FORTUNE! BUT GO AHEAD WITH YOUR STORY!
TELL ME ABOUT THE GOLDEN RIVER!
THE STORY TELLS OF HOW GLUCK WAS A VERY UNSELFISH BOY!
AND BECAUSE HE WAS SO UNSELFISH HE MADE A HIT WITH A LITTLE GNOME WHO WAS REALLY THE KING OF THE GOLDEN RIVER!
THE GNOME TOLD GLUCK HOW TO GO TO A WATERFALL AND BY A MAGIC TRICK TURN IT INTO PURE GOLD!
I LOVE THAT WORD—GOLD!
GLUCK WAS TO THROW SOME MAGIC WATER INTO THE FALLS, BUT, BEING UNSELFISH, HE GAVE ALL THE WATER TO THIRSTY TRAVELERS HE MET ON THE WAY!
SOFT TOUCH, WASN'T HE?

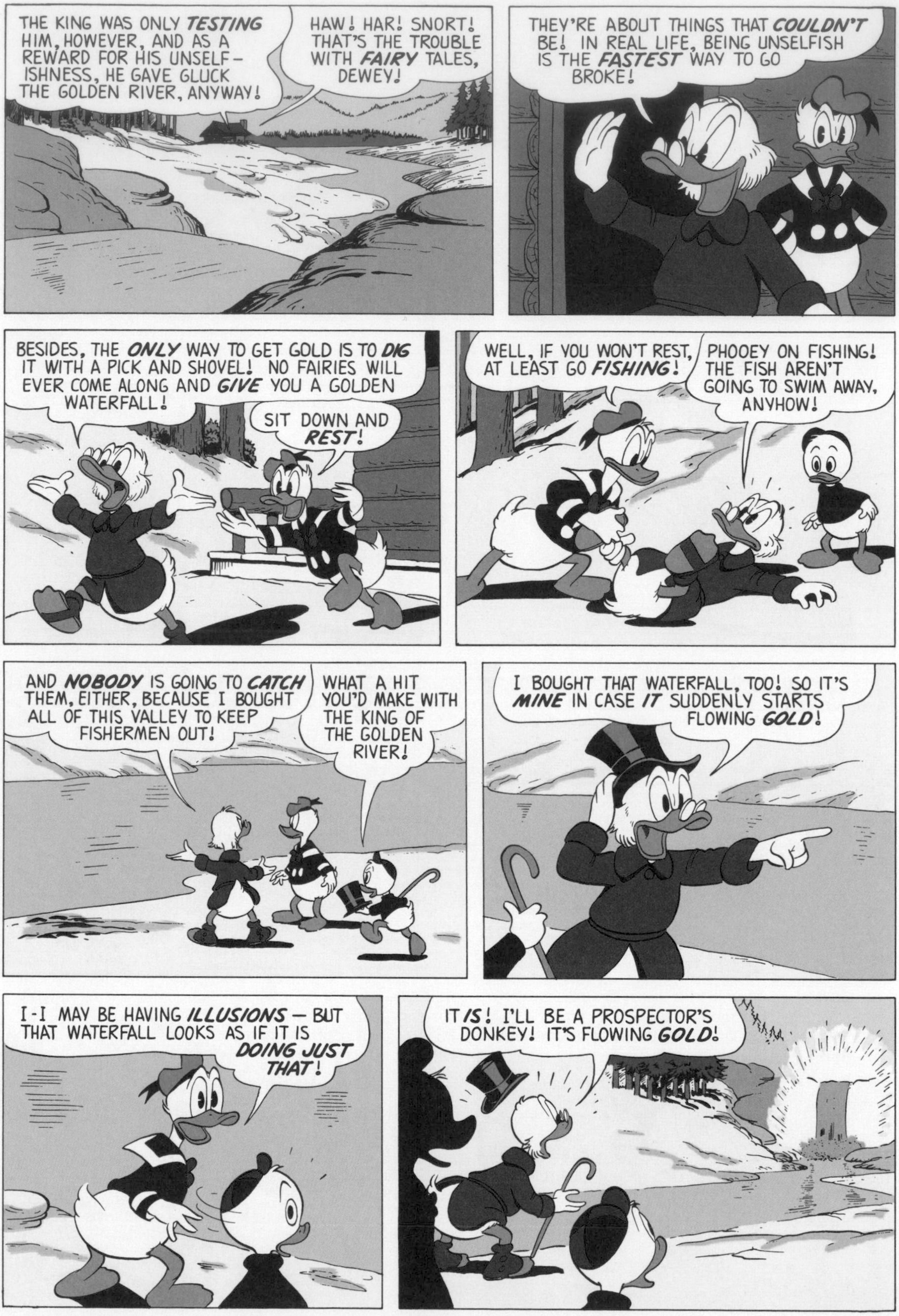

THE KING WAS ONLY TESTING HIM, HOWEVER, AND AS A REWARD FOR HIS UNSELF-ISHNESS, HE GAVE GLUCK THE GOLDEN RIVER, ANYWAY!
HAW! HAR! SNORT! THAT'S THE TROUBLE WITH FAIRY TALES, DEWEY!
THEY'RE ABOUT THINGS THAT COULDN'T BE! IN REAL LIFE, BEING UNSELFISH IS THE FASTEST WAY TO GO BROKE!
BESIDES, THE ONLY WAY TO GET GOLD IS TO DIG IT WITH A PICK AND SHOVEL! NO FAIRIES WILL EVER COME ALONG AND GIVE YOU A GOLDEN WATERFALL!
SIT DOWN AND REST!
WELL, IF YOU WON'T REST, AT LEAST GO FISHING!
PHOOEY ON FISHING! THE FISH AREN'T GOING TO SWIM AWAY, ANYHOW!
AND NOBODY IS GOING TO CATCH THEM, EITHER, BECAUSE I BOUGHT ALL OF THIS VALLEY TO KEEP FISHERMEN OUT!
WHAT A HIT YOU'D MAKE WITH THE KING OF THE GOLDEN RIVER!
I BOUGHT THAT WATERFALL, TOO! SO IT'S MINE IN CASE IT SUDDENLY STARTS FLOWING GOLD!
I-I MAY BE HAVING ILLUSIONS — BUT THAT WATERFALL LOOKS AS IF IT IS DOING JUST THAT!
IT IS! I'LL BE A PROSPECTOR'S DONKEY! IT'S FLOWING GOLD!

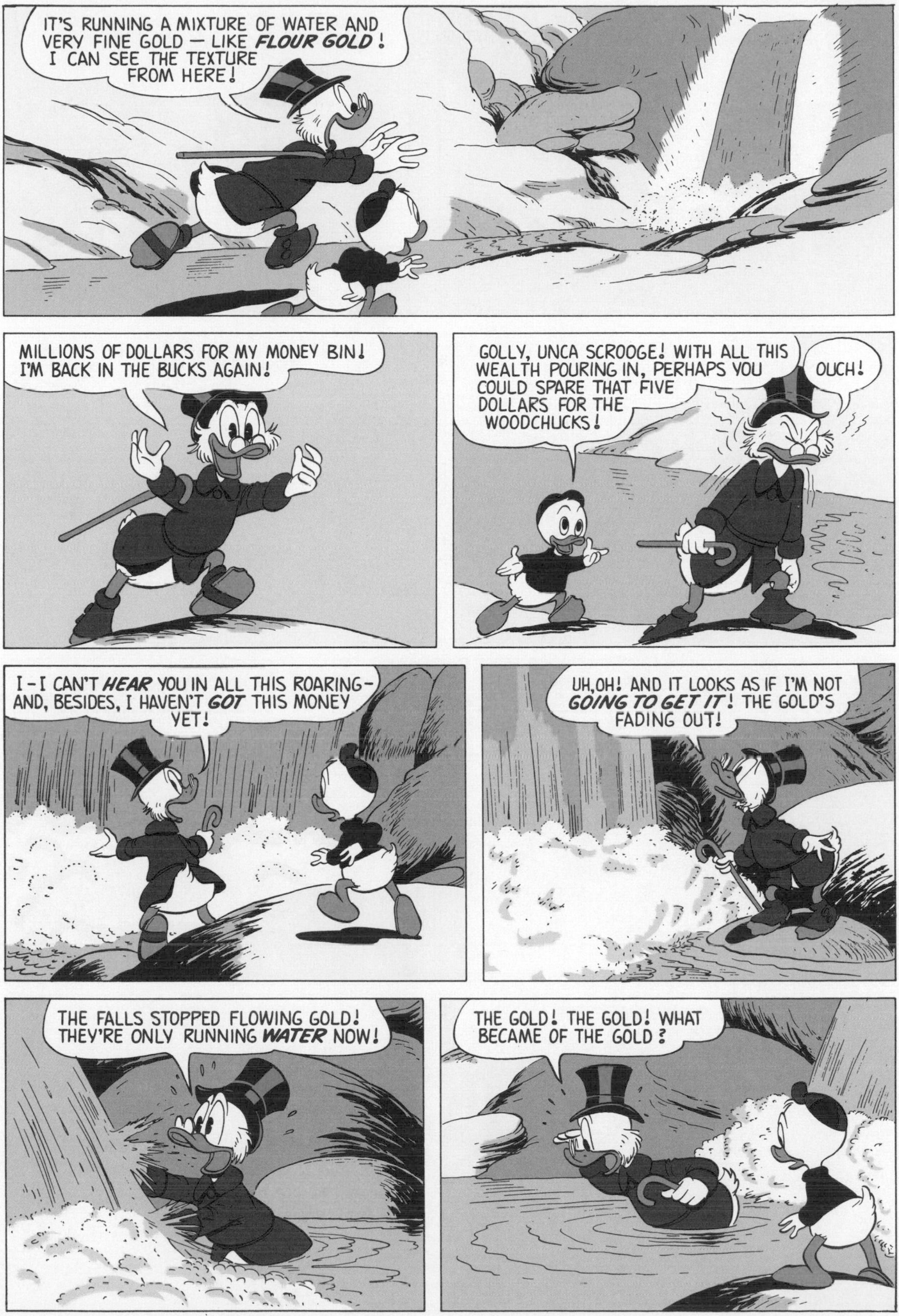

IT'S RUNNING A MIXTURE OF WATER AND VERY FINE GOLD — LIKE **FLOUR GOLD**! I CAN SEE THE TEXTURE FROM HERE!
MILLIONS OF DOLLARS FOR MY MONEY BIN! I'M BACK IN THE BUCKS AGAIN!
GOLLY, UNCA SCROOGE! WITH ALL THIS WEALTH POURING IN, PERHAPS YOU COULD SPARE THAT FIVE DOLLARS FOR THE WOODCHUCKS!
OUCH!
I-I CAN'T **HEAR** YOU IN ALL THIS ROARING- AND, BESIDES, I HAVEN'T **GOT** THIS MONEY YET!
UH,OH! AND IT LOOKS AS IF I'M NOT **GOING TO GET IT**! THE GOLD'S FADING OUT!
THE FALLS STOPPED FLOWING GOLD! THEY'RE ONLY RUNNING **WATER** NOW!
THE GOLD! THE GOLD! WHAT BECAME OF THE GOLD?

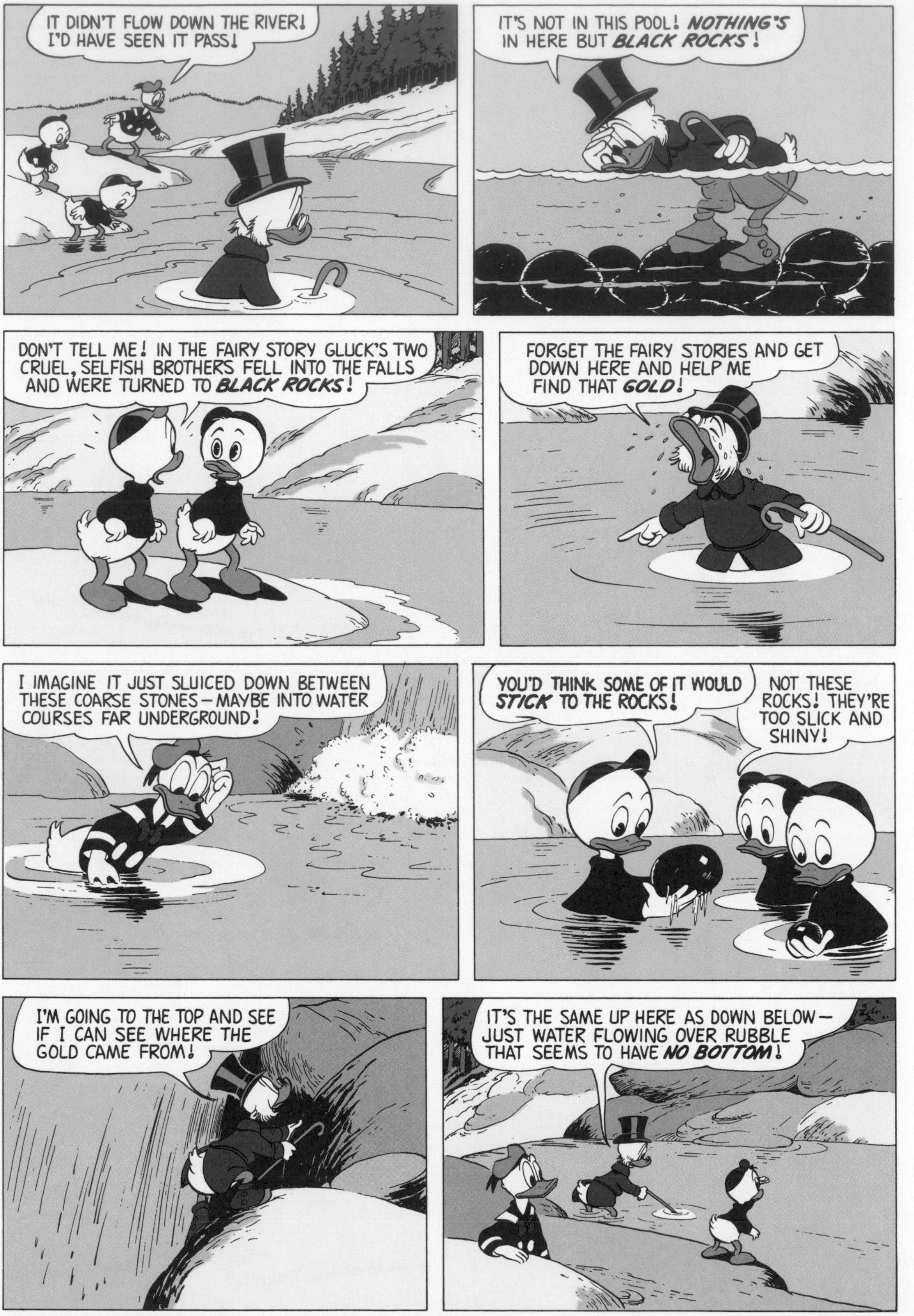
IT DIDN'T FLOW DOWN THE RIVER! I'D HAVE SEEN IT PASS!
IT'S NOT IN THIS POOL! NOTHING'S IN HERE BUT BLACK ROCKS!
DON'T TELL ME! IN THE FAIRY STORY GLUCK'S TWO CRUEL, SELFISH BROTHERS FELL INTO THE FALLS AND WERE TURNED TO BLACK ROCKS!
FORGET THE FAIRY STORIES AND GET DOWN HERE AND HELP ME FIND THAT GOLD!
I IMAGINE IT JUST SLUICED DOWN BETWEEN THESE COARSE STONES—MAYBE INTO WATER COURSES FAR UNDERGROUND!
YOU'D THINK SOME OF IT WOULD STICK TO THE ROCKS!
NOT THESE ROCKS! THEY'RE TOO SLICK AND SHINY!
I'M GOING TO THE TOP AND SEE IF I CAN SEE WHERE THE GOLD CAME FROM!
IT'S THE SAME UP HERE AS DOWN BELOW—JUST WATER FLOWING OVER RUBBLE THAT SEEMS TO HAVE NO BOTTOM!

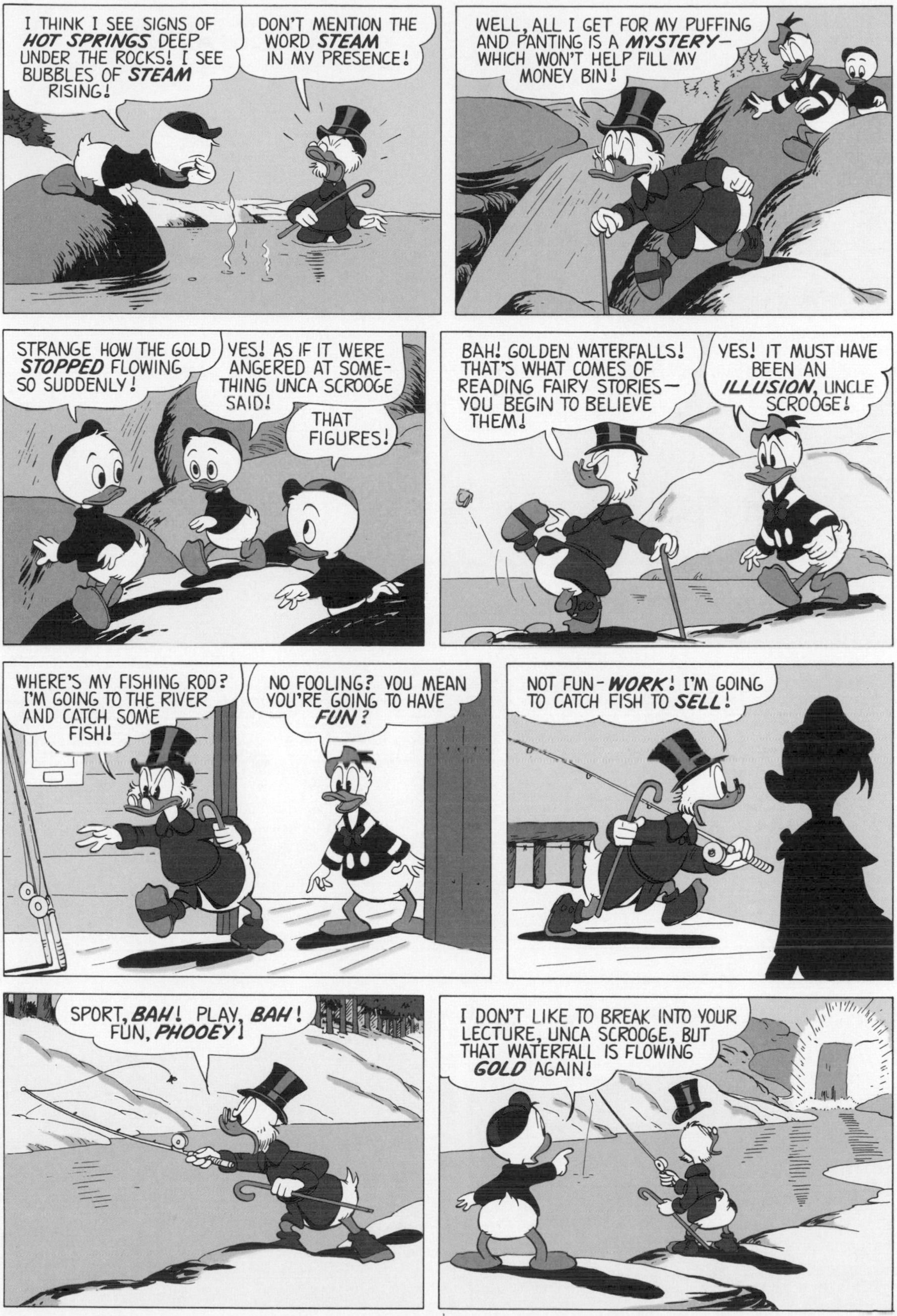
I THINK I SEE SIGNS OF HOT SPRINGS DEEP UNDER THE ROCKS! I SEE BUBBLES OF STEAM RISING!
DON'T MENTION THE WORD STEAM IN MY PRESENCE!
WELL, ALL I GET FOR MY PUFFING AND PANTING IS A MYSTERY— WHICH WON'T HELP FILL MY MONEY BIN!
STRANGE HOW THE GOLD STOPPED FLOWING SO SUDDENLY!
YES! AS IF IT WERE ANGERED AT SOMETHING UNCA SCROOGE SAID!
THAT FIGURES!
BAH! GOLDEN WATERFALLS! THAT'S WHAT COMES OF READING FAIRY STORIES— YOU BEGIN TO BELIEVE THEM!
YES! IT MUST HAVE BEEN AN ILLUSION, UNCLE SCROOGE!
WHERE'S MY FISHING ROD? I'M GOING TO THE RIVER AND CATCH SOME FISH!
NO FOOLING? YOU MEAN YOU'RE GOING TO HAVE FUN?
NOT FUN-WORK! I'M GOING TO CATCH FISH TO SELL!
SPORT, BAH! PLAY, BAH! FUN, PHOOEY!
I DON'T LIKE TO BREAK INTO YOUR LECTURE, UNCA SCROOGE, BUT THAT WATERFALL IS FLOWING GOLD AGAIN!

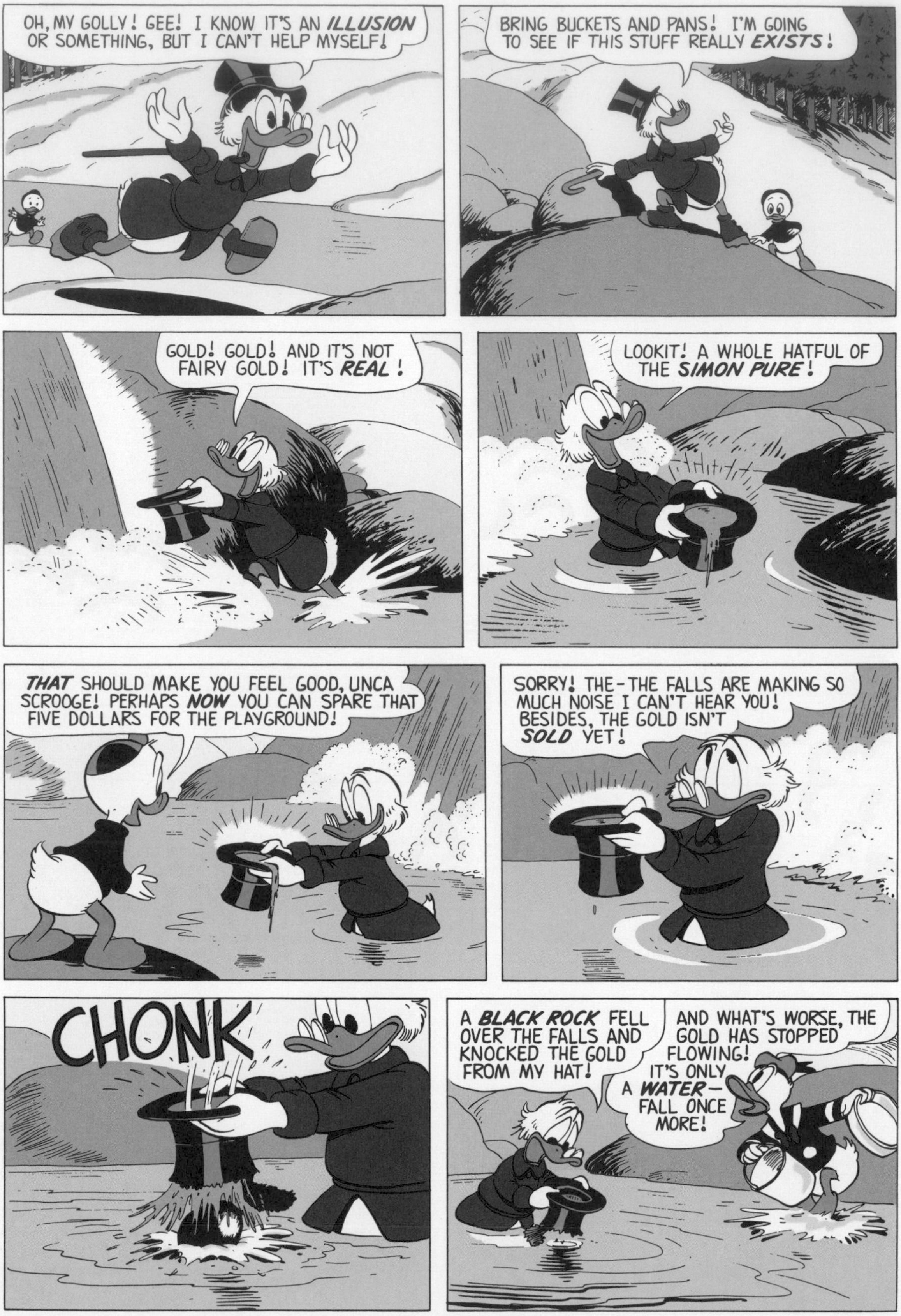
OH, MY GOLLY! GEE! I KNOW IT'S AN ILLUSION OR SOMETHING, BUT I CAN'T HELP MYSELF!
BRING BUCKETS AND PANS! I'M GOING TO SEE IF THIS STUFF REALLY EXISTS!
GOLD! GOLD! AND IT'S NOT FAIRY GOLD! IT'S REAL!
LOOKIT! A WHOLE HATFUL OF THE SIMON PURE!
THAT SHOULD MAKE YOU FEEL GOOD, UNCA SCROOGE! PERHAPS NOW YOU CAN SPARE THAT FIVE DOLLARS FOR THE PLAYGROUND!
SORRY! THE-THE FALLS ARE MAKING SO MUCH NOISE I CAN'T HEAR YOU! BESIDES, THE GOLD ISN'T SOLD YET!
CHONK
A BLACK ROCK FELL OVER THE FALLS AND KNOCKED THE GOLD FROM MY HAT!
AND WHAT'S WORSE, THE GOLD HAS STOPPED FLOWING!
IT'S ONLY A WATER-FALL ONCE MORE!

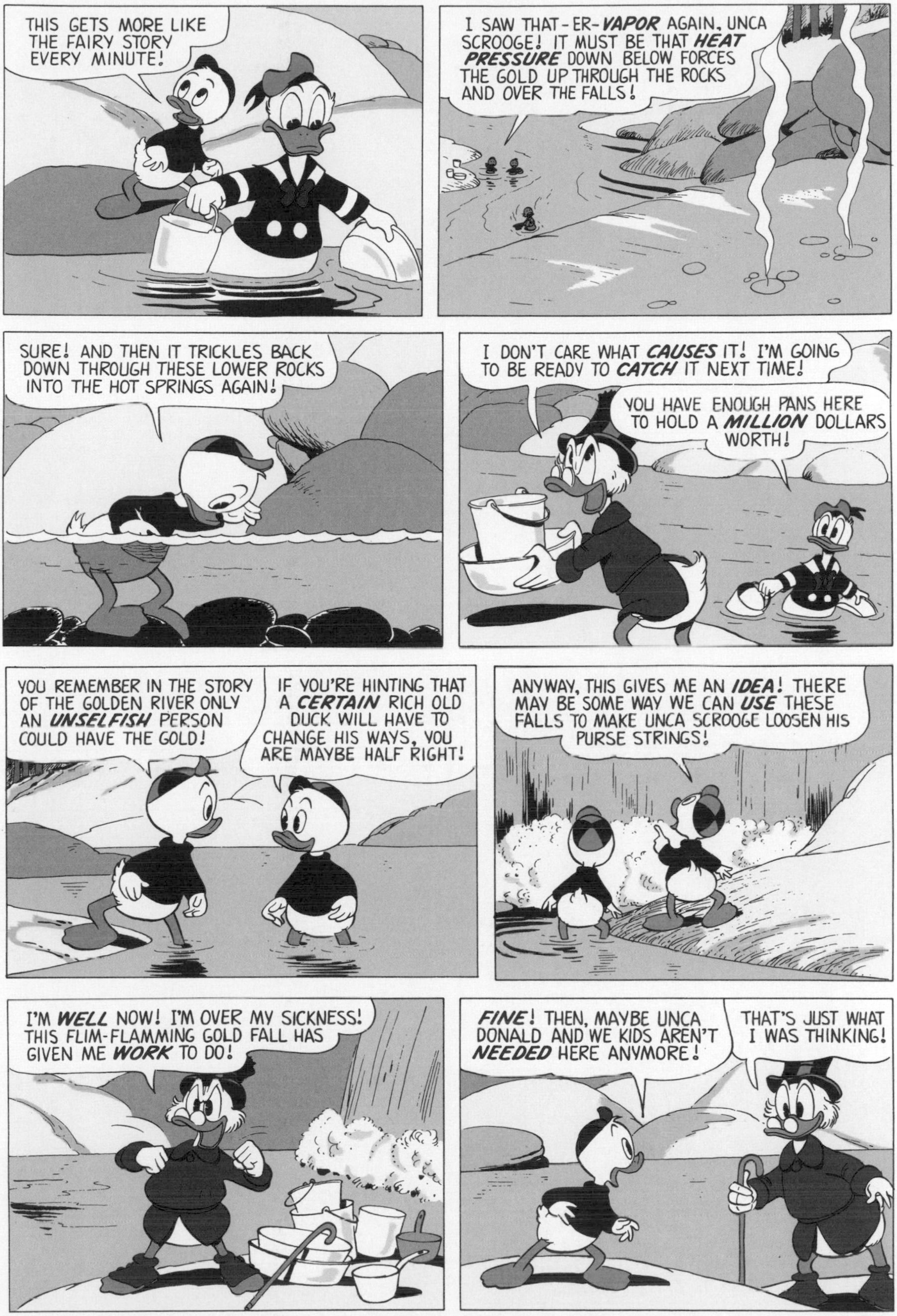
THIS GETS MORE LIKE THE FAIRY STORY EVERY MINUTE!
I SAW THAT-ER-VAPOR AGAIN, UNCA SCROOGE! IT MUST BE THAT HEAT PRESSURE DOWN BELOW FORCES THE GOLD UP THROUGH THE ROCKS AND OVER THE FALLS!
SURE! AND THEN IT TRICKLES BACK DOWN THROUGH THESE LOWER ROCKS INTO THE HOT SPRINGS AGAIN!
I DON'T CARE WHAT CAUSES IT! I'M GOING TO BE READY TO CATCH IT NEXT TIME!
YOU HAVE ENOUGH PANS HERE TO HOLD A MILLION DOLLARS WORTH!
YOU REMEMBER IN THE STORY OF THE GOLDEN RIVER ONLY AN UNSELFISH PERSON COULD HAVE THE GOLD!
IF YOU'RE HINTING THAT A CERTAIN RICH OLD DUCK WILL HAVE TO CHANGE HIS WAYS, YOU ARE MAYBE HALF RIGHT!
ANYWAY, THIS GIVES ME AN IDEA! THERE MAY BE SOME WAY WE CAN USE THESE FALLS TO MAKE UNCA SCROOGE LOOSEN HIS PURSE STRINGS!
I'M WELL NOW! I'M OVER MY SICKNESS! THIS FLIM-FLAMMING GOLD FALL HAS GIVEN ME WORK TO DO!
FINE! THEN, MAYBE UNCA DONALD AND WE KIDS AREN'T NEEDED HERE ANYMORE!
THAT'S JUST WHAT I WAS THINKING!

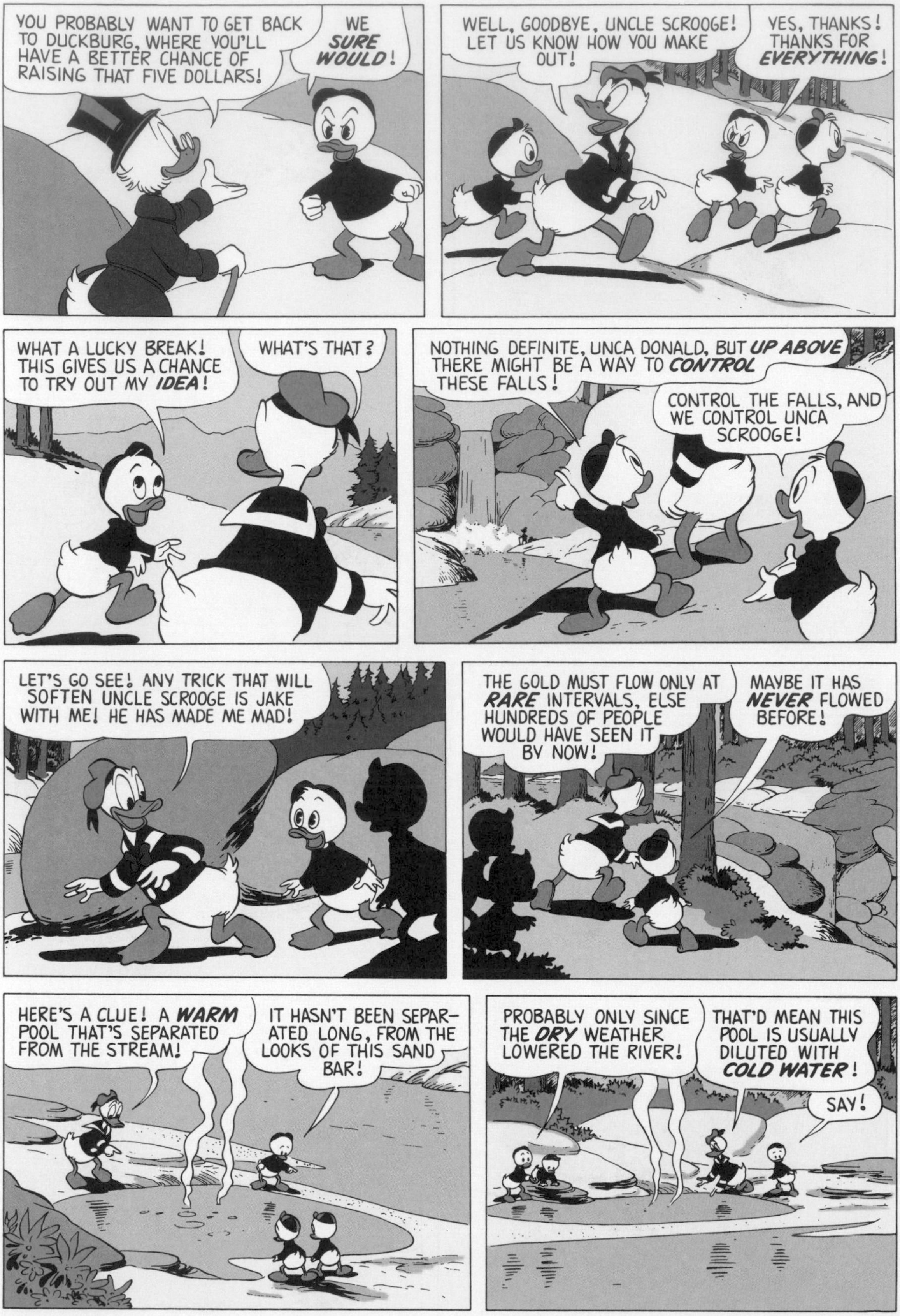
YOU PROBABLY WANT TO GET BACK TO DUCKBURG, WHERE YOU'LL HAVE A BETTER CHANCE OF RAISING THAT FIVE DOLLARS!
WE *SURE WOULD*!
WELL, GOODBYE, UNCLE SCROOGE! LET US KNOW HOW YOU MAKE OUT!
YES, THANKS! THANKS FOR *EVERYTHING*!
WHAT A LUCKY BREAK! THIS GIVES US A CHANCE TO TRY OUT MY *IDEA*!
WHAT'S THAT?
NOTHING DEFINITE, UNCA DONALD, BUT *UP ABOVE* THERE MIGHT BE A WAY TO *CONTROL* THESE FALLS!
CONTROL THE FALLS, AND WE CONTROL UNCA SCROOGE!
LET'S GO SEE! ANY TRICK THAT WILL SOFTEN UNCLE SCROOGE IS JAKE WITH ME! HE HAS MADE ME MAD!
THE GOLD MUST FLOW ONLY AT *RARE* INTERVALS, ELSE HUNDREDS OF PEOPLE WOULD HAVE SEEN IT BY NOW!
MAYBE IT HAS *NEVER* FLOWED BEFORE!
HERE'S A CLUE! A *WARM* POOL THAT'S SEPARATED FROM THE STREAM!
IT HASN'T BEEN SEPARATED LONG, FROM THE LOOKS OF THIS SAND BAR!
PROBABLY ONLY SINCE THE *DRY* WEATHER LOWERED THE RIVER!
THAT'D MEAN THIS POOL IS USUALLY DILUTED WITH *COLD WATER*!
SAY!

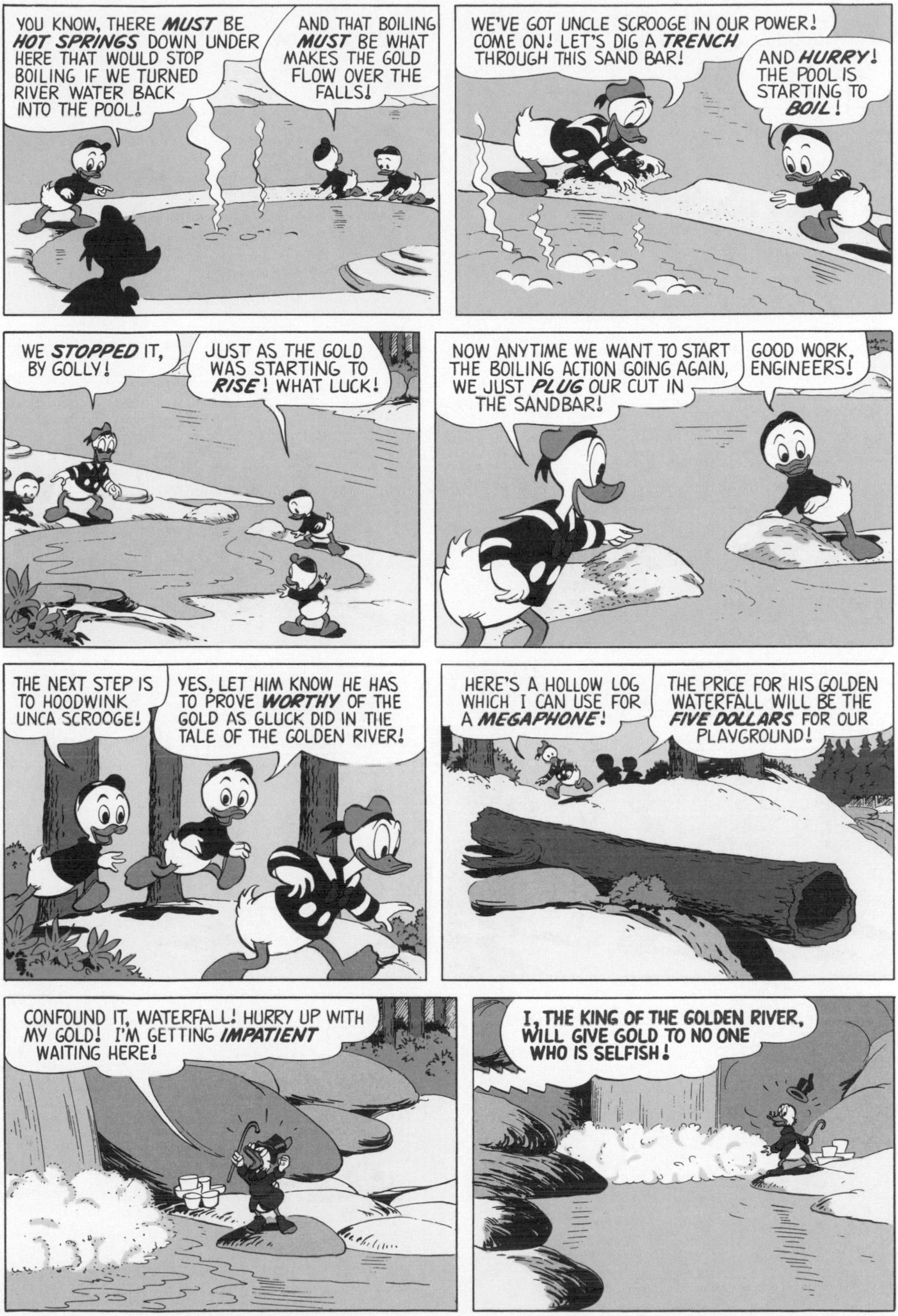
YOU KNOW, THERE MUST BE HOT SPRINGS DOWN UNDER HERE THAT WOULD STOP BOILING IF WE TURNED RIVER WATER BACK INTO THE POOL!
AND THAT BOILING MUST BE WHAT MAKES THE GOLD FLOW OVER THE FALLS!
WE'VE GOT UNCLE SCROOGE IN OUR POWER! COME ON! LET'S DIG A TRENCH THROUGH THIS SAND BAR!
AND HURRY! THE POOL IS STARTING TO BOIL!
WE STOPPED IT, BY GOLLY!
JUST AS THE GOLD WAS STARTING TO RISE! WHAT LUCK!
NOW ANYTIME WE WANT TO START THE BOILING ACTION GOING AGAIN, WE JUST PLUG OUR CUT IN THE SANDBAR!
GOOD WORK, ENGINEERS!
THE NEXT STEP IS TO HOODWINK UNCA SCROOGE!
YES, LET HIM KNOW HE HAS TO PROVE WORTHY OF THE GOLD AS GLUCK DID IN THE TALE OF THE GOLDEN RIVER!
HERE'S A HOLLOW LOG WHICH I CAN USE FOR A MEGAPHONE!
THE PRICE FOR HIS GOLDEN WATERFALL WILL BE THE FIVE DOLLARS FOR OUR PLAYGROUND!
CONFOUND IT, WATERFALL! HURRY UP WITH MY GOLD! I'M GETTING IMPATIENT WAITING HERE!
I, THE KING OF THE GOLDEN RIVER, WILL GIVE GOLD TO NO ONE WHO IS SELFISH!

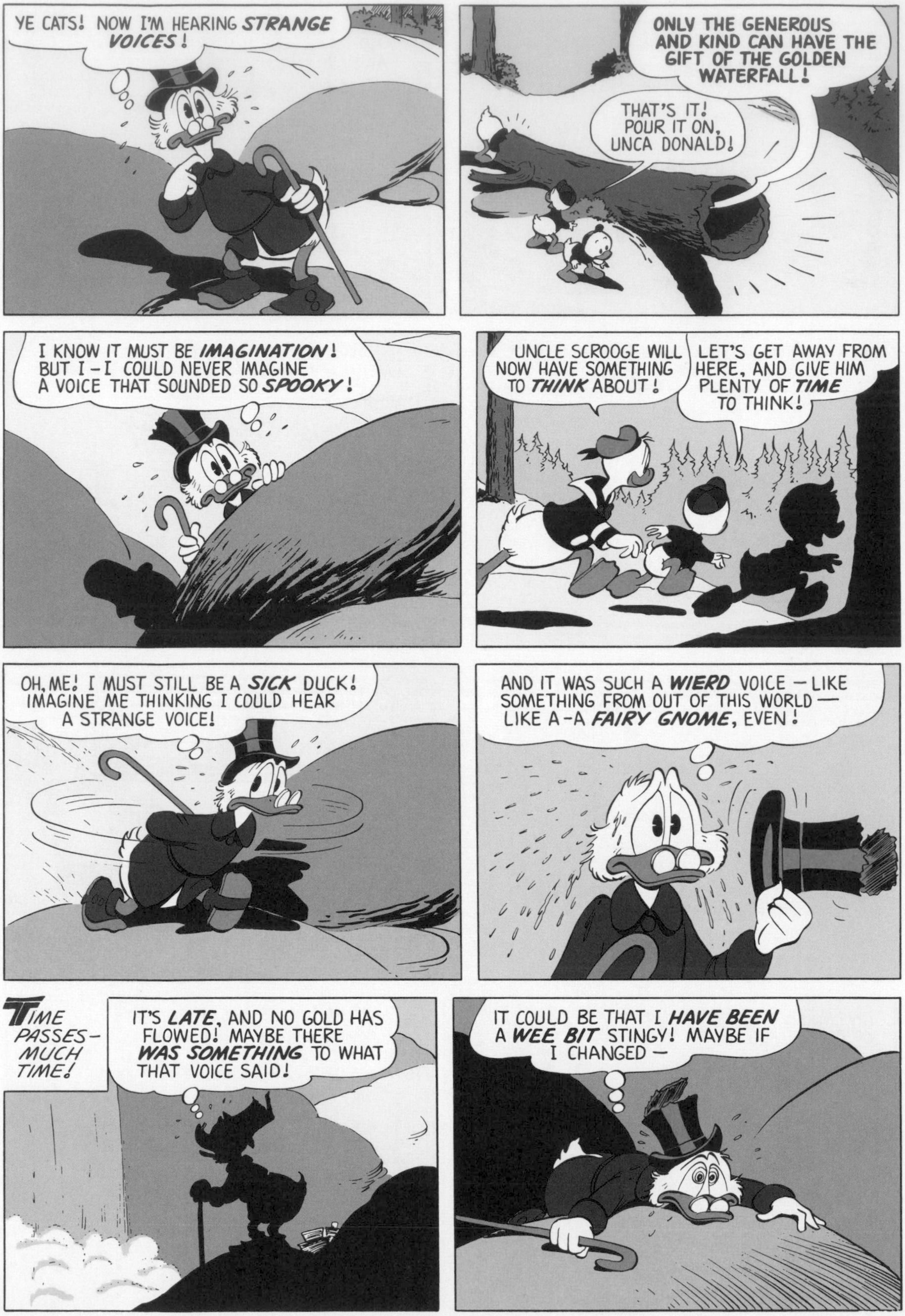
YE CATS! NOW I'M HEARING STRANGE VOICES!
ONLY THE GENEROUS AND KIND CAN HAVE THE GIFT OF THE GOLDEN WATERFALL!
THAT'S IT! POUR IT ON, UNCA DONALD!
I KNOW IT MUST BE IMAGINATION! BUT I-I COULD NEVER IMAGINE A VOICE THAT SOUNDED SO SPOOKY!
UNCLE SCROOGE WILL NOW HAVE SOMETHING TO THINK ABOUT!
LET'S GET AWAY FROM HERE, AND GIVE HIM PLENTY OF TIME TO THINK!
OH, ME! I MUST STILL BE A SICK DUCK! IMAGINE ME THINKING I COULD HEAR A STRANGE VOICE!
AND IT WAS SUCH A WIERD VOICE — LIKE SOMETHING FROM OUT OF THIS WORLD — LIKE A-A FAIRY GNOME, EVEN!
TIME PASSES-MUCH TIME!
IT'S LATE, AND NO GOLD HAS FLOWED! MAYBE THERE WAS SOMETHING TO WHAT THAT VOICE SAID!
IT COULD BE THAT I HAVE BEEN A WEE BIT STINGY! MAYBE IF I CHANGED —

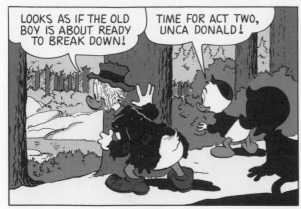

LOOKS AS IF THE OLD BOY IS ABOUT READY TO BREAK DOWN!

TIME FOR ACT TWO, UNCA DONALD!

I'LL GO OUT IN MY BEGGAR DISGUISE AND UNFREEZE HIM FROM THAT MONEY!

WE HOPE!

OH, ME! OH, MY! IF I ONLY HAD A CHANCE TO BE GENEROUS!

WELL, TALK ABOUT LUCK! OVER THERE IS SOMEBODY WHO LOOKS EXTREMELY NEEDY!

PROBABLY A POOR BEGGAR! I'LL BE GENEROUS WITH HIM AND MAYBE THE FALLS WILL FLOW AGAIN!

WAIT, POOR FELLOW! PERHAPS THERE IS SOMETHING I CAN DO TO HELP YOU!

GIVE YOU A DIME FOR A CUP OF COFFEE MAYBE!

OH, KIND SIR, I OWE MONEY FOR MY DANCING LESSONS, AND I HAD TO HOCK MY GOLF CLUBS TO PAY FOR MY NEW BOWLING BALL!

YOU SURE HAVE IT TOUGH!

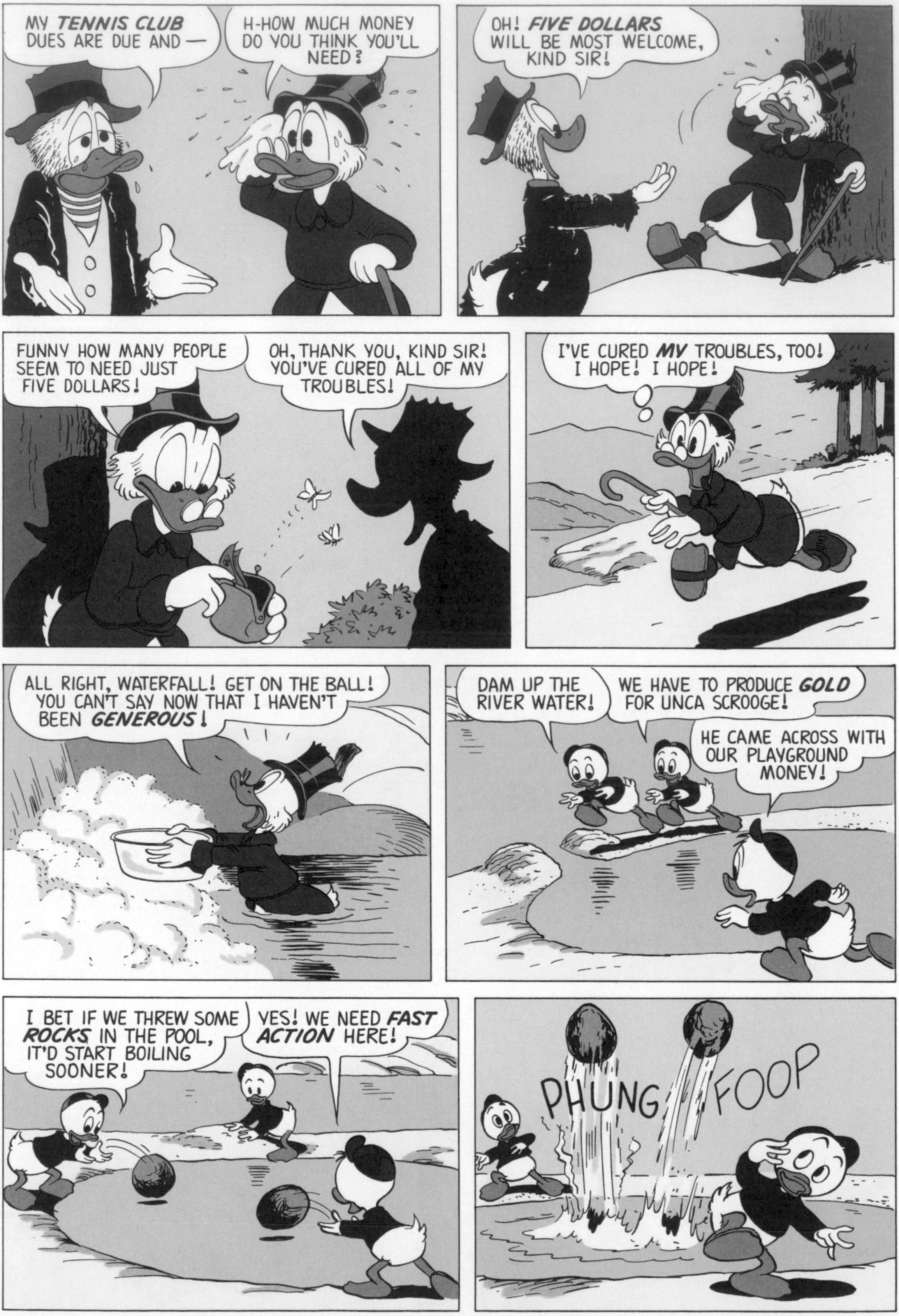
MY TENNIS CLUB DUES ARE DUE AND —
H-HOW MUCH MONEY DO YOU THINK YOU'LL NEED?
OH! FIVE DOLLARS WILL BE MOST WELCOME, KIND SIR!
FUNNY HOW MANY PEOPLE SEEM TO NEED JUST FIVE DOLLARS!
OH, THANK YOU, KIND SIR! YOU'VE CURED ALL OF MY TROUBLES!
I'VE CURED MY TROUBLES, TOO! I HOPE! I HOPE!
ALL RIGHT, WATERFALL! GET ON THE BALL! YOU CAN'T SAY NOW THAT I HAVEN'T BEEN GENEROUS!
DAM UP THE RIVER WATER!
WE HAVE TO PRODUCE GOLD FOR UNCA SCROOGE!
HE CAME ACROSS WITH OUR PLAYGROUND MONEY!
I BET IF WE THREW SOME ROCKS IN THE POOL, IT'D START BOILING SOONER!
YES! WE NEED FAST ACTION HERE!
PHUNG
FOOP

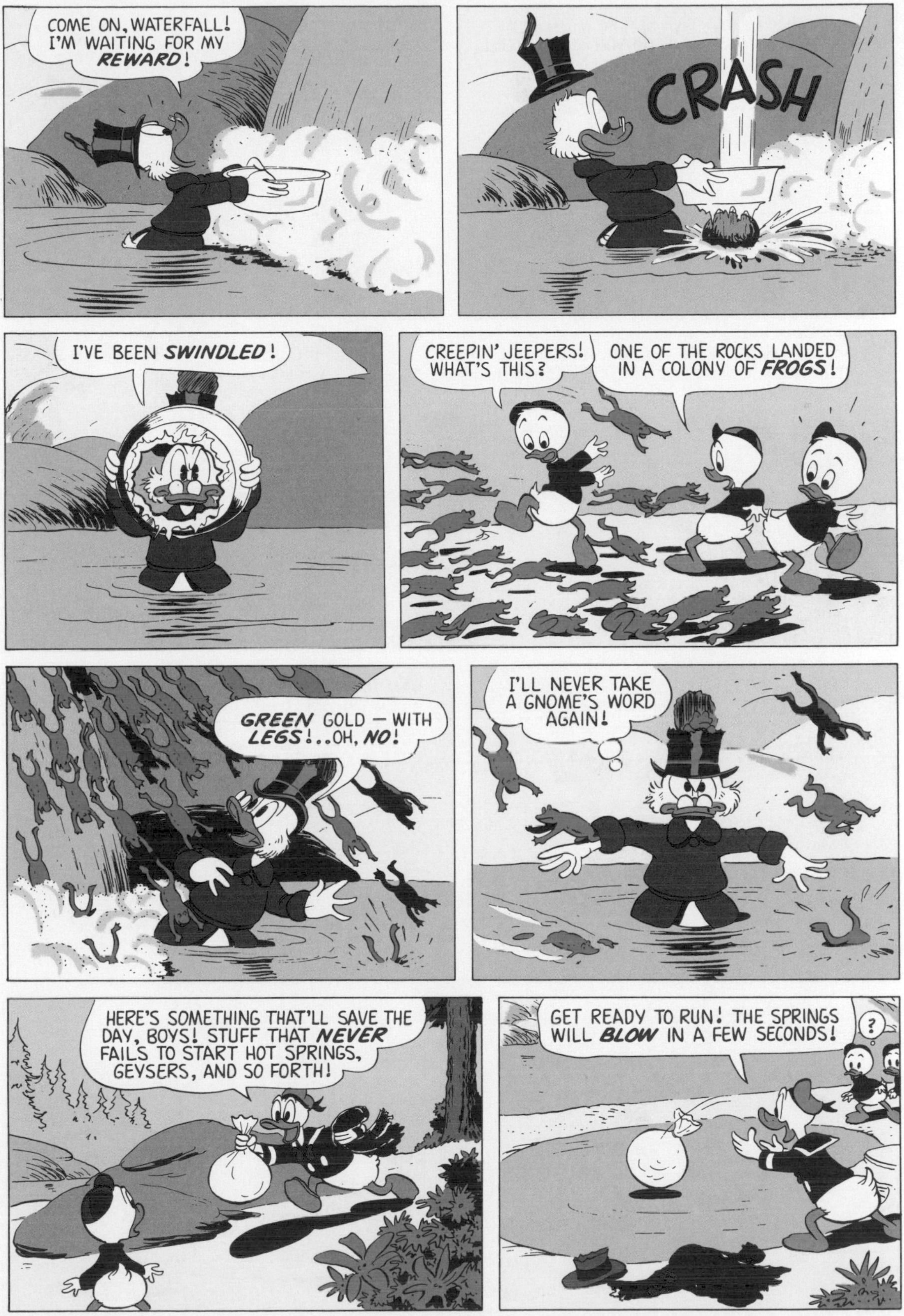
COME ON, WATERFALL! I'M WAITING FOR MY REWARD!
CRASH
I'VE BEEN SWINDLED!
CREEPIN' JEEPERS! WHAT'S THIS?
ONE OF THE ROCKS LANDED IN A COLONY OF FROGS!
GREEN GOLD — WITH LEGS!..OH, NO!
I'LL NEVER TAKE A GNOME'S WORD AGAIN!
HERE'S SOMETHING THAT'LL SAVE THE DAY, BOYS! STUFF THAT NEVER FAILS TO START HOT SPRINGS, GEYSERS, AND SO FORTH!
GET READY TO RUN! THE SPRINGS WILL BLOW IN A FEW SECONDS!
?

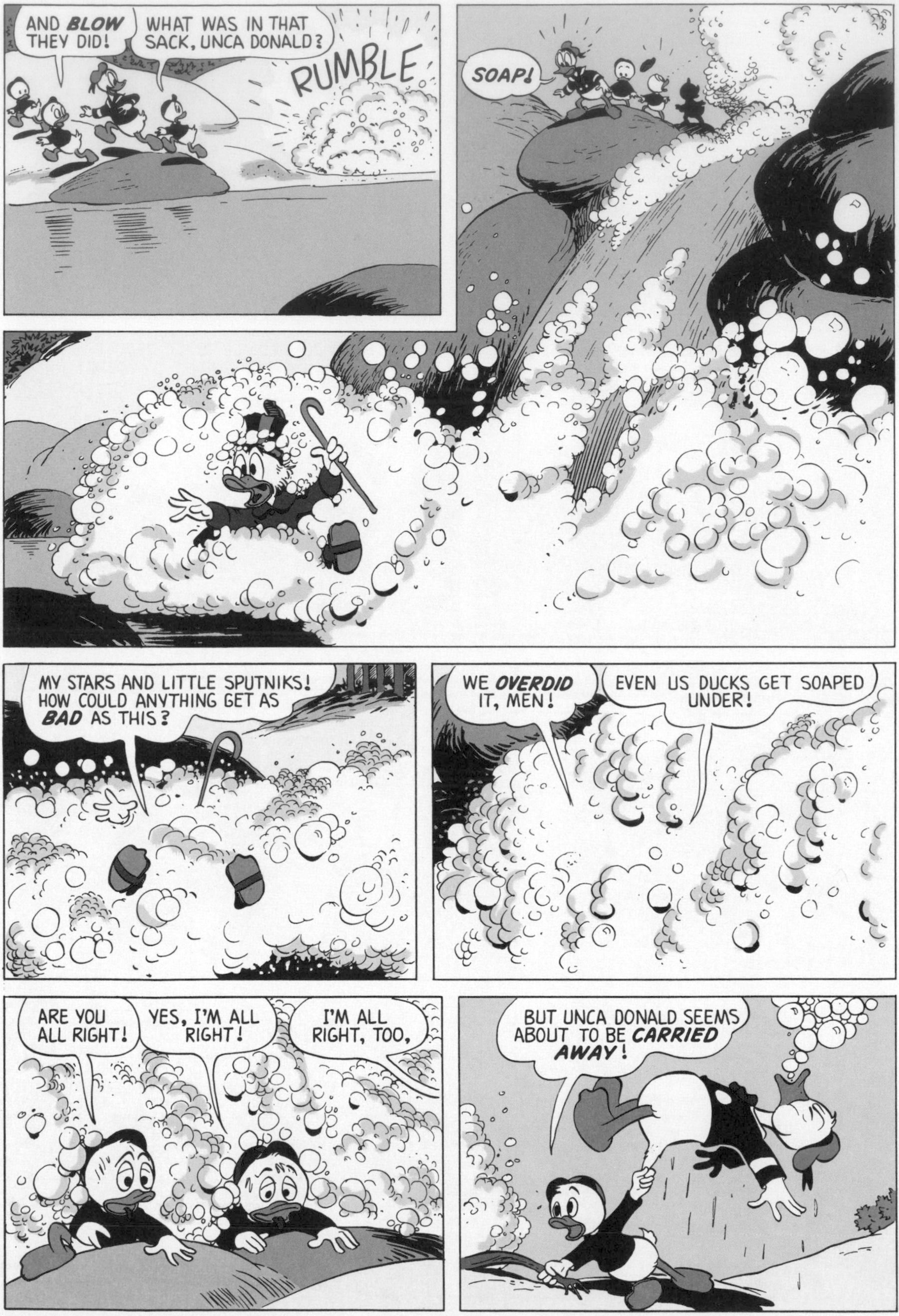
AND BLOW THEY DID!
WHAT WAS IN THAT SACK, UNCA DONALD?
RUMBLE
SOAP!
MY STARS AND LITTLE SPUTNIKS! HOW COULD ANYTHING GET AS BAD AS THIS?
WE OVERDID IT, MEN!
EVEN US DUCKS GET SOAPED UNDER!
ARE YOU ALL RIGHT!
YES, I'M ALL RIGHT!
I'M ALL RIGHT, TOO,
BUT UNCA DONALD SEEMS ABOUT TO BE CARRIED AWAY!

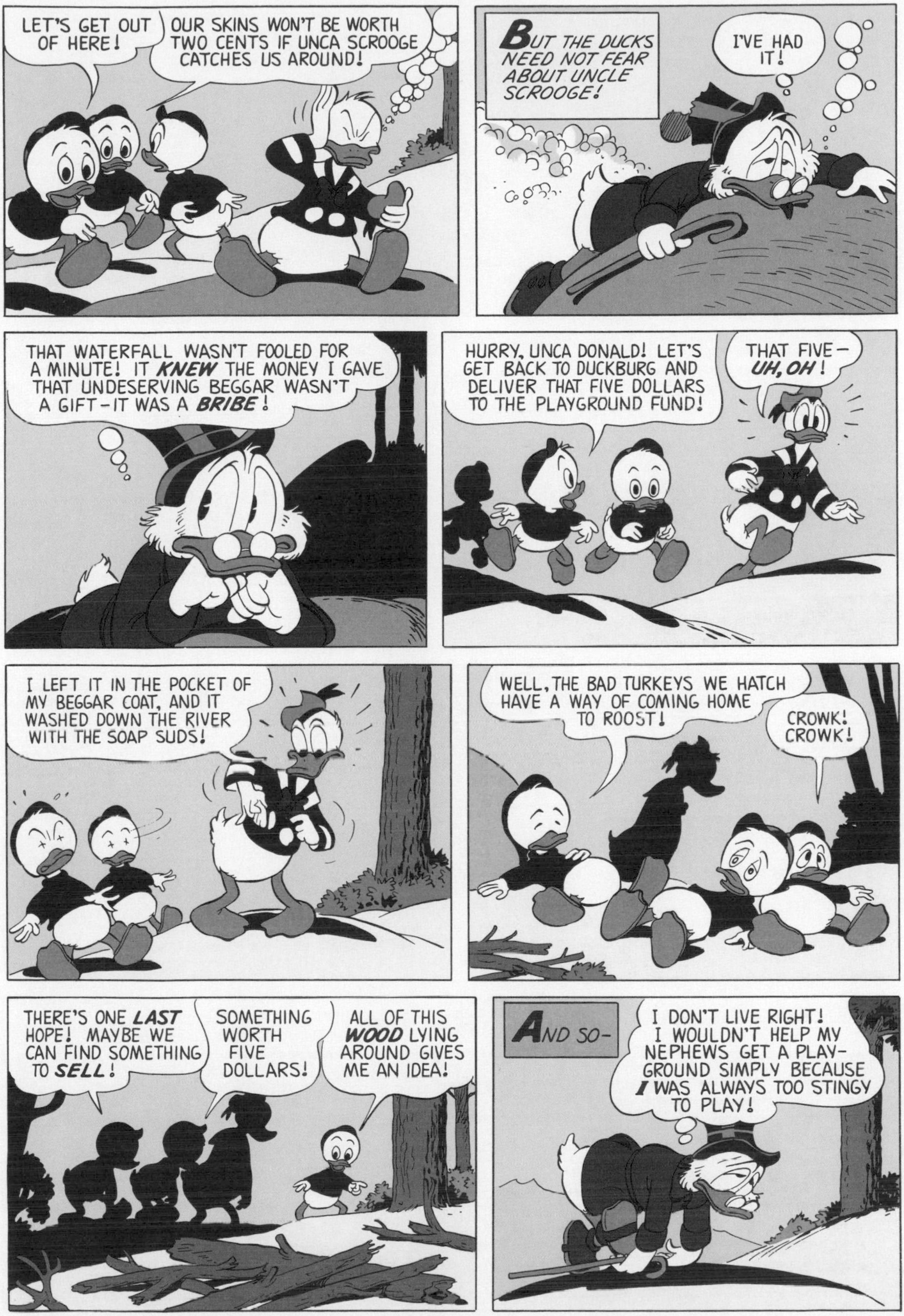
LET'S GET OUT OF HERE!
OUR SKINS WON'T BE WORTH TWO CENTS IF UNCA SCROOGE CATCHES US AROUND!
BUT THE DUCKS NEED NOT FEAR ABOUT UNCLE SCROOGE!
I'VE HAD IT!
THAT WATERFALL WASN'T FOOLED FOR A MINUTE! IT KNEW THE MONEY I GAVE THAT UNDESERVING BEGGAR WASN'T A GIFT-IT WAS A BRIBE!
HURRY, UNCA DONALD! LET'S GET BACK TO DUCKBURG AND DELIVER THAT FIVE DOLLARS TO THE PLAYGROUND FUND!
THAT FIVE- UH, OH!
I LEFT IT IN THE POCKET OF MY BEGGAR COAT, AND IT WASHED DOWN THE RIVER WITH THE SOAP SUDS!
WELL, THE BAD TURKEYS WE HATCH HAVE A WAY OF COMING HOME TO ROOST!
CROWK! CROWK!
THERE'S ONE LAST HOPE! MAYBE WE CAN FIND SOMETHING TO SELL!
SOMETHING WORTH FIVE DOLLARS!
ALL OF THIS WOOD LYING AROUND GIVES ME AN IDEA!
AND SO-
I DON'T LIVE RIGHT! I WOULDN'T HELP MY NEPHEWS GET A PLAY-GROUND SIMPLY BECAUSE I WAS ALWAYS TOO STINGY TO PLAY!

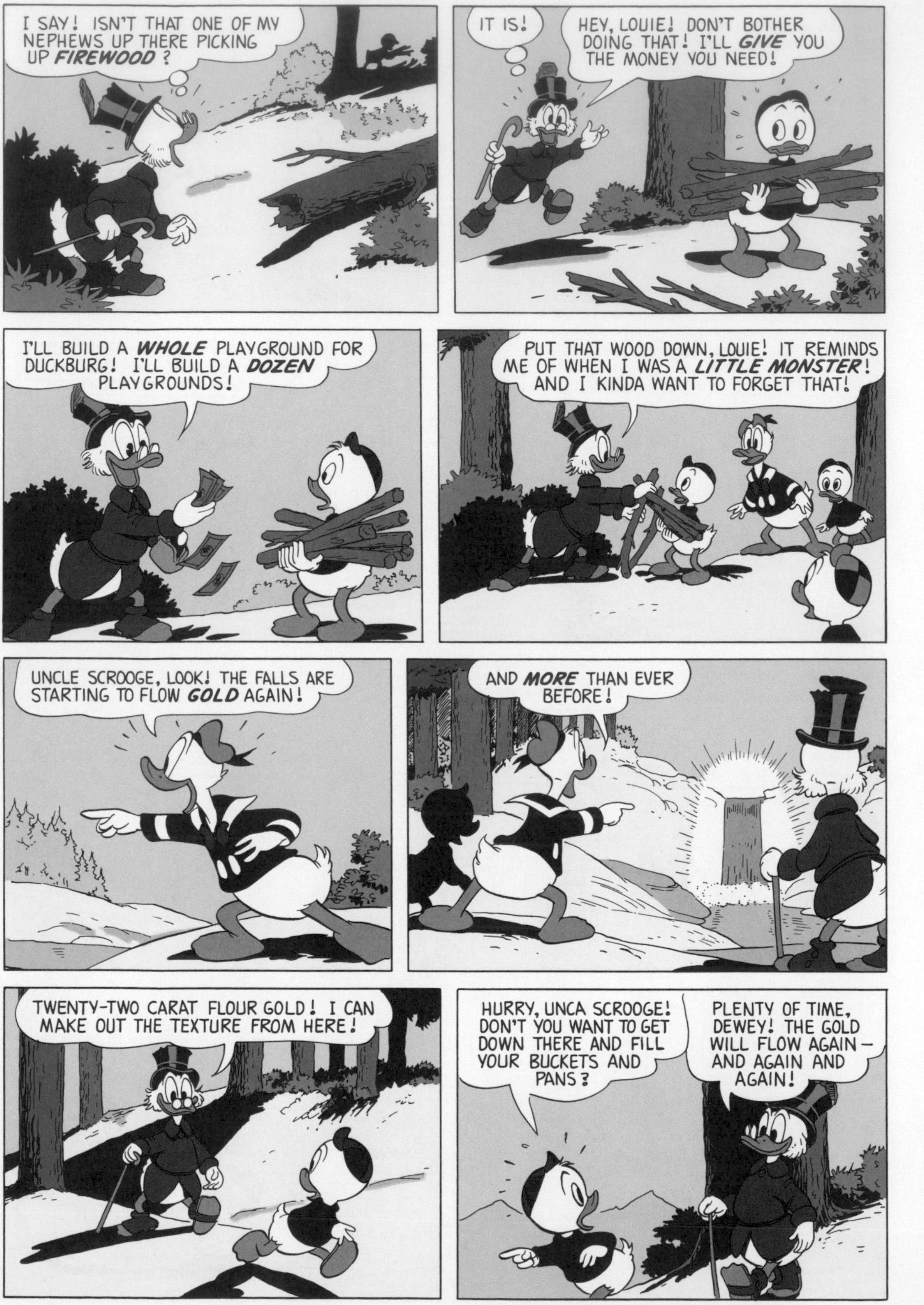
I SAY! ISN'T THAT ONE OF MY NEPHEWS UP THERE PICKING UP **FIREWOOD**?
IT IS!
HEY, LOUIE! DON'T BOTHER DOING THAT! I'LL **GIVE** YOU THE MONEY YOU NEED!
I'LL BUILD A **WHOLE** PLAYGROUND FOR DUCKBURG! I'LL BUILD A **DOZEN** PLAYGROUNDS!
PUT THAT WOOD DOWN, LOUIE! IT REMINDS ME OF WHEN I WAS A **LITTLE MONSTER**! AND I KINDA WANT TO FORGET THAT!
UNCLE SCROOGE, LOOK! THE FALLS ARE STARTING TO FLOW **GOLD** AGAIN!
AND **MORE** THAN EVER BEFORE!
TWENTY-TWO CARAT FLOUR GOLD! I CAN MAKE OUT THE TEXTURE FROM HERE!
HURRY, UNCA SCROOGE! DON'T YOU WANT TO GET DOWN THERE AND FILL YOUR BUCKETS AND PANS?
PLENTY OF TIME, DEWEY! THE GOLD WILL FLOW AGAIN— AND AGAIN AND AGAIN!

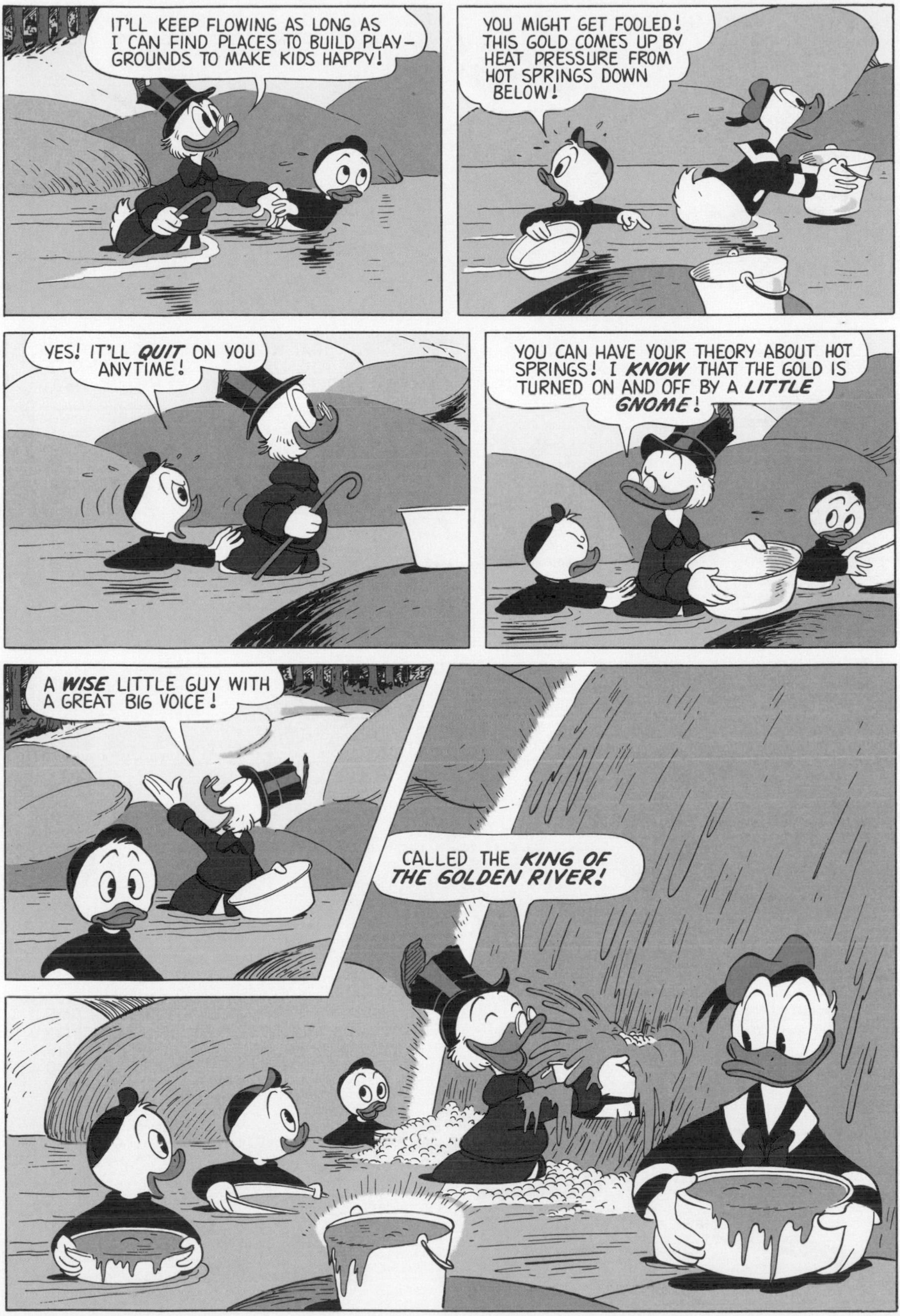
IT'LL KEEP FLOWING AS LONG AS I CAN FIND PLACES TO BUILD PLAY-GROUNDS TO MAKE KIDS HAPPY!
YOU MIGHT GET FOOLED! THIS GOLD COMES UP BY HEAT PRESSURE FROM HOT SPRINGS DOWN BELOW!
YES! IT'LL QUIT ON YOU ANYTIME!
YOU CAN HAVE YOUR THEORY ABOUT HOT SPRINGS! I KNOW THAT THE GOLD IS TURNED ON AND OFF BY A LITTLE GNOME!
A WISE LITTLE GUY WITH A GREAT BIG VOICE!
CALLED THE KING OF THE GOLDEN RIVER!

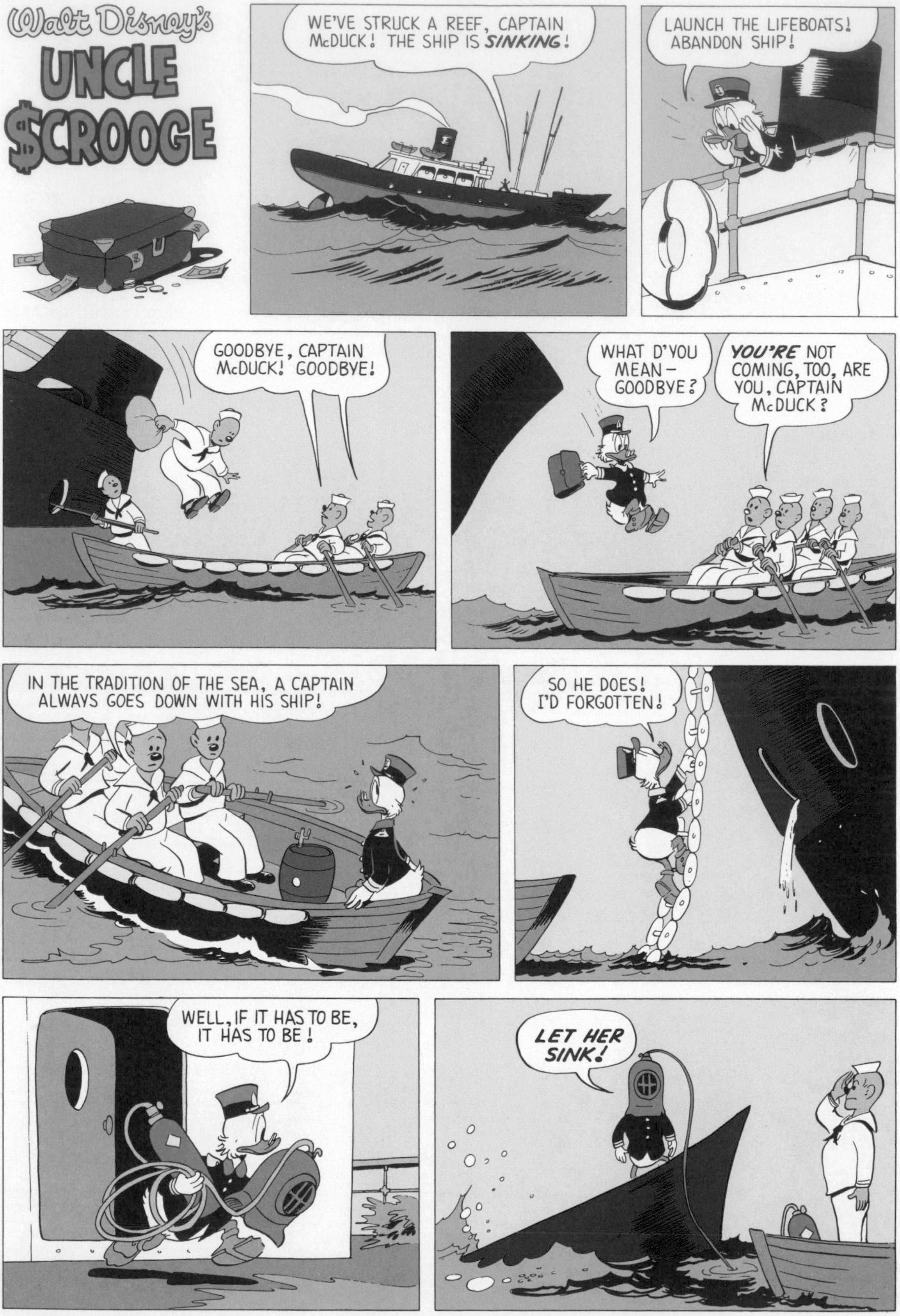
Walt Disney's
UNCLE $CROOGE
WE'VE STRUCK A REEF, CAPTAIN McDUCK! THE SHIP IS SINKING!
LAUNCH THE LIFEBOATS! ABANDON SHIP!
GOODBYE, CAPTAIN McDUCK! GOODBYE!
WHAT D'YOU MEAN— GOODBYE?
YOU'RE NOT COMING, TOO, ARE YOU, CAPTAIN McDUCK?
IN THE TRADITION OF THE SEA, A CAPTAIN ALWAYS GOES DOWN WITH HIS SHIP!
SO HE DOES! I'D FORGOTTEN!
WELL, IF IT HAS TO BE, IT HAS TO BE!
LET HER SINK!

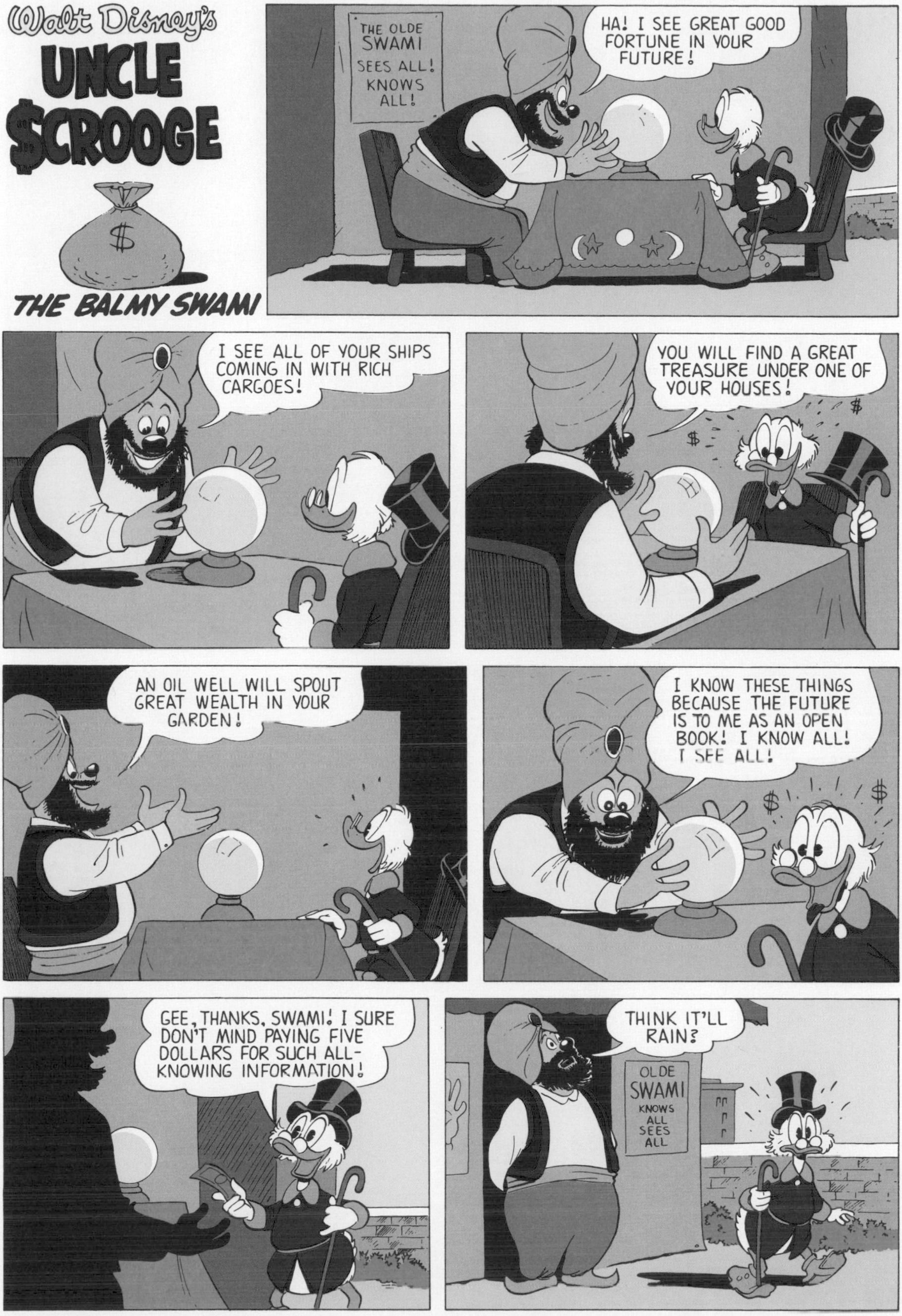
Walt Disney's
UNCLE $CROOGE
THE BALMY SWAMI
THE OLDE SWAMI SEES ALL! KNOWS ALL!
HA! I SEE GREAT GOOD FORTUNE IN YOUR FUTURE!
I SEE ALL OF YOUR SHIPS COMING IN WITH RICH CARGOES!
YOU WILL FIND A GREAT TREASURE UNDER ONE OF YOUR HOUSES!
AN OIL WELL WILL SPOUT GREAT WEALTH IN YOUR GARDEN!
I KNOW THESE THINGS BECAUSE THE FUTURE IS TO ME AS AN OPEN BOOK! I KNOW ALL! I SEE ALL!
GEE, THANKS, SWAMI! I SURE DON'T MIND PAYING FIVE DOLLARS FOR SUCH ALL-KNOWING INFORMATION!
THINK IT'LL RAIN?
OLDE SWAMI KNOWS ALL SEES ALL

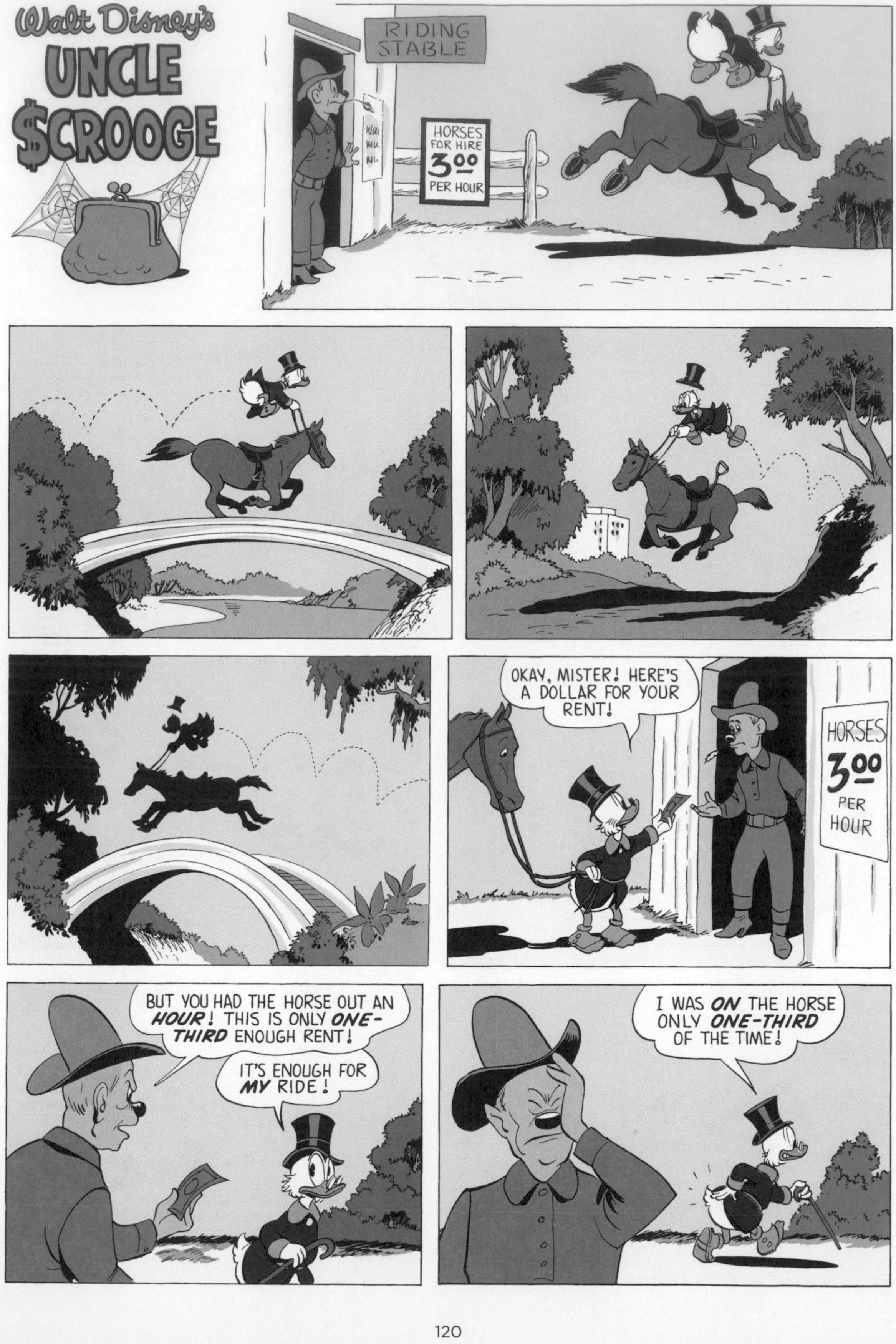
Walt Disney's
UNCLE $CROOGE
RIDING STABLE
HORSES FOR HIRE 3.00 PER HOUR
OKAY, MISTER! HERE'S A DOLLAR FOR YOUR RENT!
HORSES 3.00 PER HOUR
BUT YOU HAD THE HORSE OUT AN HOUR! THIS IS ONLY ONE-THIRD ENOUGH RENT!
IT'S ENOUGH FOR MY RIDE!
I WAS ON THE HORSE ONLY ONE-THIRD OF THE TIME!

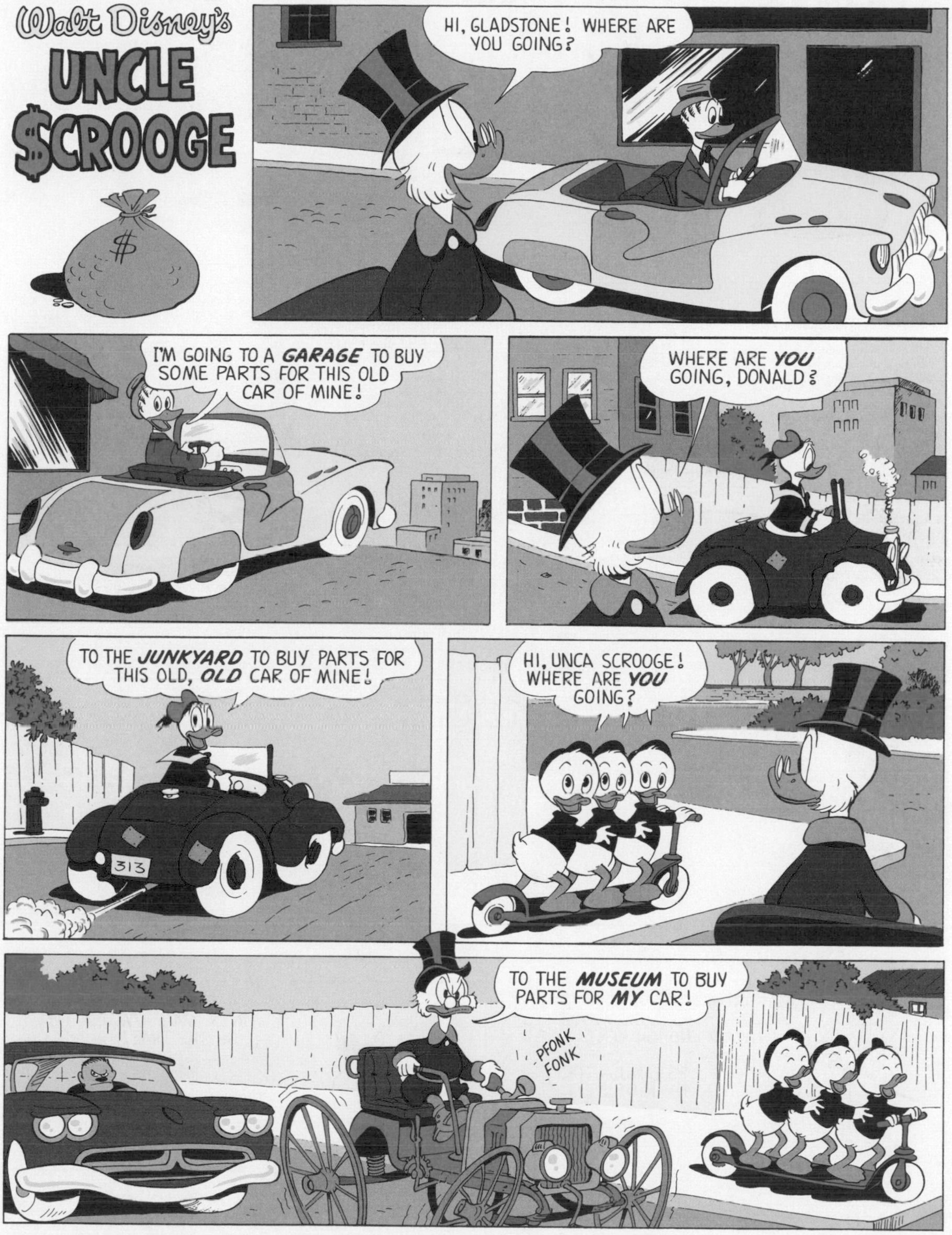
Walt Disney's
UNCLE $CROOGE
HI, GLADSTONE! WHERE ARE YOU GOING?
I'M GOING TO A GARAGE TO BUY SOME PARTS FOR THIS OLD CAR OF MINE!
WHERE ARE YOU GOING, DONALD?
TO THE JUNKYARD TO BUY PARTS FOR THIS OLD, OLD CAR OF MINE!
313
HI, UNCA SCROOGE! WHERE ARE YOU GOING?
TO THE MUSEUM TO BUY PARTS FOR MY CAR!
PFONK FONK

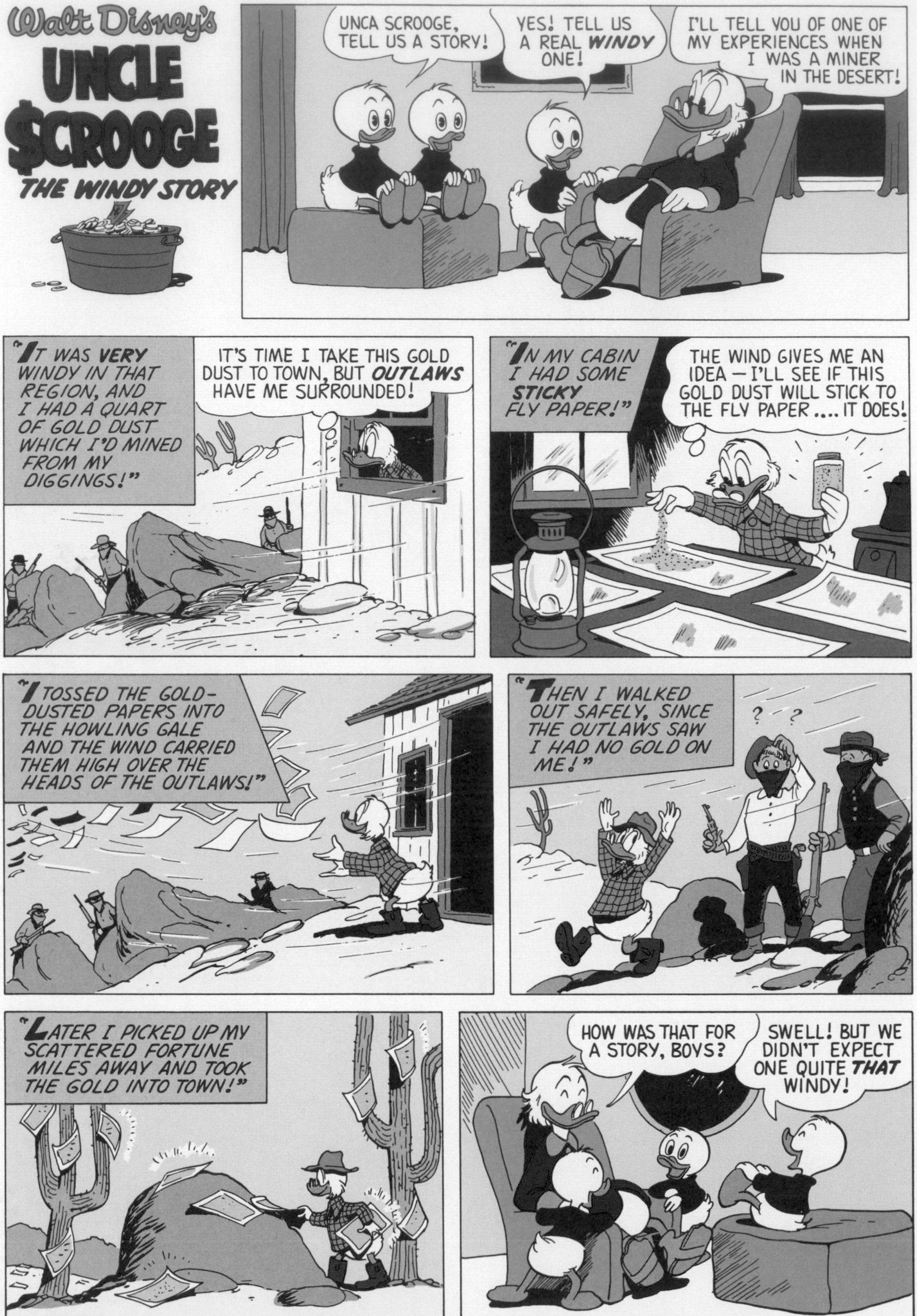
Walt Disney's
UNCLE $CROOGE
THE WINDY STORY
UNCA SCROOGE, TELL US A STORY!
YES! TELL US A REAL WINDY ONE!
I'LL TELL YOU OF ONE OF MY EXPERIENCES WHEN I WAS A MINER IN THE DESERT!
"IT WAS VERY WINDY IN THAT REGION, AND I HAD A QUART OF GOLD DUST WHICH I'D MINED FROM MY DIGGINGS!"
IT'S TIME I TAKE THIS GOLD DUST TO TOWN, BUT OUTLAWS HAVE ME SURROUNDED!
"IN MY CABIN I HAD SOME STICKY FLY PAPER!"
THE WIND GIVES ME AN IDEA — I'LL SEE IF THIS GOLD DUST WILL STICK TO THE FLY PAPER .... IT DOES!
"I TOSSED THE GOLD-DUSTED PAPERS INTO THE HOWLING GALE AND THE WIND CARRIED THEM HIGH OVER THE HEADS OF THE OUTLAWS!"
"THEN I WALKED OUT SAFELY, SINCE THE OUTLAWS SAW I HAD NO GOLD ON ME!"
? ?
"LATER I PICKED UP MY SCATTERED FORTUNE MILES AWAY AND TOOK THE GOLD INTO TOWN!"
HOW WAS THAT FOR A STORY, BOYS?
SWELL! BUT WE DIDN'T EXPECT ONE QUITE THAT WINDY!

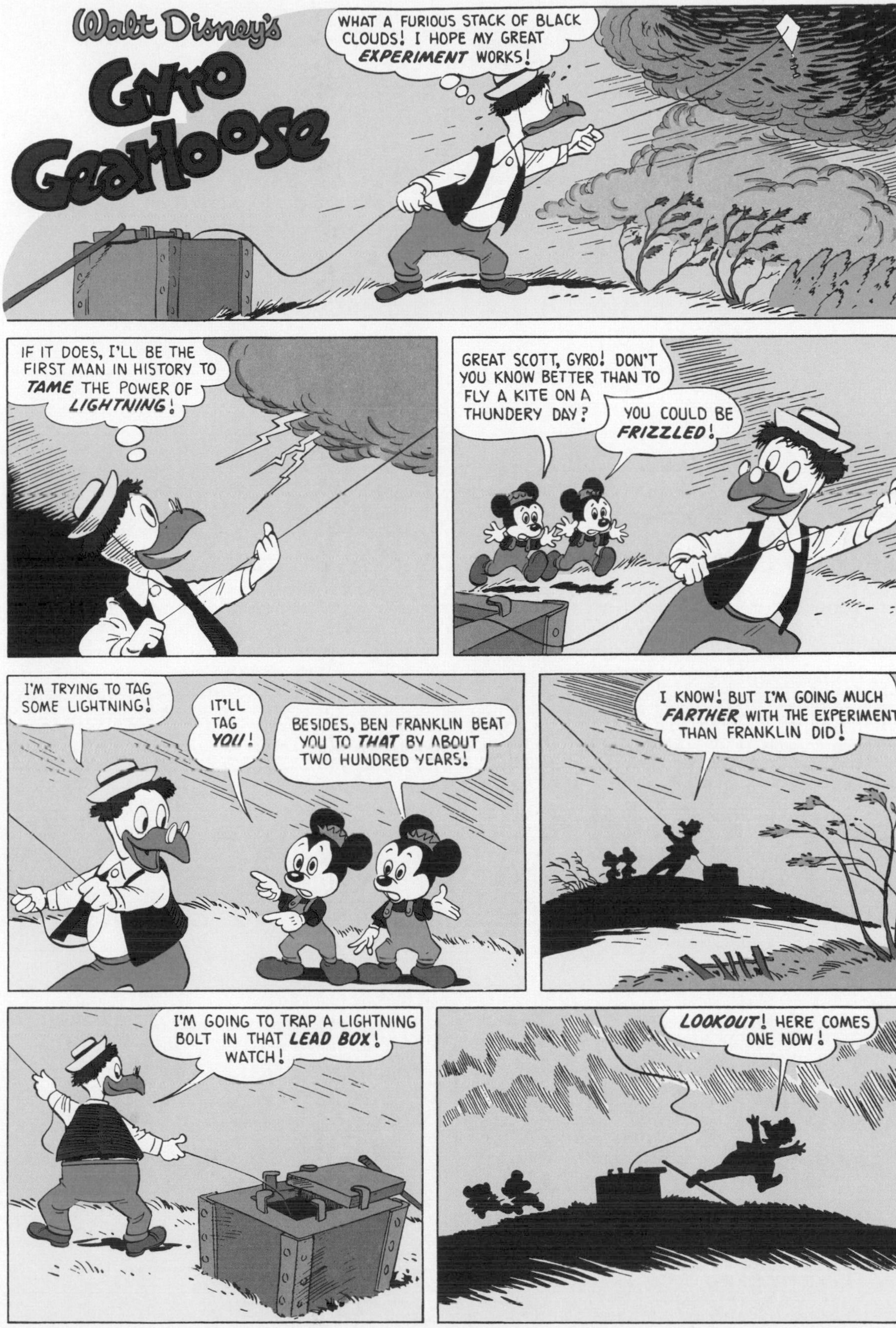
Walt Disney's
Gyro Gearloose
WHAT A FURIOUS STACK OF BLACK CLOUDS! I HOPE MY GREAT EXPERIMENT WORKS!
IF IT DOES, I'LL BE THE FIRST MAN IN HISTORY TO TAME THE POWER OF LIGHTNING!
GREAT SCOTT, GYRO! DON'T YOU KNOW BETTER THAN TO FLY A KITE ON A THUNDERY DAY?
YOU COULD BE FRIZZLED!
I'M TRYING TO TAG SOME LIGHTNING!
IT'LL TAG YOU!
BESIDES, BEN FRANKLIN BEAT YOU TO THAT BY ABOUT TWO HUNDRED YEARS!
I KNOW! BUT I'M GOING MUCH FARTHER WITH THE EXPERIMENT THAN FRANKLIN DID!
I'M GOING TO TRAP A LIGHTNING BOLT IN THAT LEAD BOX! WATCH!
LOOKOUT! HERE COMES ONE NOW!

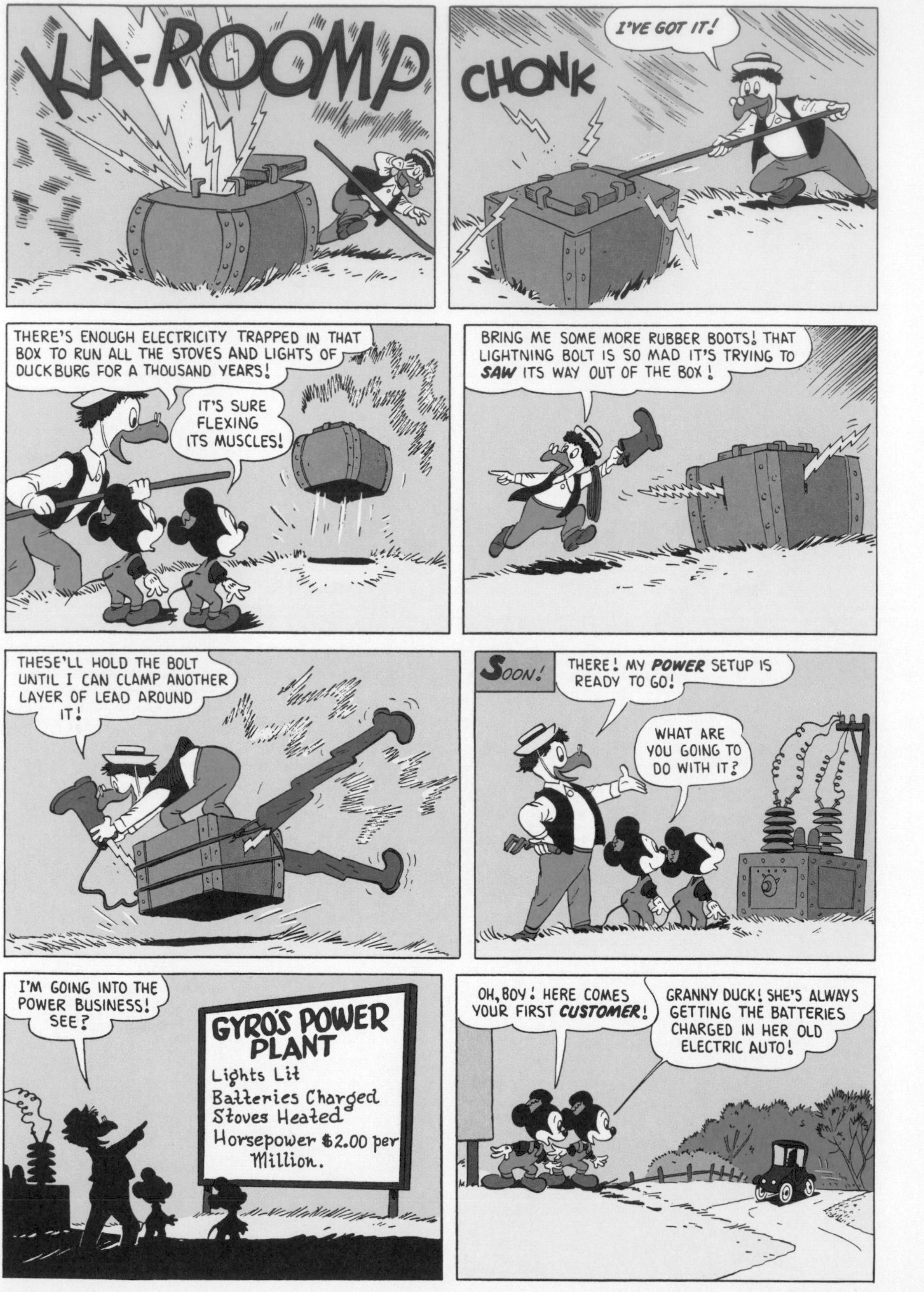
KA-ROOMP
CHONK
I'VE GOT IT!
THERE'S ENOUGH ELECTRICITY TRAPPED IN THAT BOX TO RUN ALL THE STOVES AND LIGHTS OF DUCKBURG FOR A THOUSAND YEARS!
IT'S SURE FLEXING ITS MUSCLES!
BRING ME SOME MORE RUBBER BOOTS! THAT LIGHTNING BOLT IS SO MAD IT'S TRYING TO SAW ITS WAY OUT OF THE BOX!
THESE'LL HOLD THE BOLT UNTIL I CAN CLAMP ANOTHER LAYER OF LEAD AROUND IT!
SOON!
THERE! MY POWER SETUP IS READY TO GO!
WHAT ARE YOU GOING TO DO WITH IT?
I'M GOING INTO THE POWER BUSINESS! SEE?
GYRO'S POWER PLANT
Lights Lit
Batteries Charged
Stoves Heated
Horsepower $2.00 per Million.
OH, BOY! HERE COMES YOUR FIRST CUSTOMER!
GRANNY DUCK! SHE'S ALWAYS GETTING THE BATTERIES CHARGED IN HER OLD ELECTRIC AUTO!

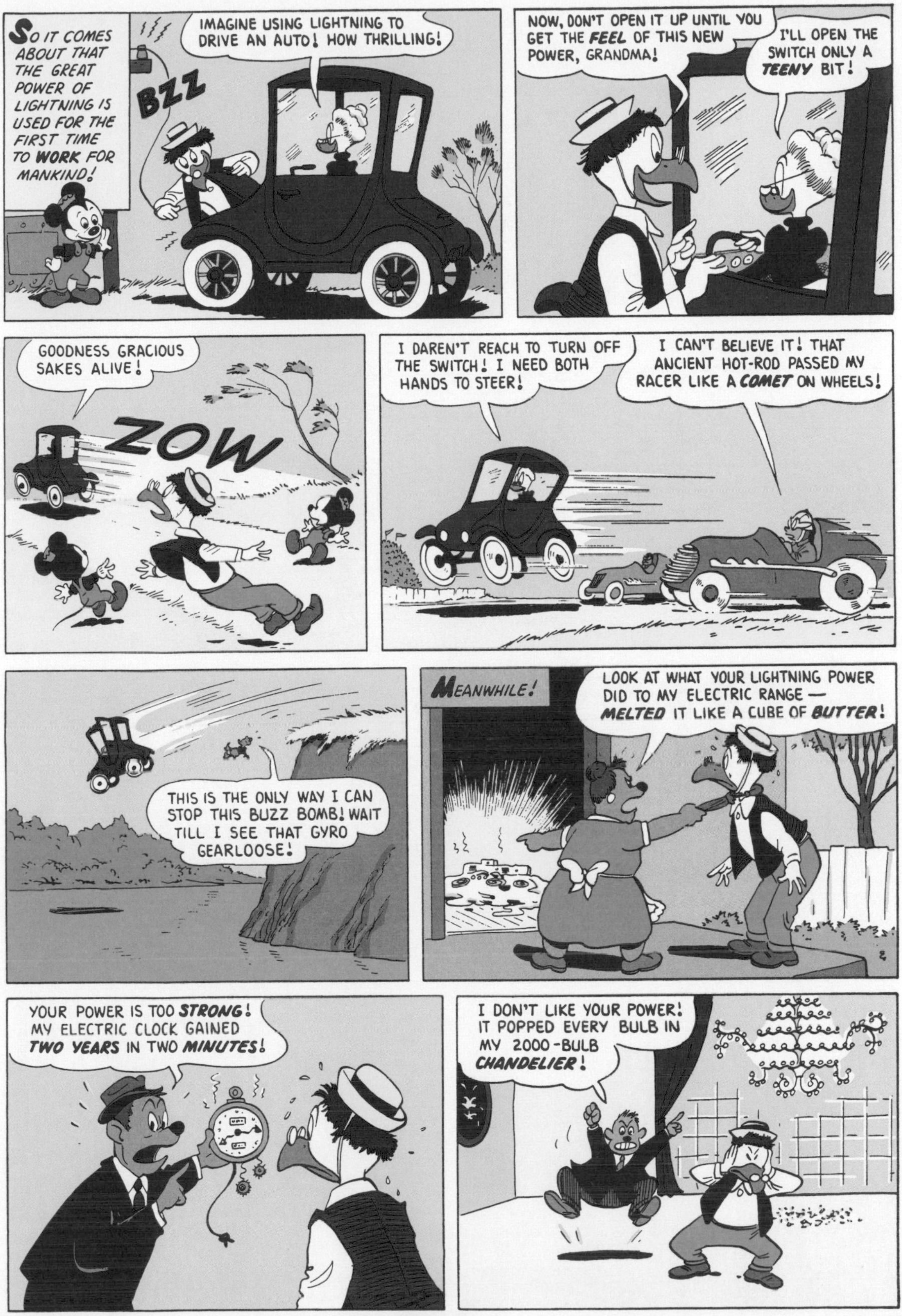
SO IT COMES ABOUT THAT THE GREAT POWER OF LIGHTNING IS USED FOR THE FIRST TIME TO WORK FOR MANKIND!
IMAGINE USING LIGHTNING TO DRIVE AN AUTO! HOW THRILLING!
BZZ
NOW, DON'T OPEN IT UP UNTIL YOU GET THE FEEL OF THIS NEW POWER, GRANDMA!
I'LL OPEN THE SWITCH ONLY A TEENY BIT!
GOODNESS GRACIOUS SAKES ALIVE!
ZOW
I DAREN'T REACH TO TURN OFF THE SWITCH! I NEED BOTH HANDS TO STEER!
I CAN'T BELIEVE IT! THAT ANCIENT HOT-ROD PASSED MY RACER LIKE A COMET ON WHEELS!
THIS IS THE ONLY WAY I CAN STOP THIS BUZZ BOMB! WAIT TILL I SEE THAT GYRO GEARLOOSE!
MEANWHILE!
LOOK AT WHAT YOUR LIGHTNING POWER DID TO MY ELECTRIC RANGE — MELTED IT LIKE A CUBE OF BUTTER!
YOUR POWER IS TOO STRONG! MY ELECTRIC CLOCK GAINED TWO YEARS IN TWO MINUTES!
I DON'T LIKE YOUR POWER! IT POPPED EVERY BULB IN MY 2000-BULB CHANDELIER!

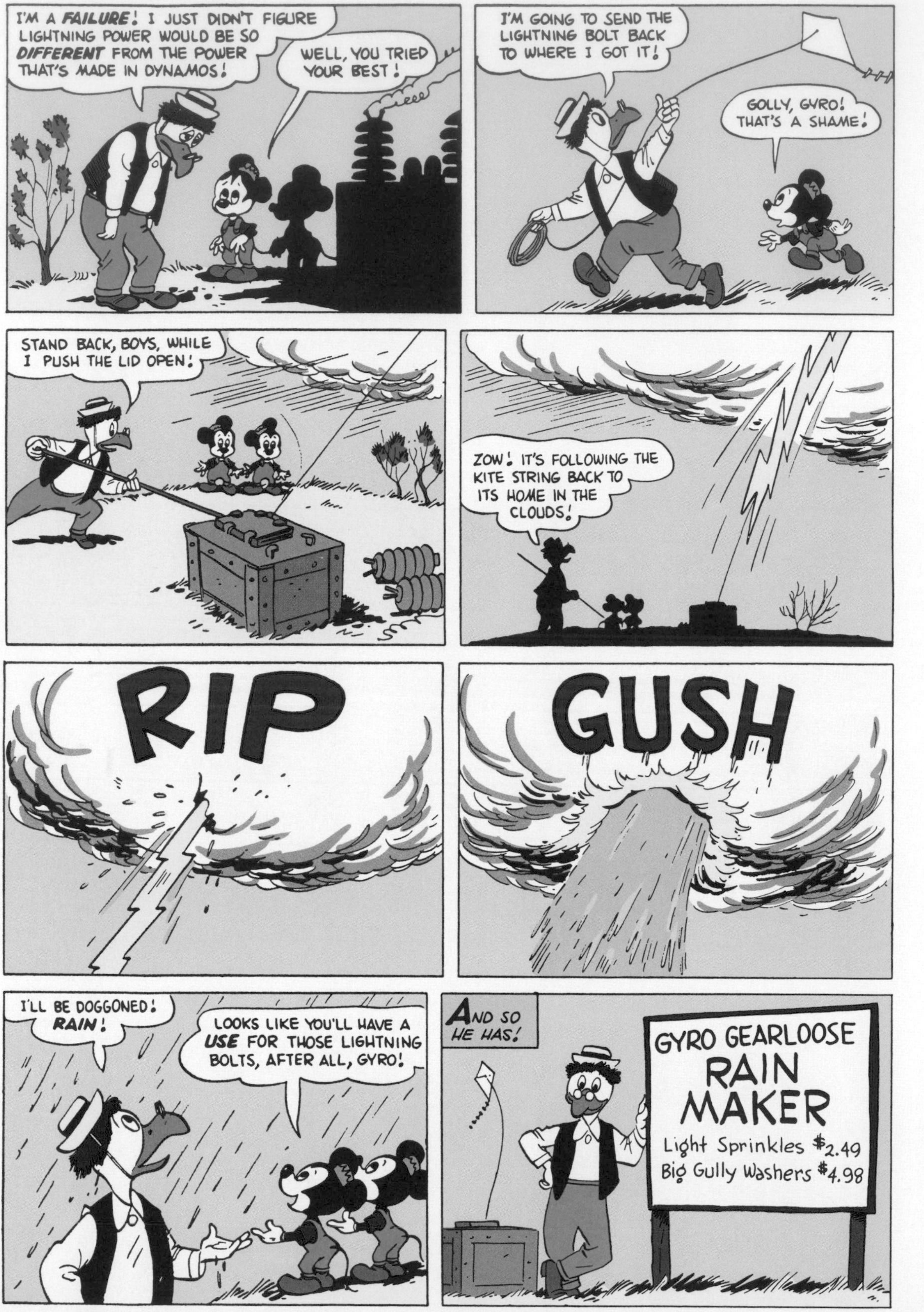
I'M A FAILURE! I JUST DIDN'T FIGURE LIGHTNING POWER WOULD BE SO DIFFERENT FROM THE POWER THAT'S MADE IN DYNAMOS!
WELL, YOU TRIED YOUR BEST!
I'M GOING TO SEND THE LIGHTNING BOLT BACK TO WHERE I GOT IT!
GOLLY, GYRO! THAT'S A SHAME!
STAND BACK, BOYS, WHILE I PUSH THE LID OPEN!
ZOW! IT'S FOLLOWING THE KITE STRING BACK TO ITS HOME IN THE CLOUDS!
RIP
GUSH
I'LL BE DOGGONED! RAIN!
LOOKS LIKE YOU'LL HAVE A USE FOR THOSE LIGHTNING BOLTS, AFTER ALL, GYRO!
AND SO HE HAS!
GYRO GEARLOOSE
RAIN MAKER
Light Sprinkles $2.49
Big Gully Washers $4.98

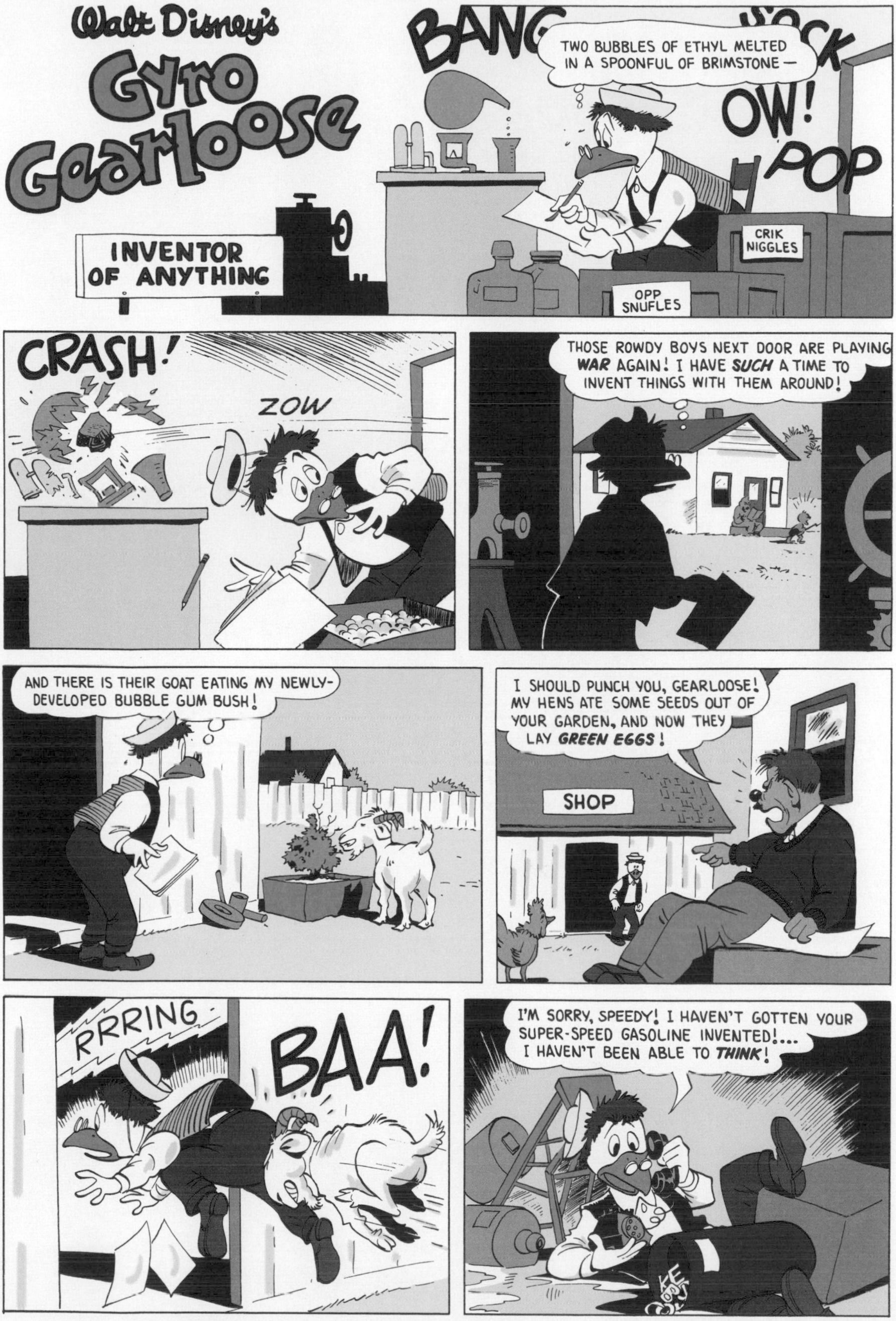
Walt Disney's
Gyro Gearloose
INVENTOR OF ANYTHING
BANG
SOCK
TWO BUBBLES OF ETHYL MELTED IN A SPOONFUL OF BRIMSTONE—
OW!
POP
CRIK NIGGLES
OPP SNUFLES
CRASH!
ZOW
THOSE ROWDY BOYS NEXT DOOR ARE PLAYING WAR AGAIN! I HAVE SUCH A TIME TO INVENT THINGS WITH THEM AROUND!
AND THERE IS THEIR GOAT EATING MY NEWLY-DEVELOPED BUBBLE GUM BUSH!
I SHOULD PUNCH YOU, GEARLOOSE! MY HENS ATE SOME SEEDS OUT OF YOUR GARDEN, AND NOW THEY LAY GREEN EGGS!
SHOP
RRRING
BAA!
I'M SORRY, SPEEDY! I HAVEN'T GOTTEN YOUR SUPER-SPEED GASOLINE INVENTED!... I HAVEN'T BEEN ABLE TO THINK!

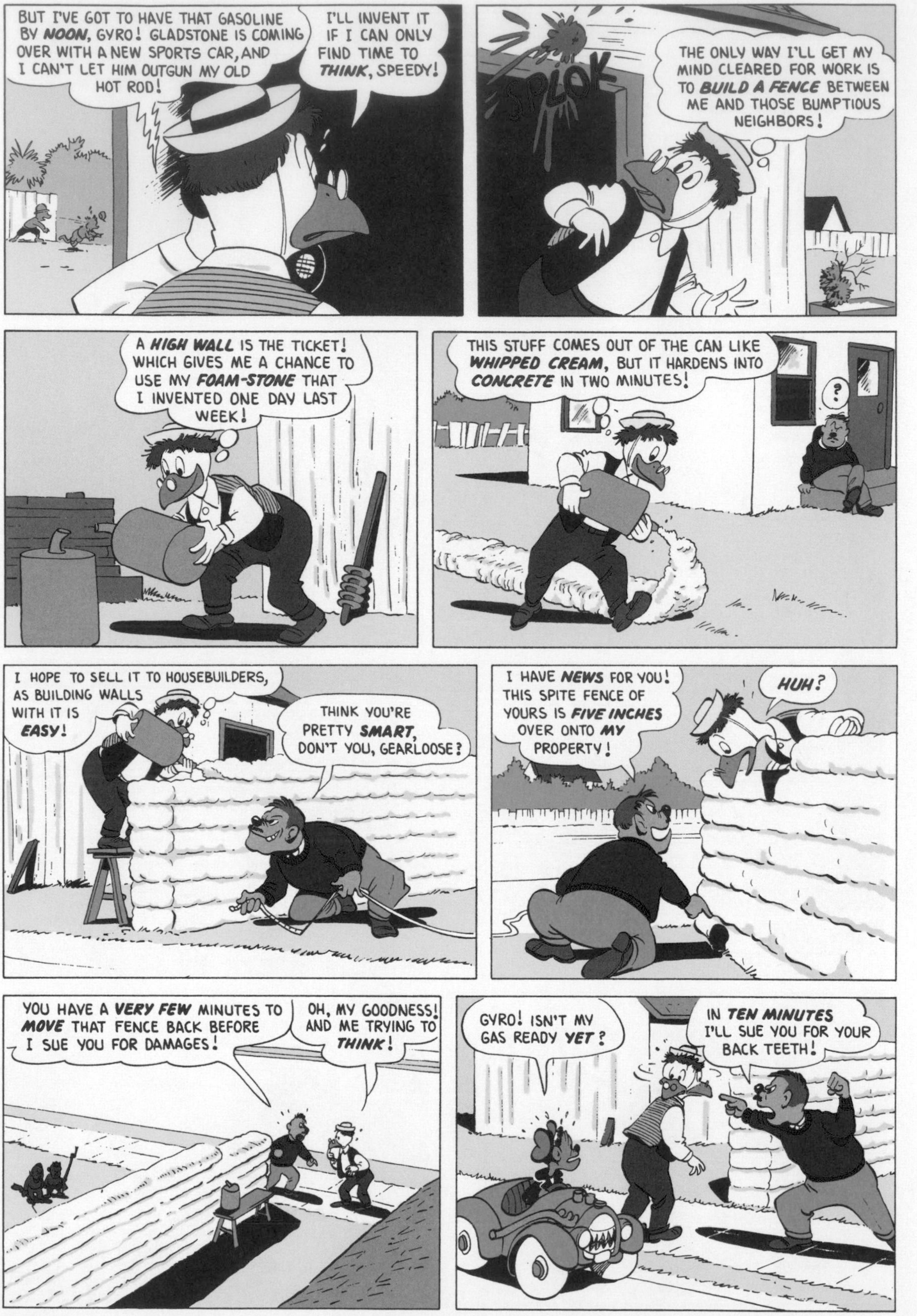
BUT I'VE GOT TO HAVE THAT GASOLINE BY NOON, GYRO! GLADSTONE IS COMING OVER WITH A NEW SPORTS CAR, AND I CAN'T LET HIM OUTGUN MY OLD HOT ROD!
I'LL INVENT IT IF I CAN ONLY FIND TIME TO THINK, SPEEDY!
SPLOK
THE ONLY WAY I'LL GET MY MIND CLEARED FOR WORK IS TO BUILD A FENCE BETWEEN ME AND THOSE BUMPTIOUS NEIGHBORS!
A HIGH WALL IS THE TICKET! WHICH GIVES ME A CHANCE TO USE MY FOAM-STONE THAT I INVENTED ONE DAY LAST WEEK!
THIS STUFF COMES OUT OF THE CAN LIKE WHIPPED CREAM, BUT IT HARDENS INTO CONCRETE IN TWO MINUTES!
?
I HOPE TO SELL IT TO HOUSEBUILDERS, AS BUILDING WALLS WITH IT IS EASY!
THINK YOU'RE PRETTY SMART, DON'T YOU, GEARLOOSE?
I HAVE NEWS FOR YOU! THIS SPITE FENCE OF YOURS IS FIVE INCHES OVER ONTO MY PROPERTY!
HUH?
YOU HAVE A VERY FEW MINUTES TO MOVE THAT FENCE BACK BEFORE I SUE YOU FOR DAMAGES!
OH, MY GOODNESS! AND ME TRYING TO THINK!
GYRO! ISN'T MY GAS READY YET?
IN TEN MINUTES I'LL SUE YOU FOR YOUR BACK TEETH!

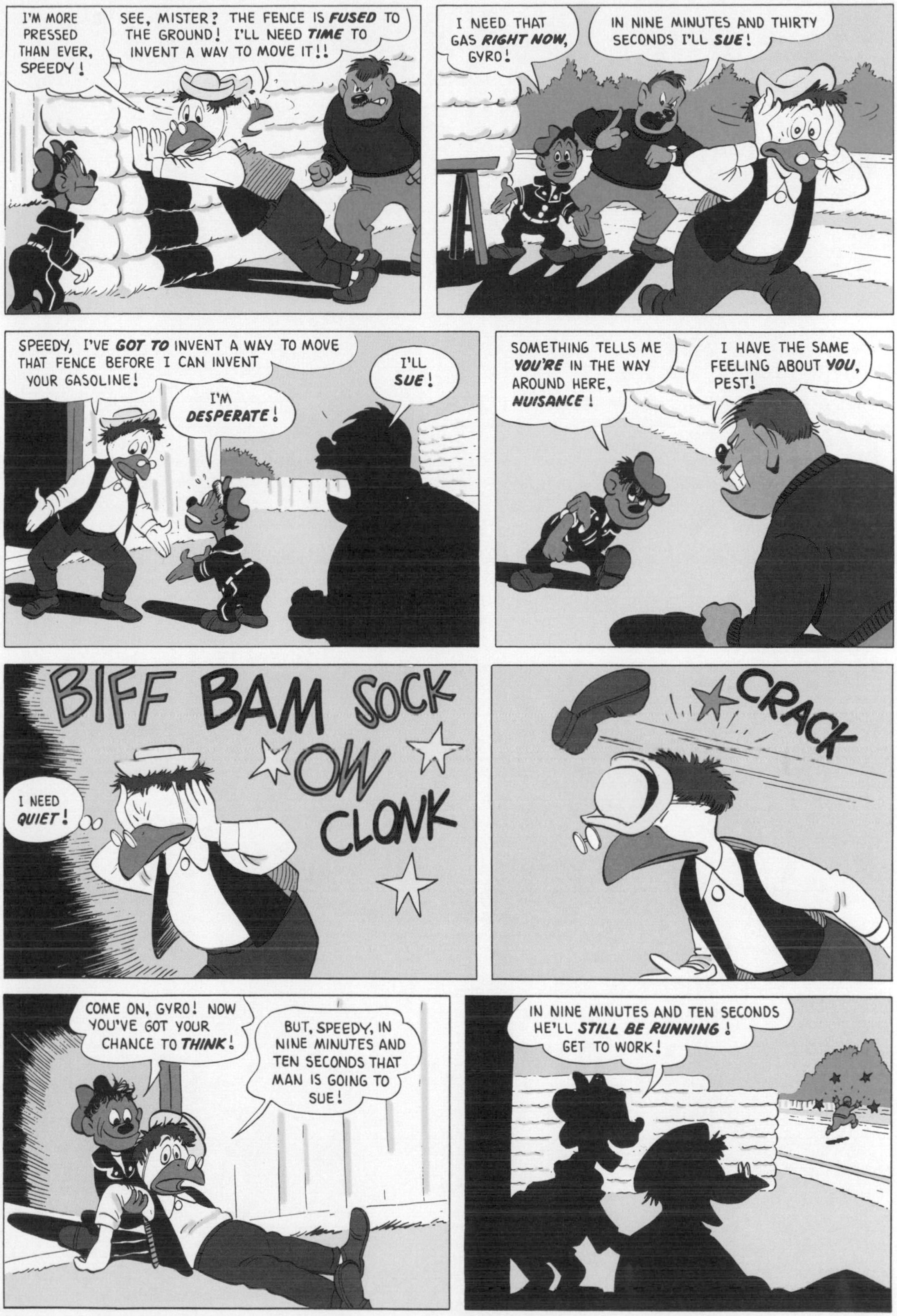
I'M MORE PRESSED THAN EVER, SPEEDY!
SEE, MISTER? THE FENCE IS FUSED TO THE GROUND! I'LL NEED TIME TO INVENT A WAY TO MOVE IT!!
I NEED THAT GAS RIGHT NOW, GYRO!
IN NINE MINUTES AND THIRTY SECONDS I'LL SUE!
SPEEDY, I'VE GOT TO INVENT A WAY TO MOVE THAT FENCE BEFORE I CAN INVENT YOUR GASOLINE!
I'M DESPERATE!
I'LL SUE!
SOMETHING TELLS ME YOU'RE IN THE WAY AROUND HERE, NUISANCE!
I HAVE THE SAME FEELING ABOUT YOU, PEST!
BIFF BAM SOCK
OW
CLONK
I NEED QUIET!
CRACK
COME ON, GYRO! NOW YOU'VE GOT YOUR CHANCE TO THINK!
BUT, SPEEDY, IN NINE MINUTES AND TEN SECONDS THAT MAN IS GOING TO SUE!
IN NINE MINUTES AND TEN SECONDS HE'LL STILL BE RUNNING! GET TO WORK!

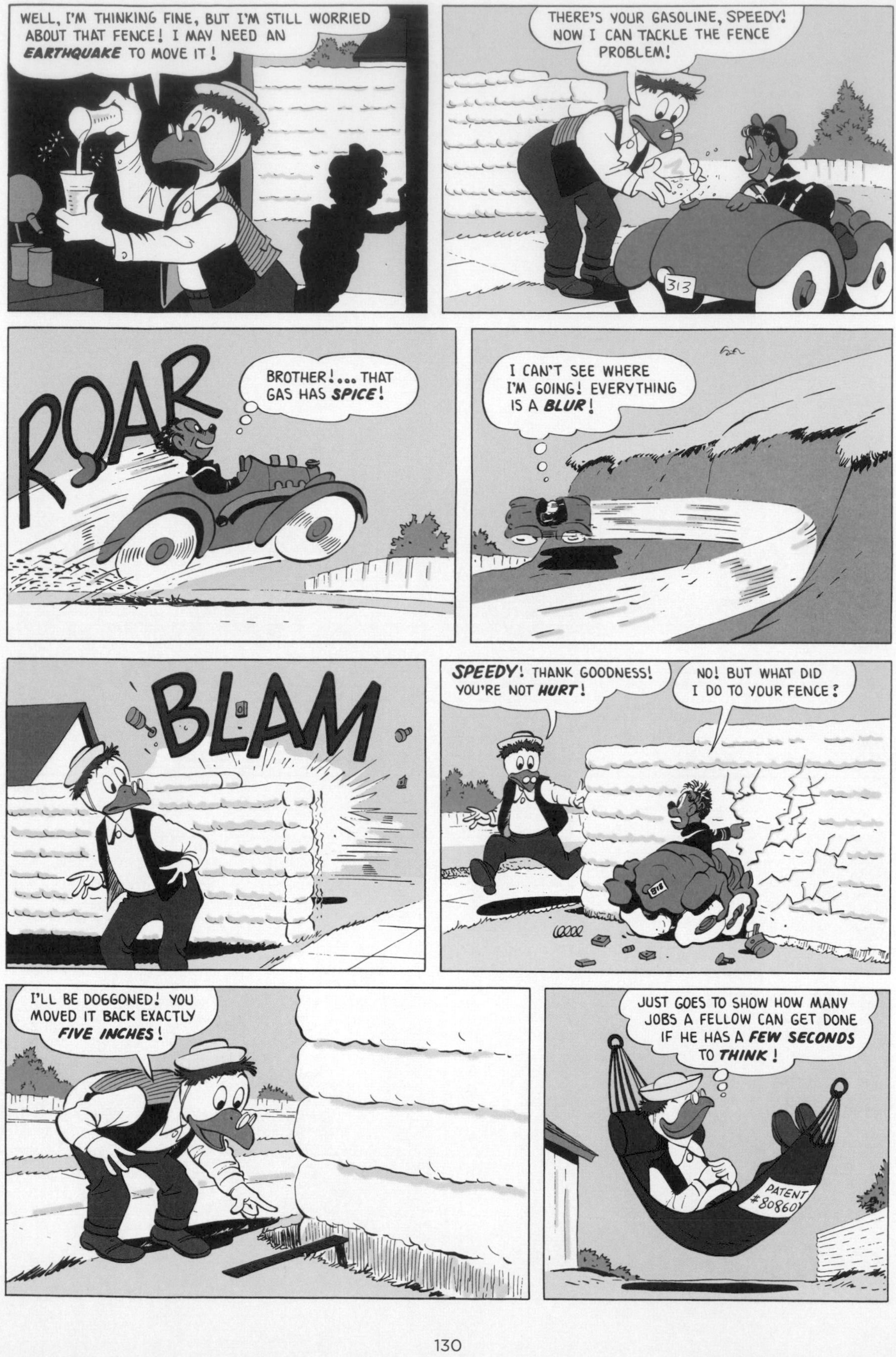

WELL, I'M THINKING FINE, BUT I'M STILL WORRIED ABOUT THAT FENCE! I MAY NEED AN EARTHQUAKE TO MOVE IT!
THERE'S YOUR GASOLINE, SPEEDY! NOW I CAN TACKLE THE FENCE PROBLEM!
313
ROAR
BROTHER!... THAT GAS HAS SPICE!
I CAN'T SEE WHERE I'M GOING! EVERYTHING IS A BLUR!
BLAM
SPEEDY! THANK GOODNESS! YOU'RE NOT HURT!
NO! BUT WHAT DID I DO TO YOUR FENCE?
I'LL BE DOGGONED! YOU MOVED IT BACK EXACTLY FIVE INCHES!
JUST GOES TO SHOW HOW MANY JOBS A FELLOW CAN GET DONE IF HE HAS A FEW SECONDS TO THINK!
PATENT #80860

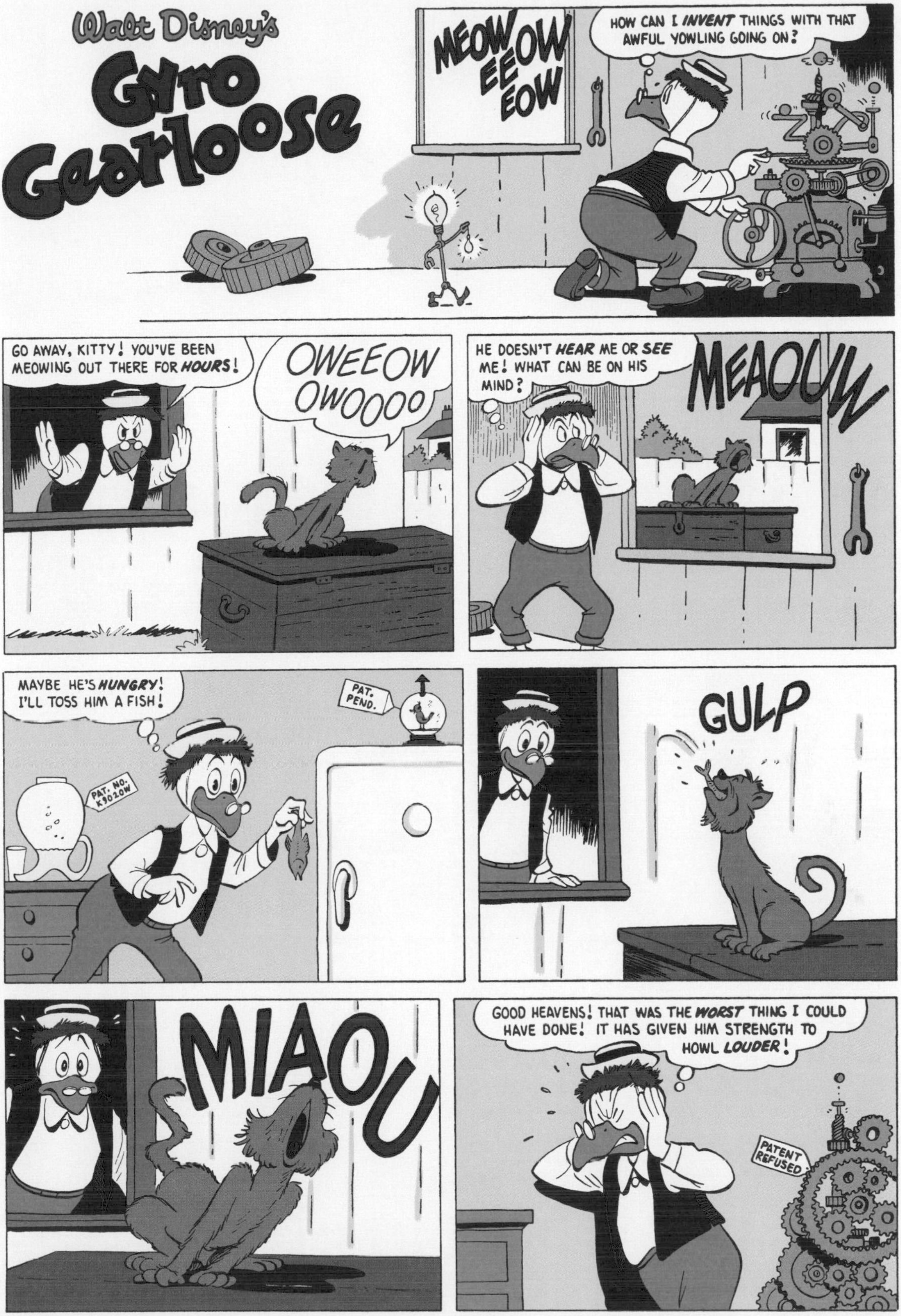
Walt Disney's
Gyro Gearloose
MEOW EEOW EOW
HOW CAN I INVENT THINGS WITH THAT AWFUL YOWLING GOING ON?
GO AWAY, KITTY! YOU'VE BEEN MEOWING OUT THERE FOR HOURS!
OWEEOW OWOOOO
HE DOESN'T HEAR ME OR SEE ME! WHAT CAN BE ON HIS MIND?
MEAOUW
MAYBE HE'S HUNGRY! I'LL TOSS HIM A FISH!
PAT. PEND.
PAT. NO. K9020W
GULP
MIAOU
GOOD HEAVENS! THAT WAS THE WORST THING I COULD HAVE DONE! IT HAS GIVEN HIM STRENGTH TO HOWL LOUDER!
PATENT REFUSED

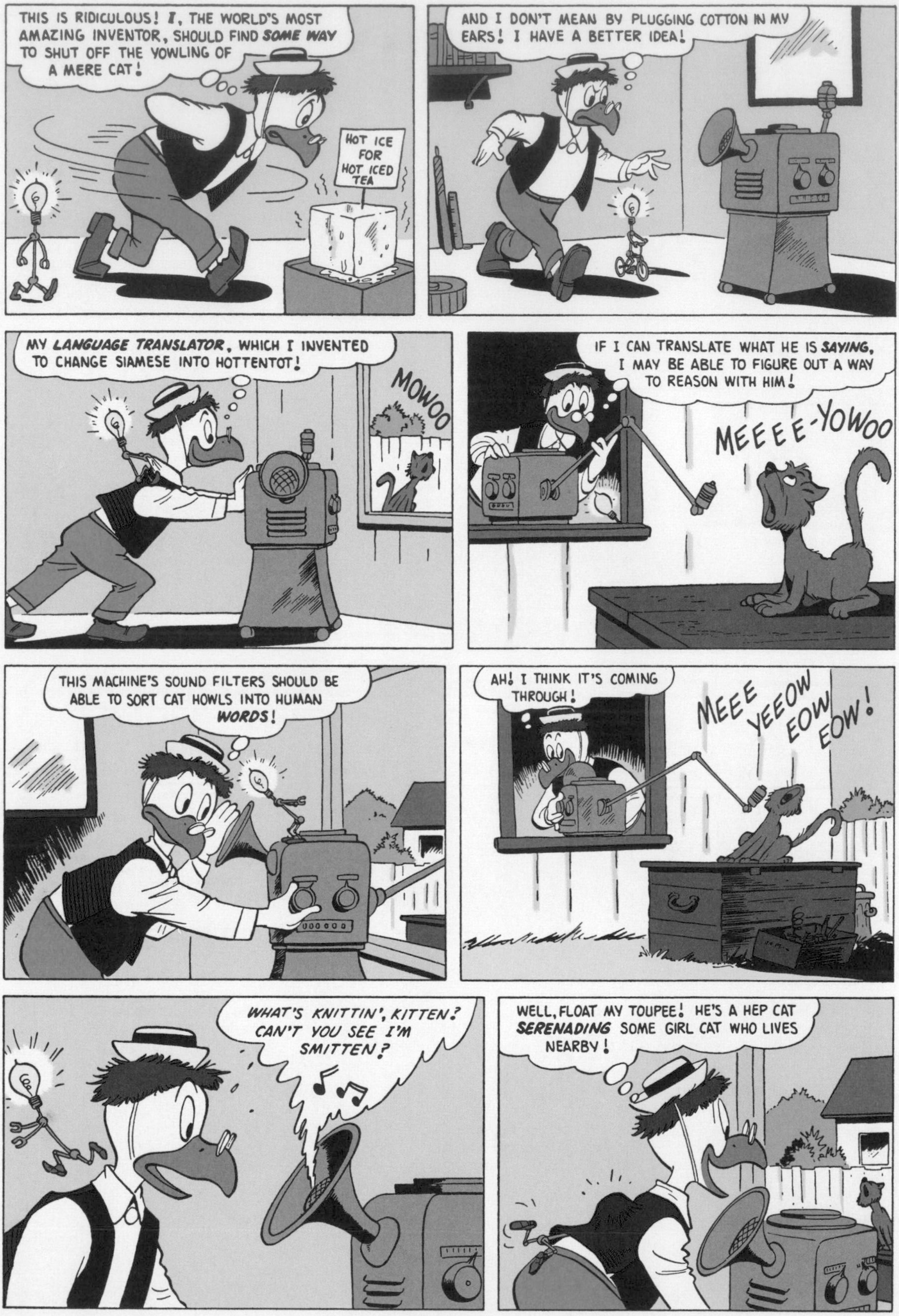
THIS IS RIDICULOUS! I, THE WORLD'S MOST AMAZING INVENTOR, SHOULD FIND SOME WAY TO SHUT OFF THE YOWLING OF A MERE CAT!
HOT ICE FOR HOT ICED TEA
AND I DON'T MEAN BY PLUGGING COTTON IN MY EARS! I HAVE A BETTER IDEA!
MY LANGUAGE TRANSLATOR, WHICH I INVENTED TO CHANGE SIAMESE INTO HOTTENTOT!
MOWOO
IF I CAN TRANSLATE WHAT HE IS SAYING, I MAY BE ABLE TO FIGURE OUT A WAY TO REASON WITH HIM!
MEEEE-YOWOO
THIS MACHINE'S SOUND FILTERS SHOULD BE ABLE TO SORT CAT HOWLS INTO HUMAN WORDS!
AH! I THINK IT'S COMING THROUGH!
MEEE YEEOW EOW EOW!
WHAT'S KNITTIN', KITTEN? CAN'T YOU SEE I'M SMITTEN?
WELL, FLOAT MY TOUPEE! HE'S A HEP CAT SERENADING SOME GIRL CAT WHO LIVES NEARBY!

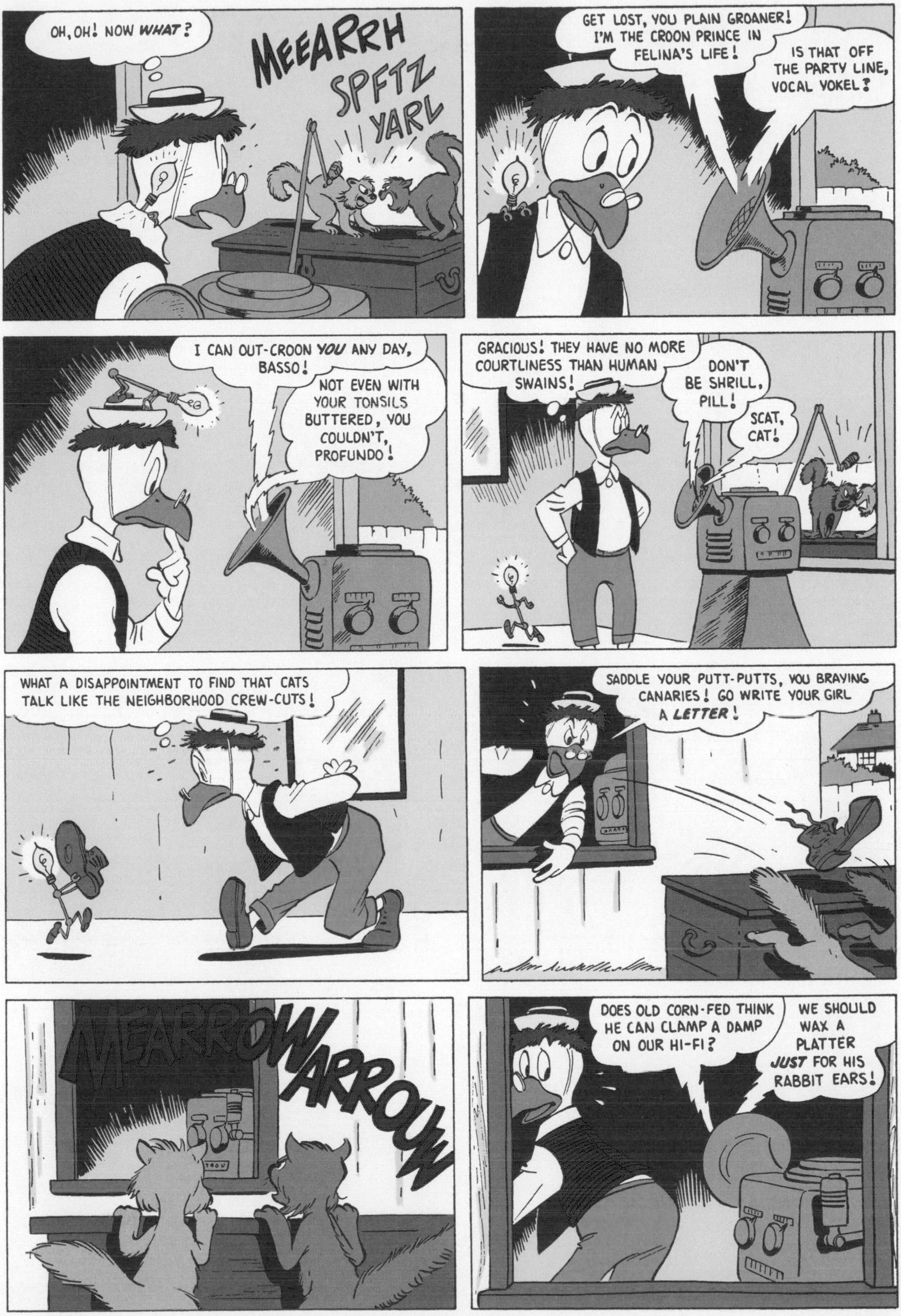
OH, OH! NOW WHAT?
MEEARRH
SPFTZ
YARL
GET LOST, YOU PLAIN GROANER! I'M THE CROON PRINCE IN FELINA'S LIFE!
IS THAT OFF THE PARTY LINE, VOCAL YOKEL?
I CAN OUT-CROON YOU ANY DAY, BASSO!
NOT EVEN WITH YOUR TONSILS BUTTERED, YOU COULDN'T, PROFUNDO!
GRACIOUS! THEY HAVE NO MORE COURTLINESS THAN HUMAN SWAINS!
DON'T BE SHRILL, PILL!
SCAT, CAT!
WHAT A DISAPPOINTMENT TO FIND THAT CATS TALK LIKE THE NEIGHBORHOOD CREW-CUTS!
SADDLE YOUR PUTT-PUTTS, YOU BRAYING CANARIES! GO WRITE YOUR GIRL A LETTER!
MEARROWARROUW
DOES OLD CORN-FED THINK HE CAN CLAMP A DAMP ON OUR HI-FI?
WE SHOULD WAX A PLATTER JUST FOR HIS RABBIT EARS!

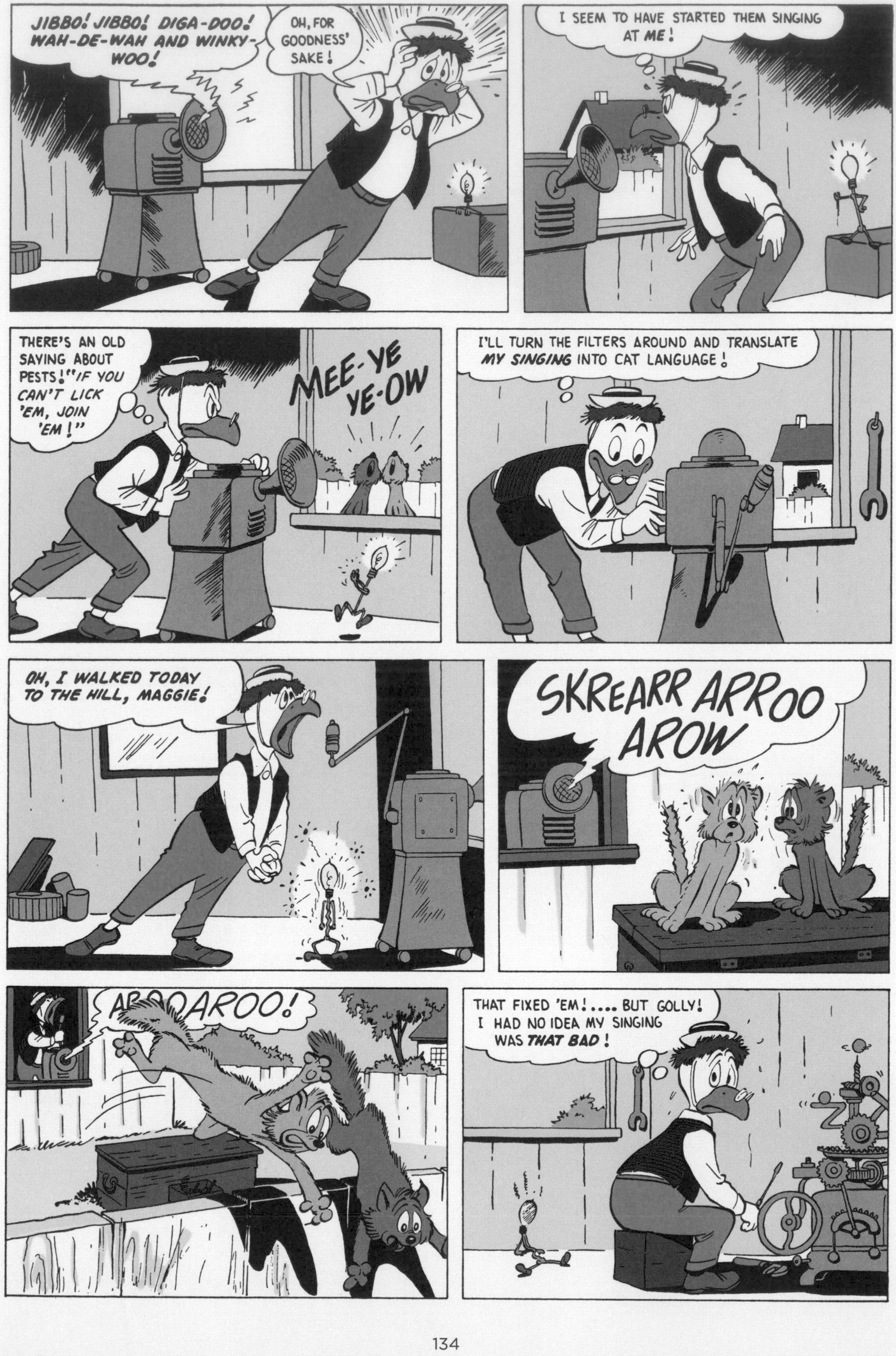

JIBBO! JIBBO! DIGA-DOO! WAH-DE-WAH AND WINKY-WOO!
OH, FOR GOODNESS' SAKE!
I SEEM TO HAVE STARTED THEM SINGING AT ME!
THERE'S AN OLD SAYING ABOUT PESTS! "IF YOU CAN'T LICK 'EM, JOIN 'EM!"
MEE-YE YE-OW
I'LL TURN THE FILTERS AROUND AND TRANSLATE MY SINGING INTO CAT LANGUAGE!
OH, I WALKED TODAY TO THE HILL, MAGGIE!
SKREARR ARROO AROW
AROOAROO!
THAT FIXED 'EM! .... BUT GOLLY! I HAD NO IDEA MY SINGING WAS THAT BAD!

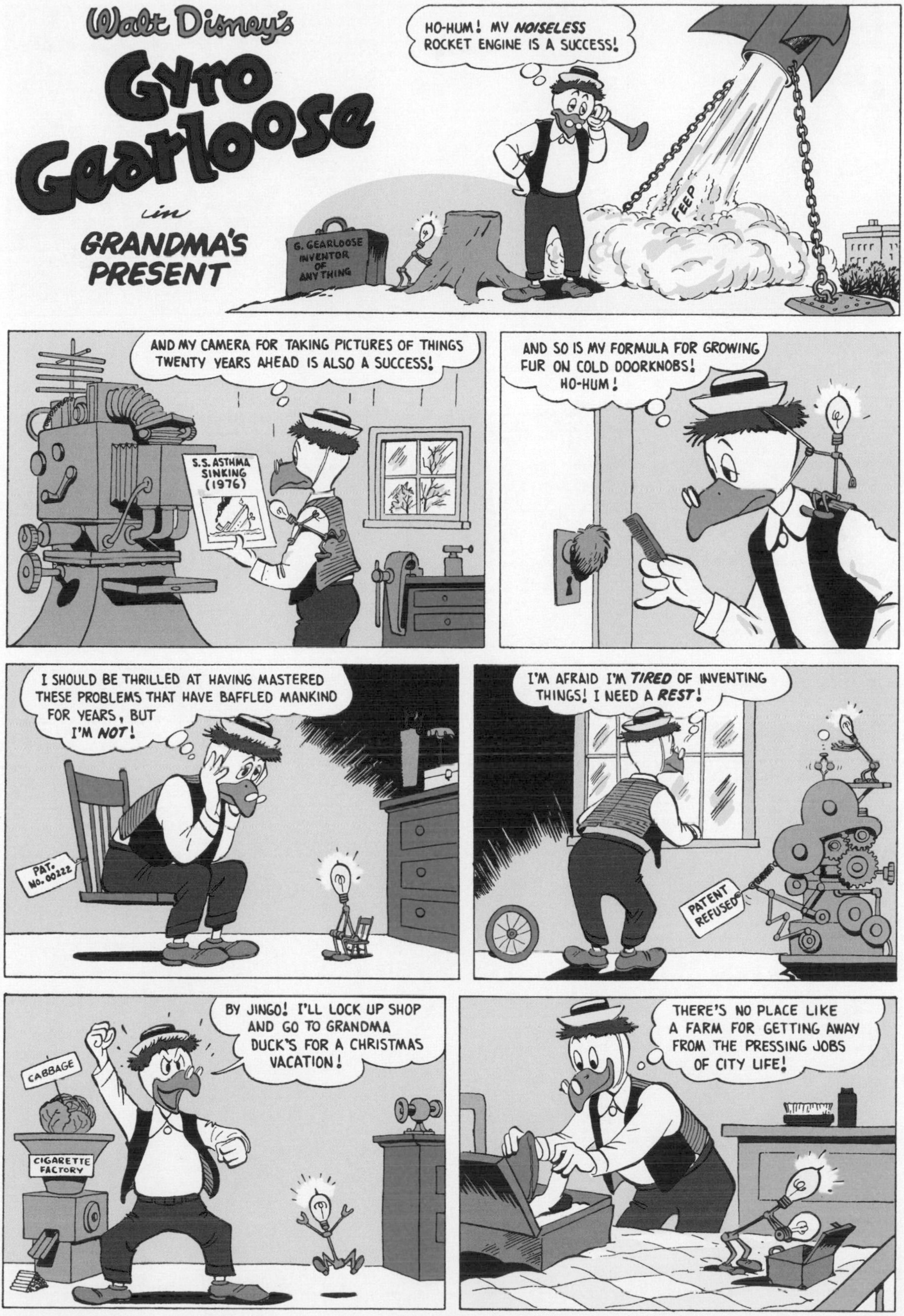
Walt Disney's
Gyro Gearloose
in
GRANDMA'S PRESENT
HO-HUM! MY NOISELESS ROCKET ENGINE IS A SUCCESS!
G. GEARLOOSE INVENTOR OF ANYTHING
FEEP
AND MY CAMERA FOR TAKING PICTURES OF THINGS TWENTY YEARS AHEAD IS ALSO A SUCCESS!
S.S. ASTHMA SINKING (1976)
AND SO IS MY FORMULA FOR GROWING FUR ON COLD DOORKNOBS! HO-HUM!
I SHOULD BE THRILLED AT HAVING MASTERED THESE PROBLEMS THAT HAVE BAFFLED MANKIND FOR YEARS, BUT I'M NOT!
PAT. NO. 00222
I'M AFRAID I'M TIRED OF INVENTING THINGS! I NEED A REST!
PATENT REFUSED
BY JINGO! I'LL LOCK UP SHOP AND GO TO GRANDMA DUCK'S FOR A CHRISTMAS VACATION!
CABBAGE
CIGARETTE FACTORY
THERE'S NO PLACE LIKE A FARM FOR GETTING AWAY FROM THE PRESSING JOBS OF CITY LIFE!

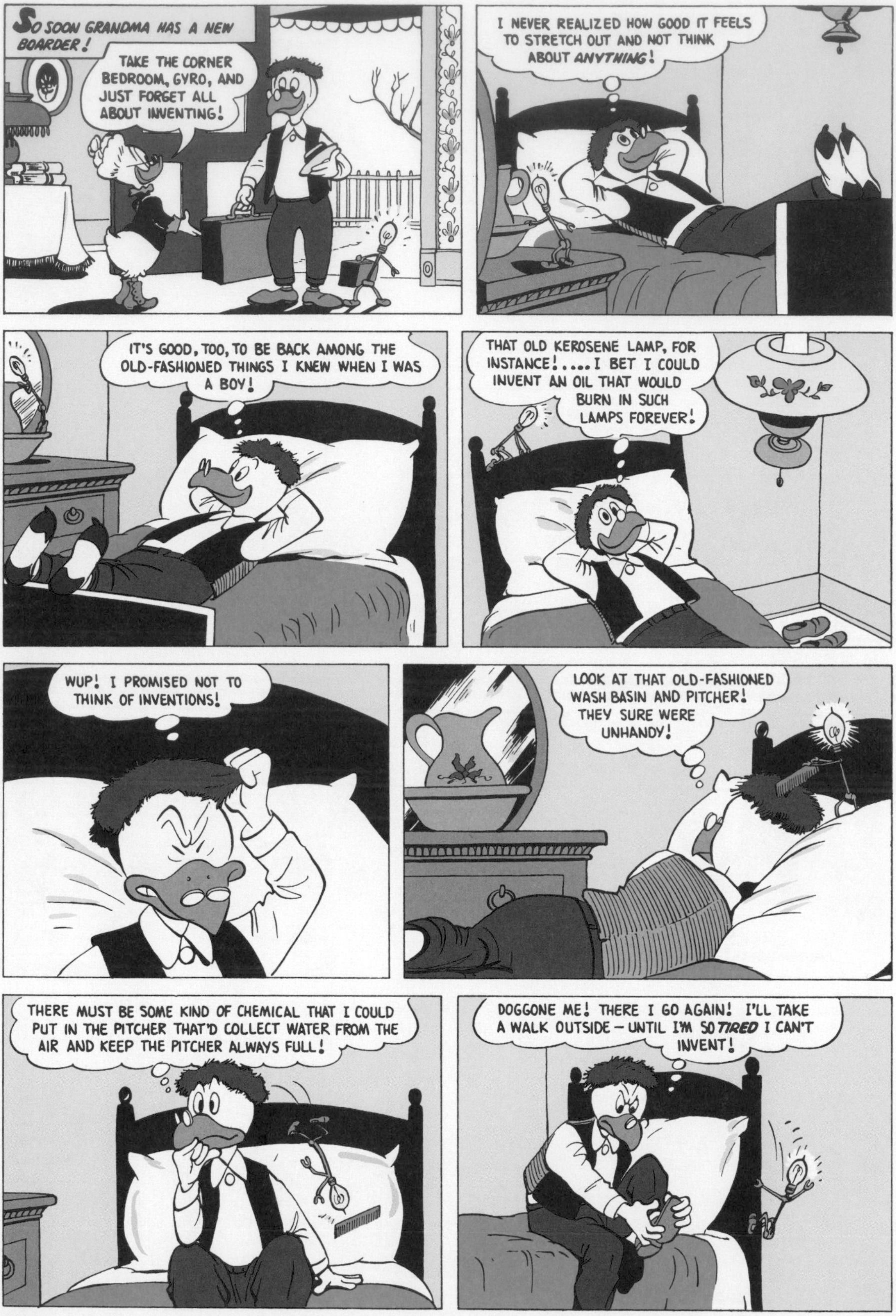
SO SOON GRANDMA HAS A NEW BOARDER!
TAKE THE CORNER BEDROOM, GYRO, AND JUST FORGET ALL ABOUT INVENTING!
I NEVER REALIZED HOW GOOD IT FEELS TO STRETCH OUT AND NOT THINK ABOUT ANYTHING!
IT'S GOOD, TOO, TO BE BACK AMONG THE OLD-FASHIONED THINGS I KNEW WHEN I WAS A BOY!
THAT OLD KEROSENE LAMP, FOR INSTANCE!.... I BET I COULD INVENT AN OIL THAT WOULD BURN IN SUCH LAMPS FOREVER!
WUP! I PROMISED NOT TO THINK OF INVENTIONS!
LOOK AT THAT OLD-FASHIONED WASH BASIN AND PITCHER! THEY SURE WERE UNHANDY!
THERE MUST BE SOME KIND OF CHEMICAL THAT I COULD PUT IN THE PITCHER THAT'D COLLECT WATER FROM THE AIR AND KEEP THE PITCHER ALWAYS FULL!
DOGGONE ME! THERE I GO AGAIN! I'LL TAKE A WALK OUTSIDE — UNTIL I'M SO TIRED I CAN'T INVENT!

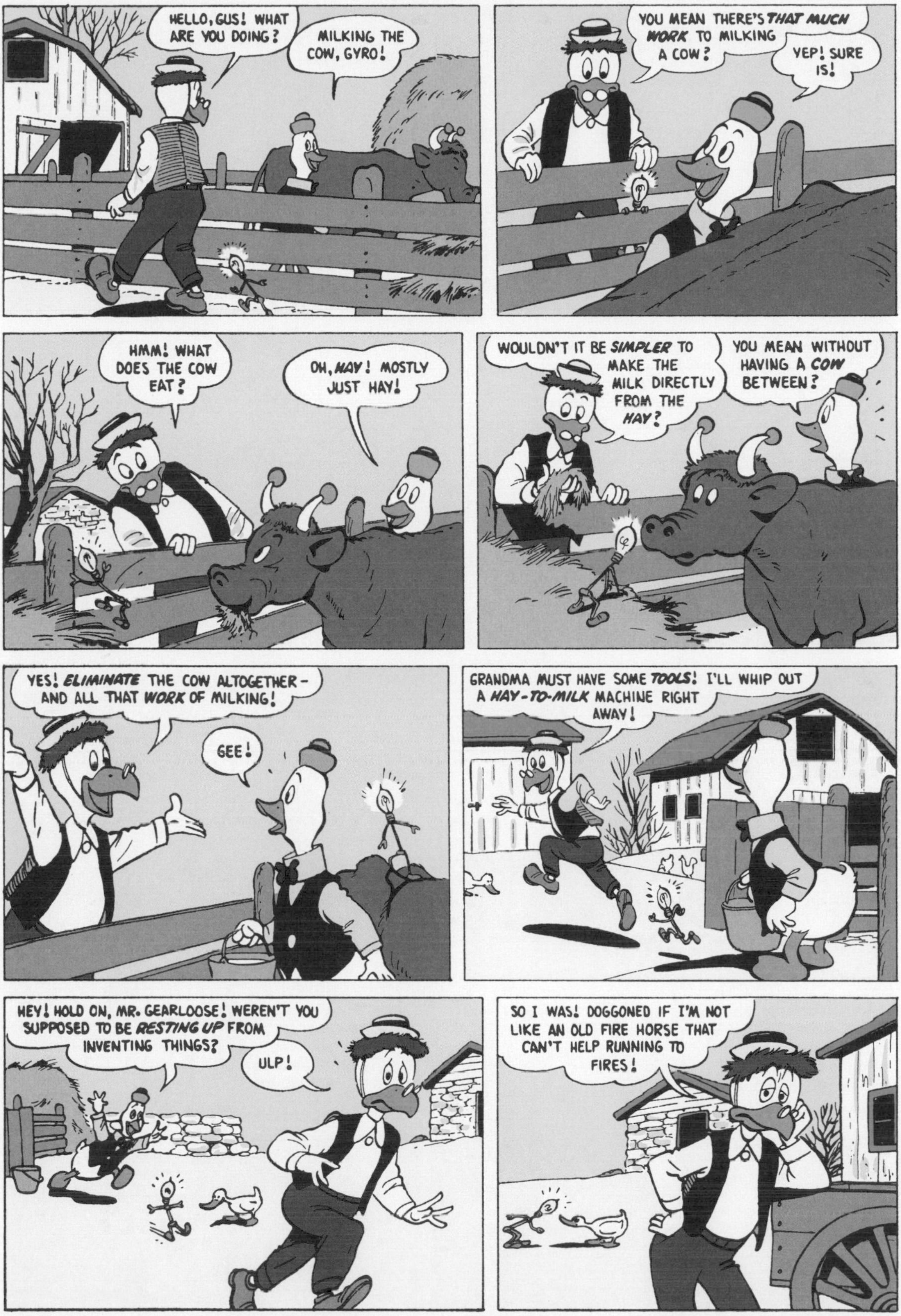
HELLO, GUS! WHAT ARE YOU DOING?
MILKING THE COW, GYRO!
YOU MEAN THERE'S *THAT MUCH WORK* TO MILKING A COW?
YEP! SURE IS!
HMM! WHAT DOES THE COW EAT?
OH, *HAY*! MOSTLY JUST HAY!
WOULDN'T IT BE *SIMPLER* TO MAKE THE MILK DIRECTLY FROM THE *HAY*?
YOU MEAN WITHOUT HAVING A *COW* BETWEEN?
YES! *ELIMINATE* THE COW ALTOGETHER- AND ALL THAT *WORK* OF MILKING!
GEE!
GRANDMA *MUST* HAVE SOME *TOOLS*! I'LL WHIP OUT A *HAY-TO-MILK* MACHINE RIGHT AWAY!
HEY! HOLD ON, MR. GEARLOOSE! WEREN'T YOU SUPPOSED TO BE *RESTING UP* FROM INVENTING THINGS?
ULP!
SO I WAS! DOGGONED IF I'M NOT LIKE AN OLD FIRE HORSE THAT CAN'T HELP RUNNING TO FIRES!

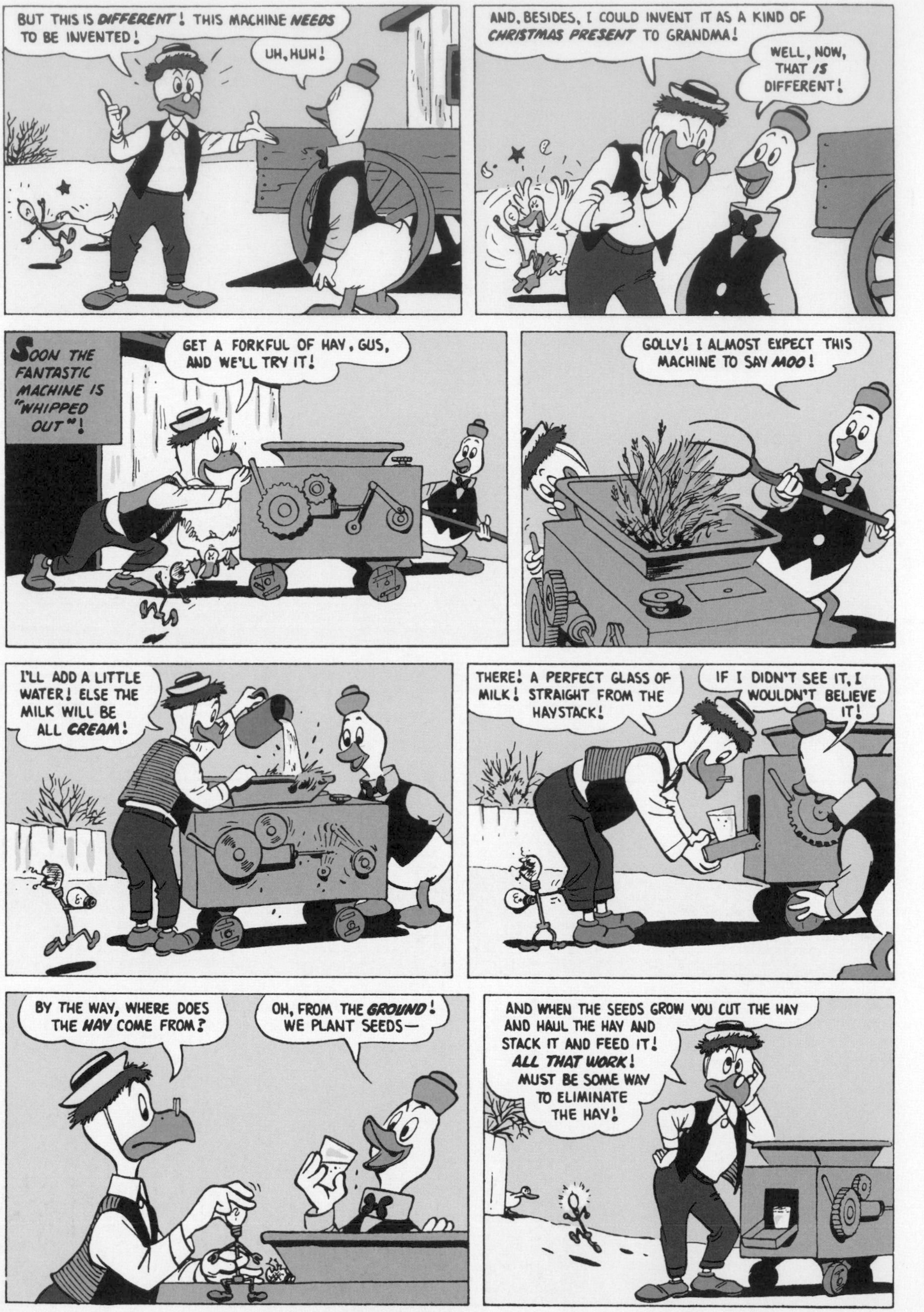
BUT THIS IS DIFFERENT! THIS MACHINE NEEDS TO BE INVENTED!
UH, HUH!
AND, BESIDES, I COULD INVENT IT AS A KIND OF CHRISTMAS PRESENT TO GRANDMA!
WELL, NOW, THAT IS DIFFERENT!
SOON THE FANTASTIC MACHINE IS "WHIPPED OUT"!
GET A FORKFUL OF HAY, GUS, AND WE'LL TRY IT!
GOLLY! I ALMOST EXPECT THIS MACHINE TO SAY MOO!
I'LL ADD A LITTLE WATER! ELSE THE MILK WILL BE ALL CREAM!
THERE! A PERFECT GLASS OF MILK! STRAIGHT FROM THE HAYSTACK!
IF I DIDN'T SEE IT, I WOULDN'T BELIEVE IT!
BY THE WAY, WHERE DOES THE HAY COME FROM?
OH, FROM THE GROUND! WE PLANT SEEDS—
AND WHEN THE SEEDS GROW YOU CUT THE HAY AND HAUL THE HAY AND STACK IT AND FEED IT! ALL THAT WORK! MUST BE SOME WAY TO ELIMINATE THE HAY!

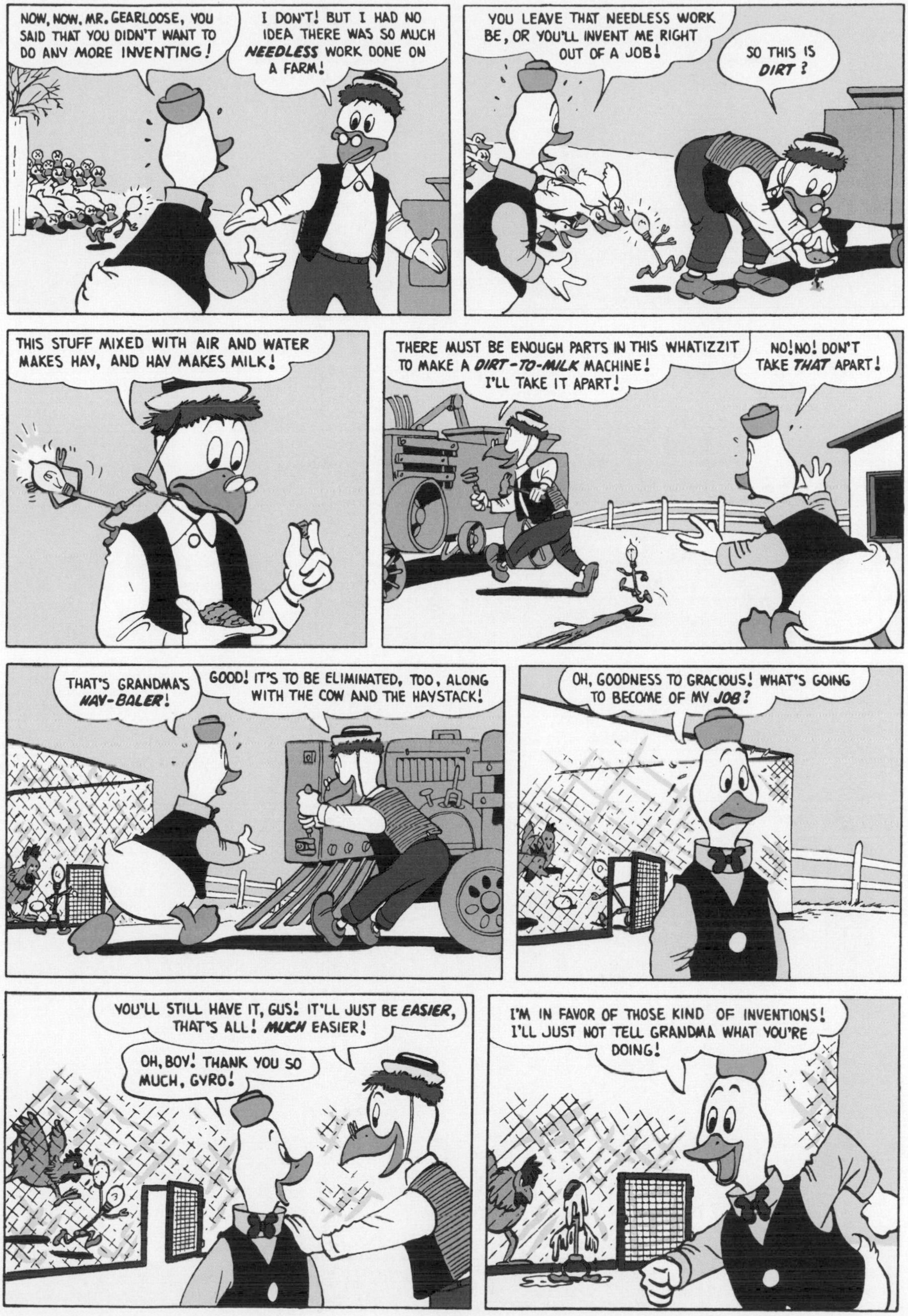
NOW, NOW, MR. GEARLOOSE, YOU SAID THAT YOU DIDN'T WANT TO DO ANY MORE INVENTING!
I DON'T! BUT I HAD NO IDEA THERE WAS SO MUCH NEEDLESS WORK DONE ON A FARM!
YOU LEAVE THAT NEEDLESS WORK BE, OR YOU'LL INVENT ME RIGHT OUT OF A JOB!
SO THIS IS DIRT?
THIS STUFF MIXED WITH AIR AND WATER MAKES HAY, AND HAY MAKES MILK!
THERE MUST BE ENOUGH PARTS IN THIS WHATIZZIT TO MAKE A DIRT-TO-MILK MACHINE! I'LL TAKE IT APART!
NO! NO! DON'T TAKE THAT APART!
THAT'S GRANDMA'S HAY-BALER!
GOOD! IT'S TO BE ELIMINATED, TOO, ALONG WITH THE COW AND THE HAYSTACK!
OH, GOODNESS TO GRACIOUS! WHAT'S GOING TO BECOME OF MY JOB?
YOU'LL STILL HAVE IT, GUS! IT'LL JUST BE EASIER, THAT'S ALL! MUCH EASIER!
OH, BOY! THANK YOU SO MUCH, GYRO!
I'M IN FAVOR OF THOSE KIND OF INVENTIONS! I'LL JUST NOT TELL GRANDMA WHAT YOU'RE DOING!

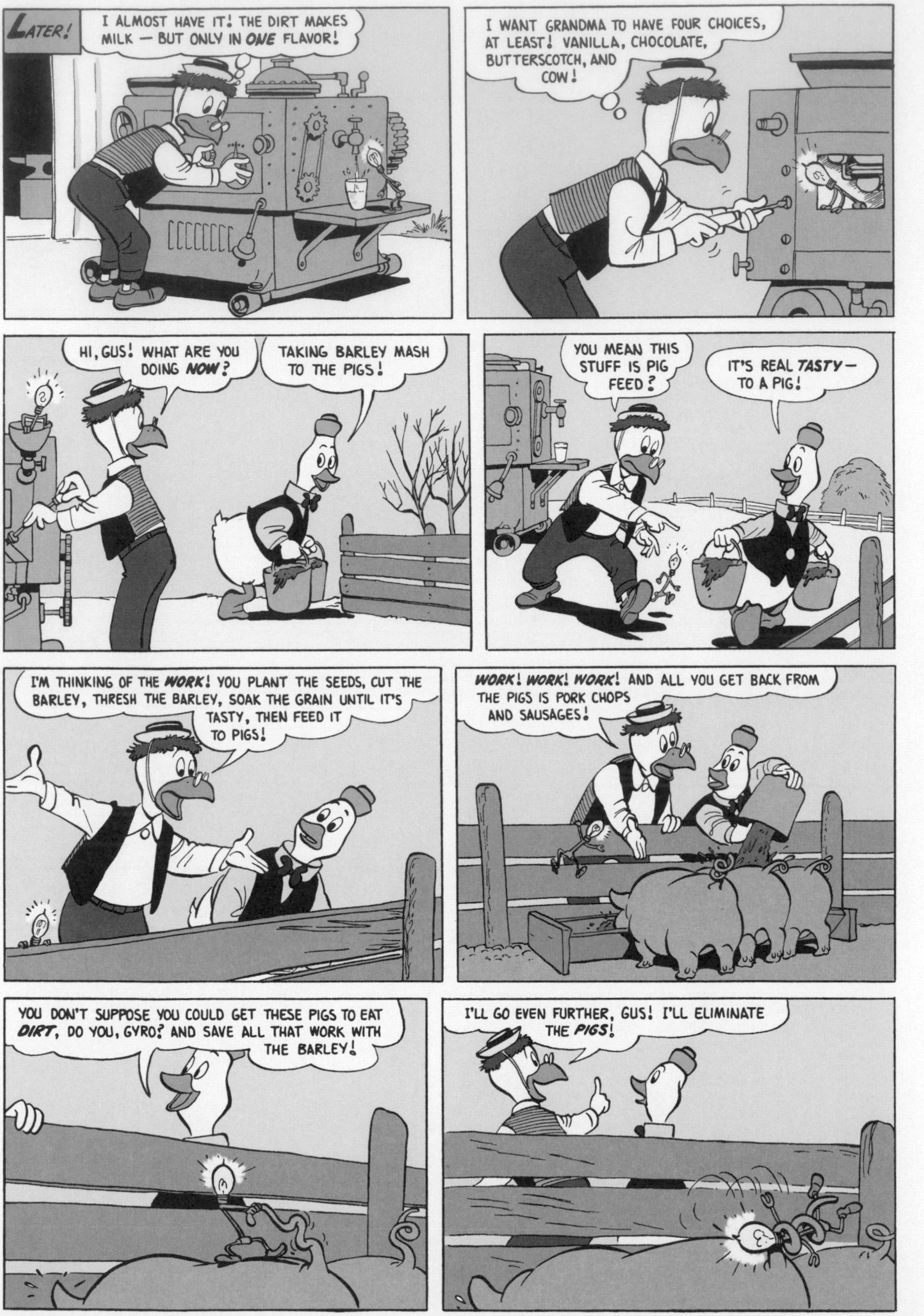
LATER!
I ALMOST HAVE IT! THE DIRT MAKES MILK — BUT ONLY IN ONE FLAVOR!
I WANT GRANDMA TO HAVE FOUR CHOICES, AT LEAST! VANILLA, CHOCOLATE, BUTTERSCOTCH, AND COW!
HI, GUS! WHAT ARE YOU DOING NOW?
TAKING BARLEY MASH TO THE PIGS!
YOU MEAN THIS STUFF IS PIG FEED?
IT'S REAL TASTY — TO A PIG!
I'M THINKING OF THE WORK! YOU PLANT THE SEEDS, CUT THE BARLEY, THRESH THE BARLEY, SOAK THE GRAIN UNTIL IT'S TASTY, THEN FEED IT TO PIGS!
WORK! WORK! WORK! AND ALL YOU GET BACK FROM THE PIGS IS PORK CHOPS AND SAUSAGES!
YOU DON'T SUPPOSE YOU COULD GET THESE PIGS TO EAT DIRT, DO YOU, GYRO? AND SAVE ALL THAT WORK WITH THE BARLEY!
I'LL GO EVEN FURTHER, GUS! I'LL ELIMINATE THE PIGS!

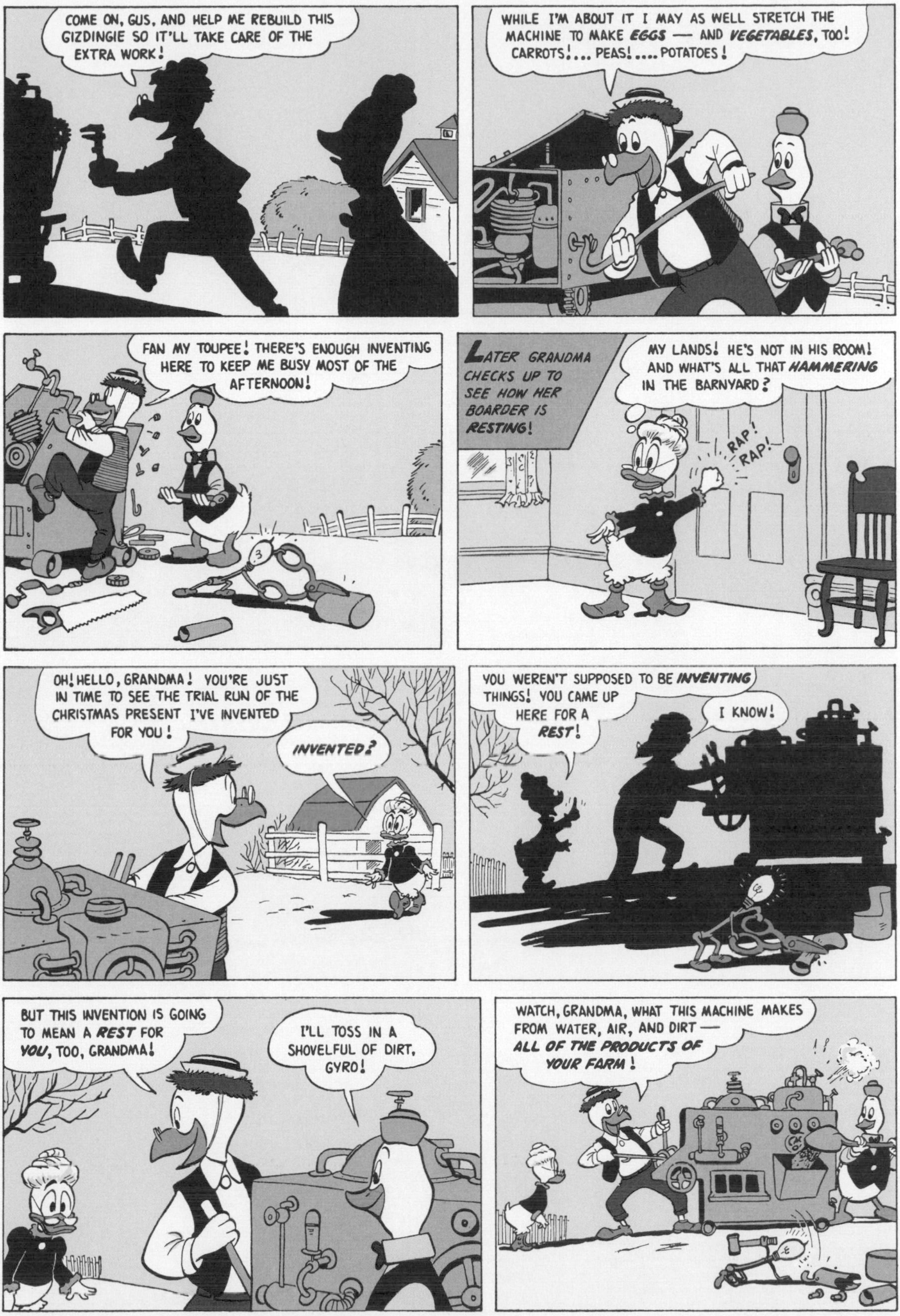
COME ON, GUS, AND HELP ME REBUILD THIS GIZDINGIE SO IT'LL TAKE CARE OF THE EXTRA WORK!
WHILE I'M ABOUT IT I MAY AS WELL STRETCH THE MACHINE TO MAKE EGGS — AND VEGETABLES, TOO! CARROTS!... PEAS!.... POTATOES!
FAN MY TOUPEE! THERE'S ENOUGH INVENTING HERE TO KEEP ME BUSY MOST OF THE AFTERNOON!
LATER GRANDMA CHECKS UP TO SEE HOW HER BOARDER IS RESTING!
MY LANDS! HE'S NOT IN HIS ROOM! AND WHAT'S ALL THAT HAMMERING IN THE BARNYARD?
RAP! RAP!
OH! HELLO, GRANDMA! YOU'RE JUST IN TIME TO SEE THE TRIAL RUN OF THE CHRISTMAS PRESENT I'VE INVENTED FOR YOU!
INVENTED?
YOU WEREN'T SUPPOSED TO BE INVENTING THINGS! YOU CAME UP HERE FOR A REST!
I KNOW!
BUT THIS INVENTION IS GOING TO MEAN A REST FOR YOU, TOO, GRANDMA!
I'LL TOSS IN A SHOVELFUL OF DIRT, GYRO!
WATCH, GRANDMA, WHAT THIS MACHINE MAKES FROM WATER, AIR, AND DIRT — ALL OF THE PRODUCTS OF YOUR FARM!
! !

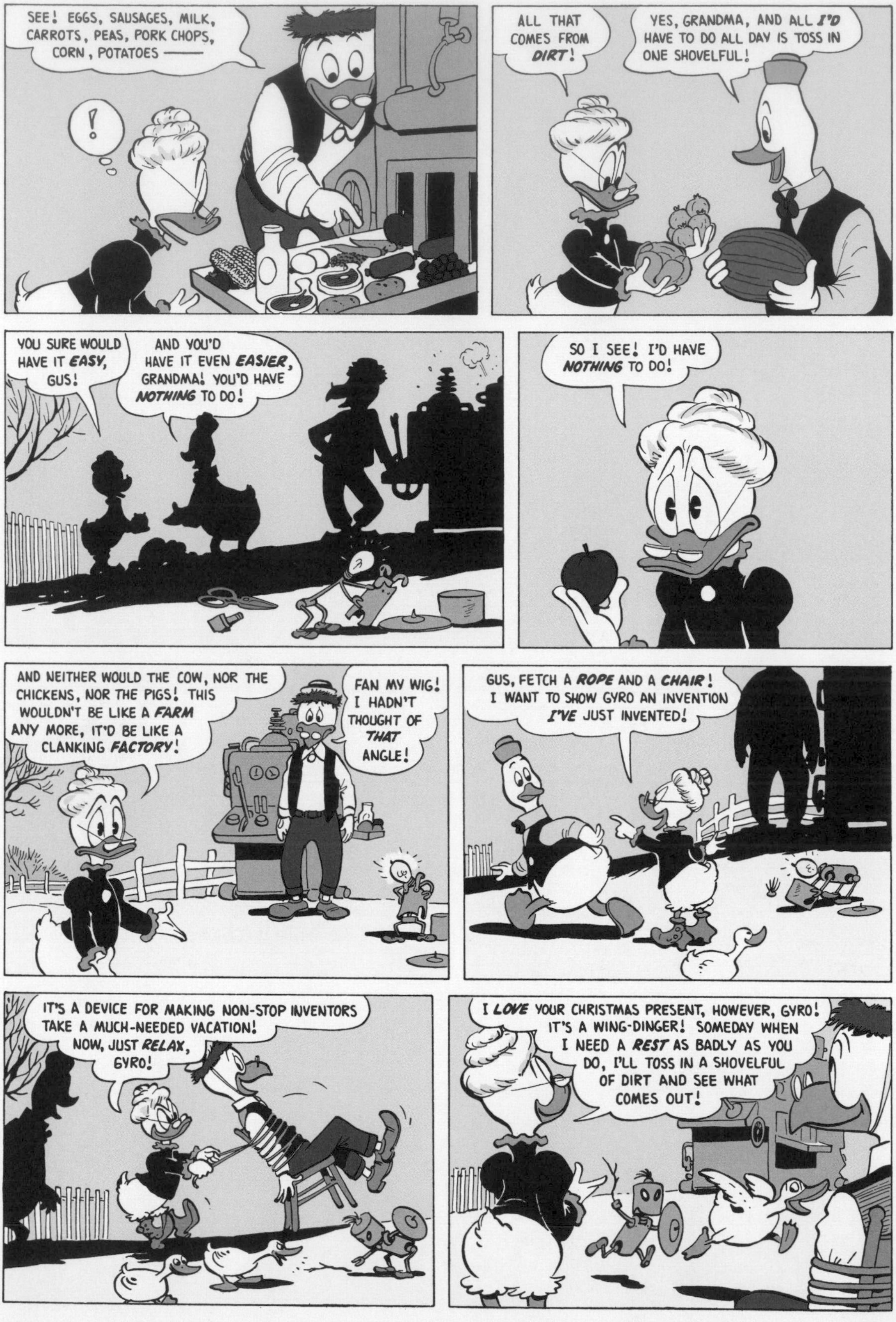
SEE! EGGS, SAUSAGES, MILK, CARROTS, PEAS, PORK CHOPS, CORN, POTATOES ——
!
ALL THAT COMES FROM DIRT!
YES, GRANDMA, AND ALL I'D HAVE TO DO ALL DAY IS TOSS IN ONE SHOVELFUL!
YOU SURE WOULD HAVE IT EASY, GUS!
AND YOU'D HAVE IT EVEN EASIER, GRANDMA! YOU'D HAVE NOTHING TO DO!
SO I SEE! I'D HAVE NOTHING TO DO!
AND NEITHER WOULD THE COW, NOR THE CHICKENS, NOR THE PIGS! THIS WOULDN'T BE LIKE A FARM ANY MORE, IT'D BE LIKE A CLANKING FACTORY!
FAN MY WIG! I HADN'T THOUGHT OF THAT ANGLE!
GUS, FETCH A ROPE AND A CHAIR! I WANT TO SHOW GYRO AN INVENTION I'VE JUST INVENTED!
IT'S A DEVICE FOR MAKING NON-STOP INVENTORS TAKE A MUCH-NEEDED VACATION! NOW, JUST RELAX, GYRO!
I LOVE YOUR CHRISTMAS PRESENT, HOWEVER, GYRO! IT'S A WING-DINGER! SOMEDAY WHEN I NEED A REST AS BADLY AS YOU DO, I'LL TOSS IN A SHOVELFUL OF DIRT AND SEE WHAT COMES OUT!

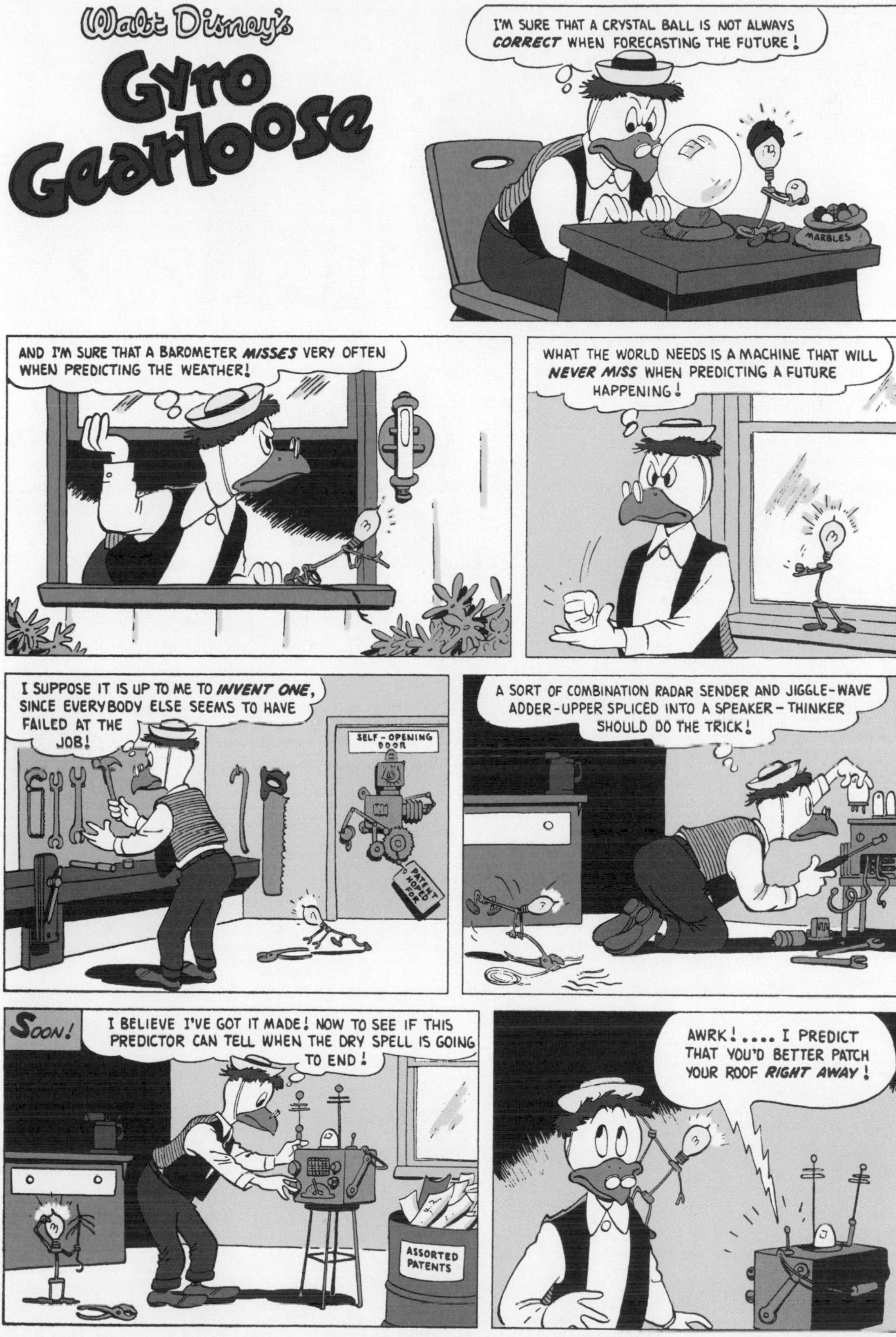
Walt Disney's
Gyro Gearloose
I'M SURE THAT A CRYSTAL BALL IS NOT ALWAYS CORRECT WHEN FORECASTING THE FUTURE!
MARBLES
AND I'M SURE THAT A BAROMETER MISSES VERY OFTEN WHEN PREDICTING THE WEATHER!
WHAT THE WORLD NEEDS IS A MACHINE THAT WILL NEVER MISS WHEN PREDICTING A FUTURE HAPPENING!
I SUPPOSE IT IS UP TO ME TO INVENT ONE, SINCE EVERYBODY ELSE SEEMS TO HAVE FAILED AT THE JOB!
SELF-OPENING DOOR
PATENT HOPED FOR
A SORT OF COMBINATION RADAR SENDER AND JIGGLE-WAVE ADDER-UPPER SPLICED INTO A SPEAKER-THINKER SHOULD DO THE TRICK!
SOON!
I BELIEVE I'VE GOT IT MADE! NOW TO SEE IF THIS PREDICTOR CAN TELL WHEN THE DRY SPELL IS GOING TO END!
ASSORTED PATENTS
AWRK! .... I PREDICT THAT YOU'D BETTER PATCH YOUR ROOF RIGHT AWAY!

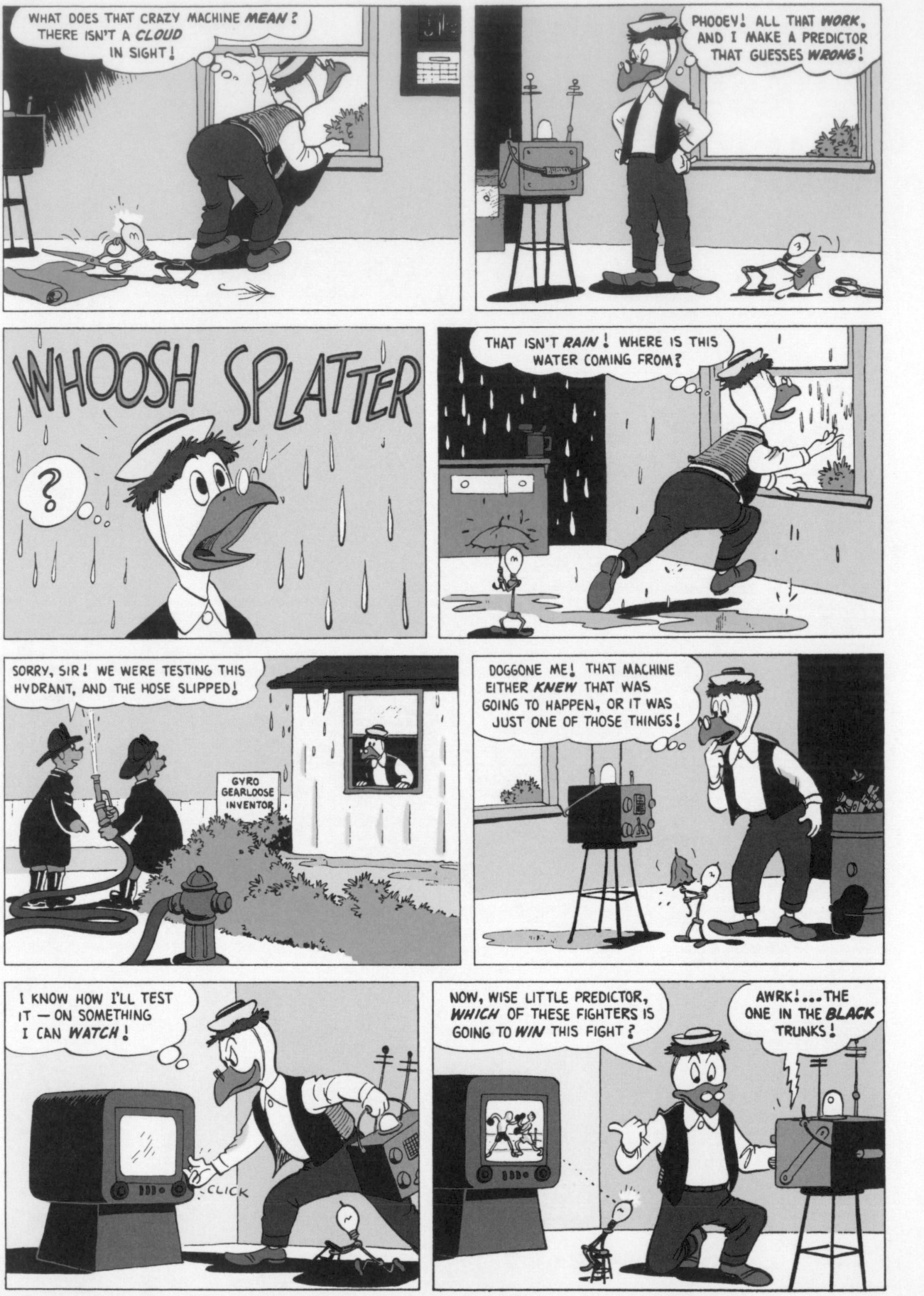
WHAT DOES THAT CRAZY MACHINE MEAN? THERE ISN'T A CLOUD IN SIGHT!
PHOOEY! ALL THAT WORK, AND I MAKE A PREDICTOR THAT GUESSES WRONG!
WHOOSH SPLATTER
?
THAT ISN'T RAIN! WHERE IS THIS WATER COMING FROM?
SORRY, SIR! WE WERE TESTING THIS HYDRANT, AND THE HOSE SLIPPED!
GYRO GEARLOOSE INVENTOR
DOGGONE ME! THAT MACHINE EITHER KNEW THAT WAS GOING TO HAPPEN, OR IT WAS JUST ONE OF THOSE THINGS!
I KNOW HOW I'LL TEST IT — ON SOMETHING I CAN WATCH!
CLICK
NOW, WISE LITTLE PREDICTOR, WHICH OF THESE FIGHTERS IS GOING TO WIN THIS FIGHT?
AWRK!... THE ONE IN THE BLACK TRUNKS!

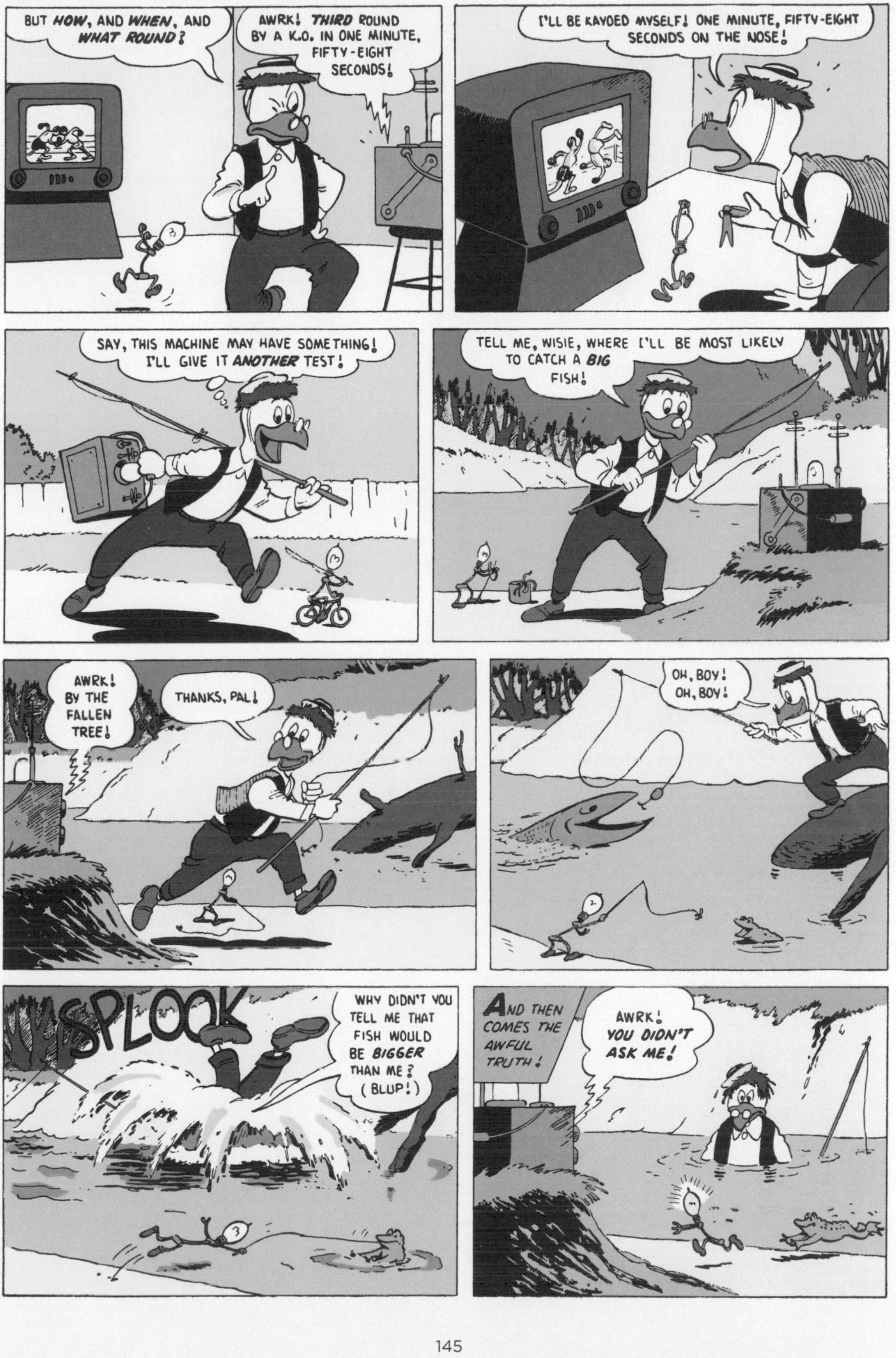

BUT HOW, AND WHEN, AND WHAT ROUND?
AWRK! THIRD ROUND BY A K.O. IN ONE MINUTE, FIFTY-EIGHT SECONDS!
I'LL BE KAYOED MYSELF! ONE MINUTE, FIFTY-EIGHT SECONDS ON THE NOSE!
SAY, THIS MACHINE MAY HAVE SOMETHING! I'LL GIVE IT ANOTHER TEST!
TELL ME, WISIE, WHERE I'LL BE MOST LIKELY TO CATCH A BIG FISH!
AWRK! BY THE FALLEN TREE!
THANKS, PAL!
OH, BOY! OH, BOY!
SPLOOK
WHY DIDN'T YOU TELL ME THAT FISH WOULD BE BIGGER THAN ME? (BLUP!)
AND THEN COMES THE AWFUL TRUTH!
AWRK! YOU DIDN'T ASK ME!

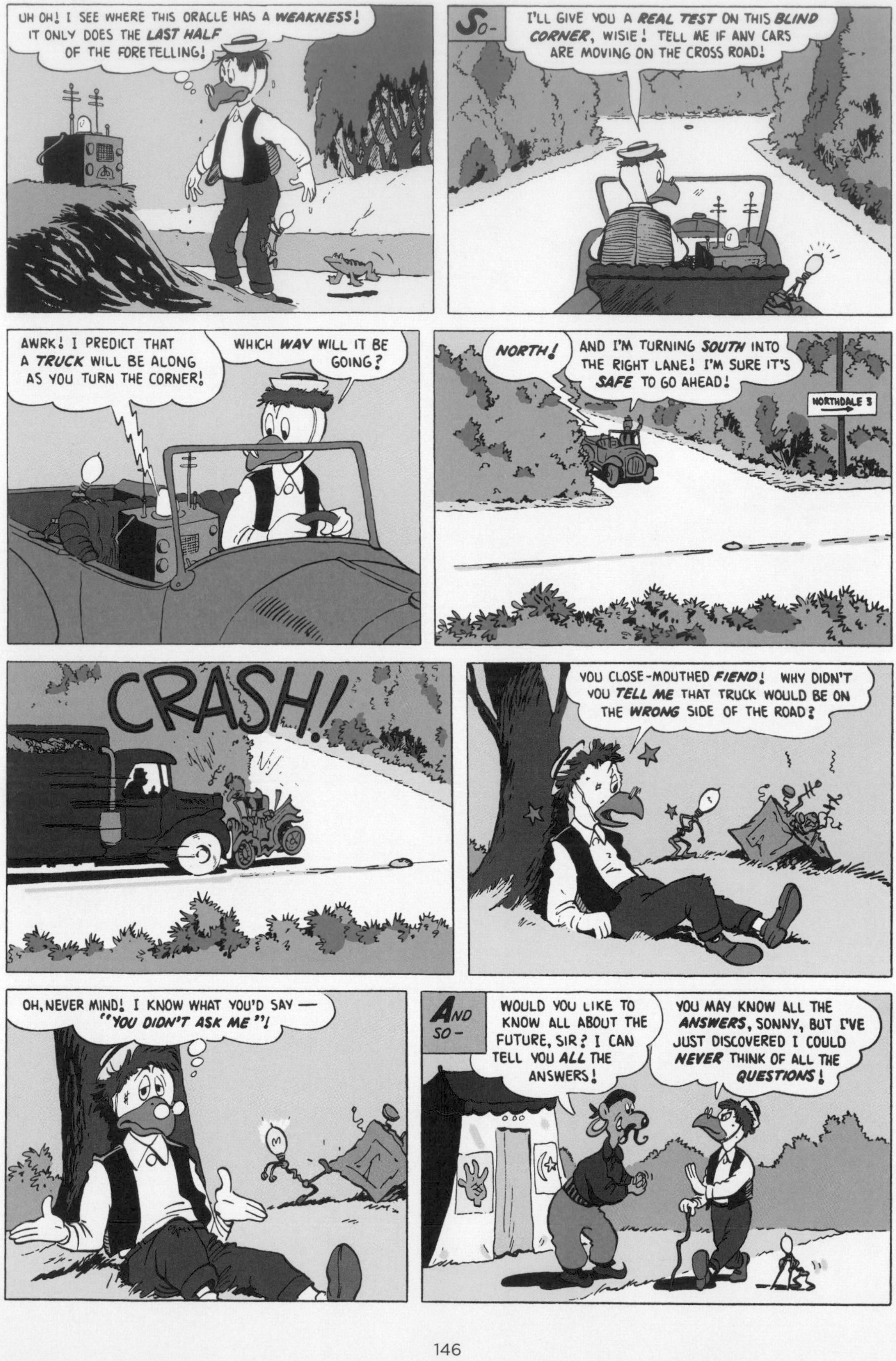

UH OH! I SEE WHERE THIS ORACLE HAS A WEAKNESS! IT ONLY DOES THE LAST HALF OF THE FORETELLING!
SO-
I'LL GIVE YOU A REAL TEST ON THIS BLIND CORNER, WISIE! TELL ME IF ANY CARS ARE MOVING ON THE CROSS ROAD!
AWRK! I PREDICT THAT A TRUCK WILL BE ALONG AS YOU TURN THE CORNER!
WHICH WAY WILL IT BE GOING?
NORTH!
AND I'M TURNING SOUTH INTO THE RIGHT LANE! I'M SURE IT'S SAFE TO GO AHEAD!
NORTHDALE 3
CRASH!
YOU CLOSE-MOUTHED FIEND! WHY DIDN'T YOU TELL ME THAT TRUCK WOULD BE ON THE WRONG SIDE OF THE ROAD?
OH, NEVER MIND! I KNOW WHAT YOU'D SAY — "YOU DIDN'T ASK ME"!
AND SO-
WOULD YOU LIKE TO KNOW ALL ABOUT THE FUTURE, SIR? I CAN TELL YOU ALL THE ANSWERS!
YOU MAY KNOW ALL THE ANSWERS, SONNY, BUT I'VE JUST DISCOVERED I COULD NEVER THINK OF ALL THE QUESTIONS!

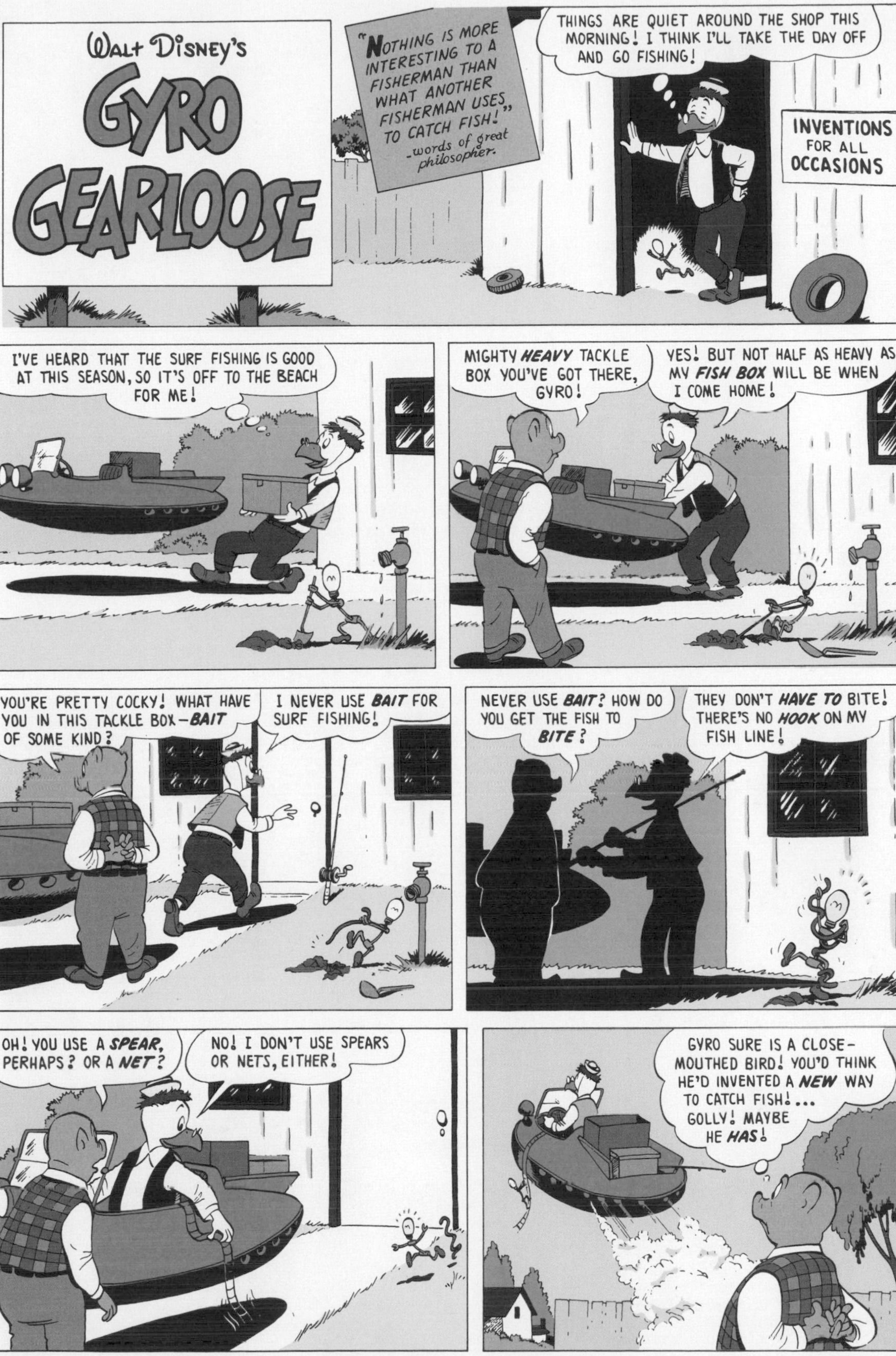

WALT DISNEY'S
GYRO GEARLOOSE
"NOTHING IS MORE INTERESTING TO A FISHERMAN THAN WHAT ANOTHER FISHERMAN USES TO CATCH FISH!" -words of great philosopher.
THINGS ARE QUIET AROUND THE SHOP THIS MORNING! I THINK I'LL TAKE THE DAY OFF AND GO FISHING!
INVENTIONS FOR ALL OCCASIONS
I'VE HEARD THAT THE SURF FISHING IS GOOD AT THIS SEASON, SO IT'S OFF TO THE BEACH FOR ME!
MIGHTY HEAVY TACKLE BOX YOU'VE GOT THERE, GYRO!
YES! BUT NOT HALF AS HEAVY AS MY FISH BOX WILL BE WHEN I COME HOME!
YOU'RE PRETTY COCKY! WHAT HAVE YOU IN THIS TACKLE BOX—BAIT OF SOME KIND?
I NEVER USE BAIT FOR SURF FISHING!
NEVER USE BAIT? HOW DO YOU GET THE FISH TO BITE?
THEY DON'T HAVE TO BITE! THERE'S NO HOOK ON MY FISH LINE!
OH! YOU USE A SPEAR, PERHAPS? OR A NET?
NO! I DON'T USE SPEARS OR NETS, EITHER!
GYRO SURE IS A CLOSE-MOUTHED BIRD! YOU'D THINK HE'D INVENTED A NEW WAY TO CATCH FISH!... GOLLY! MAYBE HE HAS!

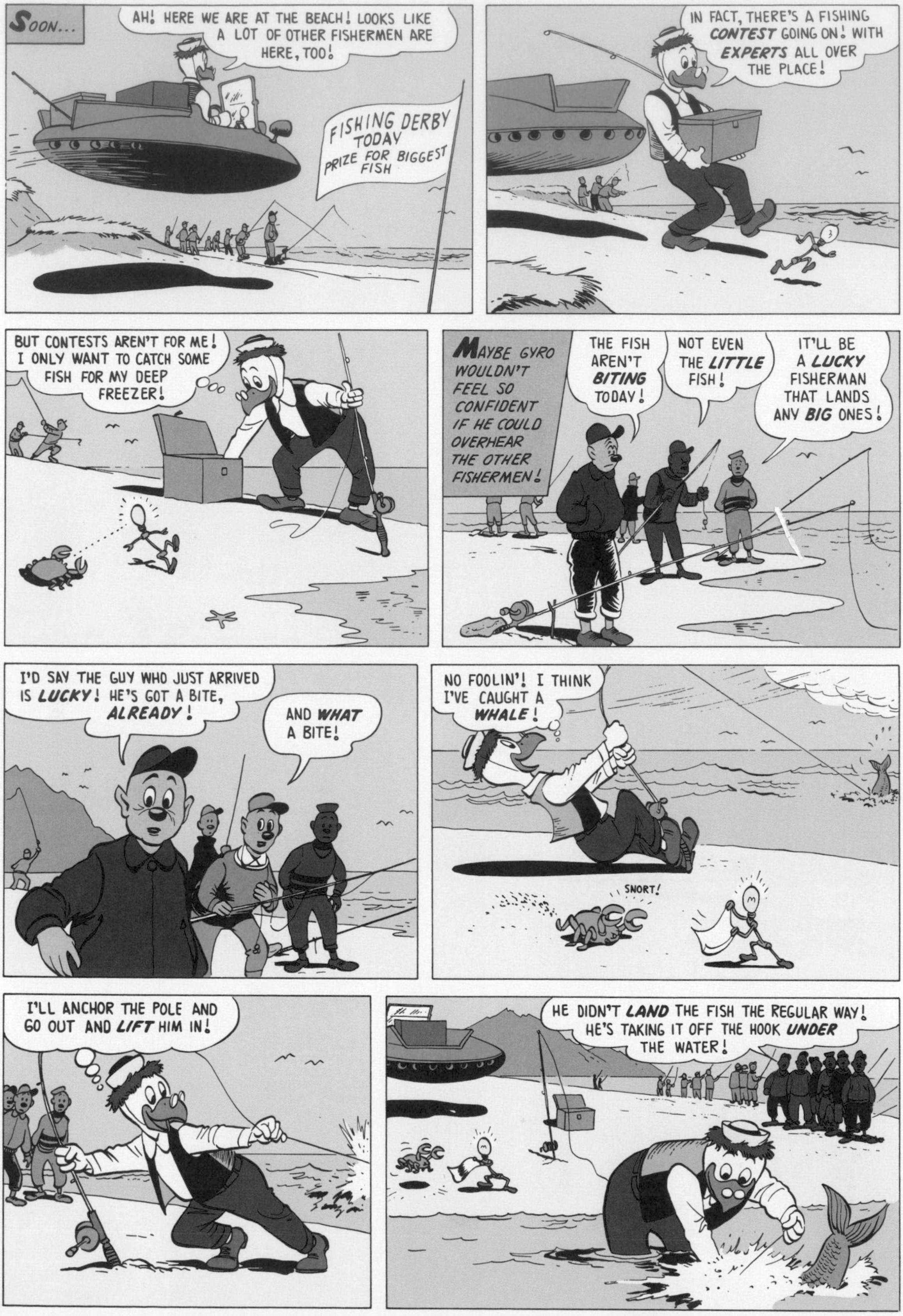
SOON...
AH! HERE WE ARE AT THE BEACH! LOOKS LIKE A LOT OF OTHER FISHERMEN ARE HERE, TOO!
FISHING DERBY TODAY PRIZE FOR BIGGEST FISH
IN FACT, THERE'S A FISHING CONTEST GOING ON! WITH EXPERTS ALL OVER THE PLACE!
BUT CONTESTS AREN'T FOR ME! I ONLY WANT TO CATCH SOME FISH FOR MY DEEP FREEZER!
MAYBE GYRO WOULDN'T FEEL SO CONFIDENT IF HE COULD OVERHEAR THE OTHER FISHERMEN!
THE FISH AREN'T BITING TODAY!
NOT EVEN THE LITTLE FISH!
IT'LL BE A LUCKY FISHERMAN THAT LANDS ANY BIG ONES!
I'D SAY THE GUY WHO JUST ARRIVED IS LUCKY! HE'S GOT A BITE, ALREADY!
AND WHAT A BITE!
NO FOOLIN'! I THINK I'VE CAUGHT A WHALE!
SNORT!
I'LL ANCHOR THE POLE AND GO OUT AND LIFT HIM IN!
HE DIDN'T LAND THE FISH THE REGULAR WAY! HE'S TAKING IT OFF THE HOOK UNDER THE WATER!

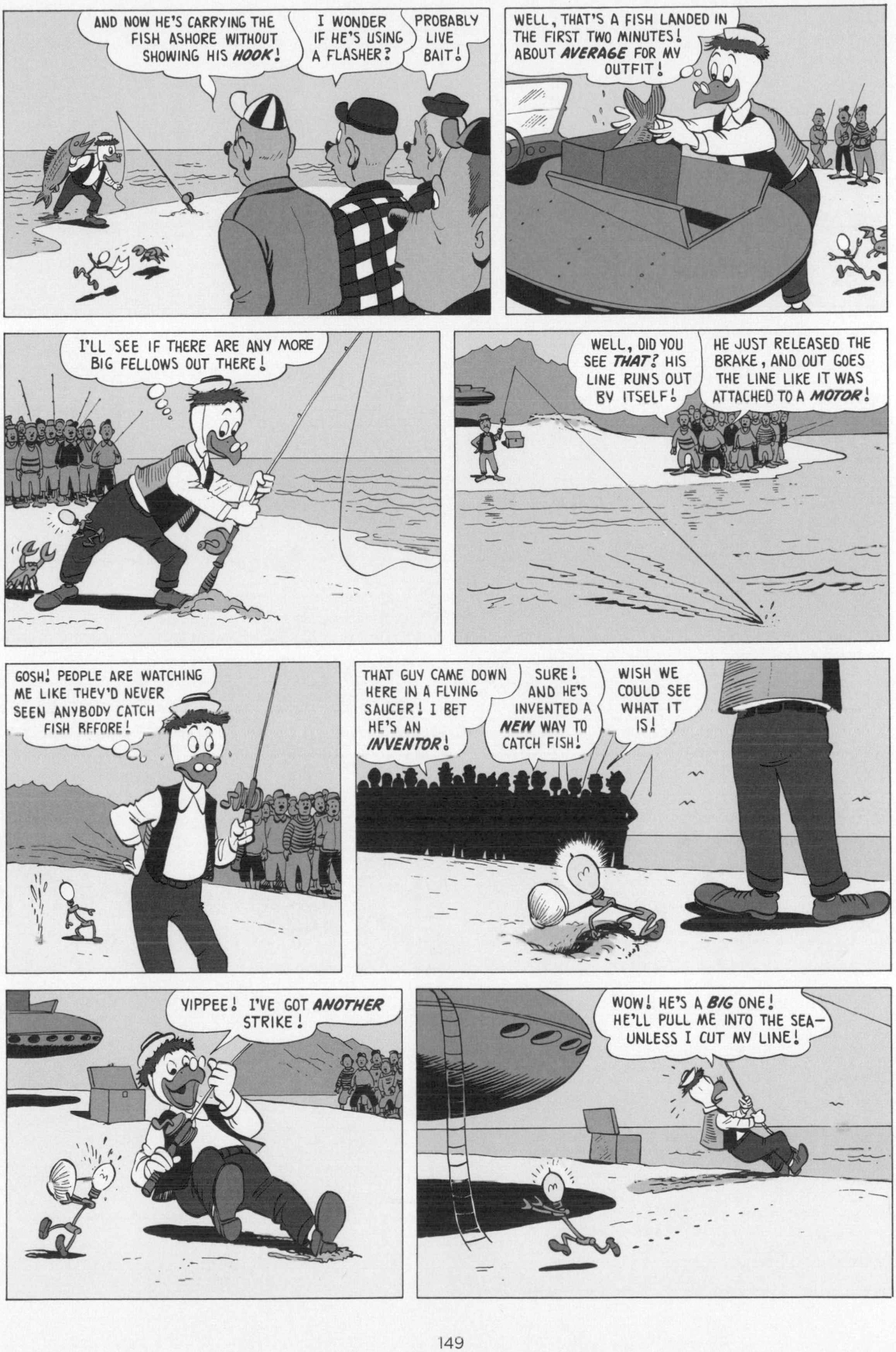
AND NOW HE'S CARRYING THE FISH ASHORE WITHOUT SHOWING HIS HOOK!
I WONDER IF HE'S USING A FLASHER?
PROBABLY LIVE BAIT!
WELL, THAT'S A FISH LANDED IN THE FIRST TWO MINUTES! ABOUT AVERAGE FOR MY OUTFIT!
I'LL SEE IF THERE ARE ANY MORE BIG FELLOWS OUT THERE!
WELL, DID YOU SEE THAT? HIS LINE RUNS OUT BY ITSELF!
HE JUST RELEASED THE BRAKE, AND OUT GOES THE LINE LIKE IT WAS ATTACHED TO A MOTOR!
GOSH! PEOPLE ARE WATCHING ME LIKE THEY'D NEVER SEEN ANYBODY CATCH FISH BEFORE!
THAT GUY CAME DOWN HERE IN A FLYING SAUCER! I BET HE'S AN INVENTOR!
SURE! AND HE'S INVENTED A NEW WAY TO CATCH FISH!
WISH WE COULD SEE WHAT IT IS!
YIPPEE! I'VE GOT ANOTHER STRIKE!
WOW! HE'S A BIG ONE! HE'LL PULL ME INTO THE SEA— UNLESS I CUT MY LINE!

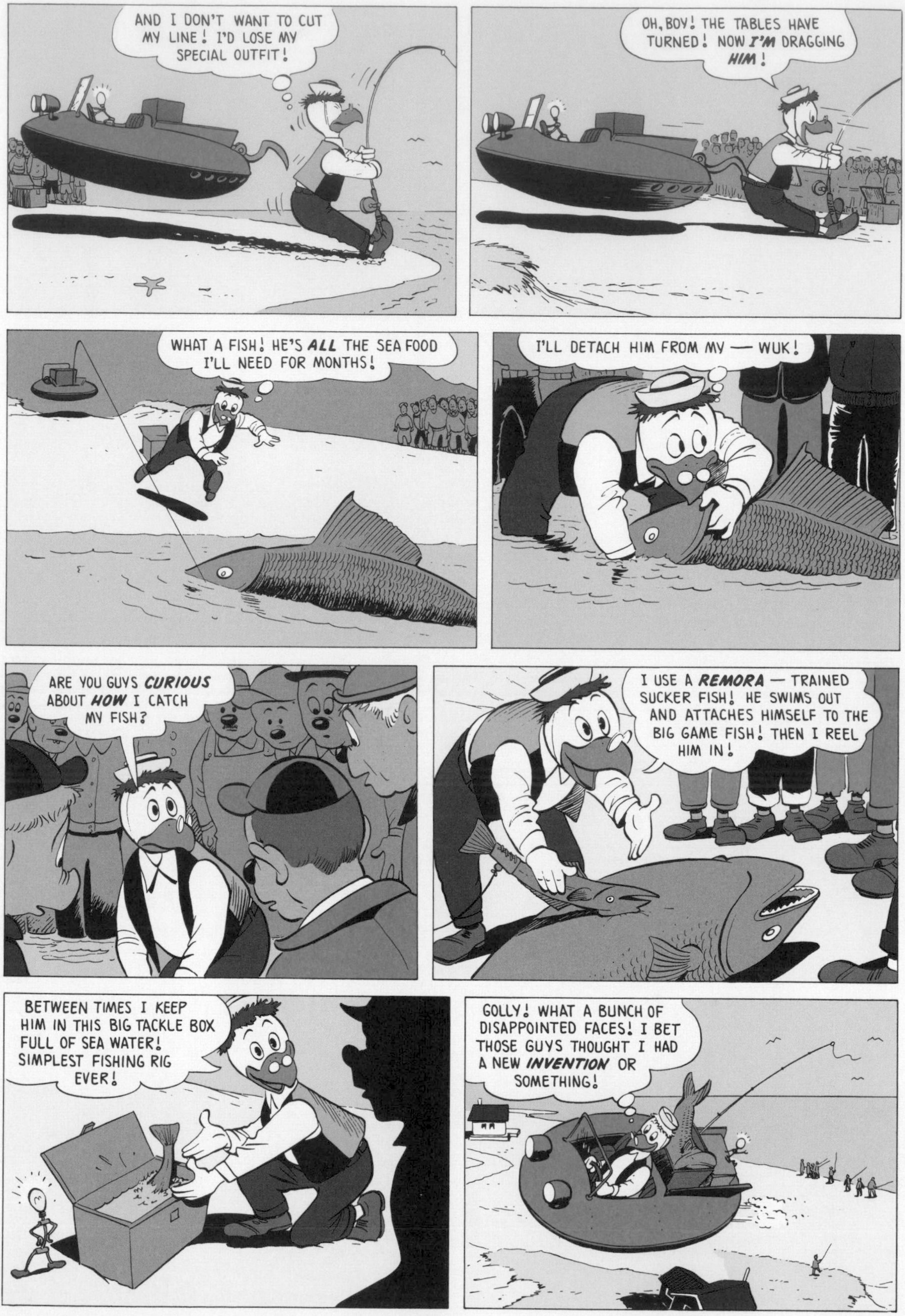
AND I DON'T WANT TO CUT MY LINE! I'D LOSE MY SPECIAL OUTFIT!
OH, BOY! THE TABLES HAVE TURNED! NOW I'M DRAGGING HIM!
WHAT A FISH! HE'S ALL THE SEA FOOD I'LL NEED FOR MONTHS!
I'LL DETACH HIM FROM MY — WUK!
ARE YOU GUYS CURIOUS ABOUT HOW I CATCH MY FISH?
I USE A REMORA — TRAINED SUCKER FISH! HE SWIMS OUT AND ATTACHES HIMSELF TO THE BIG GAME FISH! THEN I REEL HIM IN!
BETWEEN TIMES I KEEP HIM IN THIS BIG TACKLE BOX FULL OF SEA WATER! SIMPLEST FISHING RIG EVER!
GOLLY! WHAT A BUNCH OF DISAPPOINTED FACES! I BET THOSE GUYS THOUGHT I HAD A NEW INVENTION OR SOMETHING!

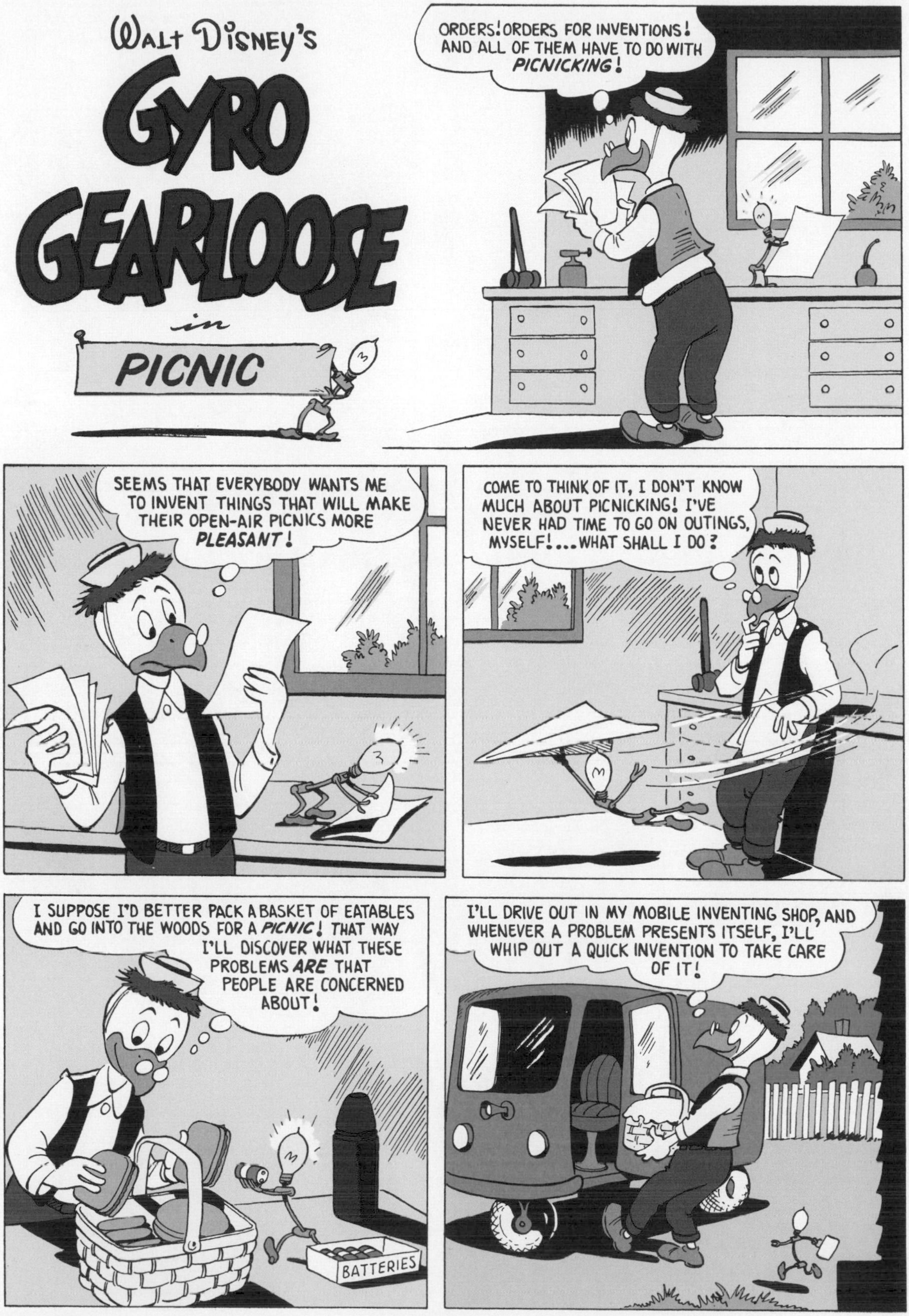
WALT DISNEY'S
GYRO GEARLOOSE
in
PICNIC
ORDERS! ORDERS FOR INVENTIONS! AND ALL OF THEM HAVE TO DO WITH PICNICKING!
SEEMS THAT EVERYBODY WANTS ME TO INVENT THINGS THAT WILL MAKE THEIR OPEN-AIR PICNICS MORE PLEASANT!
COME TO THINK OF IT, I DON'T KNOW MUCH ABOUT PICNICKING! I'VE NEVER HAD TIME TO GO ON OUTINGS, MYSELF!...WHAT SHALL I DO?
I SUPPOSE I'D BETTER PACK A BASKET OF EATABLES AND GO INTO THE WOODS FOR A PICNIC! THAT WAY I'LL DISCOVER WHAT THESE PROBLEMS ARE THAT PEOPLE ARE CONCERNED ABOUT!
BATTERIES
I'LL DRIVE OUT IN MY MOBILE INVENTING SHOP, AND WHENEVER A PROBLEM PRESENTS ITSELF, I'LL WHIP OUT A QUICK INVENTION TO TAKE CARE OF IT!

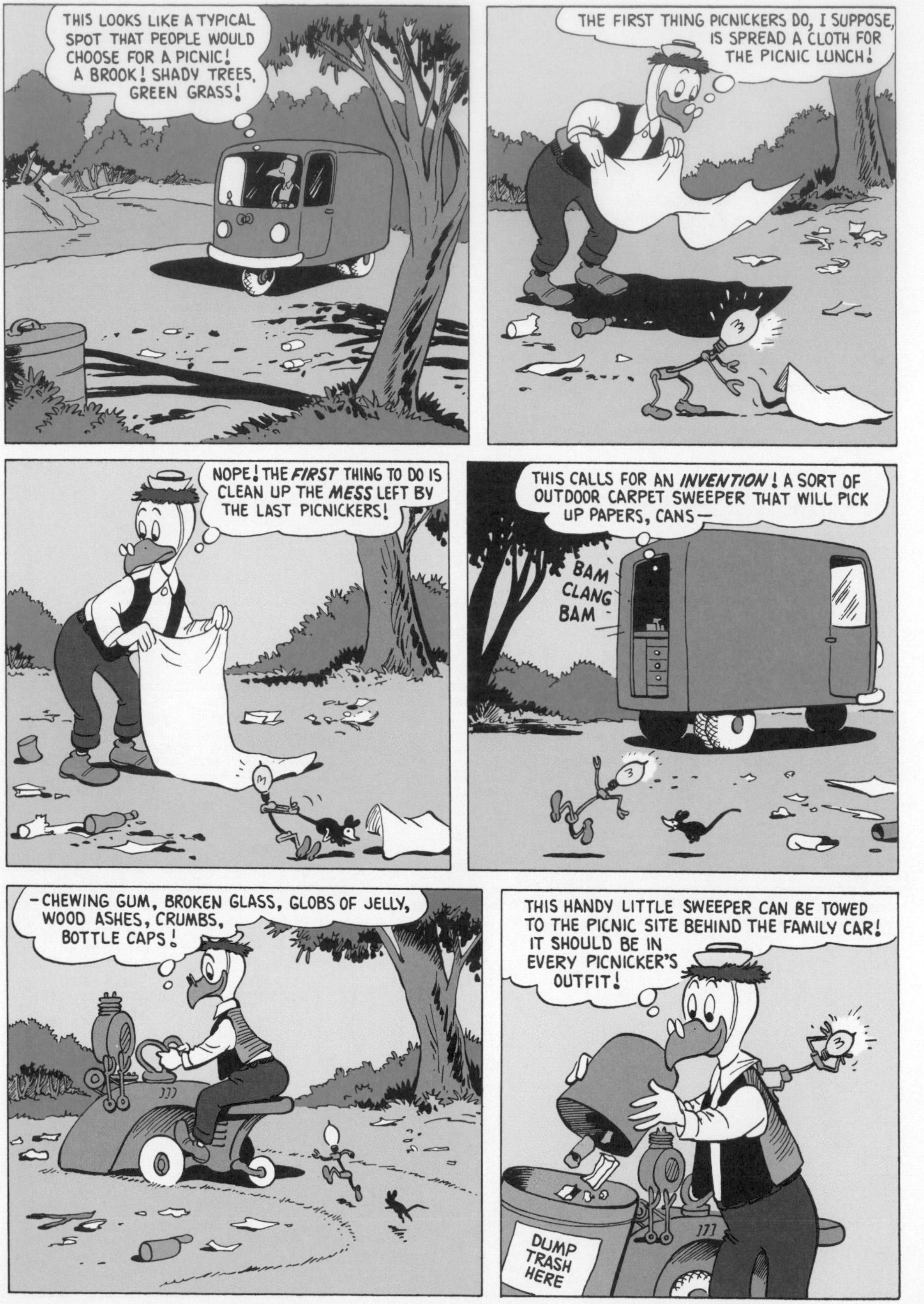
THIS LOOKS LIKE A TYPICAL SPOT THAT PEOPLE WOULD CHOOSE FOR A PICNIC! A BROOK! SHADY TREES, GREEN GRASS!
THE FIRST THING PICNICKERS DO, I SUPPOSE, IS SPREAD A CLOTH FOR THE PICNIC LUNCH!
NOPE! THE *FIRST* THING TO DO IS CLEAN UP THE *MESS* LEFT BY THE LAST PICNICKERS!
THIS CALLS FOR AN *INVENTION*! A SORT OF OUTDOOR CARPET SWEEPER THAT WILL PICK UP PAPERS, CANS—
BAM
CLANG
BAM
—CHEWING GUM, BROKEN GLASS, GLOBS OF JELLY, WOOD ASHES, CRUMBS, BOTTLE CAPS!
THIS HANDY LITTLE SWEEPER CAN BE TOWED TO THE PICNIC SITE BEHIND THE FAMILY CAR! IT SHOULD BE IN EVERY PICNICKER'S OUTFIT!
DUMP TRASH HERE

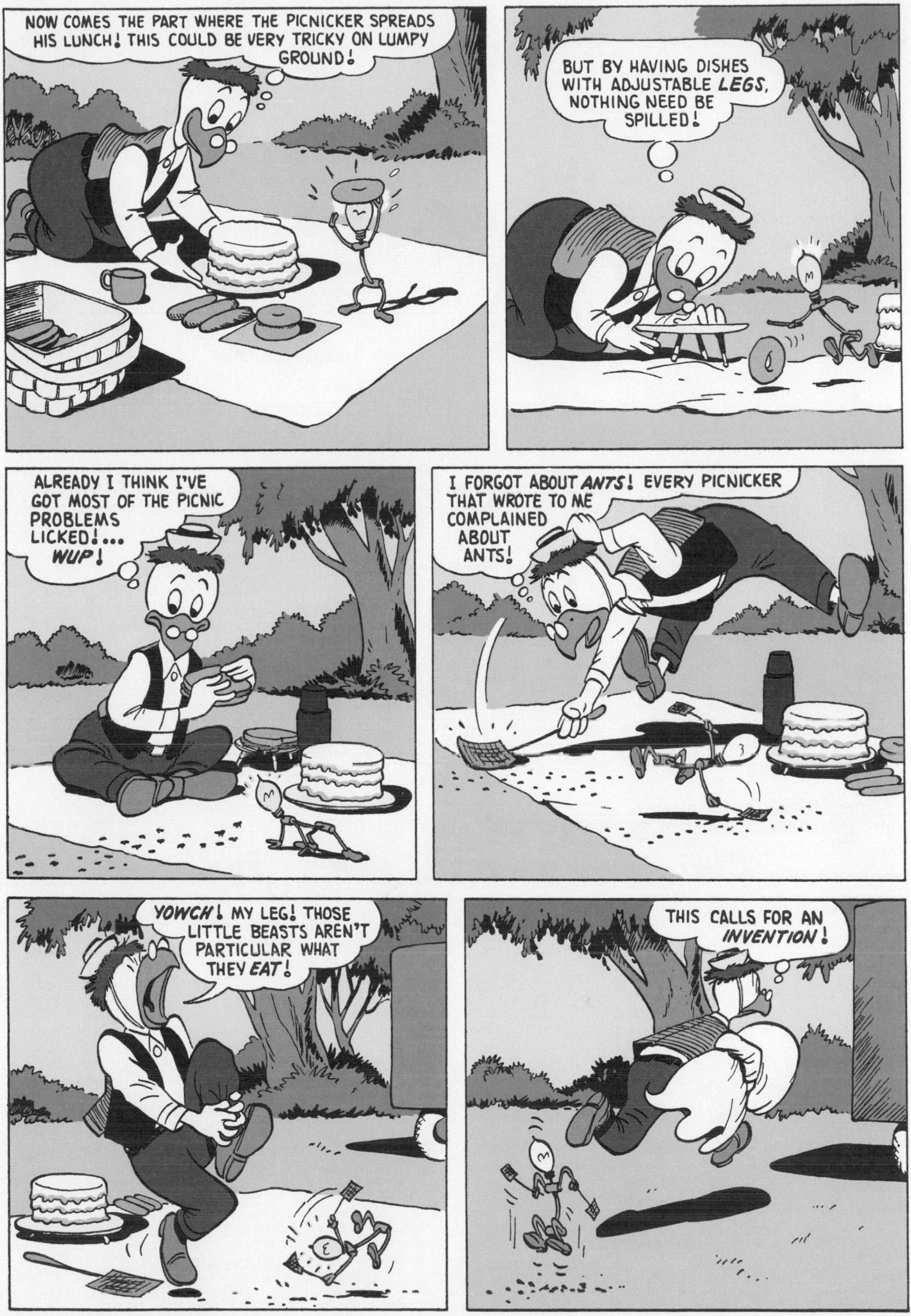

NOW COMES THE PART WHERE THE PICNICKER SPREADS HIS LUNCH! THIS COULD BE VERY TRICKY ON LUMPY GROUND!
BUT BY HAVING DISHES WITH ADJUSTABLE LEGS, NOTHING NEED BE SPILLED!
ALREADY I THINK I'VE GOT MOST OF THE PICNIC PROBLEMS LICKED!... WUP!
I FORGOT ABOUT ANTS! EVERY PICNICKER THAT WROTE TO ME COMPLAINED ABOUT ANTS!
YOWCH! MY LEG! THOSE LITTLE BEASTS AREN'T PARTICULAR WHAT THEY EAT!
THIS CALLS FOR AN INVENTION!

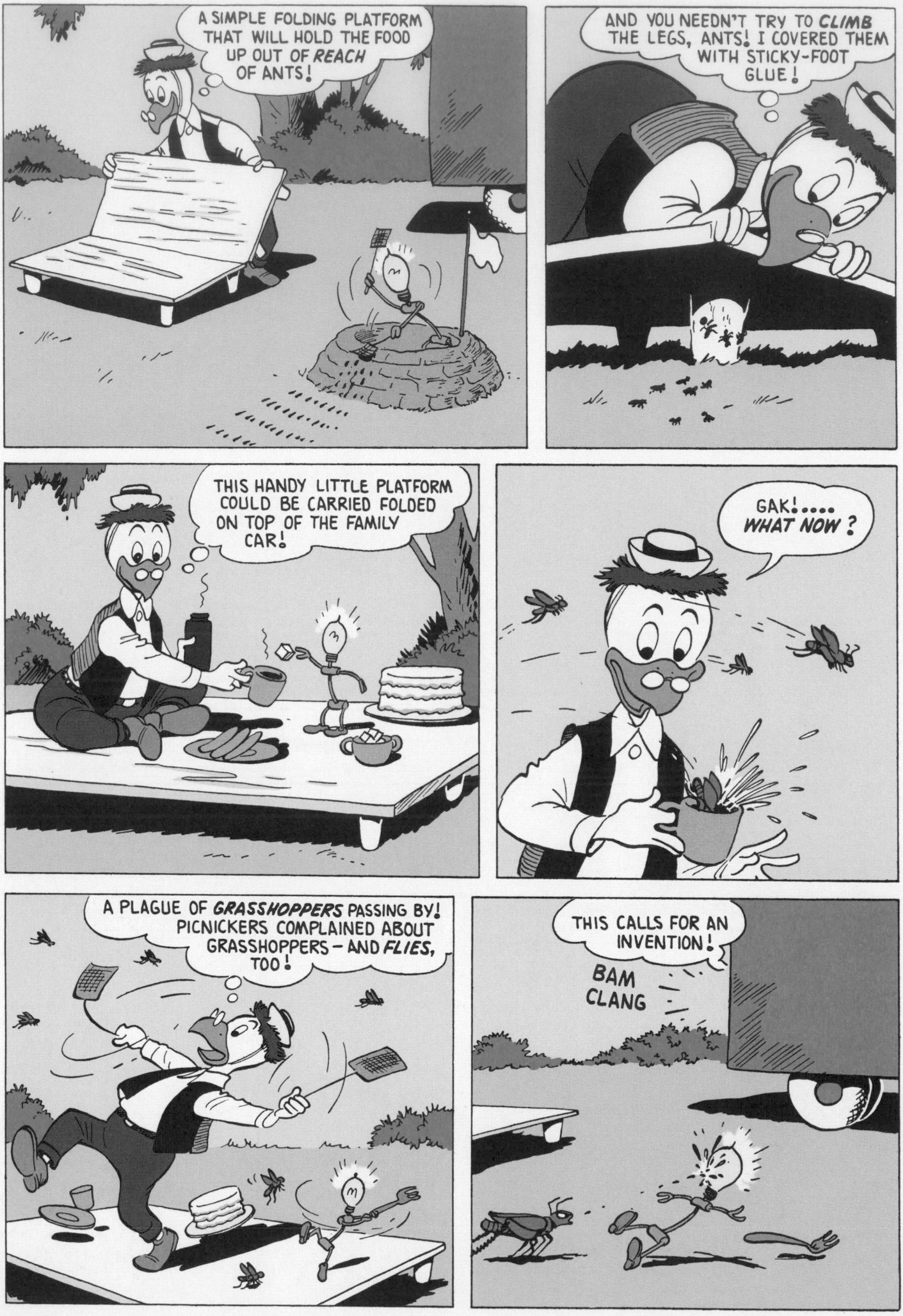
A SIMPLE FOLDING PLATFORM THAT WILL HOLD THE FOOD UP OUT OF REACH OF ANTS!
AND YOU NEEDN'T TRY TO CLIMB THE LEGS, ANTS! I COVERED THEM WITH STICKY-FOOT GLUE!
THIS HANDY LITTLE PLATFORM COULD BE CARRIED FOLDED ON TOP OF THE FAMILY CAR!
GAK!.... WHAT NOW?
A PLAGUE OF GRASSHOPPERS PASSING BY! PICNICKERS COMPLAINED ABOUT GRASSHOPPERS—AND FLIES, TOO!
THIS CALLS FOR AN INVENTION!
BAM
CLANG

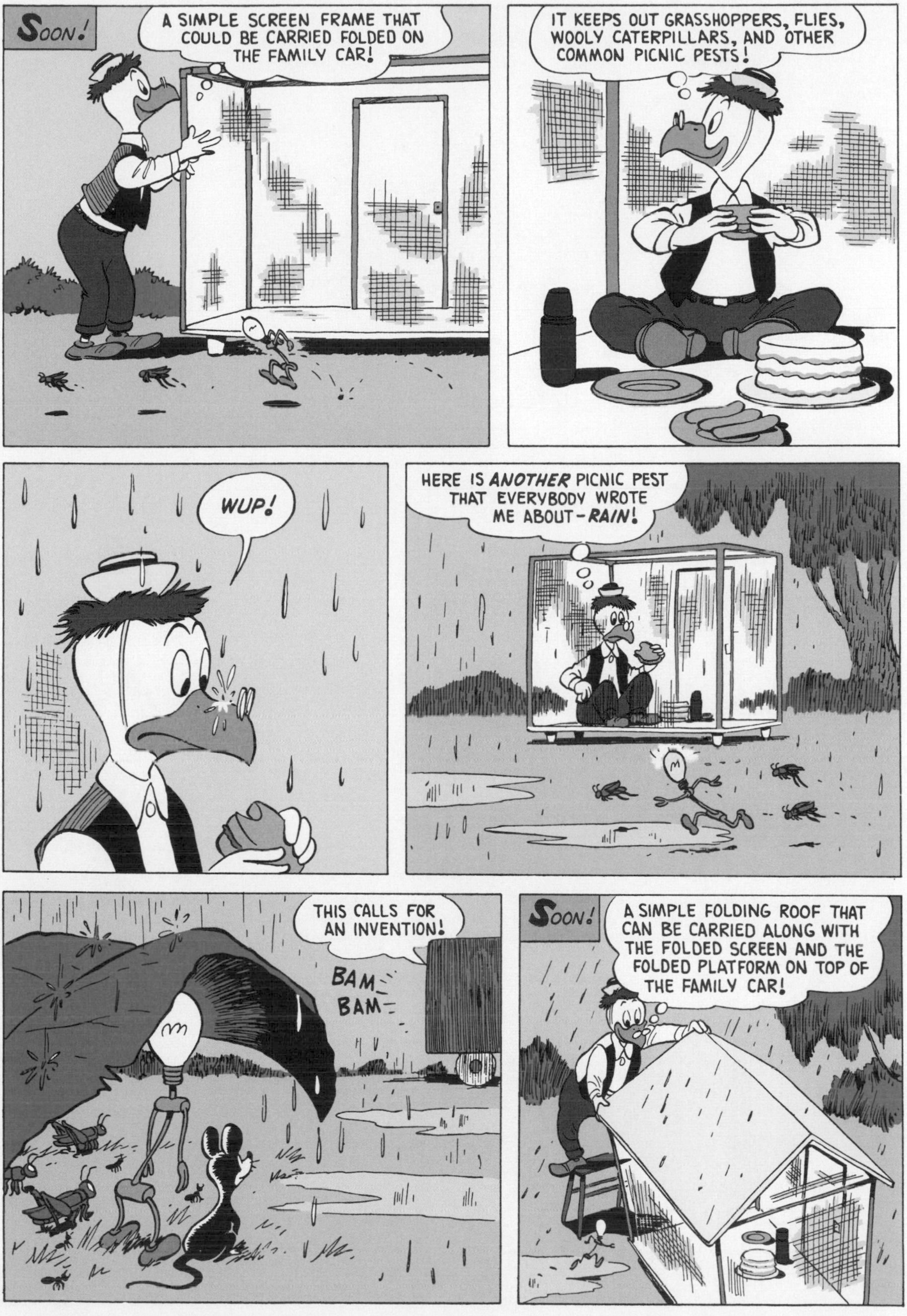
SOON!
A SIMPLE SCREEN FRAME THAT COULD BE CARRIED FOLDED ON THE FAMILY CAR!
IT KEEPS OUT GRASSHOPPERS, FLIES, WOOLY CATERPILLARS, AND OTHER COMMON PICNIC PESTS!
WUP!
HERE IS ANOTHER PICNIC PEST THAT EVERYBODY WROTE ME ABOUT-RAIN!
THIS CALLS FOR AN INVENTION!
BAM BAM
SOON!
A SIMPLE FOLDING ROOF THAT CAN BE CARRIED ALONG WITH THE FOLDED SCREEN AND THE FOLDED PLATFORM ON TOP OF THE FAMILY CAR!

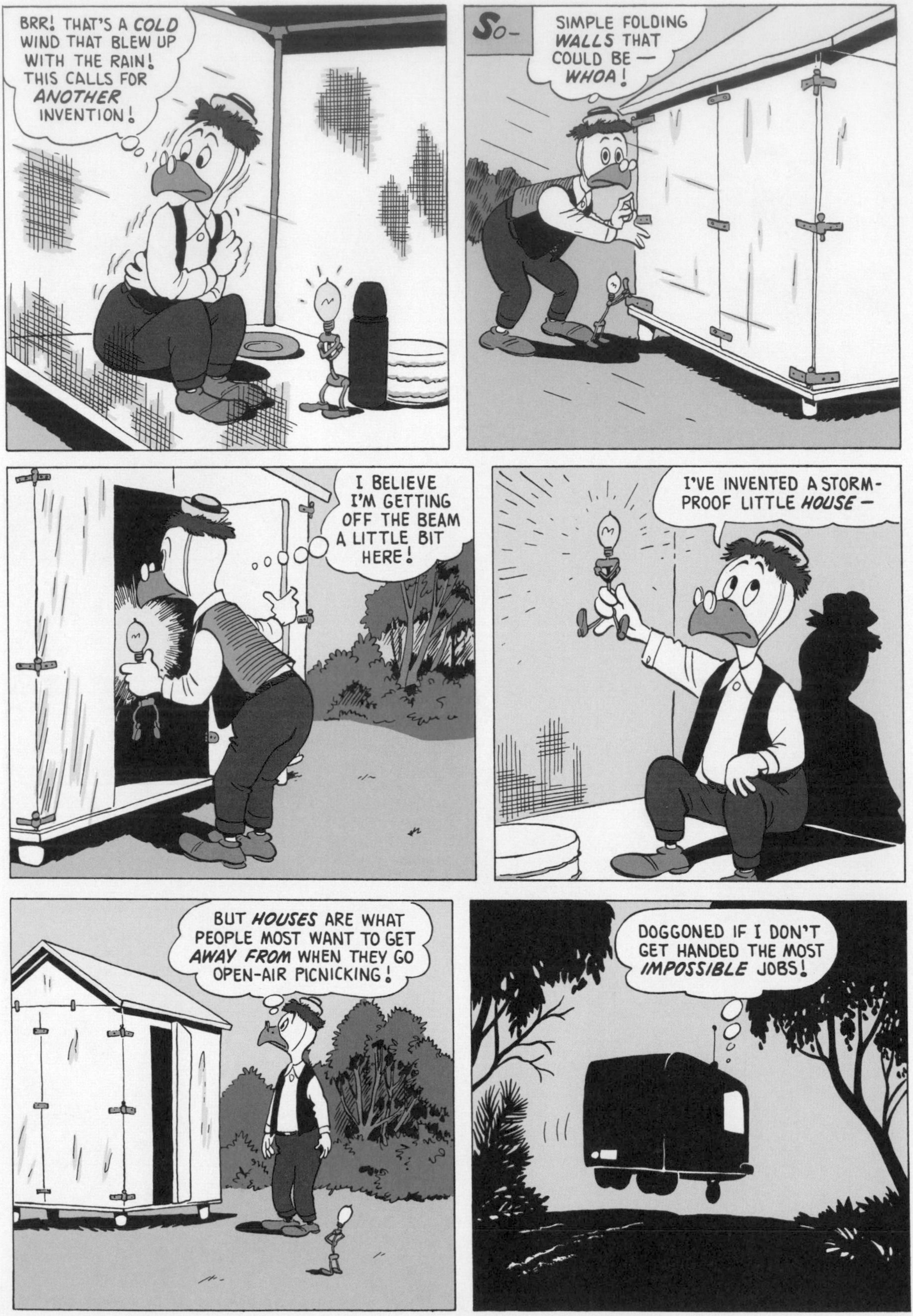
BRR! THAT'S A COLD WIND THAT BLEW UP WITH THE RAIN! THIS CALLS FOR ANOTHER INVENTION!
SO—
SIMPLE FOLDING WALLS THAT COULD BE — WHOA!
I BELIEVE I'M GETTING OFF THE BEAM A LITTLE BIT HERE!
I'VE INVENTED A STORM-PROOF LITTLE HOUSE —
BUT HOUSES ARE WHAT PEOPLE MOST WANT TO GET AWAY FROM WHEN THEY GO OPEN-AIR PICNICKING!
DOGGONED IF I DON'T GET HANDED THE MOST IMPOSSIBLE JOBS!

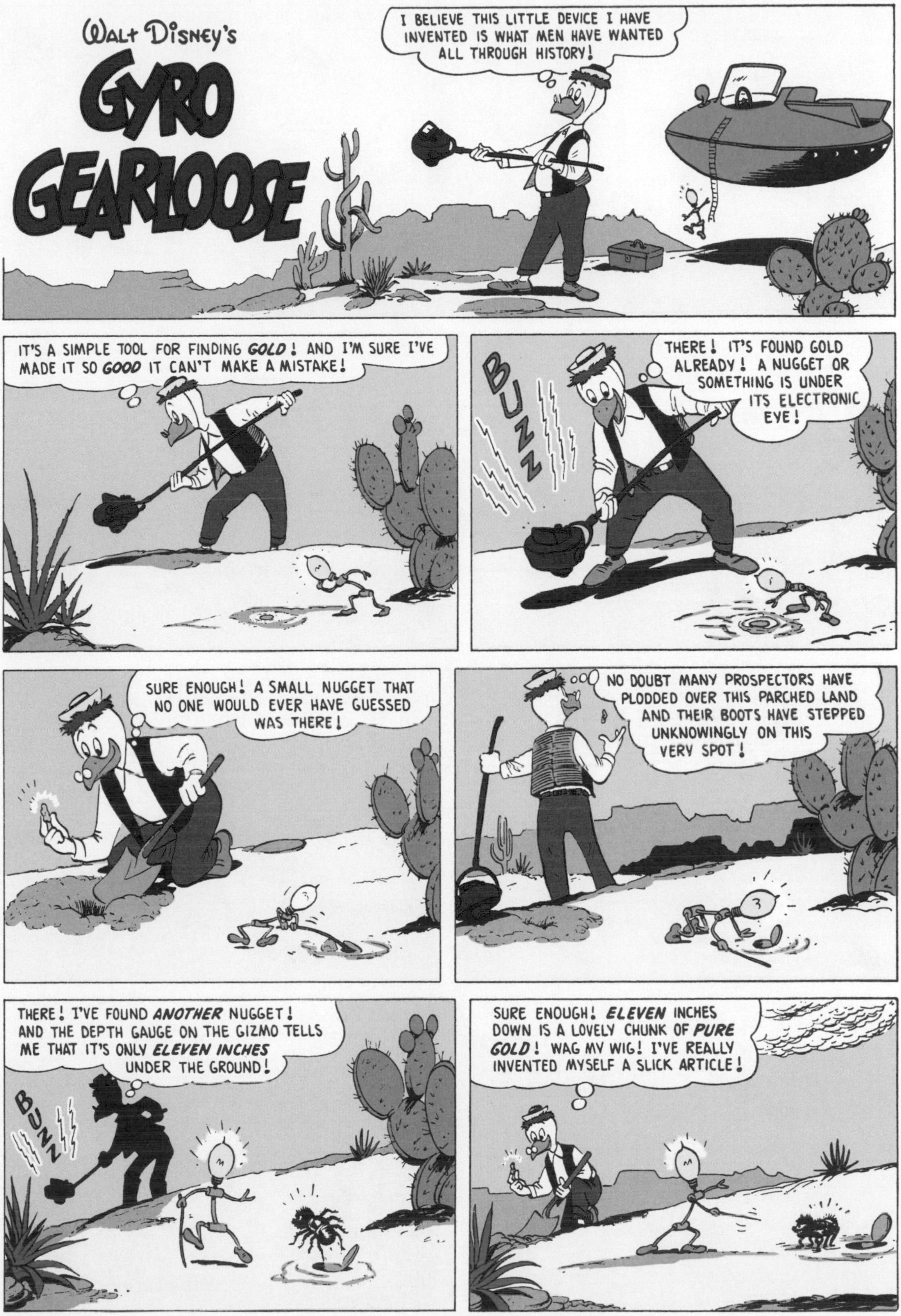
Walt Disney's
GYRO GEARLOOSE
I BELIEVE THIS LITTLE DEVICE I HAVE INVENTED IS WHAT MEN HAVE WANTED ALL THROUGH HISTORY!
IT'S A SIMPLE TOOL FOR FINDING GOLD! AND I'M SURE I'VE MADE IT SO GOOD IT CAN'T MAKE A MISTAKE!
BUZZ
THERE! IT'S FOUND GOLD ALREADY! A NUGGET OR SOMETHING IS UNDER ITS ELECTRONIC EYE!
SURE ENOUGH! A SMALL NUGGET THAT NO ONE WOULD EVER HAVE GUESSED WAS THERE!
NO DOUBT MANY PROSPECTORS HAVE PLODDED OVER THIS PARCHED LAND AND THEIR BOOTS HAVE STEPPED UNKNOWINGLY ON THIS VERY SPOT!
THERE! I'VE FOUND ANOTHER NUGGET! AND THE DEPTH GAUGE ON THE GIZMO TELLS ME THAT IT'S ONLY ELEVEN INCHES UNDER THE GROUND!
BUNZ
SURE ENOUGH! ELEVEN INCHES DOWN IS A LOVELY CHUNK OF PURE GOLD! WAG MY WIG! I'VE REALLY INVENTED MYSELF A SLICK ARTICLE!

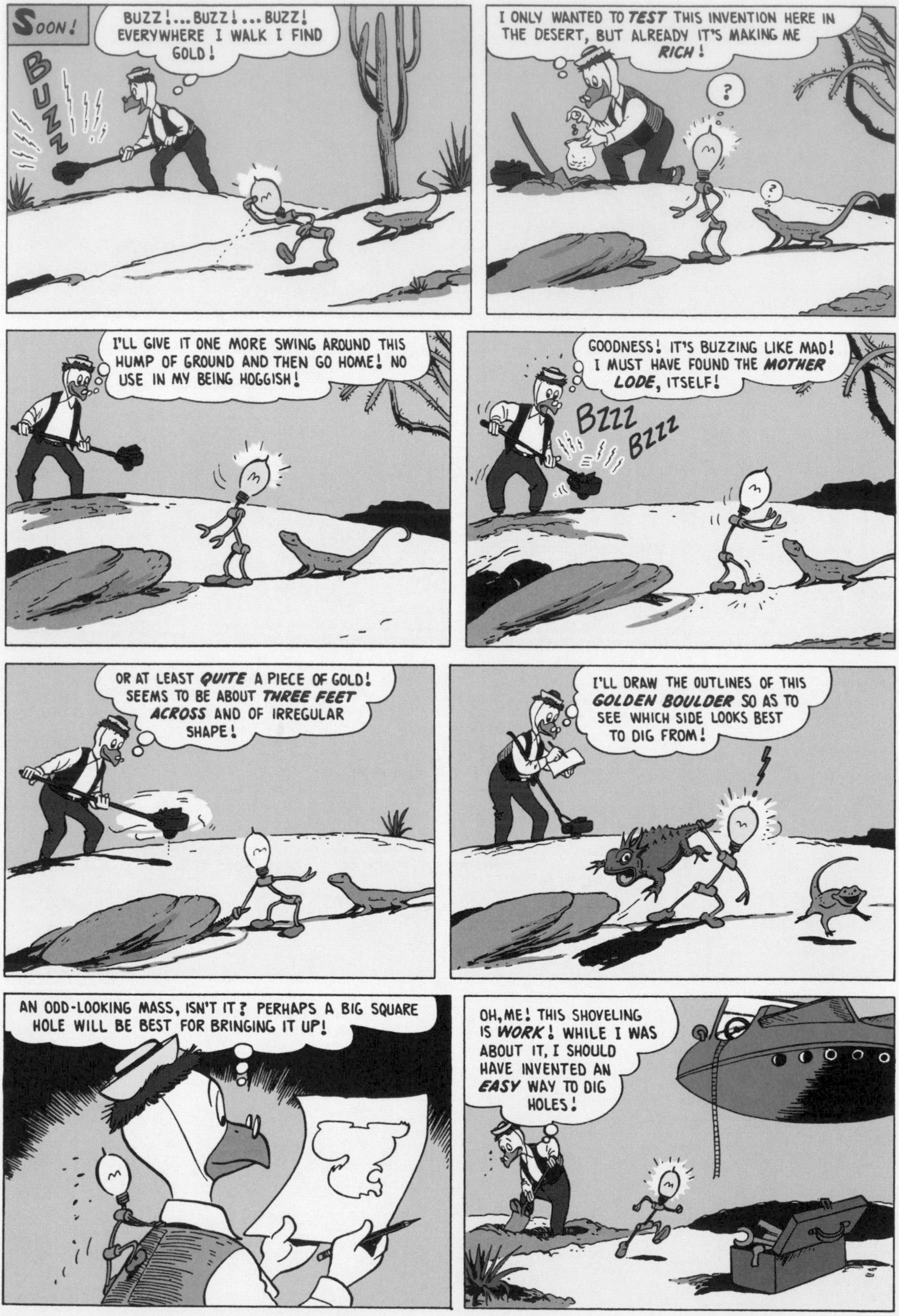
SOON!
BUZZ!...BUZZ!...BUZZ! EVERYWHERE I WALK I FIND GOLD!
BUZZ
I ONLY WANTED TO TEST THIS INVENTION HERE IN THE DESERT, BUT ALREADY IT'S MAKING ME RICH!
?
?
I'LL GIVE IT ONE MORE SWING AROUND THIS HUMP OF GROUND AND THEN GO HOME! NO USE IN MY BEING HOGGISH!
GOODNESS! IT'S BUZZING LIKE MAD! I MUST HAVE FOUND THE MOTHER LODE, ITSELF!
BZZZ BZZZ
OR AT LEAST QUITE A PIECE OF GOLD! SEEMS TO BE ABOUT THREE FEET ACROSS AND OF IRREGULAR SHAPE!
I'LL DRAW THE OUTLINES OF THIS GOLDEN BOULDER SO AS TO SEE WHICH SIDE LOOKS BEST TO DIG FROM!
AN ODD-LOOKING MASS, ISN'T IT? PERHAPS A BIG SQUARE HOLE WILL BE BEST FOR BRINGING IT UP!
OH, ME! THIS SHOVELING IS WORK! WHILE I WAS ABOUT IT, I SHOULD HAVE INVENTED AN EASY WAY TO DIG HOLES!

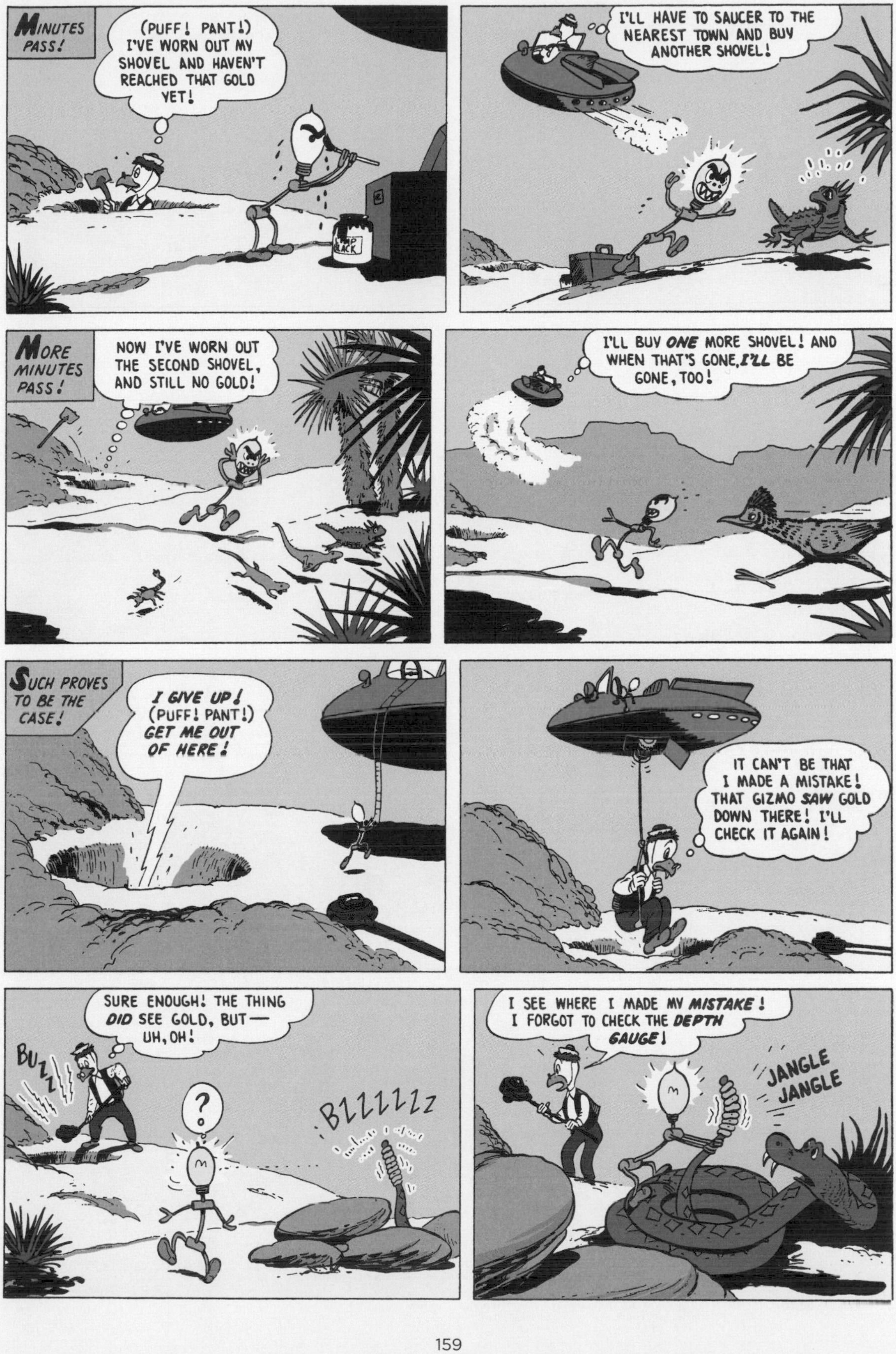
MINUTES PASS!
(PUFF! PANT!) I'VE WORN OUT MY SHOVEL AND HAVEN'T REACHED THAT GOLD YET!
I'LL HAVE TO SAUCER TO THE NEAREST TOWN AND BUY ANOTHER SHOVEL!
MORE MINUTES PASS!
NOW I'VE WORN OUT THE SECOND SHOVEL, AND STILL NO GOLD!
I'LL BUY ONE MORE SHOVEL! AND WHEN THAT'S GONE, I'LL BE GONE, TOO!
SUCH PROVES TO BE THE CASE!
I GIVE UP! (PUFF! PANT!) GET ME OUT OF HERE!
IT CAN'T BE THAT I MADE A MISTAKE! THAT GIZMO SAW GOLD DOWN THERE! I'LL CHECK IT AGAIN!
SURE ENOUGH! THE THING DID SEE GOLD, BUT— UH, OH!
BUZZZ
?
BZZZZZZ
I SEE WHERE I MADE MY MISTAKE! I FORGOT TO CHECK THE DEPTH GAUGE!
JANGLE JANGLE

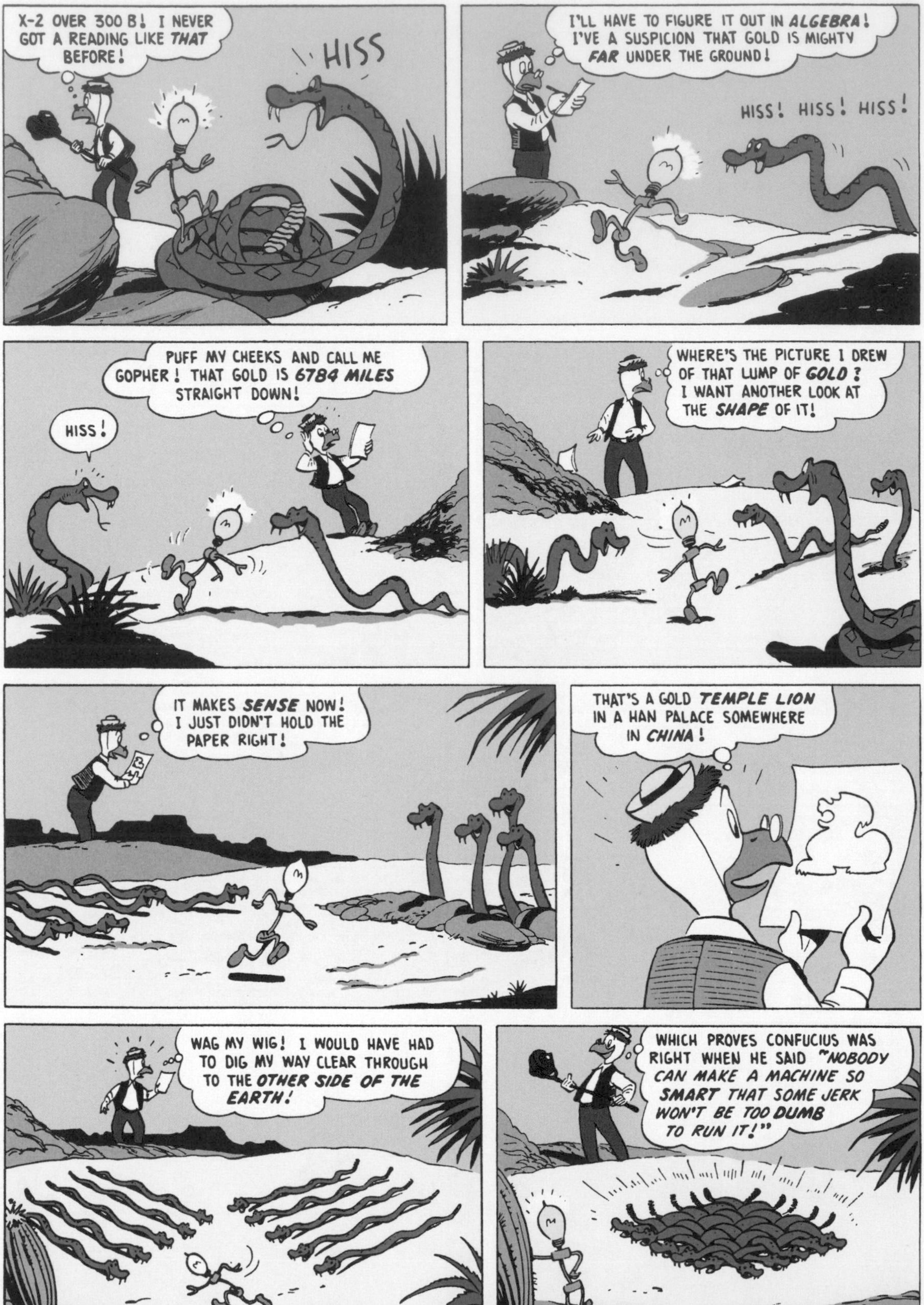
X-2 OVER 300 B! I NEVER GOT A READING LIKE THAT BEFORE!
HISS
I'LL HAVE TO FIGURE IT OUT IN ALGEBRA! I'VE A SUSPICION THAT GOLD IS MIGHTY FAR UNDER THE GROUND!
HISS! HISS! HISS!
PUFF MY CHEEKS AND CALL ME GOPHER! THAT GOLD IS 6784 MILES STRAIGHT DOWN!
HISS!
WHERE'S THE PICTURE I DREW OF THAT LUMP OF GOLD? I WANT ANOTHER LOOK AT THE SHAPE OF IT!
IT MAKES SENSE NOW! I JUST DIDN'T HOLD THE PAPER RIGHT!
THAT'S A GOLD TEMPLE LION IN A HAN PALACE SOMEWHERE IN CHINA!
WAG MY WIG! I WOULD HAVE HAD TO DIG MY WAY CLEAR THROUGH TO THE OTHER SIDE OF THE EARTH!
WHICH PROVES CONFUCIUS WAS RIGHT WHEN HE SAID "NOBODY CAN MAKE A MACHINE SO SMART THAT SOME JERK WON'T BE TOO DUMB TO RUN IT!"

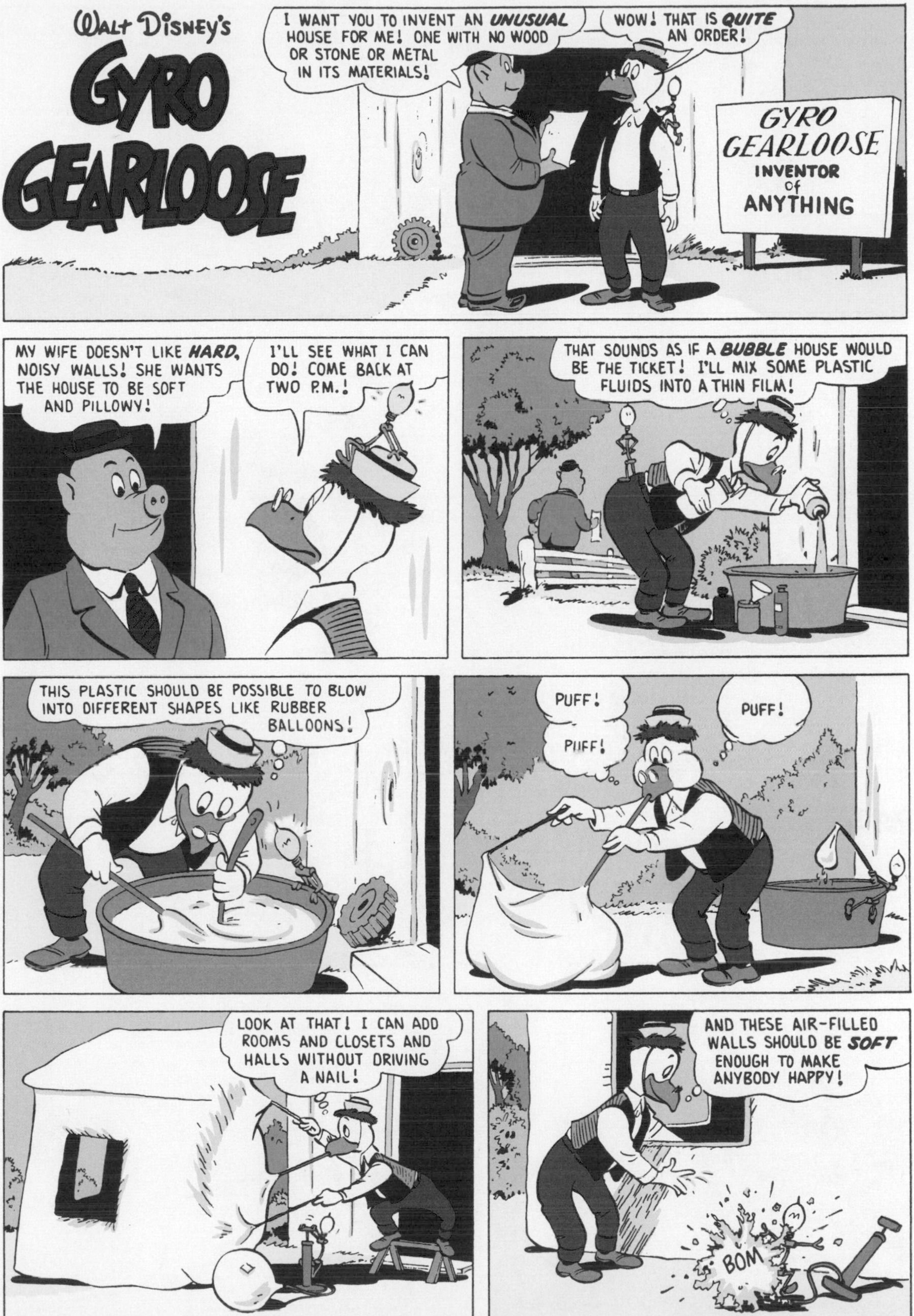
Walt Disney's
GYRO GEARLOOSE
I WANT YOU TO INVENT AN UNUSUAL HOUSE FOR ME! ONE WITH NO WOOD OR STONE OR METAL IN ITS MATERIALS!
WOW! THAT IS QUITE AN ORDER!
GYRO GEARLOOSE INVENTOR of ANYTHING
MY WIFE DOESN'T LIKE HARD, NOISY WALLS! SHE WANTS THE HOUSE TO BE SOFT AND PILLOWY!
I'LL SEE WHAT I CAN DO! COME BACK AT TWO P.M.!
THAT SOUNDS AS IF A BUBBLE HOUSE WOULD BE THE TICKET! I'LL MIX SOME PLASTIC FLUIDS INTO A THIN FILM!
THIS PLASTIC SHOULD BE POSSIBLE TO BLOW INTO DIFFERENT SHAPES LIKE RUBBER BALLOONS!
PUFF!
PUFF!
PUFF!
LOOK AT THAT! I CAN ADD ROOMS AND CLOSETS AND HALLS WITHOUT DRIVING A NAIL!
AND THESE AIR-FILLED WALLS SHOULD BE SOFT ENOUGH TO MAKE ANYBODY HAPPY!
BOM

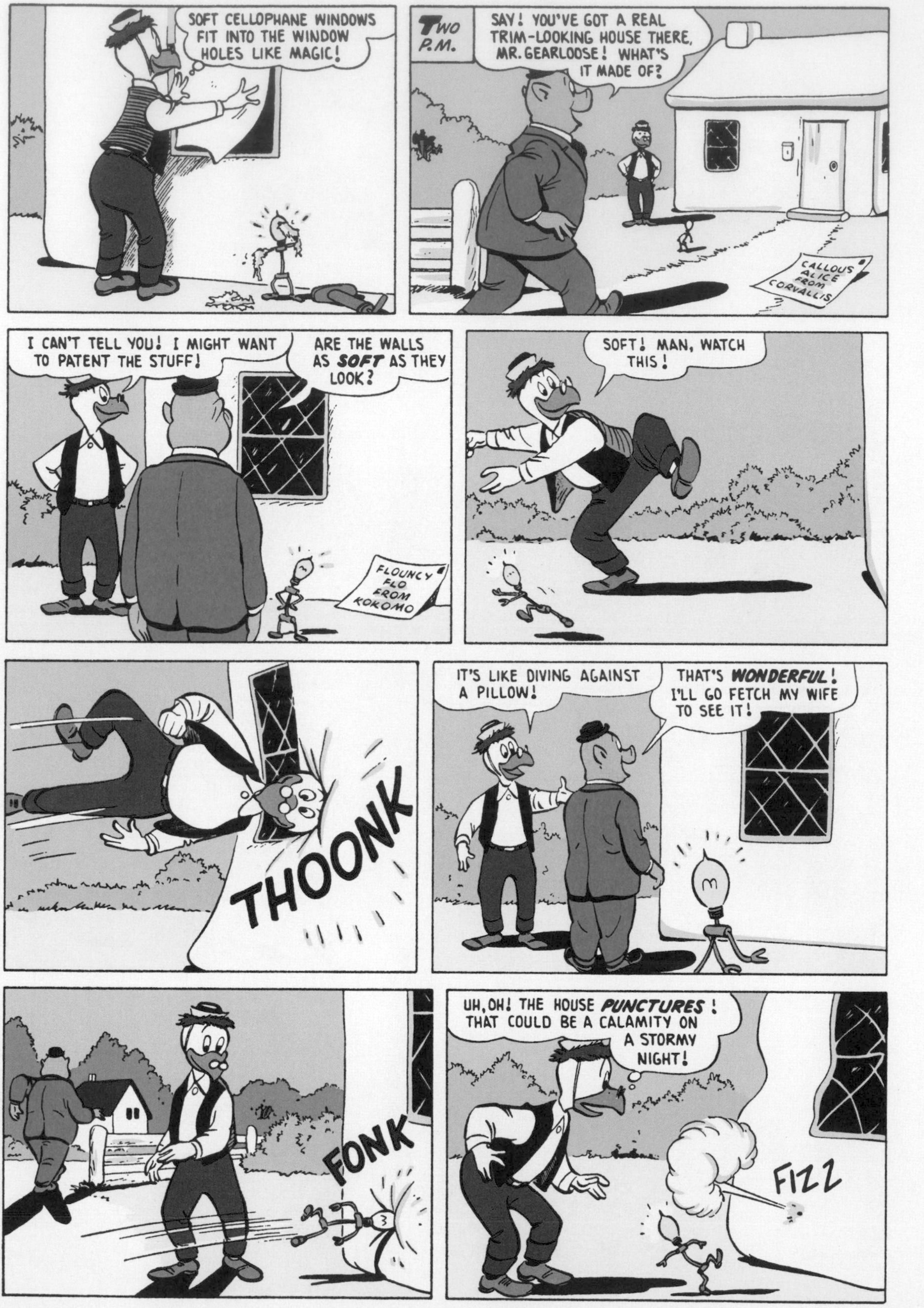
SOFT CELLOPHANE WINDOWS FIT INTO THE WINDOW HOLES LIKE MAGIC!
TWO P.M.
SAY! YOU'VE GOT A REAL TRIM-LOOKING HOUSE THERE, MR. GEARLOOSE! WHAT'S IT MADE OF?
CALLOUS ALICE FROM CORVALLIS
I CAN'T TELL YOU! I MIGHT WANT TO PATENT THE STUFF!
ARE THE WALLS AS SOFT AS THEY LOOK?
FLOUNCY FLO FROM KOKOMO
SOFT! MAN, WATCH THIS!
THOONK
IT'S LIKE DIVING AGAINST A PILLOW!
THAT'S WONDERFUL! I'LL GO FETCH MY WIFE TO SEE IT!
FONK
UH, OH! THE HOUSE PUNCTURES! THAT COULD BE A CALAMITY ON A STORMY NIGHT!
FIZZ

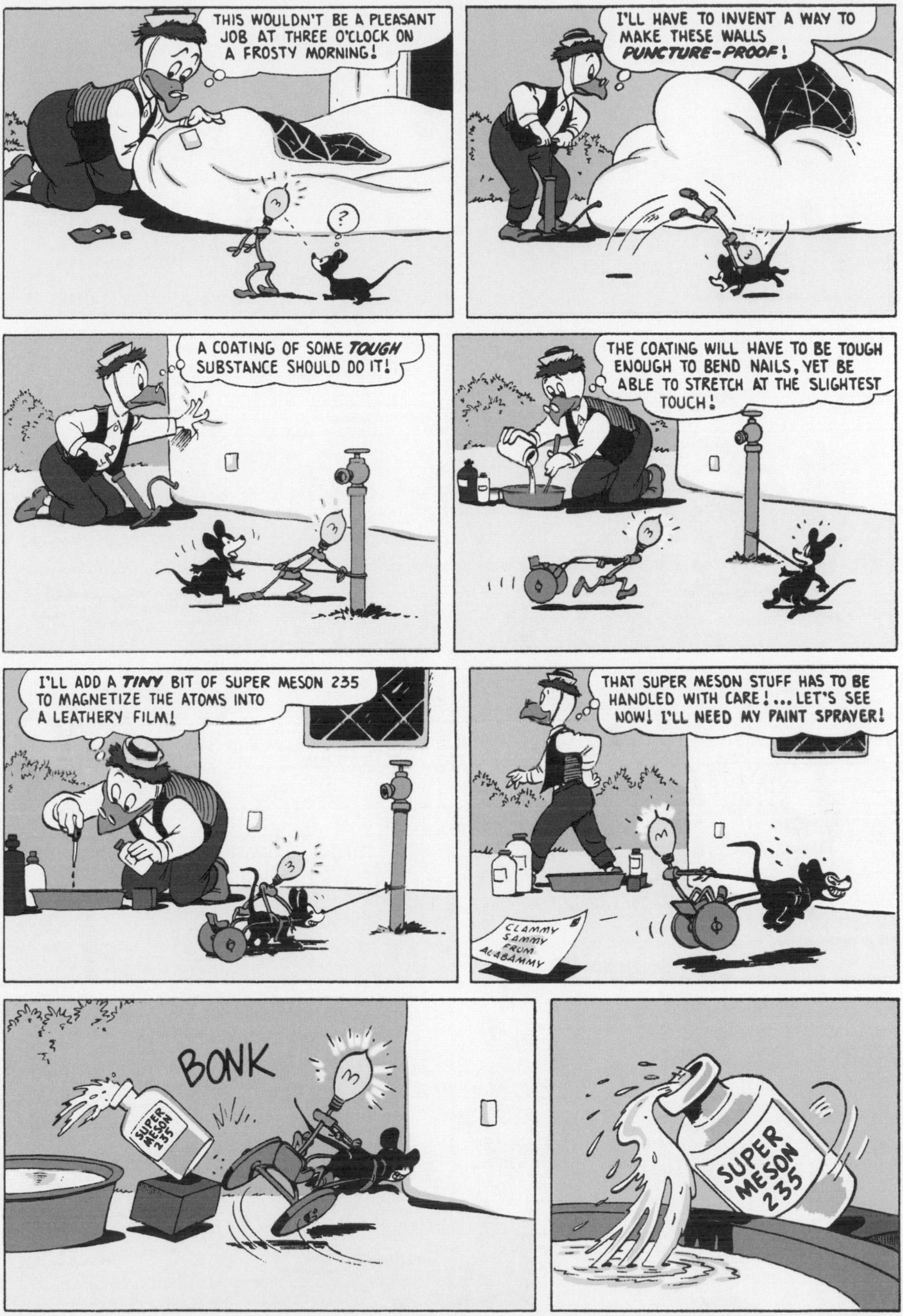
THIS WOULDN'T BE A PLEASANT JOB AT THREE O'CLOCK ON A FROSTY MORNING!
?
I'LL HAVE TO INVENT A WAY TO MAKE THESE WALLS PUNCTURE-PROOF!
A COATING OF SOME TOUGH SUBSTANCE SHOULD DO IT!
THE COATING WILL HAVE TO BE TOUGH ENOUGH TO BEND NAILS, YET BE ABLE TO STRETCH AT THE SLIGHTEST TOUCH!
I'LL ADD A TINY BIT OF SUPER MESON 235 TO MAGNETIZE THE ATOMS INTO A LEATHERY FILM!
THAT SUPER MESON STUFF HAS TO BE HANDLED WITH CARE!... LET'S SEE NOW! I'LL NEED MY PAINT SPRAYER!
CLAMMY SAMMY FROM ALABAMMY
BONK
SUPER MESON 235
SUPER MESON 235

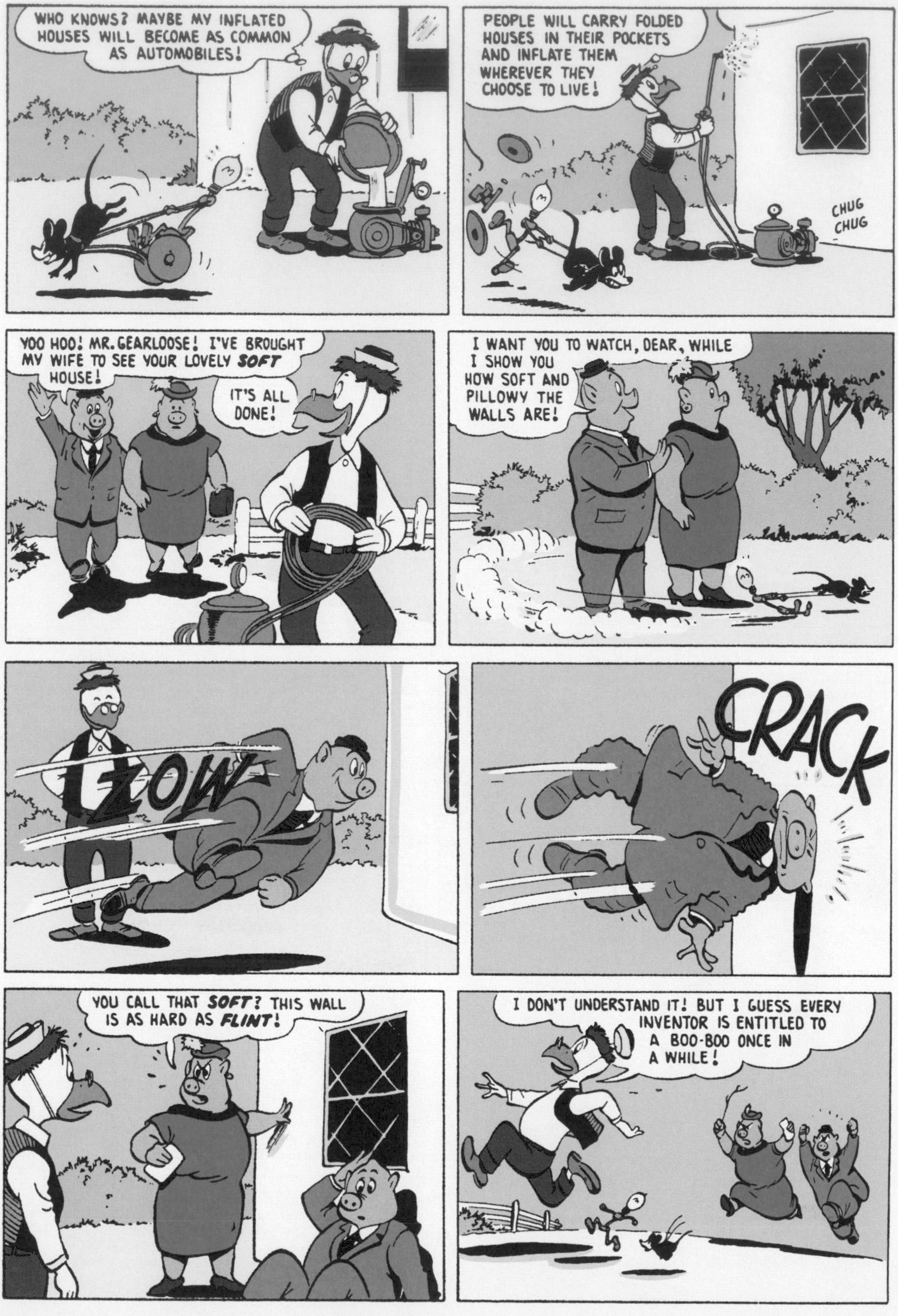
WHO KNOWS? MAYBE MY INFLATED HOUSES WILL BECOME AS COMMON AS AUTOMOBILES!
PEOPLE WILL CARRY FOLDED HOUSES IN THEIR POCKETS AND INFLATE THEM WHEREVER THEY CHOOSE TO LIVE!
CHUG CHUG
YOO HOO! MR. GEARLOOSE! I'VE BROUGHT MY WIFE TO SEE YOUR LOVELY SOFT HOUSE!
IT'S ALL DONE!
I WANT YOU TO WATCH, DEAR, WHILE I SHOW YOU HOW SOFT AND PILLOWY THE WALLS ARE!
ZOW
CRACK
YOU CALL THAT SOFT? THIS WALL IS AS HARD AS FLINT!
I DON'T UNDERSTAND IT! BUT I GUESS EVERY INVENTOR IS ENTITLED TO A BOO-BOO ONCE IN A WHILE!

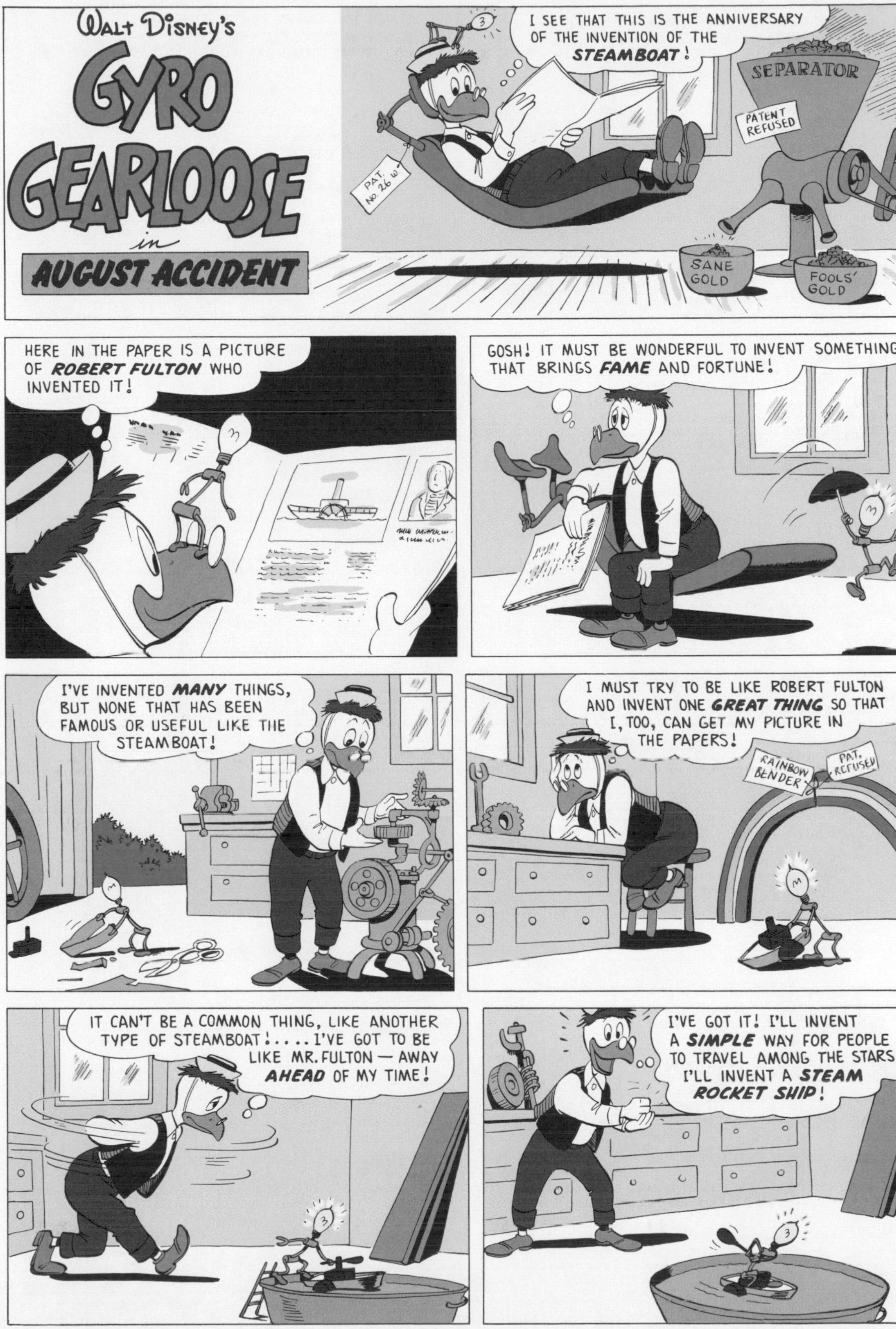

WALT DISNEY'S
GYRO GEARLOOSE
in
AUGUST ACCIDENT
I SEE THAT THIS IS THE ANNIVERSARY OF THE INVENTION OF THE STEAMBOAT!
SEPARATOR
PATENT REFUSED
PAT. NO. 26 W.
SANE GOLD
FOOLS' GOLD
HERE IN THE PAPER IS A PICTURE OF ROBERT FULTON WHO INVENTED IT!
GOSH! IT MUST BE WONDERFUL TO INVENT SOMETHING THAT BRINGS FAME AND FORTUNE!
I'VE INVENTED MANY THINGS, BUT NONE THAT HAS BEEN FAMOUS OR USEFUL LIKE THE STEAMBOAT!
I MUST TRY TO BE LIKE ROBERT FULTON AND INVENT ONE GREAT THING SO THAT I, TOO, CAN GET MY PICTURE IN THE PAPERS!
RAINBOW BENDER
PAT. REFUSED
IT CAN'T BE A COMMON THING, LIKE ANOTHER TYPE OF STEAMBOAT!....I'VE GOT TO BE LIKE MR. FULTON — AWAY AHEAD OF MY TIME!
I'VE GOT IT! I'LL INVENT A SIMPLE WAY FOR PEOPLE TO TRAVEL AMONG THE STARS! I'LL INVENT A STEAM ROCKET SHIP!

MOST ROCKETS INVENTED THESE DAYS ARE COMPLICATED THINGS! ONLY SCIENTISTS CAN FIGURE HOW TO RUN THEM!

MY *STEAM* ROCKET WILL BE SO SIMPLE THAT ANY SCHOOLBOY CAN FLY IT ANYWHERE!

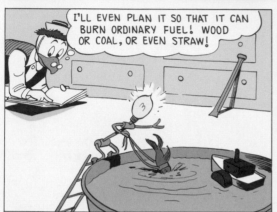

I'LL EVEN PLAN IT SO THAT IT CAN BURN ORDINARY FUEL! WOOD OR COAL, OR EVEN STRAW!

I GUESS IT'LL HAVE TO BE *COAL*! THE OTHER FUELS WOULD TAKE UP TOO MUCH SPACE!

EXTRA WATER CAN BE CARRIED IN THE NOSE CONE!

NOW TO ATTACH THE BLOWPIPE, WHICH MUST BE BOTH *SMOKE-STACK* AND *STEAM JET*!

IT'S A POWERFUL-LOOKING VEHICLE! I'LL ADD A DRIVER'S CAB, AND IT WILL BE FINISHED!

SOON!

THERE IT IS — READY TO STEAM OFF FOR THE WILD BLUE YONDER!

166

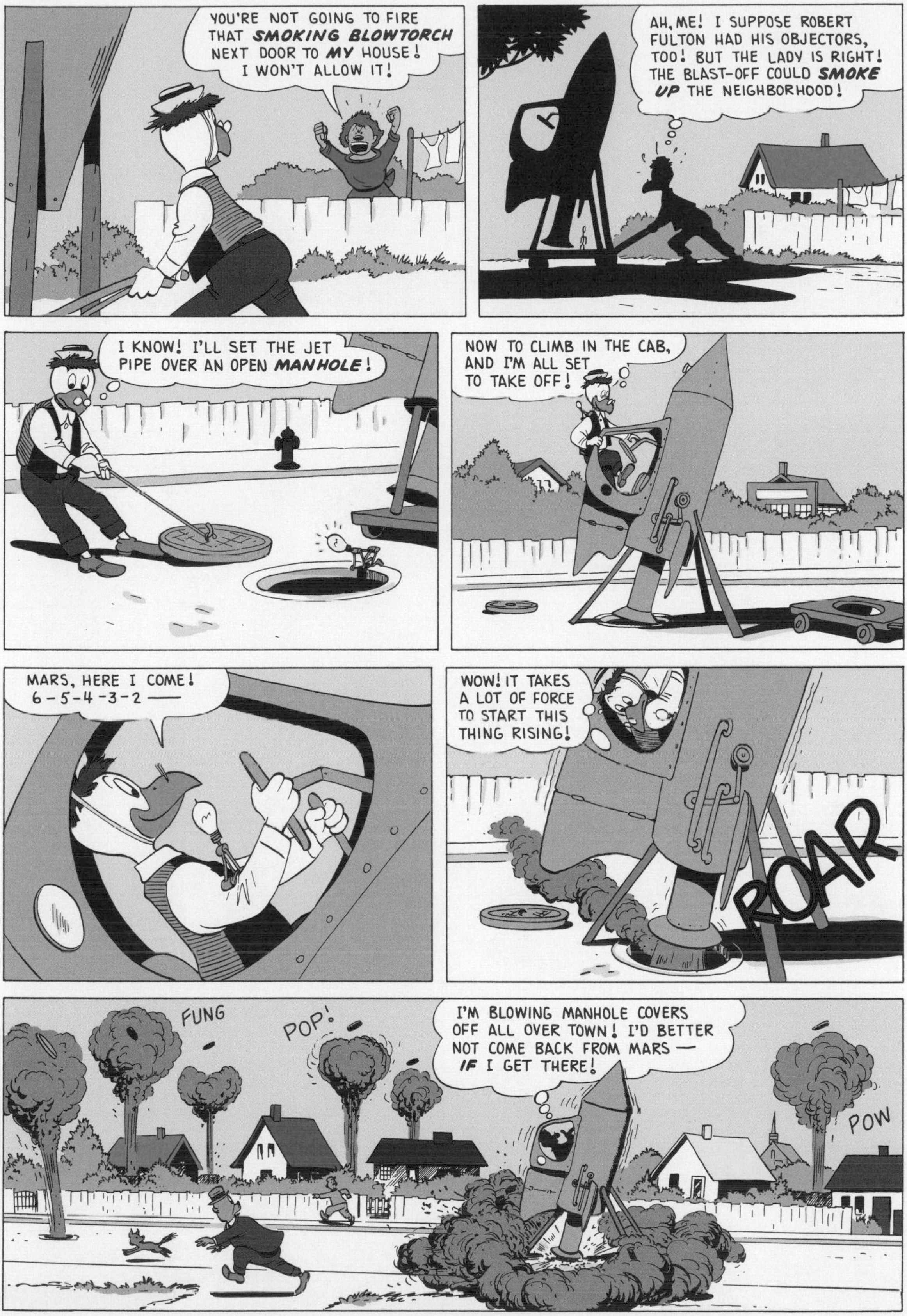
YOU'RE NOT GOING TO FIRE THAT SMOKING BLOWTORCH NEXT DOOR TO MY HOUSE! I WON'T ALLOW IT!
AH, ME! I SUPPOSE ROBERT FULTON HAD HIS OBJECTORS, TOO! BUT THE LADY IS RIGHT! THE BLAST-OFF COULD SMOKE UP THE NEIGHBORHOOD!
I KNOW! I'LL SET THE JET PIPE OVER AN OPEN MANHOLE!
NOW TO CLIMB IN THE CAB, AND I'M ALL SET TO TAKE OFF!
MARS, HERE I COME! 6-5-4-3-2 ——
WOW! IT TAKES A LOT OF FORCE TO START THIS THING RISING!
ROAR
FUNG
POP!
I'M BLOWING MANHOLE COVERS OFF ALL OVER TOWN! I'D BETTER NOT COME BACK FROM MARS — IF I GET THERE!
POW

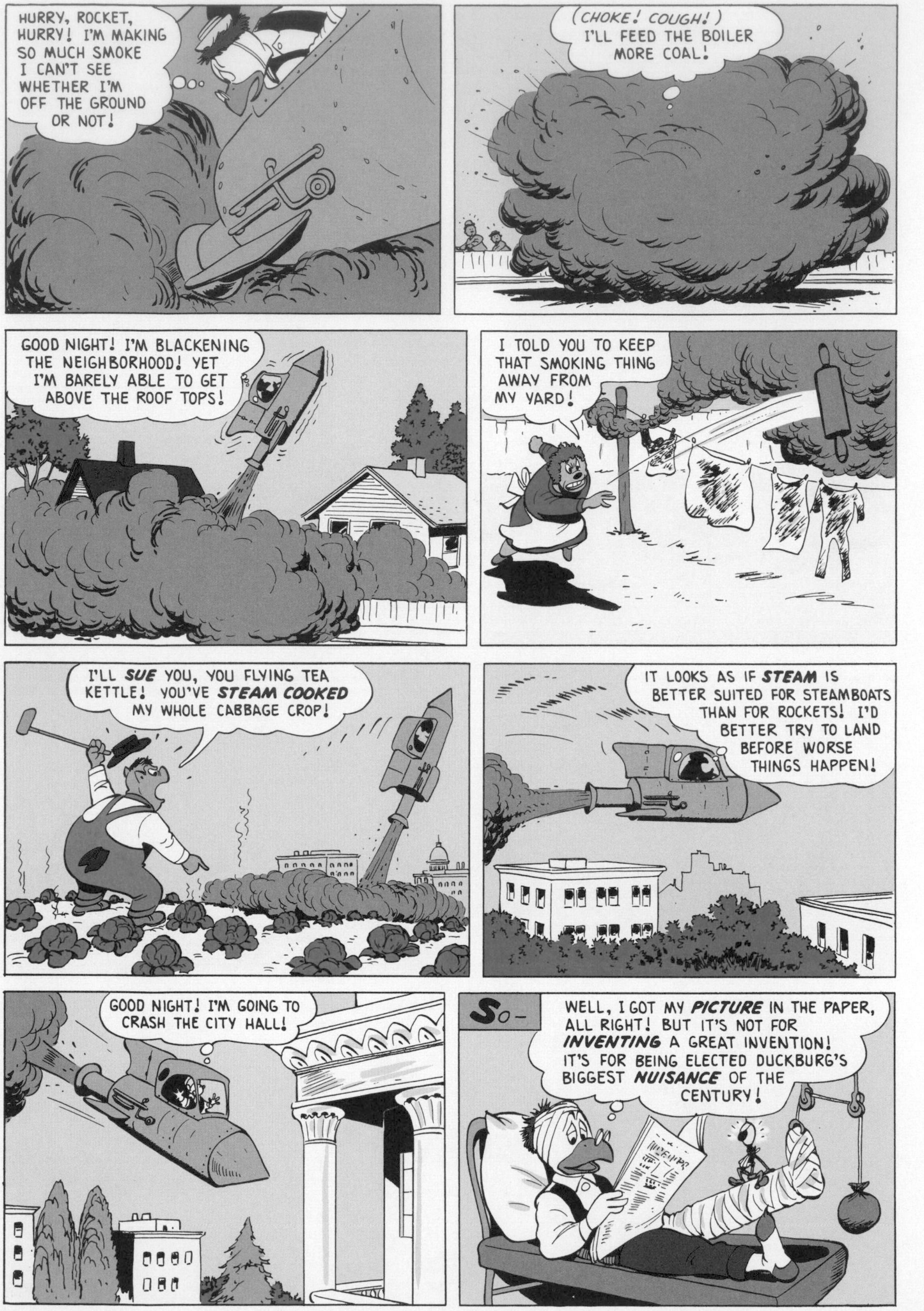

HURRY, ROCKET, HURRY! I'M MAKING SO MUCH SMOKE I CAN'T SEE WHETHER I'M OFF THE GROUND OR NOT!
(CHOKE! COUGH!) I'LL FEED THE BOILER MORE COAL!
GOOD NIGHT! I'M BLACKENING THE NEIGHBORHOOD! YET I'M BARELY ABLE TO GET ABOVE THE ROOF TOPS!
I TOLD YOU TO KEEP THAT SMOKING THING AWAY FROM MY YARD!
I'LL SUE YOU, YOU FLYING TEA KETTLE! YOU'VE STEAM COOKED MY WHOLE CABBAGE CROP!
IT LOOKS AS IF STEAM IS BETTER SUITED FOR STEAMBOATS THAN FOR ROCKETS! I'D BETTER TRY TO LAND BEFORE WORSE THINGS HAPPEN!
GOOD NIGHT! I'M GOING TO CRASH THE CITY HALL!
SO-
WELL, I GOT MY PICTURE IN THE PAPER, ALL RIGHT! BUT IT'S NOT FOR INVENTING A GREAT INVENTION! IT'S FOR BEING ELECTED DUCKBURG'S BIGGEST NUISANCE OF THE CENTURY!

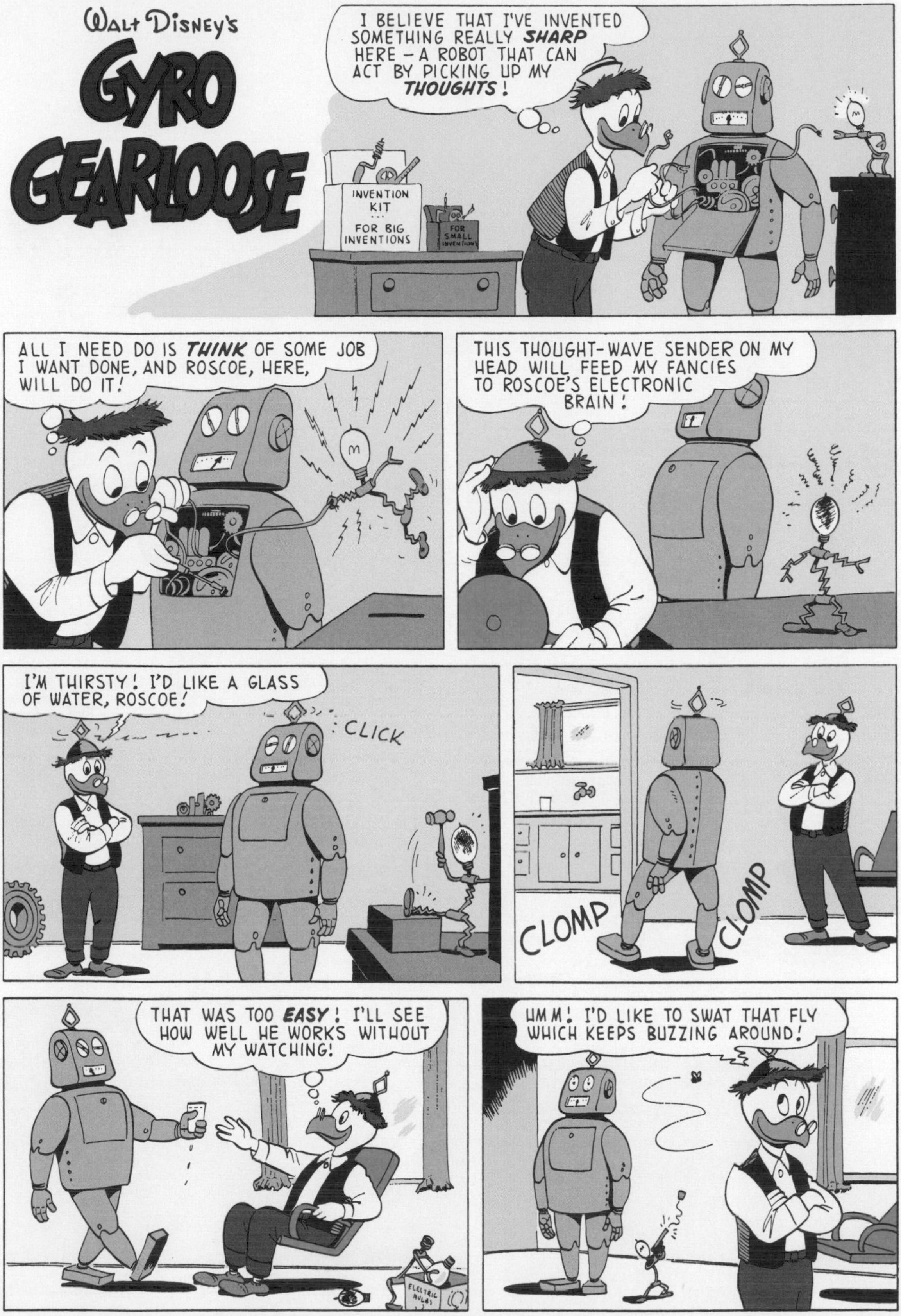
WALT DISNEY'S
GYRO GEARLOOSE
I BELIEVE THAT I'VE INVENTED SOMETHING REALLY SHARP HERE — A ROBOT THAT CAN ACT BY PICKING UP MY THOUGHTS!
INVENTION KIT ... FOR BIG INVENTIONS
FOR SMALL INVENTIONS
ALL I NEED DO IS THINK OF SOME JOB I WANT DONE, AND ROSCOE, HERE, WILL DO IT!
THIS THOUGHT-WAVE SENDER ON MY HEAD WILL FEED MY FANCIES TO ROSCOE'S ELECTRONIC BRAIN!
I'M THIRSTY! I'D LIKE A GLASS OF WATER, ROSCOE!
CLICK
CLOMP
CLOMP
THAT WAS TOO EASY! I'LL SEE HOW WELL HE WORKS WITHOUT MY WATCHING!
ELECTRIC BULBS
HMM! I'D LIKE TO SWAT THAT FLY WHICH KEEPS BUZZING AROUND!

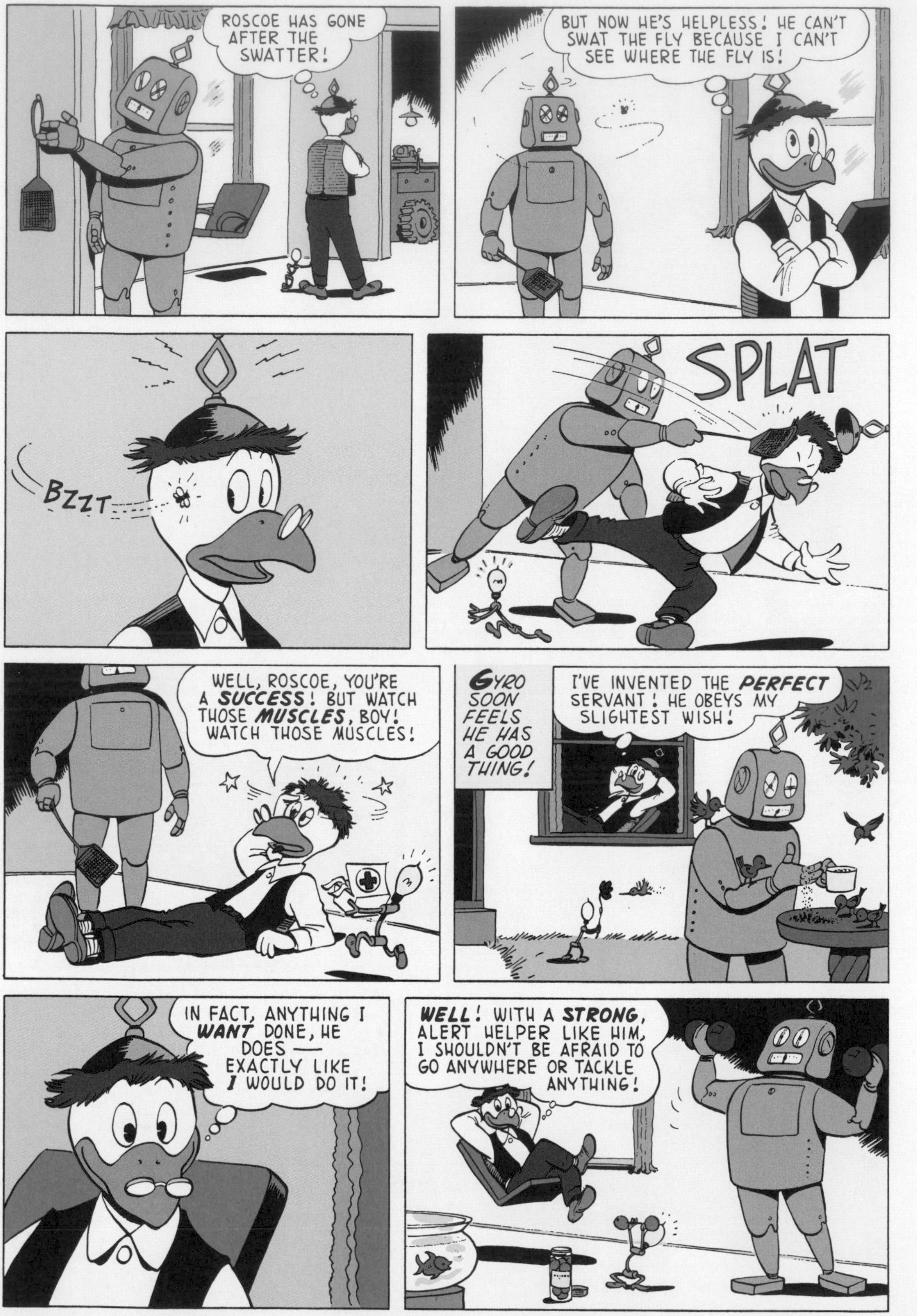
ROSCOE HAS GONE AFTER THE SWATTER!
BUT NOW HE'S HELPLESS! HE CAN'T SWAT THE FLY BECAUSE I CAN'T SEE WHERE THE FLY IS!
BZZT
SPLAT
WELL, ROSCOE, YOU'RE A SUCCESS! BUT WATCH THOSE MUSCLES, BOY! WATCH THOSE MUSCLES!
GYRO SOON FEELS HE HAS A GOOD THING!
I'VE INVENTED THE PERFECT SERVANT! HE OBEYS MY SLIGHTEST WISH!
IN FACT, ANYTHING I WANT DONE, HE DOES — EXACTLY LIKE I WOULD DO IT!
WELL! WITH A STRONG, ALERT HELPER LIKE HIM, I SHOULDN'T BE AFRAID TO GO ANYWHERE OR TACKLE ANYTHING!

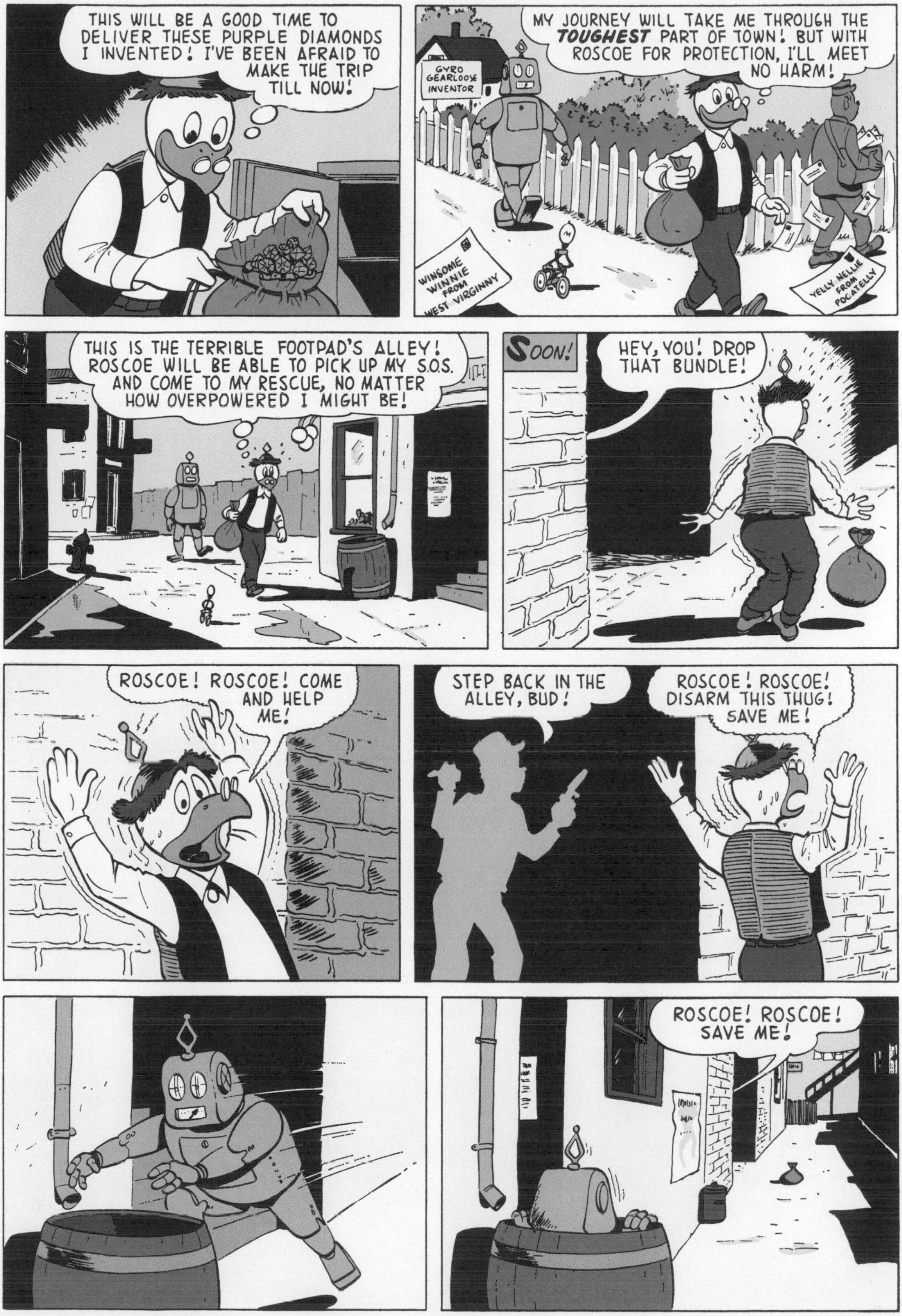
THIS WILL BE A GOOD TIME TO DELIVER THESE PURPLE DIAMONDS I INVENTED! I'VE BEEN AFRAID TO MAKE THE TRIP TILL NOW!
MY JOURNEY WILL TAKE ME THROUGH THE TOUGHEST PART OF TOWN! BUT WITH ROSCOE FOR PROTECTION, I'LL MEET NO HARM!
GYRO GEARLOOSE INVENTOR
WINSOME WINNIE FROM WEST VIRGINNY
YELLY NELLIE FROM POCATELLY
THIS IS THE TERRIBLE FOOTPAD'S ALLEY! ROSCOE WILL BE ABLE TO PICK UP MY S.O.S. AND COME TO MY RESCUE, NO MATTER HOW OVERPOWERED I MIGHT BE!
SOON!
HEY, YOU! DROP THAT BUNDLE!
ROSCOE! ROSCOE! COME AND HELP ME!
STEP BACK IN THE ALLEY, BUD!
ROSCOE! ROSCOE! DISARM THIS THUG! SAVE ME!
ROSCOE! ROSCOE! SAVE ME!

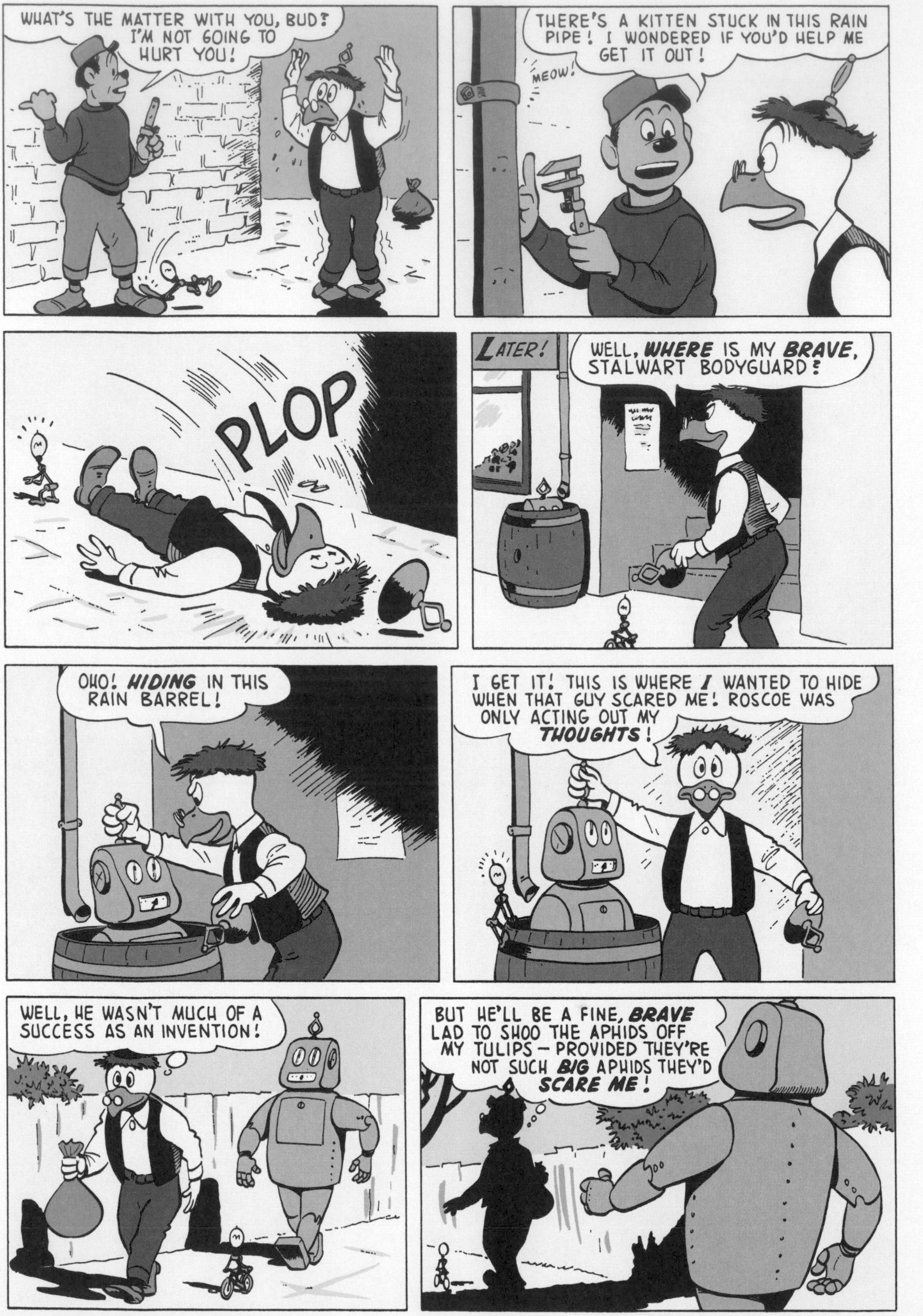
WHAT'S THE MATTER WITH YOU, BUD? I'M NOT GOING TO HURT YOU!
THERE'S A KITTEN STUCK IN THIS RAIN PIPE! I WONDERED IF YOU'D HELP ME GET IT OUT!
MEOW!
PLOP
LATER!
WELL, WHERE IS MY BRAVE, STALWART BODYGUARD?
OHO! HIDING IN THIS RAIN BARREL!
I GET IT! THIS IS WHERE I WANTED TO HIDE WHEN THAT GUY SCARED ME! ROSCOE WAS ONLY ACTING OUT MY THOUGHTS!
WELL, HE WASN'T MUCH OF A SUCCESS AS AN INVENTION!
BUT HE'LL BE A FINE, BRAVE LAD TO SHOO THE APHIDS OFF MY TULIPS—PROVIDED THEY'RE NOT SUCH BIG APHIDS THEY'D SCARE ME!

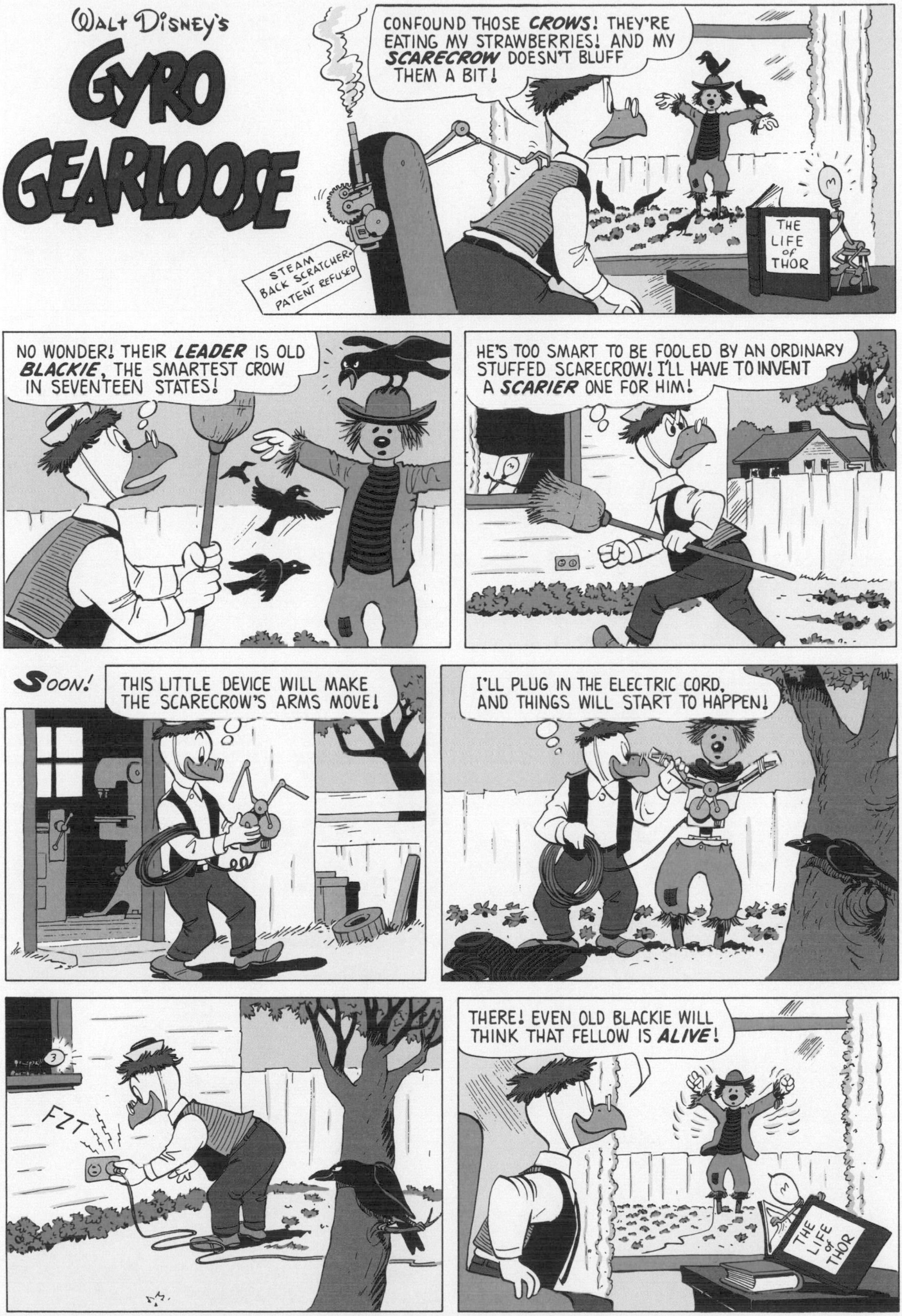
WALT DISNEY'S
GYRO GEARLOOSE
CONFOUND THOSE CROWS! THEY'RE EATING MY STRAWBERRIES! AND MY SCARECROW DOESN'T BLUFF THEM A BIT!
STEAM BACK SCRATCHER — PATENT REFUSED
THE LIFE of THOR
NO WONDER! THEIR LEADER IS OLD BLACKIE, THE SMARTEST CROW IN SEVENTEEN STATES!
HE'S TOO SMART TO BE FOOLED BY AN ORDINARY STUFFED SCARECROW! I'LL HAVE TO INVENT A SCARIER ONE FOR HIM!
SOON!
THIS LITTLE DEVICE WILL MAKE THE SCARECROW'S ARMS MOVE!
I'LL PLUG IN THE ELECTRIC CORD, AND THINGS WILL START TO HAPPEN!
FZT
THERE! EVEN OLD BLACKIE WILL THINK THAT FELLOW IS ALIVE!
THE LIFE of THOR

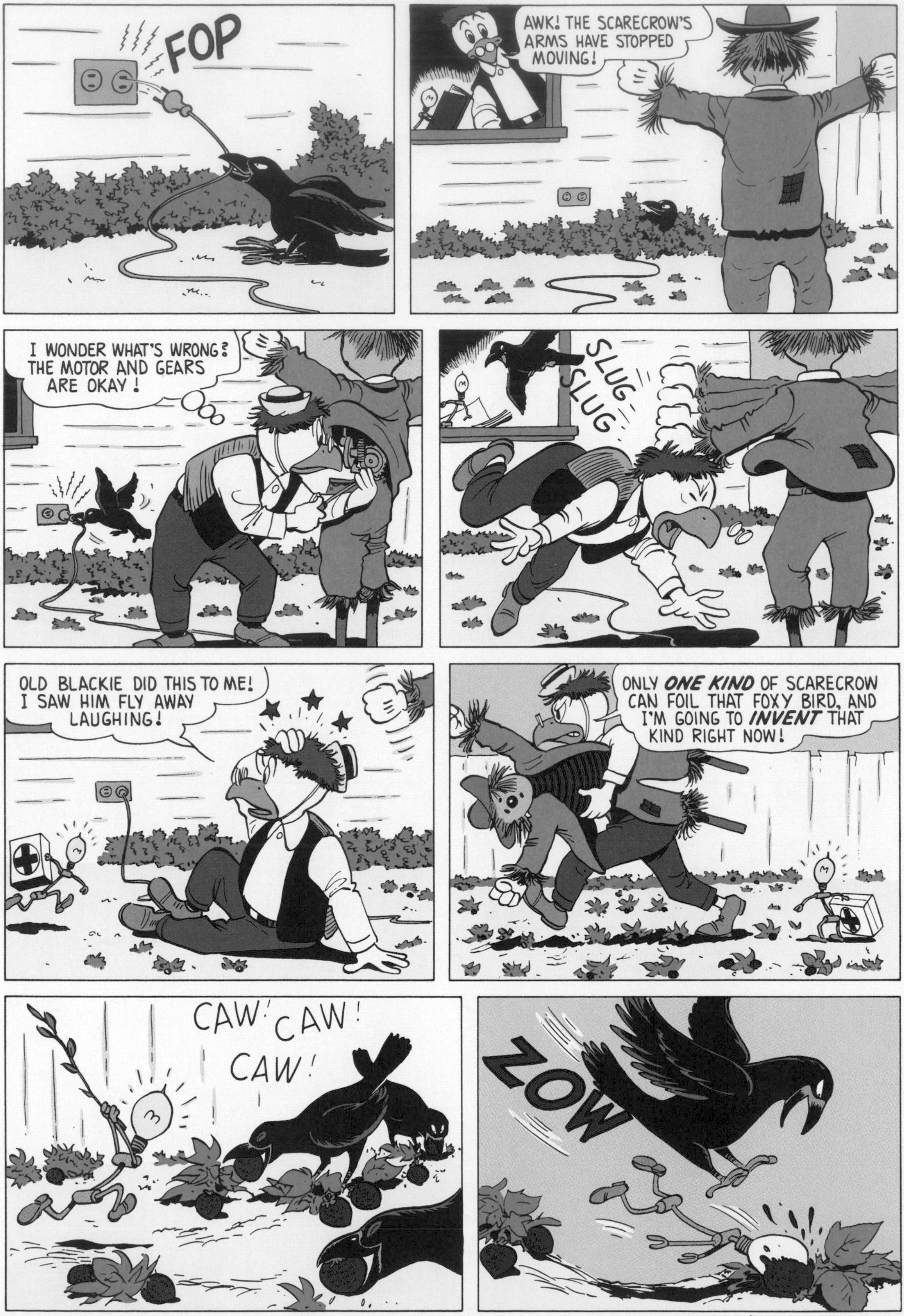
FOP
AWK! THE SCARECROW'S ARMS HAVE STOPPED MOVING!
I WONDER WHAT'S WRONG? THE MOTOR AND GEARS ARE OKAY!
SLUG SLUG
OLD BLACKIE DID THIS TO ME! I SAW HIM FLY AWAY LAUGHING!
ONLY ONE KIND OF SCARECROW CAN FOIL THAT FOXY BIRD, AND I'M GOING TO INVENT THAT KIND RIGHT NOW!
CAW! CAW! CAW!
ZOW

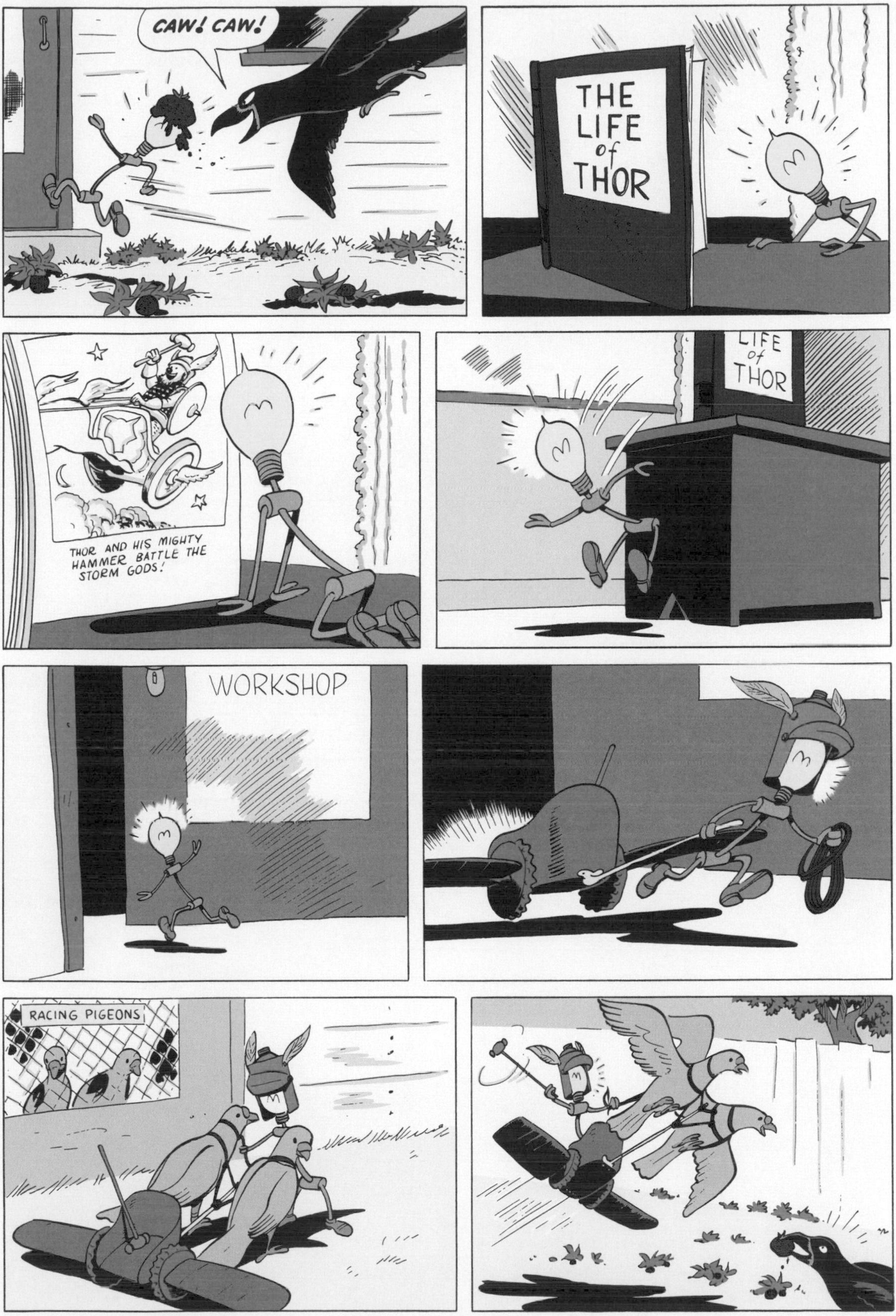
CAW! CAW!
THE LIFE of THOR
THOR AND HIS MIGHTY HAMMER BATTLE THE STORM GODS!
LIFE of THOR
WORKSHOP
RACING PIGEONS

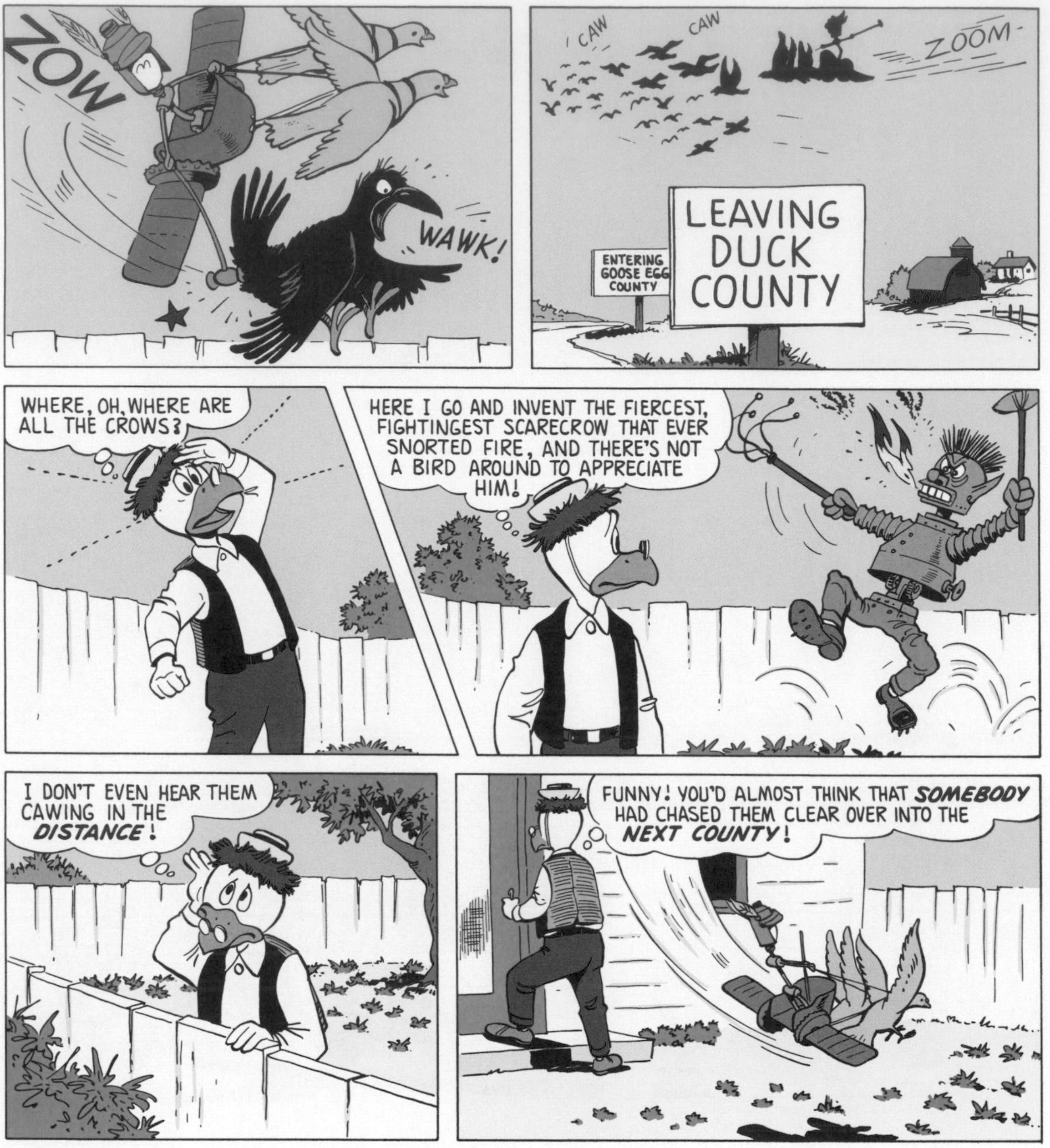
ZOW
WAWK!
CAW
CAW
ZOOM
ENTERING GOOSE EGG COUNTY
LEAVING DUCK COUNTY
WHERE, OH, WHERE ARE ALL THE CROWS?
HERE I GO AND INVENT THE FIERCEST, FIGHTINGEST SCARECROW THAT EVER SNORTED FIRE, AND THERE'S NOT A BIRD AROUND TO APPRECIATE HIM!
I DON'T EVEN HEAR THEM CAWING IN THE ***DISTANCE***!
FUNNY! YOU'D ALMOST THINK THAT ***SOMEBODY*** HAD CHASED THEM CLEAR OVER INTO THE ***NEXT COUNTY***!

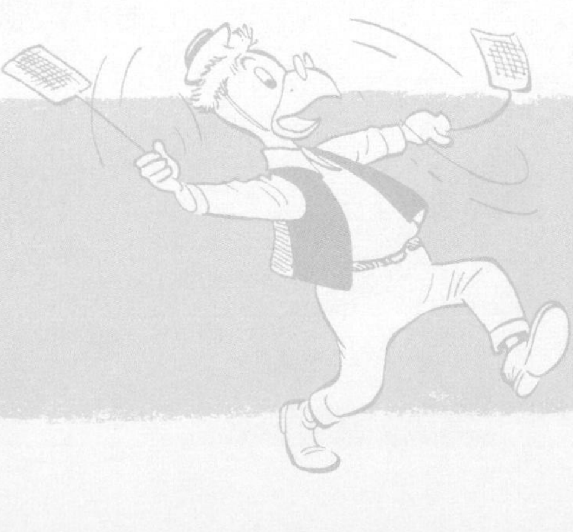

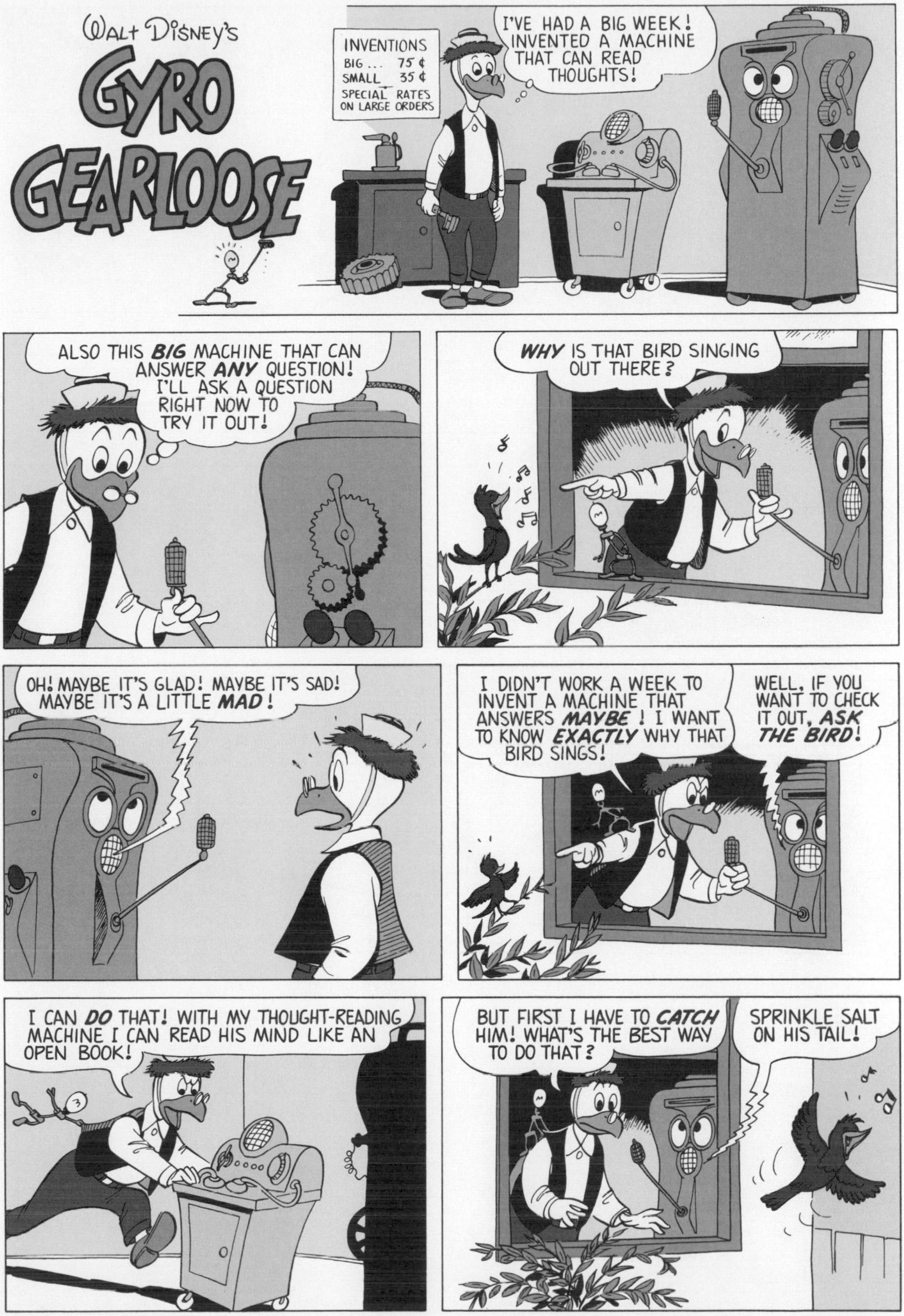
WALT DISNEY'S
GYRO GEARLOOSE
INVENTIONS
BIG ... 75 ¢
SMALL 35 ¢
SPECIAL RATES ON LARGE ORDERS
I'VE HAD A BIG WEEK! INVENTED A MACHINE THAT CAN READ THOUGHTS!
ALSO THIS BIG MACHINE THAT CAN ANSWER ANY QUESTION! I'LL ASK A QUESTION RIGHT NOW TO TRY IT OUT!
WHY IS THAT BIRD SINGING OUT THERE?
OH! MAYBE IT'S GLAD! MAYBE IT'S SAD! MAYBE IT'S A LITTLE MAD!
I DIDN'T WORK A WEEK TO INVENT A MACHINE THAT ANSWERS MAYBE! I WANT TO KNOW EXACTLY WHY THAT BIRD SINGS!
WELL, IF YOU WANT TO CHECK IT OUT, ASK THE BIRD!
I CAN DO THAT! WITH MY THOUGHT-READING MACHINE I CAN READ HIS MIND LIKE AN OPEN BOOK!
BUT FIRST I HAVE TO CATCH HIM! WHAT'S THE BEST WAY TO DO THAT?
SPRINKLE SALT ON HIS TAIL!

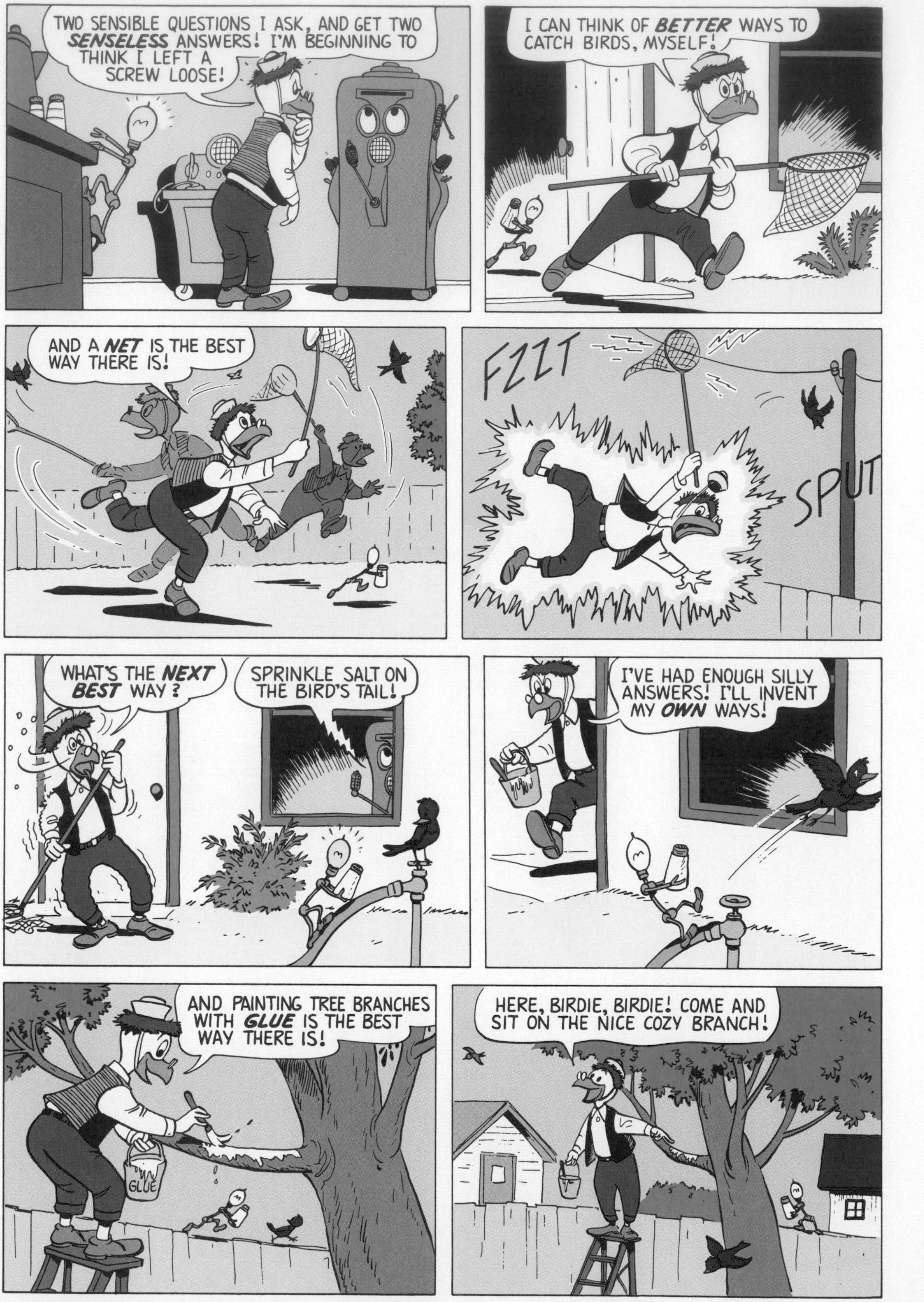

TWO SENSIBLE QUESTIONS I ASK, AND GET TWO SENSELESS ANSWERS! I'M BEGINNING TO THINK I LEFT A SCREW LOOSE!
I CAN THINK OF BETTER WAYS TO CATCH BIRDS, MYSELF!
AND A NET IS THE BEST WAY THERE IS!
FZZT
SPUT
WHAT'S THE NEXT BEST WAY?
SPRINKLE SALT ON THE BIRD'S TAIL!
I'VE HAD ENOUGH SILLY ANSWERS! I'LL INVENT MY OWN WAYS!
AND PAINTING TREE BRANCHES WITH GLUE IS THE BEST WAY THERE IS!
GLUE
HERE, BIRDIE, BIRDIE! COME AND SIT ON THE NICE COZY BRANCH!

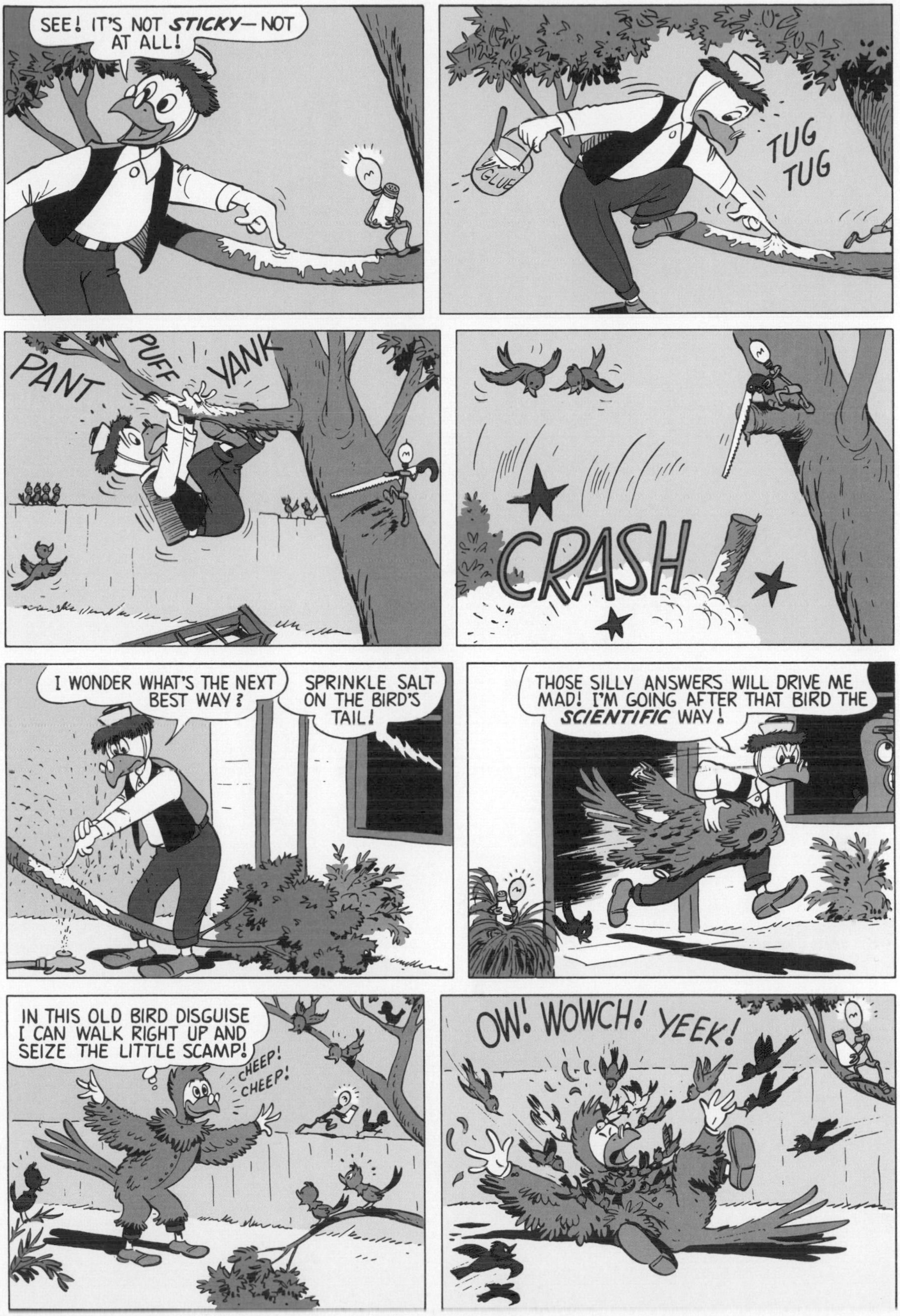
SEE! IT'S NOT STICKY— NOT AT ALL!
TUG TUG
PANT
PUFF
YANK
CRASH!
I WONDER WHAT'S THE NEXT BEST WAY?
SPRINKLE SALT ON THE BIRD'S TAIL!
THOSE SILLY ANSWERS WILL DRIVE ME MAD! I'M GOING AFTER THAT BIRD THE SCIENTIFIC WAY!
IN THIS OLD BIRD DISGUISE I CAN WALK RIGHT UP AND SEIZE THE LITTLE SCAMP!
CHEEP! CHEEP!
OW! WOWCH! YEEK!

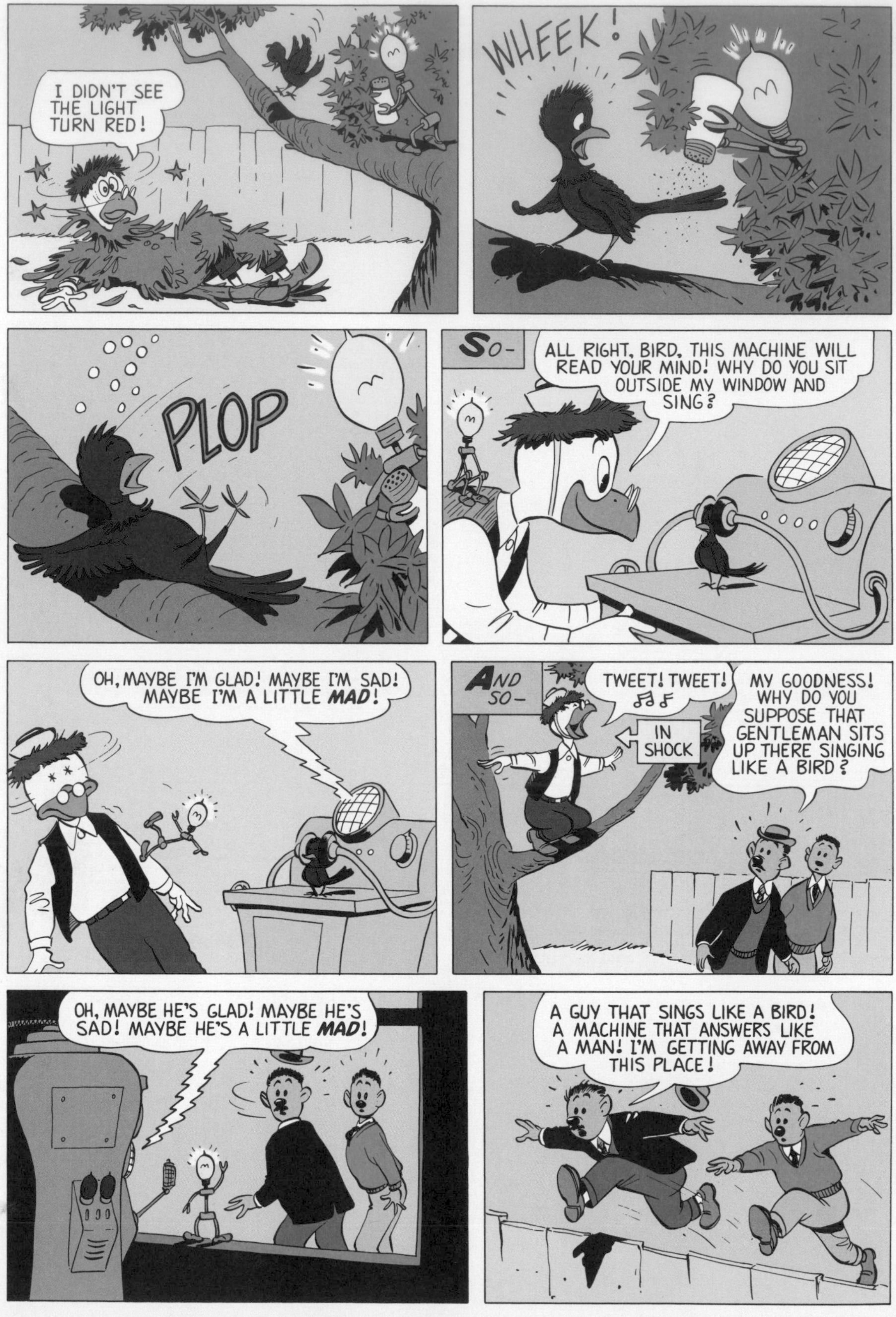
I DIDN'T SEE THE LIGHT TURN RED!
WHEEK!
PLOP
SO-
ALL RIGHT, BIRD, THIS MACHINE WILL READ YOUR MIND! WHY DO YOU SIT OUTSIDE MY WINDOW AND SING?
OH, MAYBE I'M GLAD! MAYBE I'M SAD! MAYBE I'M A LITTLE MAD!
AND SO-
TWEET! TWEET!
IN SHOCK
MY GOODNESS! WHY DO YOU SUPPOSE THAT GENTLEMAN SITS UP THERE SINGING LIKE A BIRD?
OH, MAYBE HE'S GLAD! MAYBE HE'S SAD! MAYBE HE'S A LITTLE MAD!
A GUY THAT SINGS LIKE A BIRD! A MACHINE THAT ANSWERS LIKE A MAN! I'M GETTING AWAY FROM THIS PLACE!

SEPT.-NOV.

10¢

Walt Disney's

UNCLE $CROOGE

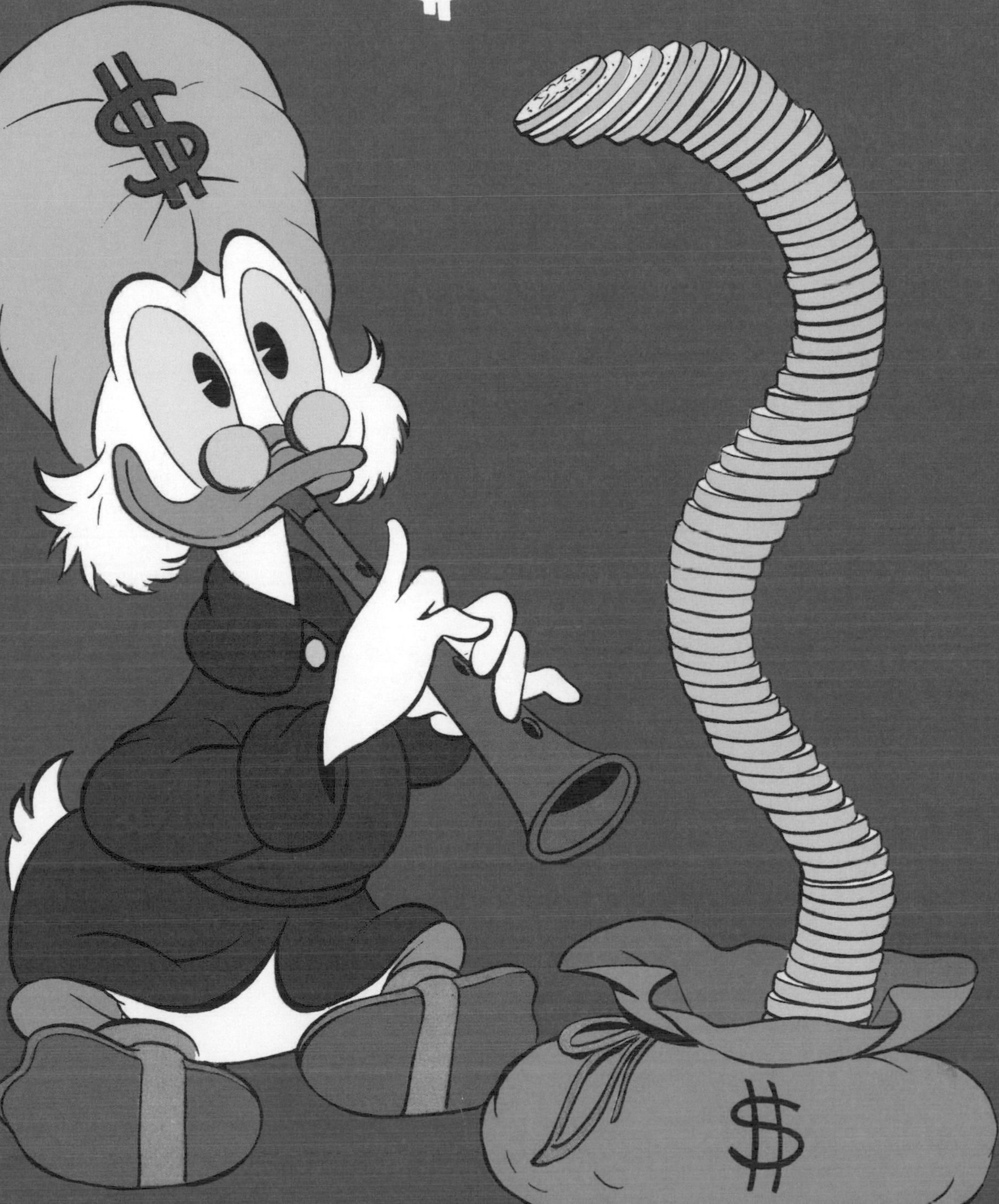

$
$

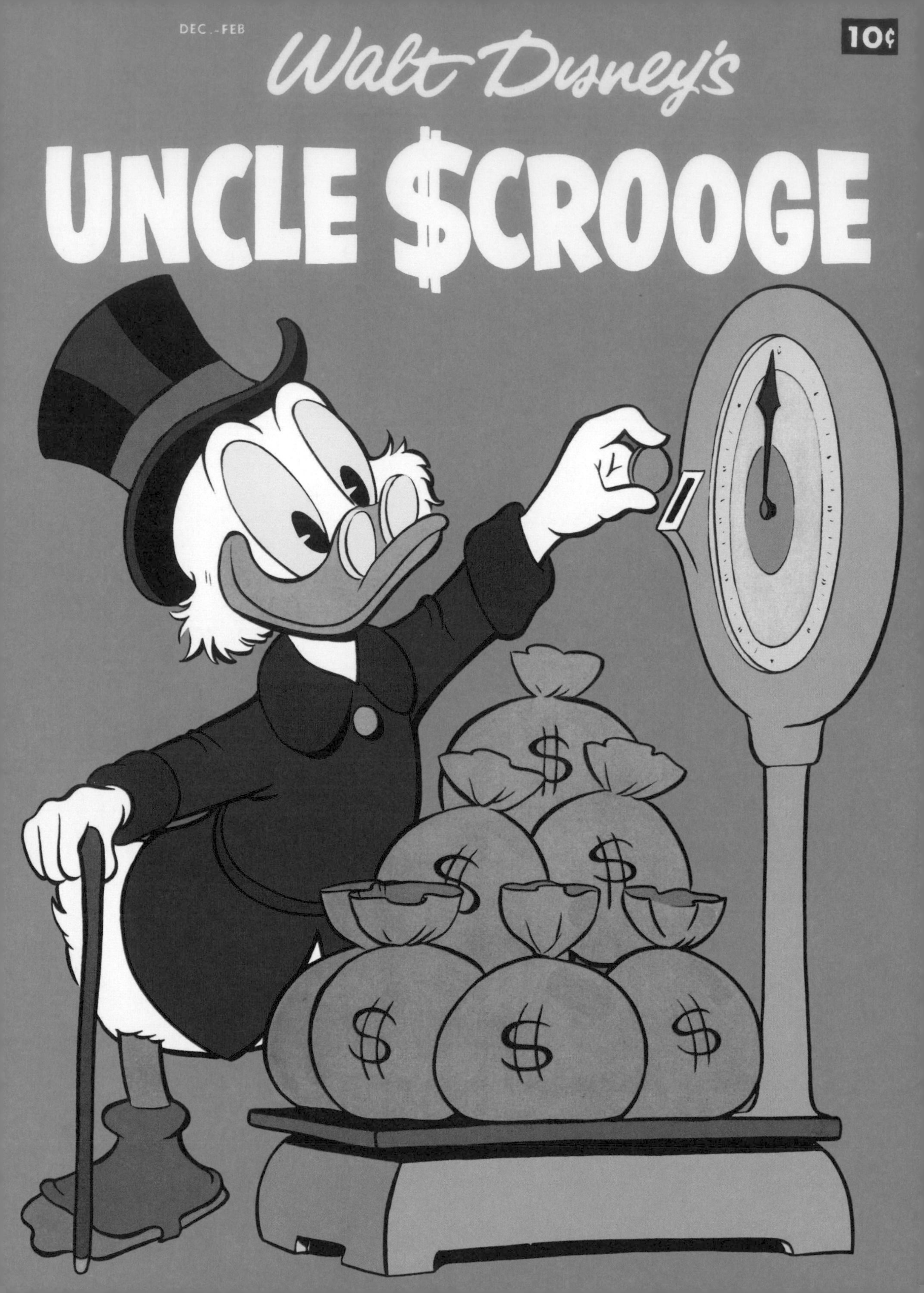
DEC.-FEB
10¢
Walt Disney's
UNCLE $CROOGE

Story Notes

THE MINES OF KING SOLOMON *p. 1*

Among Carl Barks's best stories are those in which Uncle Scrooge and his nephews travel the world in search of lost treasure. In this outing, Barks comes up with a compelling yarn based—in part, at least—on the legend of King Solomon's mines. The wise Solomon (c. 1011–931 BCE), third king of Israel and son of David and Bathsheba, built the famous temple in Jerusalem and gave his name to the copper and iron mines which were most likely located near Aqabah, in Jordan. Thus, Solomon's mines probably did exist. But it was the English writer Henry Rider Haggard who built up the legend of the fabulous gold and diamond treasure they held in his 1885 novel, *King Solomon's Mines*.

Besides being familiar with Haggard's novel, Barks had certainly seen its film versions, especially the 1950 one starring Stewart Granger as the adventurer/explorer Allan Quatermain (himself partly based on the British "white hunter" and explorer of Colonial Africa, Frederick Courtney Selous). Like Quatermain, Scrooge—accompanied, as usual, by Donald Duck and the Nephews—sets off on the quest for King Solomon's Mines while overseeing his own mines and banks around the world.

Yet, as he often does, before leading us to the Red Sea hills where the fabulous mines are reportedly located, Barks uses the first third of the story as an introduction, suggesting that two elements will be instrumental in the rest of the adventure. The first is the stack of tickets the Ducks need to travel around the world, and the second (and more important one) is the Nephews' animal whistles. In fact, both these elements will prove crucial after the Ducks' meeting with the Bedouins led by El Jackal, whose language Uncle Scrooge is perfectly able to understand and speak, since "I learned [it] when I sold lawn mowers in the Sahara," as Scrooge himself recalls on page 8, panel 3.

"Give a little whistle," Jiminy Cricket sings in the 1940 *Pinocchio* animated feature, and that is what the Nephews repeatedly do here—with mixed results, it must be said. The acme is reached when Scrooge, tooting on Louie's whistle to guide the others back to safety, unwittingly also summons a host of

COME ON, DEWEY! WHAT ARE YOU WHISTLING AT?
SQUEEK
SQUEEK
SQUEEK
JUST CALLING OUT ANY LOST MICE THAT MIGHT HAVE GOTTEN INTO THIS MOUNTAIN OF PAPER!

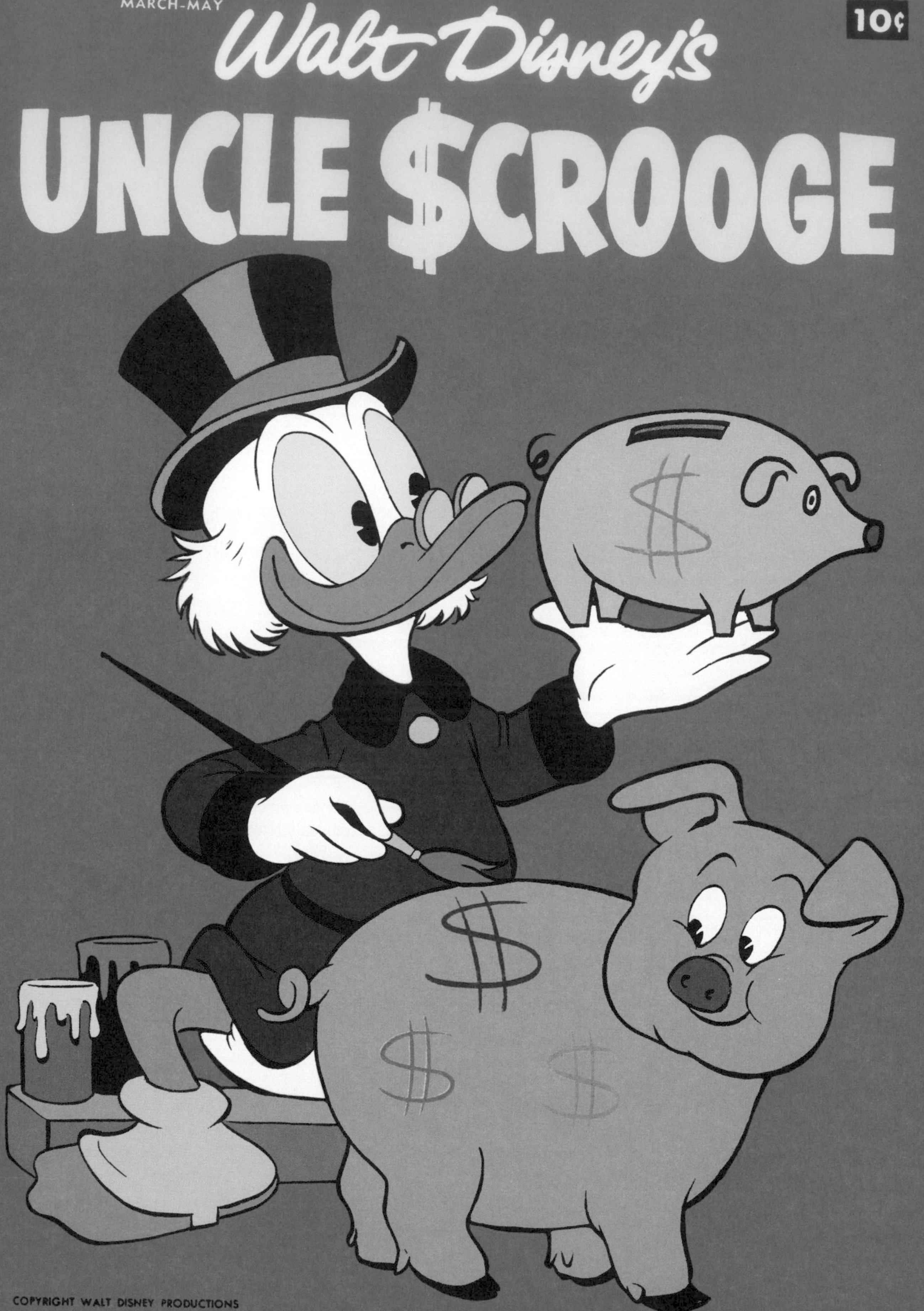

MARCH-MAY
Walt Disney's
UNCLE $CROOGE
10¢
COPYRIGHT WALT DISNEY PRODUCTIONS

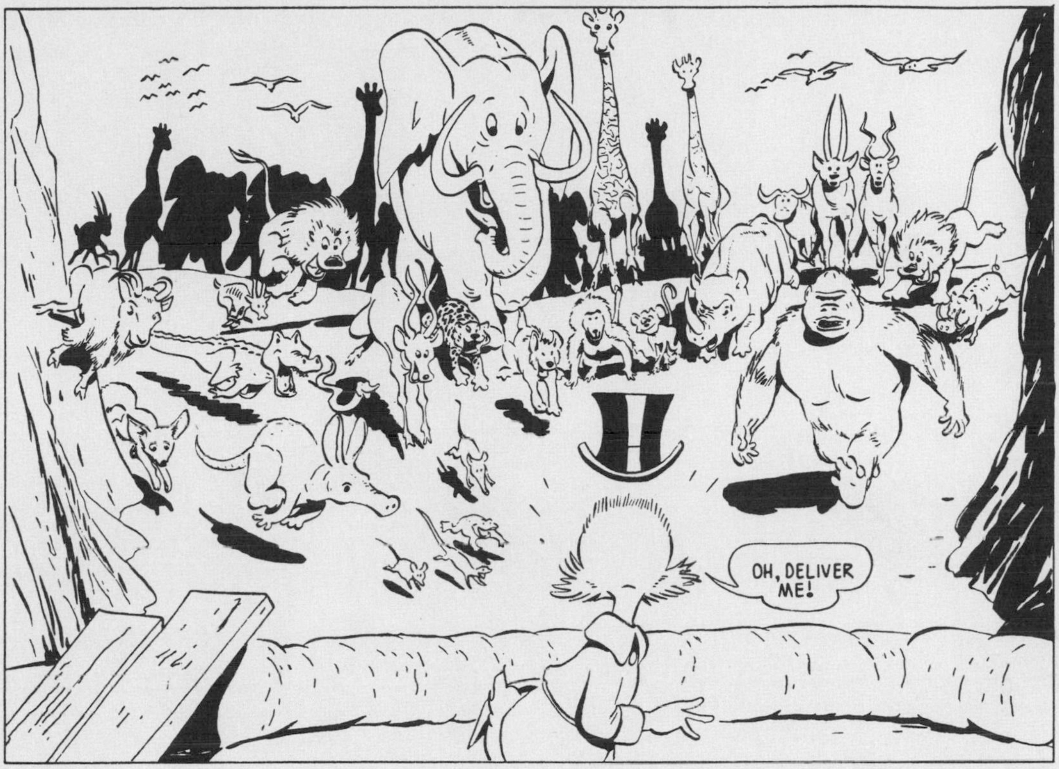
OH, DELIVER ME!

different animals (at least 50 of which can be seen, distinctly or in silhouette, on the top half of page 26) — evoking the memorable stampedes as Barks portrayed in "Donald Duck in 'Darkest Africa'" (*Walt Disney's Donald Duck: "The Old Castle's Secret,"* Volume 6 in this series) and in its partial remake, "Forbidden Valley" (*Walt Disney's Donald Duck: "The Black Pearls of Tabu Yama,"* Volume 19).

— ALBERTO BECATTINI

SEPTEMBER SCRIMMAGE *p. 31*

This short and sweet barrage of visual gags ends with referees literally throwing the rulebook at Uncle Scrooge and Jocko. The latter is the "gorilla" playing defense for Dogdale, the away team on which he turns the tables with his "old-time tricks."

Carl Barks seems to have been motivated to create this, his only story centering on football, by the structure of its publication venue, the first issue of the *Mickey Mouse Almanac* (which we'll come back to later on). The magazine contained twelve four-page stories, one for each of the twelve months of the year. Barks was assigned August, for which he came up with the Gyro Gearloose story "August Accident" (p. 165), and September, for which he decided to reflect on America's favorite autumn sport.

Literalizing a metaphorical saying as he does for the payoff was a favored tactic of Barks's. He perhaps employed it most memorably when he let colorblind Johnny the Bull loose in a china shop in "The Unorthodox Ox" (*Walt Disney's Donald Duck: "Secret of Hondorica,"* Volume 17). Here, it takes on self-reflexive irony, in that Barks clearly did not care much for football or its rules.

For one, he seems to be getting his positions mixed, using the offensive position 'fullback' to describe the clearly defensive Jocko. And you would have thought the outsized lug would have gotten Dogdale ahead by more than the six points that Dewey is worried about at the outset.

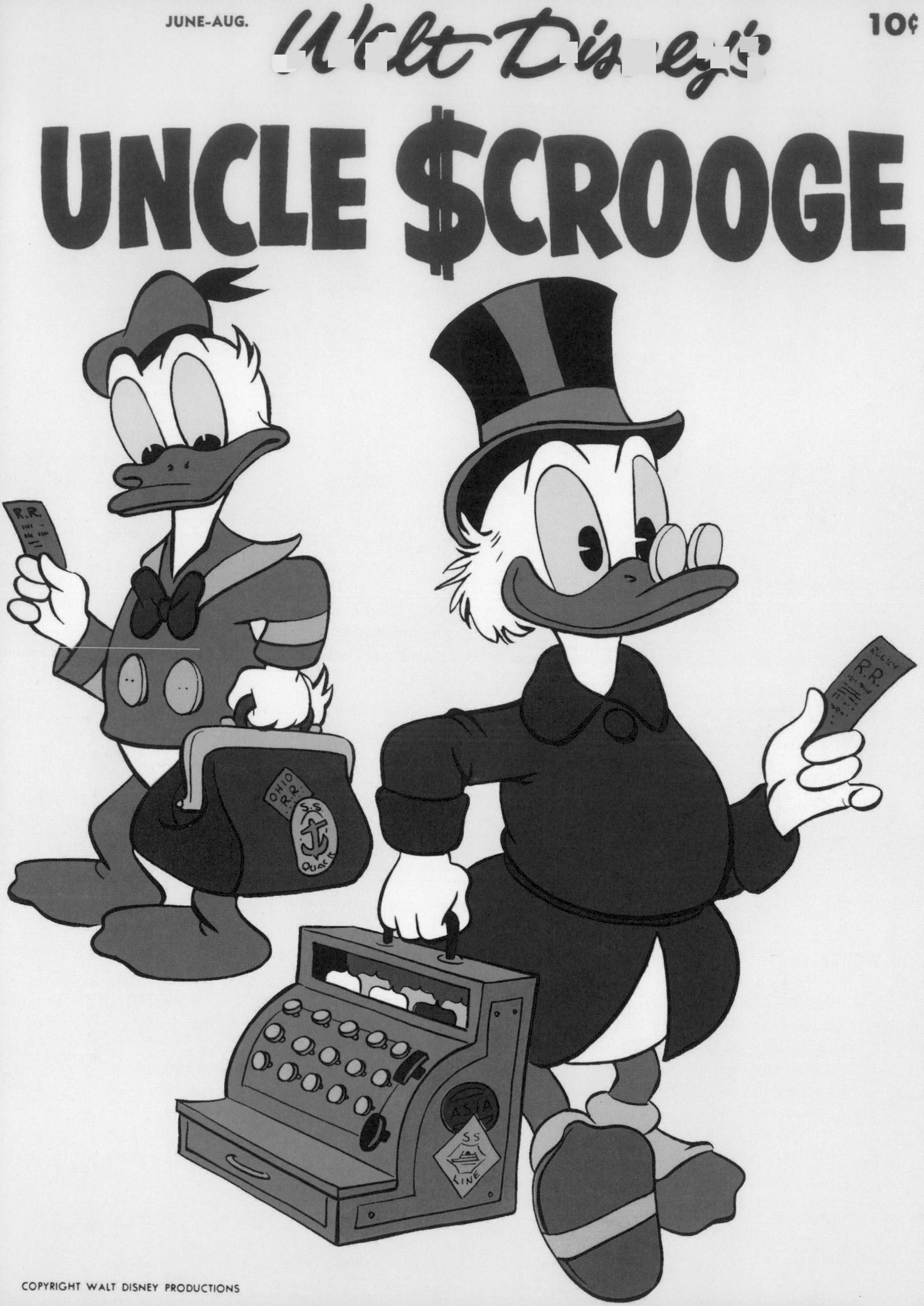
JUNE-AUG.
Walt Disney's
10¢
UNCLE $CROOGE
R.R.
OHIO R.R.
S.S QUACK
R.R.
ASIA
S.S LINE

More fundamentally, Barks's disdain for the sport is obvious in his portrayal of it as a violent free-for-all, with players routinely eliminated with broken bones. The panel of Jocko looming threateningly over Louie, his torso cropped by the panel borders, is a particularly inspired condensation, in microcosm, of Barks's familiar take on American society as a whole.

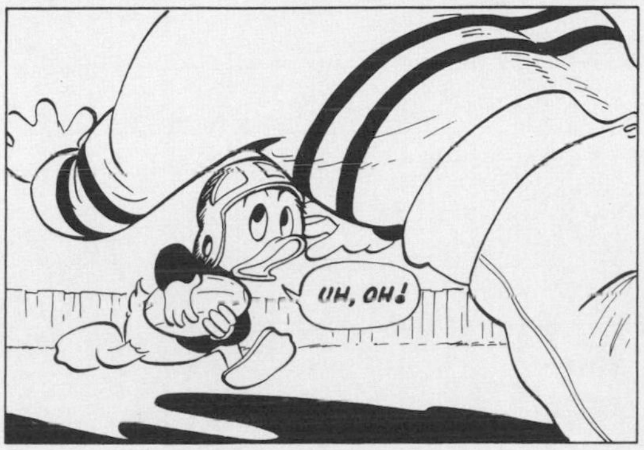
UH, OH!

And, as usual, Scrooge, the ever-ambiguous incarnation of the American Dream, was there at the game's anarchic inception. ("We'll play 1870 football!" Scrooge declares.) We can thus add another endeavor to the long list of which Barks cast Scrooge as an early pioneer: the first intercollegiate football game is usually considered to have been between Princeton and Rutgers in 1869. It would appear, for reasons unclear, that Scrooge's Webfoot Tech got involved the following year.

— MATTHIAS WIVEL

CITY OF GOLDEN ROOFS *p. 35*

"City of Golden Roofs" treads some familiar terrain. The usual ego-driven dare sends Scrooge off on another globe-hopping contest of wills, eventually enveloping the nephews in the frantic commercial colonization of yet another unfortunate, exotic locale.

The Ducks, as usual, blunder their way into a fairly peaceful "lost" city trimmed in indigenous treasures ready for plundering, or, in this case, literal liquidation. Scrooge matches wits with several adversaries including Donald, hordes of rapacious would-be sales reps, a herd of royal elephants, and the befuddled King of Tangkor Wat, Barks's lampoon of Cambodia's Angkor Wat temple complex.

When McDuck emerges triumphant, he dances in gleeful triumph at actually having sweated his profits out of the bamboozled natives and forced his frustrated nephew into a faint. Along the way, Barks skewers an eclectic bevy of targets from Elvis and Yul Brynner to calypso music and high-fidelity audiophilia. For all the running, drumming, shilling, and shouting that takes place, "City of Golden Roofs" never quite delivers the same excitement as other swashduckling postcolonial farces. In fact, it feels a bit like two half-developed scenarios quickly conglomerated into one clunky chunk of running gags and goofy one-liners.

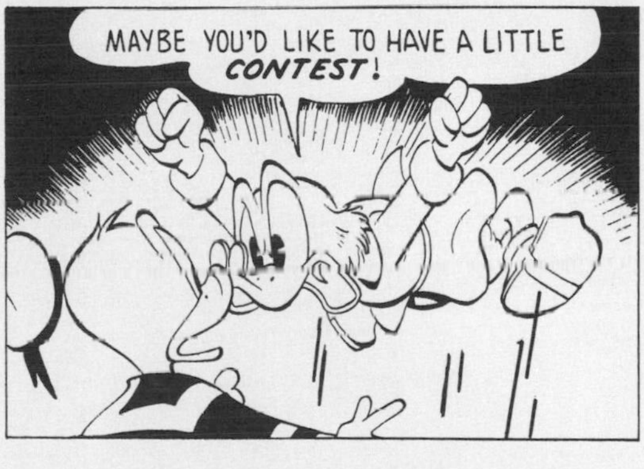
MAYBE YOU'D LIKE TO HAVE A LITTLE CONTEST!

First, there is McDuck's mad dash to obtain a lucrative position as a "cushy salesman." Scrooge's hijinks emphasize his generational rivalry with Donald as well as the driving entrepreneurial chutzpah of Duckburg's capitalist concrete jungle. In a wry nod to the many swaps and scams to come, Scrooge initially secures a ladder and pail on credit, but the established squillionaire's time-tested bag of tricks, hacks, and gambits has grown stale. False window washers and duct inspectors already clog every opportunity for advancement. There are whiffs of Sinclair Lewis's George Babbitt, Arthur Miller's Willy Loman, and John Updike's Harry "Rabbit" Angstrom in

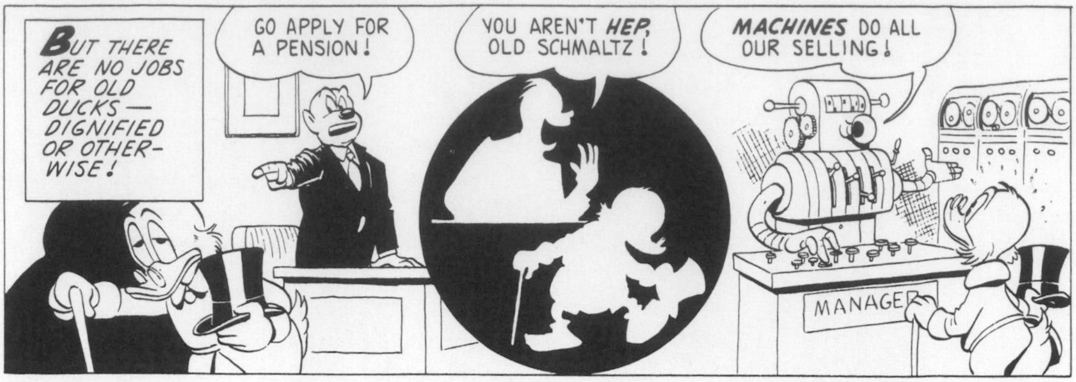
BUT THERE ARE NO JOBS FOR OLD DUCKS — DIGNIFIED OR OTHER-WISE!
GO APPLY FOR A PENSION!
YOU AREN'T HEP, OLD SCHMALTZ!
MACHINES DO ALL OUR SELLING!
MANAGER

Scrooge's moments of periodic failure, doubt, and distress, especially in Barks's mock-tragic triptych describing the elderly gent struggling through Duckburg's tough job market.

Donald — the eternal *bon vivant* — doesn't fare much better until his familiarity with tape recorders and musical fads gets him the last remaining territory in the world — the "Gung Ho River Valley" in "Indo-China" (Southeast Asia). Meanwhile, Scrooge gets saddled with "a super colossal fire belcher for heating airplane hangars in Greenland." Barks's contrast between Donald's high tech "midget" microrecorders and Scrooge's gargantuan wood stove emphasize the extreme differences in their ages, expertise, and entrepreneurial outlooks.

In the jungles of Indo-China, the story introduces some of Barks's more cringeworhty ethnic grotesques. The Ducks savor their one-sided deals with kindly, clueless natives. They rack up tiger pelts, elephant tusks, sapphires, and gold while the Indo-Chinese gladly go along, with off-putting salvos of pidgin English like "Tradee! Tradee!" Only the flustered, nap-deprived king of Tangkor Wat speaks clearly and correctly, but he, too, eventually yields to Scrooge's tactics.

The story provides Barks with plentiful opportunities to mock contemporary trends involving foreign customs such as calypso music, beatnik bongo parties, and especially Walter Lang's 1956 hit adaptation of Richard Rodgers and Oscar Hammerstein's *The King and I*. Barks's king of Tangkor Wat bears quite a likeness to Yul Brynner's King Mongkut.

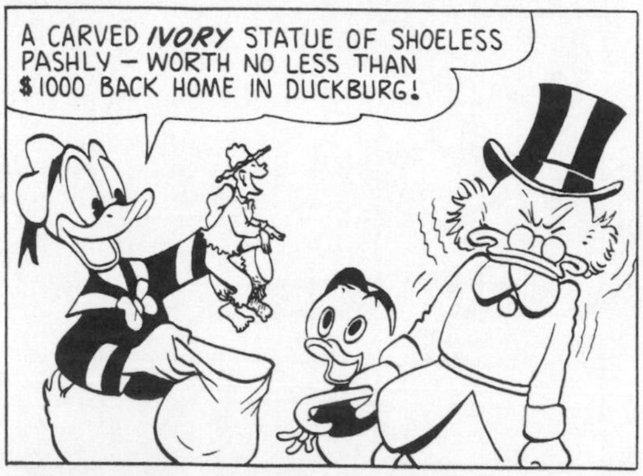
A CARVED IVORY STATUE OF SHOELESS PASHLY — WORTH NO LESS THAN $1000 BACK HOME IN DUCKBURG!

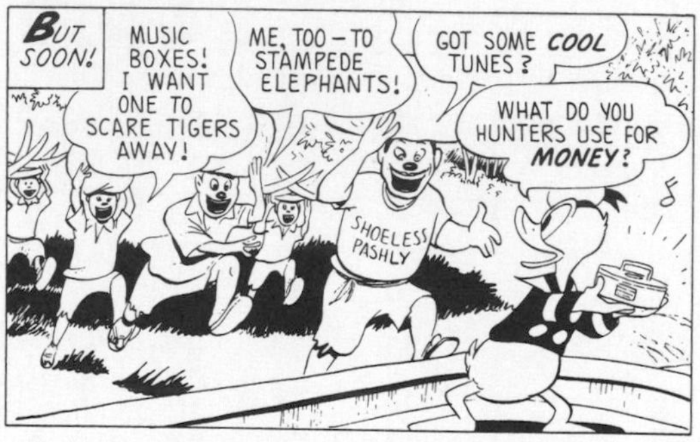
BUT SOON!
MUSIC BOXES! I WANT ONE TO SCARE TIGERS AWAY!
ME, TOO — TO STAMPEDE ELEPHANTS!
GOT SOME COOL TUNES?
WHAT DO YOU HUNTERS USE FOR MONEY?
SHOELESS PASHLY

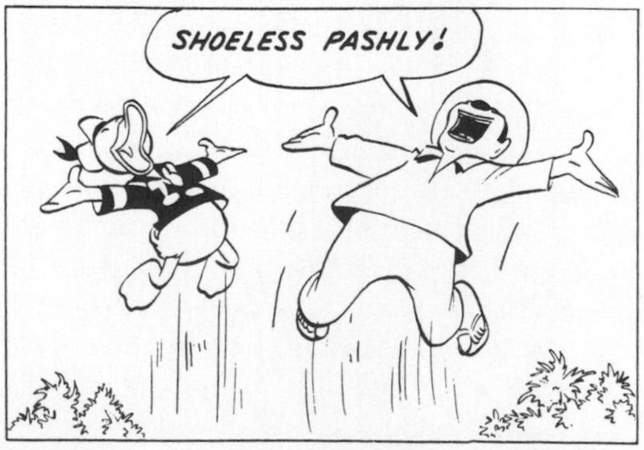
SHOELESS PASHLY!

This brings us to the story's one true gem—the bongolicious charms of Shoeless Pashly! Pashly himself only "appears" once—as the tiny ivory effigy that Donald accepts as payment for his sale, suggesting Barks's scorn for such ludicrous celebrities. An obvious phonetic corruption of rock icon Elvis Presley, Pashly's fame as "king of the bongo drums" inspires elaborate greeting rituals among his devoted fans and also initiates the calypso calamity that bankrupts Tangkor Wat. Deployed through Donald's newfangled "bongo monsters," Pashly's music confuses Scrooge, tortures the king, and completely debilitates traditional Indo-Chinese forms of dance, dress, and decorum. Barks's sequence depicting the be-bop bomb that melts the "waxen poses" of pupils in the royal dancing school and virtually compels them to gyrate in moves that are "not graceful" is an especially shrewd parody of Western cultural imperialism.

Despite a few bright spots, this particular Scrooge odyssey is more forced, dated, and intolerant than many better adventures. Shoeless Pashly, however, has endured. The name has been adopted by a number of professional musicians in both Europe and the U.S., though it will probably never top Indo-Chinese charts.

—DANIEL YEZBICK

THE MONEY WELL *p. 63*

"The Money Well" offers ample insight into how simpler and sillier Carl Barks's storytelling became just a few short years into his *Uncle Scrooge* comic book. The whole plot—a property battle of wits with the Beagle Boys—is a reworking of "Only a Poor Old Man" (*Walt Disney's Uncle Scrooge: "Only a Poor Old Man,"* Volume 12), almost to the letter in terms of pacing and staging. The grandiose scheming, warfare, and character development of that seminal story are replaced with happy accidents and the downsides of senility. (The glasses here also mirror the memory pills in "Back to the Klondike," also in Volume 12.) When the titular money well strikes and delivers Scrooge's riches to the Beagle Boys, Scrooge doesn't seem *nearly* as distraught as he should be. It's almost as if he's giving the reader a telling wink that he's seen how this has played out before.

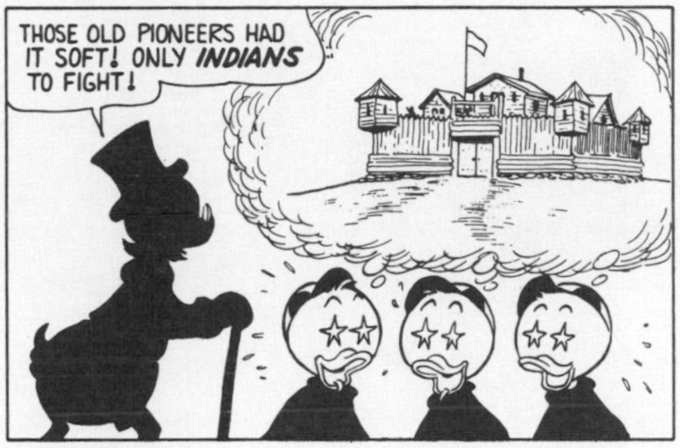
THOSE OLD PIONEERS HAD IT SOFT! ONLY *INDIANS* TO FIGHT!

While it may not be as sharp or hard-hitting as the earlier Scrooge tales, "The Money Well" still offers fine examples of how Barks enriches his characters' backstories in a wholly entertaining fashion. Scrooge had already made a passing reference that he bought the land where his money bin stands "when there was nothing within fifty miles but a fort" in "Migrating Millions" (*Walt Disney's Uncle Scrooge: "The Lost Crown of Genghis Khan,"* Volume 16), and it gets the name of "Fort Duckburg" here, proving to be an important concept to Duck Lore. The city's founders give Scrooge a ready-made solution to his Beagle Boys dilemma, and Barks establishes Scrooge's fascinating connection to Duckburg that goes back centuries, which provides him and other writers (Don Rosa, to pick an obvious example, in his "The Life and Times of Scrooge McDuck" epic) ample fodder for further historical adventures. "Only a Poor Old Man" introduced quite a bit of McDuck history, and yet Barks still finds ways to expand it using the same story elements.

We're also introduced to the present-day Grandpa Beagle, the founder of the Beagle Boys gang. He's a character Barks, sadly, never revisited, but was adopted as a crotchety leader for the Beagles by Italian writers. Just think—this degeneracy is family business that spans three generations! And thanks to "The Fantastic River Race" (also Volume 16),

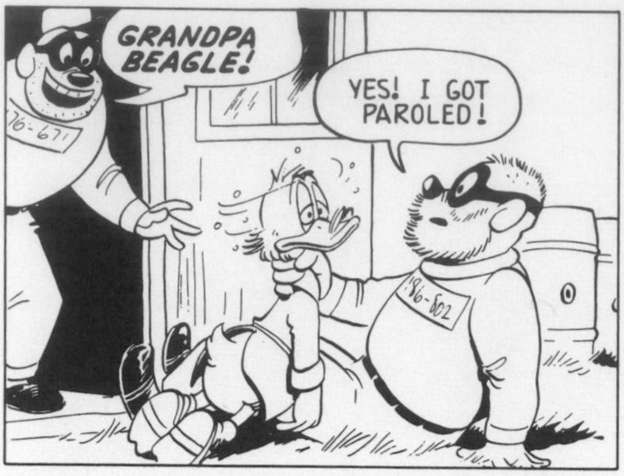
GRANDPA BEAGLE!
YES! I GOT PAROLED!

we have backstory that the Beagle Boys organization has harassed Scrooge McDuck for the better part of a century! It's obvious Barks was just having fun and not establishing any kind of "canon" for his characters. Yet since he was so gifted a writer, we can't help but not read even throwaways like Grandpa Beagle as anything but rich and colorful and worthy of continuing character status.

So while "The Money Well" is ostensibly a little too familiar, it's hard for the reader to disagree with Scrooge's conclusion: "I wouldn't have missed this bout with the Beagle Boys for anything — it was great fun!"

— THAD KOMOROWSKI

UNCLE SCROOGE AND THE GOLDEN RIVER *p. 91*

A morality play in Duckburg. A decade after creating his old miser, Carl Barks uses him in a tale of moral fall and (maybe) rise, inspired by John Ruskin's 1851 book, *The King of the Golden River or The Black Brothers: A Legend of Stiria.*

In the beginning, we see Scrooge really desperate (as often happens), but this time not because of the Beagle Boys — the dry weather is shrinking the size of his paper money, and so he thinks he's getting poorer. This makes him even stingier. He orders his employees to conserve almost everything (water, paper, pencils). And, when asked for a few dollars to help build a playground for the Junior Woodchucks, he explodes in an angry tirade against having fun. The first third of the story functions as a sort of prologue for the real adventure — as Scrooge goes to the mountains with his nephews to recover from the trauma of his money bin exploding during an attempt to reverse the paper money shrinkage.

There, the nephews read Scrooge a Barks version of Ruskin's tale, wherein holy water becomes magic water. And suddenly, they spy a waterfall that is flowing gold, just like in the story. But in the story, only those who are unselfish and generous (unlike Scrooge) can actually gather the gold.

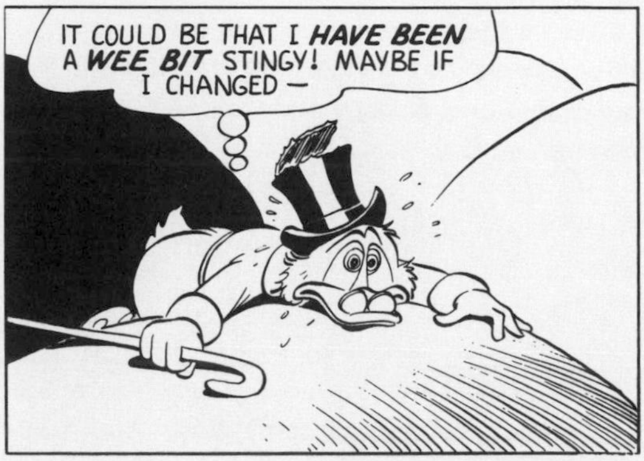
IT COULD BE THAT I HAVE BEEN A WEE BIT STINGY! MAYBE IF I CHANGED —

It is an atypical story — no treasure hunt, no Beagle Boys. Here, Scrooge is facing himself — the old miser who "never has any fun" (apart from pulling a lever that opens a trapdoor, thus expelling nuisances from his office). He is so obsessed with saving money and recalling his old times as a gold prospector in the Klondike that even his employees poke fun at him. ("That was when he did his figuring with a walrus tusk on a block of ice," says one of them sarcastically to a colleague.)

Here, Barks speaks, ironically through his creation, about the constant obsession with money. As in most Barks stories, there is a sort-of scientific explanation for the flowing of gold (the Duck Man was a rationalist), but in the end we don't know if Scrooge really does believe that a little gnome let him have the gold because he promised to buy his nephews playgrounds, thus proving his generosity.

Perhaps he does, perhaps he is just revitalized from making money once again. (Scrooge's complaint that he never has fun is untrue — he always has fun discovering new wealth and becoming richer and richer.) The old troubled Duck we saw at the beginning is long gone. Scrooge — the indefatigable gold prospector of the Klondike — is back!

Ruskin's book also inspired Italian writer Guido Martina to write "Uncle Scrooge and the King of the Golden River," with art by Giovan Battista Carpi (*Uncle Scrooge: King of the Golden River, Disney Masters* Volume 6, Fantagraphics Books, 2019), which makes for an interesting contrast to this story. Martina, who wrote many good Disney stories and translated a lot of Barks stories, kept faithful to Barks's initial unsympathetic vision of Scrooge. In Barks's story, Scrooge is redeemed (to a point), while in Martina's version, Scrooge's greed is punished.

— STEFANO PRIARONE

CARL BARKS'S ALTER EGO

Beginning in this volume, we are treated to a generous helping of short Gyro Gearloose stories (mostly 4-pagers) — a series of delightful small portraits, from various angles, of one of the most beloved of Barks's characters. Attentive readers will note that these stories feature Gyro on his own, not in conjunction with Scrooge, Donald, or any of the other well-known inhabitants of Duckburg.

In narrative terms, Gyro is a natural companion for Scrooge, backing the tycoon's entrepreneurial drive with a unique scientific and technological ability to design and build the devices that might help Scrooge reach his goal. However, in these stories, we instead see Gyro by himself, going about his own daily life. We get a glimpse of the "rest time" he gets at home between one grand Scrooge adventure and the next. We see him facing and addressing everyday mundane problems such as noisy howling cats and picnic-ruining ants, and we get to know him better as a result.

Interestingly, this way of portraying the Gyro character was not initially a stylistic choice. It was instead forced upon Barks by the U.S. Post Office (!). At the time, comics magazines mailed to subscribers under second class mailing regulations qualified for a discount on postage if the issue contained at least two stories and at least one of those stories featured characters that did not appear in any of the other stories in that issue. Why on Earth should such a combination attract a discount? Go figure! But that's why Western Publishing asked Barks to write these short Gyro solo outings.

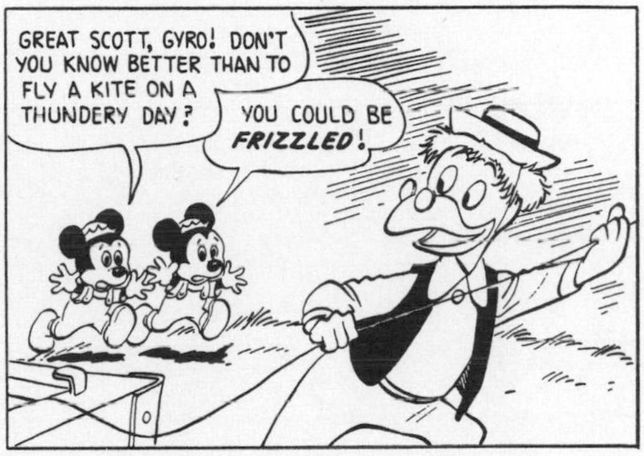
GREAT SCOTT, GYRO! DON'T YOU KNOW BETTER THAN TO FLY A KITE ON A THUNDERY DAY?
YOU COULD BE FRIZZLED!

Fortunately, Barks, being the grandmaster that he was, turned that constraint into an opportunity and came up with these wonderful little everyday portraits of his "inventor of anything." (It's also why the first of these stories, "Trapped Lightning" (p. 123), features Mickey Mouse's nephews, Morty and Ferdie. The story originally co-starred Huey, Dewey, and Louie, but it had to be redrawn because the trio was already featured in the issue's lead Scrooge adventure.)

In "The Cat Box" (p. 131), Gyro's problem is a noisy cat that disturbs his concentration. Ordinary people would find many ordinary ways to shut up the cat, starting with chasing him away, but not Gyro! He chooses to figure out why the cat is yowling and does so by means of a machine that he had already invented that can translate any language (including that of felines) into any other. Note how the capabilities of the machine depicted in those few panels (handling multiple speakers talking simultaneously, handling

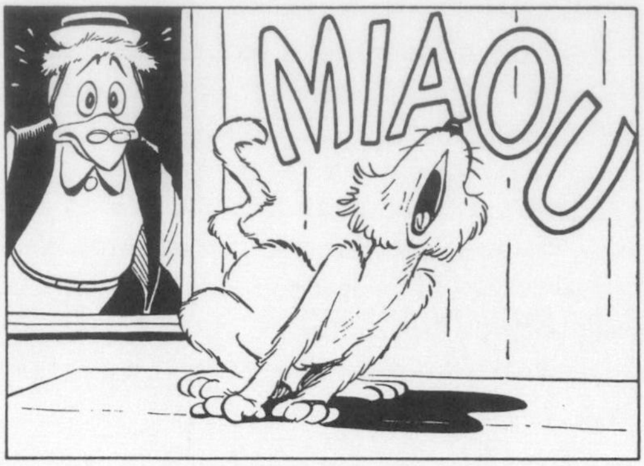
MIAOU

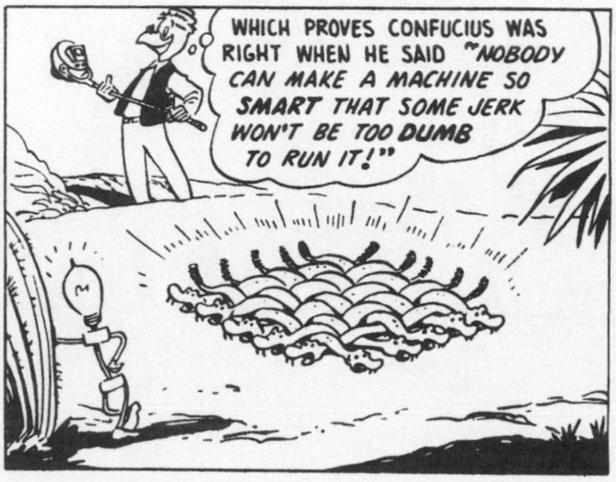
WHICH PROVES CONFUCIUS WAS RIGHT WHEN HE SAID "NOBODY CAN MAKE A MACHINE SO SMART THAT SOME JERK WON'T BE TOO DUMB TO RUN IT!"

slang, translating non-human languages, and particularly doing all that without any prior training in the source language) are so advanced that it is still impossible to build one even now, over 60 years later, despite enormous advances in machine translation, artificial intelligence, and related fields. The machine tells Gyro that the cat was merely serenading a girl cat — a trivially obvious explanation that any normal person would have guessed without the need for an advanced translation machine.

Such intellectual dualism is typical of Gyro. He's clever enough to invent a translation machine but too dumb to understand something that everyone else already knows — namely, that the yowling cat was merely in love. The translated slang of the two cats arguing with each other "like the neighborhood crew-cuts" (teenage boys of the 1950s) is hilarious, but that's just by the way. The means by which Gyro eventually defeats his feline opponents is crucial, because it's simultaneously a victory and a loss. Gyro is almost superhuman in his intellectual prowess as scientist and inventor, but the reason he manages to get rid of the cats is not because he's clever, but because his singing is so poor! This brings him down to Earth and makes him fallible and therefore more lovable as a character, something he could never be if he were flawlessly perfect.

It is part of Barks's flair as an author to mix a touch of humanity into Gyro's character, so as to allow readers to identify with him through his flaws in spite of his superior intellect. We see this in other stories in this volume, such as "Sure-Fire Gold Finder" (p. 157) — Gyro is so clever that he can invent a portable machine to locate gold anywhere, even sensing the exact shape of the lump

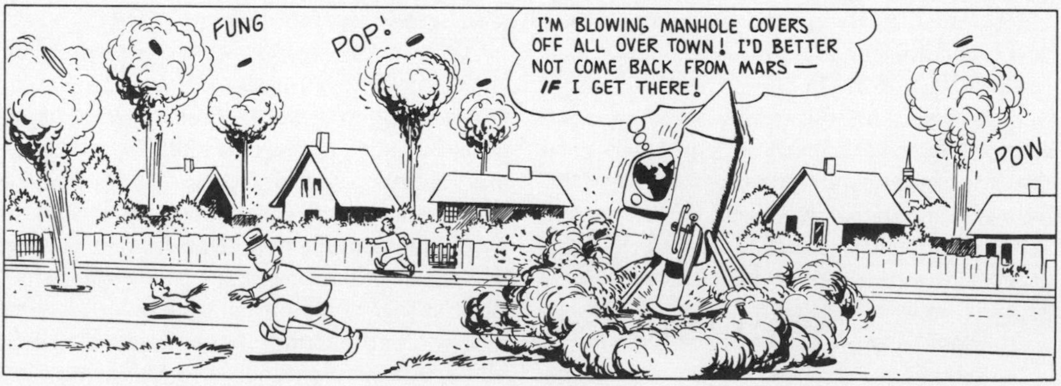
FUNG
POP!
I'M BLOWING MANHOLE COVERS OFF ALL OVER TOWN! I'D BETTER NOT COME BACK FROM MARS — IF I GET THERE!
POW

(again, something that is still technologically impossible 60 years later). But then he is so absentminded and dumb that he doesn't notice that the golden statue he's looking at is on the opposite side of the Earth. Or "August Accident" (p. 165)—Gyro is so clever that he can design and build a flying rocket in his living room, but he is so dumb that he can't foresee the damage it will cause to his neighborhood. And so on with many other stories.

Gyro is admirable for his amazing cleverness and creativity, but he is still "one of us" because he also screws up from time to time, which removes all the distance between his genius and us and makes him instantly lovable.

The true creative genius—the greatest inventor of all—is, of course, not Gyro but Barks himself, an amazing "idea man" capable of imagining the wildest and most out-of-the-box solutions to problems of any kind. Any of today's technology companies would immediately want him as their Senior Vice President of Design. Just look at the succession of machines Barks devises for Gyro in "Grandma's Present" (p. 135). First, there is a machine that synthesizes milk from hay (which is what the milk-producing cow eats). Then, bypassing the need for seeding and harvesting the hay, he comes up with a second machine to produce milk directly from soil, which is later improved to produce milk in four flavors. Finally, an even more amazing machine bypasses the pigs and produces pork chops and sausages from first principles—water, air, and dirt. All perfectly logical in their own way. And how cute it is to see Barks merrily ignore all the complex biochemistry and advanced process control required to produce such results, and instead have Gyro build the machine out of purely mechanical and hydraulic parts—Gyro's main engineering activity appears to be linking gears together in new configurations. A humorous exaggeration that amuses the adult readers and, for the primary intended audience of child readers, removes needless detail about how stuff works.

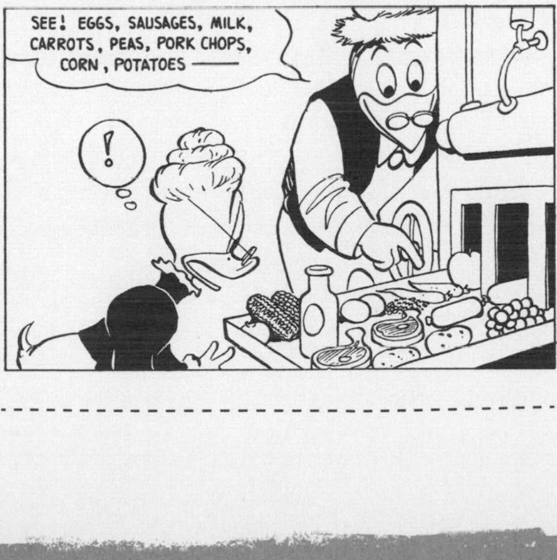
SEE! EGGS, SAUSAGES, MILK, CARROTS, PEAS, PORK CHOPS, CORN, POTATOES ——
!

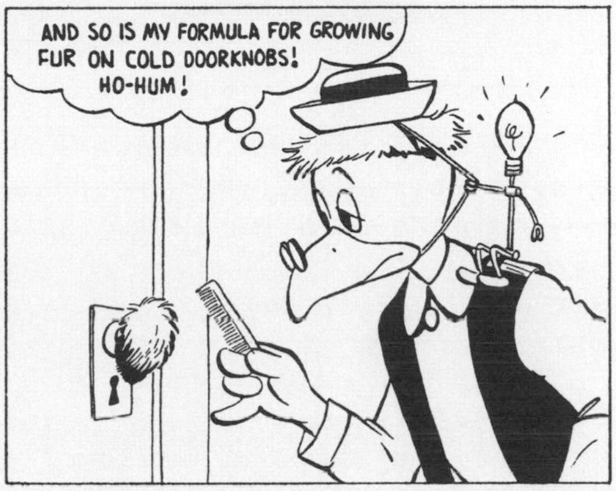
AND SO IS MY FORMULA FOR GROWING FUR ON COLD DOORKNOBS! HO-HUM!

Another aspect of these Gyro stories worth mentioning is the "silent stuff" that goes on in the background of the panels. These stories often allow the reader to follow the main plot just by speed-reading through the balloons and looking at what Gyro does. But you may enjoy them much more by going back and savoring each panel slowly, thereby discovering many ephemeral but hilarious gags such as his "formula for growing fur on cold doorknobs" on the first page of "Grandma's Present" (p. 135), or the steam-powered armchair back scratcher in the opening panel of "Getting Thor" (p. 173).

Gyro's unnamed light bulb–headed helper almost lives a parallel life in these gags, and sometimes a whole new story unfolds in the background, completely silently, while Gyro goes about his business. Sometimes (rarely) the two stories actually intersect, as in "Inventor of Anything" (p. 127) where the helper's intervention actually ruins Gyro's otherwise perfect invention, or in "Getting Thor" (p. 173) where the helper is the one

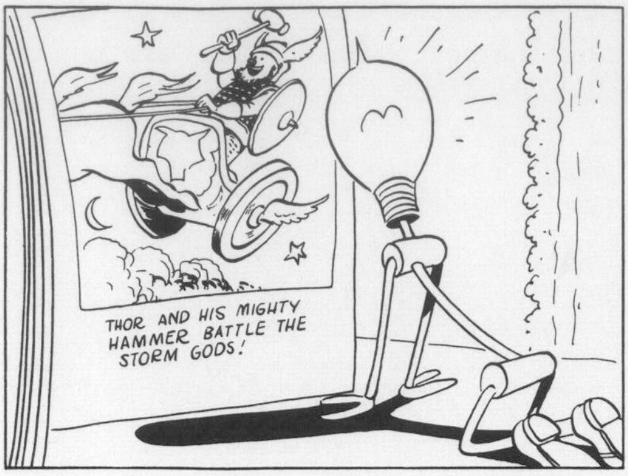
THOR AND HIS MIGHTY HAMMER BATTLE THE STORM GODS!

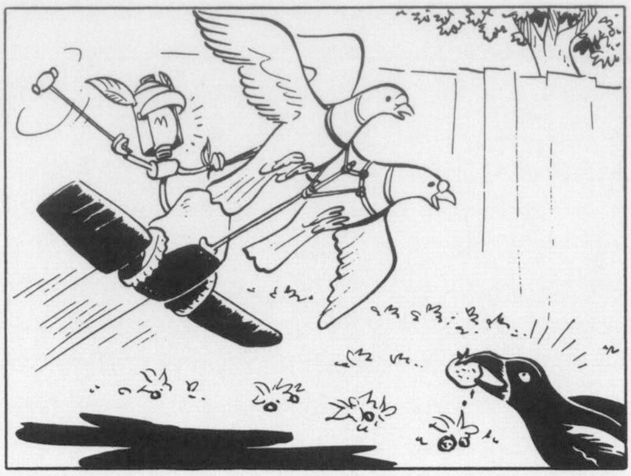

who actually solves the main problem. But in most other cases, the helper's stories remain independent. The helper is in fact a miniature version of Gyro, both in his uncanny resourcefulness and creativity and in his spectacular ability to screw up.

Barks himself was an inventor at heart and, therefore, Gyro is also, in part, a self-portrait. Co-author Frank Stajano will never forget his three-day visit to Barks in Grants Pass, Oregon, a couple of years before Barks's death, during which Barks showed him, among other things, the simple mechanical contraption Barks had built to steady his nonagenarian hand in order to be able to work on his oil paintings. At that moment, Stajano realized, as in a flash, that Barks was Gyro.

Many of Barks's stories show his profound love for unspoiled nature (think of "Land of the Pygmy Indians" in Volume 16 of this series), which may lead some to classify Barks as anti-technology. But we find instead that, in many other stories — particularly with Gyro but sometimes also with Donald — Barks visualizes the amazing possibilities afforded by technology and celebrates the joy of creating something new. Barks generally enjoys (for Gyro but also for himself as a storyteller) the superpowers of inventing, designing, and building new pieces of machinery that expand the boundaries of what humans can achieve.

At the same time, though, some of Gyro's failures can be read as a warning by Barks that technology can backfire and cannot be a universal solution — in "Picnic" (p. 151), Gyro repeatedly attempts to get rid of some classic picnic nuisances, from ants to grasshoppers, rain, and storms. At each cycle, the result is slightly better protected from the nuisances but slightly further away from the open-air experience, until eventually the original aim is completely negated. Barks the inventor-at-heart loves technology but not unconditionally. Several subtle warnings in his 1950s stories anticipate such modern themes as environmental pollution and the pointlessness of trying to fix with technology some problems that technology itself has created.

— FRANCESCO STAJANO AND LEONARDO GORI

FLEETING GENIUS

The limited nature of these Gyro Gearloose stories — that they must be four pages, feature Gyro without his Duck co-stars, and be strictly gag stories — could have easily taken them in a repetitive direction. Yet Barks used the constraints of the back-up feature to helm an already endearing side character into a compelling lead. As with Donald and Scrooge, Gyro was an appealing character because he and his brilliant mind so perfectly illustrated the capricious nature of humanity.

Gyro is never guarded with his gifts, and loves to share them with the world — even when the world so often doesn't deserve him. Indeed, the citizens of Duckburg expect too much perfection out of Gyro and aren't shy about saying so, whether it's a crowd of fishermen expressing disappointment over Gyro's "simple" fishing solution in "Fishing Mystery" (p. 147), or a piggish married couple demanding a soft, puncture-proof home in "Gyro Builds a Better House" (p. 161). "Every inventor is entitled to a boo-boo once in a while!" shouts Gyro as angry clients run him out of town. Since many Gyro stories end in that fashion, expecting such entitlement when the whole world remains very much against you might be — well, entitled.

Even Gyro himself is a regular dissatisfied customer, but not because he's a klutz. In "Forecasting Follies" (p. 143), his prediction machine can answer any question, only Gyro never thinks to ask all the questions he should. "Roscoe the Robot" (p. 169) acts out Gyro's thoughts even if it means putting its human master in danger. The "Know It-All Machine" (p. 177) really *does* know it all, despite Gyro's hasty dismissal that he inadvertently created sarcastic artificial intelligence (a *real* know-it-all). So his inventions always work, only a little too well, and always for foreseeable reasons. But Gyro *can't* foresee them due to his extravagance and excitement to build a better tomorrow, and his confidence that his genius left nothing to question. (Oh, if only Helper could talk!)

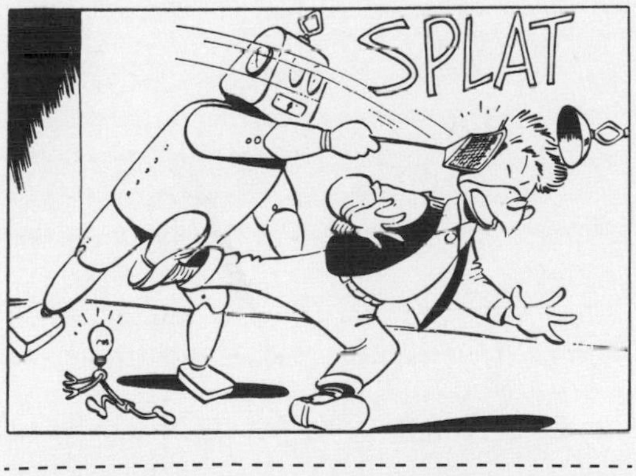
SPLAT

While Barks could have hacked these stories out, the Gyro shorts are the perfect no-frills chasers to the lead Scrooge adventures, as they still embody all of Barks's gifts for characterization and storytelling in a short and

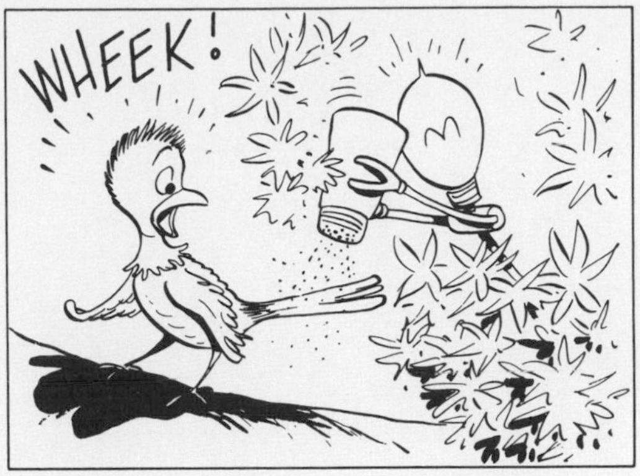
WHEEK!

sweet fashion. Gyro is a genius, but he's still human and can't avoid the most normal pratfalls — and that is what makes him the charming, enduring "MVP" of Duck back-up stories.

— THAD KOMOROWSKI

UNCLE SCROOGE ONE-PAGERS

A look at the biography of Carl Barks included in this book shows that his first work with the Ducks was done at the Disney animation studio. There, cartoons were created to exploit fraught situations and exaggerate tensions to produce raucous antics. They catered to and uproariously refined the elements of what we think of as physical humor.

In his comic books, Barks would capitalize on an even broader, deeper (if not as persistently dynamic) wellspring of comedy — human nature. Such is the case right down to the one-page gags of this volume.

For instance, "Forgotten Precaution" (p. 62) begins with that all-too familiar feeling of *knowing* something has been forgotten but not being able to remember exactly *what*, until it is too late. The special irony here, of course, is that the very thing forgotten was expressly installed to combat any act of forgetting.

Likewise, we've all been eager, grateful recipients of glad tidings even where a little reflection and circumspection would suggest the news is simply too good to be true. The ecstatic Scrooge relishes the predictions of

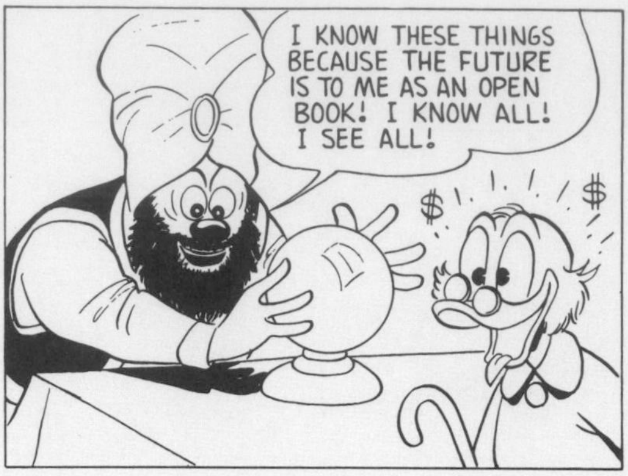
I KNOW THESE THINGS BECAUSE THE FUTURE IS TO ME AS AN OPEN BOOK! I KNOW ALL! I SEE ALL!

"The Balmy Swami" (p. 119) right up until a casual bit of small talk destroys his confidence.

Everyone has pleasant dreams. That of Scrooge's in "Windfall of the Mind" (p. 61) is tailor-made for his acquisitive obsession. Again, there's added irony in that the focus of his fantasy is precisely the subject of the lecture that his waking intelligence has forsaken.

While such mortal traits are widely shared, Scrooge's unique perspective and sensibilities put a particular spin on them. "History Tossed" (p. 28) shows the lengths he will go to retrieve a single coin. It's risked in the first place because of the very Scrooge-like insistence on seeing for oneself, testing an assertion, establishing veracity through hands-on experience. Such expended effort permits him to completely and fully appreciate Washington's proclaimed feat. Yet with that goal realized and curiosity satisfied, he remains oblivious to the fact that the confirmation involved an even more remarkable accomplishment of his own.

Similarly, admirable creativity and problem-solving à la Scrooge allow him again to recapture and retain his hard-earned riches in "The Windy Story" (p. 122), only this time under considerable duress.

"The Big Bobber" (p. 30) displays a less savory extreme. Scrooge's drive to augment his wealth, one dime at a time, monetizes childhood play. The humor present here — his immediate transition from scoffing observer to disguised participant — hinges on the remarks of the bearded onlookers to entirely understand. Barks worked scrupulously to address readers of every age, including the preliterate. The action and facial expressions in every panel, as always, carry a great deal of information, but the amusement value in this strip would be largely hidden without the ability to read.

Likewise, "That Sinking Feeling" (p. 118) depends on the spoken cue of the sailor who repeats the old saw about the captain going down with his ship (which is pretty unfunny right there). Again, what laughs are available depend upon a reader's verbal skills, although that last, unusual depiction of Scrooge is strangely striking and ludicrous on its own merits.

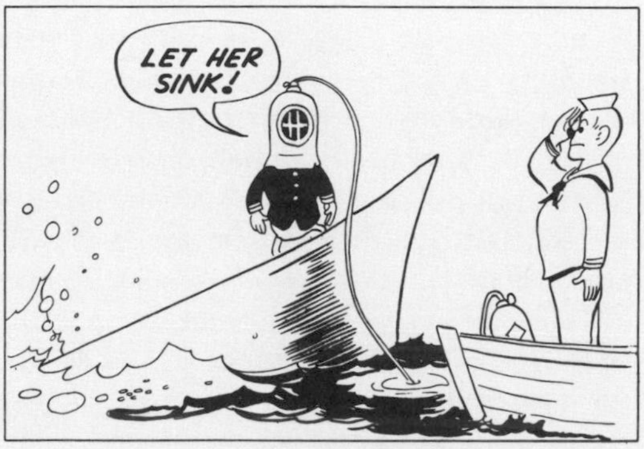
LET HER SINK!

This crucial role for words holds true as well in the more elaborate set-ups of "High Rider" (p. 120) and "Going to Pieces" (p. 121). In "High Rider," Barks goes to considerable pains to establish the rhythmic gait of horse and mount. But in the end, the rental payment and its logic make no sense if one cannot grasp Scrooge's spoken rationale. (For more on "High Rider," see "Restoring High Rider" on the next page.)

In "Going to Pieces," very young readers who can't decode the dialog will understand the visual "beats" of the succession of different vehicles leading to the humorous reveal of Scrooge's antique flivver. But they will miss the parallel construction of the spoken replies by Gladstone, Donald, and Scrooge. Without the ability to decipher the dialog in the final panel — with its disregard for age and modernity — a bit of wit is lost.

The delivery of these jokes contrasts sharply with two shorter strips, both of which are highly accessible to those who read just pictures. Scrooge's success in "Dogged Determination" (p. 89) rests on an intuitive understanding of the escalation from big dog to bigger dog. The silent "Rescue Enhancement" (p. 90) may depend on appreciating the inherent attraction of waving greenbacks, but its greatest pleasure lies in the sheer inventiveness of the international flotilla responding to Scrooge's altered mayday.

For the most part, these one-pagers were found on the inside front, inside back, and back covers of Uncle Scrooge comics. Those that are not quite as tall as a normal full page (such as "Going to Pieces," p. 121) were drawn to that slightly shorter height to allow room for the fine-print indicia that routinely ran at the bottom of the inside front cover (moved, in later years, to the bottom of page one of the comic book itself), which held necessary business and postal information.

As was the case of Barks's longer stories, some of these one-pagers were sometimes shuffled from the issues Barks had originally intended, moved for various reasons including making room for advertisements. As well as can be determined, they appear in this volume in the order in which Barks drew them.

That even includes "A Real Bargain at Last" (p. 29), a one-pager previously unnamed in English but referred to as "the blinders gag." It joins "Donald the Milkman" (*Walt Disney's Donald Duck: "The Black Pearls of Tabu Yama,"* Volume 19) and "Silent Night" (slated for an upcoming volume) as one of only three Barks stories that saw print overseas before appearing in the U.S. "A Real Bargain at Last" was first printed in Brazil and Italy in 1958, then it ran in Australia and elsewhere in Europe before eventually seeing print in the United States, more than 20 years after its creation. But some things remain timeless. Once more, Scrooge's ingenuity triumphs over an all-too human weakness — Donald's inability to resist the temptation of what others declare to be a "bargain."

— RICH KREINER

RESTORING "HIGH RIDER"

Prior to the publication of this volume, "High Rider" (p. 120), has only ever been seen as a 7-panel page. Barks's editor cut one panel at the time of its original publication to make room for a Dell Comics "Pledge to Parents" notice, assuring all and sundry that "Dell Comics Are Good Comics" of "clean and wholesome entertainment." The "Pledge" was Dell's response to the public hysteria at the time that comics promoted juvenile delinquency. You can see instances in other stories in this volume where panels were excised in order to fit in Dell's "Pledge."

But quite unexpectedly, the deleted panel from "High Rider" surfaced (and was authenticated) in late 2018, mixed in with a small group of other individual panels by other artists cut from other Dell comics for the same reason. Joakim Gunnarsson, editor at Egmont Publishing, Sweden, fit it back in, restoring this one-page story to the full 8-panel gag that Carl Barks had originally created, 61 years ago.

Our thanks to Joakim, Disney historian David Gerstein, and colorist Gary Leach for making it possible for us to publish it here, complete at last, for the first time anywhere. The restored panel? It's panel 5, the first panel on the third tier of the page (see above).

— J. MICHAEL CATRON

Restoring "Uncle Scrooge and the Golden River"

In earlier volumes of this series, we have looked at instances where Carl Barks had to truncate a story at the behest of his editor. But in this volume, we have an example of him shortening a story for his own reasons.

When Barks submitted "Uncle Scrooge and the Golden River," he held back a page in which Huey figures out how "heat pressure ... forces the gold up through the rocks and over the falls" thus giving him an idea how to "loosen [Scrooge's] purse strings." That page — page 17 — is restored to its proper place in the story in this volume (p. 107).

Barks knew he had just 26 pages to tell this story, but when he finished and looked it over, he decided it needed more gags. So he went back and inserted a new sequence — most likely, according to Barks expert Kim Weston, the bottom half of page 4 (p. 94) and the top half of page 5 (p. 95). (Skip from the top half of page 4 to the bottom half of page 5, and you'll see that the narrative still works without those panels.) To stay at 26 pages, Barks eliminated page 18 (p. 107), which is mostly exposition.

But in doing so, he realized he needed to bridge the continuity gap between page 17 and new page 18 (previously page 19). To accomplish that, he took panel 5 from old page 18 (p. 107), drew one new panel, and thus created a new two-panel sequence for the top of new page 18 (p. 108). That new panel cannot be fit back into the expanded story, both because there is literally no space for it and because it creates an alternate and contradictory reason for Donald and the boys to go off on their own.

If not for the strict page count requirement, it seems likely that Barks would have submitted "Uncle Scrooge and the Golden River" as a 27-pager, and most Barks scholars agree that the longer version, as presented here, is the preferred one.

Reproduced below is Barks's two-panel "continuity patch" as it appeared when the shortened version of the story was first printed. To get a sense of how the 26-page version looked to readers of the original comic book, read page 106, then the two panels at the bottom of this page, and then page 108, beginning with panel 3.

— J. MICHAEL CATRON

YOU REMEMBER IN THE STORY OF THE GOLDEN RIVER ONLY AN *UNSELFISH* PERSON COULD HAVE THE GOLD!
IF YOU'RE HINTING THAT A *CERTAIN* RICH OLD DUCK WILL HAVE TO CHANGE HIS WAYS, YOU ARE MAYBE HALF RIGHT!
I'M SURE YOU KIDS ARE BRINGING ME *BAD LUCK*! I WISH YOU'D GO *HOME* BEFORE YOU BRING ME MORE!
SWELL! WE'RE NOT HAVING SUCH *GOOD* LUCK, OURSELVES!

Carl Barks

LIFE AMONG THE DUCKS

by DONALD AULT

ABOVE: *Carl Barks at the 1982 San Diego Comic-Con. Photo by Alan Light.*

"I was a real misfit," Carl Barks said, thinking back over an early life of hard labor — as a farmer, a logger, a mule-skinner, a rivet heater, and a printing press feeder — before he was hired as a full-time cartoonist for an obscure risqué magazine in 1931.

Barks was born in 1901 and (mostly) raised in Merrill, Oregon. He had always wanted to be a cartoonist, but everything that happened to him in his early years seemed to stand in his way. He suffered a significant hearing loss after a bout with the measles. His mother died. He had to leave school after the eighth grade. His father suffered a mental breakdown. His older brother was whisked off to World War I.

His first marriage, in 1921, was to a woman who was unsympathetic to his dreams and who ultimately bore two children "by accident," as Barks phrased it. The two divorced in 1930.

In 1931, he pulled up stakes from Merrill and headed to Minnesota, leaving his mother-in-law, whom he trusted more than his wife, in charge of his children.

Arriving in Minneapolis, he went to work for the *Calgary Eye-Opener*, that risqué magazine. He thought he would finally be drawing cartoons full time, but the editor and most of the staff were alcoholics, so Barks ended up running the whole show.

In 1935 he took "a great gamble" and, on the strength of some cartoons he'd submitted in response to an advertisement from the Disney Studio, he moved to California and entered an animation trial period. He was soon promoted to "story man" in Disney's Donald Duck animation unit, where he made significant contributions to 36 Donald cartoon shorts between 1936 and 1942, including helping to create Huey, Dewey, and Louie for "Donald's Nephews" in 1938. Ultimately, though, he grew dissatisfied. The production of animated cartoons "by committee," as he described it, stifled his imagination.

For that and other reasons, in 1942 he left Disney to run a chicken farm. But when he was offered a chance by Western Publishing to write and illustrate a new series of Donald Duck comic book stories, he jumped at it. The comic book format suited him, and the quality of his work persuaded the editors to grant him a freedom and autonomy he'd never known and that few others were ever granted. He would go on to write and draw more than 6,000 pages in over 500 stories and uncounted hundreds of covers between 1942 and 1966 for Western's Dell and Gold Key imprints.

Barks had almost no formal art training. He had taught himself how to draw by imitating his early favorite artist — Winsor McCay (*Little Nemo*), Frederick Opper (*Happy Hooligan*), Elzie Segar (*Popeye*), and Floyd Gottfredson (*Mickey Mouse*).

He taught himself how to write well by going back to the grammar books he had shunned in school, making up jingles and rhymes, and inventing other linguistic exercises to get a natural feel for the rhythm and dialogue of sequential narrative.

Barks married again in 1938, but that union ended disastrously in divorce in 1951. In 1954, Barks married Margaret Wynnfred Williams, known as Garé, who soon began assisting him by lettering and inking backgrounds on his comic book work. They remained happily together until her death in 1993.

He did his work in the California desert and often mailed his stories in to the office. He worked his stories over and over "backward and forward." Barks was not a vain man, but he had confidence in his talent. He knew what hard work was, and he knew that he'd put his best efforts into every story he produced.

On those occasions when he did go into Western's offices he would "just dare anybody to see if they could improve on it." His confidence was justified. His work was largely responsible for some of the best-selling comic books in the world — *Walt Disney's Comics and Stories* and *Uncle Scrooge*.

Because Western's policy was to keep their writers and artists anonymous, readers never knew the name of the "good duck artist" — but they could spot the superiority of his work. When fans determined to solve the mystery of his anonymity finally tracked him down (not unlike an adventure Huey, Dewey, and Louie might embark upon), Barks was quite happy to correspond and otherwise communicate with his legion of aficionados.

Given all the obstacles of his early years and the dark days that haunted him off and on for the rest of his life, it's remarkable that he laughed so easily and loved to make others laugh.

In the process of expanding Donald Duck's character far beyond the hot-tempered Donald of animation, Barks created a moveable locale (Duckburg) and a cast of dynamic characters: Scrooge McDuck, the Beagle Boys, Gladstone Gander, Gyro Gearloose, the Junior Woodchucks. And there were hundreds of others who made only one memorable appearance in the engaging, imaginative, and unpredictable comedy-adventures that he wrote and drew from scratch for nearly a quarter of a century.

Among many other honors, Carl Barks was one of the three initial inductees into the Will Eisner Comic Book Hall of Fame for comic book creators in 1987. (The other two were Jack Kirby and Will Eisner.) In 1991, Barks became the only Disney comic book artist to be recognized as a "Disney Legend," a special award created by Disney "to acknowledge and honor the many individuals whose imagination, talents, and dreams have created the Disney magic."

As Roy Disney said on Barks's passing in 2000 at age 99, "He challenged our imaginations and took us on some of the greatest adventures we have ever known. His prolific comic book creations entertained many generations of devoted fans and influenced countless artists over the years…. His timeless tales will stand as a legacy to his originality and brilliant artistic vision."

Contributors

Donald Ault is Professor of English at the University of Florida, founder and editor of *ImageTexT: Interdisciplinary Comics Studies*, author of two books on William Blake (*Visionary Physics* and *Narrative Unbound*), editor of *Carl Barks: Conversations*, and executive producer of the video *The Duck Man: An Interview with Carl Barks*.

Alberto Becattini was born in Florence, Italy. He has taught high school English since 1983. Since 1978, he has written essays for Italian and U.S. publications about comics, specializing in Disney characters and American comics generally. Since 1992, he has been a freelance writer and consultant for The Walt Disney Company-Italy, contributing to such series as *Zio Paperone*, *Maestri Disney*, *Tesori Disney*, *Disney Anni d'Oro*, *La Grande Dinastia dei Paperi*, and *Gli Anni d'Oro di Topolino*.

J. Michael Catron is editor of *The Complete Carl Barks Disney Library* and of *Disney Masters*, which collects work by international artists working in the Disney tradition.

Leonardo Gori is a comics scholar and collector, especially of syndicated newspaper strips of the 1930s and Italian Disney authors. He has written, with Frank Stajano and others, many books on Italian "fumetti" and American comics in Italy. He has also written thrillers, which have been translated into Spanish, Portuguese, and Korean.

Thad Komorowski is an animation historian and digital restoration artist with a long-standing professional relationship with Disney comics. He is a regular contributor to Fantagraphics's Walt Disney archival collections and translates stories for IDW's Disney comic books and Fantagraphics's *Disney Masters* series. He is the author of *Sick Little Monkeys: The Unauthorized Ren & Stimpy Story* and co-author of a forthcoming history of New York studio animation.

Rich Kreiner is a longtime writer for *The Comics Journal* and a longtime reader of Carl Barks. He lives with wife and cat in Maine.

Stefano Priarone was born in Northwestern Italy about the time when a retired Carl Barks was storyboarding his last Junior Woodchucks stories. He writes about popular culture in many Italian newspapers and magazines, was a contributor to the Italian complete Carl Barks collection, and wrote his thesis in economics about Uncle Scrooge as an entrepreneur (for which he blames his aunt, who read him Barks's Scrooge stories when he was 3 years old).

Francesco (Frank) Stajano is a full professor at the 800-year-old University of Cambridge, a Fellow of Trinity College, a founding director of two hi-tech start-up companies, and a licensed teacher in the Japanese "Way of the Sword." As a comics scholar, he has co-authored books on Don Rosa and Floyd Gottfredson and written essays on many others. Over the decades, he became a correspondent and personal friend of many of his favorite Disney creators and was occasionally hosted as overnight guest by Barks, Rosa, Cimino, Cavazzano, and Ziche.

Matthias Wivel is Curator of Sixteenth-Century Italian Painting at the National Gallery, London. He has written widely about comics for a decade and a half.

Daniel F. Yezbick grew up in Detroit, Michigan, reading Carl Barks's comics in Gold Key and Whitman reprints. Since then, he has wandered the nation in Barksian fashion, pursuing a variety of odd jobs including bartender, sheep wrangler, technical writer, and college professor. He now teaches comics, film studies, and writing courses at Forest Park College. His essays on Barks and Disney comics have appeared in a variety of anthologies including *Icons of the American Comic Book*, *Comics Through Time*, and *Critical Survey of Graphic Novels: History, Theme, and Technique*. He is the author of *Perfect Nonsense: The Chaotic Comics and Goofy Games of George Carlson* (Fantagraphics, 2014). He currently lives in South St. Louis with his wife, Rosalie, their two children, and one wise, old hound.

Where did these Duck stories first appear?

The Complete Carl Barks Disney Library collects Donald Duck and Uncle Scrooge stories by Carl Barks that were originally published in the traditional American four-color comic book format. Barks's first Duck story appeared in October 1942. The volumes in this project are numbered chronologically but are being released in a different order. This is Volume 20.

Stories within a volume may or may not follow the publication sequence of the original comic books. We may take the liberty of rearranging the sequence of the stories within a volume for editorial or presentation purposes.

The original comic books were published under the Dell logo and some appeared in the so-called *Four Color* series — a name that appeared nowhere inside the comic book itself, but is generally agreed upon by historians to refer to the series of "one-shot" comic books published by Dell that have sequential numbering. The *Four Color* issues are also sometimes referred to as "One Shots."

Most of the shorter stories in this volume were originally published without a title. Some stories were retroactively assigned a title when they were reprinted in later years. Some stories were given titles by Barks in correspondence or interviews. (Sometimes Barks referred to the same story with different titles.) Some stories were never given an official title but have been informally assigned one by fans and indexers. For the untitled stories in this volume, we have used the title that seems most appropriate. The unofficial titles appear below with an asterisk enclosed in parentheses (*).

The following is the order in which the stories in this volume were originally published.

***Uncle Scrooge* #13**
(March–May 1956)
Trapped Lightning (*)

***Uncle Scrooge* #14**
(June–August 1956)
Inventor of Anything (*)

***Uncle Scrooge* #15**
(September–November 1956)
The Cat Box (*)

***Walt Disney's Christmas Parade* #8**
([December] 1956)
Grandma's Present

***Uncle Scrooge* #16**
(December 1956–February 1957)
Forecasting Follies (*)

***Uncle Scrooge* #17**
(March–May 1957)
Fishing Mystery (*)

***Walt Disney's Picnic Party* #8**
([July] 1957)
Picnic

***Uncle Scrooge* #18**
(June–August 1957)
The Sure-Fire Gold Finder (*)

***Uncle Scrooge* #19**
(September–November 1957)
Cover
History Tossed (*)
The Mines of King Solomon
Gyro Builds a Better House (*)

***Mickey Mouse Almanac* #1**
(December 1957)
August Accident
September Scrimmage

***Uncle Scrooge* #20**
(December 1957–February 1958)
Cover
City of Golden Roofs
Roscoe the Robot (*)
Rescue Enhancement (*)

***Uncle Scrooge* #21**
(March–May 1958)
Cover
Windfall of the Mind (*)
The Money Well
Getting Thor (*)
[a.k.a. Scarecrow]
Dogged Determination (*)
Forgotten Precaution (*)

***Uncle Scrooge* #22**
(June–August 1958)
Cover
Going to Pieces (*)
The Golden River
The Know-It-All Machine (*)
High Rider (*)
That Sinking Feeling (*)

***O Pato Donald* #345**
(June 17, 1958; Brazil; first publication)
The Carl Barks Library of Walt Disney's Uncle Scrooge 1952–1958
Volume 3 (December 1984; first U.S. publication in English)
A Real Bargain at Last (*)
[a.k.a. A Única Defesa; Paperino e le tentazioni; Blinders; The Blinders Gag]

***Uncle Scrooge* #31**
(September–November 1960)
The Balmy Swami

***Uncle Scrooge* #33**
(March–May 1961)
The Big Bobber

***Uncle Scrooge* #37**
(March–May 1962)
The Windy Story

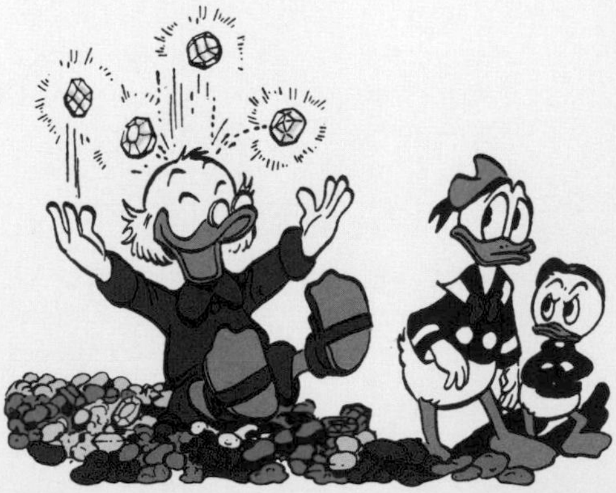